Sage could see the diaries now; all of them methodically numbered and dated, as though her mother had always known that there would come a time, as though she had deliberately planned . . .

Her hands were shaking as she opened the first diary. She didn't want to do this, and yet even in her reluctance she could almost feel the pressure of her mother's will, almost hear her whispering,

"You promised . . ."

Sage blinked rapidly to clear her eyes and then read the first sentence.

"Today I met Kit . . ."

"Kit . . ." Sage frowned and turned back the page to check on the date. The diary had begun when her mother was seventeen. Soon after her eighteenth birthday she had been married to Edward. So who was this Kit?

Nebulous, uneasy feelings stirred inside her as Sage stared reluctantly at the neat, evenly formed handwriting. It was like being confronted with a dark passage you had to go down and yet feared to enter. And yet, after all, what was there to fear?

Telling herself she was being stupid, she picked up the diary for the second time and started to read.

"A real page turner . . . one book you don't want to miss."

—*Affaire de Coeur*

"Penny Jordan is at her best in THE HIDDEN YEARS. She delivers an intense story of dark passions, bitter betrayals and the search for love."

—*Amanda Quick*

PENNY JORDAN

Popular Fiction Reader's Poll
PERSEPHONE AWARD WINNER

Born in Preston, Lancashire, Penny Jordan
now lives with her husband in a beautiful four-
teenth-century house in rural Cheshire, England. Hers is a success almost as breathtaking
as the exploits of the characters she so skillfully
and knowingly portrays. Penny has been writing for ten years, and now has more than 70
novels to her name.

Also available from Harlequin by
PENNY JORDAN

POWER PLAY
SILVER

**MORE THAN 30 MILLION COPIES OF
PENNY JORDAN'S NOVELS IN PRINT**

PENNY JORDAN

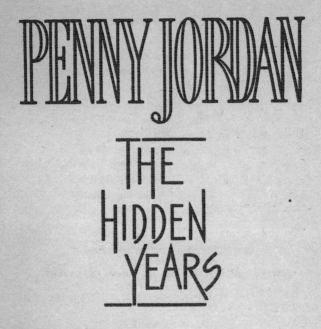

THE HIDDEN YEARS

HARLEQUIN

TORONTO • NEW YORK • LONDON
AMSTERDAM • PARIS • SYDNEY • HAMBURG
STOCKHOLM • ATHENS • TOKYO • MILAN

First published in Great Britain in 1990
by Worldwide Books.
First Harlequin North American paperback edition 1991

ISBN 0-373-97121-4

PROLOGUE

JUDGED by the laws of logic, the accident should never have happened at all.

A quiet—or at least quiet by London's frenetic standards—side-street; a clear, bright spring morning; a taxi driver who prided himself on his accident-free record; a slender, elegant woman who looked and moved like someone ten years younger than she actually was; none of the parts that went to make up the whole was in any way logically vulnerable, and yet, as though fate had decreed what must happen and was determined that it would happen, even though the woman crossed the road with ease and safety, even though the taxi driver had seen her and logged the fact that she had crossed the road ahead of him, even though the pavement and road were free of debris and frost, for some reason, as she stepped on to the pavement, the woman's heel caught on the kerb, throwing her off balance so that she turned and fell, not on to the relative safety of the pavement, but into the road and into the path of the taxi, whose driver was safely and law-abidingly not driving along its crown in the sometimes dangerous and arrogant manner of taxi drivers the world over, but well into his correct side of the street.

He saw the woman fall, and braked instinctively, but it was too late. The sickening sensation of soft, vulnerable human flesh hitting his cab was a sound he would carry with him the rest of his life. His passenger, a pinstripe-suited businessman in his early fifties, was jolted out of his seat by the impact. Already people were emerging from the well-kept, expensive houses that lined the street.

Someone must have rung for an ambulance because he could hear its muted siren wailing mournfully like a dirge... He could hardly bear to look at the woman, he was so sure that she must be dead, and so he stood sickly to one side as the ambulance arrived and the professionals took over.

'She's alive... just,' he heard someone say, and in his mind's eye he pictured the people somewhere who were still at this moment oblivious to the tragedy about to darken their lives.

Somewhere this woman would have family, friends, dependants—she had had that look about her, the confident, calm look of a woman in control of her life and those lives that revolved around her own. Somewhere those people still went about their daily business, unaware and secure.

Her mother, injured in a road accident and now lying close to death in a hospital bed—it seemed impossible, Sage thought numbly; her mother was invulnerable, omnipresent, indestructible, or so she had always seemed.

Vague, disconnected, unreal thoughts ricocheted through her brain: memories, fears, sensations. The Porsche, which had been a celebratory thirtieth birthday present to herself, cut through the heavy traffic, her physical ability to control and manoeuvre the expensive piece of machinery oddly unaffected by her mental turmoil.

There was a sensation in the pit of her stomach which she remembered from her childhood and adolescence: an uncomfortable mixture of apprehension, pain and anger. How dared her mother do this to her? How dared she intrude on the life she had built for herself? How dared she reach out, as she had reached out so very many times in the past, to cast her influence, her presence over her own independence?

She wasn't a child any more, she was mature, an adult, so why now was she swamped with those old and oh, so familiar feelings of resentment and guilt, of pain and anger and, most betraying of all, of fear?

The hospital wasn't far away, which was presumably why they had contacted her and not Faye. And then she remembered that she was her mother's closest blood relative...the next of kin. A tiny tremor of pure acid-sharp horror chilled her skin. Her mother, dying... She had told herself for so long that she felt nothing for the woman who had given birth to her—that her mother's treachery and deceit had made it impossible for any emotion other than hatred to exist between them—that it was doubly shocking to feel this dread...this anguish.

She turned into the hospital, parked her car, and climbed out of it, frowning, the movement of her elegant, lithe body quick and impatient. A typical Leo was how Liz Danvers had once ruefully described her second child: fiery, impetuous, impatient, intemperate and intelligent.

That had been almost twenty years ago. Since then time had rubbed smooth some of the rough edges of her restless personality, experience gentling and softening the starkness of a nature that weaker souls often found too abrasive. Now in her early thirties, she had learned to channel those energies which had once driven her calmer and far more self-possessed mother behind the wall of reserve and dignity which Sage had wasted so much of her childhood trying to batter down, in an effort to reach the elusive core of her personality which she had sensed her mother withheld from her; just as she had always felt that in some way she was not the child her mother had wanted her to be.

But then of course she was not, and never could be, another David. David...her brother. She missed him even now...missed his gentle wise counsel, missed his love, his understanding. David...everyone who had known him had loved him, and deservedly so. To describe his virtues was to make him appear insipid, to omit due cognisance of the essential sweetness and self-lessness of both David the child and David the man, which had made him so deeply loved by everyone who knew him. But she had never been jealous of David, had never felt that, but for him, her mother would have loved her more or better...so the schism between them went too deep to be explained away by a maternal preference

for a more favoured sibling. Once it had hurt, that
knowledge that there was something within her that
turned the love her mother seemed to shower on everything and everyone else around her into enmity and
dislike, but maturity had taught her acceptance if nothing
else, acceptance and the ability to distance herself from
those things in her past which were too painful to confront. Things which she avoided, just as she avoided all
but the most necessary contact with her mother. She
seldom went home to Cottingdean these days.

Cottingdean: the house itself, the garden, the village;
all of them her mother's domain, all of them created
and nurtured by her mother's will. They were her
mother's world.

Cottingdean. How she had hated and resented the
place's demands on her mother throughout her
childhood, transferring to it the envy and dislike she had
never felt for David. Too young then to analyse why it
was that her mother seemed to hold her at a distance,
to dislike her almost, she had jealously believed that it
was because of Cottingdean and its demands upon her
mother's time; that Cottingdean meant far more to her
mother than she ever could.

In that perhaps she had been right, and why not? she
thought cynically—Cottingdean had certainly repaid to
her mother the time and devotion she had invested in it,
in a way that she, her child, her daughter, never could.

Cottingdean, David, her father—these had been the
main, the important components of her mother's life,
and she had always felt that she stood apart from them,
outside them, an interloper... an intruder; how fiercely
and verbally she had resented that feeling.

She pushed open the plate-glass door and walked into
the hospital's reception area. A young nurse listened as
she gave her name, and then consulted a list nervously
before telling her, 'Your mother is in the intensive care
unit. If you'd like to wait in reception, the surgeon in
charge of her case would like to have a word with you.'

Self-control had been something she had learned long
ago, and so Sage allowed nothing of what she was feeling

to be betrayed by her expression as she thanked the nurse and walked swiftly over to a seat. Was her mother dead already? Was that why the surgeon wanted to see her? A tremor of unwanted sensation seized her, a panicky terror that made her want to cry out like a child. No, not yet… There's too much I want to know… Too much that needs to be said.

Which was surely ridiculous given the fact that she and her mother had long ago said all that there was to say to one another… When she herself had perhaps said too much, revealed too much. Been hurt too much.

As she waited, her body taut, her face smooth of any expression, even in repose there was something about her that reflected her inherent inner turbulence: her dark red hair so vibrant with life and energy, her strong-boned face quick and alive, the green eyes that no one knew quite where she had inherited as changeable as the depths of a northern lake under spring skies. The nurse glanced at her occasionally, envying her. She herself was small and slightly plump, a pretty girl in her way, but nowhere near in the class of the stunning woman who sat opposite her. There was elegance in the narrowness of her ankles and wrists, beauty that owed nothing to youth or fashion in the shaping of her face, mystery and allure in the colour of her hair and eyes, and something about every smallest movement of her body that drew the eye like a magnet.

Somewhere in this huge anonymous building lay her mother, Sage told herself, impossible though that seemed. Her mother had always seemed almost immortal, the pivot on which so many lives turned. Even hers, until she had finally rebelled and broken away to be her own person. Yes, her mother had always seemed indestructible, inviolate, an immutable part of the universe. The perfect wife, the perfect mother, the perfect employer—the epitome of all that her own peer group was striving so desperately to achieve. And she had achieved it against the kind of odds her generation would never have to face. Her mother was a woman thirty years ahead of her time, a woman who had taken a sick man, at one time close to death, and kept him alive for over twenty-five years. A woman who had become the mistress of a sick house and a dying estate and had turned them both into monuments of what could be achieved if one was single-minded and determined enough, if one had the skill, and the vision, and the sheer dogged will-power needed to perform such miracles.

Was this perhaps the root cause of the disaffection between her and her mother? Not that her mother had not loved her enough, but that she had always unknowingly been jealous and resentful of her mother's gifts? Was she *jealous* of her mother's achievements? Was she masking those feelings by letting herself believe that it was her right to feel as she did... that the guilt, the betrayal, the blame were her mother's and not her own?

'Miss Danvers?'

Her head snapped round as the impatient male voice addressed her. She was used to the male awareness that momentarily overwhelmed this doctor's professionalism. It was a dubious gift, this dark, deep vein of sexuality that seemed to draw men to her in desire and need. Desire but not love. Something sharp and bitter moved inside her—an old wound, but one that had never healed.

To banish it she asked crisply, 'My mother...?'

'Alive. At the moment,' he told her, anticipating her question. He was focusing on her properly now, banishing his earlier awareness of her; a tall, thin man who was probably only six or seven years older than she was herself, but whose work had aged him prematurely. A gifted, intelligent man, but one who, at the moment, looked exhausted and impatient.

Fear smothered Sage's instinctive sympathy as she waited for him to go on.

'Your mother was unconscious when she was brought in—as yet we have no idea how serious her internal injuries are.'

'No idea...' Sage showed her shock. 'But...'

'We've been far too busy simply keeping her alive to do anything more than run the most cursory of tests. She's a very strong woman, otherwise she'd never have survived. She's conscious at the moment and she's asking for you. That's why I wanted to see you. Patients, even patients as gravely injured as your mother, react very quickly to any signs of distress or fear they pick up from their visitors, especially when those visitors are close family.'

'My mother was asking for *me*?' Sage queried, astonished.

'Yes!' He frowned at her. 'We had the devil of a job tracing you . . .'

Her mother had asked for *her*. Sage couldn't understand it. Why her? She would have expected her to ask for Faye, David's wife—David's widow—or for Camilla, David and Faye's daughter, but never for her.

'My sister-in-law——' she began, voicing her thoughts, but the surgeon shook his head brusquely.

'We have notified her, but at this stage we have to limit your mother's visitors. There's obviously something on her mind, something distressing her . . . With a patient as gravely ill as your mother, anything we can do to increase her chances of recovery, no matter how small, is vitally important, which is why I must stress that it is crucial that whatever it is your mother wants to say to you, however unlikely or inexplicable it seems, you must try to find a way of reassuring her. It's essential that we keep her as calm as we possibly can.'

The look he was giving her suggested that he had severe doubts that she would be able to do any such thing. Doubts which she herself shared, Sage acknowledged wryly.

'If you'd like to follow me,' he said now, and, as she followed him down the narrow, empty corridor leading off the main reception area, Sage was amused by the way he kept a wider than necessary physical distance between them. Was he a little intimidated by her? He wouldn't be the first man to react to her like that. All the nice men, the ones with whom she might have found something approaching peace and contentment, shared this ambiguous, wary attitude towards her. It was her looks, of course: they couldn't see beyond them, beyond the dangerous sensuality they invoked, making them see her as a woman who would never need their tenderness, never make allowances for their vulnerabilities. They were wrong, though. She had far too many vulnerabilities of her own to ever mock or make light of anyone else's. And as for tenderness—she smiled a bitter smile—only she knew how much and how often she had ached for its healing balm.

'This way,' he told her. Up ahead of them were the closed doors barring the way to the intensive care unit.

Sage shivered as he pushed open the door, an instinctive desire to stop, to turn and run, almost halting her footsteps. Somewhere beyond those doors lay her mother. Had she *really* asked for *her*? It seemed so out of character, so unbelievable almost, and the shock of it had thrown her off guard, disturbing the cool, indifferent, self-protective shield she had taken up all those years ago when the pain of her mother's final betrayal had destroyed her reluctant, aching love for her.

She shivered again, trying to recognise the unfamiliar image of her mother which the surgeon had held up for her. Surely in such extremity as her mother now suffered a person must always ask for whoever it was they most loved, and she had known almost all her life that for some reason her mother's love, given so freely and fiercely to others, had never really been given to her. Duty, care, responsibility...they had all been there, masquerading under the guise of mother love, but Sage had learned young to distinguish between reality and fiction and she had known then, had felt then that insurmountable barrier that existed between them.

As she hesitated at the door, the surgeon turned impatiently towards her.

'Are you sure she asked for me?' she whispered.

As he watched her for a moment he saw the self-confident, sensually stunning woman reduced to the nervous, uncertain child. It was the dangerous allure of seeing that child within such a woman that made him say more brusquely than he otherwise might, 'There's nothing for you to fear. Your mother's injuries are all internal. Outwardly...'

Sage glared at him. Did he really think she was so weak, so self-absorbed that it was fear of what she might *see* that kept her chained here outside the ward? And then her anger died as swiftly as it had been born. It wasn't *his* fault; what could he know of the complexities of her relationship with her mother? *She* didn't really understand them herself. She pushed open the door and walked into the ward. It was small, with only four beds, and bristling with equipment.

Her mother was the ward's only occupant. She lay on one of the high, narrow beds, surrounded by machinery.

How tiny she looked, Sage marvelled as she stared down at her. Her once naturally fair hair, now discreetly tinted blonde, was hidden out of sight beneath a cap; her mother's skin, so white and pale, and so different from her own with its decidedly olive tint, could have been the skin of a woman in her late forties, not her early sixties, Sage reflected as she absorbed an outer awareness of the tubes connected to her mother's body, which she deliberately held at bay as she concentrated instead on the familiar and less frightening aspects of her still figure.

Her breathing was laboured and difficult, but the eyes fixed on her own hadn't changed—cool, clear, all-seeing, all-knowing...a shade of grey which could deepen to lavender or darken to slate depending on her mood.

She was frowning now, but it was not the quick, light frown with which Sage was so familiar, the frown that suggested that whoever had caused it had somehow not just failed but disappointed as well. How many times had that frown marked the progress of her own life, turning her heart to lead, shredding her pride, reducing her to rebellious, helpless rage?

This frown, though, was different, deeper, darker, the eyes that watched her full of unfamiliar shadows.

'Sage...'

Was it instinct alone that made her cover her mother's hand with her own, that made her sit down at her side, and say as evenly as she could, 'I'm here, Mother...'?

Mother...what a cold, distant word that was, how devoid of warmth and feeling. As a small child she had called her 'Mummy'. David, ten years her senior, had preferred the affectionately teasing 'Ma', but then David had been permitted so much more licence, had been given so much more love... Stop it, she warned herself. She wasn't here to dwell on the past. The past was over.

'It's all right,' she whispered softly. 'It's all right, Mother. You're going to be fine...'

Just for a moment the grey eyes lightened and mocked. They seemed to say that they knew her platitude for exactly what it was, making Sage once more feel a child in the presence of an adult.

'Sage, there's something I want you to do...' The words were laboured and strained. Sage had to bend closer to the bed to catch them. 'My diaries, in my desk at Cottingdean... You must read them... All of you...'

She stopped speaking and closed her eyes while Sage stared at her. What on earth was her mother talking about? What diaries? Had her mind perhaps been affected by her injuries?

She stared uncertainly at the woman in the bed, as her mother opened her eyes and demanded fiercely, 'Promise me, Sage... Promise me you will do as I say... Promise me...'

Dutifully, docilely almost, Sage swallowed and whispered, 'I promise...' and then, unable to stop herself, she cried out, 'But why me...? Why did you ask for me? Why not Faye? She's so much closer to you...'

The grey eyes seemed to mock her again. Without her knowing it, her fingers had curled tightly round the hand she was still holding.

'Faye doesn't have your ruthlessness, your discipline... Neither does she have your strength.' The voice dropped to a faint sigh.

Beneath her fingers, Sage felt the thready pulse flicker and falter and a fear greater than anything she had ever

known, a fear that overwhelmed anger, resentment, pain
and even love poured through her and she cried out
harshly, 'Mother...no,' without really knowing what
she was crying out for.

Then she heard the light, quiet voice saying reassuringly, 'I'm here, Sage. When you read the diaries, *then*
you will understand.' She closed her eyes, so obviously
exhausted that for a moment Sage thought she had actually died.

It was the surgeon's firm touch on her arm, his quiet
words of reassurance that stilled her panic.

'She wants me to read her diaries,' she told him, too
bewildered to understand her need to confide, to
understand...

'Sometimes when people are closest to death they sense
what is happening to them and they dwell on certain
aspects of their lives and the lives of those around them.'

'I never even knew she kept a diary.' Sage was speaking
more to herself than him. 'I never knew... She made
me promise,' she told him inconsequentially, knowing
already that it was a promise she must keep. A promise
she *had* to keep, and yet already she was dreading doing
so, dreading what she might read...dreading perhaps
confronting the truth and the pain she thought she had
long ago put behind her.

As the surgeon escorted her from the ward, she cast
a last, lingering look at her mother. 'Will she...?'

Will she die? she wanted to ask, even while she knew
that she didn't want to know the answer, that she wanted
to hold on to the hope...the belief that because her
mother was alive she would live.

She had often heard people say that there was no pain,
no guilt, no awareness of life passing too quickly more
sharp-edged than when an adult experienced the death
of a parent.

Her father had died while she was a teenager, his death
a release to him and something that barely touched her
life. She had been at home then. Her father, because of
his poor health, had never played a large part in her life.
He was a remote, cosseted figure on whom her mother's

whole life pivoted and yet somehow someone who was distant from her own.

Until today she had thought she had stopped loving her mother over fifteen years ago, her love eroded by too much pain, too much betrayal—and she had decided then that the only way to survive the catalyst of that betrayal was for her to forge a separate, independent life of her own.

And that was what she had done.

She now had her own career, her own life. A life that took her from London to New York, from New York to LA to Rome, to Paris, to all those places in the new world where people had heard by word of mouth of her skills as a muralist.

There were houses all over the world—the kind of houses owned by people who would never dream of wanting them to be featured in even the most upmarket of glossy publications—where one of her murals was a prized feature of the décor. She was sought after and highly paid, working only on favoured commissions. Her life was her own...or so she had thought.

Why me? she had asked, and even in extremity her mother had not spared her. Of course, gentle, tender Faye would never have been able to bring herself to read another person's diaries...to pry into their privacy. What was it, then, that made it so important that she read them...that they all read them...so important that her mother should insist with what might well be her dying breath that they do so?

There was only one way that she was going to find out.

There was nothing to be gained in putting off what had to be done, Sage acknowledged as she left the hospital. As chance would have it, she was in between commissions at the moment and there was nothing of sufficient urgency in her life to excuse her from fulfilling the promise she had made to her mother, nothing to stop her from going immediately to Cottingdean, no matter how little she wanted to do so.

Cottingdean, the family's house, was on the outskirts of an idyllic English village set in a fold of the hills to the south-east of Bath. It was a tiny rural community over which her mother presided as its loving and much-loved matriach. Sage had never felt the same love for it that the rest of her family shared—for some reason it had stifled her, imprisoned her, and as a teenager she had ached for wider skies, broader horizons.

Cottingdean: Faye and Camilla would be waiting there for her, waiting to pounce on her with anxious questions about her mother.

How ironic it was that Faye, her sister-in-law, should be able to conjure from her mother the love she herself felt she had always been denied—and yet she could not resent Faye for it.

She sighed a little as she drove west heading for the M4. Poor Faye—life had not been kind to her, and she was too fragile... too vulnerable to withstand too many of its blows.

Sage remembered how Faye had looked the day she and David married...a pale, fragile, golden rose, openly adoring the man she was marrying, but that happiness had been short-lived. David had been killed in a tragic, useless road accident, leaving Faye to bring up Camilla on her own.

Sage hadn't been surprised when her mother had invited Faye to make her home at Cottingdean; after all, in the natural course of events, David would eventually have inherited the estate. Faye had accepted her offer— the pretty ex-vicarage in the village, which David had bought for his bride, was sold and Faye and her one-year-old daughter moved into Cottingdean. They had lived there ever since and Camilla had never known any other home, any other way of life.

Sage smiled as she thought of her niece; almost eighteen years old and probably in the eyes of the world spoiled rotten by all of them. If the three of them suffered deeply in losing David then some of the suffering had been eased by the gift he had left behind him.

One day Cottingdean and everything that it represented would be Camilla's, and already Sage had seen that her mother was discreetly teaching and training her one grandchild in the duties that would then fall on her shoulders.

Sage didn't envy her that inheritance, but she did sometimes envy her her sunny, even-tempered disposition, and the warmth that drew people to her in enchantment.

As yet she was still very much a child, still not really aware of the power she held.

Sage sighed. Of all of them Camilla would be the most deeply affected if her mother... Her hands gripped the wheel of the Porsche until her knuckles whitened. Even now she could not allow her mind to form the word 'die', couldn't allow herself to admit the possibility...the probability of her mother's death.

Unanalysed but buried deep within the most secret, sacred part of her, the instinctive, atavistic part of her that governed her so strongly, lay the awareness that to have refused the promise her mother had demanded of her, or even to have given it and then not to have carried out the task, would somehow have been to have helped to still the pulse of her mother's life force; it was as though there was some primitive power that linked the promise her mother had extracted from her with her fight against death, and if she broke that promise, even though her mother could not possibly know that it had been broken, it would be as though she had deliberately broken the symbolic silver thread of life.

She shuddered deeply, sharply aware as she had been on certain other occasions in her life of her own deep-rooted and sometimes disturbing awareness of feelings, instincts that had no logical basis.

Her long fingers tightened on the steering-wheel. She had none of her mother's daintiness—that had bypassed her to be inherited by Camilla. She had nothing of her mother in her at all, really, and yet in that brief moment of contact, standing beside her mother's bed, it had been for one terrifying milli-second of time as though their souls were one and she had felt as though it were her own her mother's fear and pain, her desperation and her determination; and she had known as well how over-whelmingly important it was to her mother that she kept her promise.

Because her mother knew she was going to die? A spasm of agony contracted Sage's body. She ought not to be feeling like this; she had dissociated herself from her mother years ago. Oh, she paid lip-service to their relationship, duty visits for her mother's birthday in June, and at Christmas, although she had not spent that Christmas at Cottingdean. She had been working in the Caribbean on the villa of a wealthy French socialite. A good enough excuse for not going home, and one her mother had accepted calmly and without comment.

She turned off the motorway, following the familiar road signs, frowning a little at the increased heaviness of the traffic, noting the unsuitability of the enormous eight-wheel container trucks for the narrow country lane.

She overtook one of them on the small stretch of bypass several miles east of the village, glad to be free of its choking diesel fumes.

They had had a hard winter, making spring seem doubly welcome, the fresh green of the new hedges striking her eye as she drove past them. In the village nothing seemed to have changed, and it amused her that she should find that knowledge reassuring, making her pause to wonder why, when she had been so desperate to escape from the place and its almost too perfect prettiness, she experienced this dread of discovering that it had changed in any way.

She had rung the house from the hospital and spoken to Faye, simply telling her that she was driving down but not explaining why.

Whoever had first chosen the site for Cottingdean had chosen well. It sat with its back to the hills, facing south, shielded from the east wind by the ancient oaks planted on the edge of its parkland.

The original house had been built by an Elizabethan entrepreneur, a merchant who had moved his family from Bristol out into the quiet and healthy solitude of the countryside. It was a solid, sensible kind of house, built in the traditional style, in the shape of the letter E. Later generations had added a jumble of extra buildings to its rear, but, either through lack of wealth or incentive, no one had thought to do anything to alter its stone frontage with its ancient mullions and stout oak door.

The drive still ran to the rear of the house and the courtyard around it on which were the stables and out-buildings, leaving the front of the house and its vistas completely unspoiled.

Sage's mother always said that the best way to see Cottingdean for the first time was on foot, crossing the bridge spanning the river, and then through the wooden gate set into the house's encircling garden wall, so that one's first view of it was through the clipped yews that guarded the pathway to the terrace and the front entrance.

When her mother had come to Cottingdean as a bride, the gardens which now were famous and so admired had been nothing more than a tangle of weeds interspersed with unproductive vegetable beds. Hard to imagine that now when one saw the smooth expanses of fresh green lawn, the double borders with their enviable collections of seemingly carelessly arranged perennials, the knot garden, and the yew hedges which did so much to add to the garden's allure and air of enticing, hidden secrets. All this had been created by her mother—and not, as some people imagined, with money and other people's hard work, but more often than not with her own hands.

As she drove into the courtyard Sage saw that Faye and Camilla were waiting for her. As soon as she stopped the car both of them hurried up to her, demanding in unison, 'Liz...Gran...how is she?'

'Holding her own,' she told them as she opened the door and climbed out. 'They don't know the extent of her injuries as yet. I spoke to the surgeon. He said we could ring again tonight...'

'But when can we see her?' Camilla demanded eagerly.

'She's on the open visiting list,' Sage told them. 'But the surgeon's told me that he'd like to have her condition stabilised for at least forty-eight hours before she has any more visitors.'

'But *you've* seen her,' Camilla pointed out.

Sage reached out and put her arm round her. She was so precious to them all in different ways, this child of David's. 'Only because she wanted to see *me*, Camilla... The surgeon was worried that with something preying on her mind she would——'

'Something preying on her mind... What?'

'Camilla, let Sage get inside and sit down before you start cross-questioning her,' Faye reproved her daughter gently. 'It isn't a very comfortable drive down from London these days with all the traffic... I wasn't sure what your plans are, but I've asked Jenny to make up your bed.'

'I'm not sure either,' Sage told her sister-in-law, following her inside and then pausing for a moment as her eyes adjusted to the dimness of the long panelled passageway that led from the back to the front of the house.

When her mother had first come to Cottingdean this panelling had been covered in paint so thick that it had taken her almost a year to get it clean. Now it glowed mellowly and richly, making one want to reach and touch it.

'I've asked Jenny to serve afternoon tea in the sitting-room,' Faye told her, opening one of the panelled doors. 'I wasn't sure if you would have had time to have any lunch...'

Sage shook her head—food was the last thing she wanted.

The sitting-room was on the side of the house and faced west. It was decorated in differing shades of yellow, a golden, sunny room furnished with an eclectic collection of pieces of furniture which somehow managed to look as though they were meant to be together. Another of her mother's talents.

It was a warm welcoming room, scented now with late-flowering pots of hyacinths in the exact shade of lav-

ender blue of the carpet covering the floor. A fire burned
in the grate, adding to the room's air of welcome, the
central heating radiators discreetly hidden away behind
grilles.

'Tell us about Gran, Sage,' Camilla demanded,
perching on a damask-covered stool at Sage's feet. 'How
is she?'

She was a pretty girl, blonde like her mother, but,
where Faye's blondeness always seemed fairly insipid,
Camilla's was warm and alive. Facially she was like her
grandmother, with the same startlingly attractive bone-
structure and the same lavender-grey eyes.

'Is she really going to be all right?'

Sage paused. Over her head, her eyes met Faye's. 'I
hope so,' she said quietly, and then added comfortingly,
'She's a very strong person, Camilla. If anyone has the
will to fight, to hold on to life...'

'We wanted to go to see her, but the hospital said she'd
asked for you...'

'Yes, there was something she wanted me to do.'

Both of them were looking at her, waiting...

'She said she wanted us...all of us, to read her
diaries... She made me promise that we would.' Sage
grimaced slightly. 'I didn't even know she kept a diary.'

'I did,' Camilla told them. 'I came downstairs one
night when I couldn't sleep and Gran was in the library,
writing. She told me then that she'd always kept one.
Ever since she was fourteen, though she didn't keep the
earliest ones...'

Ridiculous to feel pain, rejection over something so
insignificant, Sage told herself.

'She kept the diaries locked in the big desk—the one
that belonged to Grandpa,' Camilla volunteered. 'No one
else has a key.'

'I've got the key,' Sage told her gruffly. They had given
it to her at the hospital, together with everything else
they had found in her mother's handbag. She had hated
that...hated taking that clinically packaged bundle of
personal possessions...hated knowing why she had been
given them.

'I wonder why she wants us to read them,' Faye murmured. She looked oddly anxious, dread shadowing her eyes.

Sage studied her. She had got so used to her sister-in-law's quiet presence in the background of her mother's life that she never questioned why it was that a woman—potentially a very attractive and certainly, at forty-one, a relatively young woman—should want to choose that kind of life for herself.

Sage knew Faye had been devoted to David . . . that she had adored him, worshipped him almost, but David had been dead for over fifteen years, and, as far as she knew, in all that time there had never been another man in Faye's life.

Why did she choose to live like that? In another woman, Sage might have taken it as a sign that her marriage held so many bad memories that any kind of intimate relationship was anathema to her, but she knew how happy David and Faye had been, so why did Faye choose to immure herself here in this quiet backwater with only her mother-in-law and her daughter for company? Sage studied her sister-in-law covertly.

Outwardly, Faye always appeared calm and controlled—not in the same powerful way as her mother, Sage recognised. Faye's self-control was more like a shield behind which she hid from the world. Now the soft blue eyes flickered nervously, the blonde hair which, during the days of her marriage, she had worn flowing free drawn back off her face into a classic chignon, her eyes and mouth touched with just the merest concession to make-up. Faye was a beautiful woman who always contrived to look plain and, watching her, it occurred to Sage to wonder why. Or was her curiosity about Faye simply a way of putting off what she had come here to do?

Now, with both Faye and Camilla watching her anxiously, Sage found herself striving to reassure them as she told them firmly, 'Knowing Mother, she probably wants us to read them because she thinks whatever she's written in them will help us to run things properly while she's recovering.'

Faye gave her a quick frown. 'But Henry's in charge of the mill, and Harry still keeps an eye on the flock, even though his grandson's officially taken over.'

'Who's going to chair the meeting of the action group against the new road, if Gran isn't well enough?' Camilla put in, making Sage's frown deepen.

'What road?' she demanded.

'They're planning to route a section of the new motorway to the west of the village,' Faye told her. 'It will go right through the home farm lands, and within yards of this side of the village. Your mother's been organising an action group to protest against it. She's been working on finding a feasible alternative route. We had a preliminary meeting of the action group two weeks ago. Of course, they elected your mother as chairperson...'

The feelings of outrage and anger she experienced were surely wholly at odds with her feelings towards Cottingdean and the village, Sage acknowledged. She'd been only too glad to escape from the place, so why did she feel this fierce, protective swell of anger that anyone should dare to destroy it to build a new road?

'What on earth are we going to do without her?' Faye demanded in distress.

For a moment she seemed close to tears, and Sage was relieved when the door opened and her mother's housekeeper came in with the tea-trolley.

Afternoon tea was an institution at Cottingdean, and one which had begun when her parents had first come to the house. Her father, an invalid even in those days, had never had a good appetite, and so her mother had started this tradition of afternoon tea, trying to tempt him to eat.

Jenny and Charles Openshaw had worked for her mother for over five years as her housekeeper and gardener-cum-chauffeur, a pleasant Northern couple in their mid-fifties. It had been Charles's unexpected redundancy which had prompted them to pool their skills and to look for a job as a 'live-in couple'.

Charles's redundancy money had been used to purchase a small villa in the Canaries. They had bought wisely on a small and very strictly controlled development and, until they retired, the villa was to be let through an agency, bringing them in a small extra income.

Sage liked them both very much; brisk and uncompromising in their outlook, they had nothing servile or over-deferential in their manner. Their attitude to their work was strictly professional—they were valued members of the household, treated by her mother, as they had every right to be, with the same respect for their skills as she treated everyone else who worked for her.

Now, once she had informed Sage that her old bedroom was ready for her, Jenny asked how her mother was.

Sage told her, knowing that Jenny would guess at all that she was not saying and be much more aware of the slenderness of the chances of her mother's full recovery than either Faye or Camilla could allow themselves to be.

'Oh! I almost forgot,' Jenny told Sage. 'Mr Dimitrios telephoned just before you arrived.'

'Alexi.' Sage sighed. He would be furious with her, she suspected. She was supposed to be having dinner with him tonight and she had rung his apartment before leaving the hospital to leave a message on his answering machine, telling him briefly what had happened, and promising to try to ring him later.

He had been pursuing her for almost two months now, an unknown length of time for him to pursue any woman without taking her to bed, he had informed her on their last date.

There was no real reason why they should not become lovers. He was a tall, athletic-looking man with a good body and a strong-boned face. Sage had been introduced to him in Sydney while she had been working there

on a commission. He was one of the new generation of
Greek Australians; wealthy, self-assured, macho, in a way
which she had found amusing.

She had forgotten what it was like to be pursued so
aggressively. It had been almost two years since she had
last had a lover; a long time, especially when, she was
the first to admit, she found good sex to be one of life's
more enjoyable pleasures.

That was the thing, of course. Good sex wasn't that
easy to come by—or was it simply that as the years passed
she was becoming more choosy, more demanding . . . less
inclined to give in to the momentary impulse to respond
to the ache within herself and the lure of an attractive
man?

Of course, her work kept her very busy, allowing her
little time for socialising or for self-analysis, which was
the way she liked things. She had spent too many
wearying and unproductive hours of her time looking
for the impossible, aching for what she could not
have . . . yearning hopelessly and helplessly until she had
made a decision to cut herself off from the past to start
life anew and live it as it came. One day at a time, slowly
and painfully like a person learning to walk again after
a long paralysis.

Sage acknowledged that her lack of concern at Alexi's
potential anger at her breaking of their date suggested
that her desire for him was only lukewarm at least. She
smiled easily at Jenny and told her that she wasn't sure
as yet how long she would be staying.

Tomorrow she'd have to drive back to London and
collect some clothes from her flat, something she ought
to have done before coming down here, but when she'd
left the hospital she had been in no mood to think of
such practicalities. All she had been able to concentrate
on was her mother, and fulfilling her promise to her.
Her mother had always said she was too impulsive and
that she never stopped to think before acting.

After Jenny had gone, she drank her tea impatiently,
ignoring the small delicacies Jenny had provided. She
admitted absently that she probably ought to eat some-

thing, but the thought of food nauseated her. It struck her that she was probably suffering from shock, but she was so used to the robustness of her physical health that she barely gave the idea more than a passing acknowledgement.

Seeing her restlessness, Faye put down her teacup as well. 'The diaries,' she questioned uneasily. 'Did Liz really mean all of us to read them?'

'Yes. I'm afraid so. I'm as reluctant to open them as you are, Faye. Knowing Mother and how meticulous she is about everything, I'm sure they contain nothing more than detailed records of her work on the house, the estate and the mill. But I suspect the human race falls into two distinct groups: those people like you and me who feel revulsion at the thought of prying into something as intimate as a diary, and those who are our opposites, who relish the thought of doing so. I have no idea *why* Mother wants us to read the things . . . *I* don't want to do it any more than you do, but I gave my promise.' She paused, hesitating about confiding to Faye her ridiculous feeling that if she didn't, if she broke her promise, she would somehow be shortening the odds on her mother's survival and then decided against it, feeling that to do so would be to somehow or other attempt to escape from the burden of that responsibility by putting it on to Faye's so much more fragile shoulders.

'I suppose I might as well make a start. We may as well get it over with as quickly as possible. We can ring the hospital again at eight tonight, and hope that all of us will be able to visit tomorrow . . . I thought that as I read each diary I could pass them on to you, and then you could pass them on to Camilla, once you've read them.'

'Where will you do it?' Faye asked her nervously. 'In here, or . . .?'

'I might as well use the library,' Sage told her. 'I'll get Charles to light the fire in there.'

Even now, knowing there was no point in delaying, she was deliberately trying to find reasons to put off what she had to do. Did she really need a fire in the library?

The central heating was on. It startled her, this insight into her own psyche... What was she afraid of? Confirmation that her mother didn't love her? Hadn't she accepted that lack of love years ago...? Or was it the reopening of that other, deeper, still painful wound that she dreaded so much? Was it the thought of reading about that time so intensely painful to her that she had virtually managed to wipe her memory clear of it altogether?

What was she so afraid of...?

Nothing, she told herself firmly. Why *should* she be...? She had *nothing* to fear... *nothing* at all. She picked up the coffee-coloured linen jacket she had been wearing and felt in the pocket for her mother's keys.

It was easy to spot the ones belonging to the old-fashioned partners' desk in the library, even if she hadn't immediately recognised them.

'The diaries are in the drawers on the left side of the desk,' Camilla told her quietly, and then, as though sensing what Sage thought she had successfully hidden, she asked uncertainly, 'Do you... would you like us to come with you?'

For a moment Sage's face softened and then she said derisively, 'It's a set of diaries I'm going to read, Camilla, not a medieval text on witchcraft... I doubt that they'll contain anything more dangerous or illuminating than Mother's original plans for the garden and a list of sheep-breeding records.'

She stood up swiftly, and walked over to the door, pausing there to ask, 'Do you still have dinner at eight-thirty?'

'Yes, but we could change that if you wish,' Faye told her.

Sage shook her head. 'No... I'll read them until eight and then we can ring the hospital.'

As she closed the door behind her, she stood in the hall for a few minutes. The spring sunshine turned the panelling the colour of dark honey, illuminating the huge pewter jugs of flowers and the enormous stone cavern of the original fireplace.

The parquet floor was old and uneven, the rugs lying on it rich pools of colour. The library lay across the hall from the sitting-room, behind the large drawing-room. She stared at the door, and turned swiftly away from it, towards the kitchen, to find Charles and ask him to make up the fire.

While he was doing so she went upstairs. Her bedroom had been redecorated when she was eighteen. Her mother had chosen the furnishings and the colours as a surprise, and she had, Sage admitted, chosen them well.

The room was free of soft pretty pastels, which would have been far too insipid for her, and instead was decorated in the colours she loved so much: blues, reds, greens; colours that drew out the beauty of the room's panelled walls.

The huge four-poster bed had been made on the estate from their own wood; her name and date of birth were carved on it, and the frieze decorating it had carved in the wood the faces of her childhood pets. A lot of care had gone into its design and execution; to anyone else the bed would have been a gift of great love, but she had seen it merely as the execution of what her mother conceived to be her duty. *Her* daughter was eighteen and of age, and therefore she must have a gift commensurate with such an occasion.

In the adjoining bathroom, with its plain white suite and dignified Edwardian appearance, Sage washed her hands and checked her make-up. Her lipstick needed renewing, and her hair brushing.

She smiled mirthlessly at herself as she did so... Still putting off the evil hour... why? What was there after all to fear... to reveal...? She already knew the story of her mother's life as *everyone* locally knew it. It was as blameless and praiseworthy as that of any saint.

Her mother had come to this house as a young bride, with a husband already seriously ill, his health destroyed by the war. They had met when her mother worked as a nursing aide, fallen in love and married and come to live here at Cottingdean, the estate her father had inherited from a cousin.

Everyone knew her mother had arrived here when she was eighteen to discover that the estate her husband had drawn for her in such glowing colours—the colours of his own childhood—had become a derelict eyesore.

Everyone knew how her mother had worked to restore it to what it had once been. How she had had the foresight and the drive to start the selective breeding programme with the estate's small flock of sheep that was to produce the very special fleece of high-quality wool.

But how her mother had had the vision to know that there would come a time when such wool was in high demand, how she had had the vision to persuade her husband to allow her to experiment with the production of that wool, let alone the run-down mill, Sage realised she had no idea, and with that knowledge came the first stirrings of curiosity.

Everyone knew of the prosperity her mother had brought to the village, of the new life she had breathed into Cottingdean. Everyone knew of the joys and sorrows of her life; of the way she had fought to keep her husband alive, of the cherished son she had borne and lost, of the recalcitrant and troublesome daughter she was herself...

No, there were no real secrets in her mother's life. No reason why she herself should experience this tension...this dread...this fear almost that made her so reluctant to walk into the library and unlock the desk.

And yet it had to be done. She had given her word, her promise. Sighing faintly, Sage went back downstairs. She hesitated outside the library door for a second and then lifted the latch and went in.

The fire was burning brightly in the grate and someone, Jenny, no doubt, had thoughtfully brought in a fresh tray of coffee.

As she closed the door behind her, Sage remembered how as a child this room had been out of bounds to her. It had been her father's sanctuary; from here he had been able to sit in his wheelchair and look out across the gardens.

He and her mother had spent their evenings in here...
Stop it, Sage told herself. You're not here to dwell on
the past. You're here to read about it.

She surprised herself by the momentary hope that the
key would refuse to unlock the drawers, but, of course,
it did. They were heavy and old, and slid surprisingly
easily on their wooden runners. A faint musty scent of
herbs and her mother's perfume drifted up towards her
as she opened them.

She could see the diaries now; far more of them than
she had imagined, all of them methodically numbered
and dated, as though her mother had always known that
there would come a time, as though she had deliberately
planned...

But *why*? Sage wondered as she reached tensely into
the drawer and removed the first diary.

She found her hands were shaking as she opened it,
the words blurring as she tried to focus on them. She
didn't want to do this... could not do it, and yet even
in her reluctance she could almost feel the pressure of
her mother's will, almost hear her whispering, You
promised...

She blinked rapidly to clear her eyes and then read
the first sentence.

'*Today I met Kit...*'

'Kit...' Sage frowned and turned back the page to
check on the date. This diary had begun when her mother
was seventeen. Soon after her eighteenth birthday she
had been married. So who was this Kit?

Nebulous, uneasy feelings stirred inside her as Sage
stared reluctantly at the neat, evenly formed handwriting. It was like being confronted with a dark passage
you had to go down and yet feared to enter. And yet,
after all, what was there to fear?

Telling herself she was being stupid, she picked up the
diary for the second time and started to read.

'*Today I met Kit.*'

CHAPTER ONE

Spring 1945

'TODAY *I met Kit.*'

Just looking at the words made her go dizzy with happiness, Lizzie acknowledged, staring at them, knowing it was impossible to translate into cold, dry print the whole new world of feelings and emotions which had opened up in front of her.

Yesterday her life had been bound and encompassed by the often arduous routine of her work as a nursing aide: long hours, low pay, and all the horrid dirty jobs that real nurses were too valuable to spend their time on.

She would rather have stayed on at school, but, with her parents killed in one of the many bombing raids on London, she had had no option but to accept her great-aunt's ruling that she must leave school and start to earn her living.

Aunt Vi didn't mean to be unkind, but she wasn't a sentimental woman and had never married. She had no children of her own, and, as she was always telling her great-niece, she had only agreed to take Lizzie in out of a sense of family duty. She herself had been sent out to work at thirteen, skivvying in service at the local big house. She had worked hard all her life and had slowly made her way up through the levels of service until she had eventually become housekeeper to Lord and Lady Jeveson.

Lizzie had found it bewildering at first, leaving the untidy but comfortable atmosphere of the cramped terraced house where she had lived with her parents and grandparents, evacuated from the busy, dusty streets so familiar to her to this place called 'the country', where everything was strange and where she missed her ma and pa dreadfully, crying in her sleep every night and wishing she were back in London.

Aunt Vi wasn't like her ma ... for a start she didn't talk the way her ma did. Aunt Vi talked posh and sounded as though her mouth was full of sharp, painful stones. She had made Lizzie speak the same way, endlessly and critically correcting her, until sometimes poor Lizzie felt as though she dared not open her mouth.

That had been four years ago, when she had first come to the country. Now she had almost forgotten what her ma and pa had looked like; her memories of them and the dusty terraced house seemed to belong to another life, another Lizzie. She had grown accustomed to Aunt Vi's pernickety ways, her sharp manner.

Only yesterday one of the other girls at the hospital, a new girl from another village, had commented on Lizzie's lack of accent, taunting her about her 'posh' speech, making her realise how much she had changed from the awkward, rebellious thirteen-year-old who had arrived on Aunt Vi's doorstep.

Aunt Vi knew how things should be done. No great-niece of hers was going to grow up with the manners and speech of a kitchen tweeny, she had told Lizzie so many times that she often thought the words were engraved in her heart.

She had hated it at first when her aunt had got her this job at the hospital, but Aunt Vi had firmed up her mouth and eyed her with cold determination when Lizzie had pleaded to be allowed to stay on at school, telling her sharply that she couldn't afford to have a great lazy girl eating her out of house and home and not bringing in a penny piece.

Besides, she had added acidly, in case Lizzie hadn't realised it, there was a war on and it was her duty to do what she could to aid her countrymen. Aunt Vi had made up her mind. The matron of the hospital was one of her friends, and, before Lizzie had time to draw breath, she was installed in the hostel not far from the hospital grounds, in a dormitory with a dozen other girls, all of them working the same long, gruelling hours, although the others, unlike Lizzie, spent their free time not on their own but in giggling, excited groups, vying with one another to present the most enticing appearance for their weekly visits to nearby barracks to attend their Saturday night dances.

They made fun of Lizzie, taunting her because she held herself aloof from them, because she was 'different', and not just because of the way she spoke.

Aunt Vi was very strict, and, even though Lizzie was no longer living under her jurisdiction, the lessons she had enforced on her made it painfully difficult for Lizzie to throw off her aunt's warnings about what happened to girls foolish enough to listen to the brash flattery of boys who 'only wanted one thing' and who 'would get a girl into trouble as soon as look at her'.

Aunt Vi had no very high opinion of the male sex, which, in her view, was best kept at a distance by any right-minded female.

She herself had grown up in a harsh world, where a single woman who managed to rise to the position of housekeeper in a wealthy upper-class home was far, far better off than her married sisters, who often had half a dozen dependent children and a husband who might or might not be inclined to support them all.

Men, in her opinion, were not to be trusted, and Lizzie had a natural sensitivity that made her recoil from the often clumsy and always suggestive passes of the few young men she did come into contact with.

This was wartime and young men did not have the time, or the necessity, to waste their energy, and what might only be a very brief life, in coaxing a girl when there were so many who did not want such coaxing.

The only other men Lizzie met were the patients in the hospital, men who had been so badly injured that it was tacitly admitted that nothing more could be done for them, and so they lay here in the huge, decaying old building, economically and clinically nursed by young women who had learned to seal themselves off from human pity and compassion, who had seen so many broken bodies, so many maimed human beings, so many tormented young male minds that they could no longer agonise over what they saw.

For Lizzie it was different. She had wondered at first when she came to the hospital if she might eventually try to qualify as a nurse, but after a year there, a year when she had seen a constant stream of young men, their minds and bodies destroyed by this thing called war, lying in the wards, when she had seen the hopelessness in their eyes, the anger, the pain, the sheer bitter resentment at their loss of the future they had once anticipated, she had known that she did not have the mental stamina for nursing.

With every familiar patient who left the wards, taken home by a family helpless to cope with the physical and mental burdens of their sons and husbands, and with every new arrival, her heart bled a little more, and she could well understand why the other girls sought relief from the trauma of working with such men by spending their free nights with the healthy, boisterous, whole representatives of manhood they picked up at the dances they attended.

That the Americans were the best was the universal opinion of her colleagues; Americans were generous and fun to be with. There were some stationed on the other side of the village, and once or twice one of them had tried to chat her up when Lizzie walked there to post her weekly duty letter to Aunt Vi.

She always ignored them, steeling her heart against their coaxing smiles and outrageous invitations, but she was only seventeen, and often, once she was safely out of sight, she would wonder wistfully what it would be like to be one half of the kind of perfect whole that was formed when two people loved with the intensity she had envied in her reading.

Lizzie was an avid reader, and a daydreamer. When she had first come to live with Aunt Vi, she had barely opened a book in her life, but, in addition to ceaselessly correcting her speech and her manners, Aunt Vi had also insisted that her great-niece read what she had termed 'improving books'.

The chance munificence of a large trunkful of books from the vicar's wife, which had originally belonged to her now adult children, had furnished Lizzie with the ability to escape from Aunt Vi's strict and sometimes harsh domination into a world she had hitherto not known existed.

From her reading Lizzie discovered the tragedy of the love between Tristan and Iseult, and started to dream of emotions which had nothing in common with the clumsy overtures of the outwardly brash young men with whom she came into contact. Their very brashness, the fact that her sensitive soul cringed from their lack of finesse and from the often unwelcome conversation and revelations of the other girls in her dormitory, made it easy for her to bear in mind Aunt Vi's strictures that she was to keep herself to herself and not to get up to any 'funny business'.

By funny business Aunt Vi meant sex, a subject which was never openly referred to in her aunt's house. As far as Aunt Vi was concerned, sex was something to be ignored as though it did not exist. Lizzie had naïvely assumed that all women shared her aunt's views, until she had come to work at the hospital. From her peers' conversations she had learned otherwise, but until now she had felt nothing other than a vague yearning awareness that her life was somehow incomplete... that some vital part of it was missing. She had certainly never contemplated sharing with any of the men she had met the intimacies she heard the other girls discussing so openly and shockingly... Until now...

She stared dreamily at her diary. It had been at Aunt Vi's insistence that she had first started keeping a diary, not to confide her most private thoughts in, but as a factual record of the achievements of her days.

It was only since she had come to work at the hospital that she had found herself confiding things to her diary that were little more than nebulous thoughts and dreams.

Kit... Even now she was dazzled by the wonder of meeting him... of being able to whisper his name in the secret, private recess of her mind, while her body shivered with nervous joy.

Kit... He was so different... so special, so breathtakingly wonderful.

She had known the moment she saw him. He had turned his head and smiled at her, and suddenly it was as though her world had been flooded with warmth and magic.

And to think, if she hadn't decided to go and visit poor Edward, she would never have met Kit... She shook with the enormity of how narrowly she had averted such a tragedy.

Edward Danvers had been with them for many months now; a major in the army, he had been badly injured in Normandy... his legs crushed and his spine injured, resulting in the eventual amputation of both his legs.

He had come to them supposedly to recuperate from a second operation, but Lizzie knew, as they all knew, that in fact he had come to them because there was nowhere else for him to go. His parents were dead, he wasn't married, and privately Lizzie suspected that he himself no longer had any desire to live. He wasn't like some of the men who came to them: he didn't rage and rail against his fate; outwardly placid and calm, he seemed to accept it, but Lizzie had seen the way he looked inwards into himself, instead of out into the world, and had known that she was looking at a man who was gradually closing himself off from that world. Willing himself to die, almost.

He never spoke about his injuries. Never complained, as some of the men did, about fictitious limbs that were still there. Outwardly, he seemed to have adjusted well to his amputations, quietly allowing the nurses to get him into a chair, so that Lizzie, or one of the other aides, could wheel him into the gardens.

Lizzie liked him, although she knew that most of the other girls found him poor company, complaining that

he never laughed or joked like the other men and that
he was a real misery.

Lizzie didn't mind his silences—she knew that he particularly liked to be wheeled round the gardens. He had
told her once that they reminded him of the gardens of
his grandparents' home.

Cottingdean, it was called, and when he talked about
it Lizzie could tell that it was a place he loved and that,
in some way, the memory of it brought him both joy
and pain. Sometimes when he mentioned it she would
see the bright sheen of tears in his eyes and would wonder
why, if he loved it so much, he stayed here, but she was
too sensitive to question him, too aware of the deep, raw
pain he kept hidden from the others.

She liked him and discovered, as the months went by,
that she looked forward to seeing him, to winning from
him his fugitive, reluctant smile.

Like her, he enjoyed reading, and when he discovered
that she had read, and now reread, everything the vicar's
wife had donated to her he offered to lend her some of
his own books. She refused, worrying about the wisdom
of leaving them in the dormitory. The other girls would
not deliberately damage them, but they were not always
as careful with other people's property as they might
have been.

Gradually, a tentative friendship developed between
them and often, on her days off, she would spend time
with Edward, taking him out in the garden if the weather
was fine, sometimes reading aloud to him when it wasn't,
knowing how much the mere effort of holding a book
sometimes tired him.

She made no mention of Edward in her letters home
to her aunt. Aunt Vi would not have approved. Edward
came from a very different world from her own and Aunt
Vi did not approve of any mingling of the classes. It
always led to trouble, she had warned Lizzie.

It made her blood run cold now to remember that,
on this particular Thursday, she had almost decided
against spending her precious time off with Edward. She
had woken up in an odd, restless, uncomfortable mood,

her mind and body filled with vague, unfamiliar yearnings, but then she had reminded herself that Edward would be looking forward to going out. The rhododendrons were in full flower in the park, and he had been looking forward to seeing them for days. The sun was out, the sky a clear, soft blue... No, it wouldn't be fair to let him down.

And so, suppressing her rebellious yearnings, she had washed in the cold, shabby bathroom which all the girls shared, allowing herself the luxury of washing her hair, and wondering at the same time if she dared to have it cut. She was the only girl in the hostel who wore her hair in such an old-fashioned style, braided into a neat coronet, which Aunt Vi insisted upon. She wondered idly for a moment what she would look like with one of the shoulder-length bobs worn with such suggestive insouciance by some of the other girls, and then sighed as she studied her make-up-free reflection in the spotted mirror.

The other girls wore powder and lipstick, and cheap perfume given to them by their American boyfriends. They curled their hair and darkened their eyelashes with shoe blacking and, if they were lucky enough to own a pair of the coveted nylons, they deliberately wore their skirts short enough to show off their legs.

As she dressed in the serviceable cotton underwear which Aunt Vi's strict teachings ensured that she spent her precious allowance of soap scrupulously washing until her hands were almost raw and bleeding, to ensure that it stayed white, she admitted that lipstick and fashionably bobbed hair were not for her.

She knew the other girls laughed at her behind her back, mimicking her accent and making fun of her clothes.

Aunt Vi had practised a lifetime of frugality and, as Lizzie had grown out of the clothes she had originally arrived with from London, the older woman had altered garments from the trunks full of clothes she had been given by her employers over the years to fit her great-niece, and, in doing so, had also turned the exercise into lessons in dressmaking and fine plain sewing.

That the skirt she was wearing now had once belonged to Lady Jeveson would have impressed the other girls in the hostel as little as it impressed her, although for different reasons, Lizzie acknowledged. The other girls would have screamed with laughter and derision at the thought of wearing something which had first been worn by a girl who was now a grandmother.

That quality of cloth never wore out, Aunt Vi declared firmly, and indeed it did not, Lizzie reflected wryly, fingering the heavy, pleated tweed.

It was a pity that Lady Jeveson had not favoured the soft pastel colours more suited to her own fair colouring, rather than the dull, horsy tweeds of which she had apparently been so fond. The blouse she was wearing might be silk, but it was a dull beige colour which did nothing for her skin, just like the brown cashmere cardigan she wore over it.

She had seen the other girls, on their days off, going out in bright, summery dresses, with thin floating skirts and the kind of necklines which would have shocked Aunt Vi, and, while she knew that she could never have worn anything so daring, this morning Lizzie found herself wishing that her blouse might have been a similar shade of lavender-grey to her eyes, and that her skirt might have been made out of a fine, soft wool, and not this heavy, itchy stuff, which was a physical weight on her slender hips.

There were no nylons for her. She had to make do either with bare legs, which the rough wool made itch dreadfully, or the thick, hand-knitted stockings her aunt had sent her for Christmas.

She wasn't sure what had made her opt for bare legs, what particular vanity had decreed that this morning she would not be sensible and wear the hated stockings, knowing that they made her slender ankles look positively thick, even if they were warm and practical.

The hostel was just across the village from the hospital, and Lizzie cycled there on an ancient bicycle. When they were on duty, the girls ate at the hospital; not the same food as the patients, but meals which the others often angrily derided as 'not fit for pigs'.

Certainly, the meals were stodgy and unappetising, and not a patch on Aunt Vi's dishes. Her aunt might almost be bordering on the parsimonious, she might make every penny do the work of two, but she was a good cook, and Lizzie missed her appetising meals, the fresh vegetables and fruit in season which she always managed to obtain by some country means of barter.

This morning, since she wasn't on duty, there would be no breakfast for her at the hostel, and, since the girls were not allowed to cook food in the hostel, that meant either whatever she could buy and eat on the way to the hospital, or an expensive and not very appetising snack in the village's one and only café.

Trying not to let herself think about her aunt's porridge, thick and creamy with the top of Farmer Hobson's milk, Lizzie told herself stoically that she didn't really want any breakfast.

All the girls were always hungry; their workload was heavy, and no matter how unappetising they found their food it was always eaten.

All of them were a little on the thin side, Lizzie in particular as she was more fine-boned than the rest, with tiny, delicate wrists and ankles that sometimes looked so frail that they might snap.

As she cycled towards the village, she could feel the sun beating down on to the back of her head and smell the fresh warm scent of late spring, mingling with the tantalising suggestion of the summer still to come.

As she rode, wisps of blonde hair escaped from her coronet and curled in feathery tendrils round her face. At first, the other girls had refused to believe her hair was naturally fair, accusing her of dyeing it.

She chose not to ride through the village but to circle round it, using a narrow side-road which meandered towards the rear entrance to the hospital.

Before the war, the hospital had been a grand house, and the lane she was using had originally been that used by the tenants and the tradespeople.

She was cycling happily down the centre of it when she heard the car, the sound so unexpected that at first she made no attempt to move off the crown of the road. The village saw its fair share of wartime traffic; the squire's wife still drove her car on Red Cross business and Lizzie was used to the imperious sound of car horns demanding the right of way, especially when they were driven by excitable young men in uniform.

She was not, though, used to them being driven down this narrow little lane which led only to the hospital, which was why, lost in her own daydreams, she did not initially react to the sound of this one until it was almost too late.

The realisation that someone was driving up behind her, that the car was one of those expensive, open-topped sporty models driven by a young man with wind-blown thick black hair, bronzed skin, and the dashing uniform of an airforce pilot, hit her in a series of small shocks as she glanced over her shoulder and saw the shiny dark green bonnet of the car, realised that there wasn't room for both of them on the narrow little road, tried desperately to turn to one side, and lost her balance at the same time. The young man stopped his car with a cacophony of squealing tyres, protesting engine and angrily bellowed complaints about her sanity.

Lying on the dusty road, her knees stinging with pain and her eyes with tears, Lizzie wished devoutly that a large hole would appear beneath her into which she could conveniently disappear.

Her face scarlet with mortification and embarrassment, she struggled to her feet, at the same time as she heard the car door slam.

'I say, are you OK? That was a nasty tumble you took... I thought you'd heard me...'

'I did...but I didn't realise... Well, no one ever drives down this road...'

She was on her feet now, her face still red, a tiny voice inside her deriding her for her vanity in not wearing the woollen stockings which would have protected her now smarting skin from the road, all too conscious of the appearance she must present to this unbelievably handsome young man who was now standing next to her, towering over her, looking at her in a way which made her loathe and castigate Lady Jeveson for ever being stupid enough to choose such unflattering clothes.

Two bright spots of colour burned on her cheekbones as she realised what was happening to her. For the first time in her life she was experiencing the dizzying, dangerous sensation of falling helplessly in love with a stranger—that sensation, that awareness... that feeling which she had heard so often described by the others.

The unexpectedness of it distracted her momentarily, her mouth half parting at the wonder of it, so that Kit Danvers found his attention caught by her, despite the awfulness of her clothes and the hairstyle that made her look like photographs he had seen of his grandmother.

If one really studied her it was possible to see that she was quite a looker, he recognised with the ease of a master long used to seeking out his quarry in the most unexpected of places.

Finding pearls hidden in dull oysters was Kit Danvers's speciality—the other men in the mess envied him for it, admiringly, if sometimes resentfully, recognising that when it came to women Kit Danvers had something, some unrecognised quality that the female sex found it impossible to resist.

Lizzie knew none of this. She only knew that as she looked into the laughing blue eyes looking back into hers, as she studied the handsome tanned face with its firm male bone-structure and its warm smile, something inside her melted and uncurled, something completely new to her and yet as old as Eve.

'You've got a smudge on your nose... There, it's gone.'

She held her breath as he leaned towards her and carelessly rubbed his thumb against her skin. A thousand pin-pricks of sensation were born where his touch had been, an odd yearning constricting her breathing, her body suddenly tense and yet languorous at the same time.

'Look, you can't ride that thing now... Why don't I give you a lift to wherever you're going...?'

'The hospital—I'm going to the hospital,' Lizzie told him breathlessly, scarcely conscious of what she was saying, unable to take her wondering gaze off his handsome, smiling face. 'I work there.'

'You do? Now, there's a coincidence. I'm on my way there too. They told me in the place where I'm staying that this road would get me there quietly and discreetly. Not supposed to be running this job really, you know,' he told her, patting the bonnet of his car. 'And she's a thirsty lady. But when you're in the forefront of a war you're entitled to a few perks. Luckily the Yanks aren't as parsimonious with their petrol as our people, and I know this Yank...' He broke off and smiled winsomely at her. 'Boring you to death, I expect. A pretty girl like you doesn't want...'

A pretty girl... Lizzie gazed adoringly at him. He thought her pretty... her heart raced and sang, and then she remembered all Aunt Vi's stern teachings and turned her head away from the dangerous potency of that warm smile, saying shakily, as she tried to pick up her cycle, 'I really must go... I'm sorry I didn't hear you coming...'

'Going to be late for work, are you? What do you do up there... nurse?'

'No, actually, I'm a nursing aide,' Lizzie told him and for some reason the surprise in his eyes hurt her a little. It had never mattered when other people spoke derisively about the lowly status of her work, but now, suddenly, for this handsome laughing young man, she ached to be able to announce that she did something very important...

'Well, we don't want you getting into trouble for being late. Not when it was really my fault. Hop in... I'll strap your cycle to the back.'

'I'm not actually working,' Lizzie told him, hesitating beside the car. It would be breaking all Aunt Vi's rules and her own to accept his offer of a lift, but she wanted to do so more than she had wanted anything else in her life. 'I'm going to visit someone...'

Immediately his glance sharpened. 'Boyfriend?' he questioned her, making her blush and shake her head.

'No, it's one of the patients... I promised him I'd wheel him out to see the rhododendrons now they're in flower. He says they remind him of his grandparents' home when he was a little boy...'

'Sensitive little thing, aren't you? A no-hoper, is he?'

Something in the careless way he spoke jarred on Lizzie's tender conscience; even though she knew that for Edward Danvers life could never ever be anything other than painful and lonely, she said quickly, 'No—no, of course not...'

Perhaps it was the stark contrast between the two men: Edward so pale and thin, old before his time, his body wasted, his manhood destroyed by the same terrible injuries which had necessitated the amputation of his legs.

It had happened in the frantic push to land on the Normandy beaches. He had been helping to organise the disembarkation, standing chest-deep in the icy cold water. Someone had got into difficulty in the water—a young private who couldn't swim—Edward had dived down to help him, and had been crushed beneath some landing equipment in the rush to get the troops ashore.

Edward's life had been saved but not his legs, and even now in his nightmares he cursed God for that cruel mercy.

In her mind's eye Lizzie saw him, so thin and wasted in his wheelchair, and compared him to this man, so fit and healthy, so insolently cheerful and careless of whatever dangers fate had in store for him, and suddenly and unexpectedly she was overwhelmed by a swift surge of protective, possessive fear, by a need to take him to herself and keep him safe... It was the first time she had ever experienced such an emotion and it stunned her, leaving her feeling too vulnerable and weak to object when he insisted on helping her into his car, and fastening her bike across its boot.

The space inside the car was so tiny that when he got in she was immediately conscious of the heat of his body, of its warm male scent, of all the differences of sex that separated them and stirred exciting *frissons* of sensation in every corner of her body, in her blood, under her skin, a tingling dangerous wave of heat that made her cheeks burn and her heart pound.

He set the car in motion, driving it with a careless recklessness that excited her even while it frightened her.

'I take it you don't have any people living locally—any family,' he enlarged, taking his attention off the road to turn and look at her. She made him feel a rare curiosity about her with her lack of any regional accent, her shyness, her total air not just of being unawakened but also of being completely unaware. He doubted that any man had ever kissed her, never mind...

'No. No, I don't,' Lizzie told him huskily. 'My... my aunt.'

'So what brought you to this part of the country, then?'

He was an expert in knowing how to approach a woman, and this one, this woman, child, green as she was, was going to drop into his arms as easily as ripe soft fruit.

All it needed was a little care, a little flattery, a little coaxing.

Lizzie gave him a surprised look. She was not used to people being interested enough in her to ask her questions. A warm glow began to spread through her body, bringing with it a dizzying surge of self-confidence and bravery.

'My... my aunt sent me here. She knows the matron in charge of the hospital.'

'Your aunt, you say... You don't have any other family, then?'

'No... not now...' Her voice dropped, her eyes darkening as she relived the shock of hearing of her parents' death. 'There was a bomb...'

While he nodded his head and made sympathetic noises, he was congratulating himself on having picked a real winner. No family to speak of apart from an aunt who, by the sound of it, didn't give a damn and anyway was too far away to be of any concern to him. He had a couple of days' leave owing to him. There was no reason why he shouldn't spend them here... Any longer than that and he would be bored out of his mind with her. As he made light conversation with her he amused himself by imagining what she would be like. She would be nervous but malleable; she would give him whatever he asked of her, just as long as he told her he loved her. He smiled cynically to himself. He was well aware of the effect his handsome face had on susceptible female hearts. He had seen that bemused, adoring look in too many pairs of feminine eyes before not to have recognised it.

Women were such fools. Tell them you loved them and they'd give you anything... everything...

'What a pity we can't pretend that you don't have to go in here,' he murmured softly to her, as the hospital came in sight. 'Then we could just keep on driving...run away together and never, ever come back. Would you like that, my sweet? Would you like to spend the rest of your life with me?'

Lizzie's heart thumped frantically with a mixture of shock and delight.

She heard him laugh and knew that she was blushing...knew that he must be able to read her feelings in her eyes.

'Shall we do that?' he continued to tease her. 'Shall I steal you away, take you somewhere where it would be just the two of us...?'

His voice had developed a deep, caressing, almost mesmeric quality. Totally unable to take her eyes off his face, Lizzie discovered that she had virtually forgotten to breathe and that suddenly her lungs were labouring desperately to take in air.

Taking advantage of her bemused state, he allowed the tone of his voice to change, to deepen with regret as he told her, 'How I wish I could do just that, but I can't, can I...? There's a war to be won.' He allowed his eyes to darken, his whole manner to become subtly infused with purposefulness; he had discovered very early on in the war that if there was one thing women fell for even more than being told he loved them, it was the suggestion that he as a man of honour had to put his country before his feelings. This one, he could see, was no exception.

Lizzie was aching inside. Soon they would be going their separate ways, and she doubted that she would ever see him again, despite what he had said. A tearing, sharp pain splintered inside her, making her catch her breath and lose her colour.

'I think you'd better drop me off here,' she told him as they approached the gate. The matron had very strict views about the girls keeping their distance both from the men and from their visitors.

'Fraternisation forbidden, is it?' he guessed, understanding at once and stopping the car.

Lizzie couldn't open the door and she watched breathlessly as he leapt over his own and came round to help her out, not opening the door for her as she had expected, but instead leaning down inside the car to lift her out bodily, so that for a brief, dazzling moment of time she was held against him, body to body, looking down into those teasing blue eyes, feeling her chest tighten and her muscles coil in heady excitement as he slowly lowered her to her feet, holding her tantalisingly and dangerously just off the ground, while he looked at her mouth and whispered to her.

'Tiny little thing, aren't you, just made to fit into a man's arms, with a mouth just made for a man to kiss? Has anyone kissed you before, sweetheart, or have you been saving yourself for me?'

Her heart was pounding so heavily, so noisily that she could barely hear what he was saying. She felt both light-headed and yet at the same time as though everything around her had somehow become dazzlingly clear and sharp, as though she was seeing the whole world with new eyes.

'You know what's happening to us, don't you?' he pressed. 'You know that you and I...' He broke off, his face suddenly tense and fierce, his hands gripping her so tightly that it almost hurt. 'I've got to see you again,' he told her with an urgency that thrilled her. 'When will you be free?'

Free... She struggled to hold on to her sanity, to reason, but they had both been swept away and were no longer of any force in her life.

This was what mattered, this sweet sharp bliss, this delirious sensation of floating above the ground, of suddenly living life to the full, of knowing beyond any shadow of a doubt that she had met the man who embodied every single facet of all her yearning daydreams, that she had in fact fallen headily and instantly in love.

'I...after lunch,' she heard herself telling him in a thick, unfamiliar voice. 'I was going to write to my aunt. I write to her every week. She has arthritis and so she can't always write back...'

'I'll pick you up here at half-past two,' he told her softly, ignoring her flurried, strangled words.

And then, as he lowered her to the ground, his lips brushed lightly against her own, the merest touch—a touch which another and more aware girl would have recognised as deliberate provocation, but which to Lizzie appeared to be a gesture of the deepest reverence and respect, the most chaste kind of embrace, as though he hardly dared to do more than merely allow his lips to touch hers. So, in her reading, had the heroes hardly dared to sully their adored ones with the male carnality of their desires, cherishing their purity, even while they ached to possess it.

Lizzie knew nothing of the real world of real emotions, of the careless urgency with which men like Kit Danvers physically possessed her sex, claiming their compliance as their right as men who daily, hourly faced death.

'And, sweetheart...'

As she looked up at him, mute and adoring, he touched her braided hair and said, 'Wear this loose, and something pretty. I like my girls to look pretty...'

Just for a moment a cloud seemed to obscure the sun, chilling her skin. His *girls*, he had said... She frowned, her dizzying, bemusing dream suddenly darkened with reality, but then he touched her face, tracing the delicacy of its bone-structure, and the clouds were burned away in the intensity of the heat that shook her...

As she waited for him to unstrap her bike, Lizzie found herself wishing that it were already half-past two, that there were no long, tense hours to wait before she could see him again...hours which would be shadowed with fears that he might change his mind...that he might meet some prettier, more appealing girl whom he might favour with his smiles instead of her, and already, though she didn't know it, she had taken her first step into a dangerous and unfamiliar new world.

She found Edward ready and waiting for her, his face set and tense.

'I'm sorry I'm late,' she apologised. Some instinct that was beginning to grow with her own maturity gave her an insight into the feelings of others which she often wished she did not have. It was hardly less painful to be so receptive to the emotional pain of others at second hand than it was for them to experience it themselves. Today she was particularly receptive to Edward's pain, her own emotional nerve-endings curling back in sensitive reaction to his anxiety.

'I thought perhaps you'd changed your mind. You shouldn't be spending your free time with me... Pretty girl like you should be out having fun.'

That was the second time in one morning a man had described her as pretty, but this time she felt none of the soaring joy she had experienced when *he* had described her thus, only a sharp anguished knowledge of Edward's own awareness that, while a woman might feel compassion for him, she could never feel desire.

As she wheeled him outside, she saw him lift his face towards the warmth of the sun. His skin had a grey, sickly undertone, the bones slightly shrunken under his flesh. He had lost weight in the long months he had been with them and her heart ached compassionately for him, as she contrasted him again with *him*.

The rhododendrons were set on a sloping bank just outside the formal gardens, and Lizzie, who had genuinely wanted to foster the tiny spark of interest she had seen in Edward's eyes the last time she had taken him there, had discovered that they had originally been planted by an owner of the house who had travelled extensively in China before the Boxer uprising. A keen botanist, he had collected various specimens in the wild and created this special area for them.

Where the formal gardens of the house had now gone to make way for vegetable plots, the rhododendrons had been allowed to remain.

Lizzie was slightly out of breath by the time she had pushed the wheelchair up the overgrown path that led to them, but her efforts were well rewarded when she turned a corner and stopped the wheelchair so that Edward could take in the full glory of the scene in front of them.

She heard him catch his breath, and, when she quickly kneeled down to look at him, she discovered that there were tears running down his face.

'They're beautiful,' he told her quietly. 'So very much like those at Cottingdean... My grandmother adored her garden.'

'Who lives there now?' Lizzie asked him, more because she sensed his need to talk about the house he obviously loved so much than out of any real curiosity.

'No one. It was requisitioned during the early part of the war, but it's empty now. It's too remote to be of any real use—on the edge of a tiny village tucked away in the Wiltshire hills. Ultimately, I suppose, it belongs now to my cousin. His father was the elder son, mine the younger. Sometimes during the night I dream that I'm back there...' A bitter smile twisted his face. 'Pure escapism. If I do go back, it won't be as a boy free to run around but as a useless cripple...'

Lizzie bit her lip, wondering if she had done the right thing in bringing him out here... wondering if she had perhaps not been kind in stirring up memories of his childhood.

Without saying a word, she turned the wheelchair round. She knew from experience that when these moods of deep despair came down on him it was best to simply

let Edward speak. Rather like letting poison drain out
of a wound, only for his particular wound there could
never be any total cleansing and healing.

They were halfway back to the hospital when she saw
the man walking down the path towards them. She recognised him immediately, her heart giving a tremendous
bound of pleasure and shock. He was walking with the
sun behind him, so that his dark hair had a golden
nimbus, his easy, long-legged stride so male, so unconsciously arrogant that her heart bled a little for Edward,
whom she could see gripping the arms of his wheelchair.

Such was her incandescent joy at the sight of him that
there was no time, no room in her mind to question what
he was doing. All she wanted to do was to fly towards
him, to feel his arms tighten around her, his man's body
press close to hers, his mouth find hers to possess and
cherish it until the tremulous joy flooding through her
burst into a wild surge.

But it wasn't her he addressed—he seemed not to
notice her at all, speaking instead to Edward, saying
casually, 'Ah, there you are, old boy. They told me I'd
find you down here somewhere...'

'Christopher...'

Christopher... His name was Christopher... It suited
him somehow... She savoured it silently, tasting it, rolling
it around her mouth, marvelling at the foresight of
parents able instinctively to choose a name so fitting.

'I'll push this for you, shall I?'

Engrossed in her bemusement, she hadn't seen him
move, and now suddenly he was standing beside her, her
body instantly aware of his, so that she longed to move
closer to him, to bathe in his body heat, to breathe in
his special scent.

She tried to look at him and couldn't, paralysed by
unexpected, awkward shyness. In front of her she heard
Edward saying, 'Lizzie...this is Christopher Danvers...
My cousin... Christopher, Lizzie is——'

'I know. Lizzie and I have already met... This morning
when I practically ran her down...'

He held out his hand and gripped hers. The pressure of his fingers against her own made her quiver with delight.

'Call me Kit,' he told her softly, while his blue eyes laughed dangerously into hers.

She was so bemused, so entranced by him that it wasn't until several seconds after he had released her hand and she had turned away from him that she became aware of Edward's tension.

And then, hypersensitive to a point where she almost felt as though she had stepped inside his skin, she could feel the pressure he was placing on his fragile muscles and instinctively moved towards him and then stopped, confused by her own actions.

For a moment she had wanted to place herself protectively between Edward and Kit. But why...? And why to protect Edward...? Kit was his cousin...

She was in love with him. He was wonderful, perfect. She couldn't understand Edward's antagonism towards him.

'You always did drive too damn fast,' Edward was saying curtly.

'Well, luckily there was no harm done, and when your ministering angel told me that she was spending her time off charitably entertaining one of her patients I had no idea she meant you.'

'What are you doing here, Kit?'

The way Edward Danvers asked the question was brusque, almost as though he disliked the other man, which startled Lizzie.

'Felt I ought to, old chap, now that the old man's finally gone. Duty. Head of the family and all that. Came to see how you were getting on. What plans you've got for when all this is over...'

'I won't be burdening you with my presence at Cottingdean, if that's what's worrying you,' Edward said stiffly.

Lizzie was beginning to feel uncomfortable. There was something here between the two men which she felt instinctively should not be aired in front of a third party.

'I... I think I'd better go,' she began uncertainly, and appealed to Kit, 'You've obviously got private family business to discuss...'

She started to move away down the path, but Kit followed her, standing between her and Edward and blocking her view of the wheelchair as he bent his head and murmured, 'You haven't forgotten about our date, have you? I shouldn't be too long with old Edward... Half-past two, remember.'

Her heart gave a tremendous thud as happiness burst into a million tiny effervescent fragments inside her.

'Half-past two,' she agreed shakily.

Both men watched her walk out of sight, and then Kit drawled, 'Pretty little thing for a skivvy.'

'She is not a skivvy, she is a nursing aide... By rights she ought to have done more years at school. She's far too bright for this kind of work.' Edward moved restlessly in his chair and cursed bitterly, 'Damn this war... Damn it to hell...'

'Steady on, old chap. Can't say I blame you, though. Tied to that thing and not able to do a thing about it, while you've got a pretty little bit like that fluttering round you. Must say, I'd feel pretty frustrated myself.' He watched in cynical amusement as he saw his cousin's skin turn dark red.

Edward always had been over-prudish, which was perhaps just as well in all the circumstances when you thought about it. Kit hadn't been looking forward to this visit. While his father had been alive he had carelessly pushed the thought of his cousin and his plight out of his mind; he had more important things to think about, such as winning a war and in the process laying as many pretty girls as he could... One of the perks of being one of Britain's bravest. As a pilot, it was virtually expected of him. Not that he found it any hardship... But now his father was dead, and his CO had made one too many comments about Edward's plight, so that he had felt obliged to drive down here and see how he was doing, and to make it plain to Edward that once this

war was over they would both have their own separate
lives to lead.

'You leave her alone,' he heard Edward saying grimly.
'She's still little more than a child. She doesn't understand the kind of rules you play by, Kit. She's an innocent...' He broke off, realising that he was only affording
the other amusement, and asked instead, 'I take it you
are still engaged to Lillian?'

'Of course. All that money, you know... Besides, I
don't have much option, do I?'

'If you don't love her——'

'Love? What a fool you are, Edward. You've been
spending too much time on your own,' he added derisively. 'I need a wife like Lillian, but that doesn't mean
I can't amuse myself in other directions.'

'You haven't changed, Kit. You never did care about
people's feelings and you never will.'

'While you always cared too much, which is why
you're in that wheelchair. If you hadn't been so damned
heroic, you'd still be a whole man, instead of a helpless
cripple,' Kit taunted him. 'You're a fool, Edward, you
always were and you always will be... And by the way,
old man, once Lillian and I are married, don't expect
to find yourself a billet at Cottingdean, will you? I dare
say I shall sell the old place anyway. Lillian wants a flat
in London, and I dare say by the time this is over
Cottingdean will only be fit for knocking down.'

Kit always had had a cruel streak, Edward reflected
silently; as a boy he had been inclined to bully and
torment. That hadn't bothered him *then*... He suddenly realised how tired and sick he felt, how helpless
and vulnerable. He felt his eyes mist with the helpless
tears of impotence and frustration, and he wished, as
he had wished so many times before, that he had the
strength and the courage to put an end to it all.

CHAPTER TWO

'GOT a date, have you?'

Lizzie flushed, even though the question was asked in a friendly enough way. The moment she had left Edward and Kit, she had collected her bike and ridden back to the hostel.

Mindful of Kit's commands, she had rifled frantically through her meagre wardrobe, looking in vain for anything that might be described as 'pretty'. There wasn't anything, of course, but she could unpin her hair from its braids, brush it until it shined and leave it hanging loose.

That it felt odd and slightly uncomfortable didn't matter. Kit had demanded it of her, and for him she was prepared to make any sacrifice...do anything that might please him.

Now though, confronted by the amused scrutiny of the other girls who also had the time off from working at the hospital, she felt acutely self-conscious, her face burning as she stammered an assent.

'Not going to go out wearing that, are you?' another girl commented, grimacing.

Lizzie blushed harder. She wasn't used to confiding in others, to encouraging intimacy with them. Aunt Vi always kept her at a distance and had taught her to do the same to others.

'I . . . I don't have anything else.'

It shamed her to admit it. She bent her head forwards, so that her curtain of hair swung across her face.

'I could lend you something,' one of the girls offered. 'We're about the same size.'

'Give over, Rosie, you might be the same height, but she's much thinner than you.'

56

'Not that much,' Rosie protested. 'She could wear that dress I got from Meg the other week. With a belt round the waist.'

'Well, I suppose she could try it, only she's going to need a bit of make-up as well, isn't she? And some decent shoes. What size do you take, Lizzie?'

Thoroughly bemused, Lizzie stood there while they argued good-naturedly and loudly all around her.

'It's a pity you didn't think to put your hair in rags last night,' one of them told her. 'Then it would have a bit of a curl to it. You're lucky to be so blonde. Men really go for that. What is he? Yank?'

'No, no, he's——'

'Here's the dress,' Rosie interrupted. 'Come on, Lizzie, try it on.'

Suddenly she was one of them, an outsider no longer, but she flinched when they laughed at her sturdy utilitarian underwear.

'Heavens, just look at it,' one of them derided as she slipped off her cardigan and blouse to reveal the heavy cotton brassière which, like the rest of her clothes, had been inherited from someone else.

Normally she tried to undress and dress in privacy. Aunt Vi had always made her feel somehow that her body was something she ought to be ashamed of and, even when she had had the luxury of her own bedroom, she had always studiously avoided looking at herself.

Now she blushed deeply as one of the older girls announced cynically, 'My God, whoever he is, he's going to get a shock when he sees that. Let's hope he's in the artillery. They're used to dealing with armour plating.'

The other girls laughed, but it was good-natured laughter, Lizzie recognised.

'You'll have to take it off,' Rosie told her decisively, and before she could protest the other girl had stepped behind her and unsnapped the fastener.

She had never stood in front of anyone before clad in only her knickers and she felt a sharp stab of shock ricochet through her system as she realised how easily she was shedding Aunt Vi's rules.

'Look at her,' someone said mockingly. 'She doesn't need to wear anything. There's hardly anything of her.'

'No, but at least what she's got is in the right place,' another girl responded.

Rosie turned to her and said kindly, 'Don't pay any attention to Mavis, she's jealous because her boyfriend says her chest is too big... Poor Mavis. She's used to them thinking it's wonderful. She needed taking down a peg or two. The rest of us were sick of hearing about how wonderful her forty inches were... Here you are, get this on,' she instructed, handing her a flimsy cotton garment.

Lizzie hesitated as she stared at the fabric, its white background rather dingy from too many washings of a poor-quality cloth. The fabric was overprinted with a too-busy design of bright red and yellow flowers that made her feel slightly dizzy, but everyone was waiting and if she refused she would offend Rosie and probably everyone else as well. They were, after all, trying to be helpful.

As she put the dress on and fastened the buttons down the front she realised how much plumper Rosie must be. The dress, which on Rosie hugged the waist, hung loosely on her, and the V-neckline was surely much more revealing on her than it was when it strained across Rosie's plump breasts.

She tried not to feel relieved as she reached for the buttons. 'It's kind of you, Rosie, but it doesn't look anywhere near as good on me as it does on you,' she said tactfully.

Although she was loath to admit it she was actually longing to get back to Lady Jeveson's cast-offs. At least in them she felt she was decently dressed. She had been horror stricken to realise that through the thin fabric of Rosie's dress it was actually possible to see not only the outline of her nipples, but also the dark shadowing of their surrounding areola.

'No, keep it on,' Rosie protested, 'all it needs is a belt. You've got a red one, haven't you, Jean...? Bring it here and let's see how it looks...'

Jean Adams was a tall thin girl, with dark hair and dense brown eyes. The belt in question was made of bright red shiny plastic and had been a present from an admiring GI.

Lizzie felt her fingers recoil from contact with the sharp shiny stuff in distaste. The only belts she was familiar with were soft leather, often worn, with the stitching gone in places, and always in dull browns and greys.

'Give it 'ere, Jean,' Rosie instructed, obviously enjoying her role as transformer-in-chief. 'Now breathe in, Lizzie, while I get it fastened... My goodness, you are thin, aren't you? Even Jean can't get it fastened on that first notch, can you, Jean? No, you can't look at yourself yet,' Rosie told her firmly as she tried to step to one side so that she could see her reflection in the dormitory's one spotted mirror.

'What you need now is a bit of colour in your face. Some nice bright red lipstick and a bit of rouge...'

'And some blacking on her lashes,' someone suggested. 'What size shoes does she take?'

'Threes,' Lizzie said weakly.

'So small...well, it will have to be Mary's white courts, then... You take a four, don't you, Mary? We'll have to stuff the toes. Where's he meeting you, love, outside?'

Lizzie shook her head. 'On the back lane to the hospital.'

'She's not walking all down there, not in my white courts,' Mary objected indignantly.

'No, well, she'll have to wear her own shoes and then change just before she meets him. Leave her own hidden—she can pick them up in the morning.'

Lizzie wanted to object that it wasn't necessary for Mary to make such a sacrifice. Aunt Vi had always told her that a lady never wore white shoes, but it was difficult to speak with Rosie determinedly outlining her mouth with what felt like sticky paste, and someone else spitting on a cake of mascara ready to attend to her eyelashes.

It was a good half-hour before they were satisfied with their efforts and ready to let her look in the mirror.

When she did, the image confronting her was so totally unfamiliar that she could only stare at it in confused disbelief. She looked so much older, so much more worldly, so... so common, a sharp inner voice derided, but with the circle of expectant faces watching her she could only swallow down her dismay and weakly thank them.

'Just you remember,' Rosie warned her, all motherly concern, 'if he tries it on, you make him wait. Show him that you expect to be treated with a bit of respect. They're all the same... All after one thing... and they'll tell you anything to get it...'

She wanted to protest that they were wrong, that Kit was different... but her feelings were too new... too precious to be shared with anyone else.

Someone, she rather thought it was Mary, provided her with a white cardigan to wear over the dress, which mercifully buttoned up to the throat, and then she was being escorted downstairs and outside, so that it was impossible for her to plead that she couldn't accept their generosity and change back into her own things.

Lizzie couldn't cycle to meet Kit, not wearing her borrowed finery, and at first she found it disconcerting to feel the freer movements of her breasts as she walked.

That the sensation of her flesh pressing against this cotton was not entirely unpleasant shocked her, as did the sudden illuminating knowledge that when Kit took her in his arms she would be able to feel his body against her own separated only by such a flimsy barrier.

Such thoughts were forbidden, disgusting, Aunt Vi would have said, but it wasn't disgust that welled up inside her. Far from it. It was the same fizzing, exciting sensation she had experienced when Kit had pressed his lips against hers, the same curling tautness deep down inside her, which made her stop walking and instinctively press the palm of her hand low down against her body, until she realised what she was doing and went scarlet with shock and guilt.

She knew all about what happened between men and women—it would have been hard not to, when the other girls gave such graphic and detailed descriptions of their boyfriends' prowess or lack of it—but she had never realised until now that the physical intimacies they had described, and which she had found rather nauseating, could be responsible for the kind of delicious ache that was tormenting her body and making her hurry eagerly to meet Kit.

She had set off in plenty of time and, when she reached the arranged rendezvous, she was able to slip out of her own brogues and replace them with Mary's white shoes, which looked very large and ungainly on her own slender feet.

The only thing she had not been provided with was a pair of the much prized stockings, and she had firmly refused to allow her helpers to draw lines down the backs of her legs in imitation of stocking seams. Her ankles looked very fragile and pale, she decided, eyeing them uncertainly, but her woollen stockings would have looked ridiculous with Rosie's dress.

Time passed. She seemed to have been waiting for hours. Her stomach tensed and she began to wonder if Kit wasn't coming after all. She had no watch and no way of telling what time it was. She couldn't stay standing here for ever, she told herself, thankful that the lane was seldom used so that there was no one about to witness her humiliation.

She could just imagine the other girls' reactions when she went back and told them that Kit hadn't turned up. Her eyes stung with tears. It had never occurred to her that this might happen. She had been so certain, so sure that Kit felt as she did...

She was just about to retrieve her shoes when she heard the sound of a car engine. Her heart bounded, her pulses thudding frantically as she froze and waited.

When she saw the familiar bonnet of Kit's car coming round the corner she almost cried with relief, unaware of how very easily he was interpreting her reaction as he brought the car to a standstill beside her and smiled warmly at her.

Old Edward wouldn't think her such an innocent now, Kit reflected cynically as he studied her. Quite a transformation.

He looked at her dark red mouth and felt a kick of sensation burst inside him. Sex was like a drug to Kit—the more he had, the more he wanted—and since he had been grounded five days ago for disobeying orders and breaking formation to chase off an enemy plane in a dogfight over the Channel, sex had been the only outlet he had had for the compulsive energy that drove him.

'Sorry I'm late,' he apologised, jumping out of the car and coming towards her.

Relief shone in her eyes, making them glitter with the tears which had been about to fall.

'You look wonderful,' he lied, making her wonder if perhaps after all the other girls had been right and that it was she who had been wrong to have had doubts about her appearance.

'So wonderful, in fact, that I've simply got to do this...'

Kit was no fool. No matter how willing the woman, they still liked all the trappings. And this one was more nervous than willing. He felt her tremble as he took her in his arms and felt his body tense with elation. It gave him an extra thrill to know that he would be the first, that no one else had ever touched her or kissed her. Her mouth beneath his betrayed her inexperience. 'No one's ever kissed you before, have they?' he said, crushing her body against his own, revelling in his power over her, her innocence, her gullibility. He placed his hand on her heart and felt its frantic beat. His fingertips were just brushing the underside of her breast, causing her both to tense and to tremble. His tongue snaked over her glossy red lips, making Lizzie shiver frantically again as his touch caressed her already sensitised flesh. She was so responsive to him, so dizzyingly aware of him. They had looked at one another and immediately she had known without words... without explanation—she had known.

Kit was biting at her mouth now, almost too roughly, but she guessed that it was because he, like her, had been overwhelmed by their love. She felt his tongue press against the closed line of her mouth and obediently parted her lips. She had heard the other girls talking about this kind of kissing, but had never thought that she herself could experience it without intense revulsion. Instead she discovered, as Kit's tongue penetrated the moist intimacy of her mouth, that the slow caressing thrusts he was making were sending her dizzy with the waves of pleasure which seemed to be rolling over her in ever increasing ferocity.

'I can't make love to you here,' Kit told her thickly. 'My God, you're dynamite, do you know that...? You and I are going to be so good together...so very good.'

To Lizzie it was a statement of commitment for their future, an avowal of love. Cynically Kit watched the effect his words were having on her, loving her vulnerability to him, his power over her. Fleetingly he wished he had more time to spend with her. There were things he could show her—teach her. His body grew hot and hard, the intensity of his desire for her catching him by surprise.

'Come on...let's go somewhere more private,' he commanded, picking her up and carrying her over to the car.

As he held her against his body, Lizzie felt the hardness of his physical arousal, and her senses thrilled to the knowledge that *she* had done this to him. She knew from the other girls' conversation what that hardness meant; what she hadn't known before was how exciting it would be to know that she could have that effect on the man she loved, nor how much she would want to press her body against his, to take that hardness deep within her own flesh so that she could prolong and intensify the fierce, aching pleasure being close to it brought.

As he lifted her into the car, either by accident or design, his hands slid up over her body, fleetingly caressing her breasts.

'Where can we go?' he demanded. 'You know this area better than I do... I'd take you back to where I'm staying but the landlady...'

Take her back to his room, he meant... She wasn't ready for that yet, Lizzie acknowledged. It smacked too much of what she had always considered to be the rather sordid intimacies of the other girls. She wanted this to be different... It *was* different, of course. She and Kit were in love with one another, and after the war... She took a deep breath, her heart pounding with the heady excitement of anticipating the future...their future, and then hard on its heels came the sharp new fear experienced by every woman whose man risked his life in the defence of his country. What if Kit should die—what if all they had was here and now? What if there *was* no future, only these few precious hours? It was a thought she could not bear to contemplate—not now—not ever.

'There is a place,' she told him huskily. 'It's just inside the hospital grounds, but no one ever goes there. We'll have to walk, though.'

The place she had in mind was a small, neglected summer-house in an overgrown glade, hidden deep in the tangled undergrowth of the neglected grounds. Even the path to it was overgrown with saplings and brambles. She had discovered it by accident and often went there when she wanted privacy. She had half contemplated taking Edward there, knowing he would enjoy it as she had... She had seen the first primroses flower there on the banks of its quiet pool, followed by wild bluebells, but the difficulties of pushing Edward's chair down the overgrown and soft earth path had made her decide against suggesting such an outing. Now she was fiercely glad, because now it would be *their* secret place, known to them alone...a sacred temple to their love.

Kit parked his car at the end of the lane. When he lifted her out of her seat Lizzie clung shyly to him, blushing as he looked down at her mouth. The red lipstick was gone now, but her lips glowed with their own colour, softened and swollen from his earlier kiss.

'Mm...innocent little thing, aren't you...? Not that I mind.' His hands slid down her back, past her waist and over her buttocks, squeezing them as he lifted her into his own body and moved urgently against her.

Dizzy with the tumult of sensations inside her, Lizzie could only cling to him, innocently offering herself to him, wanting only to please him.

When he released her, she felt disorientated and bereft.

'Which way is it...this place?' Kit was demanding, hoarsely.

As she pointed in the direction of the glade, Lizzy realised guiltily that Mary's shoes were going to be ruined. They had to cross two fields and then fight their way down the overgrown pathway to get to the glade and Mary's courts were not designed for such stuff.

Neither, it seemed, were Kit's flannels and blazer. He frowned impatiently when the brambles caught in the fabric, and complained that she might have warned him what to expect. His irritation jarred a little but Lizzie dismissed those feelings.

The path seemed more overgrown than it had been the last time she had visited the glade a few weeks ago, but at last she could see the glint of sunlight on water through the tangled undergrowth and branches and when at last they broke through into the silence of the sun-dappled clearing she asked breathlessly, 'Will this be all right?'

'Well, we certainly won't be disturbed,' Kit told her, examining their surroundings, and walking towards the dilapidated summer-house. Personally he would have preferred the comfort of a double bed, but beggars couldn't be choosers and the woman running the boarding-house where he was staying had made it plain that she did not allow her guests to bring in 'friends'.

'Pity you didn't think to bring a rug,' Kit added as he studied their surroundings.

'But it *is* private, isn't it?' Lizzie asked him anxiously, suddenly desperate to placate him and win some word of approval, knowing that she was somehow responsible for that frown of displeasure which had banished the warmth of his smile and hating herself for it.

'Oh, it is private,' Kit agreed, and suddenly he was smiling at her again so that her heart and body were flooded with warmth and love. She went eagerly towards him, feeling as though she had stepped into heaven itself when he took hold of her arm and led her inside the summer-house, and then turned her more fully into his arms.

Even with familiarity the sensation of his tongue moving erotically within her mouth didn't lose its power to make her body ache and melt, Lizzie recognised, thrilled by the way Kit was moving against her, silently telling her how much he loved and wanted her.

'You know how much I want you, don't you?' he told her thickly. She trembled, too full of emotion to speak, tremulously eager to show him how much she loved him...how much she needed him. She was still so bemused by it all, still caught up in the miracle of it all, totally blinded to reality by her innocence and her love.

In the past, a lifetime ago, had she really been a girl who had believed idiotically that the physical aspects of love were its least important, that the physical consummation of love was something unimportant and even faintly sordid, something to be endured rather than enjoyed? If so, she was discovering how ignorant she had been, how blind and unfit to be the recipient of the love of a man like Kit.

That he needed her and that he was so open and urgent in that need touched her with tenderness that bordered on the maternal. When they were apart he would have these memories of her to bring him safely back to her, and as he kissed her and held her against his body she recognised that what she was experiencing now was a world away from her girlish dreams of what love might be.

How *could* it be wrong to experience such pleasure...such joy...to feel her pulses leap as Kit kissed her face and her throat, as his hands caressed her sun-warmed body through her borrowed clothes?

'You don't need this on, do you?'

He was already unfastening the cardigan, exposing the V-neckline of her dress and the softness of her skin. She tensed a little suddenly, made nervous by the way he was looking at her and Kit, who had thought himself long beyond ever allowing his reactions to escape his own control, was almost angered by the sensation that coiled through him as the sunlight slanted across her body and he saw quite clearly through the thin cotton the shape and shadowing of her nipples. He had already known that she was naked beneath her dress, but the unexpected glimpse of her body through it was somehow more erotic, more arousing than if he had been looking at her naked body, and, as he removed the bulky cardigan from her stiff body, he was suddenly possessed by a frenzy of need so sharply intense that almost before he had finished his hands were gripping her waist, his head descending so that his mouth could find the dark-fleshed peak and punish it for its temerity in so arousing him.

Lizzie had never felt a man's hands on her body so intimately, never mind his mouth, and the sensation of Kit's teeth savaging her flesh froze her into immobility, and alarm. It was far too much, far too soon.

As he felt her tension, her resistance, Kit cursed silently. For a moment he had forgotten her lack of experience, but now her body was forcibly reminding him of it, causing his own flesh to ache with resentment. He was almost tempted to take hold of her and make her body accept his, but she was so small, so delicately made that he could hurt her easily if he did. There had been an innocent young girl once before; a pretty little thing from the village. That had been before he had learned not to play in his own backyard. Her father had complained to his parents. His father had been furious with him. He had been forced to buy her family off. It was a pity that this one happened to know his cousin.

If she chose to go running to Edward... Not that there was a damn thing that Edward could do about it... Except tell Lillian...

His mouth had grown still on her body. Relief unlocked her muscles into shaky weakness. She felt sick and tremulous. She had known that men enjoyed touching a woman's breasts, but she had not known...never dreamed...

Despite the sunshine, and the musty scented warmth of the summer-house, she suddenly felt so cold that her teeth had started to chatter.

He still wanted her, Kit recognised, and it wasn't too late to retrieve the situation. 'I'm sorry, sweetheart,' he told her, murmuring the words in her ear, so that she wouldn't see the lie for what it was. 'But you know it really was your own fault.'

When she tensed again, and turned towards him, her eyes dark with confusion, he smiled ruefully at her. 'Coming out dressed like that...tempting me like that...'

Subtly, cleverly, he shifted the responsibility, the blame, so that Lizzie, who had felt uncomfortable enough about her appearance to start with, now flushed dark red and bit nervously at her bottom lip.

'I'm sorry if I frightened you,' Kit told her, smiling at her as he saw her reaction. He could perhaps turn the situation to his advantage.

'I didn't know...I didn't realise,' Lizzie was apologising abjectly. 'I——'

'I know...I know...' Kit took her back in his arms, stroking her hair. 'The trouble is I want you so very much, and you don't have the experience...'

Immediately Lizzie tensed again, hearing the reproach in his voice, wincing beneath the implied criticism.

'Let's try again, shall we?' Kit suggested, and her heart bounded with the relief of knowing that despite her deficiencies he still wanted her.

Shyly she nodded her head, blushing harder when he added, 'Let's take this off, then, shall we?'

His fingers were already deftly unfastening the buttons on her dress, freeing her breasts to his eyes and his hands.

He wasn't going to make the same mistake this time, Kit told himself, and besides, a little holding back now, a little coaxing and persuading, would pay him handsome dividends later. What he had already seen of her body was making him urgently eager to possess her. She felt so small and soft beneath his hands, so vulnerable, her bones so fragile that he could almost believe he could break them. Would she be as small inside as her body seemed to suggest, would she...?

'Perfect...you're so perfect,' he told her thickly as he caressed her bare breasts with his hands, silencing the hesitant protest he sensed she was about to make by kissing her.

As he kissed her the memory of her earlier fear faded; there was, Lizzie recognised tremulously, something sharply pleasurable about the way he was touching her, something which, if she allowed it to grow, she sensed would lead her into a whole new world of experiences and feelings. But what she was doing was wrong, she reminded herself...this kind of intimacy...

As Kit stopped kissing her mouth and started instead to kiss the soft flesh of her throat, her thoughts became muddled and confused, impossible to hold on to in the flood of sensation that swept through her body. This time Kit held his desire in check, caressing her slowly and lingeringly until at last his mouth was once again on her breasts.

Immediately she froze, but he refused to let her push him away, whispering against her skin, 'Did I hurt you, my sweet? I'm sorry, I didn't mean to. Here, let me kiss it better.'

She was still too tense, too shocked really to enjoy what he was doing to her, her mind too full of Aunt Vi's teachings and warnings for them to be totally ignored. And yet...and yet, dimly, distantly, she sensed that there *was* a pleasure to be found in this shockingly intimate exploration of her body, if only her darling Kit had the patience to lead her to it gently and tenderly.

But tenderness and gentleness, never mind patience, were virtues that were unknown to Kit Danvers—already he was growing impatient, bored with such juvenile caresses. He pushed up her skirt, and put his hand on her thigh, sliding it upwards until he reached her knickers.

Immediately fresh tension gripped her—her up-bringing, Aunt Vi's strictures, warning against the instincts struggling for life inside her.

Kit was kissing her again, and, untutored though it was, somehow her body recognised the selfishness in his touch, the determination and the greed, and her tension increased.

'If you loved me you'd let me,' Kit was telling her angrily. 'I thought you and I had something special.'

If it weren't that the very innocence that was irritating him so much now was also exciting him, arousing him in a way he had not experienced in a very long time, he would already have lost interest in her and abandoned her, but for all her reluctance, her fear, indeed almost because of them, he felt his desire sharpen.

'I want you, Lizzie... let me show you how much. Let me show you how good it can be,' he coaxed her, kissing her again, ignoring her tension, ignoring the tremors that made her thigh muscles quiver.

'I'm not going to hurt you,' he told her, 'I only want to show you how good it's going to be between us... You do love me, don't you...?'

What could she say? Of course she loved him.

'Yes,' she whispered helplessly.

'Then let me touch you... let me love you. You're not one of those women who can't please a man, are you?' Kit asked her, abruptly changing tack and making a fresh shiver of fear ice along her spine. Of course she wasn't what he was suggesting... was she? Confused thoughts jumbled in her brain. She did love him, she knew that; so why did she feel this hesitation...this fear? Why, when she had enjoyed his kisses so much, did she feel this apprehension at his more intimate touch?

She heard the hospital village clock tolling the hour. Four o'clock already, and she was due back on the ward at five.

Mingling with her panic was a sense of relief...of escape almost, as she pushed desperately against Kit's imprisoning arms and told him huskily, 'I must go... I'm due back at work at five.'

Cursing beneath his breath, Kit released her. She was proving more of a challenge than he had expected and like green unripe fruit she was beginning to leave a sour taste in his mouth, but he still wanted her; not just because he desired her. Now anger and male pride were also spurring him on. There was something about her. Something about her vulnerability, her naïveté, that made him almost want to reach out and punish her for them.

Not a man given to introspection of any kind, he withdrew from her abruptly, uncomfortable with his own thoughts. It wasn't in his nature to give in, to back down from a challenge of any kind.

'I'd better drive you back, then,' he told her curtly, watching the effect his coldness was having on her, and smiling inwardly as he recognised her pain. Well, it wouldn't hurt her to suffer a little . . . It might even teach her a much-needed lesson, and it would certainly make her all the more eager to give him what he wanted the next time he saw her.

He walked her back to the car in a coldly remote silence that made Lizzie ache with misery and regret. Why on earth had she behaved so stupidly? Of course she loved him, and of course he had expected her to allow him to make love to her. He wasn't a boy; he was a man . . . a man who was fighting for his country, a man who could walk out of her life today . . .

She felt the tears clogging her throat and pain and the panic churning inside her stomach. Why had she panicked like that . . .? Why had she felt that tension, that apprehension? *Was* there something wrong with her . . . was she perhaps incapable of pleasing a man as he had suggested, of sharing physical desire?

It was a devastating thought and one that made her face go white with anguish as they finally reached Kit's car.

When he turned to look at her Kit was pleased to see the effect his silence had had on her. It made him relent a little towards her and cup her face with one careless hand while he demanded softly, 'When can I see you again, sweetheart?'

Lizzie's heart leaped with gratitude and relief. He still wanted her, after all. He was actually giving her a second chance—he did love her.

'I——'

'Tonight,' Kit pressed. 'What time do you finish work? I could pick you up...'

Lizzie shook her head.

'Not until late.'

'Then when?' Kit pressed her. 'Tomorrow...'

Tomorrow was her day off. Her heart started to pound, as, almost incapable of speech, she nodded her head.

'Good,' Kit told her, and then added carelessly, 'Look, I'll tell you what. Instead of picking you up, why don't I meet you at the summer-house? That way...that way we'll keep it our secret...something special just for the two of us...'

Silently Lizzie nodded her head. She had no idea how she was going to get through the interminably long hours before she could see him again, but one thing she had already promised herself, and that was that when she did see him, when he held her and kissed her, when he touched her and told her how much he wanted her, she was going to behave like a woman and not a child, she was going to remind herself of how lucky she was to have met him, and how precious this time together with him was...how vulnerable their future together when the war could sweep them apart again at any time, maybe only for a short space of time, or maybe for eternity.

She shuddered from head to foot, suddenly so cold that her teeth were chattering.

'Tomorrow, then...eleven o'clock,' Kit reminded her before they parted.

'Tomorrow,' Lizzie echoed in a whisper, her sight suddenly blinded by weak tears.

She loved him so much. She wanted to reach out to him and to say the words, to be held in his arms. To be kissed by him...to be loved by him, she recognised shakily. So why was it that when he touched her the way he had she had acted like that, tensing against him, rejecting him?

As she watched him drive away from her she shivered again, feeling more alone, more sharply aware of the precariousness of life, more confused by her feelings than at any other time in her life...

Back at the hostel there was her borrowed finery to be returned. When questioned, she kept quiet about her date with Kit in the morning. She still felt too bruised by her own stupidity, by the way she had angered him and jeopardised their love to want to discuss what had happened with anyone, so that when Rosie asked eagerly, 'Seeing him again, are you?' she made a non-committal reply, glad that the fact that she had to hurry to get to work on time made it impossible for them to question her too closely.

The evening shift was always a busy one, with the men to be settled for the night, their medication to be given to them, the wards to be cleaned and made ready for the morning.

Lizzie only saw Edward Danvers briefly as she passed through his ward.

As she helped another aide with the blackout cloths, she noticed how grey Edward's skin looked and guessed sympathetically that he was in great pain. She wanted to go across to him and ask him if he would like some extra medication, but already she knew how touchy his pride was, how he hated any reference being made to the physical agony he often had to endure.

She glanced uncertainly across the ward. The sister on duty was a woman in her late fifties who had little time for the young aides, and Lizzie knew there would be no point in her trying to have a discreet word with her to solicit her help for Edward. She was the kind of woman who genuinely believed that to endure pain was good for the soul. All the junior nurses, and even some of the doctors, were in awe of her. The aides detested her, mercilessly mimicking her and making fun of her behind her back.

'A sexless old bag,' was how Lizzie had heard them describe her. Sexless ... She grimaced over the word, exploring it apprehensively, her heartbeat quickening with anxiety. Surely *she* wasn't like that ... surely *she* wasn't that kind of woman? No, of course she wasn't ...

Then why hadn't she been able to respond to Kit's lovemaking...? Why had she felt so afraid, so tense?

Too young and far too inexperienced to know that the answer lay both in her aunt's grim upbringing and Kit's lack of true care for her, she was unaware of the danger of the destructive seeds which Kit had so cruelly sown for her.

Eleven o'clock. Lizzie tensed as she heard the chimes from the church clock. She had arrived at the summerhouse over fifteen minutes ago and now, as she waited for Kit to join her, her nervous tension made her stomach ache and her thoughts fly helplessly in a hundred different directions at once.

Before coming out she had scrupulously washed every inch of her skin, wincing at the coldness of the water, and wishing that she had something other than carbolic soap with which to scent it.

The weather had changed, clouds covering the sky, the wind cold, promising rain for later, and today she was once more dressed in her own clothes, or rather Lady Jeveson's. Perhaps they weren't as flattering as Rosie's borrowed dress, but somehow she felt more comfortable in them.

One thing she had done, though, and that was to discard her bulky, unfeminine bra.

At first she had flushed with guilt, half glancing over her shoulder almost as though she had expected Aunt Vi to materialise behind her to chastise her for what she was doing, for her wanton dress, her lack of morals.

There was a small bruise mark on her left breast where Kit had bitten her, and her nipples still felt uncomfortably tender, and yet last night, lying alone in her narrow, cold bed, when she had closed her eyes and daringly allowed herself to remember the later, more gentle touch of Kit's hands and mouth against her breasts, the tiny thrill of sensation in her stomach had made her tremble with mixed excitement and relief.

Everything was going to be all right, she was sure of it. Today she would be able to show Kit how much she loved him. Today...she took a deep breath...today she would do whatever he asked of her, if only to prove to him that she had not been lying when she had claimed to love him.

And yet she still felt nervous, ill at ease...vulnerable. She tensed as she heard someone coming down towards the pool. What if it wasn't Kit? What if it was someone else, a stranger, coming unwittingly to destroy their precious time together? But when she looked through the broken window it was Kit's tall, lithe body she saw striding towards her. Today he was dressed in his uniform and her heart was caught up in a jolt of sharply piercing sensation, a mingling of pride and dread as the reality of their situation swept in on her on an unwanted tide, reinforcing her awareness of how precious their time together was. Kit—who knew quite well how good he looked in his uniform, how very male it made him seem, how very much the epitome of all that an airman ought to be.

He paused as he walked towards her, recognising in her expression her adoration and her fear. A feeling of power, of triumph filled him.

'Come here,' he commanded softly as he walked towards the summer-house and then paused on its threshold.

Uncertainly, tremulously, Lizzie did as he instructed, and, as she felt his arms go round her, she lifted her face towards his in blind supplication of his kiss and his forgiveness for her errors of the previous day.

'That's better,' Kit told her approvingly, savouring the soft tremble of her mouth. 'Much better.'

As he slid his tongue between her lips, he pulled her closer to his body, reinforcing her awareness of his arousal, his hands moving rapidly over her back and buttocks, his own body moving urgently against hers as he sought to impress its sexual message, its need on her still innocent flesh.

When his hand slid up to cover her breast and discovered that beneath her dull sensible jumper she was naked, he told her approvingly, 'Good girl,' and then whispered thickly in her ear, 'I ought to reward you for being so thoughtful, oughtn't I? What would you like, sweetheart—what would you like me to do?'

Her mind registered the thickening of his voice and sent sharp warning signals darting through her body, so that when she squirmed in his arms it was more with apprehension than excitement, but Kit was in no mood to be patient with her. He had lain awake far too long last night with his body aching and his temper on edge to waste time this morning. He wanted her and he intended to have her.

Fighting against her apprehension, Lizzie reminded herself that this was what she wanted; that only last night she had lain in bed and thrilled to the memory of Kit caressing her breasts as he was doing now, first with his hands, and then with his mouth, and yet she still cried out with pain when he savaged their tender crests with his teeth, wanting to beg him to stop, to protest that he was hurting her, but afraid of doing so in case she angered him, in case it proved that there *was* something wrong with her, that she *was* somehow lacking as a woman. There was nothing wrong with her, she told herself despairingly, but the doubt persisted and grew, locking her muscles, and making her feel tense and uncomfortable.

Kit undressed her quickly, roughly almost, she thought, trying not to flinch when his hands almost bruised her sensitive skin, closing her mind to the hesitant but instinctive knowledge that told her that this was not the way it should be, that in some way she was being cheated.

Dark, shadowy thoughts, doubts and fears chased one another across her mind. By Aunt Vi's standards what she was doing was totally unforgivable...wrong... Her own emotions, so at war with her physical inhibitions,

confused her. She shivered, and Kit, sensing her withdrawal from him, cursed under his breath and demanded abruptly, 'What is it, what's wrong?'

Lizzie looked nervously at him. He was frowning at
her and she shivered again, but her doubts, her fears
couldn't be suppressed.

'I shouldn't be doing this,' she told him huskily, 'it
isn't right. I...'

Not bothering to hide his irritation, Kit took hold of
her. He was not having her back out on him now. He
wanted her too much, ached for her too much.

'It isn't wrong, sweetheart,' he insisted, kissing her.
'How can it be wrong when we love one another...when
we have so little time together? You do love me, don't
you?' he demanded caressingly.

'Yes...yes...I love you.' At least she was sure about
that.

'Then let *me* love *you*, sweetheart. Let me have these
memories of you to take with me when I'm up there
fighting for this country...for us...'

He had used the words so many times before that even
to his own ears they sounded like a meaningless repetition of emotions he did not feel, but they were new
to Lizzie, new and a frightening reminder of the reality
of the war...and as Kit saw the thoughts and feelings
reflected so clearly in her eyes he kissed her again and
whispered against her ear, 'Let me love you...let me
show you...' His voice thickened with excitement as he
felt the tremor of emotion go through her body, and,
taking advantage of her fear for him, he quickly removed the rest of her clothes.

No other human being had seen her completely naked
since she had been sent to live with Aunt Vi, and she
blushed hotly as Kit looked at her. Did he find her
beautiful, desirable, or had she disappointed him? She
wasn't voluptuous with an hour-glass figure, but small
with a narrow waist and hips and slender legs. Would
he, who was so much bigger, so much heavier, so very
different from her, find her too thin, too unfeminine?
She blushed again and made a small embarrassed sound

of protest in her throat as she tried to conceal herself from him, but he wouldn't let her, laughing at her as he took hold of her hands and held them behind her back.

She wasn't sure she liked being held like that; as though . . . as though she were his prisoner and as though he enjoyed holding her captive.

'There's nothing to be afraid of, old girl,' he told her thickly as he watched her, and she couldn't find the words to tell him that his careless scrutiny of her, his whole attitude towards her somehow cheapened their love, cheapened her! She had better not try to back out on him now, Kit thought resentfully. He watched her narrowly as he touched her.

Lizzie tried not to tremble. Without yesterday's sun it was cold in the summer-house, and she tried to tell herself that it was for this reason that she felt so chilled, so nervous. She couldn't possibly be nervous of Kit, could she? After all, she loved him and he loved her. So why was she finding the movement of his hands against her skin unnerving rather than arousing; why was her strongest emotion of fear . . . fear of angering and irritating him?

She tensed a little as Kit pushed her down on to the floor, her eyes wide with apprehension as he covered her body with the heavy weight of his own.

As she watched him he leavered himself away from her, fumbling with the waistband of his uniform trousers, but, instead of removing them and along with them the rest of his clothes, he simply unbuttoned them and then lowered his whole weight against her, pinning her down on the dusty floor, pushing apart her legs.

She did her best to accommodate him as he positioned himself between her thighs, confused by her own inability to communicate to him her tension and afraid of revealing to him her lack of desire.

The floor beneath her was hard and uncomfortable and she flinched as he pushed fiercely into her body and then repeated the jarring movement, cursing under his breath as he met with resistance.

'Relax, can't you?' he muttered as he held her down beneath him.

Her body's resistance both excited and irritated him, making him both want to drive hard against it, and impatient to be rid of the barrier of her virginity. She was far too tense, far too on edge.

He told her as much, angry with her for spoiling his pleasure, and when he thrust hard into her again Lizzie bit down on her bottom lip, terrified of letting him see how uncomfortable she was. She had heard, of course, that sometimes the first time it could hurt, but she had never imagined it would be like this...never imagined that her body would feel so tense and dry.

'You should have been a bloody nun,' Kit growled at her as he finally forced his way past her tense muscles.

He wasn't even looking at her any more, Lizzie realised as she winced beneath the cruelty of his words and the burden of knowing that she *had* failed him, that she had failed herself...that as a woman she was in some way lacking.

Although she knew that what was happening should be giving her pleasure, instead she was filled with pain and confusion, both physically and emotionally, so that the harsh sound of Kit's breathing, the fierce movement of his body within her own, seemed distant and apart from her. She was acutely conscious of them being not, as she had imagined, one perfect whole brought together by the intimacy of their lovemaking, but two very separate individuals.

The physical pain of his possession might have gone, but she was left with a deeper and far more hurtful emotional pain, so that when he finally collapsed on top of her, breathing erratically, she felt no relief, no pleasure, nothing other than a deep welling coldness and a searing sense of panic. She *had* disappointed him, failed him...she was not somehow a real woman, a sexual woman.

She could see the condemnation in his eyes, feel it in the way he refused to look at her as he moved away from her and kept his back to her as he fastened his trousers.

She was shivering now, her body stiff with cold.

'Come on, sweetheart, you'd better get dressed. I've got to go and see old Edward again before I leave...'

Her hands shook as she dressed herself. She felt numb inside, her throat thick with tears.

'You're leaving so soon,' she stammered, forcing back her tears.

'Have to, I'm afraid, old girl. Duty calls and all that...'

'But... I thought...' She had thought they would have longer together. She had thought there would be more time...

'Don't worry... Shouldn't be too long before I can get a twenty-four-hour pass,' Kit lied to her. The last thing he wanted right now was a tearful scene.

Already, now that his desire for her was sated, he was beginning to forget how sharply he had wanted her. Soon she would be no more than another memory... another girl to join all the others there had been. It was wartime, and a man like him who lived constantly on the edge of danger was entitled to take what pleasure he could from life.

They made their way back to where Kit had parked his car in silence. Whatever she did, she must not give way to her misery... she must not break down in tears. Men hated seeing women cry, Lizzie knew. And, besides, she must be strong now, she must send him away from her with a smile so that his last memory of her would be a good one.

She ached to plead with him not to go and see Edward but to spend what leave he had left with her, but acknowledged the selfishness of her thoughts. Poor Edward had such an unhappy life. Kit was the first visitor he had had since she had come to the hospital. She must not be demanding... greedy. After all, he had promised her that he would see her again just as soon as he could get a pass... unless of course he was sent into action.

Action. The very word made her shudder with fear. Where before it had simply been another word, a word to terrify other women, now she knew its full horror and bone-chilling danger for herself.

Now she had been admitted to the ranks of those of her sex whose loved ones were at risk and she knew the full anguish and despair of what that meant: the inescapable weight of dread and hope for the life of another human being.

From now on there would be no nights of peaceful sleep for her; never again would she hear planes overhead without her stomach churning with fear. Never again would she know a moment's peace other than for those few precious hours that Kit could spend with her. Only with him held in her arms would she know he was truly safe. Not until this war was finally over would she know true peace of mind again...the war over and Kit safely with her, the rest of their lives ahead of them for them to share and enjoy, for them to cherish their love, for her to show him emotionally and physically how much he meant to her. Her physical coldness, her inability to respond to him as she had wanted to respond—these were things she must not dwell on now. She bit her lip, wishing for the first time in her life that she had a female confidante, someone she could turn to for advice and reassurance. To listen to the other girls in the dormitory one would assume that sex was a source of huge amusement to them, a careless sharing of their bodies, in return for their lovers' gifts; from her reading she had learned that it was one of the highest pleasures two human beings could attain together, and yet for her...

She started to tremble. What was wrong with her? *Why* hadn't she enjoyed it? *Why...?*

They were standing beside the car now, as Kit moved towards her and told her lightly, 'Better not give you a lift, sweetheart. Don't want to set people gossiping, do we...? Don't want to get you in trouble with that matron of yours.'

'No. No, I suppose not,' Lizzie agreed, and then, abandoning her pride, abandoning her restraint, she threw herself into his arms and sobbed, 'You will write to me, won't you, Kit...? I'm so sorry I was a...a disappointment to you...'

She held her breath, waiting for him to deny it, to offer her some soothing panacea...but instead he simply shrugged and released himself from her, telling her casually, 'I expect you're just one of those women who isn't any good at sex... Give me your address...it will be better if I write to you first. If I'm sent into action it might be a while before your letters catch up with me. There's talk of us being posted abroad...'

'Abroad...but...'

Quickly he shook his head. "Fraid I can't say any more, sweetheart...shouldn't have told you that much. All very hush-hush at the moment...'

Lizzie had a small notebook in her handbag and she tore a leaf out of it, her hand trembling as she wrote down her address for him. As he pocketed it, and before he climbed into his car, he told her carelessly, 'Chin up, old thing, and don't worry—just as soon as I can get a pass I'll be back to see you.'

He was a man who never gave much thought to the consequences of his actions. A conscience wasn't something that bothered him unduly, but now, looking into her face, seeing the love reflected so innocently there, an odd, unfamiliar sensation flickered inside him.

It made him feel uncomfortable and irritated at the same time. Stupid girl, didn't she realise...? He glanced at her and saw the purity of her profile, the soft naturalness of her blonde hair, the clearness of her skin, and something approaching regret stirred inside him.

She was lovely, her body lissom and tender; his body began to ache and he realised with increasing resentment that he still wanted her. Characteristically he blamed her for it, reminding himself that it was her lack of expertise that had cut short his lovemaking. Even while he was resenting her, wanting to leave her, an impulse he couldn't control made him lean across to cup her face with his hand so that he could kiss her.

Lizzie's heart swelled with frantic joy. Just for a moment she had begun to doubt...to wonder...but no, she had simply been foolish. Of course he loved her just as she loved him.

'I'll write as soon as I can,' he told her thickly, knowing that he was lying and that once he was away from her he would soon forget this unfamiliar, unwanted ache she made him feel. Suddenly another thought struck him. 'Not a word about this... us to cousin Edward,' he warned her, and then, seeing her face, amended, 'at least, not yet...'

He was right, Lizzie recognised. Their feelings for one another were too new, too precious to be shared with a third party...

As he drove away she watched until the last of the dust raised by his wheels had finally settled.

Less than a mile down the road Kit suddenly frowned, an unpleasant possibility occurring to him.

It was all very well for Lizzie to have agreed now not to say a word to Edward about what had happened, but, when a few weeks had gone by without her hearing from him, would she still keep that promise?

It wasn't that he cared one way or the other what Edward thought about him, but what if Edward should attempt to get in touch with his CO on the stupid girl's behalf? It was just the kind of thing he would do, damn him!

Still frowning, he thought quickly. He had her address—a brief note sent when he got back to camp, telling her that he was being posted abroad and wouldn't be able either to give her his address or get in touch for some time... yes... yes, that should do it.

The odd letter, two or even three perhaps. He scowled to himself, cursing under his breath, already regretting his involvement.

Damn Edward for the interfering old woman he could be, but he dared not take the chance, however slight, of Edward making trouble for him. He had already received a couple of warnings and the threat that if his CO had to discipline him a third time he would be grounded permanently, and he wasn't having that.

If Kit loved anything it was flying, flying and the mixture of exhilaration and fear that came with going into action, better by far than any thrill he got from having sex.

Yes, little as he relished the idea, once he was back at camp he would have to drop the damned girl a line, carefully omitting his address, of course...

In Lizzie's heart was a mixture of joy and desolation. Joy in their finding of one another, in their coming together in a physical celebration of their love—trying to forget her own pain and shock, selflessly thinking only of Kit, of his pleasures, his needs, his satisfaction. And desolation because they had had so little time together.

Her body ached in an unfamiliar way, a faint tenderness between her legs. She placed her hand over her body, wondering uncertainly what it was that drove men so incessantly and violently to perform such an act, and why she had found that all the wonderful, singing pleasure she had been enjoying at the touch of his hands and mouth against her body had disappeared at that moment of physical joining, which should have been so wonderful—the physical completion of their love for one another.

Was there something wrong with her? She started to walk down the lane and retrieved the shoes she had left there the day before, her pace quickening as anxiety tensed her body.

Aunt Vi had always refused to discuss sexual matters; the information Lizzie had gleaned from the other girls' conversation had been varied and sometimes unappealingly frank, but she had naïvely assumed that, when two people loved, their physical union was blessed with a spiritual leavening which lifted it above the mere physical coupling she had heard described graphically and sometimes very coarsely by her companions.

Now she wondered unhappily why she had not experienced the wonderful magical pleasure of which she had read; why Kit's possession of her had not transported her to that special plane which belonged only to lovers.

She ached for Kit to be with her, so that she could talk to him, unburden herself of her doubts.

All of a sudden she felt very tired, very alone... very unhappy, her feelings in stark contrast to her earlier elation.

When she returned to the hostel, subdued, with dark shadows under her eyes, she was relieved to discover that she had the place to herself. She was glad to be alone. She didn't want to discuss Kit with the other girls; their relationship was special, sacred almost.

She had done something which Aunt Vi had always impressed on her that no decent girl did outside marriage, but she felt no guilt or remorse for having done so. These were different times from those Aunt Vi had known. Sometimes a few fleeting precious hours were all one might have. There was a recklessness in the air, a fierce determination to take everything that life offered while life still existed, because no one knew when that precious gift of life might be snatched away.

No, she felt no anguish at having loved Kit, only a terrible aching need to have him with her... close to her... holding her. He was a pilot and he hadn't needed to tell her the dangers he lived with daily.

She listened to the news bulletins... read the papers... she was an intelligent girl, and, even if she hadn't already witnessed the devastation and destruction that could be wrought on human flesh by the weapons of destruction created by mankind in her work at the hospital, and experienced in the loss of her parents, she had too vivid an imagination not to be aware that Kit could be killed or maimed every single time he went out on a mission.

That night when she came off duty, and before she went to bed, she prayed as she had never prayed in her life before, 'Please God, keep Kit safe.'

And even as she whispered the words she knew that she was only repeating what millions of other women over the country were also saying, and that for every man whose life was spared there were others whose lives were not... women whose pain she could already imagine, recoiling from it as though it were her own, frantically trying to push her knowledge of it out of her mind.

She must be strong...for Kit's sake and her own. She must be strong and brave and when she saw him again she must smile and laugh and not allow him to see her fear. Must somehow find a way of ensuring that she did not disappoint him, of hiding from him her growing dread that sexually there was something wrong with her, something that prevented her from enjoying his love-making as she wanted to enjoy it.

Just over a week after she had said goodbye to him, Lizzie received Kit's letter. She touched the envelope with trembling fingers, turning it over and over before opening it, her heart bursting with joy.

If the few scant lines on the single sheet of paper disappointed her, she forced herself to accept that a man on the verge of leaving with his squadron to fight for his country was not in a position to sit down and write a long love-letter.

Avidly reading and then rereading every single word, she soon had them committed to memory.

> Just a few lines to tell you that I shan't be able to be in touch for some time, old thing. As I warned you, it looks as though I shall be taking a 'holiday' in foreign parts.
>
> Will write again as soon as I can. In the meantime, sweetheart, think about me as I shall be thinking of you.
>
> With love, your Kit.

Lizzie pressed the final words to her lips, torn between tears and elation; elation because she had at least heard from him and because his letter held no hint of the distance and irritation with which he had left her, and fear because he was going into danger.

She frowned a little when she realised there was no address on the letter, no way she could get in touch with him, and then realised that she would probably have to wait for his next letter, since he himself probably did not as yet know just where he was to be posted.

She refolded the letter and put it back in its envelope, and then put it in her handbag. From now on she intended to carry it everywhere with her. She closed her eyes, trembling a little as she tried to visualise Kit actually writing it...his hand inscribing the words...his dark head bent over the paper.

Oh, dear God, please keep him safe, she whispered. Please keep him safe.

Lizzie and Edward paid two more visits to view the rhododendrons but Edward could tell that her heart wasn't in it. He wanted to ask her if something was wrong, but shrank from doing so.

Since he had been wounded, he had become acutely sensitive about his physical appearance, about the destruction of his manhood. He recognised Lizzie's compassion for him and sometimes at night when he couldn't sleep he ached bitterly to be a whole man again and not an empty shell of one, incapable of arousing a woman to any emotion other than pity.

Most of the women who worked at the hospital only reinforced his awareness of his physical disabilities—only with Lizzie did he feel anything approaching ease. Her patent innocence meant that she did not look at him with the same mixture of pity and contempt with which he felt the others viewed him.

Now he sensed that she was different, abstracted...lost in some private world of her own, but it didn't occur to him to associate this sudden change in her with the visit of his cousin.

Edward and Kit had never got on, even as boys. As the elder, Edward had nevertheless grown up knowing that he was the less favoured. Kit was the one who would eventually inherit Cottingdean and not him. Edward was the one who loved it...who ached for it when he was away from it, who begged his parents to be allowed to spend his holidays there...but ultimately Cottingdean would belong to Kit. He had tried not to feel resentful, but perhaps this would have been less hard if Kit had shared his love for the house and its land.

Cottingdean had been in their family since the time of Charles II. Their ancestor—penniless, landless, titleless—had supported Charles throughout his exile, fought and played at his side, and when Charles had been finally placed on the throne he had offered to reward him with a title and the exalted position of a Gentleman of the Bedchambers. Knowing how much it would cost him to maintain such an exalted position, instead of accepting the King's generous offer, he had asked that instead Charles allow him to marry the widow of a Cromwellian supporter.

The King, suspecting a love-match, had given his consent and had then been astonished to discover that the woman in question was plain and well into her thirties.

Plain she might have been, but she had provided her first husband with five healthy daughters, and the rich and well-tended flocks of sheep that grazed on the lands that had been her dowry from her parents.

Philip Danvers had reasoned that a woman so evidently and bountifully fertile could well provide him with the sons he wanted, and the rich pastures her first husband had carefully nurtured during the years of the Protectorate would yield far more profit than an empty title.

The widow had no option but to accept this second husband with as good a will as she could muster. It was the King's command that she marry his friend. She was under no illusions; Cottingdean was a rich property to a man who owned nothing but the clothes on his back and the sword at his side. Oh, no, she knew quite well why she was being married, and it was not to provide her lusty new husband with a bedmate.

Thus it came as something of a surprise to discover how attentive her new husband was in bed, and continued to be even after the birth of their first and then their second son.

Philip Danvers had quickly realised that his plain, dull wife, whom he had married for her wealth and for sons, had a sensual gift that many a courtesan would have welcomed and flaunted, and because he was a man with a sense of humour, he laughed to himself sometimes in the privacy of their bedchamber while they rested in one another's arms, sated and relaxed, and when she asked him why he would tell her that it was because, in giving her to him, the King had given away one of the rarest treasures in his Kingdom.

It was not of his ancestors, however, that Edward was thinking as he sat motionless in his wheelchair, staring into space, but of those generations as yet to come... as yet unborn. Kit would marry and one day produce sons who would inherit Cottingdean, and he hoped they would love and cherish it as he had always longed to have the right to do.

Now, though, he was forced to admit that even if his father had been the elder... even if he had inherited, he would never be able to father sons for the house. Almost violently he clenched his hands and wished as he had wished so often that he might find the courage to end this dull misery that was his life.

Kit had made it plain to him that there would be no sanctuary for him at Cottingdean. He had even talked of selling up, damn him... of living permanently in London, as though Cottingdean was nothing more than a burden he wished to be rid of. How he resented him for that. How he almost hated him for it!

CHAPTER THREE

'SAGE, I'm awfully sorry to interrupt you, but Alexi is on the phone and he's insisting on speaking with you.'

Sage stared so blankly at her that for a moment Faye wondered if she had actually heard her.

The large, comfortably upholstered chair which had replaced Edward's leather chair when Liz had taken over the library had been pushed away from the desk, and when she had opened the door Sage had been curled up in the chair, her knees drawn up into her body, a silky wing of hair falling across her face, so deeply absorbed in what she was reading that for a moment Faye had been reminded of that much younger and far more vulnerable Sage she had known when she herself first came to Cottingdean.

Now, though, as Sage raised her head, the illusion was shattered and Faye wondered to herself if Sage actually knew how very commanding and autocratic she could look when that cool, distant reserve shuttered her expression.

'Alexi?' she queried now, almost as though the name meant nothing to her.

She glanced involuntarily at the open diary she was holding and Faye felt a tiny flutter of apprehension stir in her own stomach. What was in the diaries that was so compelling that Sage was still here reading them hours after she had first walked into the room? The fire had burned low in the grate, and, apart from the pool of light cast by the reading lamp on the desk, the room was heavily shadowed; sombrely shadowed, Faye thought, shivering in a faint stirring of unease.

'Yes. He was most insistent about speaking with you... Oh, and when you didn't come out for your evening

meal—we didn't like to disturb you—I rang the hospital
again. Liz is still holding her own...'

Holding her own... Sage slowly closed the diary,
wincing as she felt pins and needles prickling her legs.
She had been curled in her mother's chair in a semi-
foetal position for so long that her body had gone numb
without her even noticing it.

She glanced at her watch, half shocked to discover it
was gone midnight, and remembered that she had intended to ring Alexi at eleven, thinking that by that time
she would have had more than enough of her mother's
diaries with their clinical, businesslike description of how
she had run her life.

The reality couldn't have been a greater contrast to
what she had expected. In some ways she found it hard
to believe that the girl who had written so openly and
painfully in the diaries, pouring out her deepest emotions
and vulnerabilities, was her mother. Even more aston-
ishing was that her mother had wanted her to read them.

Would she in the same circumstances have been able
to sanction such an intrusion into her past, into her life?

Perhaps if she had thought that she might be dying...if
this might be her last chance to reach out...to explain.

She shivered suddenly. When Faye had interrupted her
she had been so reluctant to stop reading, so very reluctant that initially she had resented her intrusion...but now, sharply, she didn't want to read any
more, didn't want to...to what? What was she afraid
of discovering?

'Alexi,' Faye reminded her diffidently.

Poor Faye. No doubt Alexi had been extremely rude
to her, demanding that Sage be brought to the phone.
Alexi was a very demanding man; despite his veneer,
inwardly he still believed that man was infinitely su-
perior to woman and that it was woman's duty to pander
to man's needs and desires.

'I'm sorry, Faye,' she apologised now as she stood up,
replaced the diary in the desk drawer and automatically
locked it.

As she had anticipated, when she picked up the receiver Alexi was seething. 'You said you'd ring this evening,' he challenged her. 'Where were you?'

Sage had an obstinate streak in her make-up which she herself considered to be a childish flaw and one which she had long ago mastered, but abruptly it resurfaced as she heard the arrogant challenge in Alexi's voice. Suddenly those things which initially she had found amusingly attractive in him began to grate.

'I said I'd *try* to ring you, Alexi,' she corrected him flatly. 'As it happens, I've been too busy. I'm sorry I had to break our date at such short notice...'

She could tell he was fighting to control his breathing and with it his temper, and she felt a brief resurgence of mocking contempt.

Poor Alexi, he must want her very much if he was prepared to tolerate her defiance. But his tolerance wouldn't last very long or go very far. She had no illusions; Alexi desired and intended to dominate her, to subjugate her if he could. In bed he would be a powerful, commanding lover, and ultimately a selfish one. He would have no doubts or hesitancy about his prowess; her eagerness for his lovemaking, her desire to please him sexually would be things he would expect as his due. Oh, at first he would be prepared to indulge and coax her, but once he was sure of her...

It was a game she had played so often before...and yet suddenly she was tired of it, sickened by it just as though she had suffered a surfeit of a once favourite food, her nausea tinged with faint self-disgust.

Why? Because of the innocent outpourings of a girl so naïve, so trusting that to read them had brought into sharp focus the girl she herself had once been and the woman she now was?

Or was it simply that the times and their low-key sexual climate, their caution, their emphasis on separate contained lives geared for high materialistic achievement, were at last beginning to have their effect on her?

Whatever the reason, she suddenly knew that she was bored with this game she was playing with Alexi, and with that knowledge came a faint twinge of self-dislike because she knew that she would have gone to bed with him, probably simply to prove to him that in bed or out of it he couldn't dominate her...certainly not because she was overwhelmed by physical desire for him. Which made her stop and think, and try to remember the last time she had felt like that...the last time she actually wanted the man rather than merely the act of sex, as a means of demonstrating her power over him...and over her mother, and the strict morality with which she had seemed to live her life. Was that what it had been all about...the men, the sexual freedom...? Had it *not* just been because, having loved so desperately and then lost that love, she had turned herself into a woman for whom sex was simply an appetite which she appeased whenever the need seized her? Was it an outright act of defiance, chosen deliberately to shock and hurt her mother?

'Sage, are you still there?'

Now Alexi wasn't bothering to control his irritation. Once that would have made her smile, the small secret triumphant smile that she knew drove her lovers mad, but now she merely dismissed the knowledge that she had annoyed him, as uncaringly as though it meant nothing to her...which it didn't, she realised tiredly.

Suddenly there was an unpleasant taste in her mouth, a tiredness in her body and her mind, a weariness with her life and everything it embraced.

'Yes. I'm still here, Alexi,' she responded. 'I'm sorry if you're annoyed. I should have rung you, but——'

'It isn't your telephone call I want, Sage. It's you, you...here with me...filling my bed, the way you've been filling my mind. You know I want you, Sage, you know how good we'd be together. Let me come down there now and drive you back to London. Your sister-in-law told me that your mother's condition is stable. You can do nothing for her down there...here you would be closer to the hospital, in any case. Let me take care of you, Sage. You know how much I want to...'

How caressing his voice was, low and deep, soft as velvet, and how he knew how to use it, she acknowledged absently.

'No, I'm sorry, Alexi, that's impossible. I'm needed here.'

Or rather *she* needed to be here, she acknowledged. Admitting it was like discovering a small piece of grit on an otherwise smooth surface, irritating...challenging...absorbing...so absorbing that she missed what Alexi was saying to her.

Suddenly she was irritated both by him and by herself. She didn't want him; she had probably never really wanted him. The contrast between her own behaviour and that of the young untried girl in the diaries was sharply painful. Whatever else her faults might be, they did not include self-deception. She was, she realised, measuring herself against her mother, just as she had done so often during her formative years, and once again she was discovering how far she fell short of her mother's standards and achievements, how far she fell short of her own ideals.

She didn't want Alexi, so why was she playing this unnecessary and unrewarding game with him?

'It's no use, Alexi,' she told him flatly, 'I'm not coming back to London tonight, and, even if I were, it would be to sleep alone in my own flat. Find someone else, Alexi. The game's over.'

She let him bluster and protest, and then when he started to become angry and abusive she simply ended the conversation by replacing the receiver. After she had done so, she discovered that she was shaking. It wasn't the first time a man had grown angry with her...not the first time she had been on the receiving end of the insults Alexi had just voiced. But it was the first time she had recognised in them a hard core of truth, the first time she had acknowledged that her own behaviour had been responsible for such a reaction.

When she stepped into the hall, it was half in darkness and silent. She paused outside the library door, her hand reaching for the doorknob before she realised what she was doing. If she started reading again tonight, she would probably be up all night. Tomorrow she would have to visit her mother in hospital, call in at her office, make arrangements to have her messages relayed here to Cottingdean. It had been a long day and a traumatic one, which her body recognised, even if her mind refused to admit just how difficult it had all been.

She stepped back from the door. The diaries weren't going to go away; after all, they had waited for over forty years already. Forty years...how many other revelations did those silent pages hold?

Her mother's first love-affair, described so rawly...so openly in the pages she had read tonight, had been written so honestly and painfully that it had almost been as though she was reliving...suffering...

She had never imagined...never dreamed... And now there were questions clamouring for answers...questions which she half dreaded to have answered...and the most urgent one of all was why, why had her mother chosen to do this...to reveal herself and her past like this...to open a door into her most private and secret life, and to open it to the one person who she knew had more reason than anyone else to want to hurt her?

It was as though silently, deliberately, she was saying, Look, I too have suffered, have endured, have known pain, humiliation, and fear.

But why now, now, after all these years...unless it no longer mattered, unless she thought she was going to die?

Sage stopped halfway up the stairs, her body suddenly rigid with pain and a frantic, desperate fear.

She didn't want her mother to die, and not just selfishly because she didn't want the burden of Cottingdean, or the mill: those would fall on other shoulders anyway; that inheritance was surely destined for Camilla, the granddaughter who was everything that she, Sage, was not.

She wanted her mother to live...she needed her to live, she recognised, overwhelmed by the knowledge of that discovery, overwhelmed by the discovery that some-

where inside her mature, worldly thirty-four-year-old self,
a small girl still crouched in frightened terror, desperately yearning for the security represented by the presence
of her mother.

She slept badly, her dreams full of vague fears, and
then relived an old nightmare which she had thought
had stopped haunting her years ago.

In it she was endlessly trying to reach the man she
loved. He was standing at the end of a long, shadowy
path, but, whenever she tried to walk down it towards
him, others stepped out of the shadows in front of her,
preventing her from doing so.

Always in the past these others had had familiar faces;
her mother's, her father's, sometimes even David's; but
on this occasion it wasn't her love she was striving to
reach, but her mother, and this time the motionless figure
turned so that she could see her mother's face quite
clearly, and then she started to walk towards her.

In her dream a tremendous feeling of relief, so strong
that it almost made her feel giddy, encompassed her, but
even as she experienced it the shadows masking the path
deepened so that she couldn't see her mother any longer,
and couldn't move towards her, couldn't move at all, as
invisible bonds held her immobile no matter how much
she struggled against them.

It was only when she woke up, sweating and shivering, after some time that she realised that in all the
years she had experienced the dream before, out of all
those times, never once had her lover turned and walked
towards her as her mother had done. It was a simple,
small thing, but it was like suddenly being confronted
with a stranger in the place of a familiar face. She
shivered, recognising a truth she didn't really want to
know. A truth she wasn't ready to know.

As she sat up in bed, dragging the quilt round her to
keep her warm, she wondered if it was reading about
her mother's first love-affair, and recognising in it the
raw, painful fact that the man, Kit, had never really loved
her mother as she had so naïvely believed, that had made

her recognise that she too had made the mistake of loving too well a man who could not match that commitment.

She moved abruptly in mute protest at her own thoughts, her own disloyalty. The two cases were poles apart. Her mother had been callously and uncaringly seduced by a man who had never felt anything more than momentary desire for her.

She and Scott had been deeply, agonisingly in love. Physically that love never had been consummated, which was why... She bit down hard on her bottom lip, a childish habit she had thought she had long ago outgrown.

She had loved Scott... He had loved her... They had been cruelly and deliberately torn apart, and why? Was it because her mother had wanted to put the final social gloss on her own success... had wanted her to marry the only son of a peer? An impoverished peer, it was true, but possessed of a title none the less. And had she wanted that marriage for no better reason than to be able to boast of 'My daughter, Lady Hetherby'? Sage remembered accusing her of as much, angrily and bitterly, flinging out the words like venom-tipped knives, but as always her mother's reaction had been calm and controlled.

'Jonathon would make you an excellent husband,' she had said quietly. 'His temperament would complement yours——'

'Not to mention his father's title complementing your money,' she had snapped back.

'In my view you're still far too young for marriage, Sage,' was all her mother had said.

'In your view, but not in the law's...which is of course why Scott's father had him dragged back to Australia... We love each other... Can't you see...? Don't you understand...?'

'You're nineteen, Sage—you might think you love Scott now, but in ten years' time, in *five* years' time you'll be a different person. You're an intelligent girl... You know what the odds are against marrying at your age and having that marriage last.'

'You married at eighteen...'

'That was different... There was the war...'

'Which was virtually over when you married Father... Oh, what's the use—you're determined to keep us apart, you and Scott's father. I hate you, I hate you both,' she had finished childishly, racing upstairs to collapse in tears of anger and impotent and helpless emotion.

No, Scott might not have been able to stop his father taking him back home, but later...later, surely, he could have got in touch with her...come back for her...?

Now for the first time she was confronting a truth she had sought desperately and successfully to avoid for a long time.

If Scott had loved her, loved her with the intensity and passion she had felt for him, he would have found a way of coming back to her.

Never mind that he was his father's only child...never mind the fact that he had been brought up from birth in the knowledge that one day he would be solely responsible for the vast sheep station owned and run by his father, and for all the complex financial investments that had stemmed from the profits made from those sheep. Never mind the fact that he had always known that it was his father's dearest wish that he would marry the daughter of a neighbouring station owner, thus combining the two vast tracts of land. Never mind the fact that until he'd met her, Sage, he had been quite content with this future. Never mind anything that had stood between them. He had told her he loved her and he had meant it, she knew that. He had loved her as she loved him. He had wanted to marry her, to spend the rest of his life with her.

Or had he...? Had he had a change of heart back there in Australia? Had he somehow stopped loving her, stopped wanting her, blocked her out of his mind, started hating her for what she had done? She shuddered, remembering how his father had refused to see her that night at the hospital, how he had also given instructions that she wasn't to be allowed to see Scott. He had blamed her for the accident, she knew that, but surely Scott,

Scott who had loved her, understood her, been a part of her almost, surely he could not have blamed her? Even though ... even though she deserved to be blamed!

She knew he had married ... Not the neighbour's daughter, but someone equally suitable from his father's point of view. The daughter of a wealthy Australian entrepreneur. *She* ought to have been his wife ... the mother of his children. But she wasn't, and until now she had blamed her mother and his father for that fact. Now, abruptly, she was being forced to recognise that Scott's love might not have been the all-consuming, intensely passionate, unchangeable force that was her own.

After the nightmare she did not get back to sleep properly and she was awake at seven when Jenny knocked on her door and came in with a tray of tea, served, she noticed, on one of the pretty antique sets of breakfast boudoir china that her mother had collected over the years. When her friends expressed concern that she should actually use anything so valuable Liz always smiled and replied that the pleasure of using beautiful things far outweighed the small risk of their being damaged by such use.

Sage frowned as Jenny put the delicate hand-painted breakfast set on her bedside table, and then said abruptly, 'Jenny, that Sèvres boudoir set my mother likes so much—I'd like to take it to the hospital with me ... I think once she's feeling a little better she'd appreciate having something so familiar.'

'Yes. That particular set always has been her favourite. She used to say that that special first morning cup of tea always tasted even better when she drank it from the Sèvres.'

She used to say ... Sage felt her stomach muscles clench anxiously. Unable to look at the housekeeper, she said huskily, 'Has there ...? Have the hospital ...?'

'No, nothing,' Jenny quickly reassured her. 'And as they always say, no news must be good news. Don't you fret ... if anyone could pull through that kind of accident it would be your mother. She's such a strong person. Emotionally as well as physically ...'

'Yes, she is,' Sage agreed. 'But even the strongest among us have our vulnerabilities... Faye and Camilla, are they up yet?'

'Camilla is; she's gone out riding, she said she'd be back in time for breakfast. I'm just about to take Faye her tea. I don't think she'll have slept very well... These headaches she gets when she's under pressure...'

Faye... Headaches... Sage frowned. No one had ever told her that Faye suffered bad headaches... But then, why should they? She had long ago opted out of the day-to-day life of the house and its occupants. Long, long ago made it plain that she was going to go her own way, and that that way was not broad enough to allow for any travelling companions.

It was a perfect late spring morning, with fragile wisps of mist masking the grass, and the promise of sunshine once it had cleared.

The telephone was ringing as Sage went downstairs. She picked up the receiver in the hall, and heard a woman whose name she did not recognise asking anxiously after her mother.

'We heard about the accident last night, but, of course, we didn't want to bother you then. And it's very awkward, really. There's this meeting tonight about the proposed new road. Your mother was going to chair it... I doubt that we'll be able to get it cancelled, and there's no one really who can take her place...'

The action committee Faye had told her about. Sage suppressed a sigh of irritation. Surely the woman realised that the last thing they wanted to concern themselves with right now was some proposed new road...? And then she checked. Her mother would have been concerned; her mother, whatever her anxiety, would, as she had always done, have looked beyond the immediate present to the future and would have seen that no matter how irritating, no matter how inconvenient, no matter how unimportant such a meeting might seem in the face of present happenings, there would come a time when it would be important, when it would matter, when she might wish that she had paid more attention.

'Faye and I have already discussed the problem,' she said now, suppressing her impatience. 'She suggested that I might stand in for my mother, as a representative of the family and the interests of the mill. I believe my mother had files and reports on what is being planned. The meeting's tonight, you say...? I should have read them by then...'

She could almost hear the other woman's sigh of relief.

'We hate bothering you about it at such a time, but your mother was insistent that we make our stance clear right from the beginning, that we fight them right from the start. The Ministry are sending down a representative to put their side of things, and the chairman of the contractors who'll be doing the work will be there as well... If you're sure it's not going to be too much trouble, it would be wonderful if you could take your mother's place.'

Sage could hear the relief in her voice and wondered a little wryly if her caller would continue to place such faith in her abilities to step into her mother's shoes once they had met.

'No trouble at all,' she responded automatically, as she made a note of the exact time of the meeting and promised to be there fifteen minutes earlier so that she could meet the rest of the committee.

'Was that the hospital?' Faye asked anxiously, coming downstairs towards her. If anything her sister-in-law looked even more drawn this morning, Sage recognised, turning to answer her, and even more frail.

Why was it that when confronted with Faye's ethereal, haunted delicacy she immediately felt the size of a carthorse and twice as robust? And, even worse, she felt rawly aware that as her mother's daughter *she* ought to be the one who looked harrowed to the point of breakdown.

'No, it was a Mrs Henderson; she's on the committee for the protest against the new road. She was ringing about this evening's meeting. It's just as well you'd mentioned it to me, otherwise I shouldn't have had a clue what she was talking about. I've arranged to be there fifteen minutes before the meeting starts. I'm afraid that means I'm going to have to spend the afternoon reading through Mother's papers and files, which means that you'll be left to field telephone calls and enquiries.

'Jenny was telling me when she brought my tea that virtually half the village came round yesterday to ask how Mother is. If you're finding all this a bit much, Faye, and you'd like to get away for a few days...'

Immediately Faye went so pale that Sage felt as though she'd threatened her in some way and not offered her an escape route from the pressure she was undoubtedly suffering. She was so sensitive that the constant enquiries about her mother's health, the constant reminders of how slim her actual chances of full recovery were, were obviously proving too much for her.

'Oh, no... I'd rather stay here... but if I'm in your way...'

'In my way!' Sage grimaced. 'Faye, don't be ridiculous, nor so self-effacing; this is your home far more than it has ever been mine. I'm the one who should be asking you that question. In fact I was going to ask if it would be too much of an imposition if I moved myself in here for the duration of Mother's recovery. And, before you say anything, that means all the extra hassle of my clients telephoning here, and I'm afraid I'll have to sort myself out a workroom of some sort. I can take some time off but...'

'But if Liz does recover, it's going to be a long, slow process,' Faye finished bleakly for her.

'Yes. I was thinking about that this morning. Last night, in the euphoria of knowing that she was at least alive, one tended to overlook the fact that being alive is a long way from being fit and healthy...'

'I suppose deep down inside I wasn't ready to acknowledge then that Liz might not recover. I've leaned on her for so long...' Faye pulled a small face. 'I wish I could be more like you—independent, self-sufficient... But realising how dangerously ill Liz is brought home to me how much I've come to rely on her...'

So that was the reason for her sister-in-law's wan face—well, there was one issue on which she could re-assure her right away, Sage decided, and said bluntly, 'I can't promise you that Mother will recover, Faye, but if you're worrying about the practicalities of life...well, should the worst happen, then please don't. Cottingdean will always be your home. Knowing my mother, she'll have done the sensible thing that so few of us do and already drafted her will. I'm quite sure that in it she will have made it plain that Cottingdean will eventually belong to Camilla...' She saw that Faye was going to object and stopped her. 'No...please don't think I should mind. I shouldn't... If anything, I'm the one who is the intruder here, who doesn't belong, and, please, if you'd rather I went back to London and left you to manage here without me, don't be afraid to say so.'

'That's the last thing I want,' Faye told her honestly. 'I couldn't possibly cope on my own, and as for this not being your home...' She went a faint and pretty pink with indignation. 'That's nonsense and you know it.'

'Is it?' Sage asked her drily, and then concluded, 'Heaven knows how long you're going to have to put up with me here, but I want you to promise me that if there are any problems caused by my presence you'll come right out and tell me. I'm not very good at being tactful, Faye, nor at reading subtle hints of displeasure. If I'm responsible for something happening that you don't like, just tell me.'

'I think Jenny's the one you ought to be saying that to, not me.' Faye smiled at her. 'She's the one who's really in charge.'

Sage had turned to walk towards the small sunny breakfast-room where Jenny had said she would serve their breakfast, and, as Faye fell into step beside her, the latter asked hesitantly,

'And Alexi—will he mind that you'll be living here and not——?'

'What Alexi minds or doesn't mind no longer matters,' Sage told her crisply. 'And if he rings up and makes a nuisance of himself, Faye, just hang up on him. I'd planned to visit the hospital this morning and then I ought to call in at the office—there'll be a few arrangements. I'll have to have my calls and post transferred here... Would you and Camilla like to come to the hospital with me, or would you prefer to visit Mother on your own, now that the doctor says visits are allowable?'

'No, we'll come with you, if you're sure that's all right...'

They were in the breakfast-room now. It faced south and was decorated in warm shades of yellow with touches of fresh blue.

Outside, Jenny's husband was already working in the garden. The breakfast-room had french windows which opened out on to a small private terrace with steps leading down to a smooth lawned walk flanked by double borders enclosed by clipped yew hedges that carried the eye down the length of the path to focus on the statue of Pan at the far end of the vista.

When her mother had first come to Cottingdean, neither the borders nor the vista had existed, just a wild tangle of weeds. What faith she must have had in the future to plan this mellow green perfection out of such chaos, and yet how could she have had? Cottingdean had been a decaying, mouldering ruin. There had been no money to restore it, and certainly no money to spend on creating an elegant and useless garden; she had had a husband whose health was uncertain, a baby on the way... no family, no friend, no one to help her, and yet in her first summer at the house she had sat down and planned this view, this garden, knowing that it would take years to mature.

Why? In the past Sage had always attributed her mother's vision to stubborn pride, to a refusal to let anything stand in the way of her will, and yet now, illuminatingly, she suddenly saw her actions as the kind of wild, impulsive, desperate thing she might have done herself: a fierce battling against the weight of burdens so crippling that one either had to defy them or be destroyed by them.

'Sage, are you all right?'

As Faye touched her arm in concern, she turned to look at her, unaware of the stark anguish and pain that shadowed her eyes.

'I was just thinking about Mother's garden,' she said shakily, 'wondering what on earth gave her the faith to believe it would ever come to fruition.'

She could see that Faye didn't understand: why should she? Faye hadn't, as yet, read the diaries, and stupidly Sage was reluctant to suggest that she should, not yet... not until... Not until what? It was ridiculous of her to have this sensation of somehow needing to protect her mother, to make sure that... That what? It was her mother's wish that they all read what she had written... all of them...

'Here's Camilla,' Faye announced, breaking into her too introspective mood. She turned to her daughter as she hurried into the breakfast-room via the terrace and reproached her gently, 'Darling, I think you ought to have gone upstairs and changed before breakfast, I'm sure Sage doesn't want to eat hers sitting next to someone who smells of horses...'

'Gran never minded,' Camilla said fiercely, as though daring Sage to object.

They had always got on well together, she and this child of David's, her niece, but now Sage could see in her eyes a shadow of uncertainty and rejection. Because Sage was taking her mother's place... Because Camilla had known of the lack of love between the two of them, and felt resentful on her grandmother's behalf. She was such a fiercely loyal child, so deeply emotional and sensitive.

'Neither do I,' Sage responded equably, and then asked, 'Did you enjoy your ride? I rather envied you when Jenny told me you'd gone down to the stables.'

She sat down, taking care to avoid the chair which had always been her mother's, the one which afforded the best view of the garden.

Without seeming to be, she was aware of Camilla watching her, aware of the younger girl's faint relaxation as Sage said calmly to Faye, 'I think you're going

to have to take over Mother's job of pouring the coffee,
Faye. I never did get the knack of doing it without
dripping the stuff everywhere...'

'Gran told me that it used to be a test that would-be
mothers-in-law set for their sons' girlfriends: to make
them pour the tea,' Camilla informed them.

Sage laughed. 'So that's why I've never managed to
get myself a husband. I've often wondered.'

They all laughed, the atmosphere lightening a little.
Sage left it to Faye to inform Camilla that they were all
going to visit the hospital together. While she was doing
so, Jenny came in with a cardboard box, full of news-
paper-wrapped shapes, which Sage realised must be her
mother's Sèvres breakfast set.

'I've put in a packet of her favourite tea, Russian
Caravan, and some of those biscuits she likes so much...'

'Is that for Gran?' Camilla asked Jenny curiously.

'Yes, Sage thought that Liz would enjoy having her
tea out of her favourite Sèvres breakfast set and she asked
me to wrap it up so that she could take it to the hospital.'

'Oh, yes... Gran loves that set, she always
said...says...' Camilla faltered, darting a quick, anxious
look at her mother '...that it makes her tea taste extra
specially good.'

'Well, it will be a long time before she can actually
use it,' Sage warned her, not adding the words all of
them felt—a long time, if ever...

'Sage will want to make an early start,' Faye informed
her daughter. 'She's standing in for your grandmother
at tonight's meeting of the action committee and she
wants to spend later this afternoon going through Liz's
files, so as soon as you've finished your breakfast I
suggest you go upstairs and get changed.'

'And then I think that perhaps from tomorrow you
can go back to school,' Sage suggested quietly but firmly,
pretending not to see the grateful look Faye gave her.

When asked for her opinion Camilla had objected to
being sent away to boarding-school, and instead had
asked her mother and grandmother if she could attend
a very good local day school. She was now in her A level

year, with a good prospect of getting to Oxford, if she worked hard, and on this subject at least Sage didn't need to wonder what her mother would have wanted Camilla to do.

'I know you'll be anxious about your grandmother,' she continued, seeing the words already springing to Camilla's lips, 'but if you're honest with yourself, Cam, you'll know that she'd have wanted you to continue with your school work. She's so proud of you... Every time I see her she tells me how thrilled she is that you'll probably be going to Oxford. The last thing she'd want would be for you to neglect your studies—and don't worry. We'll make sure that you get to visit her, even if it means my taking you in to London myself.'

'I wish she were closer to us... Can't she be transferred to Bristol or Bath?'

'Not at this stage,' Sage told her, adding gently, 'She's in the best possible place, Camilla... The facilities at St Giles's are among the most advanced in the country. Perhaps later when she's recuperating...'

She wondered if she ought to do more to prepare her niece for the visual gravity of the intensive care ward with its machinery and tubes, its high-tech austerity and the shocking contrast of one pale, frail human body among all that alien machinery, and then decided not to do so. Camilla was of a different generation, a generation for whom machinery, no matter how complex, was accepted as a matter of course. Camilla might not necessarily find the sight of the intensive care ward shocking as she had done, but rather reassuring, taking comfort from the knowledge that the most advanced techniques were being used to support the frail thread of life.

Sage was driving through the heavy London traffic when Camilla suddenly asked her, 'How are you getting on with the diaries...? I meant to ask you last night, but I'd gone to bed before you'd finished.'

'I haven't finished the first one yet,' Sage lied, know-ing that she was making an excuse for not yet having passed the diary on to Faye as they had arranged.

'What's in it? Anything interesting?'

Sage had no idea what to say. Her fingers tensed on the wheel and as she fumbled for words, for something to say, Faye unwittingly came to her rescue by telling her daughter, 'Liz wanted us all to read the diaries sep-arately...to learn from them individually...'

'Yes, that's right, she did.'

'Will you finish the first one tonight, then?' Camilla pressed.

It was almost as though she sensed her caution, her reluctance to discuss the diaries, the fact that she was deliberately withholding something from them, Sage recognised.

Only she knew how much she had been tempted to go back downstairs last night to go on reading... As for finishing more of the diaries tonight... She had no idea how long the meeting would go on for, but what she did know was that she would be expected to make copious notes...to record faithfully every detail of what had taken place for her mother's later assessment, if not for the rest of the committee.

Odd how, now, when her mother could not physically or emotionally compel her to act in the way she con-sidered right and proper, she was actually compelling herself to do so... The details of her own work, her own commitments, she carried around with her in her head, much to the irritation of her secretary—she had never been methodical, never been organised or logical in the way she worked, always taking a perverse and contrary delight in abandoning routine and order to follow a seemingly careless and uncontrolled path of her own.

And yet here she was meticulously planning to follow in her mother's orderly footsteps, as though in doing so she was somehow fulfilling some kind of sacred trust, somehow keeping the flickering flame of her mother's life-force alive.

Ridiculous...emotional, idiotic stuff...and yet so powerful, so strong, so forceful was its message within her that she was compelled to listen to it and to obey.

CHAPTER FOUR

'I HADN'T realised—it was almost as though Gran wasn't there at all.' Camilla shivered, despite the centrally heated warmth of the hospital.

'She's heavily drugged, Cam,' Sage told her gently. 'The nurse said that it was to give her body a chance of getting over the shock of the accident and her injuries...'

Camilla swallowed visibly, suddenly a child again as she pleaded anxiously, 'She isn't going to die, is she, Sage...? I don't want her to die...'

Sensing the hysteria lurking beneath the plea, Sage turned to her and took her in her arms. 'I can't answer that question, Cam. I only know, as you do, that if anyone can survive this kind of thing your grandmother will do so...'

Sage was wondering if they had been wise allowing Camilla into the intensive care unit. She had seen the compassion in the nurse's eyes when Camilla had visibly reacted to the sight of her grandmother hooked up to so much machinery, her body still, her eyes shuttered, to all intents and purposes already gone beyond any human help.

'Please, let's go... I can't...'

'I have to wait to see the specialist,' Sage reminded her quietly. 'But you can go and wait in the car if you'd prefer... Perhaps your mother...?'

She turned to Faye, who was if anything even more visibly affected than her daughter, but Faye shook her head and said doggedly, 'No, I'll stay with you.'

Handing Camilla the car keys and watching her walk a little unsteadily down the corridor, Sage nibbled ferociously on her bottom lip.

'I hadn't realised,' Faye was saying unevenly beside her. 'I knew she was very ill, but I hadn't...' She swallowed. 'Oh, God, Sage, I'm so scared... I can't bear the thought of losing her... I thought... I thought the worst was over and that it was just a matter of time...of recuperation, but now... And I'm being so selfish. She's your mother and not mine...'

'And because of that I must love her more?' Sage smiled grimly. 'How naïve you can be sometimes, Faye. You know the situation between Mother and me. We don't get on; we never have. Oh, as a child I wanted her love, craved it almost until I realised I simply was not and never could be the child she wanted—or another David... I don't blame her for that... After David, I must have come as a deep disappointment to her. I don't suppose you can understand. The whole world adores my mother... adores her and respects her...'

'I do understand.'

It was said so quietly that Sage almost didn't hear it. She turned to look at her sister-in-law and surprised such a look of raw pain in her eyes that she had to turn away again. It was as though she had momentarily opened the door into a private, secret room, and she withdrew from it with the instinctive speed of a nature that hated to trespass or impinge on anyone else's privacy because she valued her own so much.

'Sage——'

The fierce urgency with which Faye said her name caused her to look at her again, but just as Faye was about to speak the door opened and the specialist she had seen before, Alaric Ferguson, walked in.

If anything he looked even more exhausted, Sage recognised. He gave her a distant glance before focusing properly on her, saying as he recognised her, 'Miss Danvers, Sister will have told you that we have had to sedate your mother in an effort to lessen the physical shock of her accident, and until we're completely happy that that has taken place we won't be able to do anything further.'

'Her injuries—what exactly are they?' Sage demanded urgently.

He paused, looked at her thoughtfully for a moment and then said bluntly, 'We suspect there's some pressure on her brain—how much we can't as yet tell. In case you don't understand the seriousness of this, perhaps I should explain...'

When he did so, outlining in brutal detail the small, very small chance of her mother actually recovering, Sage discovered that she was gripping the inside of her mouth sharply with her teeth to prevent her lips from trembling. Behind her she heard Faye give a low, shocked cry. She reacted to it immediately, spinning round to reach out to her, but the specialist had moved faster and as Sage turned towards Faye he was already reaching out to grip her arm and steady her.

He wasn't the kind of man who appealed sexually to Sage—oh, he was tall, and probably well enough built if one discounted the exhausted hunch of his shoulders and the stoop that came from working long hours. True, his skin was pale from lack of fresh air, his eyes bloodshot, his dark red hair untidy and badly cut, but underneath his lack of outward physical gloss there was such an obvious aura of male strength and reliability about him that Sage was astounded to see Faye stagger back from him, her face white with deathly fear, her mouth contorted almost in a grimace of atavistic rejection.

Sage knew that her sister-in-law preferred to keep the male sex at a physical distance, but she had never seen her react like this before, never seen her make a movement that was uncoordinated... never seen any emotion across her face as intense and primitive as the defensive rage which now etched it.

For a moment she was too shocked to speak or intervene. The specialist looked as shocked as she felt, and then Sage saw shock give way to a mingling of curiosity and concern as he quickly withdrew from her.

'It's perfectly all right,' he told her quietly. 'I'm sorry if I alarmed you.' With that he turned on his heel and left them alone.

In the strained silence of the empty room, the harsh battle Faye was fighting for control of her body and breathing was painfully audible. Sage dared not reach out to her, dared not speak to her, never mind touch her. Her eyes had gone wild, feral almost like an animal's when the primitive instinct of panic overcame every trace of domesticity. It was almost as though, if Sage did reach out to touch her, Faye might sink into her hand the teeth she had bared in that shocking sharp snarl of rejection.

Her skin, usually so pale, was now burning with colour. She started to shake violently, her eyes slowly focusing on Sage, their brilliance dimming as recognition took the place of rage and then gave way to flat, open despair.

She was shaking so much that she could barely stand up, and very gently, very cautiously, Sage reached out to her and, when she let her take hold of her arm, led her gently over to a chair.

Much as she longed to ask what was wrong, she suppressed the words, knowing by instinct that she wouldn't get an answer.

'I'm so sorry,' Faye was whispering painfully. 'So very sorry... It was just the shock...'

Of hearing about her mother's slender chances of recovering, or of being touched by the specialist? Sage wondered silently.

'He could have broken the news rather less brutally,' was all she allowed herself to say. 'It's just as well Camilla decided not to stay...'

The look of mingled agony and gratitude Faye gave her made her wince inwardly for her own lack of strength. Had she been her mother, there was no way she would have allowed the incident to be passed off like this... She would have insisted on routing out the real cause of Faye's reactions... Would have told herself that, no matter how much pain talking about it might cause Faye, in the end she would feel better for unburdening herself of whatever it was that had caused such a violent response.

But she wasn't her mother... She avoided encouraging people to confide in her, to lean on her. Selfishly she didn't want their problems... their confidences. She was almost glad that Faye had withdrawn from her, that she was keeping whatever it was that troubled her so desperately to herself.

'I think perhaps I'd better leave calling at my office until tomorrow. It's been a traumatic visit for all of us. We can't do anything to help Mother by staying here, no matter how guilty we might all feel about leaving her. The sister said they'd ring us immediately if there was any change in her condition...'

'If she dies, you mean,' Faye said bitterly. 'Have you noticed how even here in a hospital, where they're dealing in death every day, they refuse to use the actual word? Not at all well... but never, never dying...'

Watching Faye pound her fists helplessly against the arms of her chair, Sage wished she could give vent to her feelings as easily.

She too was frightened, she recognised... No, her fear wasn't the same as Faye's... But it was there none the less. Hers was a selfish fear, she thought in self-contempt. Hers was a fear of having to shoulder the burdens her mother had carried... Of having to step into shoes which had never been designed for her... which she knew instinctively would cripple and hobble her. And already it was happening... already Faye was turning to her. How long would it be before she started to lean on her the way she had leaned on David and then on her mother?

Shocked and almost disgusted by the selfishness of her own thoughts, Sage took hold of Faye's arm and gently pulled her to her feet. 'Camilla will be waiting,' she reminded her.

She had always liked Faye, albeit with the same kind of affection she might have felt towards a favourite pet, and it came as a shock to find herself almost close to hating her, to feeling as though Faye had set in motion a trap which was starting to close around her. Faye wasn't the clinging type in the accepted sense of the word. On the contrary, she visibly and painfully struggled not to be so, and yet one was always aware of her desperate need for the strength of others, for the companionship and caring of others. Why she had never married again was a mystery to Sage. She so obviously needed the strength and devotion of a husband, of another David... but then men like David were hard to find, even if one looked, and Faye did exactly the opposite of that, preferring to shut herself off from the rest of the world rather than go out to meet it.

She couldn't go on like this, Faye recognised as she followed Sage down the corridor. For a moment there in that small stuffy room she had virtually destroyed everything she had worked so hard to create... for a moment there with that male hand reaching out towards her, she had stupidly, recklessly come perilously close to throwing everything away, everything she had spent her entire adult life trying to achieve.

Why had she been so careless? Why had she overreacted so dangerously? She could put it down to the shock of realising how very ill Liz was, but that was no excuse.

Thank God Camilla hadn't been there to see... She swallowed hard, her mouth full of nervous saliva. She glanced sideways at Sage.

Her sister-in-law was far too astute not to realise that it was more than mere shock at Liz's condition which had made her react so violently, but thank God she had not tried to question her, to dig and delve as others might have done. Surely after all these years she ought to have more command over herself, more self-control? Why had she behaved like that, and to a man so obviously unthreatening, so obviously well-intentioned? How on earth would she ever be able to face him again? She had seen the shock, the concern, the curiosity shadowing his expression as he looked at her, and no wonder... She wished that he weren't Liz's specialist, that there would be no occasion for her ever to have to see him again, but how could she refuse to visit her mother-in-law? How could she allow Sage to shoulder the burden of visiting her mother alone? How could she abandon Liz to the

cold efficiency of the machinery which was keeping her
alive when she owed her mother-in-law so much? How
could she put her own welfare, her own needs before
theirs? She couldn't do it... She could only pray that
the specialist would accept, as Sage seemed prepared to
do, that her shock had been so great that it had led to
her idiotic behaviour. A psychiatrist of course would have
recognised immediately—but Liz's specialist wasn't a
psychiatrist, thank God... he would have no inner
awareness, no realisation... It was stupid of her to feel
this panic, this fear, this anxiety. No one could, after
all, compel her to talk about the past. To revisit and
relive it...

She ached to be back at Cottingdean, to be safe, protected, within the haven of its womblike walls. By the
time they reached the car she was trembling inwardly as
though she had been running frantically in flight, a stitch
in her side caused not by exhaustion but by tension, by
her grimly clenching her muscles until they ached under
the strain she was imposing on them.

Running, running... sometimes it felt as though she
had spent her entire life in flight. Only with David had
she felt safe, protected... Only with David, and with
Liz, who knew all her secrets, knew them and protected
her from them.

Liz... This was so wrong. She ought to be thinking
of Liz, not herself—praying for her recovery, not because she needed her so much, but for Liz's own sake.
Please God, let me be strong, she prayed as she got in
the car. Give me the strength I need—not for myself,
but for Liz and for Camilla... and perhaps as well for
Sage, she added, glancing at her sister-in-law, and wondering if the latter had yet recognised within herself the
same fierce will-power that was Liz's particular gift. And,
like all gifts, a two-edged sword which could be honed
in use for the benefit of others for the greater good, or
sharpened on the dangerous edge of self-interest and used
against other, weaker members of the human race.

Thank God for Sage: without her... She closed her
eyes and leaned back in her seat, physically and men-

tally exhausted, longing only for escape, for peace of mind, and knowing how little chance she had of attaining either.

'Did you manage to get through everything in Liz's files on the proposed motorway?' They were having tea, produced by Jenny, who stood sternly over them until it was safely poured, ignoring their protests that they weren't hungry. Even *in absentia* Liz's habits still ruled the household. Perhaps all of them in their separate ways were clinging to those habits, in an instinctive need to believe that in keeping them alive they were keeping Liz herself alive, Sage thought.

'Mmm...' she answered, responding to Camilla's question, her forehead furrowing. She had read them, but nothing in them had given her any clue as to how her mother had hoped to prevent the construction of the new motorway. Far from it.

'You don't think we'll be able to stop them, do you?' Camilla guessed astutely.

'It's too soon to say, but it doesn't look very hopeful. If the road was being constructed near a site of particular archaeological significance, or special natural beauty, then we'd have something to work on, but as far as I can see——'

'Gran would have found a way,' Camilla told her, almost belligerently. 'But then I suppose you don't really care anyway, do you? I mean, you don't care about Cottingdean...'

'Camilla!' Faye objected, flushing a little. 'That's most unfair and untrue...'

'No, she's right,' Sage said as calmly as she could, replacing her teacup in its saucer. 'I don't feel the same way about Cottingdean as the rest of you. It's a beautiful house, but it is only a house—not a sacred trust. But it isn't just the house that's at risk; it's the village as well, people's livelihoods. Without the mill there'd be no industry here to keep people in jobs; without jobs the village would soon start to disintegrate—but I don't expect that the planners in Whitehall will be inclined to put the needs of a handful of villagers above those of road-hungry motorists.'

'Gran has offered them another site on the other side of the water meadows...'

'Yes, on land which is marshy and unstable, and which will require a good deal of expensive drainage and foundation work on it before it can be used, as well as adding countless millions of pounds to the cost.'

'I don't know why you're going to the meeting, when it's obvious that you don't care——'

'That's enough, Camilla,' Faye reproved.

'I *do* care, Cam. I just don't know how Mother planned to persuade the authorities to reroute the road... I've no idea what she had in mind, and I can't find out from what I've read in the files. I've no doubt she had some plan of action in view, but whatever it is only she knows... The best I can hope for is to use delaying tactics and to hope that somehow or other a miracle will occur enabling Mother to take over before it's too late.'

Since all of them knew just how much of a miracle would be needed for that, the three of them fell silent.

She wasn't looking forward to the evening's meeting, Sage acknowledged later as she went upstairs to change. She was not accomplished at using guile—she was too blunt, too tactless. She did not have her mother's gifts of subtle persuasion and coercion. She had no experience of dealing with officialdom, nor a taste for it either. She remembered that David had once tried to teach her to play chess and how he had chided her in that gentle, loving way he had had for her impatience and lack of logic, her inability to think forwards and to plan coolly and mathematically. No, the skills of the negotiator were not among her gifts, but for tonight she must somehow find, somehow adopt at least a facsimile of her mother's mantle.

She recognised with wry amusement how much she was already changing, how much she was already tempering her own beliefs and attitudes—even her mode of dress.

Tonight she was automatically rejecting the non-chalant casualness of the clothes she bought impulsively and sometimes disastrously, falling in love with the richness of their fabric, the skill of their cut or simply the beauty of their colour and then so often finding once she got them home that she had nothing with which to wear them.

Not for her the carefully planned and organised wardrobe, the cool efficiency of clothes chosen to project a certain image...

But tonight she would need the armouring of that kind of image, and as she rifled through her wardrobe she recognised ruefully that the best she could manage was a cream silk shirt worn with a fine wool crêpe coffee-coloured skirt designed by Alaia. If it clung rather more intimately to her body than anything her mother might have chosen to wear, then hopefully that fact would be concealed by the table behind which she was bound to be seated.

An elegant Chanel-style knitted jacket in the same cream as the shirt would add a touch of authority to the outfit, she decided, taking it off its hanger and glancing at her watch.

Seven o'clock...time she was on her way. She thought fleetingly of the diaries, acknowledging something she had deliberately been pushing to the back of her mind all day.

At the same time as she was eager to read more, to discover more about this stranger who was her mother, she was also reluctant to do so, afraid almost... Of what? Of finding out that her mother was human and fallible, and in doing so finding out that she herself was no longer able to hold on to her anger and resentment? Why should she want to hang on to them?

Perhaps because they added weight and justification to her refusal to allow her mother into any part of her life, her determination to sever the emotional ties between them and to keep them severed—to continue to punish her mother. But for what? For failing to love her as she had loved David? For destroying her happiness—

for allowing Scott to be taken from her? Or was she simply still inside an angry, resentful child, kicking at her mother's door, demanding that her attention and her love be given exclusively to her...?

Exclusively... She frowned at her reflection in the mirror. Had she wanted that? Had she wanted her mother to love her exclusively...? Surely not. She had always known that love must be shared. Or had she? Had she perhaps always inwardly resented having to share her mother with anyone else, refusing to ac- knowledge her right to love others, just as she had re- fused to acknowledge Scott's right to share his for her with his father, to feel that he owed his father a loyalty, a duty that went before even his love for her?

They had quarrelled about that, and bitterly, Scott insisting that before they could marry he had to return to Australia and explain the situation to his father. He had wanted her to go with him but she had refused. Why should she subject herself to his father's inspection when they both knew that he would reject her? Why couldn't Scott see that there was no need for them to bow to his father's will, that they could make a comfortable life for themselves away from his father's vast acres, that they did not need either his father or her mother?

'But can't you see,' he had asked her, 'they need us?'

She had lost her temper then... They had quarrelled angrily, almost violently on her part. When Scott had slowed down the car, she had reached for the door, surely never really intending to open it and jump out; but in the heat of the moment... her unforgivable, relentless temper had driven her so hard. Ridden her so hard.

Anyway, now she would never know what she might or might not have done, because Scott had reached across her to grab the door-handle and in doing so had failed to see the oncoming car.

Ironically it had been his arm across her body that had protected her from greater injury and prevented him from saving himself, so that he took the full brunt of the collision, so that he suffered the fate which should by rights have been hers...

Oh, God, she couldn't start thinking about that now... Not now. Hadn't she paid enough, suffered enough, endured enough guilt to wash away even the blackest sin?

Downstairs the grandfather clock chimed the quarter-hour. Thankfully she abandoned the painful introspection of her thoughts and hurried downstairs.

'We've put you next to the man from the construction company,' Anne Henderson told Sage once their mutual introductions were over. 'I don't seem to have a note of his name... Our secretary's little boy has been rushed into hospital for an emergency appendix operation... quite the worst possible time for something like that to happen but what can you do...? Fortunately I do have records of the names of the two people from the Ministry. They're a Mr Stephen Simmonds and a Ms Helen Ordman. They're all due to arrive together. I hope they won't be late. The meeting's due to start at seven forty-five.'

The village hall had been a gift to the village from her mother, or rather from the mill. It was originally an old barn which had been in danger of falling down, and her mother had had it rescued and remodelled to provide the villagers with a meeting place and somewhere to hold village jumble sales and dances.

Meticulous in everything she undertook, her mother had seen to it that the half-gallery of the original building had been retained, and whenever a dance was held the band was usually placed up on this gallery. Tonight it was empty, the stairs leading to it closed off. Glancing round the familiar beamed interior, Sage reflected that a stranger entering it would never guess that behind the traditional wattle and daub lay a modern purpose-built kitchen area, or that one third of the floor space could be elevated to provide a good-sized stage, much prized by the local drama group. Her mother had thought of everything; even the chairs now placed in neat rows were specially made, in solid wood, with comfortable, practical seats.

'People are starting to arrive already,' Anne Henderson told her. 'The vicar's wife rang to warn me that the vicar might be a few minutes late. He's on the committee as well. Your mother had hoped to persuade our local MP to join us tonight, but I haven't heard anything from him.'

The other committee members were a local solicitor and a local GP, both of whom had very strong views about the proposed road, and both of whom were extremely articulate.

They would need to be to make up for her deficiencies in that direction, Sage reflected, as they came in and she was introduced to them.

For tonight at least the most she could hope for was to act as a figurehead, representing her mother's stand against the new road, rather than contributing any viable arguments to the proceedings.

Her role was rather like that of a regimental standard: there simply to show that the regiment's strength existed, rather than to take any part in the fight. She was there simply as a representative of her mother...a focal point.

The hall was beginning to fill up, and from the look on the faces of the people coming in it was obvious that they were taking the threat to their rural peace very seriously indeed. Feelings were going to run high, but whenever had emotion been enough to batter down logic? If it had, why had she not been the victor in so many arguments rather than the vanquished?

There was a flurry of activity over by the door and Anne Henderson excused herself, saying, 'I think that must be the opposition. I'd better go over and introduce myself.'

Sage watched them walk in. A man and a woman: the woman a slender elegant brunette in her early twenties who had dressed in the kind of suit which the glossy magazines and upmarket newspapers were continually pushing as a working wardrobe for the modern woman. Yes, Sage thought drily, provided she could afford to buy the simple and so expensive designer garments they lauded. And this woman, despite the businesslike clothes she was wearing, came across to Sage not as a dedicated career type, but as a sensual, almost predatory female

who to Sage's eyes had dressed herself not so much with
the meeting in mind, but for a man. The plain silk
shirt that was seemingly so carelessly unfastened just
enough to hint at a provocative tempting cleavage. The
flannel skirt, short and straight to reveal slender silk-
clad legs, the hair and make-up, both elegant and discreet, but both very definitely sensual rather than
businesslike. A woman, of course, could recognise such
things immediately—men were rather different, and Sage
wondered in amusement what on earth it was about the
rather nondescript, jeans-and-windcheater-clad man at
her side that had aroused such predatory instincts.

At first sight he seemed ordinary enough: average
height, mid-brown hair, wearing, rather surprisingly for
a Ministry man, the kind of casual clothes that made
him seem more like one of the villagers than anything
else. He was talking earnestly to his companion as Anne
shepherded them towards the raised stage.

Sage stood up as they reached her, shaking hands with
both of them and introducing herself. She could see the
younger woman assessing her, and hid her own
amusement. She really had nothing to worry about—
Sage was not in the least interested in her quarry.

The man from the Ministry attempted to take the next
seat to her own, but Anne stopped him, informing him,
'I thought we'd let the chairman of the construction
company sit there...'

'Oh, yes, I ought to have mentioned,' his companion
chipped in, 'I'm afraid he's going to be a few minutes
late. He suggested that we start without him, as he's attending the meeting primarily to answer people's questions about the actual effect of the construction of the
road.'

'Isn't that rather premature?' Sage heard herself in-
tervening coolly. Helen Ordman looked coldly at her and
waited. 'You are rather presuming that the road will go
ahead, which is by no means certain as yet.'

Stephen Simmonds looked uncomfortable and shuffled
his feet, and Sage was surprised to discover how much

satisfaction it gave her to see the brunette's immaculately made-up face darken to a rather unbecoming red.

Sage rather suspected that she was the kind of woman who traded very heavily on her looks, using them to bludgeon those members of her own sex who were less well-favoured into a state of insecurity and those of the opposite sex into helpless submission.

'Well, the feasibility of the proposed new road is what we have come here to discuss,' Stephen Simmonds interrupted quickly. 'Naturally we can understand the fears of the local residents, and, of course, it's our job to assure them that full consideration has been given to their situation and that the work will be undertaken with as little disruption as possible to their lives.'

'And after it's been completed?' Sage asked drily. 'Or don't you consider that having a six-lane motorway virtually cutting the village in half is a disruption to people's lives? I suppose you could always provide us with a nice concrete bridge or perhaps even a tunnel so that one half of the village can keep in touch with the other without having to drive from here to London and back to reach it——'

'Don't be ridiculous! Naturally, provision will be made to allow for normal daily traffic,' Helen Ordman interrupted acidly, treating Sage to the sort of look that suggested that she thought she was mentally defective.

'I think we'd better start,' Anne Henderson whispered on Sage's left. 'People are beginning to get restless.'

Sage opened the meeting, introducing the guests and then handing over to Anne Henderson, as she was naturally more familiar with the committee's running of the affair. From her mother's meticulous research and the minutes of the earlier meeting, Sage did, however, have a very good idea of what to expect.

This one followed much the same pattern: a calm speech from the man from the Ministry aimed at soothing people's fears and making the construction of the road appear to be a reasonable and unalterable course of vital importance to the continuing existence of the country.

Anne Henderson gave a far less analytical and logical speech against the road's construction, and it was plain from the audience's reaction where their feelings lay.

The questions followed thick and fast, and Sage noted cynically how carefully things were stage-managed so that Helen Ordman always answered the questions from the men in the audience, turning the full wattage of her charm on them, as she skilfully deflected often very viable points with the warmth of her smile and a carefully objective response which never quite answered the question posed.

These were early days, the first of a series of skirmishes to be gone through before real battle was joined, Sage recognised. Having studied her mother's files, she was well aware of how much help could be gained in such cases from the ability to lobby powerful figures for support.

Was that why her mother had been in London? There had been a time when it had been suggested that she might stand for Parliament, but she had declined, saying that she felt she wasn't able to give enough time to a political career. Even so, her mother had a wide variety of contacts, some of them extremely influential.

Engrossed in her own thoughts, Sage frowned as the hall door opened and a man walked in.

Tall, dark-haired, wearing the kind of immaculate business suit she had rather expected to see on the man from the Ministry, he nevertheless had an air of latent strength about him that marked him out as someone more used to physical activity than a deskbound lifestyle.

One could almost feel the ripple of feminine interest that followed him, Sage recognised, knowing now why Helen Ordman had dressed so enticingly. Not for her companion but for *this* man walking towards the stage, *this* man who had lifted his head and looked not at Helen Ordman but at her. And looked at her with recognition.

Daniel Cavanagh. The room started to spin wildly around her. Sage groped for the support of the desk, gripping it with her fingers as shock ran through her like electricity.

Daniel Cavanagh... How long was it since she had allowed herself to think about him, to remember even that he existed? How long was it since she had even allowed herself to whisper his name?

She felt cold with shock; she was shaking with the force of it, the reality of the reasons for his presence immediately overwhelmed by the churning maelstrom of memories that seeing him again had invoked.

Memories it had taken her years to suppress, to ignore, to deny... memories which even now had the power to make her body move restlessly as she fought to obliterate her own culpability, to ignore her guilt and pain— and yet after that one brief hard look of recognition he seemed so completely oblivious to her that they might have never met.

She heard Anne introducing him, was aware of the low-voiced conversation passing between him and Helen Ordman and, with it, the undercurrent of sexual possessiveness in the other woman's voice, and bewilderingly a sharp pang of something so unexpected, so shockingly unwanted, so ridiculously unnecessary, stirred inside her that for a moment her whole body tensed with the implausibility of it.

Jealous... jealous of another woman's relationship with a man she herself had never wanted, had never liked even... a man she had used callously and selfishly in anger and bitterness, and who had then turned those feelings, that selfishness against her so remorselessly that her memories of him were a part of her life she preferred to forget.

So many mistakes... her life was littered with them— she was that kind of person—but Daniel Cavanagh had been more than a mistake... he had been a near-fatal error, showing a dangerous lack of judgement both of herself and of him, a turning-point which had become the axis on which her present life revolved.

He was taking his seat next to her, the economical movements of his body well co-ordinated and efficient, indicative of a man at ease with himself and with his life.

Now, without the softening influence of youth, the bones of his face had hardened, the outline of his body matured. He was three years older than she, which made him about thirty-seven.

A faint ripple of polite applause broke into her thoughts. She watched him stand up and recognised almost resentfully that his suit was hand-tailored, as no doubt were his shirts. He had always been powerfully built, well over six feet and very broad.

She tried to concentrate on what he was saying, but could hear only the crisp cadences of his voice, stirring echoes of another time, another place, when he had been equally concise, equally controlled, equally clinically detached as he had stripped her pride to the bone, ripped her soul into shreds, destroyed the very fabric of her being and then handed the pieces back to her with a cool politeness which had somehow been even more demeaning than all the rest put together.

'I pity you,' he had told her, and he had meant it. He, more than anyone else, more than Scott even, had been responsible for the destruction of the hot-headed, headstrong, self-absorbed girl she had been and the creation of the cautious, careful, self-reliant woman she had made herself become.

Perhaps she ought to be grateful to him... Grateful...that was what he had said to her, flinging the words at her like knives.

'I suppose you think I should be grateful...'

And then he had turned them against her, using them to destroy her.

All these years, and she had never allowed herself to remember, to think, cutting herself off from the past as sharply as though she had burned a line of fire between her old life and the new.

She was still cold, desperate now to escape from the hall, to be alone, but she couldn't escape, not yet—people were clamouring to ask questions. Whatever Daniel Cavanagh had said, he had stirred up a good deal of reaction.

She ought to have been listening. She ought to have been able to forget the past, to forget that she knew him...she ought to have been concentrating on what he was saying. That after all was why she was here. Sage closed the meeting without being aware of quite what she had said and the world came back into focus as Anne was saying something about the vicar having suggested that they all went back to the vicarage for an informal chat and a cup of tea. She shook her head, fighting to hold on to her self-control, to appear calm.

'I'm sorry, I can't.'

'No, of course, you'll be wanting to get back... Has there been any more news from the hospital?'

Sage shook her head again. It was beginning to ache dreadfully, a warning that she was about to have the kind of migraine attack she had long ago thought she had learned to control.

All she wanted to do was to shut herself away somewhere safe and dark, somewhere where she wouldn't have to think, to pretend, somewhere where there was no tall, dark man standing at her side making her remember, making her feel.

She was the first to leave the hall after the meeting had broken up, her footsteps quick and tense, her nostrils flaring slightly as she got outside and was able to breathe in the cool fresh air.

Her Porsche was parked only yards away, but she doubted her ability to drive it with the necessary degree of safety. Her stomach was churning sickly, her head pounding... It wasn't unheard of for her to actually black out during these migraine attacks.

If she had any sense she would telephone the house and ask Jenny if someone could come and collect her, she recognised, but to do that would mean lingering here, and inviting the possibility of having to face Daniel.

Already she could hear his voice behind her, and the softer, almost caressing one of his companion.

Had the woman no pride? she asked herself savagely. Didn't she realise how obvious she was being, or didn't she care? Daniel was not your ordinary straightforward

male... Daniel knew all there was to know about the
female psyche. Daniel...

'Sage... I hear that, like me, you aren't able to join
the others at the vicarage...'

He was standing next to her—good manners, good
sense, demanded that she turn round and acknowledge
him, but she couldn't move, couldn't even turn her head,
couldn't even open her mouth to respond.

'Daniel, must you go? There's so much we need to
discuss...'

Thank goodness for predatory women, Sage thought
in relief as Helen Ordman came between them, possessively taking hold of his arm.

'Yes, I'm afraid I must. I've got a board meeting in
the morning, and a mountain of papers to read
through... Sage, I suspect that scarlet monstrosity must
be yours. You always were an advocate of conspicuous
consumption...in all things...'

He left her as he had found her, speechless and immobile, staring after him with, as she discovered with
sick chagrin, eyes that were stupidly filmed with angry
tears.

She deliberately waited until Daniel Cavanagh had
driven off, in a steel-grey vintage Aston Martin, which
she knew quite well had cost far more than her new-
model Porsche, before walking away from her own car
in the direction of Cottingdean.

The house was only a couple of miles from the village,
not far at all, and a pleasant walk on such a warm spring
evening. As a teenager, before she had learned to drive,
she had travelled those two miles sometimes several times
a day and thought nothing of doing so.

Then, though, she had not been wearing three-inch
heels, nor had her body been reacting as violently as
though it were suffering the most virulent form of viral
flu.

What had happened to the life of which she had felt
so powerfully in control? When had that control started
to disintegrate? With her mother's accident...with the
knowledge that the strictly controlled physical and

emotional involvements which were all she allowed herself to share with the opposite sex were designed to appease an appetite she no longer had...

The chain had begun to form long before tonight, long before this unwanted resurgence of old memories, but she couldn't deny that seeing Daniel Cavanagh again had formed a link in it, so strong, so fettering that she doubted that she could break it open and slip free and safe back to her old life.

She saw the car headlights coming towards her, and instinctively walked off the road and on to the grass verge, only realising when the car swept past her that it was Daniel's grey Aston.

She could hear it slowing down and stopping. Panic splintered into sharp agony inside her. She desperately wanted to run, to hide herself away from him... Not because she feared him as a man... No, she well knew she had nothing sexual to fear from him. No, it was her own memories she wanted to flee, her own pain, her own self-condemnation.

She heard the car door open and then close, and knew that he had seen her. If she walked away now, if she ran away now... Pride made her stand stiffly where she was, but nothing could make her turn to face him as he walked towards her.

'I thought you were driving back.'

'I decided I preferred to walk.'

'In high heels?'

He always had been far too observant.

'There isn't a law against it,' she told him sharply. 'Although, of course, if you get your way and you run a six-lane motorway through here, the days of walking anywhere will be over for all of us.'

'The motorway will run over a mile from here. You won't even see it from Cottingdean. It won't interfere with your lives there at all. But then you always did prefer emotionalism to logic, didn't you, Sage?'

'What are you doing here, Daniel? You're on the wrong side of the village for the motorway and London...'

'Yes. I realise that. I took a wrong turning and had to turn back again.'

She had the odd feeling that he was lying, although what he was saying sounded plausible. Was it because of her knowledge of the man, her awareness that taking a wrong turning in anything was the last thing he was likely to do, that she found it hard to believe him?

He was watching her, she realised, refusing to give in to the magnetic pull of his concentration. His eyes were grey, the same metallic colour as his car, and she didn't need to look at him to remember how powerful an effect that intense concentration could have. He also had the most ridiculously long curling lashes. She remembered how she had once thought they gave him a look at times of being almost vulnerable. More fool her; 'vulnerable' was the very last description that could be applied to him. He was solid steel all the way through.

The sick pounding in her head, which had started to ease a little as she walked, had returned. Automatically she raised her hand and pressed her fingers to her temple.

'Migraine?'

She stared at him, forgetting her resolve not to do so, surprise momentarily widening her eyes.

'How did you...?'

The ironic look he gave her made her stop, the swift colour burning up under her skin stripping away the veneer of fifteen years of sophistication and reducing her once again to the girl she had once been.

'I've got a retentive memory,' he told her drily.

'You must have,' she agreed bitterly.

'I'll give you a lift. It isn't safe for a woman to walk alone at night these days... Not even out here.'

'No, thanks, I'd prefer to walk. I need the fresh air...'

'So go and walk round Cottingdean's gardens once you get home. You should be safe enough there...'

His calm assumption that she would allow him to make her decision for her infuriated her. 'I don't want a lift,' she repeated tightly, but he had already taken hold of her arm and was walking her towards his car.

Thankfully the thickness of her jacket muffled the sensation of his fingers on her arm, and his touch, although firm, wasn't constraining.

It was easier to go with him than to argue, she decided weakly as he opened the passenger door and waited politely until she was safely inside before closing it on her.

'You really needn't have done this.'

'I know,' he agreed as he set the car in motion.

He was a good driver, careful, controlled.

'Odd,' he mused, as the gates to the house appeared, 'you're the last person I'd envisage chairing a committee for environmental protection.'

'I'm not,' Sage told him stiffly. 'I'm simply standing in for my mother.'

'Really? The Sage I knew would have taken that as a heaven-sent opportunity for sabotage rather than a sacred bit of family flag-waving.'

Sage felt herself stiffening. This was what she had been dreading from the moment she had set eyes on him. Being reminded of the past, of its pain, of its shadows...and most of all being reminded of the person she had been...

Was it reading her mother's diaries which had thrown so sharply into focus the differences between them, made her so sharply aware of her own shortcomings, of her own faults, not just of omission but of commission as well?

'No comment?' Daniel asked her softly as he brought the car to a halt.

'Did you ask me a question?' Sage challenged him acidly as she reached to open her door. 'I thought you were simply making a statement. How I live my life has nothing to do with you, Daniel...it's my own affair.'

'Or affairs,' he murmured cynically, making her forget that she was still wearing her seatbelt, so that she pushed open the heavy door and tried to get out, only to discover infuriatingly that she was still trapped in her seat.

'Still the same old Sage. Impatient, illogical. So damn used to getting her own way that she doesn't even have the sense to avoid any obstacles.'

He opened his own door, and was round her side of the car almost before she had finished unfastening her seatbelt.

She discovered that she was trembling as she got out of the car, not with dread any longer, but with anger... anger, and something else, something that fuelled her adrenalin and banished the pain from her temples.

'Thanks for the lift.'

'You're welcome.'

His face was in the shadows, but as he turned away from her to walk back to the driver's door his expression was briefly illuminated by the moon, and for an instant he might have been the old Daniel she had once known so well, only to discover she had not really known him at all.

Daniel Cavanagh... Why had he come back into her life, and now of all times, reopening doors—wounds— she had thought long since sealed?

Daniel Cavanagh... She discovered she was shivering again as she walked towards the house, fighting against the threatening avalanche of memories she was only just managing to keep at bay.

CHAPTER FIVE

IT WAS no use—she wasn't going to sleep tonight, Sage acknowledged, sitting up in bed. She didn't want to sleep... she was actually afraid of going to sleep, afraid of the memories which might be unleashed once she was no longer in complete control of her own mind.

She moved restlessly in her bed, and stared at her watch. Two o'clock. She might as well be doing something constructive as lying here like this, trying not to think, not to remember... something constructive such as... such as reading the diaries?

What was she hoping to find there? Or was she simply using them as a panacea, a deterrent, a means of holding her own thoughts at bay?

She went downstairs, the house making the familiar creaks of an old building. She opened the desk drawer and extracted the diary she had been reading, taking it back up to bed with her, plus a couple of apples from the fruit bowl in the kitchen. They were the slightly sour, crunchy variety she had always preferred, different from the soft juicy red fruit both her mother and Faye loved.

Her mother always explained away her sweet tooth by saying it was a result of the war, of being deprived of sweet things. When she made this explanation she was always slightly defensive; it was a small enough weakness in an otherwise very strong woman. Sage felt an unfamiliar twinge of guilt over the way she had often childishly and sometimes cruelly drawn attention to it. Children were cruel, she acknowledged wryly—they had no compunction about using whatever weapons fell into their hands, no guilt, no remorse... especially when driven by a sense of righteousness as she had been.

How old had she been when she had first started to blame her mother for her father's indifference to her?

Eight, nine...even younger. Certainly it seemed when she looked back that she had always been aware of the fact that, while David had always been free to approach their father directly, when she had tried to do the same thing her mother had always come between them, so that all her contact with her father was made either through or in the company of a third party, and that invariably that third party was her mother.

Anger, bitterness, resentment; she had felt the destructive lash of all those emotions, and yet why had her mother felt it necessary to stop her from becoming close to her father? Surely not because she had feared that such a closeness would threaten her own relationship with him?

He had adored her mother, loved her with an intensity which as an adult Sage herself recognised *she* would have found too possessive. She remembered how her mother had scarcely been able to leave the house without first explaining where she was going and how long she would be.

Sage tensed, her own body automatically reacting to the thought of so much possessive love. *Possessive* love? She frowned, recognising reluctantly how much she would have resented the burden of that kind of love, how much her freedom-loving nature would have kicked and fought against him. She tried to imagine how she would have reacted to her father's possessiveness had she been her mother. She would have left him, probably, she recognised grimly. But she was not her mother. Her mother was far too saintly, far too morally perfect to put her own needs above those of someone as dependent and helpless as her husband had been.

Sage's frown deepened as she realised that this was the first time she had ever looked closely at her parents' marriage, ever questioned a relationship which for years she had seen enviously as an ideal, feeling both resentful and envious of her mother's role as the pivot of her father's life. The first time she had seen it as a relationship which she as a woman would have found both stultifying and caging.

And yet her mother had obviously not done so. She shrugged the thought away—she and her mother were two different women, two very different women. They had nothing in common other than the fact that they were mother and daughter, an accident of birth which had brought them together in a relationship which neither of them enjoyed, even if her mother was rather better at concealing her antipathy than she was herself.

And yet despite that, despite everything that had happened between them, despite her resentment, her bitterness, there was still a part of her that was drawn compulsively towards the girl she was discovering in the diaries.

Which was why she was here at gone two in the morning, turning the pages of her mother's diary, pushing aside the memories which had kept her from sleeping. Memories stirred up by that unexpected and unwanted meeting with Daniel Cavanagh.

Daniel Cavanagh. For a moment she closed her eyes, trying hard not to feel as though the living, breathing man had somehow or other forced his presence into the room with her.

Daniel Cavanagh, what was he after all? Only a man. Nothing more. Just a man, like so many others.

She opened her eyes and quickly turned the pages of the diary, to find the place where she had previously stopped reading, resolutely pushing away all thoughts of Daniel Cavanagh and the past, and instead concentrating on her mother's record of her life.

A week passed and then another and still Lizzie hadn't heard from Kit. Every day she waited hopefully for a letter, but none came, and then one morning when she woke up the world swung dizzily around her, her stomach heaved and a vast welling nausea had her running desperately to the bathroom where she was violently and painfully sick.

That the reason for her sickness didn't immediately occur to her was due in the main to the prudery which ruled her great-aunt's life.

Lizzie had been sick before, when she had first come to work at the hospital, when her stomach had revolted against the unappetising diet, and, if she had any time to spare from her aching longing to hear from Kit and her constant daydreams about him to dwell on the nausea which seemed to be plaguing her, she simply assumed that it was a return of that earlier sickness.

That was until one of the other girls heard her one morning and accidentally enlightened her, assuming that she must already know the reason for her sickness.

A baby... No, not just a baby, but Kit's baby. Hard on the heels of her first thrill of appalled recognition of the fact that in her great-aunt's eyes she had now joined that unmentionable band of her sex who had 'got themselves into trouble', and was therefore now a social and moral outcast, came a tiny pang of pleasure. Kit's baby. She was having Kit's baby.

Alone in the dormitory, she sank down on to her bed, trembling slightly, clasping her hands protectively over her stomach. She felt dizzy but not sick any longer. Rather the dizziness sprang from elation and joy.

Kit's child... A sudden urgency to share her news with him, to be able to marvel with him over the new life they had created together, overwhelmed her. Kit! How much she longed to see him.

She sat staring into space, lost in a wonderful daydream in which Kit suddenly appeared, sweeping her off her feet and announcing that they must get married immediately... that he loved her to distraction.

He would take her away with him in his shiny little green car, and they would be married secretly and excitingly. She would live in a tiny rose-smothered cottage hidden away from the world, but close enough to where he was based for her to see him whenever he was off duty.

She would wait there for the birth of their child... a son, she knew it would be a son, and they would be so blissfully happy...

It took one of the older and far, far more worldly-wise girls in the dormitory to shatter her daydreams with brutal reality.

Donna had been nominated by the others to talk to her. Kind girls in the main, they found Lizzie's attitude baffling. Had they found themselves in her condition, they wouldn't be sitting around waiting for Mr Wonderful to turn up and make things right. Didn't the poor sap realise what had happened? Didn't she know what would happen to her when the hospital authorities found out about her condition?

Donna Roberts was the eldest of a family of eight, five of them girls; she had seen her mother pregnant far too often to have any illusions about the male attitude to the careless and unwanted fathering of a child, but even she quailed a little when faced with the childish luminosity of Lizzie's unwavering belief that he, whoever he was, was going to come back and marry her.

'Look, kid,' she began awkwardly. She was dating an American airman and had picked up not just his habit of chewing gum, but something of his accent as well. 'We all know about the fix you've got yourself in... I know it isn't easy, but you've got to face up to it... You don't want to end up like Susan Philpott, do you?'

'Susan Philpott.' Lizzie stared at her. 'But she went home.'

'Like hell she did,' Donna told her inelegantly. 'God knows where she is right now, but she hasn't gone home. Told me that herself—said her dad would kill her for getting herself in trouble. Of course when the dragon found out it was the end for her here. Probably on the street somewhere now,' Donna added, explaining explicitly what she meant when Lizzie looked uncomprehendingly at her.

'He isn't going to come back. They never do,' she told her with brutal honesty. 'And you're going to have to do something about that...' she added, gesturing towards Lizzie's still flat stomach.

'Do something?' Lizzie questioned, puzzled, focusing on her, ignoring her comments about Kit. Donna didn't

know Kit... Donna didn't realise how she and Kit felt
about one another, how much in love they were. She had
known it the moment they met, had seen it in Kit's eyes,
had felt it, she remembered almost maternally, in the
roughness of his possession, his inability to control his
passion, his desire for her.

'What do you mean "do something"?' she questioned softly.

She could see the pity in Donna's eyes, feel it in the
waiting silence of the others in the dormitory. She could
feel their rough sympathy enveloping her, sense their affinity with her, and yet she felt outside their concern,
untouched by it, in no need of it. She knew they meant
to be kind, and she herself was too gentle, too sensitive
to rebuff them directly.

Donna sighed and lifted her eyes to heaven. This was
going to be worse than she had thought. Why was it
always these idiotic naïve ones who got themselves into
this kind of trouble? she wondered. Hadn't they got the
sense...? But she already knew the answer to that
question, had heard it often enough in her mother's slow
Dorset voice, as she repeated over and over again warningly to her eldest child, showing her, by the example of
her own life, just what happened to girls foolish enough
to believe in the lies told by men. She had been sixteen
when she had conceived her first child, and at thirty-
five, when Donna had left home, she had looked and
moved like a woman of twice her age, worn down by
too many pregnancies, too much hardship and poverty.

The war had come as a welcome escape for Donna,
releasing her from having to follow in her mother's footsteps, from early marriage and too many children, and
she had been glad to go. Glad to leave the damp, insani-
tary farm worker's cottage where she had shared a
bedroom and a bed with her sisters, glad to escape from
the bad temper of her father and the rough manners of
her brothers. Glad to cut herself free of too many pairs
of clinging hands and too many demanding voices.

'You're going to have to get rid of it, aren't you? Look,
I know what you think but he isn't going to marry you.

They never do,' she said bluntly. Her own life had not
given her tact or sensitivity. As far as she was concerned
the best thing she could do for the silly little fool was
to make her see sense and then, if it wasn't already too
late, to sit her in a bath of near-boiling hot water, and
pour as much gin into her as they could get their hands
on in the hope that it would bring on a spontaneous
abortion.

Sometimes it worked, sometimes it didn't... There
were other methods, but they were too risky, and anyway,
by the looks of it, they were going to have a hard time
persuading her to do what had to be done.

She looked so pale and raw, so childlike almost, but
Donna wasn't deceived. That type could have the will
of a donkey... and the stupidity.

Lizzie stared at her in shocked disbelief. Get rid of
Kit's child... She recoiled from Donna as though she
thought the other girl was going to physically attack her,
her arms crossing protectively over her belly.

'Look, you little fool,' Donna repeated grimly, 'he
isn't going to come back for you. They never do, no
matter what they tell you. Did he give you his address?
Did he tell you anything about himself other than his
name? Do you even know that that's real? You know
what's going to happen to you when it gets out that
you're carrying, don't you? You'll lose your job and
you'll be sent back home...'

Sent back home... To her aunt... For the first time
fear chilled Lizzie's heart. She gave a deep shudder,
totally unable to accept what Donna was saying to her,
and yet at the same time terrified by the mental pictures
Donna was drawing for her. Just for a moment she tried
to imagine what her life would be like if she did have to
return to her aunt, pregnant and unmarried. Her aunt
would never have her back—she would turn her from
her door, and disown her. She started to shiver, suddenly cold and shocked. But why was she afraid?
Nothing like that was going to happen to her. Kit was
going to marry her—she knew it. There was nothing for
her to fear. All she had to do was to hold on to that

truth, to have faith and courage, to remember that Kit loved her.

'Come on, kid—be sensible. You can't be that far along... with any luck, we could get rid of it.'

'No,' Lizzie told her firmly, and then added with quiet dignity, 'Even if you are right about Kit not loving me— and I know you aren't—I still could not destroy my child.'

Donna knew when she was defeated. Muttering under her breath about the folly of her own sex, she withdrew.

Let the little fool learn, then—and she would... It was all right now claiming that she wanted the brat, but let her wait until she was homeless, penniless, disgraced, without a job, without anyone to help her... Then she would sing a different tune. She, Donna, had seen it happen so many times, and to so many girls.

Just for a moment she thought savagely and angrily of the burdens carried by her own sex, and hungered for a time when things would be different, when women would have the right and ability to govern their own lives. But to do that they would have to cast off the emotional shackles they seemed to be born with, to cease loving and depending on men... She herself had no illusions about the male sex. She never intended to marry and she certainly never intended to burden herself with the responsibility and pain of children.

It was many weeks since she had heard from Kit... Weeks during which she had slowly grown accustomed to the fact that she was carrying his child. The end of the war in Europe caused nationwide celebration, but for Lizzie what was happening within her was more important. Kit had not been in touch and she had no way of knowing if victory in Europe had brought him safely home or if he was still in danger somewhere. Until she knew, there could be no celebration for her. Her eighteenth birthday, too, passed without any celebration apart from a card and small present sent by her aunt.

Sometimes, in bed, she pressed her hands to her still-flat stomach in wonder, in love, and sometimes, shamingly, in panic. She knew that Kit loved her, of course she did, but she needed to hear from him, and, even better, to see him... She knew that it was Kit and men like him who were fighting so hard to protect their country, and that she, like countless thousands of other women, must wait in patience and anxiety for his safe return, but she longed so much for the reassurance of his presence, needed him so desperately to ward off the pitying looks of the other girls, for the knowledge that she was now set apart from them, that all of them were silently thanking God that they were not in her shoes, was undermining her courage and faith.

Edward had noticed her withdrawn mood and been concerned about it. But he had not questioned her, believing it was because she found his company a burden.

He had been told by his doctor that, with care, and if he lived as an invalid, his lifespan could stretch for another twenty years, and it was a prospect that made him shudder in horror.

Another twenty years like this... There were mornings when living another twenty hours seemed too great a burden.

Lizzie, normally so sensitive to the moods and feelings of others, was unaware of Edward's despair. She still spent time with him, but her attention to his attempts at conversation had become perfunctory, her concentration narrowed down to the child she carried and her love for its father.

The weather turned colder, with squally winds and showers of rain; her cycle ride to work often left her wet and shivering on her arrival, and, despite the fact that she was pregnant, Lizzie began to lose weight.

She tried desperately hard not to allow her anxiety, her natural fears for the future and her need to be with Kit, to affect her appetite, telling herself that she must eat, if not for her own sake then for her child's, but, no matter how stern she was with herself, once the unappetising plate of food was in front of her her tender stomach rebelled.

Edward was disturbed to see how frail she was becoming. That she had somehow or other found a place in his heart was something he had already come to accept. Nothing could come of it, of course, he acknowledged bitterly. She was a young and potentially very beautiful girl with her whole life ahead of her once this damnable war was over, while for him the future stretched merely painfully into nothingness... A permanent invalid with nothing whatsoever to offer any woman. Bitterly he contrasted himself with his cousin.

A letter had arrived for him in the morning's post. It was from the family firm of solicitors, and he hadn't opened it as yet, suspecting that it was probably a formal warning from Kit to him not to expect to make his home at Cottingdean once Kit was married.

It would be typical of Kit's selfishly egotistical attitude to life to do something like that. What did his cousin think he would do? he wondered savagely as he stared at the envelope—force himself on him? He'd end it all before he'd do that... be forced to live as Kit's pensioner, forced always to be grateful for his contempt, forced to see Kit and Kit's children thriving while his own life dwindled into nothing.

Lizzie was on duty this morning. As always he was looking forward to seeing her. She had promised him an outing into the park. He looked through the window. It was raining and he could see the wind bending the trees. Normally that wouldn't have deterred her, but she was looking so pinched and thin these days. He suspected that none of them, neither the aides nor the nurses, ever really had enough to eat, and they worked desperately hard.

There was a bustle lower down the ward which heralded the change of shifts. He stuffed the letter into his pocket unopened and tried not to search too eagerly for Lizzie's familiar face.

It had rained heavily during the night, and Lizzie had accidently stepped into a huge puddle on her way inside the building. Her shoes were soaked and she was shivering; the last thing she felt like doing was going out again, but as she hurried on to the ward the girl relieving her whispered derogatively, 'I hope you've brought your

mackintosh with you. His nibs is ready and raring to
go...' She tossed her head in Edward's direction, and
Lizzie's heart sank as she saw that the protective blanket
and covering had been pulled over Edward's chair.

Edward saw the tiredness in her eyes as she walked
up to him, and said quickly, 'Ah, Lizzie... I'm sure you
won't want to go out today... It's been such a wet
morning...'

Without wanting to, Lizzie heard the wistful note in
his voice, and wondered how she would have felt cooped
up in here, never breathing in fresh air, never seeing anything other than the grim walls of the ward; she fought
down her own tiredness and cold, and said, as brightly
as she could, 'It is wet, but it has stopped raining now...'

Out of the corner of her eyes she saw Sister giving her
an approving nod as she took hold of Edward's chair
and wheeled it towards the doors. Once outside she
shivered, and Edward, who felt the faint vibration,
frowned.

That coat she was wearing—little more than a jacket
really—was far too thin for this weather. What she
needed was something warm and thick in a good tweed,
he thought protectively. He remembered his mother had
had a coat like that with a huge fur collar.

Edward had a favourite place in the grounds: a small
quiet garden with a stone seat overlooking what had once
been a large circular fishpond with a fountain. The
fountain no longer worked, and the water was choked
with weeds. What goldfish were left were huge and fat,
and somehow rather frightening, Lizzie felt—or was it
simply that she couldn't help contrasting their overfed,
lazy obesity with her own sharp, constant hunger?

She had been feeling more than usually ill this
morning. The sickness had lasted longer than normal
and had left her feeling weak and shaky. As she put the
brake on Edward's chair and sat down on the bench,
she discovered that she was trembling. This morning
when she woke up her face had been wet with tears. She
so desperately needed to hear from Kit. She was so
alone... and, yes, she was beginning to feel frightened

as well. Not that he would desert her—never that—but what if something had happened to him? But whatever happened she would never give up her baby. Never.

Edward saw that she was close to tears, her eyes dark and misty with them, her face surely even paler than ever. He ached to be able to help. He had the sudden presentiment that something was very wrong. As he watched he saw one tear and then another roll down her face, and immediately turned away, wanting to spare her any intrusion into her privacy.

As he turned awkwardly in his chair, he felt the crackle of the envelope in his pocket, and immediately felt for it, keeping his head averted from her as he opened it, wanting to give her time to recover from whatever it was that was upsetting her so much.

He knew virtually nothing about her private life, and had never felt he could ask, frightened of trespassing too much on her kindness, not wanting to burden her with his loneliness, his deep-seated need to form a bond with her that was based on more, he knew, than could ever exist between them.

She was not like the others. She didn't treat him with their rough pity, their feminine contempt for his incompleteness. She was tender and gentle, and he, after all, had his pride, his self-respect.

He removed the letter from the envelope and read it impatiently, stopping suddenly as he realised what it contained, and then rereading it slowly, absorbing the shock of its contents.

At his side, Lizzie was grateful for his tact. She would have died if he had asked her what was wrong. It seemed so improbable that this man should be related by blood to the child she was carrying. He and Kit were so different... What would he say if he knew? Somehow she knew that he would not denounce her, that he would not, as the girls had done, laugh at her and tell her brutally that her child was something she should want to be rid of, a burden, a punishment for having allowed Kit to love her.

She had no idea why she was behaving like this, breaking down into stupid tears. Perhaps it was something to do with the fact that she had received her aunt's monthly letter this morning. It was as chilly and disapproving as all her aunt's missives, cautioning her to work hard and behave herself, warning her against falling into bad company, reminding her that, no matter what kind of immoral standards were set elsewhere, in her household there was only one law, and that was 'Thou shalt not...'

If only she dared ask Edward about Kit, but how could she when she had promised Kit that she would not? Beside her she suddenly heard Edward say in a low voice, 'Oh, my God.'

And immediately she pushed her own problems to one side, turning to him, retrieving the letter he had let fall, and asking anxiously, 'What is it? Are you unwell...? Are you——?'

'No, no, it's nothing like that...'

His hand closed over hers, surprisingly warm and firm, even though the skin itself was soft like a woman's, not hard and slightly scarred as Kit's had been... Kit... Kit...

'It's Kit...my cousin. You may remember he visited me here... I've just heard. He's...he's dead... Killed in action. I must get back...there will be things I'll have to do, arrangements I'll have to make for Cottingdean... I'll have to write to his poor fiancée, too... Poor girl, but I dare say she'll soon find someone else, and she's well out of it... Kit would never have made good husband material——'

He broke off, exclaiming in concern as he saw Lizzie's face. He had never seen anyone lose so much colour. It was as though every drop of blood had drained out of her skin, leaving it as white as though she were a corpse. In fact for a moment he wondered frantically if she was actually still alive—her chest barely seemed to move, her lips, normally so warm and curved, drawn together, only her eyes showing any signs of life, as they glittered with shock and disbelief.

She was trying to say something to him—her mouth opened, but no sound emerged. She was shivering like someone he had once seen in the grip of a malaria attack, her teeth chattering, her body shaking.

He was desperately afraid that she was going to collapse. He should never have insisted on coming out this morning. It was too cold, too wet—he had been selfish.

All his old frustration with his immobility, his wounds, came sweeping over him in a dark, bitter tide. He would have given everything he possessed right now, and that included Cottingdean, to be able to get up and take hold of her, to be able to act as a man, and not as a decaying lump of flesh. As it was all he could do was pray that somehow or other they could get back safely to the hospital.

Furious with himself for his inability to help her, he said awkwardly, 'You aren't well. I should have realised... We must go back...'

Later Lizzie realised that she must have heard the words, because she did reach out and take hold of the chair, did release the brake and turn it round in the direction of the hospital, but she was unaware of doing these things. Unaware of anything at all, other than the raw agony of what was happening inside her.

Kit dead... Kit gone, taken from her... But worse... far, far worse than that was that other knowledge, that frightening, unbelievable knowledge she had been handed so casually, so accidentally almost...

Kit had been engaged to someone else.

'I'll have to write to his poor fiancée...' Edward had said, and she knew, no matter how much she tried to escape from those words, that there was simply no way she could have imagined them. They were real enough—too real, she thought dully.

She had no idea they had reached the hospital until she heard Edward calling out anxiously to a passing nurse, 'Can you help Lizzie? She's unwell...'

She opened her mouth to deny it, but everything was wavering around her, turning crimson and then black, opening up to swallow her in a terrifying, pain-filled void.

Edward fretted anxiously all afternoon, asking everyone he could how Lizzie was, and what was wrong with her.

In the end nurses grew impatient with him, and Sister came bustling down the ward, her mouth prim.

'Now, then, Major Danvers, there's no use your working yourself up into a state. There's nothing wrong with Miss Bailey. Nothing that you need blame yourself for, anyhow,' she added grimly. Really, these girls...you'd think they'd have more sense than to get themselves into that sort of trouble. Well, this one would be sent packing just as soon as the doctor discharged her and from the talk she had had with matron, who knew the girl's aunt, she'd receive scant sympathy from that quarter. Sister's bosom heaved beneath her starched apron.

She was fifty-four and unmarried. These girls with their stupidity and their man problems infuriated her. Normally she could tell which ones were going to give her trouble. Never in a hundred years would she have thought that this girl—but there you were, it just went to show.

Her mouth pursed again, and Edward sensed uneasily that something was being withheld from him.

'Come on, now, Major Danvers—it will soon be time for your medicine...'

Sister thought she was being kind. After all, what could it mean to a man like this that the stupid girl had gone and got herself in trouble? That kind of thing could no longer be any part of his life.

All night Edward fretted. No matter whom he asked, no one would tell him what was wrong with Lizzie.

Lizzie herself, banned from returning to her hostel, was lying in bed, under the grimly disapproving eye of a nurse.

She had been told immediately the doctor had discovered her condition that she was to be sent home. At first, in the anguish and misery of discovering that Kit was dead, that Kit, no matter how much he might have loved her, had been engaged to someone else, she had had no thought in her head for what was happening to her.

But now, lying sleepless and frightened, the reality of her situation was beginning to seep into her. She was going to have a baby, a baby whose father was now dead and to whom she was not married... Just for a moment she conjured wildly with the idea of pretending that she and Kit had been married... but that would be dishonest. She knew she could not do it, which left her with having to face Aunt Vi. Always providing that the latter would allow her into the house once she knew why she was being sent home.

She lay shivering in bed, dreading the morning, crying silent tears of pain and fear.

Edward too could not sleep. A nurse on her late-night rounds saw how he twisted and turned and, being new to the ward, sent for the doctor.

'Something bothering you, old chap?' the doctor asked. He was overdue for retirement, thin and exhausted by the stress of trying to do the work of four much younger men. He had seen so much pain and suffering during the years of the war that he had developed a self-protective distancing mechanism, without which he suspected he might well have lost his sanity, but there was something about Edward that had always reached out to him.

'It's about Lizzie, Miss Bailey,' Edward elucidated when he frowned. 'She became ill this morning when we were out... No one will tell me what's wrong with her.'

The doctor wasn't a narrow-minded man. One look at the pale, tragic face of the young girl Sister had summoned him to see had told its own story. He had felt desperately sorry for her, and angry with her at the same time. They were such fools, these young girls, and the more innocent they were, the more foolish.

Now, looking at his patient's tense face, he decided that if he hadn't known that Edward was an amputee he might almost have suspected... after all, presumably there was still a chance, albeit a very faint chance, that he could father a child.

'Silly little fool's gone and got herself into trouble,' he said brusquely. 'That's the problem with these young girls... Their heads get turned by some young man, he tells them a few lies, says he loves them...pity, but there's nothing to be done about it. Rules are rules. She'll have to be sent home. Only got an aunt to go to, and by the sound of it she's a bit of a tartar, a friend of matron's who probably won't treat the poor child too well—but what can you do? We aren't running a home for silly young girls...'

Edward stared at him in shock.

Lizzie...little Lizzie pregnant...he couldn't believe it...he wouldn't believe it...

'The man,' he demanded. 'The father...?'

The doctor shook his head.

'Dead, so I understand... Matron managed to get that much out of her, although she wouldn't give his name. An airman, by all accounts. Probably never intended to marry her anyway, they never do, although she'd never believe that, poor soul...'

Lizzie pregnant, Lizzie who was little more than a child herself... So pure and so innocent, that he could have sworn...And then suddenly he knew the truth.

Lizzie, his Lizzie was carrying Kit's child. He didn't question how he knew, or why he should feel this possessively fierce emotion towards Lizzie herself; he only knew that from the deep welling emotion inside him came two sure facts. The first was that Kit, his hated cousin, had destroyed Lizzie's innocence, had deceived and defiled her, had no doubt lied to her and deserted her, and the second was that he had to see Lizzie, to talk to her...

He was awake for the rest of the night thinking and planning. The doctor had inadvertently let slip the fact that Lizzie was being sent home in disgrace in the morning. Always an imaginative man, Edward had grasped all that the doctor was not saying and, having grown up in a small enclosed community himself, he knew quite well how Lizzie and her child would be treated, if she was allowed to remain with her aunt.

That could not be allowed to happen. Lizzie did not deserve to suffer that kind of pain, that kind of rejection. Her child... He stopped suddenly. Lizzie's child would be his nephew, his heir...Lizzie's child would one day inherit Cottingdean. There could be no other heirs. After all, Kit was dead, and he... well, he might as well be for all the use he was...

But he could be of use to Lizzie... He was still a man... in the eyes of the law at least... and not just any man. He was a man who now owned the house which would one day belong to Lizzie's child.

Once, long ago, it would have been his responsibility to marry and provide heirs, heirs for the land and the house. Lizzie, though, already carried such a child, the only child of Danvers blood there could ever be. His brain spun with ideas, urgent and clamouring. If he were to marry Lizzie...

His ears were buzzing. He felt curiously light-headed, as though he had suddenly discovered a wonderful and mystical secret, as though he had suddenly been admitted into an awareness that life could still hold hope, anticipation, a future.

And as he lay back against his pillows, exhausted by the enormity of his thoughts, his plans, it came to him that fate might just possibly have relented, that she might after all have turned the tide and be handing him the lifeline he needed so desperately to hang on to if he was to make anything of the worthless remnants of his shattered life.

He already had Cottingdean—what was to stop him having everything else as well? He had Kit's inheritance—why should he not have Kit's child? In his hands, under his care, with his love that child would, after all, grow to maturity with far, far more than Kit would ever have given it.

And last, but most definitely not least, he would have Lizzie, gentle, beautiful Lizzie who walked through the

dull greyness of his days like a rainbow, bringing them
to life, giving them colour and substance.

But would Lizzie want to marry him? She was young,
beautiful, desirable...what if she would marry him now
and then at some later stage leave him? She was so
young—was it even fair of him to think in terms of marriage? Why not simply offer a home, a haven?

Was it just because he knew how people would gossip,
especially once they saw she was having a child, or was
it because secretly all the time this was what he had
wanted?

Lizzie couldn't sleep either. The closer it got to morning
the more afraid she became.

Matron had left her in no doubts as to what her aunt's
reaction to her condition was going to be. The enormity
of the future that lay ahead for her was slowly breaking
through the anguish of losing Kit. Kit who, she was just
beginning to realise, had never been hers in the first
place.

Her heart started to beat painfully fast...she felt so
frightened and alone. Even more than she had done when
she had first been sent to live with her aunt.

For the first time she found herself almost wishing
there was no baby, but she suppressed the thought,
ashamed of her own weakness. How could she deny Kit's
child? Her hands closed protectively on her stomach as
she begged the growing foetus to forgive her. Of course
she wanted it, of course she loved it, of course any
hardship she had to bear would be more than worthwhile.

And then she remembered what it was like for the one
or two women she knew who had given birth to illegitimate children—how they were shunned by the village
women and sniggered at by the men, how their children
were treated by their peers—and she felt her eyes burn
with tears. One of them, a girl of her own age, had even
taken her own life rather than face the gossip. She shuddered sickly, mortally afraid for her child and for herself.

Oh, Kit... How could you leave me? I need you so
much, she whispered silently in her thoughts. But Kit
had left her, she was alone, and Kit had never really

been hers anyway. Kit had been engaged to someone else. He had deceived her—and she had believed him. The bright, strong love she had thought so precious had been nothing more than the base metal of lust. She shuddered, remembering how little she had enjoyed Kit's sexual possession of her, accepting it only because of her love for him.

Edward waited until the change of shift. There was always confusion around this time when the night shift went off and the morning shift came on.

He commandeered another patient to wheel him to the small side-ward where Lizzie was lying.

She heard his chair and turned to look at him, her face flooding with embarrassed colour.

Pity and anger filled him as he watched the way she almost cringed back from him. Already she was being marked by the stigma of his cousin's defilement. Already she had lost her fresh look of innocence. Already her body looked strained by the burden of the child she was carrying.

Lizzie turned her head away as Edward reached her. The other man had gone, leaving the two of them alone after a muttered conversation during which Edward asked him to return for him in ten minutes.

Tears burned her eyes. She couldn't bear to look at Edward. She knew from his face that he knew. Now, when no amount of anger and shock from others had been able to make her feel shame, Edward's quiet face did.

He saw the way her shoulders heaved and fresh anger struck him. He could have killed Kit for this alone.

'Lizzie, don't,' he said gently, touching her shoulder. 'It's Kit, isn't it? Kit, my cousin, is the father of your child. And it's my fault that you're here like this now. My clumsiness yesterday...'

'Is it true that he was engaged to someone else?'

Edward froze. He should have anticipated this. She had loved him, poor child...he had realised that instantly, knowing that Lizzie was not the kind to give herself to any man without believing that.

For a moment he was tempted to tell her the truth, but he couldn't. 'Yes,' he said and then added quickly, 'But he told me the last time I saw him that he intended to break the engagement...'

It wasn't perhaps entirely a lie. He knew that Kit had had every intention of marrying his fiancée but he had certainly never loved her. Privately Edward doubted that he had ever loved anyone other than himself, but he was not going to tell Lizzie this.

'Look, I've only got ten minutes and I must talk to you. Please try to listen. I know how much you must be suffering, but it's important, not just to you, but to your child.'

He felt the tension in her body and although she didn't turn round he knew he had her attention.

'You realise, don't you, that this child, Kit's child will one day be my heir—that he will inherit Cottingdean from me, as I have now inherited from Kit. I know from Dr Marshall that you are to be sent home today to your aunt, and I suspect from what he tells me that she won't make you very welcome. Lizzie, you know as well as I do that I shall be an invalid for the rest of my life, dependent on the care of others, that it's very doubtful that I shall have a child of my own—but your child, Kit's child, has a right to be brought up at Cottingdean... after all, one day it will be his. I wish I could offer you the protection of my home as my cousin's widow, I wish we could freely acknowledge your relationship with him and the child's, but I'm afraid that that isn't possible. I want to take you and the child to Cottingdean with me, Lizzie. After all, it's his right and yours. If Kit had lived he would have married you and taken you there himself.'

He was sure it wasn't true and that Kit would not have done any such thing, but he couldn't bring himself to tell her as much.

'I want you to come to Cottingdean with me, Lizzie... I want you to marry me.'

Lizzie sat up in bed and stared at him.

Was she dreaming, or had Edward just proposed to her? She swallowed a hysterical desire to burst out laughing, more in agony than amusement. She had dreamed so long of Kit asking her to marry him, of being Kit's wife, that now to be asked to marry Edward struck her as such a parody of her dreams, such a mocking cruelty of fate that she almost didn't know how she could stand it.

Marry Edward... Edward, nice and kind though he was, was an invalid, as he had said himself. Edward could never be a husband to her nor would she want him to be—not sexually. That part of her life was over. She would never again allow another man to love her as Kit had.

Edward could never take Kit's place, but Edward could protect her, a small inner voice told her. Edward could throw a cloak of respectability around her and her unborn child. Edward could stop her being sent home to face her aunt.

No, Edward was not Kit, but what man ever could be? She shuddered sickly, trying and failing to imagine even wanting to share with another man the intimacies she had known with Kit. Intimacies which even with the man she loved she had found painful, and distasteful. Intimacies which, if she was honest, she would be only too pleased to have completely removed from her life.

Marry Edward. She ought to have already said no, so why hadn't she?

'Think of the child,' Edward pressed, sensing all that was going through her mind. Her face was so clear, her thoughts so readable in her eyes.

'Think,' he urged. 'I know what a sacrifice it will be for you, but it's what Kit would want for his child, his son—that he should grow up at Cottingdean.'

He knew that Kit wouldn't have given a damn about his child, son or daughter, but he was never going to tell Lizzie that.

'Marry me, Lizzie,' he demanded, suddenly bold and decisive, reminding her sharply and painfully of Kit, so that for a moment she was confused and lost.

She felt so weak, so helpless...she had been so frightened, and now here was Edward offering her sanctuary, escape. Hope for herself and her child. And he was right, she acknowledged, taking a deep breath. Her son, Kit's son should be brought up in his father's old home, should be saved from the slur of illegitimacy.

'It's what Kit would want,' Edward repeated firmly.

'What Kit would want...' Yes, of course it was... Suddenly everything was so simple, so easy—she must do as Edward said, she must marry him.

They would be safe then. She and her baby, safe for ever. The baby from the cruelty of others because of its illegitimacy, and she from the greed and pain of male sexuality.

Once married to Edward she would be safe, protected from other men's desire. She would be Edward's wife and Edward would never be able to demand of her the physical intimacy she now feared so much.

She was just eighteen years old but suddenly felt as though she were close to eighty.

CHAPTER SIX

TODAY Edward and I were married. Lizzie stared at the words, as though they were written in a foreign language and meant nothing to her. How flat and metallic they tasted in her own mind. How devoid of the euphoria and joy with which she had written of meeting Kit. Everything had happened so quickly. Edward had had to get her aunt's permission for the marriage, as she was under age. She still wasn't sure how he had accomplished it, since her aunt had flatly refused to have anything more to do with her. Now she was Mrs Danvers. Pain spiralled through her. Mrs Edward Danvers, when she ought to have been Mrs Christopher Danvers. Her eyes felt dry and gritty. She had cried too many tears already. She had none left.

All at once she couldn't wait to leave the hospital, to escape to the new life that Edward had promised her. He was as excited as a small child about the prospect of returning to his childhood home. He had painted it for her in such glowing colours that already she could see it in her mind's eye. She wondered a little doubtfully how she would fit into such elegant surroundings. She had visited such houses with her aunt, and had always felt intimidated by them. All those pretty, delicate antiques, all that fragile china . . . those silky pastel carpets, and those polished, shiny floors.

But at Cottingdean it would be different. Cottingdean would be her home. She would be its mistress, her child its heir. Her child . . . not just her child any more, but hers and Edward's.

The only person to try to talk her out of it had been Dr Marshall. Had she really thought about what this marriage would mean? he had asked her gruffly—not just immediately, but for the rest of her life. Did she

157

realise how long Edward could live? he had pressed when she stared apathetically at him, and then had added roughly, angrily almost, 'For heaven's sake, child, you must know the man can never be a proper husband to you. Right now you might not mind that too much... women in your condition seldom do... but afterwards, and in all the years to come...'

When his meaning had sunk in Lizzie had flushed, not with embarrassment, but with guilt. Guilt, because all she could feel was relief and a sense of revulsion at the thought of such intimacy with any man. If she had not enjoyed sex with Kit then how on earth could she ever possibly enjoy it with any other man? No, she obviously was one of those women designed by nature to be sexually unresponsive. After all, Kit himself had hinted as much. Now she realised that he had been right.

Dimly she was aware of Edward's kindness and concern for her, his attempt to protect her, but so vast was the ocean of pain that engulfed her, so all-consuming her misery and inability to focus on anything other than the knowledge that she must somehow endure the anguish of losing Kit for the sake of the child they had created together, that there was no room within her to comprehend anything else.

By some alchemy to which the female sex genetically held licence she had managed to transform Kit from the selfish, arrogant, uncaring man he had been into someone he was most definitely not. Already in her memory he was enshrined as a perfect human being, her one and only true love. Edward, her marriage to him, the kind of life they would live together, they were only dim shadows when compared to the bright glitter of her love for Kit.

The vicar, who had performed during the years of this war more brief wedding ceremonies than he cared to remember, had been shocked by the appearance of this particular couple: the bride so young—too young, surely—the groom, so much older, so obviously very, very ill.

Lizzie had been surprised to discover that Edward had arranged for a photographer to record the moment they left the church, watched by a largely silent group of onlookers.

'It's for the child,' he had explained to her later. The child. Lizzie frowned, suddenly jealously anxious to protect Kit's rights to his son. This was his child she was carrying within her. Kit's child. And one day when he was old enough she would tell him all about his father...she would tell him. Her thoughts stopped abruptly, as she realised how little she could tell anyone about Kit, how little she had actually known of him, how dependent she would be on Edward to supply those details, that information...but Edward wanted to bring the child up as his own. He had already told her as much, and she had listened, too shocked in the aftermath of learning of Kit's death to do anything else.

'If we don't marry there will be gossip,' he had warned her. She shivered suddenly, goose-bumps lifting under her flesh, and she stood stiffly beside Edward in the thin cotton dress he had insisted on her buying. She had been uncomfortable and embarrassed when he had handed her the coupons and the money, awkwardly insisting that she was to buy herself something pretty. It had been on the tip of her tongue to tell him that she would rather use his gift to buy something for the baby, but something, some feminine caution that was unfamiliar to her warned her not to. The only dress she had been able to find was too big, its fabric cheap and flimsy, and no protection against the cold wind howling round the small churchyard.

As they passed between the ranks of onlookers, Lizzie was suddenly conscious of the desolate, melancholy air of the whole place, the gravestones, bearing silent witness to the many, many generations that had come and gone, and now were no more. Kit had no gravestone—there was nothing to mark his passing. She shivered again and turned impulsively to Edward, begging huskily, 'Edward, could you...? Is there a church at Cottingdean? Could you...could you have something there for...for Kit...?'

Edward patted her hand, pity warring with jealousy. She was so young still, so vulnerable, and yet at the same time, because of her youth, so hardy and protected that she still had no real idea of what Kit had been. He could almost read in her heart how she intended to cherish his cousin's image there. Even in death it seemed that his cousin still intended to dominate his life.

He was not a cruel man—the blows life had dealt him had taught him great compassion for the weaknesses of others. Lizzie was young and malleable; more importantly, she was carrying the child who would one day inherit Cottingdean, and he had no wish to alienate her, to destroy her dream, to take away from her what might be a necessary crutch. But nor was he going to allow the child, his child, to be brought up to worship the fictitious image of his cousin.

His child...Kit's son would be his child in all the ways that mattered. He looked at his new bride. There would be plenty of time later for him to acquaint Lizzie with his determination that no one other than themselves must ever know the child's true parentage... Plenty of time. He loved her, and one day maybe...

There was no reception. There was rationing, and besides, the matron of the hospital was furious about the way she believed Lizzie had cunningly contrived not only to get herself out of the disgrace she had so wantonly fallen into, but also to elevate herself socially at the same time. Edward Danvers might be an invalid, he might not have more than two pennies to rub together, but he was still one of Them...the élite, mysterious hierarchy of the upper classes, even if his family's feet were only on its lowest rungs. The matron scorned Lizzie. She had no backbone; she was far too soft, too easy with the patients, and yet...and yet she had managed to go and get herself married to one of Them...scheming, conniving little hussy...

They left the hospital with nothing more than a suitcase apiece, Edward's an old battered leather one, with his father's initials still on it, and Lizzie's much the same, only hers had not been handed down to her by her father, but had originally been the property of Lady Jeveson, just like the heavy tweed suit she was wearing as protection against the cold, squally weather.

The village's one taxi deposited them at the station. The platform was already crowded, filled in the main with American servicemen from nearby. Most of them had girls with them: pretty girls, wearing bright red lipstick and shiny American nylons.

The train was crowded, even in the first class carriage which Edward had insisted on. Lizzie had never travelled first class before. She had expected the other people in the carriage with them to be like the families her aunt had occasionally visited: stiff, arrogant dowagers, with their cowed daughters and daughters-in-law, their grandchildren, and their dogs, the latter normally being more indulged than any child of the house ever was, but the other occupants of their carriage were a group of American servicemen and their girls. One of the men in particular reminded her of Kit, not so much in his looks, but more in his manner, causing a sudden sharp feeling of despair and desolation to sweep over her.

At her side Edward sat silently in his chair. Neither of them had spoken since getting on the train, and Lizzie was shamefully aware of how little she actually wanted to talk to Edward. All she wanted was to be alone with her memories of Kit, and all the time the one thing she had to hold on to was the knowledge that she was to have his child. She felt disorientated and confused. Too much had happened and too fast for her to take it all in.

Opposite the Americans and their girls were all laughing and smoking. One of the men, the one who reminded her so sharply of Kit, reached towards his girl, clasping her waist while she giggled and protested. 'Aw, come on, babe, you weren't so reluctant last night,' Lizzie heard him saying, as he grinned at his companion, and then, in front of Lizzie's shocked eyes, openly slid his hand into the bosom of her dress.

Inside her stomach something twisted sharply, something uncomfortable and painful, some hidden memory of her own that made her, just for one compelling second, see in the other couple not two strangers, but herself and Kit. And her body tensed with rejection of their sexuality.

She shivered suddenly, and one of the other girls asked solicitously, 'You all right, ducks?' Lizzie nodded. 'Your dad doesn't look so good, though. He's fallen asleep now... best thing for him.'

Lizzie stared at her. The other girl thought that Edward was her father. Lizzie knew how old he was... just thirty. It seemed old to her, but he had been only a few years older than Kit, she recognised dizzily... Of course, he did look much older: his hair was so grey, his body so twisted with pain. But her *father*...

Out of the corner of her eye she saw that the soldier who reminded her of Kit was now kissing his girlfriend, pressing her back against the dusty seat with such explicit sexuality that Lizzie had to look away. She felt a surge of relief that she would never be subjected to male desire, would never again have to pretend... Her growing revulsion towards sex was something she accepted as a flaw in her own nature, never even considering laying it at Kit's door for his lack of sensitivity, his lack of love, or at her aunt's for bringing her up to regard intimacy between men and women as something to be endured rather than enjoyed. Too young to be able to form her own opinion and values, she took those of others as being implicitly and absolutely true.

Something, some impetus she couldn't entirely understand made her focus on the girl who had addressed her and say quickly as she looked down at the worn weddingring Edward had given her, the one which had belonged to his mother and which was too big for her, 'Edward isn't my father... he's my husband.' Bravely, she looked straight at the other girl, defying her to offer pity or shock, and although she herself didn't recognise it she had taken her first step towards maturity.

Edward was not asleep. He was in far too much pain to sleep. He had seen and heard everything, and he wondered bleakly just what the future was going to hold. Was he mad, crazy, to have married Lizzie? At the moment she was still in a state of shock, still too distressed by Kit's death to care what happened to her. A small part of her was grateful to him, because he had offered her a means of escape from her aunt, from poverty, from the stigma of bearing an illegitimate child. But once that shock had gone, once she had to face up to the reality of what marriage to him would mean, how would she feel then? Would she still be grateful to him, or would she grow to hate him, to look on him as a burden? She was just eighteen. Far, far too young to be tied to a man like him. But he loved her so much...needed her so much.

In Bath they had to change trains and wait over three hours for the slow-moving local one, which would take them to Cottingdean. Lizzie could see that Edward was exhausted and, she guessed, in considerable pain. Dr Marshall had given her Edward's medication, and a letter to be given to Edward's own doctor. He had also warned her of the dangers to Edward's health, and how vulnerable he was. Her husband would always have to live as an invalid, he had reminded her, and Lizzie had accepted the knowledge without comment, without really being aware of what it meant.

As the local train wound its way through a succession of small villages she could see that the only thing sustaining Edward was the knowledge that he was returning to somewhere where he had once been happy.

She had tried to visualise Cottingdean from the mental pictures he had painted for her, but, despite his obvious love for it, all she had been able to see in her mind's eye was a formidable and unfriendly sprawl, the kind of house which she and her aunt had only ever entered via the back door. Now she was going to be Cottingdean's mistress. The knowledge made her shiver, and by the time the train actually stopped at the small overgrown station she was both tired and nervous, the queasy feeling in her stomach intensifying once she and Edward were alone on the platform.

Edward had telegraphed ahead to warn the elderly couple looking after the house that they were arriving, but there was no taxi waiting for them, and it was Lizzie who had to walk into the dusty booking office and find the clerk, an elderly, gnarled man, who frowned uncomprehendingly at her as she tried to make him understand what she wanted.

'A taxi... There's none around here, missie...' he told her, shaking his head. 'Most folks use old John Davies's trap if they're wanting to go anywhere... Either that or their own legs,' he added. 'The only person who has a car round here is the doctor, and he's over at Miller's farm delivering Maisie Miller's fifth...'

Lizzie went back to Edward to report what she had learned. Seeing him abruptly as she emerged from the booking office, she was struck by the greyness of his skin, the weary exhaustion that made her realise just why the girl on the train had assumed he was so much older.

Seeing him away from the familiar surroundings of the hospital she noticed with a sudden start of disquiet just how frail he was. Somehow at the hospital she had taken it for granted...but now comparing him with other men, men like the Americans, and even the old clerk, with his leathery, weathered skin with its healthy, ruddy colour, she was sharply aware of just how ill Edward was.

'How far is it to Cottingdean?' she asked him.

'About two miles.'

'Oh, well, that's nothing, we'll walk,' she told him, trying not to let him see how discouraged she felt, how frightened and alone, as it suddenly came home to her that it wasn't only Kit's baby who was now her responsibility, but Edward as well. Edward, her responsibility... But she was his wife, he was her husband... It should be the other way round. Suddenly she felt very frightened, very alone...

Behind her Edward was protesting, but she could see how tired he was, how much he was longing for his home. Telling herself that it would probably take less time in the long run to walk than it would to find some means of transport, she reminded herself that she had pushed Edward's chair just as far on previous occasions... But then she had not been pregnant. Then she had not been alone, isolated from any means of help. Then she had not been Edward's wife.

They had arrived at the station late in the afternoon—the village was deserted, its one street just as picturesque as she had visualised. It had a pretty, welcoming air about it, enhanced by the rich verdancy of the summer countryside. Edward directed her towards a track that ran at right angles to the main road. The land either side of the track was heavily cultivated, poppies providing brave patches of colour in the waving corn, dog roses flowering palely in the hedgerows. The track itself was overgrown with coarse grass, and plainly unused. It also ran uphill at a slight angle, and she was soon out of breath from pushing the heavy chair. Pushing it along this rutted track with its sharp stones hidden in the grass, its bumpy surface and deep ruts, was nothing like pushing it around the grounds of the hospital. She ached to stop, her legs felt weak and had started to tremble, her arm muscles straining with the effort of pushing the chair, but something inside her refused to allow her to stop.

It was as though she was locked in some fierce inner battle... as though she must persevere... as though she must reach Cottingdean without giving in to her physical need to rest. It was as though something inside her was warning her that it was time for her to shed her vulnerabilities, her fears, both physically and emotionally, and that she must take hold of her life and control it for herself, no matter how hard she might find it.

Lost in her own strange thoughts, she had stopped looking at her surroundings until Edward called out excitedly, 'Look, Lizzie, there it is. There's Cottingdean...'

There was such pride and joy in his voice that at first Lizzie automatically looked beyond the low huddle of buildings with its tall, crooked chimneys, instinctively searching for something more imposing, more in keeping with the mental images Edward had drawn for her, only slowly realising that there was nothing else, that that huddle of steeply pitched roofs, those chimneys which looked as though they were in imminent danger of collapse, did actually belong to Edward's beloved Cottingdean.

Later she was glad that Edward had not been able to see her face, that in addition to everything else he had to cope with he did not have to cope with the realisation of her shocked disbelief that anyone could possibly love such a forlorn, unkept, decaying collection of stone and slate.

'There it is!' Edward called out triumphantly. 'Cottingdean.' And she could tell from the pride and excitement in his voice that he did not see it as she saw it; that he did not see the neglect, the desolation, the sagging roofs, and damp lichen-covered walls. The lane petered out and ahead of them lay open a pair of dilapidated wooden gates, to either side of which ran stone walls. The gates seemed to perplex Edward. He stared at them as Lizzie fought to control her own shock. This was Cottingdean ... this ruin of a building with its sagging roofs and tell-tale damp marks on the walls, its blind yawning windows, many of them without glass, its tangles of weeds and poor, unproductive fields. This was the nirvana which Edward had described so lyrically to her. This was the Eden to which her child was heir.

She could hardly believe what she was seeing. She looked at Edward, expecting to hear him mirror her own shock, but he seemed oblivious to the neglect. On his face was a blind, rapt look of joy. 'Cottingdean ... at last. I suppose the gates went towards new tanks—a pity, but perhaps things will improve now after the war.' Lizzie was astonished that he could think of such things. What concerned her now were their immediate needs. Food, rest, somewhere to spend the night. Because she was sure they could not spend it here in this ruined and uninhabited place. Where were the couple Edward had told her were looking after the house?

Lizzie had come prepared to be overwhelmed by the house, by its history, by its richness, its traditions, its staff, and yet it was plain to her from the moment she set eyes on the place that her new home was nothing more than a desolate shell. 'I wonder what's happened to the Johnsons?' Edward said, frowning, as Lizzie attempted to push the wheelchair down the overgrown drive. 'Kit told me that they'd agreed to stay on until he could sell the place. It was requisitioned at the beginning of the war, and then never used. No, none of the family has actually lived in it since my grandmother died.'

Was he beginning to see, to realise the vast difference that lay between his memories and reality? Lizzie wondered. Suddenly she had almost a motherly urge to protect him, to allow him just a little longer to cling on to his dreams. She knew well enough what it was like to lose those dreams. The only thing she had left to cling to now was Kit's child...Kit's son.

They were within sight of the front door now, and Lizzie's heart sank as she saw how it yawned open. No one lived here, no matter what Edward had been told. No one had lived here for a long time. As she stopped the wheelchair, she waited for Edward to suggest that they walk back to the village, that they find somewhere to spend the night, but he said nothing and as she went to look at him, she saw that his face was crumpled like a child's, shadowed with shock and grief.

'I don't understand... Where are the Johnsons? Why isn't there anyone here? The house seems almost deserted...'

In his voice she could almost hear his plea that she contradict him, but Lizzie couldn't. Neither, she found, could she tell him, as she knew she should, that they would have to go back, that it was pointless going inside to see what further desolation awaited them. Instead she heard herself saying brightly, 'Well, we'd better go in...'

The front door was rotten in places, and festooned with cobwebs. Beyond it lay a dark, stone-floored hallway—so dark, so polluted with the rank scent of damp and disuse that she recoiled from it automatically. Her pregnancy had sharpened her sense of smell, and the odour now assaulting her nostrils made her body quiver with rejection. It was the smell of decay and death, the smell of darkness, of hidden underground places shut off from light and warmth. But Edward was waiting for her to push him inside, and as she did so she realised that the lack of light was due to the blackout covers crudely fastened to the windows.

As her eyes grew accustomed to the dimness she saw the outline of a huge stone fireplace. On the opposite wall were the stairs, a gallery above them, behind which was obviously a large window. The walls of the hallway had obviously once been panelled, but now the panelling was rotting away, had been torn away in places, she recognised.

Several doors led off the hallway, and as she stood in silence, surveying her surroundings, a large rat ran across the floor, squeaking angrily as it saw them, invaders in what was plainly its territory. 'Well, that's one thing we'll need to do,' she said briskly, sounding more like her aunt than she knew.

'What's that?' Edward asked painfully. He looked as though he could not believe his eyes, and, while originally she had felt angry with him for his refusal to see the house as it really was, now she felt the opposite. She wanted to protect him, to tell him that things weren't as bad as they seemed.

'Get ourselves a good farm cat to sort out those rats...'

'I suppose Vic the shepherd will know where best to get one... That's if we still have a shepherd, or any sheep. What's happened to this place? I don't understand.'

His shoulders sagged. He looked old...careworn, and yet almost childish at the same time, Lizzie recognised.

Instinctively she went to comfort him, kneeling down beside his chair and taking one of his hands in hers. 'It won't be so bad, you'll see... It just needs a bit of a clean-up. It seems worse because there's no one here. When the Johnsons get back and we find out what's going on——'

Edward laughed harshly. 'Use your head, Lizzie. The Johnsons aren't coming back. Look at the state of this place. No one could live here. No one *has* lived here. I just don't understand.'

'Maybe some of the other rooms are better,' Lizzie suggested brightly. 'Let's go and have a look, shall we?'

Half an hour later she and Edward stared at one another in silence. The house plainly had not been lived in for years. Everywhere there were signs of decay, of damp and mould...in every room. None of the rooms was really habitable, and even if they had been clean and sound there was still the small matter of the lack of furniture. Lizzie fought down a wild desire to laugh, remembering the antiques, the exquisite china, the silks and damasks she had visualised. These rooms, with their clothing of cobwebs and moulds, their once expensive wallpapers peeling from the walls, their broken windows covered in cheap blackout fabric, their panelling torn from walls, their ceilings crumbling away...these rooms were nothing like that. There was no furniture other than a collection of trestle tables and battered chairs, which had plainly been intended for the use of the men who might have been stationed here when the house was first requisitioned.

Only the kitchen bore some resemblence to the house she had visualised. It had, as she had suspected, a huge old-fashioned range, a worn deal table, two rockers either side of the range, and a large dresser with its complement of dirty pottery and copper. In one corner stood a deep sink with one tap. She turned it on experimentally, grimacing at the dirt, and watching cautiously as water started to spurt into the sink, testing it carefully with her finger and then sucking it. The water tasted clear and sharp and was icy cold, suggesting that it came from an underground spring.

As she stared around the room, although she didn't know it, Lizzie was judging it by the standards given to her by her aunt. She had already seen that the range, if it worked, must heat the domestic water, that its ovens could be used for cooking and baking and that its warmth, with its door opened, might just, just be enough to warm this large, cavernous room.

Somewhere outside in the jumble of outbuildings surrounding the yard must be a fuel store... If there was

any fuel. She heard a sound and turned her head. Edward
was slumped in his chair, his head in his hands. The
sound she could hear, the noise tearing into the silence
of the house, was the sound of his grief, she recognised
dispassionately. Edward, as she had already done, was
crying for his lost love, for the love which had sustained
him for so long and which he was now seeing cruelly
revealed in all its stark reality.

It was impossible for them to stay here, and yet it was
impossible for them to go, for her to push the chair back
to the station, for them to wait for another train to take
them—where? To Bath? To do what?

Although Edward now owned Cottingdean, there was
very little money. He had already explained that to her.
The flock, which had once produced Cottingdean's
wealth, had suffered through sickness during the last
years of his grandparents' lives, and there had not been
the money to replace the sheep.

And there had been the war; bad investments by his
grandfather had further impoverished the estate. The
only money Edward had came from his pension and a
small trust fund. 'My God, what have I done to you?'
she heard him saying harshly behind her. 'Kit must have
known about this. Damn him!' A protest came to her
lips, but she swallowed it. Now was not the time to
champion her love. Edward was like a man who suddenly discovered that his lover had been false to him.
He was beyond logic, beyond reason, beyond accepting
that the extent of the decay meant that the house had
fallen into disrepair long before Kit could have inherited
it...

'We can't stay here...'

'I think we'll have to,' Lizzie told him gently. 'For
tonight at least. If I can find some fuel I could light the
range. There might be mattresses upstairs. If they were
going to use the house to quarter men here, it is possible.
We... I could bring two down. If we aired them in front
of the range...'

'Sleep here?' Edward stared at her as though she had
taken leave of her senses. 'We can't... It's impossible.'

Suddenly she could feel herself losing her temper, losing her self-control. 'We don't have any option,' she told him fiercely. 'Edward, don't you understand? I can't push you back to the village. Who knows when we would get a train, and then where would we go? To Bath? To do what? You said yourself there was no money... You said we'd have to learn to be as self-sufficient as we could; grow our own food, maintain a smallholding on the land...' When he'd said those things she'd envisaged a life filled with the kind of food served by her aunt. Milk from a Jersey cow...fresh green vegetables...soft fruits in season...eggs from their own hens. Remembering the overgrown wilderness lying either side of the drive, she knew bitterly that it would be a long, long time before such a garden could be tamed to yield any kind of food crop.

'But I didn't know it was going to be like this,' Edward whispered. He looked tired and broken, more of a child than a man. A very, very old child, who suddenly looked frighteningly frail.

To keep her mind off her own desolation, Lizzie forced herself to sound cheerful. 'Look, you wait here... I'll go outside and see if there's any fuel. If we can get the range lit...'

'We!' Edward laughed bitterly. 'We!' But Lizzie wasn't listening. She was unbolting the back door and stepping outside into the yard.

The outbuildings were in much the same state of decay as the rest of the house. She had little hope of finding any fuel. She suspected now that the panelling had been used at some stage to feed a fire, which must suggest that there was no supply of wood. Even so, she searched methodically through several small, dark sheds, before coming to the stable proper, empty now of its occupants, although it still retained a rich earthy smell of hay, manure and leather. A large tarpaulin covered something in one corner, and it was curiosity more than anything else that made her lift it. To discover beneath it an enormous pile of neatly cut and split logs was like discovering gold. At first she could hardly believe she

wasn't just seeing things. She stood and blinked and then
blinked again, and when the logs refused to go away she
looked round quickly for something to put them in, in
the end using a large galvanised bucket.

When she staggered into the kitchen with them Edward
barely looked around. His skin looked grey and pinched,
and he was rubbing his hands together in a way he had
whenever something troubled him deeply. She had seen
other patients at the hospital doing the same thing, and
knew that it was not a good sign. She spoke to Edward,
trying to sound positive and cheerful, but when he looked
at her it was as though he no longer saw her.

When she asked him for his matches he stared blankly
at her, and in the end she had to remove them gently
from his pocket. She had no paper with which to light
the fire and had seen no axe with which she could split
up some of the logs for sticks, but there was the blackout
fabric yawning from the kitchen window. She could use
that, she decided ruthlessly.

As she opened the door to the range and then discovered that whoever had last lit a fire in it had not
bothered to remove the ash, she reflected that at least
that was one fear removed. She had dreaded discovering
that the chimney was blocked off and that no fire could
be lit.

She had to stand in the sink to reach up to rip down
the blackout fabric. She saw Edward frowning bewil-
deredly at her as she did so. She gave him a reassuring
smile, but said nothing. The best thing for him now was
time...time and peace and quiet for him to come to
terms with the reality of Cottingdean.

Strangely, now that she was actually doing something
she felt much better, far less helpless and afraid. It was
as though the mere activity, the simple task of lighting
the range had somehow restored to her the right to
control her own life. As she waited for the blessedly dry
logs to catch she realised wonderingly that for the first
time in her life she actually was her own mistress, that
there was no aunt, no matron, no one other than Edward
to direct her life. And poor Edward. How could he do

that when it was so desperately obvious that he was going to be the one to lean on her?

How she knew this she had no real knowledge. It was something that might have been growing on her slowly, something that she might have subconsciously perceived without being aware of doing so. All she knew was that here, now, in this place, she had suddenly realised that she was going to have not one life dependent upon her, but two. And she realised something else as well—a simple truth that her parents and then her aunt had inculcated into her: nothing in life came free. Everything had a price to be paid for it. Fate had given her Kit and then had demanded Kit's life in payment. It had given her Kit's child...a bonus. It had given her Edward and marriage...respectability and a home. It had given her child a future, even if now she was forced to accept that the only home, the only future her child would have would be one that she could make for it, and that the price she must pay for the privilege of doing so would be her duty towards Edward. Her duty to cherish and protect him, her duty to turn Cottingdean back into his dream of how it had once been.

Quite how she knew all this she had no idea. It was a vague, loose chain of thoughts no more than half formed, no more than vague sensory awareness slipping through her mind like fine veils of cloud, while her hands were busy feeding the fire, checking the damp; while she was going outside watching the smoke rise; while she was talking to Edward, telling him that they would soon have the kitchen warm and that she must go upstairs to see if she could find a couple of mattresses, and to check to see if the range did, as she hoped, heat the hot water supply. If not, she had already seen the massive kettles on the dresser and the tin bath hanging up behind the scullery door.

Outwardly totally absorbed by the practicalities of their situation, inwardly she was aware of feelings so strong that she wondered if they were engendered by her pregnancy rather than by her own emotions. Her strongest awareness was one of knowing that she must

seize hold of her own life, that she must take charge of
it and make it into something strong enough to withstand whatever blows fate raised against it, and at the
bottom of this awareness lay a peculiar conviction that
somehow her ability to do so was interwoven with this
house and its desolate decay; that in taking hold of the
house and breathing life into it she would also be taking
hold of her own life and banishing from it the desolation of losing Kit.

Was it because of her child, Kit's child? The child who
would one day inherit Cottingdean? Was it for him that
she felt this urge, this need to take hold of the house,
to cherish and love it, to restore it to what it must once
have been? Or was she simply giving in to some foolish,
impossible-to-achieve daydream?

It was impossible for them to use any of the bedrooms.
They had to sleep in the kitchen on mattresses she had
managed to salvage, wrapped in blankets she had aired
over the range. The mattresses were single ones and as
she lay sleepless within the cocoon of her own blankets,
while Edward slept several feet away from her, she remembered how earlier Edward had made an awkward
attempt to embrace her, out of gratitude, she knew, and
not desire, but the sensation of his dry lips moving
against her cheek had caused such a surge of revulsion
inside her that she had only just managed to conceal
from him what she was feeling...

Now, curled up in her thankfully solitary bed, she relived that small incident, shuddering inwardly. Her reaction to Edward's touch only reinforced her conviction
that for her sexual intimacy was a part of married life
she was more than pleased to have to do without.

How lucky she had been to find Edward, she thought
naïvely. How fortunate to marry such a kind, consider-
ate man, who was willing not only to accept her child
as his own and to provide them both with a home, but
was also a man who would never be able to criticise her
lack of sexual responsiveness to him in the way that Kit
had.

It was not perhaps a conventional beginning to their marriage, but nevertheless she was determined to make Edward a good wife, to give him all the care and devotion he might need, to love and cherish him as her husband, even if that love could never be sexual. As she fell asleep she promised fervently that from now on she would do everything she could to show Edward how grateful she was to him for what he had done for her. Somehow between them they would find a way of making Cottingdean habitable, a true home, a home filled with warmth and love, because that was what she wanted for her child. A proper home, the kind of home she herself had never really had ... not after she had gone to live with her aunt.

CHAPTER SEVEN

'TODAY we heard officially that Japan has surrendered and the war is over.'

Liz stared down at what she had written, knowing guiltily that since she had come to Cottingdean her life had been so full of so many obstacles, so many small and intensely immediate problems, that somehow the war had lost its prominence.

Their isolation didn't help; they had no radio, no delivery of a daily paper, and they seldom had visitors.

At first she had attributed this latter lack to herself; but those visitors they had had quickly if unknowingly reassured her.

It amazed her that people here should so readily accept her as Edward's wife, ignoring her youth and the disparity of that youth and his ill health, although she had seen the way even the vicar had uncomfortably avoided looking directly at Edward for too long. Only the doctor, Ian Holmes, a bracing Northerner in his mid-fifties, seemed prepared to acknowledge Edward's infirmities.

It was true that the locals, the villagers, still treated her with reserve, but not, she was coming to realise, because they had guessed the truth about her. No . . . it was simply that both she and to some extent Edward himself were strangers to them.

It was from the doctor that they learned that the couple who were supposed to have been taking care of the house had left it over twelve months ago. Edward suspected that Kit must have been aware of the situation, but it was impossible now to question his cousin about his reasons for allowing the house to fall into such a state of neglect.

It hadn't taken Liz more than twenty-four hours in the house to realise how much she was going to need all the skills her aunt had taught her. What she was slower to recognise was how much of the older woman's indomitable will had also been passed on to her. No one who had any real alternative would ever choose to live in such a place, she had acknowledged despairingly the first morning, when she woke up in Cottingdean's kitchen, her body stiff and uncomfortable from the still-damp mattress, her nose wrinkling up at the stale smell of the air.

But then what alternatives had they had? She had seen the shock and bewilderment in Edward's eyes when he too woke up, the despair and the humiliation, and in that moment she had unknowingly picked up the burden she would carry for the rest of her life...

It had been an effort to persuade Edward into a more cheerful frame of mind, to insist on pushing him down to the village so that they could buy a few supplies, find out what had happened to the Johnsons, visit the doctor and present the letter from the hospital.

It had surprised her when Edward referred to her as Liz instead of Lizzie, but after a while she had decided she rather liked it. It seemed more adult, more mature. It made her feel less of a helpless child.

Somehow or other, with some help from the doctor, who had given them the names of several local farmers who might be able to spare the odd pair of hands for half a day or so, they had managed to make a small part of the house habitable; just the kitchen, on which Liz had worked ceaselessly for a week, scrubbing and re-scrubbing its floors, walls and shelves with as much hot water as the range could provide, and the coarse yellow soap she had found in the stable, until she was satisfied that it was, if not clean enough to match her great-aunt's standards, then at least a great improvement on what it had been.

Downstairs, the cleanest and driest of the rooms had received the same treatment to turn them into temporary bedrooms, and if the uncomfortable trestle beds and thin mattresses, obviously intended for the use of whoever the house had originally been requisitioned for, were even less appealing than her bed in the hostel, then at least they were somewhere to sleep, and she was so tired at night that not even the discomfort of the lumpy mattress kept her awake. Edward was another matter. She had been disturbed at first when Ian Holmes had prescribed a sleeping potion for him, but she had to admit that after a week of proper sleep Edward did look better.

If they hadn't had a sudden spell of good weather, enabling her to take Edward outside in his chair while she worked on the house, she didn't know what she would have done.

It was plain that the shock of discovering the neglect and deterioration of the place he remembered had affected Edward deeply. At first he seemed sunk into such despondency that Liz began to wonder if she was doing the right thing in staying at Cottingdean, if Edward might not recover his spirits better if he wasn't confronted by the reality of the house's downfall. But where else could they go?

They were at Cottingdean almost a month before she had enough free time to explore further afield than the immediate garden.

It was the discovery of an old estate map in one of the cupboards that sparked off her decision to see more of the estate. She showed the map to Edward, suggesting that they might hang it above the fireplace in the room which he referred to as the library, but when she saw the look of pain darken his eyes she knew she had said the wrong thing. Inwardly she cursed herself for her insensitivity.

The library had been the room Edward had described to her in the most glowing terms of all. In his memories, it was a mellow, warm room, full of firelight, the scent of leatherbound books, and tobacco. Rich velvet curtains had hung at the window, and his grandfather's desk had been a huge island of polished wood. Two huge chairs had stood either side of the fire. There had been a fender high enough for someone sitting in those chairs to rest their feet on. His grandmother had always had a bowl of fresh flowers standing on his grandfather's desk, and to be allowed into the room had obviously been regarded by Edward as an extra-special treat.

Now, no one walking into it would recognise it from Edward's description. None of the furnishings he had described so lovingly to her remained; even the book-shelves themselves had been ripped out in places—whether by accident or design, Liz didn't know. Their contents, those books whose smell Edward remembered so clearly, lay in scattered disorder on the floor, their spines broken, their pages mildewed and chewed into nests by the colony of mice who had seemed to make this room their favourite domain.

Liz had done what she could to restore the room to some kind of order, feeling that if she could somehow recreate for Edward in this one room some faint shadow of what it had once been, it might help to soothe the anguish she could see he suffered.

Hardly a day went by without him blaming himself for what had happened, without him saying he should never have married her, never have brought her here. He seemed to hate seeing her work, although Liz herself was surprised to discover how much she was enjoying it. To her there was no hardship in the gruelling task of scrubbing and rescrubbing, of searching diligently through piles of assorted rubbish, just to make sure that nothing of value was discarded. Even when she could see no possible use for an article, she still meticulously put it on one side just in case, at some later date, when Edward was able, he might discover it to be some long-lost childhood treasure.

No one seemed to know what had happened to the original contents of the house. Liz was an intelligent girl, but, while suspecting that the Johnsons had disposed of it, she had no idea that Edward was allowing her to believe that rather than allow her to know the truth, which was that he thought that Kit had sold everything he could that was of value, and that for some reason of his own he had decided to allow the house itself to fall into disrepair. Had not only allowed, but for some reason had almost encouraged it.

It was Edward who discovered the desecration of the small cellar his grandfather had painstakingly built up, and, together with the debris of bottles and broken glasses, other evidence that the parties Kit had brought here to drink the rich clarets and rare vintages had not been comprised of only male friends.

Edward kept this information from Liz. It was bad enough that he had deceived her so much already. She had believed she was coming to a comfortable home, where she and her child would be cared for and cosseted. Instead...instead, she was down on her hands and knees scrubbing filthy floors...

Edward hated seeing her do that. He was an old-fashioned man, who had been brought up by distant, formal parents. In his eyes Liz was a precious and fragile creature, who should never have to demean herself with such tasks.

Liz did not share his views. Some part of her was almost enjoying the challenge of the house, now that she had overcome her initial shock. Now, with her pregnancy well advanced, she was no longer having to deal with her earlier enervating sickness.

One of the farmers, introduced to them by Ian Holmes—the one who had grudgingly allowed them to pay for the services of four of his labourers to repair the worst of the damage to the roof—also, and equally grudgingly, passed on to Liz the information that the best thing she could get for her garden was a pair of goats.

'They'll give you good milk as well. Not that it's to everyone's taste...'

Liz received this information cautiously. It seemed almost too good to be true. An animal which would clear the wilderness that was the garden, and leave it ready for digging over for the spring, and who would be at the same time providing them with milk.

She would have liked to ask Edward's advice, but she had quickly discovered that he knew nothing about farming, nor, it seemed, did he wish to learn. Where *she* was discovering an eagerness to find out just what kind of hens it was which produced the big speckled brown eggs that Mrs Lowndes had generously slipped to her the first time she had plucked up her courage and sought out the farmer, Edward seemed to think such interests unsuitable for a lady.

A lady... Just for a moment Liz had been tempted to laugh, to remind him that she wasn't a lady—but she knew to do so would hurt his feelings.

She was beginning to discover things about Edward that she had not noticed before. That he was perhaps a little snobbish... not in any unkind way, but that such things as the social distinctions between the classes, between himself and, for instance, the farmers—even though the latter were far, far more comfortably off than Edward himself—were important to him, and, because she was his wife, it was equally important to him that she maintain his standards. To Edward that meant preserving a certain distance from other people, a certain aloofness, which Liz found did not sit comfortably on her shoulders.

She wanted to please Edward but she wanted to be herself as well. She felt equally uncomfortable when the farm labourers referred to her as Mrs Danvers while she, so much younger than they, had to call them by their given names.

Through her marriage to Edward she had stepped into an unfamiliar world... a world where, she was beginning to discover, money was not the main criterion of a person's social standing. It was the world described to her so fondly by her aunt, but now she was seeing it from the other side of the green baize door which in her aunt's day had separated the servers from the served.

Another piece of useful information she elicited from Jack Lowndes was the surprising fact that some of the lush, crop-filled fields to the other side of the village did in actual fact belong to the estate.

'Water meadows, they be,' he told her. 'Rented from the old master by Jimmy Sutton these forty year or more... Paid a good rent for them, Jimmy did, but since the old master died, and that son of his took over...'

Liz knew a little of the ways of country folk, having observed them in her aunt's village.

Cautiously she asked Edward if he knew anything about the receipt of rent monies on some of the land.

This was another facet of the man who was now her husband she was coming to know. She realised how sensitive he could be, how proud and touchy on some subjects, and she knew that he would not welcome being told his business by a member of the class which, she suspected, he tended to despise, deep down.

She was right to be cautious. He frowned over her question and demanded to know what made her ask it. She said, as innocently as she could, that she had noticed from the estate map which she had rescued that the estate seemed to include some land along the river.

It wasn't entirely untrue. The estate map did show the water meadows, but she doubted that she would have looked for them without the farmer's tip.

She watched as Edward shifted uncomfortably in his chair. He hated being confronted with facts that were unknown to him. Liz, who was beginning to recognise his small tell-tale gestures of discomfort, tried to smile and appear unconcerned. They were so desperately short of money. Edward had told her that much. If there were rents due to the estate...

'Perhaps your late uncle's solicitor might be the best person to ask,' she suggested hesitantly.

Edward seized on her suggestion thankfully. The shock of discovering the dilapidation of the estate had been a blow he was finding difficult to throw off. The knowledge that he had inherited Cottingdean—so much loved, so completely lost to him—the knowledge that he would marry Liz, and that he would after all have an heir, a child to pass that estate on to, had filled him with such unexpected euphoria that the reality had seemed an even crueller blow.

He felt lost, bewildered, almost resentful both of Cottingdean and at times of Liz herself. And yet she was working so hard, doing so much... He had no right to feel resentment. She was wonderfully kind to him, always putting his comfort before her own, and if she treated him like an old and infirm uncle, well, what had he expected? He had always known that she would never feel desire for him, and even if she had... He saw the anxiety darkening her eyes, saw how her face had fined down, grown inexplicably more mature, so that now for all her youth she was truly a woman and not a child any more, and he felt the burden of his guilt increase intolerably.

It was he who had done this to her, who had brought her here, who had made her in his way just as many false promises as Kit had in his.

Only Ian Holmes knew the truth about the child she carried. He too had known Kit and he had shaken his head over Edward's insistence that Liz was to be allowed to retain her untarnished image of his cousin.

'She's a very intelligent young woman. Sooner or later she'll realise. He wasn't popular in the village... Right now they're keeping quiet. They don't know her well enough to say anything, but, sooner or later, it's going to come out. He used to come down here, you know... bring women with him...' Ian Holmes pulled a disgusted face. 'I know it was wartime and that men under the kind of pressure he was under need a release, but with him...'

No, let Liz keep her illusions for as long as she could. She had precious little else to sustain her, poor child.

Edward looked at her, and saw her red, swollen hands, swollen from scrubbing floors, her skin scratched from where she had spent an entire afternoon picking soft fruit from the tangle of canes in what had once been the kitchen garden... He remembered his mother and his grandmother, with their soft white hands. And cursed himself again.

'I'll write to Peter Allwood,' he promised her. 'His family have been our solicitors since my great-grandfather's time—but don't get your hopes up too high, my dear.' What he didn't want to say to her was that Kit might well have sold off any land that was of value, and that that could be why there was no rental income from the water meadows she seemed to think belonged to the estate, but he had always been a cautious man and he didn't wish to disappoint her unless he had to.

It was the discovery of the water meadows that prompted Liz to make her tour of the estate.

She set off early one afternoon, having checked that Edward was comfortable. She had cleaned out the library as best she could, but nothing would induce Edward to use it. He complained that he felt the cold and preferred the warmth of the kitchen and its range, although Liz knew quite well that he abhorred the necessity for them to practically live in this room. Kitchens were for servants, in his view, and she suspected that until now he had never done anything more than walk through one in his life.

Her pregnancy showed now, all the more so perhaps because the rest of her was so slender.

Food was short and money even shorter. It broke her thrifty housewife's heart to see so much wastage in the garden, when they were so badly in need of food.

She had persuaded Mrs Lowndes to sell some of her hens, but as yet these temperamental birds had not started to lay for her, and she was beginning to be concerned that they would cost her more in food than they would ever produce in terms of eggs.

As to the goats ... she was making discreet enquiries about these beasts, although no one locally, it seemed, knew where they might be obtained.

The best person to advise her would probably be her own shepherd, Mrs Lowndes had told her.

This had surprised Liz. She had met young Vic, as he was called, only once. He had arrived at the house three days after they had moved in, apparently having heard on the grapevine of their arrival. Liz, who had from Edward's description visualised the shepherd as a gnarled old man in his seventies, had been taken off guard by the arrival of a tall, dark-haired stranger, only a handful of years older than she was herself, and at first, intimidated by the height and breadth of him as he stood at the kitchen door, had automatically stepped back from him, forgetting that she was a wife and soon to be a mother, and conscious only that she was being confronted by a healthy young male animal, who in some complex and illogical way was bringing something threatening into her life.

When he had asked uncertainly for Edward, she had been forced to admit him into the kitchen, but she had stood guard behind Edward's chair as fiercely as a young vixen with a single cub while he introduced himself, and Vic, who knew almost as little about women as Liz did about men, knew enough about the female of the species to recognise that her silent aggression concealed fear... fear for herself and resentment on behalf of her husband.

Vic had been orphaned as a very young child, and had spent his growing years almost exclusively in the company of his grandfather.

Since he had spent all this time either with his flock or his dogs, Victor had grown up isolated from his peers, a quiet, intense boy, who had quickly absorbed everything the older man taught him and who in addition to those skills had an additional gift which his grandfather had quickly recognised.

'A natural, he is,' he would boast to his cronies, on his rare visits to the Lamb. 'Got a rare feel for the beasts... Loves them like a woman, he does, big softie. Seems to know when one of them's ill...'

It was this sensitivity that allowed him to see past Liz's rejection of him, to sense her fear and feel compassion for it. He could also sense her spirit, her strength, and he knew as instinctively as he knew when one of his flock ailed that it would be this woman who would hold together the inheritance of the man she stood guard over.

His grandfather had died the previous winter, and since then Vic had been living alone in the small farmhouse which had always been the shepherd's private domain. Once the Cottingdean flocks had been famous for their wools, but over the years the stock had deteriorated, decimated by sickness and disease. Now, despite the care he lavished on them, the sheep were in poor heart. In the evening, with nothing else to do, Vic read avidly. He had learned a good deal about the art of cross-breeding sheep. It was his dream to produce a flock which would give the richest fleece of any breed, a fleece that would be prized the world over... But for that he needed a decent ram, not the services of Tim Benson's old ram, whose progeny were stringy and good for neither meat nor fleece.

But good rams, the kind of ram he had in mind, cost money. They were experimenting now in Australia and New Zealand, producing beasts from the old hardy British stocks, but more disease-resistant, capable of much heavier fleece yields, and a different kind of fleece, one far more suited for modern machinery.

Let others dream of producing a beast that gave the maximum meat. A softie, his grandad had called him, and perhaps he was, but no lamb of his rearing would be fattened and then slaughtered, when it could instead be allowed to live, and every year reward his care and patience with a fine rich fleece.

This was Vic's dream: that one day his flock, his ewes, his ram would be talked about in tones of awe and respect everywhere where men of sense and knowledge gathered to discuss such things. But one look at Edward had told him that this man would never share such a dream. That Edward could never have any conception of what such a dream might mean. He felt heart-sorry for Edward, witnessed his wounds and disabilities not with shock but with compassion, and saw also that something in his life had also wounded the man's spirit.

He knew too with a knowledge he neither questioned nor wondered at in any prurient manner—it was simply a matter of knowing—that the child his wife carried could not be his. That, though, was their affair and not his, nor anyone else's.

Edward looked at the young shepherd and felt an instant *frisson* of aggression and resentment...but his sprang from causes very different from Liz's. His aggression came from the knowledge that in Vic he was looking at a man who was the finest of his species, a man whose goodness, whose essential spirit shone out of him, a man who would never allow life to destroy him, because he would never blame life for that destruction.

His resentment sprang from looking at Vic and seeing a whole man, a healthy man, a young man.

A man who ought to have been serving his country in recent years, not looking after sheep. He said as much, and waited for Vic to react.

Vic smiled at him. Strangers often asked him that question, with varying degrees of aggression. He never resented their curiosity, understanding quite well what lay behind it.

He'd had rheumatic fever as a child which had left him with a weak heart. The army had rejected him when he first tried to join up, and, as Dr Holmes had gently told him, he would never be fit for that kind of active service.

Sometimes in the spring when they were lambing, when he worked exhaustingly through the day and night, his chest would grow tight and pain would tingle in his arm, but then he would rest for a while and the pain would go, and he was too content with what he was doing to concern himself about something over which he had no control.

He said as much, explaining his disability without apology or self-pity.

It was impossible not to believe him. Truth, honesty, shone out of him.

And now, although Liz knew quite well that it would have been the easiest thing in the world for her to ask Vic to show her round the estate, to explain to her the working of the flock, to advise her on how best she might restore some sort of order to her garden, and turn it into the healthy, productive plot she had glimpsed on her one brief visit to his farmhouse, she held back from doing so. Not just out of reserve, but out of resentment as well, she acknowledged.

It was wrong of her to resent Vic. Without his care, she had been told, the estate flock would have disappeared long ago. She suspected humiliatingly that his wages had not been paid since Edward's grandfather's death, but it was a subject she felt unable to broach with Edward ... Perhaps when the solicitor came they would know more.

She spent the afternoon exploring the estate, using as a guide the map she had copied from the one she had found, and taking care to avoid Vic and his flock, without knowing why she felt this need to do so.

A part of her recognised that he was essentially a kind and gentle man whom she had no need to fear, but then there was his maleness, and her awareness of it ... an instinctive female awareness of him as a man.

The visit from the solicitor was illuminating. The estate did still own the water meadows and he was shocked to discover that rents were not being paid on them. He would, he advised Edward, recommend that the matter was dealt with straight away.

Peter Allwood was a small, thin man, with a dry, precise way of speaking. If he found the state of the house a shock he hid it well. If he found the fact that she was married to Edward and expecting a child a shock he hid that equally well.

Once he had gone, Edward consulted Ian Holmes on the best way to deal with the matter of the outstanding rent. He was beginning to trust Ian, Liz recognised. She too liked the North Country doctor with his forthright manner.

She was now approaching the seventh month of her pregnancy and Liz's body was inexorably preparing itself for the birth. She had an odd wish that her child might have been born in the spring at the start of nature's life-cycle, and not in January, the heart of its life's end. Although she did not wish to alarm Edward, she was dreading the coming winter. Already in November there were signs apparently that they would have snow. The stock of logs in the stable was dangerously depleted. She had seen on her walks that there were trees which should be cut down for wood, but who was to do it? They could not continually rely on the help of their neighbours, and Edward was so sensitive about his inability to do anything.

After Ian Holmes had offered to ensure that Jim Sutton received the message that his landlord wished to see him to discuss the matter of his outstanding rents, he asked Liz how she was feeling.

Although the pair of them had managed to survive through the summer and the autumn, he was not sure they could continue to do so over the winter.

He had said as much to young Vic, when the doctor had seen the shepherd in the village the previous day. What they needed was a young and reliable farm labourer, someone to chop wood, and clear the kitchen garden, someone to ensure that the range was lit every morning without Liz herself having to do it. Someone adept at doing all the small running repairs on a property like Cottingdean, which had suffered too much already from neglect.

He also mentioned this to Edward, gently suggesting that the rental income from the water meadows might be put to this use.

'We need someone,' Edward agreed, but then said doubtfully, 'But there's no good labour to be had...'

'There are men returning from the war who will need jobs,' Ian reminded him.

Liz hoped that the seed Ian had planted would take root. She herself had longed to make a similar suggestion but she knew Edward well enough now to accept that he had an old-fashioned reservation about accepting such ideas from her. She was a woman. Her place was in the drawing-room, supervising the house and its staff. That was the image Edward had of her role, never mind the fact that the drawing-room was a damp, mouldering room in which the plaster was falling from the ceiling, and the paper from the walls ... Edward had certain fixed ideas which he was almost afraid to let go of. Afraid because he was frightened that, if he did so, his whole world might fall apart, Liz recognised compassionately, and so she said nothing and hoped that Ian's words would bear fruit.

She was excluded from the interview with Jim Sutton, a large, swaggering man whom she instinctively disliked, and who she suspected had presented himself at the house driven more by the weight of public opinion than by any recognition of his omissions as a tenant.

What was said between him and Edward she was not told, merely that the arrears of rent were to be paid, although Edward did not say how much these would be, and Liz suspected that Edward had quite probably allowed himself to be cheated of their rightful due.

No matter, if they had some money. Enough to pay the wages of one man...but Edward had made no mention of taking anyone on, and Liz was reluctant to bring up the subject.

They had their first fall of snow at the end of November. Liz woke up one morning alerted to its arrival by the unfamiliar brightness beyond the window.

She and Edward slept in separate rooms on the ground floor, sharing the facility of a large, draughty bathroom. Only Liz knew how much she dreaded any kind of physical intimacy between them and how ashamed and guilty this made her feel.

Edward had regained some measure of independence since their arrival at Cottingdean and no longer needed help in getting dressed. He had learned to operate his wheelchair to get him around the ground floor of the house, but on days when it was cold and wet the pain in his amputations made him irritable and withdrawn, and so Liz sighed as she realised what the unusual clarity of the light meant.

Once—and it seemed a very long time ago indeed—her first sight of snow had thrilled her beyond measure. She had never totally lost that wondering awe at this ability of nature to completely transform the landscape overnight, but now practicalities outweighed wonder. They were running desperately short of fuel. The hens would need to be cooped for the winter, and as for the goats—she had resigned herself to not getting them.

She was downstairs lighting the range when she heard the shrill barking of the dogs, her spine tensing as she realised what the sound meant.

The only dogs at Cottingdean belonged to young Vic, and as she stood up and walked stiffly over to the window she saw him walking into the yard, his back bent under the strain of the sledge he was pulling.

Frowning, Liz opened the door. Despite the cold, his skin looked warm, glowing with life and health. He seemed not to feel the cold which iced into her own body. Like his dogs, he seemed impervious to the thick flakes of snow.

'I've brought down the logs,' he told her quietly. 'I'll stack them in the usual place, shall I? Sorry they're a bit late, but I've had some trouble with one of the ewes. By rights they should be stored until next winter to burn really well.'

While Liz stared at him he dragged the sled across to the stable, and removed the cover. She saw that it was piled high with neatly spliced logs. Enough of them to feed the boiler throughout the entire winter.

Tears shimmered unexpected in her eyes, clogging her throat. She realised as she fought against them how long it had been since she had cried, how long it had been since she had wept ceaseless tears for her dead love. Kit…she seldom allowed herself to think about him now. What was the use? Kit was dead. He would never hold her in his arms again, never tell her how much he loved her, never…

She had no idea that Vic had worked all through the night to cut down and prepare the logs, no idea, from his casual, matter-of-fact attitude, that the provision of them was not something he did as a routine matter of course, but rather was something done by him for her, out of compassion for her weakness and respect for her strength.

The sled was half empty before she managed to force herself to walk out to the stable with a mug of tea for him, and a slice of her homemade bread.

The smile he gave her was warm and natural, his appreciation of her thoughtfulness making her realise again what a truly kind person he was, even while she felt uncomfortable within his masculine presence.

He brought the empty mug back to the kitchen when he had finished unloading the logs. 'Best get back to the flock,' he told her matter-of-factly as she thanked him for them.

The overnight fall of snow soon melted, but it was a warning of the winter to come, a winter they weren't really prepared for, Liz acknowledged as she shivered in her cold bedroom.

During the second week in December they had an unexpectedly fine spell, when the sun shone and for some inexplicable reason Liz experienced an overwhelming need to be outside.

In the autumn she had started trying to restore the panelling in the hall to what it must once have been, but in recent weeks she had grown too bulky to feel comfortable working on the lower portions of it, and every time she walked through the hall it seemed to reproach her for her lack of diligence.

Only that morning she had received a visit from the vicar's wife, tactfully enquiring about her preparations for the birth of her baby. In these days of clothing coupons, shortages and rationing, and without any close family for her to turn to, it must be difficult for her to get a layette together, she had suggested.

She was right; Liz had spent hours searching through the trunks full of clothes stored away in the attic, wishing she had a sewing machine she could use so that she could make more use of the yellowing linen sheets and old-fashioned baby clothes.

She had also found a cradle up there, covered in cobwebs and dust and too heavy for her to get down unaided.

She mentioned this fact to Louise Ferndean, who promptly said that she would send her gardener round to help and that Liz must on no account attempt any kind of heavy lifting.

As for the sewing machine, she had one Liz could borrow, she offered, hiding her pity. She was so young, and her husband so badly injured. A tragic couple really, and so very brave... Look at the way they were living in this desolate, decaying house. The vicarage was bad enough, but at least it was sound and dry.

Liz knew better by now than to tell Edward about the vicar's wife's helpfulness. She was well acquainted with the stiffness of his pride and the fact that he hated their dependence on others and his jealousy when she sometimes made friendships which did not include him. She disliked this possessiveness she sensed in him, but she put it to the back of her mind, having neither the energy nor the desire to dwell on it. She found it easier to bear that way, although she sympathised with him. Financially things must now surely be a little better with the rents coming in from the water meadow land, but times were hard, for everyone, and for some more than others.

There was a mood of unrest in the village as men slowly came home from the war. Wives complained that their husbands were different, changed... that they couldn't seem to settle... and as yet Edward seemed to have done nothing about finding someone they could employ.

As she walked away from the house, taking the narrow track that led up into the hills, Liz reflected on how very much her life had changed in one short year.

It frightened her sometimes that Kit, who had been responsible indirectly for so many of those changes, should have become such a shadowy figure in her memory. Often at night she woke up, her face wet with tears from her struggles to picture him in sharper detail. She still loved him, of course she did... nothing would ever change that, but the sharpness of her memories of him seemed to be slipping away from her.

Cottingdean, the problems of her life here with Edward, Edward himself and her more immediate problems overshadowed her memories of her dead love.

And now Cottingdean itself and Edward with it were being pushed to the back of her mind by the demanding force of the child growing within her. Somehow without

her knowing how it had happened she had ceased to think
so passionately of the child as Kit's and instead it was
as though both the child she carried and the house had
somehow become entwined, as though both the birth of
her son and her determination to breathe new life into
Cottingdean itself were inextricably linked.

CHAPTER EIGHT

THE path climbed more steeply than she had realised, causing her to stop to ease the nagging ache in her side. No one in the village knew just when she and Edward had been married; the fact that she had known him for some months beforehand had made it easy to allow people to assume their marriage was well established, and if they wondered what had made such a young girl marry a man like Edward they were too polite to say so. Some of them, Liz assumed, must think that she had perhaps married Edward before he was injured, and neither of them had said anything to correct that impression.

She knew that it was important to Edward that her child was accepted as his, and, because she felt—despite the hardness of her life—that it was better than bringing up her child on her own in shame and completely alone, she was grateful enough to him to accept his need.

Besides, she knew with female wisdom and growing maturity that for her child's sake it was far better that Edward should want to accept him wholly as his own rather than to be reminded that he had been fathered by his cousin.

Edward had resented Kit. She had come to learn that much, and for all their sakes she must take care that none of the resentment was passed to her child.

The climb was more tiring than she remembered from her first walk along this path. But that had been three months ago, on a warm autumn afternoon. Now, up here, it was cold despite the sunshine, and she was only wearing a flimsy coat, but from the top of this hill she knew she would have a panoramic view of both Cottingdean and the land around it. Quite what was driving her to come up here she had no real idea; she only knew that she had felt a need to do so.

Towards the top the hill was bare of grass, rough and stony with poor, thin soil on which little grew. Liz was panting by the time she reached it, her legs and back aching. She knew she had perhaps come too far, but the summit was in sight now and determinedly she pressed on.

When she stepped unsuspectingly on a patch of loose shale she could do nothing to save herself, falling heavily to the ground, the shock of losing her balance so immediate and intense that she could only lie there frozen with it, deprived of any ability to think or reason as her body trembled and her heart pounded.

It was several minutes before she dared to move, to stretch out her arms and legs to discover in relief that they were not injured.

It wasn't just her own safety she had risked, she acknowledged as she started to move cautiously downhill. It was her child's as well.

Now, abruptly, she could not understand why she had attempted something so reckless. Her need to be back within the safe confines of Cottingdean was like a frantic pulse beating inside her. She had to force herself to walk slowly and carefully, not to break into a frantic lumbering run. Not to keep on touching the huge mound of her belly in reassurance both to herself and her child.

As she walked she talked softly to it, telling it what a foolish mother it had, begging its forgiveness. She had fallen into this habit quite a lot recently, even sometimes sitting beside the empty cradle which the vicar's gardener had brought down from the loft and taken away with him, only to return it several days later, marvellously cleaned and equipped with a full set of bedding, which the vicar's wife had told her was a small gift...

What she had not told her was that she had shamelessly cajoled her own sister-in-law to beg the items from her daughter, who had just had her third child and who had sworn she was not going to have any more.

She was halfway down the hill, and just beginning to breathe a little more easily, to relax her tense muscles, when the first pain struck, sharp enough to make her stand still and quiver with the intensity of it. Sharp enough for her to know even while she formed the comforting words that it was not merely a stitch.

Doggedly she walked on, faster now. After all, what need was there now to walk slowly? Doggedly she pleaded with her child to wait. Bitterly she chastised herself for what she had done. Grimly she told herself that she was panicking for nothing, that her baby wasn't due to be born for at least another four weeks, and then, just when she had managed to reassure herself that panic was all it had been, the pain came again.

Vic saw her coming down the hill and frowned. She had no business straying so far from the house, not in her condition. She reminded him of one of his young and skittish ewes, unused to the burdens of motherhood.

As he watched, he saw her stop and clasp her stomach. Too far away to see her expression, he could nevertheless visualise it, so graphically telling were her actions.

He discovered that he was walking, almost running towards her without realising he had made the decision.

She was over two miles away from Cottingdean and half a mile from the farm. As he moved he summoned his dogs, setting them to guard the flock.

Liz hadn't seen the shepherd. She was too caught up in her own physical needs, in trying to cope with the waves of pain that battered her. She knew she must reach Cottingdean, but each succeeding wave of pain slowed her down, confusing her, so that when Vic reached her, she was crouched over, hugging her arms around her body, her eyes wide with pain and shock. She saw him and yet did not see him, too engrossed in her fear to be aware of anything other than her immediate needs.

Vic spoke her name and took hold of her arm gently, hesitantly, watching her as she focused on him, pain giving way to the realisation of his presence, shock giving way to relief...

As she recognised him, Liz felt her animosity towards him evaporate in the relief of knowing she wasn't alone any longer. She let him take hold of her and guide her down the path, struggling against the pain to tell him through chattering teeth, 'Vic...the baby...'

He looked indulgently at her. She was so very strong that sometimes he forgot how young she was as well. Too young to be married to Edward... He frowned. Those were thoughts he should not be having. They were married. She was Edward's wife.

'I must get back to Cottingdean. In...'

Vic had seen how close together her pains were. He knew already that there would not be time to reach Cottingdean. There might not even be time to reach the farmhouse. He knew that it was unusual for a first birth to happen so quickly, and that often when it did it could be followed by heavy, sometimes fatal bleeding. It always caused him concern when one of his first time ewes went into too speedy labour. Now, as he silently guided Liz towards the farmhouse, that concern was intensified tenfold.

When she realised where he was taking her, Liz stopped dead and stared at him, fear clouding her eyes. 'No, Vic. I must get home...the baby——'

'Will come too soon for us to get there,' he told her quietly. 'The farmhouse is closer...'

Liz felt her heart jump in her breast. What was he saying? How could he know? And yet sharply she knew that he was right, and panic struck through her. 'Dr Holmes...'

Vic saw the fear in her eyes and pity washed through him. He didn't tell her what he knew: that there would be no time to summon the doctor, no time for anything other than allowing the child to be born, but something in his touch on her arm reassured her, and numbly she allowed him to urge her over the last few yards of the track and across the farmyard.

She had never been inside the small farmhouse before. The kitchen was pin-neat, its table scrubbed as clean as her own; the homely smell of stew cooking in the range reached her nostrils. She was surprised to discover that she felt hungry, and then abruptly the pain struck her again, fierce and compelling, turning her mind in upon itself, so that she had only a dim perception of Vic guiding her upstairs and into the small cold bedroom where his grandfather had once slept, and which was now bare of everything but its bed.

Liz felt the mattress dip beneath her, was aware of firm hands removing her smock, of a quiet, firm voice speaking calmingly to her, as the pain raged and tore at her, only to retreat and then rage anew with jagged tearing force.

She heard herself cry out and someone answer, she felt the force of the new life inside her demanding its own autonomy, she felt the fear of the peril of giving birth both for her child and for herself. She realised she must have cried out those fears, because someone answered them, reassuring her, calming her.

Outside it grew dark, the winter's afternoon fading into dusk: Vic had seen more births than he could remember, but each one was something special, something magical . . . a moment out of time when a man might feel immortal to witness such a wonder . . . but never more so, never more intensely, or more humbly than this moment when he witnessed the birth of this boy child.

Any embarrassment she might have imagined feeling in such circumstances had long ago faded. Liz felt nothing but gratitude and a rare, intense moment of bonding that went beyond any form of words as Vic handed her her child. She felt no awkwardness or self-consciousness when he placed the child against her breast, so matter-of-fact, so tender, so wholly instinctive were his movements. When he told her that he must lift the bed, she accepted it without question, not aware, as he was, of the heavy flow of blood caused by the child's birth.

From somewhere he had produced a sheepskin in which to wrap the child, telling Liz that it would preserve his body heat.

'I think I shall call him David . . .' she told Vic sleepily.

'It's a good name,' he agreed quickly. 'A royal name...'

She was tired, her body drained and exhausted, and yet the euphoria of having given birth made her cling determinedly to consciousness.

Vic, not wanting to alarm her, sat with her, silently monitoring the dangerously weakening loss of blood. It had slowed, but not stopped. He suspected that she would need stitches where the birth had torn her. By rights he ought to leave her and summon help. Edward must be frantic with worry.

He said as much, but she clung to his arm. 'No... Please stay with us... There's so much...' She stopped, frowning, shaking her head in negation of her own thoughts, her own needs. What was it she wanted to say to him, to share with him? He was a stranger to her, even more so than Edward, and yet they had shared something so special, so intimate that for the rest of their lives the three of them would be inextricably linked. She shivered suddenly. 'Talk to me...' she said. 'Tell me what you want out of life, Vic...'

And so he did, watching her while he talked, not allowing her to see his relief when the bleeding slowly stopped and the colour started to seep back into her face.

She would make a good mother, he saw approvingly, watching the easy, instinctive way she handled her child. He, at least, was healthy, well formed despite his early arrival, tugging eagerly at her breast.

This was the look of a Madonna, he recognised, watching as she smiled down at her child and reached out to touch his cheek. A sharp stab of envy tore through him. Suddenly it was not enough that he had his hopes and his plans. Suddenly he wanted more—suddenly he wanted her, he recognised, trying to push the knowledge away from him, to deny it before it was born, but already it was too late and the knowledge that there could never be a time when she would lie in his bed nursing his child was like a sore place in his heart.

'Go on,' Liz instructed him, lifting her gaze from her son. 'You were saying—about getting a new ram...'

*   *   *

Edward was thrilled with his son. He even approved of the name she had chosen for him, but Liz suspected that he could not quite forgive her for allowing David to be born so intemperately, and in such a horrible place— with only a shepherd in attendance.

He was a little short with Vic for several weeks after David's birth, which Liz felt guiltily was her fault, suspecting that it was really at her that his anger was directed, not realising that Edward was exhibiting an instinctive male awareness of another man's interest in his mate.

Ian Holmes was full of praise for all that Vic had done, treating the circumstances of David's birth so matter-of-factly that Liz was intensely grateful to him.

'You were lucky that Vic was on hand. You couldn't have asked for a better midwife. After all, he's had far more experience of birth than I . . .'

Edward didn't like that comment, saying distastefully that sheep were a far different thing from ladies.

'Not when they're giving birth,' Ian told him forthrightly, not adding that, but for Vic's prompt action, Liz might very well have bled far more seriously than she had.

As it was she made a speedy recovery from the birth, and was now glowing with health and pride. Her child too was thriving . . .

From somewhere someone had produced two goats, and these were now providing the rich milk that Liz was forcing herself to drink for David's sake. Ian had warned her that the poor diet they were all forced to endure might result in her milk not being sufficient to nourish her baby.

CHAPTER NINE

AROUND the time David was six months old three things happened which were to have, in varying degrees, a profound effect upon their lives.

The first of them arrived in the form of a totally unexpected visitor who presented herself at Cottingdean's unused front door at precisely four o'clock on a warm early June afternoon, just when Liz had settled both David and Edward down for the nap which had become part of their daily ritual. If she was ever forced to count her blessings, foremost among them must be Edward's love for their son. It surprised her how easy it was for her to think of David as 'theirs'. From the very first moment he had set eyes on him Edward had loved the little boy, handling him with a tenderness and wonder that always made Liz herself marvel.

Any doubts she had had about the wisdom of her marriage had faded the moment she'd looked into Edward's eyes and seen in them the pure shining love of a father for his child, and known that it was a love that would never tarnish.

If it hurt her to remember the laughing, handsome man who had given David life, then she was determined that only she would know it.

David was Edward's son. He fussed over the baby far more than she did. At first she had seen that he disliked the fact that she was feeding the baby herself. In his world ladies simply did not do that sort of thing, but Ian Holmes had some radical ideas and beliefs springing from his tough Northern upbringing and, as he ruthlessly pointed out to Edward, Liz's milk was a far more economical and, in his view, far more healthy way of feeding the child than any amount of shop-bought formulae.

It was true that David had thrived marvellously, and now, at six months, he was a placid, plump baby, with a shock of dark hair, serious blue eyes that were slowly changing to grey, and sun-warmed skin from the long hours his mother spent working in her garden with David tucked into a basket at her side.

The goats had done their work, and someone—she suspected it was probably either Ian Holmes or young Vic—had prevailed on Jack Lowndes to spare her two of his men early in the spring to do the heavy digging and clearing in the kitchen gardens.

Conscious always of their lack of money, Liz had insisted on retaining what had once been the escaliered fruit trees around the walls, and these had been pruned back as hard as she dared, in the hope that they might with care and nourishment be persuaded to grow and fruit. Now, in June, when she walked in this garden that was her own special province, early in the morning, after she had fed the hens and checked that the goats hadn't escaped from their tethers, her heart swelled with achievement as she studied the neat rows of growing produce.

With her aunt's thrifty training, she was already planning ahead to the autumn, when she would bottle, preserve and make jam with as much of the soft fruit as she could, looking to the winter ahead.

Visitors of any kind were a rare enough occurrence. The village believed in keeping itself to itself, and Liz was too conscious of being neither fish nor fowl in the social pecking order to make overtures of her own. To have a visitor therefore on a Monday afternoon, when any housewife of good sense must surely be engaged in thankfully completing the task of her Monday wash, was surprising enough; but one who presented herself at the front door, which was never used, caused Liz to frown as she wiped her hands on the overall she was quickly removing.

The only downstairs room that was really habitable was the kitchen. Edward now seemed resigned to the fact that they were virtually living in it and had made

no comment when Liz, with Vic's help, had dragged
down from the attic two ancient armchairs, their covers
worn and damp but their springs still intact.

All through the spring evenings she had worked hard
on her borrowed Singer making loose covers for them
from an old pair of damask curtains she had found in
the attic.

The flagged floor now gleamed with cleaning and pol-
ishing, the pewter winked shiningly from the bare
scrubbed floors, and the range always gave off a welcoming warmth.

As she walked through the hall, Liz grimaced. She
had fallen into the habit of using the back stairs, which
were more convenient for the kitchen, and since David's
birth she had not had any time to spend trying to restore
any more of the house to some sort of order. Now, with
the warmth of the summer sun and its strong light
pouring into the hallway, she was freshly conscious of
its state of dilapidation.

Never mind, she told herself grimly as she struggled
with the heavy bolt. If her unexpected visitor chose to
arrive at the front door, then he or she would just have
to face the consequences.

As she pulled the door open, she blinked a little at
the sunlight and then stared in astonishment at her
visitor. A tall, bone-thin woman, with a shock of grey
curly hair and skin as sunburned as a gypsy's, stood in
front of her. She must be somewhere in her late sixties,
Liz recognised, as she smiled uncertainly at her visitor
and invited her in.

'Harriet Fane,' the older woman announced, extending her hand and, to Liz's surprise, grasping her
own and subjecting it to an almost mannish handshake.
Her fingers were long and bony, the skin toughened by
outdoor work. 'From Fane Place,' her visitor continued
as she stepped into the hallway, barely giving its dilapidation a glance. 'Live there with m'brother, you know.
At least, used to. Buried him last week. Best thing,
really... shot to pieces at Dunkirk. Should have made

an end of him then. That's why I'm here. Heard about your husband. Never met him, but I know the family...'

Liz listened in amazed confusion. She had heard of Harriet Fane, or, more properly, Lady Harriet Fane, from Ian Holmes, who had mentioned during his last visit that her brother Lord George Fane had recently died. The Fanes were known in the village as an eccentric couple, whose home, Fane Place, was if anything in even more of a dilapidated state than Cottingdean. Neither of them had ever married. Lady Harriet, it was said, lived for her horses and her garden, a mannish woman who spoke plainly and was inclined to be unwittingly tactless. The vicar's wife had once told Liz that she felt vaguely sorry for her.

'Beneath her brusque manner I think she's rather shy. They live a very isolated life in that huge empty house, and her brother is confined to bed, and very often in considerable pain. They've no family to speak of, and very few friends.'

Remembering this, Liz explained a little uncomfortably to her visitor that they were virtually living in the kitchen, and led the way there. She was wishing that Edward weren't having his afternoon rest, feeling that she could have coped far better with her visitor with his support.

'Smells good.'

Liz gave the older woman a hesitant smile. Edward was a picky eater, and had to be tempted and coaxed to eat what she considered to be a good meal. On Monday washdays, in her aunt's household, cold meat, bread and pickle had been the only meal available, but this morning Liz had got up early to make a fresh batch of bread and in the range was a chicken which she was casseroling for Edward's dinner.

As she invited her guest to sit down and offered her a cup of tea, Harriet Fane announced, 'Tell you why I'm here. It's about Chivers.'

Liz waited uncertainly. She had no idea who or what Chivers might be, and wondered if perhaps it was one of Lady Harriet's horses who might have escaped.

'Chivers?' she repeated politely.

'Yes—George's batman. Been with him for years. Virtually kept him alive. Best nurse a man could ever have, George always said. Can turn his hand to anything. Got to find a place for him now that George is gone. Heard you were looking for a man...'

Enlightenment dawned. Liz felt her heart sink. It was true that she had finally persuaded Edward to do something about employing someone to take over the burden of her heavier chores. Her housewifely mind hated the deterioration and sheer wastage she saw around the house and its grounds, especially when she knew that with a little effort, a little ingenuity and hard work, much could be done to put things right at a minimal cost. All it needed was a pair of willing, deft hands. She had hoped that they might find among the men returning home from war someone with small skill at carpentry and building work, who would not mind turning his hand to giving her some help in the garden when necessary, in addition to doing things such as keeping the range supplied with wood. But what she had had in mind was a young, strong man...not some aged retainer who would probably turn up his nose at being expected to help with such menial tasks. And besides, the wages they could pay would not be very generous. As she remembered this she gave a small sigh of relief. Quickly she explained the position to her visitor.

'Oh, that's all right,' Harriet Fane told her, confounding her. 'Chivers don't want much. George never paid him in his life, I dare say. No, it's more a matter of finding a suitable billet for him. Got no one of his own. And one feels a sense of responsibility. Can't go on for ever. Chivers is a good sort.'

This was, Liz began to recognise, a matter of *noblesse oblige*. She hunted wildly in her mind for a suitable excuse, but the only one she could come up with was a weak, 'Well, it's very good of you to think of us. But it would of course be Edward——'

'Just what your husband needs, my dear. Chivers will do him the world of good.' Harriet stood up. 'Glad that's all sorted out. I'll send Chivers round in the morning.'

'In the morning...' Liz stared at her, and grasped her last straw. 'But your—Chivers—he may not want to work for us.'

'Nonsense!' Lady Harriet boomed. 'Just what he needs. He's been moping himself to death since George went. Must go now. Horses need feeding...'

Totally floored, Liz escorted her back through the house and watched as she settled herself in an ancient Morris which started with a cough, its engine rattling the rusting bodywork. After she had gone she made herself a cup of tea and sat down. Edward would be furious, of course, and rightly so... but nothing she had been able to say had been able to deter her visitor.

She waited until after dinner before informing Edward of what had happened. He was not as annoyed as she had expected, and she realised as she watched him that there were still many aspects of the social code which governed the class to which her husband belonged that she still did not understand. Unlike her, Edward did not seem to think it in the least odd that the late Lord George's batman should be passed from one household to another like a parcel. On the contrary, he almost seemed to be flattered that Lady Harriet should consider them a suitable household to receive him. Almost as if in doing so she had bestowed a favour on them. Which, she suspected, she most certainly had not, Liz reflected grimly.

This opinion was reinforced in the morning when Lady Harriet arrived with Chivers. He was a small, rotund man, with baby-smooth skin and a bald head. He could have been any age from forty to sixty, Liz reflected as she greeted him a little stiffly. She had been up early trying to prepare a room for him, hoping all the time that he would take one look at the household and announce that it was impossible for him to stay.

As she led him through the front door, she saw him studying the panelling she had been attempting to clean.

The raw scrubbed wood was now badly in need of nourishment. Linseed oil would have been an ideal method of bringing it back to life, but who could obtain that or anything else in these times of shortages and rationing?

She had told Edward that, if they were to retain Chivers, then it must be his decision, and so she led her unwanted companion through to the clean but bare library, where Edward was waiting for him. She had lit a fire in the grate but made no other concessions to comfort. Let him see the house the way it really was...let him see how they actually lived.

Even so, despite her dislike of the situation she felt she had been forced into, her aunt's training held sway, and it was impossible for Liz not to return to the kitchen and prepare a tray of tea, complete with some of the plain, almost sugarless biscuits that were all she was able to make with the meagre supplies available to her.

It took Liz just three days to change her mind about Chivers and to marvel that Harriet Fane had felt able to live without him.

When the vicar's wife heard what had happened she came round to Cottingdean and exclaimed enviously to Liz, 'You've got Chivers, you lucky thing! How on earth did you manage it?'

'I didn't,' Liz assured her, and proceeded to explain.

It was left to Chivers himself to unravel the mystery of how he came to be at Cottingdean when Liz found him on his hands and knees, lovingly soaking the hall panelling with something that smelled suspiciously like linseed oil.

When she said as much he told her calmly that it was, tapping his nose mysteriously as he added that he was unable to reveal his sources of supply for the amazing variety of things that had suddenly begun to appear at Cottingdean. The hole in the stable roof, which she had despaired of ever having repaired, had suddenly, magically almost, gone, the rotting sections of the book-shelves in the library were somehow magically exchanged for new ones...

'Chivers, you're wasted here,' Liz told him admiringly. 'You ought to be running the country.'

'Wouldn't thank you for it, madam,' he told her. He always addressed Liz as 'madam'; he had never once, as she had originally feared, indicated that he was aware that she had been born into a lower class than her husband's.

'It seemed to me, when I heard about all you was doing here, that this would be a good billet for me. And then you having the baby put the seal on it, so to speak...'

He didn't say why, and Liz knew better than to ask. Harriet Fane might have been a rather unlikely fairy godmother, but the gift she had given them in the shape of Chivers was certainly priceless...

Suddenly life was becoming a little easier. She found she was laughing more, singing when she worked in the gardens. She found there were days, sometimes days at a time when she no longer thought of Kit.

Her birthday came and went, the occasion marked by a cake baked by Chivers, and by an astounding collection of unexpected gifts.

And then, one bright sunny morning, just as she was beginning to feel at ease with her new world, she had a second unexpected visitor.

This one too was female, and she also knocked at the front door. But beyond that she was as different a woman from Harriet Fane as it was possible to be.

Liz opened the front door, unable to help admiring the soft sheen of the polished panelling, a smile curving her mouth. Her smile vanished into startled astonishment as she saw the woman standing there. Tall and slim, she had a smooth, elegant chignon of dark hair. Her face was perfectly made-up, and if there was a certain hardness around her eyes then Liz charitably pretended not to notice it. She was smoking a cigarette, with quick, impatient movements, and her clothes were obviously new and expensive, as were the gold and diamond wedding and engagement rings she was wearing.

She looked like something out of one of the magazines which Louise Ferndean sometimes received from her married daughter: expensive, brittle, and very, very out of place in Cottingdean's sunny hallway.

Behind her, drawn up in the drive, was a huge shining motor car, again obviously new, and as though she sensed Liz's bewilderment she gestured towards it and said almost acidly, 'A gift from my new husband. Nice, isn't it? May I come in? I'm Lillian Chalmers, by the way.'

Liz was mystified. The other woman plainly expected her to recognise the name.

'I was engaged to Edward's cousin, before he went and got himself killed...'

She stubbed out her cigarette almost viciously and said under her breath, 'Probably the best favour he ever did me... Did you know Kit, by the way? I've been in the States for simply ages, and I only got to know of your marriage when I came back. Mummy mentioned it to me, and now that Lee and I are married... Well, I thought I'd come down here before I fly out to New York... for old times' sake, you know. Kit had some pretty wild parties here in the old days. Not that I was invited, of course. They weren't the sort of affairs a man invites his fiancée to, especially when he's only marrying her for her father's money...'

Liz felt her head spin. An odd sense of *déjà vu* swept over her, an awareness of being dragged into a dark place of pain and despair.

'I'm sorry,' she said again. 'I'm afraid...'

This woman had been engaged to Kit, had loved him, she recognised bleakly. Had been hurt by him...

It was like being frozen into a nightmare from which there was no escape. The other woman plainly had no idea that she herself had ever been involved with Kit; she was not directing her poison, her invective at her personally, Liz realised. She was simply looking for a way of ridding herself of its taint; a kind of emotional cleansing before turning her back on her past and walking forward into her new life.

'I loved him, you know,' she said bitterly as she followed Liz into the kitchen and immediately lit another cigarette. 'That was the pure hell of it. I loved him. And for a while he allowed me to think he loved me too... Just long enough to get me into bed with him. To him it was all a game. He knew I'd never break it off with him. It amused him to hurt me... to tell me that he was just marrying me for the money.'

Liz wanted to cry out to her to stop, to tell her that she didn't want to hear, that her words were destroying her own dreams, her precious memories.

Chivers had taken Edward and David into the village. He had managed to fix an old bicycle basket on to the wheelchair, which enabled him to push them both. It would be ages before they returned.

'Even knowing what he was... I thought afterwards, when he was dead, that I'd die too. There seemed no point in doing anything else.' Her red-painted mouth twisted. 'I even wished I were having his child. Ridiculous of me. That would have been the last thing Kit would have wanted. There was a time once, when I thought... He was furious...blamed me for it...even though I knew nothing and he was the first.' She bit her lip and stopped, dragging deeply on her cigarette, while Liz fought back her own nausea. She didn't want to hear this. It was too much... She discovered that she was shaking and cold. Why...? Why had this had to happen? Why couldn't she have been left in ignorance?

'He gave me an address. I went... It was a filthy place...and the woman there...' She gave another shudder. 'Thank God it was all a false alarm. I learned afterwards from a friend that several of the women who had been to her had died...

'Kit hated women,' she announced. 'Oh, you'd never have known it... he had all the charm in the world, all the right words...but underneath he hated us. He liked hurting people. Edward told me that once, but I wouldn't listen. I thought Edward was just jealous of him—Kit had so much, and Edward so little. Even before he was wounded, he could never compare with Kit. Everyone— every woman who met him adored him. Perhaps that was the trouble. Perhaps he could only despise us for our weakness in wanting him. I don't think he cared about anyone other than himself in his whole life.'

She grimaced. 'As soon as his father died, he stripped this place of everything of any value in it. Brought his drunken pals and their girls down from London and let them run amok. The couple his father paid to look after the house left. Poor Edward. It must have been more of a burden than anything else when he found he'd inherited. Of course, what money there was in the family went to Kit...

'You're very young to have married a man like Edward. So badly wounded...'

The blue eyes weren't friendly, and Liz heard herself saying quietly, 'I knew Edward before...before...'

'And afterwards, when they sent him back to you, you felt you had to go through with whatever promises you'd made him. How noble of you. What's it like...marriage?'

Liz stared at her. She was frightened, she recognised. Underneath the paint and expensive clothes she was scared.

'It's like life,' she told her wryly. 'It's up to you what you make of it.'

Instantly the hard mask was back in place. 'Really?' she drawled. 'Well, I shall have to see what I can do, then, shan't I? At least Lee is rich enough to provide me with a good settlement if we decided to call it quits and divorce. The boot is now on the other foot, so to speak, you see,' she added with a brilliant, glittering smile. 'My father has lost his money, and I've married Lee for the same reason Kit wanted to marry me. I've shocked you, haven't I? I—I suppose you think that after being treated the way I was by Kit...'

'It isn't for me to sit in judgement,' Liz told her quietly. How much of her attitude, her hardness had been caused by Kit? How much destruction and pain had he been responsible for?

Only later would she realise that never once had she questioned the other woman's revelations...never once had any kind of denial of what she was saying risen au-

tomatically to her lips...and she recognised that it was
almost as though a part of her had known, had always
known what Kit was, but that she had clung to her
dreams like a child afraid of the dark.

'I must go—I don't really know why I came down
here...'

'To exorcise a ghost?' Liz suggested compassionately.

After she had gone, Liz sat for a long time simply staring
into space. She had sensed all along that Edward had
not cared for his cousin, and because of that, because
she was sensitive enough to realise that Edward wanted
her memories of his cousin kept in the past, she took
care never to refer to Kit. Not even in her most private
moments with her son. She already knew how jealous
Edward could be.

She had promised Edward...given him her word that
David would be his son, and she had never once broken
that word. Now she was glad...glad that her child would
grow up in ignorance of what his blood father had
been...glad that whatever had guided her life had pushed
her in Edward's direction. Glad that she had been
fortunate enough to marry him. She shuddered, remembering the other woman's brief but graphic description
of the place Kit had sent her to, and she thanked God
that she had never been given the opportunity to tell Kit
of her own pregnancy.

As the afternoon wore on and she sat locked in her
thoughts, although she didn't realise it she was finally
closing a door on her youth...Closing it and sealing it
as she vowed that for the rest of her life she would strive
to repay Edward for all that he had done for her. David,
Edward and Cottingdean...From now on they were the
boundaries of her life.

Kit had already robbed her of her right to her sexuality, although she didn't realise it; now he had destroyed her dream as well...

Just one final time, and as a punishment not a
panacea, she allowed herself to remember each second
of time she had spent with Kit...each whispered
word...each embrace...but this time she stripped from

them her own naïveté and innocence. This time she saw
them for what they were and felt sick with self-disgust.
How could she have been so deceived? Kit had never
loved her...would have laughed in her face if he had
ever guessed how she had felt.

Now her body forced her to remember how it had not
been pleasure she had felt at the moment of possession,
but pain...pain and fear.

She felt no regret at the knowledge that her life with
Edward would be celibate. She had her son, she had a
husband who was compassionate and caring, she had a
home which she would one day restore to what it had
once been. To cherish and protect these three would be
her goal, her destiny.

She was just nineteen years old.

The third surprise did not arrive in the form of a visitor,
but by letter. A typed letter, addressed to her personally,
and which she opened and then read with a deepening
frown.

'Something wrong?' Edward asked her.

They were eating breakfast in the small sunny room
which she and Chivers had managed to clean and re-
furnish from items they had found in the attic.

The attic was proving to be a treasure-house. Much
of the furniture stored there was old-fashioned and
broken, but Chivers's magical fingers always found a
way of effecting a repair, and Liz was gradually coming
to find that she actually preferred the rich patina of these
old, often shabby pieces to the modern utility furniture
that seemed so ugly in comparison.

'No,' she replied to Edward's question. 'It's a letter
from my aunt's solicitors.'

Liz had written regularly to her aunt since David's
birth but had never received a reply. It was a shock to
discover that her aunt was dead, and that, moreover, she
had decreed that Liz was not to be told until after the
funeral. What came as even more of a surprise was the
news that her aunt had willed to her her entire estate:
the small house and its contents, and a sum of money
that made Liz gasp with shock.

'Just over a thousand pounds! Well, it's a nice little sum,' said Edward.

'It's a fortune,' Liz retorted indignantly, but Edward merely smiled and shook his head.

He was more content than he had ever dreamed of being. His wounds still bothered him, but now he had something he had never had before. Now he had hope... Now he had Liz, he had David and he had Cottingdean, and he loved them all. He had promised himself, though, that he would never burden Liz with his feelings. What was the point? He could never be a husband to her in any physical sense. And yet jealously he watched her, wondering if there might one day come a time when she would yearn for a physical relationship with some other man. When she would fall in love with some other man!

'What shall we do with it?' Liz asked him. She was thinking of perhaps buying a small car, if they could find one... Something that would make life easier and more enjoyable for Edward.

But when she said as much he frowned and told her curtly, 'No, Liz, that money's yours. You should spend it on something for yourself—some pretty clothes,' he added vaguely.

Liz laughed. Pretty clothes... What need had she for anything like that? Even if she could buy them... Men really had no idea, and besides, she had been thinking recently that if she could *buy* a second-hand sewing machine—she couldn't keep borrowing Louise's—she could utilise so much more of the vast amount of fabrics and clothes stored away in the attic. However, she had already mentioned to Chivers that a sewing machine wouldn't come amiss and when one mysteriously appeared she wasn't surprised. She had stopped asking where he managed to find the articles he produced, and now was merely grateful for them.

Spend it on yourself, Edward had said, but later on that day as she stood in her garden looking out towards the hills she suddenly knew exactly what she was going to do with her aunt's bequest...

'But—a ram...' Vic stared at her.

'Not just any ram, Vic. We want the best, the very best there is. If you could go anywhere in the world to buy him, where would you go?'

'Australia,' he told her promptly. 'They've been doing some cross-breeding there...I was reading about it a while ago.' He shrugged. 'But it's impossible.'

'No...no, it isn't,' Liz corrected him.

It took a great deal of effort to persuade him, and even more to convince Edward, but in the end she had her way. For a fee, a neighbouring farmer agreed to run the flock with his own while Vic was away, and letters were written, arrangements made.

'It's like Jason looking for the golden fleece,' Liz teased him.

'Aye...you're not wrong. Gold is what our fleeces will be worth if I can bring one of Australia's finest rams with me. It won't be easy to buy one, though...'

'No,' Liz agreed, and smiled at him. 'But you'll do it, Vic.'

Half of her almost envied him the adventure which lay ahead of him, but she had her own world. Cottingdean was her world, and if sometimes it seemed small and enclosed...well, she put those thoughts out of her mind and reminded herself how much she had to be grateful for.

CHAPTER TEN

A SHADOW chased across the face of the moon, and out across the fields the vixen paused, sniffing the air. Her cubs were independent now, but she had grown used to feeding them...caring for them. She was lean with the leanness of a diligent mother, her own hunger coming second to that of her young.

In her sleep Sage frowned, her dreams jumbled and confused. The diary lay face down on the carpet beside her bed where it had slipped when she'd fallen asleep, too exhausted to read on, and yet so enthralled, so gripped by what she was reading that she had fought off her need to sleep as long as she could.

In her dreams she was standing in the hallway of the house, but it was not the hallway as she had always known it, mellow and graceful with its polished panelling, its heavy oak antiques, its rich Persian rugs... This hallway was empty, its panelling stained and damp, its halls festooned with cobwebs, just as her mother had described it in her diary.

Outside the vixen howled, a mournful sound that penetrated Sage's dreams. It was the eternal sound of the female yearning for her mate—for succour...for companionship...for love. In her dreams she wept and then cried out.

'Scott...no...no, don't leave me...' But the once-familiar face of her lover was already fading, vague, and suddenly its image was overshadowed by those of other men...more men than she cared to remember...so many men that she would not allow herself to remember. Men whom she had taken to her bed, but never to her heart. Men who had served for a little while at least to make herself forget how she had been abandoned...rejected. Men who had been more than willing to share with her the physical pleasures she and Scott had never been allowed to know... ⌐

How easy it had been to fool them, to let them believe that they mattered to her. How stupid they were, how vain.

All of them. But no...not all of them...there had been one, one who had seen through her, had recognised... Who had rejected her. Who had recognised the false coin she was offering and who had thrown it back at her.

She could see him now, towering over her, furiously angry; so angry that for a moment she had thought he might actually hit her.

That he hadn't done so had been to his credit and not hers; she had watched as he had battled against his rage, fought it and won that inward battle, and as he walked away from her she'd had a stupid impulse to call him back, to...to what? Apologise?

In her sleep she moved impatiently, as though seeking an escape from her own dreams, from the knowledge which was shattering the barrier she had always kept between herself and others. And the root cause of the destruction of that barrier was her mother's diary...the new perspective she was getting on her mother, not as a parent, but as a woman, a vulnerable, courageous, likeable woman...the kind of woman she would have welcomed as a friend.

In her narrow hospital bed Elizabeth Danvers surfaced briefly from the drug-controlled sleep. A nurse, alerted to her awakening, hurried to her bedside. It was imperative at this stage that their patient was kept sedated and calm.

With quick expertise she soothed the distressed movements of Elizabeth's hands, while monitoring the technological battery of life-saving equipment surrounding the bed.

Elizabeth opened her eyes, knowing instinctively that she was somewhere alien and unfamiliar...knowing there was something she must do...someone she must see...something important that awaited her at-

tention... but already the nurse was deftly sliding the
needle into her skin, injecting the drug, and then
watching the ever-wakeful monitors.

Only when they told her that her patient was once
again locked in a calm, protective sleep did she leave her
bedside.

Faye couldn't sleep. It was always like this on the first
Monday night of the month, and sometimes for several
nights before and afterwards. Sage had given her the
first of Liz's diaries. She had started to read it when she
came to bed. For a while it had distracted her.

The young Liz, her hopes and dreams, her belief that
she was loved, had touched a tender place in her own
heart. Unlike Sage, it had not come as an abrupt shock
to her to discover that Edward had not been David's
physical father.

She loved Liz and she always would do. Liz had given
her the best things her life had ever held, both directly
in her son, and indirectly, through him, her own precious
daughter. And more. Liz had given her love... and not
just love. Liz had taught her to distance herself from
her past, to stop blaming herself for its dark places... to
see herself not as the catalyst of all its pain, but as the
victim of events she could not control.

To discover that Liz too had known pain and
betrayal... to learn that she too had sinned against the
moral code of her peers, only made her feel closer to
her mother-in-law.

To discover that David, wonderful, precious David
who had brought her so much happiness, wasn't
Edward's son did nothing to alter her love either for him
or for his mother.

And yet, as it had Sage, the diary gripped her with
the compulsive need to discover more about its author's
fate, although from a very different viewpoint from
Sage's. And at three o'clock she put it to one side, and
opened the drawer in the table beside her bed.

Inside it the familiar bottle winked tormentingly in
the lamplight.

Her fingers twitched, curling convulsively as she forced herself not to reach out for it. She knew that the sleeping tablets inside it would put an end to the darkness and her fears...that, once taken, just one of them would ensure a dreamless night's sleep. Just one... But no...she was not going to go back down that road.

After David's death, when Dr Palmer had first prescribed them, she had taken first one...and then later, when their effect became diminished, another...and then still another, until she was spending her time in drug-induced lethargy.

It had been Liz who had taken them from her, who had insisted gently but firmly that she must not allow herself to be swept into oblivion on a tide of indifference, Liz who had reminded her that, even though she had lost her husband, she still had his child...her daughter...a daughter who needed her mother very much.

Night after night Liz had sat up with her, talking to her, listening to her, and it had been in those dark days after David's death that she had fought more desperately than she had ever fought anything in her life—and with Liz at her side she had won.

But Liz wasn't at her side any longer, and suddenly tonight the dark shadows...the fears...the panic she had never completely conquered were back in monstrous force, stealthily stalking her...laughing at her weakness and her vulnerability.

Normally on these nights Liz was there, knowing without her having to say anything how afraid she was... But now there was no Liz...and there might not be any Liz ever again.

Already her heart was beating fast, panic clenching her muscles. She felt sick, dizzy... She tried to force herself to breathe deeply, to remind herself that her symptoms were self-induced. And, after all, there was no compulsion on her to go, no real need. Nothing...other than her own guilt, her own belief that in forcing herself to go through this monthly ordeal she was somehow or other appeasing any jealous gods...that she was somehow or other protecting her daughter...that in return for her willingly carrying her burdens of fear and guilt her precious Camilla would be spared all that she herself had to endure.

Downstairs in the kitchen was the jar of herb tea which she and Liz drank together on those nights like this one when she couldn't sleep, when her mind was tormented by the past.

She looked at the bottle again, her fingers bent into stiff claws as she willed herself not to reach for it. It was three o'clock...only a few hours now. This time tomorrow it would be all over. For another month.

Shivering, she pushed back the bedclothes and picked up the pretty cotton robe lying on the bed. David had teased her about this need she had always to keep her body covered. He had teased her about it, but he had never tried to force or dissuade her from that need.

Only when they made love had she allowed him to remove her nightdress, and then afterwards had come the ritual bathing, done secretly and guiltily at first until he had reassured her that he understood... After that a clean nightdress, and then back to bed...

She had once asked David if he minded that no matter how gentle he was, how caring and understanding, she could never distance herself from the past enough to do any more than merely accept his possession of her body.

'I love you... you, the person,' he had told her softly. And then, with that illuminating, wonderful smile of his, he had added, almost self-mockingly, 'And anyway, I'm not highly motivated sexually, Faye. In another age I suspect I could quite happily have settled to life as a celibate. As it is, I don't have the religious motivation for the priesthood, otherwise... You and I are a pair... what happens within the privacy of our relationship is our affair and no one else's, and perhaps if it weren't for the fact that we both want a family...'

A family. Yes, they had both wanted that. They had both been overjoyed when she had first conceived; and both equally devastated when she lost that child.

Although David had tried his best to reassure her that
it was not so, she had seen it as a sign that she was being
punished... When she had conceived and then carried
Camilla full term she had hardly been able to believe it.
Then, for an all too short period of time, she had known
true happiness.

And then had come David's death. Another blow.
Another reinforcement of her guilt.

The letter had come a month after David's death. Liz
had found her with it in her hand, half hysterical with
shock. She had told her then, all of it, sparing herself
nothing...

Downstairs she boiled the kettle and found the jar of
herb tea. It wasn't the same drinking it alone. She felt
so afraid... but she had to go. It was her punishment
and she must not avoid it... For Camilla's sake, she
must go.

Alaric Ferguson glanced at his watch. Officially this was
his day off, but there had been an emergency just as he
was leaving the building.

He could have left the man to be operated on by his
intern, but Alaric had a Scots Presbyterian grandfather
on his mother's side, and duty, responsibility, putting
work before play and others before himself were ingrained soul-deep in him.

Jancis had said to him that he enjoyed playing the
martyr... that he liked the demands his job placed upon
him. Other surgeons didn't behave as he did, she had
told him. They found time for their wives, their
families... to enjoy themselves... and still managed to
advance their careers far faster than he had done his.

'Look at yourself,' she had commanded acidly. 'How
many of those who qualified with you are still stuck in
a run-down NHS hospital, living on a pittance, working
all the hours God sends—and for what? You were top
of your year, Alaric. And look at what you've done with
that—nothing...'

And behind her anger he had sensed her frustration
and seen more clearly than he had ever seen before how

much marriage to him had embittered and disappointed her.

She had been a medical student herself when they'd first met. He had just qualified, and he had been both bemused and flattered when she'd begun to show an interest in him. His stark and sometimes hard upbringing had left him with little time to play.

His mother had been widowed young, and, while she had supported him devotedly in his determination to become a surgeon, both of them had had to make sacrifices so that he could attain that achievement. It hadn't been easy, and to have this pretty, blue-eyed, blonde-haired young woman flirting with him, teasing him had opened a door into a completely new world.

When he had married her six months later, he had been fathoms deep in love with her, content to allow her to direct the mutual course of their lives, laughing gently at her when she told him what she wanted . . . what she hoped for . . . when she told him that he was going to become a world-famous surgeon, that they would live in a beautiful house, and she would entertain his colleagues and famous patients . . .

He had thought then that she was simply indulging in fanciful daydreams. He had no idea that what she was telling him was that these were her expectations of him, and by the time he did understand it it was too late. Even if he had wanted to, he could not have changed himself by then. The lifestyle she wanted was so diametrically opposed to the one he'd envisaged for both of them. And when he had come home early one day and discovered her in bed with one of his colleagues— the kind of clever, determined man who already had his sights firmly set on private and lucrative practice pandering to the vanity of women idiotic enough to believe that the skilled hands of a surgeon could magically transform their lives at the same time as they transformed their faces and bodies—he had known that their marriage was finally over.

He didn't blame her. She had been as deceived in him as he had been in her. That her deception was deliberate and his not, he preferred not to dwell on. He was thankful that they had no children. His mother had been very upset.

He was almost forty-two. Every time he saw her, his mother told him that he ought to remarry. He smiled and said nothing. If he was lonely at times, well, it was by his own choice. He was a brilliant and dedicated surgeon. Wasted outside private practice, so many of his colleagues considered, but Alaric felt he had a duty, a responsibility towards the sick and weak . . . a duty to use his skills to the advantage of the majority and not the minority, and sometimes, like now, he worked far longer hours than he should. If sometimes weeks, months went by when he was barely aware of a larger, more free world outside his own, he had no real regrets.

He had given up the large, uncomfortable house they had bought together when Jancis had left him, and had bought a small, convenient service flat instead.

If it rarely felt like a home, well, he hardly spent enough time in it for that to matter. If he sometimes woke up from a deep sleep aware of a need, an ache almost for the comfort and intimacy of having someone next to him in the large bed, he had only to remind himself of the disaster of his marriage to Jancis . . . the reality of modern relationships which meant that rarely did they involve the kind of almost spiritual intimacy and oneness which his Celtic spirit sometimes craved.

It was eight o'clock in the morning before he was able to leave the hospital. The man who had been brought in, the victim of a stabbing, was now recovering on the ward. He would have a long curving scar to show for his injury but nothing else. He had been lucky: the knife had just missed causing the kind of internal injury no surgeon, however skilled, could ever repair. There was such a lot still to be learned about the human body . . . so much that frustrated and angered Alaric, taunting him with his inability to help everyone who came into his hands. That woman upstairs, for instance.

He had never thought she would survive. And yet she had . . . Soon she would be strong enough for him to operate, to remove the pressure on her brain. What was it that gave some people the will to live no matter how severe their injuries, while others...?

Sighing faintly, he left the building. Outside it was light, the sky pearled with the promise of a clear day. As he got into his car, the same ordinary model he had driven for the past four years, he remembered that it was a long time since he had last visited his mother. She was living on the south coast now, in a small, lazy seaside town where the pace of life was slow and calm, and where most of the residents were retired. Sometimes when he went there he found the place faintly depressing, and yet his mother loved it.

After the council flat in one of Manchester's worst areas of deprivation he supposed her small bungalow in its neat complex of protected retirement homes was the kind of sanctuary she must often have dreamed of finding.

He felt guilty sometimes, aware of the barrenness of her life. As a child and then a student, he had been conscious of the small and large sacrifices she made for him, the pinching and scraping which had allowed him first to accept the scholarship he had won, and then later to follow his dream of becoming a surgeon.

As soon as she could he had repaid her. He had bought the bungalow for her; he gave her a monthly allowance to ensure that she never again had to go without any of life's material comforts. She asked nothing from him, not even, as other parents did, his time and attention.

As he drove towards the south coast, he wondered if there had ever been a time when she had wanted more from life, when she had hungered for a man to take the place of his father, other children, a more physically comfortable lifestyle... If she had, she had never allowed him to see it.

On impulse, just before he left the city, he pulled up outside a florist's, parking on the yellow line with unfamiliar disregard for the law. Inside the shop a girl was placing huge, still dew-fresh bunches of flowers into large vases. She smiled at him as he walked in.

Fifteen minutes later, feeling both awkward and a little foolish, he went back to his car, his arms full of the flowers he had just bought. The girl who had just sold them to him watched him, sighing romantically, wondering if her lover would ever think to stop and buy her market-fresh flowers . . . not in a single bunch, but by the armful, as her customer had just done.

When Sage got up, Faye had already gone. When she asked Camilla if she knew where her mother was, Camilla glanced at her watch and said absently, 'Oh, it's her day for that monthly WI thingy that she and Gran always go to...'

Sage frowned. It was true that she was out of touch with her mother's day-to-day routine, but the news that Liz, who thrived on the challenges of single-handedly controlling the reins of a busy business whose product was known in every part of the globe where people had the money and the inclination to buy clothes made from the famous Cottingdean Wools, should have the time to give up a whole day each and every month to spend involving herself in the affairs of a local Women's Institute surprised her.

'Where exactly has your mother gone?' she questioned Camilla.

'I don't know. I've told you, Ma and Gran took off like this one day a month for ages. Ask Jenny, she might know...'

Sage was still frowning when Jenny came in carrying their breakfast. Breakfast for two, Sage noticed.

Yes, Jenny confirmed willingly when Sage questioned her. Liz and Faye always left early on the first Tuesday in the month, generally not returning until early evening, but no, she had no idea where they went.

Plainly these Tuesdays, wherever they were spent, were such an accepted part of life at Cottingdean as to provoke no curiosity. But Sage *was* curious, and her curiosity was like a tiny piece of grit rubbing against a tender place. It seemed so out of character that Faye, who was so obviously devoted to Liz, should disappear for a whole day without leaving any indication of where she had gone, or how she might be contacted in case of an emergency.

Not that she was going to have much time to worry about Faye's whereabouts, Sage acknowledged. The local paper had arrived with the post, and there was a write-up in it about the planned motorway. The paper was printed in Siddington, five miles away, where it was obvious that opinion as to the effects of the new motorway was divided.

There were those who believed it would bring new prosperity to the small market town, who claimed that in the wake of the motorway would come new industry, bringing in its turn much needed jobs for the school leavers, who at present often had to leave home for the large cities in order to get work.

Others, like Liz, were concerned about the effects of such a motorway on their environment and lifestyle.

Protest groups had sprung up in each small village affected by the road; as she read the list of them and how to contact their organisers, Sage gnawed at her bottom lip, wondering cynically if Daniel would attend each and every one of the meetings or only those where Ms Ordman was representing the Ministry. She suspected she already knew the answer. Although why blame Daniel? He was no hunting, aggressive male in the mould of Alexi, despite his obvious sexuality. Rather, she suspected, in this case it was Ms Ordman who was doing the hunting. Telling herself that she was allowing herself to be distracted down avenues which were as unprofitable as they were idiotic, Sage gathered up her post, poured herself a second cup of coffee, told Camilla that she would drive her to school . . . and acknowledged mentally to herself that she was likely to have to spend the rest of the day in her mother's study, not, as she would have liked, avidly reading the diaries to which she had become almost compulsively addicted, almost as though she was searching for something, or someone, from them, but instead trying as conscientiously as she could to stand in her mother's shoes and protect

Cottingdean from the onslaught of Daniel Cavanagh's
bulldozers.

Faye reached the outskirts of the town at nine o'clock.
She always arrived far too early, something which Liz
good-humouredly accepted. Generally they would spend
the time before visiting time drinking cups of tea in one
of the many old-fashioned seaside cafés.

Fellingham was a town that catered well to the needs
of its inhabitants. Not for them the brash modernity of
hamburger bars and pubs; Ye Olde Tea Shoppes and
Copper Kettle Cafés were the order of the day, all of
them boasting Earl Grey tea and home-made
confectionery.

Earl Grey or not, Faye decided that tea was the last
thing she wanted. Her stomach was already churning
nauseously. Driving had at least given her something to
do, something on which to fasten her mind.

She had automatically parked on the sea-front facing
out to sea. Today the Channel was calm, reflecting the
clear sharp blue of the sky. Already Fellingham's residents were filling the neat pathways running alongside
the immaculately maintained flower-beds between the
road and the sea-front. Why was it that so much order,
cleanliness and neatness should have such a depressing
effect? she wondered idly as she tried not to focus on
the car's clock, silently marking the passage of time.

Why did she always do this—arrive so early? It wasn't
as though she was anxious to see... She could restart
the car now, turn around and go home. No one would
know. Just for a moment the temptation overwhelmed
her, and then she checked it. She was a grown woman,
not a child. She was here now...here, yes, but the ordeal
still lay ahead of her. Five to ten. Time now surely to
go. If she walked slowly...

She got out of her car, a small, slender woman whose
comparative youth was glaringly out of place among
Fellingham's residents. Several of them stared at her with
envy and a touch of resentment, until they saw where
she was going.

The house was one of the largest in the quiet road. Once a private home, now it was discreetly protected from the outside world with iron railings which were not merely decorative, and a security system which meant that Faye had to wait a dozen or more agonising moments before the gate opened to let her in.

This was one of the worst moments...this awareness that once she stepped inside she was a prisoner, trapped...and yet the immaculate orderliness of the gardens was surely anything but threatening. She remembered when she had first come here with Liz, how she had gently pointed out to her the pleasantness of their surroundings.

She walked up to the front door. The woman who opened it to her might have been any well-built, slightly reserved middle-aged housewife, and yet to Faye there was something immediately self-betraying about her. Or was it just that she, with her guilt and her fears, could too easily sense the purposefulness, the steely-eyed determination that no one who should not do so should pass through those doors? That knowledge should have comforted her, but instead she shrank from it like a child shrinking from an unacceptable fact of life.

The woman greeted Faye by name, smiling warmly at her. 'I think you'll find that we're having one of our better days today. It's the weather, I think. Always seems to cheer them up.'

She was looking over Faye's shoulder as she spoke, and, sensing that she was looking for Liz, Faye said quickly, 'I'm on my own today. My mother-in-law has had an accident.'

She heard the few quick words of professional sympathy and knew she must have responded to them, but already it was beginning...the panic, the sickness, the fear...and most of all the anger. The sheer weight of it pressed down on her, suffocating her...threatening her. She could feel her knees buckling under the pressure of it. She could feel it building up inside her like a scream...the kind of scream she had learned to suppress.

'Would you like someone to go up with you, then?'

The woman's voice was carefully neutral. God knew how many times a day she must ask the same questions...how many other tortured souls came here with the same reluctance and guilt that brought her...

She gave her a too-bright smile and shook her head. 'No, that won't be necessary...'

After all, she wasn't violent, wasn't dangerous... wasn't likely to hurt her. Not like some of the women here. She heard them sometimes, screaming and crying, the noise like so many darts of fire in her flesh.

They couldn't help it, poor souls, one of the nurses had once said to her. They didn't know what they were doing...thank God in his mercy for that at least...

She had been an Irish girl, young and raw, unaware that, for so many of the visitors who came here, the thought that their relatives were free of the knowledge of what was happening to them was the smallest particle of comfort in a vast sea of anguish and misery.

Call it what you liked, explain it away how you wished...madness was what it was, plain and simple. A madness that attacked and destroyed, the madness sometimes of old age, sometimes not...and no one could witness it without suffering, without asking why it was that the human race should be punished in this way...asking what it had ever done to merit this unholy destruction of all that was in humankind that made it what it was.

Faye went up to the top floor, ignoring the lift, wanting to delay the moment of confrontation as long as she could.

Outside the door stood a nurse. She smiled warmly and approvingly at Faye.

This visitor was one of the better ones. She hadn't just stuck the woman away in here, ignoring her existence. She was one of their most regular visitors, always insisting on seeing her, no matter how bad a day she was having. Still, she wasn't the worst of their patients...not violent, not like some of them...pathetic it was to see her sometimes, crouching in a corner like a baby, gibbering away to herself, screaming and crying when they tried to get her to her feet, to clean her up... Hard it had been, at first, to realise what could happen to the human mind and with it the human body. Old people with strength you'd never expect, behaving like helpless babies. And some of them... violent and foul-mouthed like you'd never believe, and when you tried to help them... She had scratches the like of which you'd never imagined.

She'd stuck it out, though. The pay was good. This wasn't one of your run-down NHS homes. This one was private—and expensive... Each patient had her own room, and bathroom. Not that most of them bothered to use it.

When it had first opened all the bedrooms had had carpet, she'd been told by one of the other nurses, but that hadn't lasted long. Replaced the lot now, they had, with washable floors and rugs. Some of them even had to have disposable sheets on their beds.

Still, it wasn't their fault. They didn't know what they were doing most of the time. And when they did...

'Like me to come in with you?' she asked Faye, shrugging when she shook her head. Hated coming here, this one did. You could see it in her eyes. Pretty woman, too. Didn't know how she could stomach it. In her shoes...

As she unlocked the door, Faye hesitated, and then, summoning all her strength, she walked in and said brightly, 'Hello, Mother. How are you today?'

As she heard the door close behind her, heard it being locked, she tried not to acknowledge the sound but instead to concentrate on the small, frail figure sitting in the window. Her head turned. She focused on her, but Faye knew that she hadn't recognised her. She never did. That was what made it all so stupid... This woman whom she called Mother...this woman who had given her birth...this woman for whom she felt such a huge burden of responsibility, and such an enormity of guilt and hatred, no longer knew her.

She smiled up at Faye, a timid, hesitant smile, her eyes watchful and frightened, and as Faye went towards

her she flinched back in her chair, tiny mewling noises
of frantic fear bubbling in her throat.

Instantly Faye was gripped by the familiar mixture of
anger and anguish, rendered at once helpless by her
inability to do anything to reach out and reassure
whatever awareness still lived within the blanked-off
emptiness of her mother's mind, and seized by a fierce,
overwhelming surge of angry resentment that this
woman—her mother—should be able to escape from
their shared past when she herself could not.

And yet nothing of what she was feeling showed in
her face. She had schooled herself long ago not to allow
it to do so. Those interminable, awful, painful sessions
with the psychiatrist who had counselled her had taught
her the impossibility of confronting the reality of what
her mother had become with the agony of her own past.

To grow strong and guilt-free for herself, for David
and for Camilla—that had been her aim. Some strength
she had found...but to rid herself of the guilt the
psychiatrist had told her she had no need to feel—that
was different, and entwined with all that guilt, a living,
breathing serpent twined with it, was her anger, her resentment and, yes, her hatred... And yet what had her
mother ever done? Wasn't she as much a victim as she
herself had been? But, even while she tried to analyse,
while the dull questions she might have addressed to a
stranger, any stranger, fell automatically and unanswered from her lips, she was remembering, resenting...filled with anger and bitterness.

In her mother's shoes, would she...? But no, she had
told herself long ago that she would have maimed,
killed...fought with every part of her mind and flesh
to prevent anyone from hurting Camilla. However, she
and her mother were two different creatures. She had
never had to contend with the life that had been her
mother's. It was unfair of her to blame, to make comparisons. And besides, what good did it do? There was
no going back...no altering the past. She had lived
through it... She had found David. She had had Camilla.
She had found a goodly measure of peace and con-

tentment... And in these visits she had the means to ensure that her daughter, her precious child, would never, ever know the torment that she had known. If the price of that knowledge, that security was these monthly visits to this place, the monthly reality of facing the woman who had given her birth and who had also betrayed her, then so be it.

She stayed for four hours, talking quietly to her mother of this and that, using her voice to soothe her fear enough for her to relax and watch her timidly, but never once was there any sign in her mother's eyes that she knew who she was... that she recognised her.

Before Faye left there was the ritual of lunch, watching her mother toy with her food, crumbling it into small pieces. Unlike many of the people here, her mother was physically able to take care of herself. She had not degenerated, as so many of them had, into an appalling second childhood that was a grotesque parody of all that a childhood should be.

The sounds and smells from some of the rooms when one passed by the briefly open doors were stomach-rendingly nauseating. Faye had seen other relatives leaving this place harrowed by what they had seen and heard, and yet knowing that here their money was buying their mothers, their aunts, their grandmothers the very best care there was.

In these locked rooms, encased in their too strong bondage of flesh and bone, were women who had given life to others and then unwittingly destroyed that life, as their illness, their dependence had inexorably destroyed their offspring's lives.

Her mother's dementia was different, its cause mental rather than physical, its sources easy to find. Unlike the majority of the visitors here, Faye did not have the harrowing fear of being confronted by her own future. She did not see, in the tormented features at once familiar and yet frighteningly unrecognisable, a terrifying shadow of her own face.

It was mid-afternoon when she left, her head pulsing with the onset of a migraine, her body trembling visibly as she headed for the sanctuary of her car.

There was a pedestrian crossing in front of the house. A car drew up to it and stopped for her to cross. She gave the driver a blind, glittering smile that made him frown. He had recognised her as she walked towards the crossing. The daughter-in-law of the woman in ICU, but looking very different from the last time he had seen her.

Then she had been shocked, fearful, as so many of the relatives of his patients were, but those emotions had been controlled, at least until he had reached out to touch her. As he watched her now his trained eye saw someone in a dangerous state of near collapse. Someone who, he suspected, if he hadn't stopped for her might easily have simply stepped in front of his car. The road was quiet, no traffic waiting for him to move off, so he watched curiously as Faye walked towards the sea-front and her car.

He frowned as he watched her unlock the door. In the interests of safety she should not be allowed to drive, but to his relief she made no attempt to do so, and he could see quite clearly the way she was slumped in the passenger seat.

He glanced back towards the house she had just left, frowning again as he saw the discreet plaque set into one of the stone supports of the gate.

There were many such establishments in Fellingham; this one, as he recalled, was rather better than most and had a good reputation. It specialised in taking women suffering from advanced stages of Alzheimer's Disease, or senile dementia as it was more commonly known, and no one who had ever witnessed its devastating effects both on the sufferer and on those who tried to nurture and support that sufferer could wonder at the need for such homes.

Faye had struck him as a frail, dependent sort the first time he'd seen her. She had not seemed the type to have the strength to visit somewhere like this . . . Her sort normally turned their backs, made excuses, installed their relatives somewhere conveniently too distant from their own homes to allow regular visiting...

He told himself that it was in the interests of safety that he drove his car a short distance away from Faye's and parked it discreetly where he could watch her. After all, if she made any attempt to drive in her present condition she would be a liability to herself and, more importantly, to others. It would be his duty to stop her, to caution her...

Faye was oblivious to him. She felt spent, drained... weak to the point where she felt as though if she closed her eyes the life would simply flood from her. She felt sick, light-headed, weak in the way she had when she had given birth to her aborted foetus. She shivered, suddenly cold, knowing that she should move, that she ought to get into the driver's seat and start her car, but she had no will to do so... no will to do anything other than simply crouch in the passenger seat, barely daring to breathe, panting like a hunted creature on guard for the killer stalking it.

Why couldn't she let go of the past? It was all so long ago, over, part of another life... And yet she could not let go... could not forget. Images, sharp and clear, danced through her head, feelings, memories clearer by far than those she had of David... sharper than any of the happier images with which she sought to overlay them.

Incest. It was a word few feared to use these days... and yet to Faye it smouldered with the sulphurous smell of hell, conjuring up such images, such pain that she felt as though it was written in flames of fire.

As a child she hadn't even known such a word existed. She had, in her innocence, her naïveté, imagined that no one else in the world had been bad enough to suffer what she was forced to suffer. That there were no other bad girls who had to be punished as her stepfather had punished her... That there were no other six-year-olds who lay awake in such fear that when eventually the dreaded footstep came... when eventually the hurting male hand cajoled and then demanded... when the disgusting intrusion of that alien, adult male body made her want to scream and scream again, it was almost a relief to have it actually happen, because she knew that afterwards she would be allowed to sleep, to escape from her fear.

It was because she was a bad girl that he had to do these things to her, he always told her. He used to whisper the words over and over again, telling her how bad she had been as his flesh pushed and tore and his hand clamped over her mouth, stifling her with its scent and heat.

It was because she was such a bad girl that her own father had died...and he had married her mother because God had wanted him to punish her... But she was not to tell anyone about what happened, because if she did God would be very angry with her, and would take her mother away from her.

Eventually there had come a time when her intelligence had told her he was lying to her...when she was old enough to understand properly what was happening. When every night she'd prayed that her mother would find out what he was doing to her and make him stop. Because even though she knew by then that her father had died of cancer and that it was for his own pleasure that her stepfather abused her, he had told her that the authorities would take her away from her mother and lock her up in a children's home if she dared to tell anyone what was going on.

She had known that that was true. There were children in her class at school who lived with foster parents, who had been taken away from their own parents.

Later, as she grew older still, the threat had been that her mother would be sent to prison, and with the development of her body come the sickening self-realisation that she was, as he had always told her, bad...that it was bad and wrong to have let him do to her what he had. She heard the other children at school making jokes about sex, talking about girls who did 'it', and her self-revulsion grew, but she could not stop his visits to her room...to her bed...

She'd fantasised about her mother discovering him with her and sending him away. Every day she'd prayed that it would happen...but no matter how much noise he made her mother remained deeply asleep.

And then had come the final catalyst. On the morning of her fourteenth birthday she had woken up and immediately been violently sick. For over a week she had kept on being sick, and she had seen the nervous way her mother's eyes flicked over her when she came out of the bathroom, her own dark with misery...pleading for her to say something, to notice something... But she hadn't.

Others had, though. She never knew which of her teachers guessed that she was pregnant. She was sent for by her headmistress, and questioned gently but firmly. Which boy was it who had got her into trouble? A lecture had followed about her age, about the law, about the irresponsibility of both herself and the boy concerned, but it wasn't until the headmistress had threatened to send for her parents that she had broken down and told her what had happened...

Now she knew that she had been lucky. The older woman had accepted what she had told her, and had acted swiftly to protect her. She had not, as so many others in the same circumstances had, been sent back home with a note to her parents about her telling lies.

The child she carried was aborted, the staff at the hospital kind and caring, but nothing had been able to take away her horror, the pain, the shock of her brutal emergence from childhood into the world of women.

She had been taken into care, and had discovered that it was not after all the prison-like life she had been told. Her foster parents were kind and caring, and chosen especially for their experience in dealing with damaged children. She was given her own room, with a door that locked and her own bathroom. No one came into her room without being invited, and Mr Masters—Uncle Bob—never made any attempt to touch her in any way. Her nightmare was over, or so it had seemed.

And then had come the court case, and the shock of discovering that her mother had known all along what was happening. Had known and done nothing, nothing at all to help her.

Faye had been too young to understand then, as she had come to understand later, that some women were incapable of standing up to men like her stepfather. But it was in that courtroom that her fear, her pain, her agony had given birth not just to shock, but also to anger, resentment and bitterness against her mother.

CHAPTER ELEVEN

LOOKING back, Faye acknowledged that she had been lucky, in some ways at least. Her foster parents had been marvellous, giving her far more love than she had ever been able to give them. In some ways it was as though the shock of discovering that her mother had known all along what was happening to her, had known and done nothing to help her, to save her, had traumatised her to such an extent that that part of her which had once responded emotionally to others had been totally destroyed.

She was conscious of the love and care she was being given, but it was as though an invisible wall separated her from other people, preventing her from reaching out and responding to them.

Shockingly perhaps in some ways, her anger and bitterness against her mother were far stronger than her feelings against her stepfather.

For the remainder of her teens she lived in a kind of limbo... a state of nothingness during which she went to school—a new school where no one knew what had happened to her—worked hard, and did so well in her exams that she was able to apply to go to university.

During those years she knew that on the surface she must have made all the right responses, done the normal things, but inside—inwardly... Ah, that was a different story. No doubt from the best possible motives, her past and what had happened to her was something that was never discussed by her foster parents, and so as she grew towards maturity, and her male peers made advances towards her, Faye had no way of dealing with the disgust and fear she felt towards these boys.

If she went out at all it was only with a group of girls, and only when she was completely sure that she was not going to be paired off with someone.

Only once since she went to live with her foster parents did she allow anyone male to touch her, and that was by accident at the eighteenth birthday party of a school-friend, when she was caught off guard and found herself in the clumsy embrace of a fellow pupil, who attempted to kiss her.

She went rigid in his arms, paralysed with fear and sick disgust. Fortunately he was too inexperienced to be aware of her feelings, and when she pushed him away he let her go.

She went home immediately afterwards, locking herself in her bathroom, showering and scrubbing her body, until her flesh was almost raw.

Up until then she had not allowed herself to think about her future... about what her life would be; but now for the first time she did, and, lying in bed, the glimmer of the night light she could not bear to be without illuminating the darkness, she allowed herself to confront the truth.

She could never be as other girls; she could never tease, flirt, or indulge in sexual experimentation. She could never make love. Make love... the very words made her want to scream with savage fury.

None of them, not one single one of her friends when they giggled over who had done what and with whom and what it had been like, and what it would be like really to 'do it', had any idea of what sex actually was...of how men used it...of how filthy and degrading the whole thing was... How could any woman actually like it, actually *want*...?

Faye was an intelligent girl. She read widely; after all, she had the time... when other girls were out on dates and she was on her own. She knew that her view of men, of sex, was warped by her experiences. She knew that what she read, what she heard could not all be made up, but the thought of allowing anyone, any man at all to do to her what her stepfather had once done made her sick with loathing and disgust.

But worst of all was her own feeling of guilt, her destructive inner belief that somehow she had been responsible for what had happened, that somehow she had invited it, encouraged it... As though somehow deep inside herself she was bad, wicked... as though those heated, thick, disgusting words her stepfather had moaned as he punished her for her wickedness were the truth.

It was while she was at university that other people first started noticing her aloofness towards men.

When she discovered what was being said about her— that she was frigid, that she was a lesbian—she withdrew further and further into herself, concentrating on getting her degree.

While she was in her final year her foster parents were killed in a car crash. She mourned their deaths, knowing how much they had genuinely cared for her, yet unable to feel anything more than a distant regret. That was the trouble, she acknowledged: she was unable to feel anything, anything at all.

Halfway through Faye's final year at university, one of her tutors left. His replacement, Jeremy Catesby, was thirty-five years old, married with two young children.

Right from the start Faye felt uneasy with him without being able to specify why. There was nothing in his manner towards her to make her feel threatened or uncomfortable. On the contrary. And unlike some of the male tutors he made no attempt to conceal his married state. There were family photographs on his desk, and he talked about his wife and children with warm affection.

Her fellow female students considered him dreamy and talked daringly about what it would be like to go to bed with him. As always during this sort of discussion Faye kept silent. She had a tutorial with Jeremy Catesby in the morning. She was beginning to dread them, but she was determined to get a first-class degree. She would need it in order to get a good job, since she was going to have to support herself through her life. Marriage was not for her. Nor children...

That latter knowledge hurt, but she dared not allow herself to dwell on why. Logic told her that it would have been impossible for her, a fourteen-year-old, to have brought up the baby she had conceived...that the decision of her doctor and social worker had been the right one...and yet she knew that something inside her would always ache for a child. Not just because of that child, but because it was an essential part of her nature. She had a deep-rooted need to nurture, to protect...and being denied the ability to satisfy that need brought yet another burden of bitter resentment.

Her tutorial went smoothly enough; she was a conscientious worker and once she obtained her degree she hoped to find work as an archivist, preferably in a capacity that meant she could withdraw from other people as much as possible.

When the tutorial was over she got up, collecting her books and papers as she did so. She was just walking towards the door when Jeremy Catesby said softly, 'No, don't go yet, Faye. There's something I want to discuss with you.'

Immediately she started to tremble, some deep prescient knowledge alerting her to danger. She wanted to run to the door and fling it open but she couldn't move.

Jeremy had come round from behind the desk and was standing in front of her. He was a tall, heavily muscled man with large sharp teeth which gave him a predatory, dangerous look, and he moved lithely and quietly. He smiled at her as he held out his hand.

'Come and sit down,' he invited her.

She wanted to refuse, ached to be able to do so, but he was standing between her and the door. If she didn't move he could easily reach out and touch her. The very thought made her shudder sickly, her knees almost buckling as she obeyed his instructions, picking the chair furthest away from any of the others.

'There's no need to look so apprehensive,' he told her, smiling at her, and then added, 'You know, Faye, you puzzle me. You're one of my best pupils. Conscientious...a hard worker. Normally when one of my students looks at me the way you're doing, it's because they know they're about to get a lecture on the standard of their work; but there is another side to being a tutor...a side concerned not so much with a student's academic life...but more with personal issues...'

He knew. Somehow or other he knew... Faye had started to sweat heavily, her heart pounding with sick horror. This was the fear she had carried around with her almost all her life. That somehow, someone would find out the truth about her and would use it, in the same way her stepfather had used it.

'You're a pretty girl, Faye...a beautiful girl, in fact, and yet...how shall I put this...? Well, let's just say that you appear to live the life of a nun.'

Faye felt her face burn. She wanted to scream out in protest at his invasion of her privacy... She hated the way he was looking at her...the rueful and yet calculating male smile that curved his mouth... A smile that suggested that her supposed nunlike state was a situation he had the power to remedy, and that she would be grateful to him for doing so.

'As your tutor—or one of them—I feel that it is my responsibility to ensure that my students derive much more from their time here at university than mere academic knowledge, and if they have any problems, any difficulties that prevent them from doing so then naturally I am concerned for them, and want to do all I can to help them.'

Faye couldn't bear to look at him. She felt hot and cold at the same time, burning up with hatred and anger, and yet frozen with fear. She wanted to hiss and spit at him like a small cat, to tell him just how wrong he was, to throw in his face the information that she wasn't the ignorant virgin he seemed to think; to tell him just how she had gained her sexual knowledge and how the gaining of it had made her feel about his sex; and yet at the same time she wanted to run from him and go on running, to hide herself away where she could be safe... where no one could pry and poke into her past... her pain.

'Sometimes in life we get ourselves into a situation through no fault of our own which becomes irksome... Sometimes we become the butt of unintentional, perhaps, but nevertheless cruel comment, and when we're young and just beginning to find our feet in the world, that's when we're most vulnerable. Especially in matters to do with sex...'

He was looking at her, Faye knew, but she could not bring herself to look back at him. She was terrified that if she did she would see in his eyes the same look she had seen so often in her stepfather's. She could hear already in his voice the purposefully mesmeric domination of the sexually aroused male, thick and hot like the male emissions of sex; and like those emissions the sound of his own voice seemed to give him immense pleasure.

'Of course you find it embarrassing... shocking perhaps to discuss such problems... even perhaps with your friends... You feel that they might laugh at you... make fun of you, and your virginity, which perhaps you've been brought up to think of as something you must retain until marriage at all costs, becomes a burden.

'What can you do? You're an intelligent girl. You know that among the male students there are bets being laid as to who could be the first to have you, and yet you've become aware that once you leave here... once you move out into the wider world, your virginity will become more irksome than ever.

'There is a solution.'

Faye could hear the amusement in his voice, the certainty, the assurance, the confidence... and beneath it she could also hear the hot feral note of male desire.

Somehow she managed to stand up, but as though he anticipated her he moved faster, coming to stand in front of her, to grasp her shoulders so that they were standing body to body.

Her books slipped from her hands, panic and nausea overwhelming her as he lowered his head towards her.

She reacted instinctively, raking his face with her nails, not once, but over and over again, so that he let her go almost immediately, swearing at her.

Faye barely heard him. She ran to the door, wrenching it open, almost colliding with the man coming down the corridor towards her. Behind her she heard Jeremy Catesby saying thickly, 'You stupid little bitch!'

But it didn't matter what he called her. Nothing mattered other than that she had escaped... that he hadn't done to her what her stepfather had done... that he hadn't touched her... hurt her... punished her.

In her room, she collapsed on her bed, shivering with reaction. She had made herself a dangerous enemy, she knew that. Jeremy Catesby was a vain man and wouldn't forgive her for what she had done, nor for rejecting him. But she didn't care. The thought of him touching her body... of anyone touching her body was so nauseating that anything was worth enduring to prevent that from happening.

Jeremy Catesby did punish her, tormenting her subtly and not so subtly. She heard a rumour circulating that she had propositioned him and that he had had to reject and reprimand her. She became the butt of the kind of jokes that made her soul cringe, and she was relieved rather than anything else to discover that she had been transferred to another tutor.

She was spending more and more time on her own, wanting only to get her degree and then to be free to conceal herself somewhere where no one could ever hurt or damage her again.

She met David for the first time four days after sitting her finals. She was in the university library looking up something when he came in and, obviously mistaking her for a member of the staff, asked her if she could help him.

Despite his height and breadth of shoulder, there was something about him that instantly reassured her.

Something at once so gentle and unthreatening that she was drawn to it, like someone drawn to a soft cool breeze on an overheated day when the air was thick with sulphur and the promise of a storm.

Without even being aware of how it happened, Faye took a step towards him and then another.

He was looking, David told her, for books on medieval England with particular reference to village life. He went on to explain that it was a subject which particularly fascinated his mother and that he had promised her when he took up his lectureship that he would root around the university library to discover if there was anything which might be of interest to her.

So he was a lecturer. He didn't look like one. In fact, he didn't look like anyone she knew, Faye recognised. There was something about David that set him apart from others... something special... something she couldn't analyse, except to say that for the first time in her life she found herself wanting to reach out to another human being.

After she had directed David towards the appropriate shelves, she watched him discreetly and curiously, wondering what on earth it was about him that drew her so powerfully.

When he had his books he smiled at her again and thanked her, leaving her to wonder what magic he possessed that made him seem so different from other men.

She soon discovered that she wasn't alone in thinking him 'different'. 'Saint David' was his nickname among the students, who seemed to regard him with a mixture of contempt and affection.

His subject was geography, something which surprised Faye. She had automatically assumed that he must lecture in something like philosophy, without really knowing why.

What she didn't realise was that he had been the man she had almost run into when she escaped from Jeremy Catesby's room. David had recognised her, though, quickly realising his mistake in believing her to be one of the library staff. He too had heard the rumours circulating about her, but he knew of Jeremy Catesby's bad reputation at Oxford, and he also knew that his departure from his previous teaching post had been brought about by the rumoured pregnancy of one of his students.

Jeremy wasn't alone in having a penchant for teaching his female students more than mere academics, but there was a brutality about the man, a selfishness, a desire to dominate and inflict mental pain that went way beyond sexual desire.

David had heard about Jeremy's womanising at Oxford, where as a student his scope to indulge in his vice had been limited. Now, as a tutor... He felt sorry for Faye and viewed the circulating rumours with distaste and a growing dislike for Jeremy.

Unlike his colleague, David had no taste for seducing his students. One day he would marry. Cottingdean would need an heir... He smiled a little to himself at this thought. Cottingdean, so important in the lives of his parents, so much loved and cherished. One might almost have supposed he was the heir to a feudal kingdom, from his parents' attitude towards the house and its land.

Once, very gently, when he was in his teens, he had pointed out to his mother when she had been talking about the future, about the children he would have, that it was not essential that he should marry... that there was after all Sage, and that *her* children could just as easily inherit Cottingdean as his own.

His mother's reaction had been instantaneous and revealing. No, she had told him. Only *his* children... his son must inherit. Her vehemence had made him feel uncomfortable. He knew, of course, that he was her favourite child... knew it, and felt uncomfortable with that knowledge, doing everything he could to make up to his younger sister for the disparity in their parents' attitude towards them.

Yes, one day he would marry, and when he did he would like his wife to have the same cool reserve exhibited by the girl in the library. He sometimes found modern young women a little overpowering, especially sexually.

There had been a time when David had wondered if his lack of the sharply keen sexual hunger of his fellows sprang from some unadmitted preference for his own sex, but no matter how much he searched his heart and mind he could find no indication that this was so. There had never been a time when he'd felt any kind of emotional or physical desire for another man.

He liked women, and he admired them. It amused him sometimes listening to his students. He often compared them with his mother, who had done so many of the things they now dreamed of doing, and at a time when women were not expected to make careers for themselves, to be innovative and energetic in the world of commerce.

He had lost his virginity at university to a fellow student, who had teased him about his ignorance and who had been only too pleased to enlighten him. He remembered her with affection and gratitude, while acknowledging that he was no partner for a woman with a highly motivated sex drive.

Perhaps his parents' marriage was partly to blame for that. It was obvious to him that, no matter what their relationship might have been in the past, now his parents did not have a sex life; but what impressed him far more than their apparent mutual celibacy was the fact that his parents' marriage, based not on mutual sexual desire but on friendship, respect, compassion, had thrived and survived where the marriages of their peers had not, although the strain of having an invalid husband had shown from time to time in his mother's controlled face.

David knew that he was out of step with his own generation, and its determination to break through the social barriers which had contained and ruled every previous generation.

Perhaps it had something to do with the fact that there were so many of them; that they, those children born so closely after the end of the war, were by far the largest single element of the population, and so by their might, by sheer force of numbers, could make their voices heard.

It interested him to see if this trend would continue; if the teenagers of the sixties with their music, their ideals, their refusal to bow to convention would continue all through their lives to attract attention, to rule and dominate.

Faye was as unlike the women of his own time as it was possible to be. She had none of their determination, their aggression, their belief in their right to be as sexually active as they wished, whenever they wished, where they wished and with whomever they desired. She roused within him a deeply protective instinct, a need to nurture, that he had never previously experienced.

He discovered that he was actively seeking her out, talking with her, coaxing her out of the shell she had withdrawn into.

To Faye, David was a wholly new experience. She had never known that men like him could exist. He was kind, gentle...completely non-threatening. He talked to her, not at her, and when she answered him he listened.

He told her a lot about himself...about his home and his family, and she found herself envying him, wishing almost fiercely that she could exchange her own past for one like his...one where parents were protective and caring...one where childhood was something to be looked back on with affection and pleasure.

She was careful never to mention her own family until one day by accident she was caught off guard and spoke of her foster parents. Tense with apprehension, she waited for David to comment, to question...but he seemed not to have noticed, not to be aware of the panic gripping her.

The more she got to know David, the more she liked him, and the more she knew that she could never reveal to him the truth about herself...that she could not bear to see the disgust in his eyes...to watch him withdraw from her as though she were unclean.

Faye did not think of David as a potential lover; to do so would almost have been a sacrilege, even if she had been able to contemplate herself in such a physically intimate situation without fear. He was a friend, someone she looked up to...revered almost. Someone whose kindness she treasured, whose compassion drew her almost compulsively to him.

She knew their friendship could only be short-lived. Soon she would be leaving university. David's post was only temporary. Ultimately he would be returning home, he had told her, to take over the management of the factory begun by his mother.

Faye found it difficult to picture David's mother; David plainly adored her, but to Faye she sounded formidable...overpoweringly so. She knew their burgeoning friendship couldn't last, that soon she and David would go their separate ways, and so she treasured the time they spent together, the almost casual meetings which always seemed to lead to long, intimate discussions.

She knew people were amused and curious about their relationship but she didn't care. David never made her feel threatened in the way that other men did. And even though she had never actually been alone with him—he was scrupulous about never inviting her back to his rooms or suggesting she invite him to hers—she knew that, if he did, she would be as safe as though they were in the middle of the university's crowded Student Union.

And then the blow fell. The examination results were posted, and Faye discovered that instead of getting the coveted first she had hoped for, she had barely got an indifferent third.

She walked away from the noticeboard almost physically reeling with shock. One tiny corner of her mind, still working logically, told her that in some way this was Jeremy Catesby's revenge, that he was responsible for her poor degree, even while the rest of her mind rejected the thought. The blame was hers... Somehow or other she must have misjudged the quality of her own work... Somehow or other she must have allowed her standards to slip. It was impossible...unthinkable that a tutor, someone in such a position of trust and responsibility, would actually use his power so corruptly.

David saw her crossing the quadrangle, her face white with shock. By the time he had fought his way through the mass of students tumbling out of the buildings she was almost out of sight. Heading for the library, he recognised.

He caught up with her halfway down the deserted corridor, reaching out from behind her to grasp her arm. He felt the shock that ran through her as though it was an electric current, her frantic 'Don't!' a shock of pain, fear and anger so intense that he felt them as though her emotions were his own. And then she saw him and her face flooded with colour.

'David,' she said weakly. 'I . . .'

'What's wrong?'

She shook her head, almost unable to speak.

'Come on, we can't talk here. We'll go to my rooms.'

Numbly Faye allowed him to guide her along the maze of corridors. His rooms were bare and neat, almost monklike, their very austerity somehow reassuring. She allowed him to guide her gently into a chair.

'What is it?' he asked her again. 'Your degree . . . ?'

'A third,' she told him sickly. 'I needed a first. I thought . . .'

David frowned. It was common knowledge that Faye should get a first . . . and then he remembered overhearing a small snippet of conversation between Jeremy Catesby and one of Faye's other tutors. It hadn't meant anything to him at the time, but now . . . Jeremy wouldn't be the first tutor to punish a pupil by misusing his authority over them, but he must hate her a great deal if he had actually dared to withhold her rightful degree.

His face very grim, he told Faye, 'Wait here.'

Faye never discovered what exactly it was David said to Jeremy Catesby . . . how he threatened him . . . and she was sure he must have done so, but when he eventually came back all he said was, 'It's all right, I've seen the Dean. There's been a mistake. It does happen sometimes. You were right. You've got your first...congratulations.'

At first Faye refused to believe it, but David was insistent, and when he finally had convinced her the relief was so great that she felt almost light-headed...almost euphoric.

'So what will you do now?' David asked her.

Faye shook her head. 'I don't really know. Look for a summer job while I try to find something more permanent...'

'A summer job—perhaps I might be able to help there... The library at Cottingdean is badly in need of cataloguing. Dull work, I'm afraid, and not all that well paid, but it would give you time to look round for something better. We aren't too far from London...'

Faye stared at him. Work at Cottingdean... The Cottingdean about which she had heard so much... Live in David's home, meet his parents... At once she felt two equally strong and conflicting emotions.

The first was an intense longing to accept, an intense wave of pleasure that David should actually want her in his home, that he should consider her worthy of it; the second was a sickening awareness of how unworthy she actually was...of how David would react to her if he knew the truth about her...of how his kindness, his generosity, his friendship would turn to contempt and rejection if he ever discovered...

'You'll need time to think things over,' David was saying to her. 'Well, don't worry, there's no rush. Take as long as you like. Term isn't over yet, and if something more appealing comes along...well, don't feel embarrassed about saying so.'

Something more appealing? What *could* be more appealing? Faye was beginning to realise that there was a part of her that asked nothing more from life than that she be allowed to stand in the sheltering protection of David's friendship for the rest of her life. His friendship... She swallowed as she made her way back to her own room. Not even with David could she contemplate the intimacy of sex. Sex turned men into violent destroyers, into cruel and sadistic inflictors of pain and humiliation. But David wasn't like that. David was different. And if he knew the truth about her he would surely turn away from her in disgust. She shivered. Her past had become a double burden, a guilty secret she had to hide from the rest of the world. And she intended that it should remain her secret.

Someone else, though, had other ideas. Jeremy Catesby was a vain man and, like all vain men, he could be extremely malicious when his vanity was bruised.

He had enjoyed punishing Faye for her idiotic reactions to his advances. The scratches alone had taken weeks to heal, and his wife, who was no longer under any illusions about him, had told him viciously that she hoped they would leave scars.

They hadn't, of course, but they had caused him to be the butt of his colleagues' mirth.

It had been easy to get Faye transferred to another tutor, and even easier to subtly ensure when it came to marking her examination papers that she got only a third.

He felt no compunction about what he was doing. The stupid bitch needed teaching a lesson, and as for her degree... Well, she would marry and have a parcel of brats and never use the damn thing. It was a waste of time educating women, although there were certain aspects of it that he personally found extremely enjoyable. The naïveté of his female students constantly amused him. They were so eager to fall into his arms, into his bed... They deserved all they got. Jeremy Catesby did not really like women.

To be confronted by David Danvers demanding to see Faye's papers, threatening to expose him to the Dean if he did not retract that third and announce that there had been an error, had been an unpleasant shock.

Jeremy had never liked David, and it galled him now that he was forced to give in. His wife would have something to say if he was dismissed from a second lectureship. She was already bitter and vituperative about his failure to secure one of the higher-status chairs. She had had her sights set on Oxford when she had married him, and so had he. If it hadn't been for the fact that her father was an Oxford don he would never have married her. She was too domineering, too demanding, too sure of herself to have any real appeal for him. Now he couldn't afford to divorce her, either socially or financially, and so he took his revenge against her and her whole sex in a series of amusing little relationships with his female students, leaving his stamp on them, so to speak, in the corruption of their ideals and the destruction of their belief in themselves as women, both sexually and intellectually.

Jeremy Catesby was a destroyer by nature, and he longed more than anything else to destroy Faye.

He soon found the way. A chance remark by the Dean about how well she had done considering her unfortunate start in life prompted some discreet enquiries into her background. It was easy to trace her adolescence back to her life with her foster parents.

What he uncovered after that took longer, but the results far more than repaid the effort.

Gloatingly he dwelt on what he had learned. The clever little bitch...all that pretence about being a virgin...about being so cool and untouchable. Saint David would have a shock when he learned the truth. He laughed to himself. Saint David and his whore...because that was what the girl was. No one could tell him that she hadn't encouraged the poor sod whose life she had destroyed. They all did it...all women were the same. Some of them just started earlier than others. You could see it all the time...provocative little teases, the lot of them, leading a man on, then protesting about it when they got what they deserved. And she must have enjoyed it, too...must have done to have done it for all those years. If she hadn't got herself pregnant no doubt she'd have gone on enjoying it, as well. Trust a woman to try and pin the blame on someone else...

He discovered that he was sweating, his body suddenly hard with a mixture of arousal and violent energy. This was when he enjoyed sex the most: when his ap-

petite was aroused to such a pitch that it became a
pleasure to physically subdue the woman lying beneath
him. It was even better if they protested. Then they gave
him the excuse to punish them a little, to accuse them
of leading him on, to enter them quickly, even violently
so that he could concentrate exclusively on his own
pleasure.

He wiped his hand over his damp forehead, suppressing his physical arousal. Just wait until he told Saint
David all about his precious Faye.

He set the scene for the dénouement well, chivvying
his wife into organising a small cocktail party for his
departing students.

Faye was invited along with David. She wanted to
refuse to go, but pride wouldn't let her. She had her
degree, and nothing Jeremy Catesby could do or say
could take that away from her.

As a student on a grant with no parental support, Faye
was always short of money, and certainly had none to
spare for fashionable clothes. Her working uniform of
pleated skirts and thick jumpers in winter, jeans and
thinner tops in summer comprised the entire contents of
her meagre wardrobe.

She had no idea what on earth she was going to wear
for the cocktail party. Instinct told her it would be a
formal affair. It had been a hot summer, so hot that she
had recklessly allowed herself to buy a soft gathered
cotton shirt and a couple of short-sleeved T-shirts to
supplement her jeans.

Faye never wore clothes that revealed anything of her
body. Actually almost too slim, she always chose clothes
that added bulk to her slender frame, enveloping her
figure so that she seemed almost shapeless. Make-up was
restricted to the merest touch of lipstick, her hair
invariably tied back off her face. The other girls had
grown used to her lack of vanity, her refusal to make
the most of herself, but when she joined the others on
the immaculate lawns of the Catesbys' large detached
house on the day of the cocktail party Faye was uncom-

fortably conscious of the amused and contemptuous glances of her peers.

It was David, dear, kind, thoughtful David who came to her rescue, not touching her, and yet somehow comforting her with his presence at her side as he smiled warmly at her and asked what she thought of the Catesbys' garden.

Faye did not like it. There was something hard and unappealing about the rigorously pruned and arranged rose-beds, the earth bare and weedless beneath the soulless display of, to her, over-hard blooms, the roses themselves set out with mathematical precision.

'I don't like it,' she confessed to David. 'It seems so...so regimented.'

'Good girl,' he approved. 'My mother is going to like you. She hates this kind of garden. Wait until you see the gardens at Cottingdean.' He smiled at her again, and the strangest sensation raced through her body, a combination of warmth and gratitude...an awareness of him as a person...as a man...a tentative, hesitant need to lean towards him, to touch the smiling curve of his mouth so that she could capture the wonderful essence of his smile.

As she stood there staring at him, completely overwhelmed by the unexpectedness of her feelings, Jeremy Catesby joined them.

'Well, well. Saint David and his devoted handmaiden. What a charming picture. So...innocent and unworldly...and of course so misleading. I really do admire you, David. I must say I think I would fight a trifle shy of a young woman with Faye's past. After all, as they say, there's no smoke without fire. Do you have much contact with your stepfather these days, Faye?'

David heard the small sound that tortured her throat, saw the way her skin turned livid and then white, felt the shock-waves that burned through her body...felt her panic and fear and reacted instinctively to them, closing the distance between them, guarding her...protecting her.

'You *do* know about Faye's past, don't you, David?' Jeremy continued with merciless pleasure. 'Or is it a little secret she has kept from you? Shall I tell him for you, Faye? I can understand your embarrassment. To have laid claim to virginity so determinedly and so solidly makes it very difficult for you to admit that, not only are you not a virgin, but you've already had one pregnancy terminated. She's quite a bundle of surprises, you know, David. Sleeping with her own stepfather, and then getting him sent to prison for it ... Even her own mother rejected her, and no wonder ... it's enough to make anyone turn away in disgust. Seducing her stepfather and then——'

'No ... no ... no!'

In the distance Faye heard someone screaming, the sound beating into her head until she ached for it to stop ... until her whole body vibrated to the appalling agony of that unearthly sound of another human being's pain.

The garden, with its garish, hard colours, twisted violently around her, pain exploding inside her, as the world turned into a fierce ball of red and black agony, a fire dragon with gaping jaws that devoured her into its darkness.

'Faye ... it's all right. It's all right now ...'

She opened her eyes. She was sitting in the passenger seat of David's car, or rather half sitting in it and half lying on David's lap. His cool hand rested on her forehead, gently stroking her skin, while the other hand monitored the frantic pulse in her wrist.

'David ...'

She swallowed automatically as saying his name burst against the rawness of her aching throat.

'David ...'

'Are you all right ...?'

Faye raised her head and stared out of the car window. There was a man on the other side looking back at her. There was something familiar about him, although it took her several minutes to place him.

The surgeon from the hospital... Her heart leapt in shock. Liz... something had happened to Liz. Still confused and half in shock, she didn't stop to analyse that he could not have come in person to talk to her about Liz, that he could hardly have known where to find her.

'Mrs Danvers... are you all right?'

She opened the window, her movements made awkward with haste and shock. He had wrenched her so brutally out of the past that for a moment she had been totally disorientated.

'Liz... my mother-in-law...'

Alaric Ferguson realised instantly what she was thinking and cursed himself for interfering. Why on earth hadn't he simply left her alone? It was so unlike him to intrude on someone's else's privacy, but he had been worried about her.

'No—no, there's nothing wrong,' he assured her.

Nothing wrong... then why...?

He could almost feel her withdrawing from him, her eyes shadowed and wary.

'I'm sorry, I shouldn't have intruded. I thought perhaps you were ill...'

'A headache,' Faye told him shortly. It wasn't, after all, untrue.

'I'm sorry. Perhaps a cup of tea...? There's a place a few yards down the road, and I have it on good authority—my mother's—that it serves excellent tea.'

Faye opened her mouth to refuse. The last thing she wanted to do was to sit politely with this stranger drinking tea. She ought to be on her way home—it was getting late. She shivered.

Alaric saw the look in her eyes and cursed himself under his breath. She obviously thought he was trying to pick her up. Was there no end to the vanity of women? he wondered cynically.

Without any surprise at all he heard her saying quickly, her voice high and strained, 'Thank you, but no... I must be on my way. My daughter will be wondering where I am.'

But not where she had been. He was too used to the traumatic effect mental illness could have on the people closest to its victims to question the state in which he had seen her leaving the house. But, since it did affect her so badly, what was she doing here alone? He paused for a moment, torn between irritation and concern...not specifically for her. If she was stupid enough to think he had been trying to pick her up, then... Then what? She didn't deserve his concern...his compassion?

Was it something within himself that was causing this slow brutalisation of his humanity, or was it simply a symptom of the malady of modern-day life?

Faye watched him, wishing he would go away. He had seen her at her most vulnerable and unprotected; that made her feel threatened and frightened. By what appalling coincidence had he had to be driving past the gate just as she'd opened it?

She heard him saying stiffly, 'Well, if you're sure you're all right...'

'I'm fine,' she lied. Why didn't he just go away? Couldn't he see she didn't want him there?

He tried one final time. 'You know, if you're not...not feeling well, it might not be wise for you to drive...'

Faye seldom lost her temper, but she was on the verge of doing so now, a backlash against the pent-up anxiety and fear, an emotional and unreasoning reaction that made her eyes flash and her body tense.

'You're Liz's doctor, not mine,' she told him bitingly. 'I don't need your advice...'

'And you don't want my company. Fine. I'll leave you to it.'

She could see that he was angry too, and guilt touched her momentarily as she watched him walk away.

Alaric had driven several miles before he realised that he was exceeding the speed limit. He slowed down automatically, trying to unclench his taut muscles. Stupid woman...and stupid him for trying to help her. God, did she really think if he had found her attractive he wasn't capable of letting her know it with a little bit more finesse?

If he found her attractive... He scowled to himself, not wanting to admit his contradictory feelings towards her. After all, he barely knew the woman. Barely knew her at all...

CHAPTER TWELVE

SAGE frowned. She had intended to spend the morning working on some preliminary sketches for one of her commissions. Her reputation for innovative work had not been gained overnight, and she could not afford to completely abandon her work, no matter how much she would have liked to spend the time on other things.

Such as reading her mother's diaries. She put down her pencil but did not reach for a fresh one. What was it about the diaries that made them such compulsive reading?

Reading them was like opening a door into an unknown world... The world of her mother as a young woman... as an equal with problems and pressures to which she herself could so easily relate. Why, when she had never been able to get close to her mother, was she now discovering that beneath the label of 'mother' and 'devoted wife' which she had pinned to her there was a fellow woman, someone for whom she could feel compassion and understanding? Did her mother know how much was revealed in her diaries? Not through the words themselves, but through the awareness that was coming to Sage of the feelings of the less central characters. Had her mother known then how very deeply dependent on her Edward was—that he loved her even if that love could never have any physical reality?

She stared at her drawing-board. She had been commissioned to provide her own interpretation of a suitably Italianate seventeenth-century garden on the walls of a newly built extension to house a swimming pool. Nothing particularly adventurous; she suspected these particular clients simply wanted the cachet of telling their friends that they had commissioned her. It should have been easy, but for some reason the formal avenues and statuary refused to form beneath her pencil and instead she was drawing cottage garden borders, overflowing with a wanton tumble of flowers, set against a backdrop of crumbling mellow brick walls.

Her mother's garden, she recognised irately.

Perhaps she ought to do something else, she acknowledged, staring at her drawing in disgust.

The problem of the new road was nagging at her. With so much heavyweight influence balanced against them, it was hard to see how any campaign the villagers mounted could be successful. Taking a more distant view, it was obvious that the road must go somewhere, and must cause some havoc wherever it eventually went.

In the case of Cottingdean, though, the road could avoid the village altogether if it was diverted across the marshland beyond the water meadows, thus looping its way around the village instead of straight through it.

The cost of such a detour would be a major factor against it; it wasn't just the extra length of road required, it was also the fact that the marsh would have to be drained, and adequate foundations built, all of which would cost a great deal of money.

She got up, frowning, and walked round to her mother's desk, picking up the file she had prepared.

In it were various clippings her mother had assembled, dealing with other rural objections to various building programmes, one section relating to those which had succeeded and another to those which had failed. The former was depressingly thin in comparison to the latter, even though in these far more enlightened and ecologically aware times people were fighting harder to protect their environment.

Sage had bought herself a large-scale map of the whole county and she had copied an outline of this on to black paper, putting in only the major towns and existing motorways. She grinned to herself as she unrolled it and pinned it to her drawing-board. At school the major complaint against her was that she had a good brain, but was lazy about using it. Privately she considered that her teachers had been equally at fault, since theirs had been the inability to motivate her... Once motivated, once challenged... She grimaced a little over her own turbulent and sometimes difficult personality, knowing how often her enthusiasm had been aroused by something only to wane just as quickly until she had taught herself, forced herself to grimly follow through and complete a project, no matter how arduous and dull. Before then her life had been littered with unfinished detritus of hundreds of rejected interests.

It was the fatal flaw of her character, this inability to follow things through, to stick to one course, and it had only been once she had tasted the pleasure of actually completing a set task that she had begun to fight free of its taint.

She had changed so much in these last few years... Matured. She grimaced to herself—in some ways perhaps but not in others; inside parts of her still held all the rebellious disorderliness of the old Sage.

Sage... what a name to choose for her... Had her mother done so in the hope that her name might influence her wayward personality? Hardly. She could not have known then what a trial she was going to be to her...

Had she welcomed her conception, her birth in the same way as she had David's? David... who was not after all Edward's child... but who had been so greatly loved by both her mother and by Edward. Not, she was learning, because of his parentage... but because of the person he was.

She had often wondered if her father's detachment from her had been caused by the manner of her own conception. If the fact that she had been a child born of one of modern medicine's very early miracles, rather than through the mystery of the physical union between two people, had been responsible for this... She must have been wanted at some stage for her parents, especially her mother, to have allowed her to be conceived...

Sage moved restlessly around the room, frowning as she came to rest in front of the windows that overlooked her mother's favourite part of the garden.

There was no sun today, the sky a soft English grey which seemed to melt perfectly with the equally muted colours of her mother's flowers.

She had stood in front of this window many, many times. Normally staring mutinously out of it while listening to yet another of her mother's reasoned and calm lectures on one or other of her failings, and yet today it was as though she was seeing the garden for the first time, marvelling at the perfect blending of lilacs, pinks, blues, and whites, marvelling at how on earth her mother had ever found the time to plan such a perfection of colour and form, and not just the time but the knowledge as well. Her mother was an incredibly gifted woman. Strong and determined when it came to her business, cutting through red tape and waffle with the precision of a skilled surgeon, and yet somehow at the same time refraining—as Sage knew she herself had never learned to do—from bruising tender male egos.

Her mother had been a pioneer as far as being a woman in control in a man's world went, and she had achieved this without endangering either her femininity or her values. Her mother had never, she recognised, played on the fact that she was a woman, had never used it, as Sage had seen so many many women do, and yet nor had she become a token male, eschewing her womanliness, contemptuous of her own sex. Somehow she had found and followed her own way, remained true to her own self. Her mother was rather like this garden, Sage recognised in surprise: at first glance perhaps too quiet and muted. It was only when one looked closer, observed in more detail, that one became aware of the true beauty and perfection, of the true skill and knowledge that made up the whole person.

Suddenly Sage had a sharp, aching longing to have her here. She was frightened, she realised...not just frightened of losing her, this woman whom she was only just beginning to discover—to value, she accepted humbly—but frightened of not being able to live up to her standards, her ideals...

The road, with all its complexity of problems, had somehow become a symbol of all that was lacking in their relationship. The sheer grind and perseverance required to even get as far as mounting a proper campaign against it required all the fine detailings of character that were not in her gift. Her skills were different. Not perhaps of less value, but different. She did not, she decided despairingly, have those abilities which made her mother such a master tactician... but it was to her that the role of stepping into her mother's shoes, of protecting Cottingdean, had fallen. And if she failed...

She shivered suddenly, briefly seeing, not Cottingdean as it was: a perfect, almost magical, living, breathing reincarnation of the house as it must have been centuries ago when it was first built, lovingly preserved and cosseted by her mother—cosseted not as a museum, but as a home, a home that was so evocative of its own past that to step into it was to walk into a small piece of history—but Cottingdean as it could tragically become: its gardens destroyed, the house itself neglected...

Stop being so stupid, she told herself—the road was not going to come anywhere near the house itself. It was the village which was at risk, and of course to her mother the village and the people in it were an extension of her field of responsibility. She would see it as her duty to protect them. Now that duty was hers...

Restlessly she moved back to the desk, absently glancing at the framed estate map above the fireplace as she did so, and then something caught her eye.

The map had different coloured sections to represent different kinds of land; that which was not owned by Cottingdean was coloured charcoal-grey, and there, to the north of the village, right next to the proposed site for the new road, was a large block of charcoal-grey. Sage paused and studied it, trying to visualise the actual land. Her mother had more modern maps of the estate somewhere... Sage found one neatly filed in an appropriately marked file and sighed a little for her own confused mess of paperwork on her own desk. Orderly she

was not, as her secretary often complained, but she liked
her disorder—it felt comforting, right.

As she unrolled the map she sat down, looking for
the boundaries of their own land, trying to isolate that
section of charcoal-grey. Whoever owned it would stand
to make a good deal of money from the new road. That
piece of land, if she remembered correctly, was right
where one of the existing A roads would join the new
motorway. An ideal spot for future development... The
kind of development which would eventually run into
and swamp Cottingdean itself.

She soon found the appropriate section, and saw that
it was marked neatly in her mother's handwriting with
the name of the owner.

Agnes Hazelby... she nibbled the side of her finger,
remembering that her mother had surely mentioned that
the elderly woman had been seriously ill and had needed
to sell in order to move into a nursing home.

Had she done so? The best way to find out was to
speak to her mother's solicitor, which reminded her that
sooner or later someone, either herself or Faye, was going
to have to go down to the mill to see Henry Brading.

He was perfectly capable of running the mill side of
the business without any interference, but he had made
anxious enquiries about her mother's health, and she
knew that in her shoes her mother would have been quick
to reassure him.

She picked up the phone and dialled the number of
her mother's solicitor.

He had no idea who owned the land in question, he
told her, but it should not be too difficult to find out.
He remembered that her mother had wanted to buy it,
but that it had gone to auction, and that the bidding
had risen way above the price she had decided upon.

'I know it went for way, way above the price for agricultural land. How is your mother, by the way? Any
further news?'

'She's holding her own,' Sage told him, the words
falling almost automatically from her lips—she had repeated them now so many times to so many anxious en-

quiries. 'They're hoping to operate soon... Once she's stable. There's still some pressure on her brain...'

She heard her voice faltering as she said the words, knowing what they concealed. Her mother's hold on life was so very fragile, a fine, fine thread that could so easily be broken.

'Don't worry, Sage,' he comforted her. 'Your mother's a fighter. If anyone can pull through something like this, she will... I'll ring you back just as soon as I've got that information. Hopefully it shouldn't take too long.'

While she was waiting for him to ring back, Sage studied her files again, trying to analyse what it was that the successful campaigns had had in common.

A certain amount of influence in the right places, the ability to bring their campaign to the attention of the media, and gain the maximum publicity—but what stood out most of all was that all of the successful campaigns had had something in their favour other than the fervent desire of the campaigners not to have the road or development on their territory: generally something of historic importance, although there was a small village which had been saved from the planners by virtue of the fact that it was an area of outstanding natural beauty— one of only three places in the country where a certain species of rare wild flowers grew.

Sage pushed her hand into her hair. As far as she knew, no wild flowers of spectacular importance nor birds of rarity made their home in Cottingdean or its environs, and the house and village, although old, were not of any particular historical importance.

Looking at their case from an entirely unbiased viewpoint, there was no reason why Cottingdean should not have its unwanted new motorway other than the fact that—albeit with considerable extra expense and work— the road could be diverted to run harmlessly several miles away.

The phone rang as she was mulling over what she had just read.

'I've managed to discover who now owns the lands,' the solicitor told her drily. 'I suppose it shouldn't have come as quite the surprise it did. Does the name Hever Homes mean anything to you?'

'No,' Sage told him truthfully. 'Apart from the fact that they're obviously builders.'

'Mmm...they have a reputation in the City for snapping up first-rate building sites—not for large estates; they seem to specialise in small developments of individually designed homes, and as builders they have a surprisingly good reputation. However, that's not the interesting point. Hever Homes is in actual fact a small division of a much larger company—Cavanagh Construction.'

Sage gripped the receiver.

'But that's Daniel Cavanagh's company—the one building our section of the new motorway.'

'Exactly... Too much of a coincidence, wouldn't you say, that Mr Cavanagh just happens to buy a piece of land, as yet without planning permission for the type of development favoured by his company, but very conveniently placed for the new motorway and its feeder road? And with the Government's present attitude to the releasing of agricultural land for house building, I shouldn't think Mr Cavanagh will have too much difficulty in getting the planning permission he needs.

'Very astute of him, of course, to have got in ahead of the field, so to speak, and snapped up the land, and quite a risk. If another route had been chosen... As it is, he, or rather his company, stands to make a good deal of money from such a venture. If they can break Agnes Hazelby's stipulation about leaving the Hall intact. The motorway will encourage people to move further out of London, and the appeal of moving to a brand new luxury house on the outskirts of a village like this one will add to that attraction. Of course it will mean that the village will cease to exist in its present form... I know your mother hopes to fight off the road proposal, but she's got an awful lot of power ranged against her...'

And a good deal of influence, Sage recognised sickeningly, remembering that possessive feminine hand on Daniel's arm. Which had come first, she wondered cynically, his purchase of the land or his relationship with the woman from the Ministry?

As she thanked the solicitor for his help and replaced the receiver, she wondered why it was that she should feel so shocked by what she had just learned. She ought if anything to feel contempt, especially when she remembered the arrogant way in which Daniel had once thrown at her accusations of duplicity, of deceit, of using others for her own ends.

She was prowling restlessly round the room when the door opened and Camilla came in.

'Ma not back?' she enquired. 'That's odd—she and Gran are normally back by this time. You don't suppose something's happened to her, do you?' she asked, outwardly nonchalant, but Sage had seen the shadow of apprehension darkening her eyes, and guessed with intuitive sympathy that the shock of Liz's accident had left the young girl feeling vulnerable and insecure.

'I'm sure she's fine. She probably got involved—I expect people will have asked her what's happened to Mother, and that's probably delayed her... Where exactly are these meetings?' she asked, glad to have something to distract her from dwelling on the subject of Daniel Cavanagh. Why did it have to be his company that was involved in building this section of the motorway? It would have made her role in all of this far easier if she didn't have to deal with him, but rather with an anonymous and unknown stranger.

'I don't know.' Camilla frowned. 'In fact, I don't really know where they go... it's just sort of something that always happens. Neither Ma nor Gran talks about it really.'

Sage watched her curiously. In other circumstances, with a different woman, and if Faye hadn't always been accompanied by Liz on these trips, she might have imagined from the secrecy that shrouded them that Faye was meeting a lover; and then she checked a tiny frown scoring her forehead, wondering why it was that she should feel with such certainty that Faye would not have a lover.

Surely not because she chose to play down her beauty, to wear dull clothes and little make-up? Surely she was not so stupid as to believe that men only found attractive women who made an effort to attract them?

She had seen for herself on enough occasions, surely, the effect of a woman who to the rest of her sex might appear ordinary, even plain, and yet who had that certain indescribable something that drew men to her like flies to amber? Yet Faye did not have that unmistakable sex appeal, she was quite sure of it. But Faye had been married when she was still a comparatively young woman . . . had had a child, and, although Sage was prepared to admit that no one outside a marriage truly knew what went on inside it, she was reasonably confident that her brother was not the kind of man who, for whatever reason, would treat a woman—any woman, but especially his wife—in such a way that after his death the memory of their relationship was so abhorrent to her that she now eschewed any kind of relationship with another member of his sex. Neither did she believe the opposite: that, having loved David and lost him, Faye could not endure the idea of putting another man in his place. She might not wish to remarry, but sexually. . .

A mature woman would have to have a powerful ability for self-deceit indeed if she truly believed that it was impossible to feel sexual desire without being deeply in love. And if there was one thing that Sage prided herself on it was her honesty.

She was not Faye, though, as she was the first to recognise, and the idea of Faye stealing away to spend time in the arms of an unknown lover was so impossible to imagine that she instantly dismissed it.

So why did she have this niggling, nagging feeling that there was more to these monthly disappearances than there seemed? The very fact that her brain should automatically pick on the word disappearance underlined that feeling.

She looked at her niece. Camilla was still looking worried, and she immediately tried to reassure her. 'As I said, Cam, I'm sure that your mother has merely been delayed. I promise you bad news always travels fast. If there'd been an accident...' She saw Camilla wince, but went on firmly '...if there had been an accident we'd know about it by now.' What she didn't say was that she was surprised that Faye hadn't said anything to her about her plans—that she hadn't suggested leaving a telephone number where she could be contacted, especially in view of her anxiety about Liz—but Faye was an adult, not a child, and certainly Sage did not feel that she had any right to question her movements.

'What's that?' Camilla asked, glancing at the map she had unrolled.

'I wanted to check up on who had bought that piece of land,' Sage told her.

'Oh, that...yes. Gran tried to buy it when it came up for auction.'

'Mmm.' If Daniel Cavanagh did plan to build houses on that land, he would be even more obdurate about any change in the proposed route of the road. Sage was pretty sure that Ms Ordman would take whatever view Daniel wanted her to take, but as she mulled over these thoughts it occurred to her that the right kind of publicity campaign could do a great deal of damage to the apparently pristine reputation of Daniel's companies.

She wrinkled her nose, knowing immediately that her mother would have vetoed such a suggestion as being underhand...but what was Daniel himself, purchasing the land in the first place? Sometimes one had to fight fire with fire. As this thought formed, she also realised uncomfortably that some old scars had not entirely healed and that there was a certain pleasure in anticipating throwing back at Daniel some of the insults he had once so bitterly tossed at her, in heaping on him the same kind of scorn and contempt he had once made her suffer, in taking exactly the same kind of high-minded and infuriatingly arrogant moral stance. Yes, she would enjoy making him squirm...and perhaps, after all, there need not be a public battle... Perhaps the mere suggestion that they had the information, that such a publicity campaign could be mounted against him...

She closed her mind to the fact that her knowledge of him, fifteen years or more out of date though it might be, did not incline her to believe that he would readily back down to any kind of pressure. It would do no harm to make a phone call—to suggest a meeting, to test the water, so to speak. And certainly it would do no harm to let him know that his purchase of the land had been discovered.

Behind her she heard Camilla making some comment about going riding and nodded as she picked up the file again and opened it, quickly searching for what she wanted.

Yes, there it was, the name and address of Daniel's London head office and, of course, its telephone number.

As she punched the number into the phone she discovered that her stomach muscles had become unexpectedly tense. Nervous... of speaking to Daniel Cavanagh...? How ridiculous. Why, she could remember when...

The cool, efficient tones of the girl answering the phone stopped her train of thought. She asked for Daniel by name, giving her own and adding crisply, 'I wanted to have a word with him about the proposed new motorway contract...'

'Sage... What can I do for you?'

To be put straight through to him caught her a little off guard, as did the unexpected jerk of sensations deep inside her body—the shocking familiarity of hearing him speak her name, almost as though some hidden part of her had remembered exactly that intonation, that timbre, when there could be no reason for it to have done so.

Infuriating that her brain should have logged Daniel's voice so accurately, when despite all her striving she could no longer even hear a faint echo of Scott's in her memory.

'I think we ought to have a meeting, Daniel...'

The very quality of his silence made her face burn, almost as though she had been guilty of propositioning him. Her fingers curling round the receiver, she forgot about tactics and said acidly, 'This is business, Daniel.'

'But of course.' He sounded so urbane, so polite, and yet she could have sworn there was laughter beneath the calm words...and not just laughter either.

You fool, she derided herself. What an idiotic thing to say—of course it was business...how could it have been anything else?

'What exactly was it you wanted to discuss?'

'I...we need to meet. It isn't something we can discuss over the phone...'

What the hell was the matter with her? She sounded like a teenager trying to make a date. Infuriated with herself and with him, she was almost tempted to ring off and abort the whole idea. It was typical of her, she acknowledged bitterly, that she had leapt in without proper planning...without proper thought. In her shoes, her mother would have made notes, carefully calculated what she could and could not say. Her mother would have trailed some bait, and waited cautiously until it was taken up before betraying anything. She, on the other hand—she was a fool, she derided herself, grinding her teeth in vexation.

There was another telling pause, and then a thoughtful, 'I see... Well, in that case, I believe I have half an hour free tomorrow, if you could be at my office for——'

His office. No way. This wasn't something she was going to tackle on his territory, giving him the advantage...

'I'm sorry, that's impossible,' she told him quickly. 'My sister-in-law is away at the moment and I can't really be out of touch with the hospital.'

Not strictly true, but it was the best excuse she could come up with.

'I see...and this matter you wish to discuss with me appertaining to the new motorway is urgent, I take it... Something that can't be dealt with through the usual channels of your committee?'

He sounded so suave...so polite...so under-standing...so why did she suddenly feel threatened, exposed?

'I think you'll find that it's better if we deal with it on a one-to-one basis,' she told him ignoring the faint *frisson* of wariness cautioning her, adding with what she hoped was a suaveness to match his own, 'It would certainly save us both time.'

First the threat and then the palliative... wasn't that the way it was done?

She had little experience of this kind of thing. It ran counter to everything she believed in. Deceit was not her currency. She did not have the mind for it.

'Well, of course, in that case... Perhaps if I were to drive down this evening to Cottingdean...? Or would you prefer a more—anonymous rendezvous...?'

Why was it that the words 'anonymous' and 'rendezvous' made her nerves prickle so uncomfortably? Was it because she had so recently been thinking them herself, but in a different context? There was no reason, was there, why she should suspect that Daniel was deliberately trying to undermine her, to use the words of lovers rather than adversaries?

'There's no reason why we shouldn't talk here at Cottingdean,' she told him crisply. 'At least from my point of view...'

There, let him see how he liked a taste of his own vile suggestiveness. She certainly had nothing to hide in meeting with him... while he, on the other hand... Ms Ministry had been extremely possessive... She hesitated, wondering if she dared imply that he might not want the other woman to know he was meeting her, and then regretfully abandoned the idea as too dangerous. The last thing she wanted to do was to alienate him to the point where he refused to meet with her.

'Generous of you, especially when you need to be so close to home in case the hospital need to get in touch.'

Sage stared bitterly at the receiver, wanting to tell him exactly what she thought of him and his sneaky purchase of the land, but knowing that the last thing she could afford now was to lose her temper. So many, many times in the past she had done exactly that, to spectacular and certainly momentarily satisfying effect, but afterwards . . . well, on more occasions than she cared to remember afterwards had come the humbling and often soul-destroying realisation that her temper had cost her dear. Too dear . . .

'We normally finish dinner around nine,' she told him, fighting to sound calm and unmoved.

'Nine it is, then,' came the courteous and yet somehow unnerving response, followed by an even more unnerving, 'Until then, Sage. I must say I'm rather looking forward to it . . . It isn't often one gets the opportunity to cross swords a second time with an old adversary . . . I warn you, though—I do hope your blade is well honed. I seem to recollect that on the last occasion you rejected science in favour of passion. Never a wise decision——'

Sage hung up on him, not trusting herself to speak. How dared he . . . ? How dared he allude to that . . . ? How dared he imply that what had happened in the past had any relevance at all to the present? That had been personal—extremely personal. This was different—very different, and this time . . . this time *what*? She was going to be the victor. She certainly hoped so!

CHAPTER THIRTEEN

As HE replaced the receiver, Daniel stared across his office. It was a handsome room, its walls cloaked in the seventeenth-century pine panelling he had rescued from a demolition site, its floor covered in a very masculine dark green wool carpet to complement the traditional tapestry weave fabric which covered the two large wing chairs either side of the room's fireplace.

The board had been dubious when he had turned down the opportunity to site the company's head office in a prestigious modern city block, opting instead to purchase one of the four-storey seventeenth-century houses in a square in what had then been a very unfashionable part of London.

He had overruled them though. Not by force, but by discreetly working on them as individuals, bringing them round to his point of view, and it had been worthwhile, not just for the aesthetic advantages of working in such pleasant surroundings. This once unfashionable part of the city was now highly sought after. To the original house they had added those on either side, so that their share of the square, which outwardly retained the façade of three separate dwellings, now housed the entire administrative side of the business.

He considered himself to be a builder, not merely by trade, but by inclination as well—building bridges between people was as much as his forte as building homes for them to live in, but when it came to Sage Danvers he doubted that he would ever to be able to construct foundations strong enough to bridge the divide between them.

The last thing he wanted right now was a confrontation with her, and yet quite plainly she was spoiling for a fight. What on earth did she want to see him for? He was quite certain it wasn't to talk over old times.

Old times. His mouth hardened cynically. Ever since the shock of seeing her so unexpectedly at that damned meeting he had been fighting to hold back the memories.

Perhaps it was time to stop fighting them. Perhaps it might even be therapeutic. He prided himself on having a fairly comprehensive knowledge of what motivated him, on being able to look within himself and analyse what he found there. Unlike many of his sex, he did not dismiss the need to understand more about himself, nor did he normally ignore his own intuition. So why start now?

His desk was between the room's two high windows, facing the fireplace. Above it hung a portrait of his mother's second husband. Robert Cavanagh, the man who, on his marriage to Daniel's mother, had also given the teenage boy his surname. Daniel had commissioned the painting after his death. The artist had worked from photographs and had managed to portray an extraordinarily lifelike and vigorous image of Robert Cavanagh.

Strange how much he missed Robert even now. Their paths in life had crossed so very briefly and yet that crossing had had a cataclysmic effect upon him, just as had his brief passage of arms with Sage. In many ways they were two of the most important pivots on which his whole life had turned.

As he stared at Robert Cavanagh's portrait, he pondered on what this man would have made of the new bullish attitude being displayed by builders and developers. An attitude that cut right across the entire field, from the small builder of the odd pair of houses to the mighty giants of construction who were responsible for laying down the new motorways. He had a foot in both camps.

The company he had inherited from Robert Cavanagh was now heavily involved in civil engineering, had gone public, and was no longer his private concern, a move dictated by market demands, by the threat of takeovers and asset-stripping exercises. In his role as chairman of the new public company he had in many ways lost touch with the reality of the industry and spent what seemed like the vast bulk of his time in series after series of often emotive meetings. When it came to new motorways, everyone thought they were a wonderful idea, everyone saw the necessity of them, everyone wanted to use them— but no one wanted to live next to them.

The route for this latest part of the road network had been particularly contentious. He frowned again. He still wasn't entirely sure... But the D of E... He realised he was doodling on his blotter, and grimaced a little when he saw what he had sketched; the outline of an old, traditionally E-shaped house... He threw the pencil down in disgust, recognising the sketch for what it was. He was worse than a baby with a dummy, he reflected acidly, reverting to the sketch like a child to a comforter. What was the matter with him? He wasn't afraid of seeing Sage, was he?

He moved violently in his chair and then got up, going to stand under the portrait. In winter a fire burned in this grate; or at least the application of a modern science allowed one to believe that it did. In summer the same firm that planted up and took care of the carefully co-ordinated window-boxes which lined the windows of the company's headquarters provided fresh flowers daily for the huge urn that filled the fireplace.

As he glanced at the arrangement of country-style flowers, his eyes became hooded, lending austerity to his features. His mother had loved fresh flowers. Not that she had ever been given much opportunity to do so... At least not until...

Was it because of his mother that he had refused to see the truth about Sage, that he had believed...? He closed his eyes briefly and then opened them again, flicking a switch on his intercom and when his secretary answered telling her, 'I'm going to call it a day, Heather. If anything urgent crops up I'll be in the flat, but only if it is urgent. Oh, you can go early yourself if you like.'

The flat, as he casually termed the upper two storeys of the middle property, which he had redesigned for his own use, could be reached only via a private lift tucked away discreetly in the main octagonal hallway, or via a set of stairs, hidden behind a false piece of panelling.

Using the stairs, Daniel emerged on to a cream-walled hallway, the plasterwork details picked out in authentic period colours, the rug adorning the polished floor a valuable antique which he had picked up at a country house sale, long before anyone else had realised the potential of such items.

Inside, the flat was furnished with antiques he had collected in a similar fashion. His drawing-room overlooked the trees and railed-off garden which ran the length of the small square. Behind the drawing-room was a good-sized dining-room, large enough for entertaining, and adjacent to that a comfortable kitchen with access to a small roof garden.

Daniel had no live-in help, preferring to fend for himself and to preserve his privacy. When he entertained he hired caterers, and none of the women who had shared his life had ever spent more than a succession of separate nights under his roof. None of them had ever been invited to move into the flat with him. He was not a man who considered himself to be a sexual stud, or who had any desire to do so.

He liked women; he enjoyed their company, their conversation, their personalities and their minds as much as he enjoyed their bodies. From time to time, when they were short of something to print, one or other of the gossip columns would run a piece on him, naming his latest lady, speculating on whether or not this time he would marry. He was not against marriage. Or at least not against the theory of it ... but its practice was fraught with so many pitfalls. What he was against was divorce, especially when there were children involved.

He walked over to a large breakfront bookcase, opening one of its drawers and extracting from it a bottle of whisky and a glass, and then, frowning, he put them both back, resolutely closed the door and went through into the kitchen, opening the fridge and extracting a bottle of mineral water instead.

For a man of thirty-seven, who spent long hours seated round boardroom tables, he was extremely fit. He wasn't obsessive about punishing physical exercise, hours spent sweating in a gym or pounding through Hyde Park, but he spent as much of his free time as he could in the country, riding, and walking, and he also used the pool at a local health club two or three times a week.

He shed his jacket and picked up his mineral water, the muscles in his back and arms hard under the fine cotton of his shirt.

Opening the door, he walked out on to the roof garden, putting down his glass and going to lean against the railings, looking over the roof-tops of London.

As a child growing up in one of the worst slum areas of Liverpool, the kind of luxury he enjoyed now had been something he could not even have imagined, but his mother had loved beautiful things, telling him about the furniture in the houses she cleaned, the people who lived there, and he had known then with the impotent misery of childhood that his mother wasn't happy, that it wasn't just because they did not live in one of the houses she was telling him about that he could hear the sadness in her voice.

His mother was Welsh, a pretty dark girl from the valleys with a voice so melodic that it caught at your heart. His father was Irish, a huge burly bear of a man who got work whenever he could, and when he couldn't spent his day in the pub drinking. He was their only child, and he had heard from his mother of how she had met his father when he had come to work on the new road which had opened up the valleys, how they had married and come to live here in Liverpool, where his father's family had lived for the last two generations.

They were from County Cork originally, and, despite their years in Liverpool, had remained resolutely and defiantly Irish. His grandparents had raised seven children in the tiny shabby terraced house down near the docks; a rowdy, noisy gathering of Ryans, who had eventually spilled out of the parental nest to marry and produce Ryans of their own.

Sometimes Daniel thought that Liverpool was populated entirely with his cousins. But he wasn't like them. It was something to do with Mam being Welsh. The others, unlike his father, had all married good Irish girls, and although nothing was ever said in his presence, Daniel sensed that his family was different. For a start there was the way that Nan Ryan never quite looked at his mother, and then there was the way that all the others, all his aunts and uncles, had produced several children apiece, while his parents had only him.

For some reason he felt that this failure had something to do with him... that the reason his father never picked him up or hugged him the way Uncle Liam did his boys or the way Uncle Joe did his had something to do with the fact that it was his fault he was the only one.

One thing he did know, and that was that for a Ryan to produce only one child was a failure of some kind. His mother sensed it too...otherwise why did she always change so much when they paid their Sunday visit to Nan's? When it was just the two of them on their own, although sometimes she was sad, there were other times when she laughed, sang, when she told him stories in her little Welsh voice—stories of dragons and heroes that made his eyes grow as round as saucers and his heart clench with fearful excitement.

But on Sundays his mother was different... just as though somehow all the life had drained out of her.

And then there was the mystery of Mam's parents. Daniel knew that they lived in Wales, but they never went to see them, and only at Christmas did they hear from them. A Christmas card, and a pound for his savings book.

He often wanted to ask Mam about them. It was a strange thing that, although she talked about Wales and her girlhood, she never talked about her family.

Daniel longed to ask about them, but her silence on the subject stopped him. He was a sensitive child, smaller and more frail than his Ryan cousins, who taunted him and called him a sissy. Daniel was wary with them; the boys he could cope with, but not the girls, for they pinched and tormented, and then screamed as though he had been the one to torment them. Their screams would bring one of the adults to see what was happening.

'It were that Daniel,' one of them would claim tearfully. ''E pinched me...'

And Daniel would get a cuff from whichever adult had been roused from an enjoyable gossip in the parlour to see who had caused the noise.

'That Daniel of yours is a real troublemaker,' he had once heard Nan caustically telling Mam. He had wanted to protest, to claim that it wasn't true, but there had been a huge lump in his throat, because he had known that Nan wouldn't believe him, that for some reason it pleased her to call him the cause of the trouble. He couldn't understand that, just as he couldn't understand why he was never pulled on to her lap for a cuddle, why whenever the precious sweets were being handed out he was invariably forgotten, why his uncles never picked him up and tossed him up into the air the way they did the other boys.

Even his own father seemed to prefer the others to him. Scowling at him when they were out, ignoring him when they were at home... Not that Daniel saw much of him.

He didn't come home at teatime like the majority of the other men, but went straight to the pub, often not coming back until Daniel was in bed. He would hear him returning, cursing and swearing as he hammered on the door, shouting at his mother, demanding to know where his supper was.

It was at times like this that Daniel winced and pulled the bedclothes up over his head. Other fathers raised their voices—he had heard his uncles do it to their offspring—but somehow or other when his father raised his... Daniel shivered. He was reasonably sure that he didn't love his father, at least not in the same instinctive, elemental way he loved his mother, and he suspected that his father didn't love him either, and that gave him a funny pain inside, a sort of sad, soft pain that was sharp as well.

When Daniel was eleven years old he sat the state Eleven Plus examination along with all his peers.

When the results were published and they learned not only that he had passed the examination but also that he had won a free place to a prestigious fee-paying local school, his mother was delighted.

Not so his father.

He came home late, reeking of beer. Daniel and his mother were in the kitchen when he arrived. As his father walked into the kitchen, Daniel saw the way his mother tensed. It suddenly struck him how small she was. He had been growing and now he was practically as tall as she was, both of them dwarfed by his father's heavy six-foot-odd frame.

His father was in a bad mood—Daniel could tell that immediately. He was swearing and complaining about Dick Fogarty, the foreman of his gang, and Daniel felt his heart sink. Work wasn't that easy to come by in Liverpool, and his father had already been sent off too many jobs, had too many fights with the other men. He had heard his uncles discussing it, seen them exchanging significant looks.

Quickly his mother produced his father's meal. He liked to eat the moment he came home. Personally Daniel thought that his father ought surely to go upstairs and get washed before sitting down to eat. His fingers were ingrained with dirt, the nails black and broken. Daniel and his mother had fish-paste sandwiches for their meal, but she had managed to scrape enough together from her meagre wages as a cleaner to buy enough stewing steak to make his father a pie.

Although nothing was ever said, Daniel knew quite well that his father did not always give his mother any money and that often all she had to spend on food and pay the rent was the money she earned cleaning. It grieved Daniel to see her walking down the street sometimes. She looked so tired, her shoulders bowed, her eyes dull...just the way she looked whenever his father came back late like this and drunk.

Daniel heard him swear as she served him the pie, complaining that it was no meal to put in front of a working man.

'Some of me mam's stew, that's what I want...and that's what I'm going to have,' he snarled, pushing away his plate and getting up. 'You know what the trouble with you is, don't you?' he added from the door. 'You think yourself so high and mighty, but you don't know how to treat a man. Well, think on this: if it wasn't for me, you and that brat of yours——'

'John...John, please wait a moment...'

Daniel heard the desperation in his mother's voice and hated his father. Hated him for what he was doing to his mother.

'Daniel...Daniel's won a place to the Drapers School. Isn't that wonderful...?'

For a moment there was silence, and then Daniel saw his father turn and stare at him. There was cruelty in his eyes and malice as well. The venom of the look he gave him almost took away Daniel's breath.

He had known that his father didn't love him, but this...this hatred, this enmity...

'Wonderful... Is that what you think? Well, I don't think it, and I'll tell you this—no son of mine is going to some poxy posh school. No. He'll go to Mile End, same as his dad, same as his cousins.'

Mile End...the largest and worst secondary school in the district. Daniel knew all about Mile End, about the fights, the gangs. His eldest cousin ran one of them. Daniel shivered.

'No, John...please... You don't understand—this is a wonderful opportunity for Daniel. If he does well he could go on to university. He could——'

'He could do what? Set himself up above his father and his cousins?'

His mother was clinging to his father's arm as she pleaded with him. The tension in the small kitchen seemed to smoulder with suppressed emotions, the strongest of them his own fear, Daniel recognised.

He dared not speak to his father, dared not try to plead with him.

'John, please,' his mother begged. 'He must have his chance.'

An ugly look crossed his father's face. 'Oh, he must, must he? He's my son, Megan. You just remember that. He's my son, and he'll get his schooling where I say. The trouble with you is that you've only got him to worry about. You know that Father Leary says...'

Daniel watched as his mother gave his father a fearful look. Daniel knew all about the priest. He visited Nan's every Sunday and he spoke to everyone apart from Mam and himself. But they weren't Catholics. His mother was Chapel, and had stayed in the faith of her childhood even after her marriage to his father.

Initially it had puzzled Daniel when he had not gone to church like his cousins, but then he had discovered about Mam being Chapel and had assumed that it had something to do with this.

Now, as he saw the nervous look his mother gave her father, something inside him contracted. He wanted to go up to her and put his arms round her, to protect her.

'John, please,' his mother begged again, and Daniel tensed as his father pulled away from her, shaking her off as easily as though she were a child, half pushing and half throwing her across the small kitchen, so that she fell against the stove.

'He's not going and that's that. What does a Ryan want with a fancy school? And who's going to pay for it? Soon as he's old enough he's out on a building site same as his cousins, earning his keep.'

His mother was leaning against the stove, her face tight with pain, her hand gripping her left hip. Daniel watched in silence as his father pushed past her and went out.

He didn't come back until Daniel was in bed. It was the sound of his raised voice that woke him. That, and his mother crying.

The next morning for the first time his mother didn't come in to wake him for school, and when he got up he discovered that she was still in bed, lying motionless in the small stuffy room, her face turned into the shadows.

'No, don't open the curtains,' she told him. Her voice had lost its lilt. It sounded heavy and sore somehow and suddenly Daniel was frightened without knowing why. There was no sign of his father and his mother was still in bed when he left for school. She had a bit of a headache, she told him, but she would be fine by and by.

When he got home from school the house was empty. There was a note from his mother to say she would be late getting home but he wasn't to worry.

After six when his father came in, early for once, she still wasn't back. Watching the way his face glowered at him as he demanded to know where she was, Daniel felt a strong current of antipathy and fear run through him.

'Still thinks she's going to persuade me to let you go to that fancy school, is that it? Well, you can tell her that she can think again. No money of mine's going to be wasted on posh schooling—uniforms, expensive books...'

'Where are you going?' Daniel asked his father nervously as he opened the back door.

'Nowhere that's any of your business. God knows a man's entitled to a bit of comfort, even the priest says that.'

It was seven o'clock before his mother returned. She looked both elated and frightened.

'Sorry I'm so late, but I missed the bus and then it was busy.'

'Did you have to work late?' Daniel asked her.

'What? Oh, yes...yes, I did...'

There was a livid bruise along her cheekbone and she was moving very stiffly as though her body hurt. When Daniel asked if she had had a fall, she turned her back on him and started cleaning the already clean sink.

'Yes...yes, I slipped on the stairs this morning after you'd gone to school. Must have been half asleep still, I suppose. I've got a nice bit of haddock for your tea. Mrs Silverstone gave it to me... Seems she bought it for her husband and he was eating out somewhere and she doesn't like it.'

Beneath his mother's bright chatter, Daniel could sense her tension. He gave her his father's message and watched her anxiously.

'It's all right,' she told him softly. 'You'll be taking up that scholarship, my lad—but not a word to your dad, mind.'

'But what about money?'

'Don't you worry your head about all that. It's all arranged. Your Nan's going to help out, and with what I earn——'

'Nan?' Daniel blinked at her. 'Nan's going to help? But she doesn't like me, not as much as she does the others. On Sundays——'

He saw his mother bite her lip. 'No, not your Nan Ryan, Danny. I was speaking of your Nana Rees. I...I telephoned her today from Mrs Silverstone's. It was all right. She had given me permission but I wanted to wait until the cheap rate after six o'clock.'

'Nana Rees...' Daniel stared wonderingly at his mother. 'But——'

'No, no questions, Danny...and remember, nothing to your dad, not a word.'

Daniel had been almost sixteen when his father had been killed on a building site. He couldn't mourn him. He hated him too much by then. He might not have been able to stop his son taking up his scholarship, but he had certainly made his mother pay for it, and not just with periodic beatings Daniel was sure he gave her, even though his mother herself always denied it, always claimed stoically that she had had a fall, that she had been clumsy.

So often Daniel had ached to ask her why she stayed, why she didn't leave. He knew she couldn't love him. How could any woman love a man who treated her the way his father treated his mother? It wasn't just the beatings, it was his whole attitude towards her. Daniel knew enough about his father's religion now to know that there could be no divorce. No Ryan ever divorced—and he also knew from listening to the conversations of his cousins and his uncles that his father had another woman whom he visited regularly, sometimes staying overnight with her.

'Course, it's her who I blame,' he had heard Liam's wife, Sheila, saying. 'If she'd been a proper wife to him, she'd have kept him at home. I mean, it's obvious they're not sleeping together...they've only got Danny.'

The thought of his mother having to endure the sexual attentions of his father was something that revolted Daniel. He could hardly bear to comprehend that his very life force had come from that coupling, that he owed his entire existence to his rough, brutish father's coupling with his mother.

He still did not know if his father knew where the money came from that kept him at school. He knew, though, and he was determined that as soon as he was able he was going to repay his mother for all the sacrifices she had made on his behalf—and not just his mother, there was his unknown grandmother to thank as well.

Many times he asked his mother why they never went to Wales, why they never saw her family. He knew now that both her parents were alive, that she had a married brother, that he had Welsh cousins.

The cousins didn't concern him. There was no love lost between his Irish cousins and himself. They considered him to be an outsider, different, set apart from them by virtue of his Welsh blood. The Welsh bastard, they called him, and he stoically endured it because he had told himself that never, ever would he do to a human

being with his fists, in violence and out of a desire to
damage and inflict pain, what his father had done to his
mother. That he would never, ever in his life raise his
hand to a fellow human being. He stuck to that decision
all through the early painful years at school when he had
been very much an outsider among the other pupils from
their privileged, comfortable homes...

The scholarship brat was what *they* called him, but
eventually had come at least some acceptance, and now
with his father's death had also come a lifting of the
joint burden of fear and anger he carried with his
mother—her fear, his anger.

At his funeral, watching his grandmother sob noisily
for the loss of her precious son, he wondered why it was
that he could feel nothing, no emotion—that he could
find no memories of past tendernesses to hold on to in
this the moment of committal of his father's body to its
grave.

When at last the coffin was covered, and her sons were
leading away the grieving mother, she turned to Daniel's
mother and said savagely, 'You were responsible for this.
You killed him with your stuck-up ways. You... He
should never have married you—aye, and never would
have done so if you hadn't tricked him...'

His mother, trick his father... It must surely have been
the other way round? He couldn't understand why any
woman would want to marry a man like his father, and
yet still he felt guilt and shame that he was unable to
feel any grief, any sadness, any loss.

For a while after his father's death their lives continued much as they had done before, only now they
were free of the burden of his father's presence. They
were poor, but now his mother had started singing
again... She smiled and she laughed too, and on
Saturdays and Sundays, when she wasn't working and
Daniel wasn't at school, they would visit the city's
museums and galleries, or sometimes take the train to
somewhere like Lytham St Anne's where he could gaze

in awe at the posh houses and smile while his mother told him that if he did well at school one day he would own a house such as these.

If he did, she would be living in it with him, Daniel promised himself. He wanted to give her all the things his father had not. He wanted to see her wearing pretty clothes. He wanted to stop her from working so hard and looking so tired.

And then, at the beginning of the summer holidays, three months after his father's death, there was another death, and one which changed his life completely.

CHAPTER FOURTEEN

THE letter arrived first thing on Monday morning, the handwriting unfamiliar and male.

It was from her brother, Daniel's mother told him, opening it, her face suddenly paling.

'It's your grandfather... He's dead...they buried him last week, and now Gareth, your uncle, wants us to go home, just for a visit... Mam needs me.'

No other explanations, and something in her voice told him not to ask for any.

They travelled by train to Aberystwyth, and from there by bus to the small village overlooking Cardigan bay.

To Daniel, whose only experience of the coast was Liverpool with its docks and the flat wasteland of Lytham St Anne's, the beauty of the rolling Pembroke coastline was breathtakingly wonderful. Even when the bus stopped in the small dusty square and his mother got up, he followed her, but kept his eyes on the view first seen through the bus window.

The square was empty and silent; alien after the bustle of Liverpool and the choking petrol-laden air of the street where they lived.

In the square the bus moved off, continuing its journey along the coast road; another road plunged downhill towards the sea itself, and from its crest where he stood with his mother Daniel could see the harbour and the fishing boats.

'This way,' she told him, touching his hand lightly. On the bus he had been fascinated by the accents of the other passengers, and now suddenly his mother's speech was like theirs, more lilting, more...more Welsh, he recognised as he turned to walk with her.

The narrow road was empty, but here and there Daniel noticed the discreet twitching of a lace curtain, and then, just as his mother was directing him off the road and into the lane that ran between two of the houses, a car came racing towards them, stopping abruptly.

The man who climbed out was a little over medium height, with sharp brown eyes and curly hair—there was something oddly familiar about him, although Daniel didn't realise what it was until later.

At his side his mother made an odd sound in her throat, and then the man was coming towards them, arms open wide as he smiled at them.

'Gareth...' his mother breathed tearfully. 'It's been so long. I never expected you to meet us...'

'I would have been here sooner, only Becky Saunders started with her fifth... You remember Becky, she was at school with us. She married Simon Carruthers. His father farms over near Haverfordwest... and this must be young Daniel... Well, my boys are going to have their eyes put out when they see him. Barely sixteen, isn't he, and mine now seventeen and at least a head shorter than him. Anyway, come on inside the car with the both of you. Mam's waiting in a fret of worry that you weren't going to turn up.'

'How is she, Gareth?' Daniel heard his mother asking.

'Bearing up well. You know Mam, and as we both know he wasn't always an easy man to live with.'

'Daniel, you get in the front with your uncle,' his mother instructed.

His uncle... so this Gareth was his mother's brother. Daniel inspected him thoughtfully as he got into the car, trying not to be overawed by its luxury. No one in the Ryan family owned a car, although Daniel was used to the sight of his schoolfriends being dropped off outside the school gates in a variety of expensive models.

This one was a large Volvo estate car with new registration plates.

'I wanted to let you know before the funeral, but Mam said not, said that it wouldn't have been what Dad wanted.'

Daniel heard the note of apology in his voice and wondered why her father would not have wanted his

mother at his funeral. He had already realised that for
some reason his mother was estranged from her family,
and, without knowing the cause, or feeling able to discuss
it with her, since she had never voluntarily raised the
subject, had assumed that it was perhaps something to
do with his parents' marriage and that her family had
disapproved of the union as much as he now realised
the Ryans did.

'Well, now, we hear it's a clever lad you've got yourself
here, our Megan...a good scholarship, and good reports from his school, so Mam tells us... Been boasting
about him all over town, she has.'

It was said with such affection and such a lack of resentment or contempt, the smile his uncle gave him so
very different from the bitterness he was used to seeing
in his father's eyes, that Daniel stared at him, unaware
of the thoughts running through Gareth Rees's head.

Poor little sod, he was thinking. Just as well that father
of his went and got himself killed. And that Pa's gone
too. He should never have treated Megan the way he
did... If he himself hadn't been working away in America
at the time... Well, it was all in the past now. John
Ryan was dead, and their father as well, and as for the
lad, well, although he had what he knew to be the Ryan
looks with his dark hair, it seemed that there was
blessedly little else of his father in him.

'You know that Sarah and I moved into the house
when Dad retired. He and Mam bought a bungalow on
a new development.'

'Yes. Mam wrote me about it. Said that the stairs at
the house had been getting too much for Dad anyway.'

'Yes. His heart had been weak for years, and that
temper of his didn't help.

'Well, here we are,' he announced, bringing the car
to a halt, slowing down and then turning into a drive
thickly edged with rhododendron bushes. The house at
the end of the drive was stone and solid-looking, with
large windows either side of the front door.

Daniel stared at it in amazement. Was this where his
mother had grown up? He thought of their home, the

small terraced house with its stained bath and sink, its cracked linoleum floors, its front door that opened straight out on to the street and the back one which opened into a minute back yard.

This house had what seemed to be an enormous garden—he could even see what looked like a tennis court.

The front door of the house opened and a slim, dark-haired woman came hurrying out. As his mother stepped out of the car she was already embracing her, drawing her towards the open door.

This must be his uncle's wife, Daniel realised, studying her. She was probably around the same age as his mother, maybe even older, but she looked so different... Her clothes were different, for one thing, and she didn't look tired the way his mother always did. Her nails weren't broken from scrubbing floors and her hair was thick and glossy.

'Megan ... it's been so long. Come in. Mam's waiting for you ... I've sent the boys over to a friend's for to-night, thought it would give you time to get settled in a little. You'll be staying at Mam's of course, but we thought ... well.'

'Don't forget this young man, Sarah,' his uncle was saying, one hand resting comfortingly on his shoulder as though he knew how alien he felt, how unsure of himself and awkward.

'Of course not ... Come on in, Daniel. Mam's been driving us all mad telling us how clever you are.'

Somehow or other they were marshalled inside, through a shabby large hallway cluttered with heavy furniture and into a warm sunny room, equally over-furnished, and yet somehow warm and welcoming.

A small still dark-haired woman was sitting in a chair, her face turned towards the door.

She didn't get up as they walked in, and Daniel realised that she was actually in a wheelchair and that her hands were gnarled and twisted, the knuckles and joints badly swollen.

'Mam...' He heard the emotion in his mother's voice and felt tears prick his own eyes as she hurried towards the wheelchair and its occupant.

'There, there, Megan, my lovely. There's no need for tears... Come and sit down here beside me and tell me why it's taken you sixteen years to bring my grandson to see me.'

'I couldn't, Mam... I just couldn't, what with Da and John...' Her voice broke, and, remembering the bruises he had seen on her face, the fear he had seen in her eyes, Daniel felt a sudden hot resurgence of his hatred for his father, and for all men like him, who used violence against others weaker than themselves. What kind of man had his grandfather been, that he had not known how his daughter had suffered, that he had not cared enough to find out what her life was?

'Daniel, come here and say hello to your grandmother.'

Obediently he went to his mother's side.

'So this is Daniel...' Clear grey eyes the same colour as his own searched his face, and one twisted hand covered his own. The skin felt paper-thin and hot to his touch, and he knew without knowing how that those swollen joints ached and burned with pain, and that behind her calm smile this woman who was his grandmother had known many hours of emotional and physical suffering.

'He's a fine boy, Megan. A fine boy, and a clever boy as well.'

Daniel felt himself flushing with embarrassment. He had never felt able to forget that it was his mother's hard work and his grandmother's generosity that had made it possible for him to take up his scholarship, and yet now, when he wanted to thank her, when he wanted to tell her how conscious he was of that debt, there were no words... He could only stand there feeling awkward and foolish.

'You'll be staying for a while?' Daniel turned his head as his uncle addressed his mother.

'Well, we'd like to...'

'You've always got a home here, Megan, you know that. You always have had.'

Daniel saw his mother shake her head. 'No, not while Da was still alive. I couldn't... I hurt him so badly when I married John.'

'Well, he had such high hopes for you... He wanted you to follow in Gareth's footsteps, to become a doctor.'

His mother, a doctor... Daniel stared at her. He had never known, never guessed when she had spent those long hours helping him with his school work, encouraging him... His mother, a doctor...

She could have had so much... but she had married his father instead.

Daniel was no fool. He was sixteen years old and he could count. He had been born five months after his parents' marriage. His heart bled for his mother. How had she felt when she discovered that she was pregnant, when she had known that she must marry his father? She must have loved him then, unthinkable though it seemed now.

His grandmother was saying something about a drink of tea before they left for her bungalow. Sarah was exhorting them to stay for their evening meal. Daniel let their conversation flow over him, going to stand by the window and stare outside.

'All right, son?'

The kind voice and gentle touch of his uncle startled him.

'Yes—yes, I was just wondering if you could see the sea from here—it's so different here from at home...'

'You can see it from the attic windows. I'll take you up there some time. I'm sorry about your father. I never knew him——'

'I'm not.'

The denial came thick and bitter, causing him to flush and clench his fists, this uncomfortable sign of impending manhood, the startling change of his voice from boyhood to manhood, embarrassing him, just as other manifestations of his adolescence also did.

He held his breath, fearful that his uncle would question him, knowing with an instinct that needed no definition that his mother would not want the painful bones of her marriage to his father laid bare before the compassion of her family, knowing that her pride would never allow her to tell them just what kind of husband John Ryan had been.

They had been staying with his grandmother for just over a week. He had become firm friends with his uncle's twin sons and had begun to feel as though he had finally found a place where he was actually accepted, when he looked up from the book he was reading at his grandmother's kitchen table to hear her exclaiming in a pleased voice, 'Here's Robert Cavanagh—he must be over to visit Nora's folk. Daniel, get up and let him in, will you? Your legs are younger than mine.'

As he got up, Daniel happened to see his mother's face. It had gone the colour of old putty, drained of all the healthy warmth which these last few days had put into it.

The transformation within his mother had amazed and delighted Daniel. Since coming home she had seemed to shed years... She laughed and sang as she worked in his grandmother's kitchen, her eyes shone and she even moved differently, as though a weight had been lifted from her shoulders, and now in the space of half a dozen seconds she had once again become the woman she had been in Liverpool—cowed, nervous, frightened. Why?

He opened the door before the man approaching it could knock. Tall, dark-haired, he had the lightest, most piercing blue-grey eyes Daniel had ever seen. His skin was weatherbeaten and tough like that of a man who worked out of doors, and yet he was dressed in a dark suit and crisp white shirt and he looked as though they were the kind of clothes he wore all the time. He wore them with the same ease which Daniel had already noticed in the fathers of his schoolfriends, as casually as his own father had worn his own workclothes. This was no suit donned for a special occasion. This man had wealth and power, Daniel recognised. He also recognised that for some reason his arrival had terrified his mother.

She had her back to the door now and was busy scraping potatoes for their lunch. He saw the man smile at his grandmother and then stiffen slightly as he saw his mother. A second's hesitation before he walked in and embraced his grandmother, saying calmly at the same time, 'Megan. What a wonderful surprise. I had no idea you were back.'

'She's only been here a week, Robert, and this is her son, Daniel.'

'Daniel.'

The firm handshake, the man-to-man smile, the cool, brief meeting of their eyes told Daniel a lot and yet kept a lot hidden from him as well. This man was astute, astute and cautious. Daniel could not sense the hot-headed streak of violence which had been so powerfully obvious in his father. This man was obviously well liked by his grandmother, and yet he could almost feel the waves of fear emanating from his mother as she resolutely kept her back towards the visitor.

Robert Cavanagh didn't stay long. Just long enough to commiserate with Daniel's grandmother on the loss of her husband and to refuse the proffered cup of tea.

In all he could hardly have been in the house more than ten minutes, and during that time, although she had finished scraping the potatoes soon after he had walked in the door, Daniel noticed that his mother kept herself busy at the sink, refusing to join in the conversation despite both her mother's and Robert Cavanagh's attempts to include her.

Only when he had gone did she make any comment, asking in a voice that was unfamiliarly hard and flat, and which fell sharply and discordantly against Daniel's sensitive ears, 'And where was his wife, then—I see he doesn't bring her to visit with her folk...'

'Heavens, Megan, didn't I say? Poor Nora's dead. Her bad spells had been getting much worse recently. She'd gone into hospital again for more treatment and it was while she was there...she just walked out and went straight under a lorry... Instant, it was, the doctor said. Of course Robert blamed himself but there was nothing he could have done, poor man. A good husband he'd been to her. There's many a man who would not have stuck by her the way he has. It was losing the child, of course. She was never the same after that. There's many a time when they were here that your father was called out in the night to her. And she was such a pretty little thing when they married, and both of them so young.'

When they were on their own Daniel asked his mother, 'What was wrong with Mr Cavanagh's wife?'

What he really wanted to know was why his mother was frightened of the man and why no one seemed to be aware of it but him.

They had gone for tea to his uncle's, and when his grandmother had mentioned Robert Cavanagh's visit, immediately both his uncle and aunt had been full of enthusiasm and praise for the man.

It seemed that his father had been the local builder, and that on his death Robert Cavanagh had taken over the business and built it up into a much larger concern. So large in fact that he had moved to Cardiff where he had become very successful indeed.

'He hasn't forgotten his home, though,' had been Sarah's comment. 'When the chapel roof needed replacing Robert sent a gang of his men over and virtually did the job free.'

'She had a baby, a little girl,' his mother told him quietly. 'A pretty little thing, she was. I think I must have been about fifteen at the time. She and Robert still lived here then. She was a pretty girl, Nora... always one to like a bit of a laugh and a joke with the boys... Bit of a flirt, like, some said.

'Anyway it seems she'd gone for a walk along the cliff and she'd taken the baby with her in the pram. Only while she was up there she'd met this lad, whether by accident or on purpose I don't really know. They got chatting and she must have forgotten to put the brake on the baby's pram, because the next thing they knew it was rolling towards the edge of the cliff. They tried to stop it, but it was too late. It was a full tide, and a good two-hundred-foot drop over the cliff there... The poor little mite had no chance really...

'Totally changed Nora, it did... Took to wandering along the cliff top late at night crying and wringing her hands. She had to be sent away for a while to a special hospital...' She gave a brief shake of her head. 'It's a terrible thing to happen to a woman, that... Poor woman, indeed. God willing, she's at peace now.'

'And Robert—Mr Cavanagh. How did he...?'

'Well, Robert was heartbroken... Fair doted on the child he did and no mistake, but it's different for a man...'

'And did they have any more children?' Daniel wanted to know. His mother shook her head.

'She couldn't, see... something went wrong when she had the first and the doctors told her then that there wouldn't be any more. That's what made it so hard for her.'

It was only later that Daniel recognised that this conversation with his mother had marked a turning point in his life: that she was now treating him as a co-adult and not a child, that with the removal of his father from their lives he had now become the man of the family.

Later, looking back, that summer in Wales was one of the happiest in his life.

The twins, his cousins, Andrew and Anthony, although almost two years his senior, welcomed his company.

The small town had no senior school, there weren't many other young adults in the town, and their nearest friends lived in Aberystwyth.

A bike was found from somewhere for Daniel and the three of them would sometimes cycle into Aberystwyth to meet up with a gang of the twins' friends, and to spend the afternoon watching the girls on the beach and the pier, occasionally throwing out flirtatious remarks to them, talking light-heartedly about what they would do, if they were lucky enough to get one of the girls to take up their vocal invitations.

In the end, and much to his own surprise, it was Daniel who aroused the most interest in the groups of girls who gathered on the beach ostensibly for the purpose of sun-bathing, but in reality in order to amuse themselves by teasing the boys.

He had his first amateurish kiss in the shadows beneath the pier, experienced his first unsteady and half shocking thrill of groping clumsily with the clothing of the girl wriggling in his arms as she exhorted him, 'No, not like that... it unfastens here like this, see?'

Perhaps because of his height and the breadth of his shoulders, perhaps because his voice had now well and truly broken, and his jaw was already shadowed with his first beard, or perhaps simply because the twins were older and he was accepted as being their peer, the crowd all seemed to assume that he was older than his sixteen years.

For the first time in his life he had found genuine acceptance and he blossomed under it, quickly learning to retaliate to the girls' smart back-chat, quickly shedding the burdens of caution and apprehension caused by living with his father.

When he and his mother returned to Liverpool at the end of the summer, he was two inches taller, several inches broader, and had developed muscles in his arms and chest from rowing the twins' boat, was brown from day-long exposure to the weather, and was actually having to shave... if only infrequently.

He missed Wales... He missed the twins, and the long days at school seemed to drag. He had always purposefully kept himself slightly aloof from his fellow pupils, knowing that he was different, knowing that he was there under sufferance, that his parents were not wealthy and middle-class like theirs, but his stay in Wales had given him a new self-confidence, an awareness that there was another side to him that did not embrace the culture of the Ryans. That he had an uncle who was a doctor and a mother who could have been... That he had no reason whatsoever to feel ashamed or embarrassed about his origins.

302		THE HIDDEN YEARS

His grandmother had made his mother promise that they would return to Wales for Christmas, but before that, halfway through the term, they had an unexpected visitor.

When he returned from school one day to find Robert Cavanagh standing in the kitchen talking to his mother, his first thought was to protect her, but, totally unexpectedly, it wasn't fear he could see in her eyes as she stood facing the older man, but pleasure. Her face was pink and flushed, her hair, which she had had cut in a new style, curling prettily around her face. She looked younger these days and happier, and there was a little bit more money coming into the house, from his uncle, Daniel suspected.

He himself had a weekend job working in a local supermarket stacking the shelves, and he insisted on giving the majority of these small earnings to his mother.

'Daniel,' Robert Cavanagh smiled, extending his hand towards him. Daniel took it automatically, listening as he explained how he had happened to be in Liverpool on business and had decided to call on them.

'I was just saying to your mother that I should like to take you both out for a meal.'

Robert Cavanagh stayed in Liverpool for over a week and on each and every evening of that week he took them out. His mother liked him, Daniel could see that; it was only when Robert occasionally mentioned his father that he saw his mother's face tighten and her body tense.

The afternoon before he was due to leave, Robert picked Daniel up from school. The unexpectedness of seeing him there waiting for him in his dark red Jaguar saloon made Daniel hesitate before climbing into it beside him.

'I wanted to have a word with you in private, Daniel... Man to man, see. I love your mam, and I want to marry her. I haven't said so to her yet. I wanted to talk to you about it first, let you know what was in my mind, see... You're a good boy, Danny, and I want you to know that if your mam and I do marry, you'd be to me like my own son. I know you didn't always have an easy time with your own father, and I can understand that you might not want another man in your mother's life. The Ryans haven't treated her as they ought... I'm going home tomorrow, but I'll see you both at Christmas when you come to Wales... I shan't say anything to your mam until then... I don't want to rush her, see.'

'And if I don't want you to marry her?' Daniel asked stiffly.

Robert turned round in his seat to face him, his face stern and grave.

'Well, that's your prerogative, Danny... but it isn't your permission I'm asking, see—it's your mother who'll tell me yes or no. One day when you're a man yourself you'll understand that when a man loves a woman the way I love your mam she's more important to him than anything else in the world. I want us to be friends, Danny—whether you want us to be or not is up to you...'

His mother and Robert Cavanagh were married in the spring. Robert had bought his mother a house outside Cardiff and it had been arranged that Daniel, who had taken his O Levels and obtained a respectable ten passes, would transfer to a school in Cardiff for his final two years studying to take his A Levels. But this time he would be attending as a fee-paying pupil.

It was going to be a new life for all of them, and Daniel wasn't sure quite how he felt about it. He liked Robert Cavanagh and yet at the same time he resented him... resented his intimacy with his mother... He resented the way her whole face softened and lit up when she looked at him. He was jealous, he recognised, acknowledging that his behaviour was irrational and yet unable to help it.

He spent the first summer of his mother's new marriage with his grandmother. The twins were now both at St Andrews studying medicine, but both of them were home for the holidays, and this time there was far more experience and intent to the way the three of them trawled the surprisingly rich waters of Aberystwyth looking for girls.

Daniel was well past the awkward fumbling stage now thanks to some intensive coaching from one of the girls from a local convent school. He was seventeen now, and Robert had given him a small car, so while he was staying with his grandmother he used some of the money he had earned during the term to pay for a course of driving lessons.

His aunt and uncle took him with them when they and the twins went to Brittany for three weeks on a camping holiday, and for the first time Daniel discovered the delights and dangers of foreign girls. He was maturing rapidly. Unlike the twins, he still had no idea what he wanted to do when he left school. He was hoping to get a degree in economics, but beyond that he had no thoughts.

Robert had offered to take him into the business, which was thriving and expanding, but Daniel wanted to be independent. Besides, the building trade reminded him too much of his father, of his aggression and violence.

He arrived home at the house in Cardiff two days ahead of schedule, the twins having decided to return early to St Andrews to attend a 'start-of-term bash'.

He used his key to unlock the front door. His own key had been given to him by Robert as soon as they had moved into the new house.

His mother loved her new home. It had been built at the end of the previous century by a railway baron, and overlooked the sea. It had high-ceilinged, plain, square rooms that let in plenty of sunlight, and a large rambling garden which his mother worked in on sunny days.

Now she was the one employing a cleaner instead of doing the cleaning, and a gardener came twice a week to weed the borders and mow the lawns. His mother looked happier than Daniel had ever seen her look, and yet sometimes in repose there was a sadness about her face, an uncertainty in her eyes that worried him.

He still wasn't entirely sure about Robert—there was an awkwardness between them, a barrier which Daniel was careful to keep in place.

It wasn't that he didn't like Robert; he did, and sometimes the burden of his own guilt that he should in so many ways prefer Robert to his own dead father weighed heavily on him.

The hallway smelled of roses; there was a huge bowlful of them on the table. He smiled when he saw them. His mother had confessed to him that having enough money to actually buy fresh flowers was to her the epitome of luxury.

Dropping his case in the hall, he went upstairs intending to shower and change, but as he passed his mother's bedroom door a sound from inside the room made him check.

He heard his mother's voice, low and haunted, and then Robert's, the words indistinguishable, and then agonisingly his mother cried out, a guttural, mortal sound of agony.

Daniel didn't stop to think. He thrust open the door and rushed in, one thought and one only in his mind. Robert was hurting his mother...hurting her as his father had once hurt her.

Robert and his mother were lying on the bed, Robert's naked body lean and tanned, apart from his buttocks which were paler.

He had turned his head towards the door, his body shielding that of his mother, Daniel recognised, just as he immediately recognised something else.

Robert had not been hurting his mother, he had been making love with her...that sound he had heard... Daniel had enough experience of sex himself now to know that it was a pleasure that sometimes came perilously close to agony.

He felt his face start to burn with embarrassment; heard himself stammering an apology as he backed out of the room.

Robert and his mother...he had known, of course, but had tucked the knowledge somewhere to the back of his mind, had allowed himself to believe that their marriage was made out of companionship and friendship, even though Robert had told him how much he loved her.

When he got to his own room he discovered that he was shaking, that he felt sick and somehow betrayed. He felt wretchedly uncomfortable with the knowledge of his mother's sexuality and guilty about his own stupidity.

Unable to face either of them, he went out and spent the rest of the day and well into the night wandering round Cardiff.

It was late when he got back but there was a light on in the hall and in the sitting-room.

As he unlocked the front door and went in, Robert came out of the sitting-room and said quietly, 'Before you go to bed, Danny, I'd like to have a word with you.'

Funny how Robert was the only one who called him Danny... almost as though he were a little boy still, he thought truculently as he followed the other unwillingly into the sitting-room.

'If it's about this afternoon,' Daniel began aggressively, 'I thought...'

He broke off, shaking his head in confusion, unable to admit what he had thought, afraid of making himself look an even bigger fool than he already had done.

'What did you think, Danny? That perhaps I was hurting your mother the way John did?'

Daniel felt his face blaze with colour. He couldn't meet Robert's eyes, felt as though somehow he was tarred with the same brush as his father, tainted with the same aggressive inability to control either his temper or his reactions, guilty of using his strength to hurt others weaker than himself.

'I know all about how John hurt your mother, Danny.'

'I couldn't stop him—I wanted to but...I was afraid...' Daniel stopped, not knowing where the words had come from, not knowing until now how much it had hurt him that he hadn't been able to protect her.

'No, of course you couldn't. And besides...'

He hadn't seen Robert move, but he must have done so because now he was standing beside him, gripping his arm consolingly, as though he understood... 'It's probably just as well that you didn't interfere, Danny... It might only have made a bad situation worse. It wasn't entirely John's fault. I was as much to blame as anyone... Come and sit down, Danny. There's something I want to talk to you about. Something your mother and I should have told you when we got married, but I wanted time—time for you to get to know me before you judged me. However...'

Daniel stared at him, not knowing what he was talking about or why he should look so grave.

'You know, don't you, that I was married before I met your mother?'

'Yes...'

'Well, after we lost our child Nora had a nervous breakdown. Our doctor thought it might be best if she stayed with her own family for a while, so she moved back with her parents, while I lived alone down at the yard. I knew your mother vaguely. Gareth and I had been at school together. He brought her down to the yard with him one day when he came on some errand... Introduced her to me... She was just seventeen by then, prettiest girl I've ever seen. Shyest as well, but when she smiled...well, it was so rewarding making her smile that I clean forgot what it was Gareth had wanted from me, and since he had gone on into town leaving Megan with me I said I'd better walk up to the house with her and ask him again just what it was.

'On the way there she told me about how she was going to be a doctor. She was at school in Aberystwyth then... That's where she met your father; he was working on the new road they were constructing. He'd seen her, taken a fancy to her as any man might, and pestered her into having a coffee with him after school. She was a little bit afraid of him even then, I think...

'After we'd said goodbye I found myself thinking about her more and more, and even worse making excuses to call at your grandfather's so that I could see her. I found out that she liked walking, so I persuaded your grandmother to let me take her out for the day to walk along the coastal path from St David's. It was a hot summer, with the air so still and the sky so blue... I haven't any words to explain to you why I did what I should not have done... She was still a child, I was a man and a married man at that, but when I kissed her she responded so sweetly it took my breath away and my self-control.

'I'd never intended to make love to her. I swear it... All I wanted to do was to see her smile... and afterwards, well, I was so stunned by what I'd done, by how I'd felt... I considered myself an experienced man... There'd been one or two other girls before I married Nora, but your mother... She was upset, of course, and so was I. I wanted to tell her how much I loved her, how much I wanted her, but how could I? I took her home, intended to call back the next day and talk to her, apologise... but that night I had a phone call from Nora's mother to say that that afternoon Nora had tried to commit suicide and that she was back in hospital.

'Of course I had to go to her. She was a very sick woman, mentally and physically, and the doctors told me that it would help if I took her away somewhere where there were no memories of our child.

'We went to the South of France for four months... When I came back your mother was already married to John Ryan, with a child on the way, or so the gossips had it.

'I realised then how much I loved her. I was searingly, bitterly jealous. I think I almost hated her for giving herself to someone else.

'I didn't ask for the details of how she had met him, of who he was... I only found out later that your grandfather had been completely opposed to the marriage, that he had only given his permission when Megan told him that she was pregnant. He vowed never to speak to her again as long as he lived. He was that kind of man; very strict, very stern, and Megan was his favourite child... Over the years I heard occasional reports about your mother. I tried not to listen. I couldn't endure the thought of her happiness with someone else. Time softens some pains but it can't extinguish them entirely. And then Nora died and your father... I walked into your grandmother's kitchen, saw your mother, and knew I had never stopped loving her.'

'But she looked so afraid of you...'

'Not of me, Danny,' Robert told him gently. 'What she was afraid of was that I would look at you and see that you were not John Ryan's son but mine.'

Daniel felt the room spin round him. He must have made a sound because Robert's hand gripped his shoulder, his voice raw with emotion as he offered, 'I'm sorry, son...it's a shock for you, I know...it was a shock for me as well, to learn that your mother had suffered years of desperate unhappiness to protect me, that she had married John Ryan because she was carrying my child... Because she knew the scandal would destroy me... I like to think that if I had known I'd have done the right thing, divorced Nora and married your mother. I'd certainly have wanted to, but, as your mother says, how could I have deserted poor Nora? And yet when I think of how much your mother has suffered, how much you've suffered...but you are my son, Daniel. There's nothing of John Ryan in you...you're *my* son...'

Robert's son. He was still trying to assimilate the shock of it, but strangely he felt no urge to deny it, no desperate inability to believe what he had been told—rather it was as though another burden was sliding from his shoulders with the knowledge that he need never fear he would become a man in John Ryan's image of violence and cruelty. And yet there was pain and confusion as well, the pain of knowing that it had been for his sake that his mother had suffered her marriage, the pain of realising that assumptions he had made about himself and his heritage were totally false, that he was not a Ryan...he was a Cavanagh and...a stranger to himself.

'Don't think too badly of me, son. All of us at some times in our lives do things we regret, act without thought or caution. My deepest regret is the pain I've brought on your mother—that she has had to carry the burden of my sin. The fact that I fathered her child I consider to be one of the greatest achievements of my life, and that that child is you, Danny, one of its greatest gifts. I don't ask that you love me as your father—why should you? It's much easier for me to love you as my son, but I *am* your father, and I swear to you now that there is nothing I wouldn't do to spare your mother the slightest hurt, nothing . . .'

He was Robert's son...not John Ryan's but Robert's. Not a Ryan but a Cavanagh...not half Irish and half Welsh but entirely Welsh... As he lay in bed Daniel closed his eyes, trying to come to terms with what he had learned, wondering bleakly if he ever would.

have been somewhere on the campus. What he did know was that within a very short space of time every single sentence Scott uttered seemed to contain the name 'Sage'.

He was three years older than Scott, and just cynical and worldly enough to be slightly amused by the younger man's very obvious devotion.

He hadn't met her yet, but when he did he suspected that he would discover that this paragon of all the virtues would be just another immature first-year female student, clad in the shrouding uniform of long, droopy garments favoured by the majority of the female student population. She would be thin and waiflike; Scott constantly spoke of her in terms that suggested he considered her vulnerable and fragile. She would have pale skin and kohl-rimmed eyes, and she would be studying something arty and potentially useless.

When he actually did meet her it came as a shock to discover how wrong he had been.

For a start, there was that wild banner of dark red hair vibrantly flaunting itself in the still breeze of Alcester's High Street, as Scott spotted him and dragged his obviously reluctant companion over to introduce her.

When he shook her hand he discovered that her grip was surprisingly strong, her fingers long and thin, her wrist supple. She was taller than he had expected, too, only about four or five inches shorter than Scott, who was an inch or so short of his own six feet two, and she was not wearing droopy clothes.

Nor, he realised with some amusement, did she like him. What he suspected was normally the feral stare of her extraordinary eyes had been tamed to return his scrutiny, but quite obviously only with a supreme effort, and it occurred to him to wonder what on earth it was that ordered human fallibilities so disastrously, in causing Scott, who was so placid, so organised, so insistent on order in all he did, to fall in love with this obvious termagant of a girl, whose nature, he suspected, was as unruly as her hair. Even her teeth were sharp and challenging, the apparent softness of her full mouth deceptive perhaps to the inexperienced eye which might see in it compliance and gentleness. He knew better. She was no mate for Scott and yet she plainly adored him.

Because he could see in her eyes that she wanted Scott to herself, that she didn't want his company making up a threesome, he said casually to Scott, 'I'm just on my way to the Crown. Why don't you join me...?'

He could feel the anger she was directing to him without having to look at her.

Scott, completely oblivious to it, responded eagerly, 'Great... Sage was just saying that she fancied a drink...'

Sage... Daniel wondered how he managed not to laugh. Whoever had thought up that name for her must have had good cause to regret it over the years, or had they perhaps been hoping against hope that the bestowal of such a name might go some way to alleviate the burden of temperament fate had bestowed upon her?

She was certainly not to his taste, and he could only marvel at Scott's blindness to what she really was.

He preferred his women smooth and sleek, blonde preferably, with more than a hint of the cool refinement that came from protected upper-middle-class backgrounds. The typical choice of the street-wise kid from a working-class background, he frequently taunted himself with derision, and yet to all intents and purposes he wasn't that kid. He was the only son of a man whom even the serious heavy papers were beginning to mention in their financial pages as one of the decade's most successful and innovative developers. Robert was now a millionaire, on paper at least, and outwardly if nothing else he, Daniel, had all the trappings and advantages the son of such a man could expect.

What had been left of his Liverpool accent had been completely extinguished during his last two years at school; Robert paid him well for the work he did for him during the summer, as well as sending him abroad for several weeks at a time, ostensibly to see how things were being done in other countries.

He had visited Germany and France, Spain, Italy, and, most recently, America and Canada.

In addition to his grant Robert paid him a generous allowance, and provided him with a car; the British racing green Morgan Robert had given him for his twenty-first birthday to replace the one he'd given him at seventeen was garaged safely at home and only used during the summer months. Now, with them well into the autumn term, Daniel was driving the small BMW which had originally been his mother's, but which had been passed on to him when Robert had bought her a new one.

All in all he was in a very fortunate position, but no more fortunate than many of his fellow graduates. Alcester had a growing reputation as a small but good university, not of Oxford's standard, of course, and not for those destined to grace the computer industry—for them there was Cambridge—but Alcester was spoken of in academic circles as a university with more than its fair share of upper- and upper-middle-class students.

No, there was no reason at all for him to feel either guilty or uncomfortable about his financial security. Scott received a very generous allowance from his father, and he expected that this girl did too, for all that she was looking at him with all the contempt of a newly converted communist for a dyed-in-the-wool capitalist.

'I really wanted a cup of coffee,' she was saying to Scott now, holding on to his arm, and staring defiantly at Daniel.

Possessive as well as passionate, he reflected idly, smiling back at her.

'The Crown serves coffee,' he assured her dulcetly, pretending to be unaware of the real reason she had chosen to object to his suggestion.

He could see that she was half inclined to argue, and was cynically amused that she should have so little understanding of her lover's temperament. Didn't she realise how much Scott liked peace and harmony in his life? Of all men, he was the least likely to appreciate the tantrums and fireworks which he guessed she was more than capable of exhibiting.

He marvelled inwardly at her ignorance and self-conceit that she should think that it was simply enough for her to love Scott and for him to love her in return.

She was so arrogant, this untamed, tempestuous child who looked at him with her angry defiant eyes that told him she wanted Scott to herself. So arrogant and so potentially vulnerable. Couldn't she see that ultimately Scott would turn away from her, that he would tire, not of her, but of her restless moods and her emotional highs and lows?

When she eventually became a woman she would need a man who challenged her; led her, matched her and evoked the deepest intensity of her passion.

She would find none of those things with Scott, and when she eventually made that discovery she would be the one to be the more badly hurt, he recognised. Scott's very temperament would protect him always from the highs and lows of emotions which would torment her.

He stepped back to allow her to precede him as they changed direction and headed for the pub, Scott apparently sublimely unaware of the tension crackling between them as he talked enthusiastically to Daniel about a lecture he had recently attended.

Though he listened to Scott, it was Sage on whom his attention was fixed. She moved like a young colt, he thought wryly, all jerky, uncoordinated movements which curiously had their own peculiar grace. As they passed people turned their heads to look at them. To look at her.

She was not beautiful in the strictest sense, but there was something about her: a clear message composed of sensuality, vulnerability, danger and that air of wildness that had first struck him. Temptation to any man, a dangerous temptation arousing his instinctive need to stalk and hunt, to capture and tame... He had never seen a woman who aroused his most basic male instincts as this one did, he acknowledged, finding the knowledge both amusing and enlightening.

He wondered what she was like in bed, and didn't even apologise to Scott in his mind for doing so. This was a woman whom no man could look at without asking himself that question. And yet there was nothing about her that was overtly sexual. No contrived come-ons, or deliberate underlining of her sexuality. Rather she almost seemed ashamed of it, and angered by it. Was that why she had chosen Scott—was she perhaps secretly afraid of what might happen to her if she allowed herself to want a man who matched her passion for passion, need for need, desire for desire...?

With Scott, all that was wanton and reckless within her would be safely damped down, cooled and controlled, because Scott's was not a nature that would ever reach those haunting and tormenting heights and depths of intensity. Scott would never know the almost divine sensation, the almost too painfully heightened state of awareness of self and oneness that came from such passion, and neither, mercifully, would he ever know the depths of degradation it could drag its victims down into.

But she would know those things, maybe already did, for all that she looked so clean and scrubbed, so fresh, and in some odd way almost innocent. Until one looked into those Lilith-given eyes and at that violently passionate mouth.

He wanted her, Daniel recognised. He had seen her, known her for only five minutes and yet it was more than long enough for him to recognise what was causing the deep gut-ache burning his body.

That wanting both amused and amazed him. She was not his type—too turbulent, too troublesome, too much like hard work. He liked his women sleek and complaisant, and he made no apology for doing so.

When the time eventually came for him to find a wife and settle down, it wouldn't be passion that motivated him. That was something he had already decided. He had seen what passion brought, how it destroyed and maimed. John Ryan must have loved his mother once, must perhaps also have sensed that she did not love him, must have found himself caught in a trap that constantly chafed at him. It had made him violent...abusive...

He might not be John Ryan's natural son, but he was deeply conscious of the effects of witnessing such behaviour, of the seeds of destruction it might have sown within himself... Given the same kind of circumstances, put in a situation where he loved too much and was not loved in return, might not he too resort to violence, to the social conditioning of his early years? It wasn't a risk he was prepared to take. He would marry—he had no roving bachelor instincts; he enjoyed sex but he also enjoyed cerebral foreplay just as much as physical. When he married it would be to a woman he could respect and who would respect him in return. Perhaps there would always be between them the kind of distance that came when two people married for reasons that were sensible rather than passionate, but they would have a good life together; a home, children, security... and in the meantime he satisfied the sexual hunger of his body with relationships designed to give both him and his partner pleasure without any emotional pain.

This woman would never in a thousand years understand any of that. She would be as rapacious as a famine and twice as deadly. She would want everything a man had to give and then some more. She would demand his exclusive attention, his total concentration, and she would probably drive him out of his mind into the bargain.

And despite knowing all that, Daniel recognised as he held open the pub door for her, right now, standing within two feet of her, breathing in the female scents of her skin and hair, he would take every risk there was simply out of his need to take her to his bed, and make love to her until those feral green eyes no longer glowered at him, but grew huge and soft with satiation, until her body tensed in sexual ecstasy beneath his, until she cried out his name in anger and passion, until he had made her want him with the same intensity with which he wanted her.

Luckily, he was experienced enough to conceal what he was thinking from her and from Scott.

It shocked him a little that he should so easily and so casually dismiss the claims of loyalty to his younger friend. He had never been the type to take pleasure or find a thrill in poaching on other men's preserves, especially when those men were his friends. Besides, there had never been any need. Daniel was the kind of man to whom women were instinctively attracted. So much so, that he had long ago developed a method of deflecting them without hurting or damaging them.

He liked women, but not this one... He didn't like her, and she most certainly did not like him. Sardonically he wondered how long it would take her to recognise that beneath her antipathy towards him ran this sexual awareness and need. And, when she did, whether she would admit it even to herself.

He was not an unkind man; she couldn't be much over eighteen, but he doubted that Scott was her first lover. A girl like that would have matured early, become aware of her own potent sexuality early. Unless she had been immured in a convent for the last four years, he doubted that she could have been an innocent untried virgin when she came to Scott's bed, and yet curiously she seemed not to recognise, as he would have thought a woman with any sexual experience would have recognised, that beneath the surface of her antagonism and his bland response to it lay this deeper, darker vein of emotion.

He deliberately kept them both in the pub with him for longer than he had intended, insisting on buying them lunch, and then suppressing the laughter that sprang to his eyes as she looked at him as though she wanted to rake her nails down his face, or throw her unwanted lunch at him.

Scott, oblivious to all this, was genuinely pleased to have his company, and he felt the first sharp spiralling of irritation with his friend. If he didn't watch out he was very quickly going to lose his girlfriend—other men wouldn't be as reluctant to take her from him as he was.

Or would it after all be so easy? he wondered, frowning as he saw the almost desperate way Sage had pulled her chair closer to Scott's, nestling up against him as though he was her only protection, her only security, in a world which terrified her. Sage, terrified... Impossible—she wasn't the type, and yet for a moment he had glimpsed something vulnerable and afraid in her eyes as she looked at her lover.

Observing them, he recognised how reluctant she was to so much as allow Scott out of her sight... how her whole face lit up when he came back to her side after going to the bar... how she forcibly had to stop herself from reaching out and touching him... how the whole of her fiery pride and arrogance became tamed and dimmed when she looked at the young Australian.

It was almost as though he had alone satisfied some deep psychological need within her, as though Scott and only Scott could complete her and make her whole, as though she herself felt that without him her life had no pivot on which it could turn, as though without him she was only a shadow of reality...

To recognise in someone else that depth of insecurity, that level of dependence, made his frown deepen. For the first time he wondered about her background, about her life, about what had shaped and moulded her to give rise to those vulnerabilities, and why in someone like Scott she should apparently have found the antidote to them.

He needed, he discovered, to know more about her... Much, much more.

He waited until he could get Scott on his own. The younger man had been commenting that he was not entirely happy with his room, and although in the past Daniel had been wholly against inviting another student to share with him, not even allowing his lovers to move into the small house, he invited Scott round one evening, with the suggestion that since he had a bedroom to spare Scott might like to consider moving in with him.

It was the evening they attended their debating society. Scott had thanked him eagerly, and then added a little uncomfortably, 'I mustn't stay too long, though. I promised I'd see Sage later...'

'Possessive, is she?' Daniel asked him, already knowing the answer. 'Careful, Scott, possessive women can be the very devil. Even ones as attractive as Sage. If you'll take my advice you'll tread warily there—she's a very turbulent lady.'

'She...she hasn't had an entirely happy home life,' Scott countered quickly. 'It makes her prickly and defensive, but underneath...underneath she's the sweetest girl really.'

Sweet... Daniel wondered how on earth Scott could deceive himself. Sage was pure gall and brimstone—the only sweetness about her was the aftertaste you got from drinking poison.

When he deliberately kept Scott longer than the younger man had intended he told himself that he was in reality doing them both a favour; that Sage would have to learn sooner or later that everything in life couldn't run her way. Despite Scott's claims that she had had an unhappy childhood Daniel still perceived her as an indulged, cosseted child who had never known either emotional or material hardship or paucity.

When Scott moved in with him, he waited half impatiently, half cynically—the latter emotion directed at himself for his almost obsessive interest in her—to see how Sage would react.

They had met several times now, meetings carefully stage-managed by him although neither she nor Scott was aware of it, and Daniel knew that she resented his influence over Scott.

She wanted Scott to be all in all to her and she to him, Daniel recognised, but Scott did not have her passionate nature, her fierce possessive desire, and he doubted that the romance would last. When it eventually did end... He frowned to himself—Scott was his friend, but Sage, he was beginning to recognise, was a woman he desired with an intensity he could rarely remember ever feeling before.

One weekend at the beginning of the third term she took Scott home with her to introduce him to Cottingdean. When they came back Scott talked enthu-

siastically of her home and her mother. 'A truly wonderful woman, although she and Sage don't seem able
to get on... A pity—she's so very special in some way...'

Daniel watched him. Surely Scott wasn't falling out
of love with Sage to fall in love with her mother? He
could well believe that any woman who had produced
Sage must be both beautiful and strong, and Scott, who
had never had a mother, could be fatally attracted to
that kind of woman.

'Does she have red hair?' he asked Scott flippantly.
The latter shook his head.

'No, she's blonde. We were lucky to find her at home.
She'd just come back from Hong Kong. She's been out
there selling the wool they make. It's unbelievable really
what she's achieved, and all through her own endea-
vours. By all accounts Sage's father has been an invalid
all through their marriage.'

'Not that much of an invalid if he managed to father
Sage,' Daniel pointed out drily.

Scott shook his head.

'No, no, he didn't... Sage did have a brother, ten years
older than her, but he died when she was in her last year
at school. He was killed in an accident, but Sage told
me herself that she was conceived through artificial insemination. Sage doesn't say much about it—understandably she's a little sensitive on the subject. She says
she feels that her father has never really accepted her,
never really considered her his child...'

Daniel frowned, wondering irritably if Scott was aware
of how much Sage would resent him passing on her confidences, how very hurt she would be if she knew he had
shared her secret with someone else, and then he reminded himself that it was not his role to protect the
woman—that she was perfectly capable of doing that
for herself.

It had piqued him a little that Sage never called at the
house, that she always arranged to meet Scott outside
it. What he did know, though, was that Scott never spent
the night with her. He tried to visualise himself, if he

was her lover, leaving her alone in her bed, to return to sleep alone in his own, and failed.

If he was her lover... but he wasn't. She loved Scott... or thought she did.

Four days after Scott and Sage returned from their visit to her family home, Scott received a telegram from Australia, announcing that an emergency on the sheep station meant that he would have to return home almost immediately.

Daniel had always known that for Scott it was not necessary that he obtain his degree, that his time in England was more a mind-broadening exercise than anything else, and as he waited while Scott put a call through to his home to find out exactly what had happened he wondered if Scott had thought yet about how Sage was likely to react to his departure.

Infuriatingly for Scott, his telephone call yielded very little extra information. His father's housekeeper could tell him very little other than that the foreman had had a heart attack and that he was at present in hospital undergoing tests. All she could tell him was that his father expected him to make his return just as soon as he could, since in the foreman's enforced absence Scott was needed to take over the running of the vast sheep station.

It was a role Scott had been bred for from birth, and one which held no fears for him—he was more than content to follow in his father's footsteps, but now, as he promised he would be on the first flight he could arrange and replaced the receiver, Daniel asked him quietly, 'What about Sage?'

'Sage...'

For a moment it was almost as though Scott had forgotten who she was, and then he frowned anxiously. 'I'll have to tell her, of course. I must go round and see her... She'll understand... I wish I could take her back with me, but...'

Sage, living in the vast Australian outback... Daniel wondered if either of them had ever given any real thought to the future. Sage was too brittle, too fine-drawn, too short of any inner resources to sustain her

to be able to endure the loneliness of that kind of life.
If she married Scott and went out to Australia with him
she would leave him within a year.

And as for Scott... Did Sage really think he would
be happy living here in this country, when all his life he
had known he must one day step into his father's shoes?
Must and wanted to. They said that love was blind...
Blind and self-destructive in Sage's case, and Daniel was
nearly sure that although Scott did undoubtedly love her,
it was not with the single-minded, passionate, blind
intensity with which she loved him.

'I'll go and see her now,' Scott announced.

Daniel listened as Scott drove off in his MG. Scott
had a generous father, but perhaps a possessive
one... certainly a determined one. The kind of father
who would have clear-cut, definite ideas about the kind
of girl he wanted his son to marry, and he doubted if
that girl bore any resemblance to Sage.

When midnight came and went and Scott hadn't returned, Daniel looked up from the book he was studying
and frowned. It had been eight o'clock when Scott left—
four hours was surely long enough for him to have made
his explanations and say his goodbyes, no doubt adding
to them promises that he would quickly return, that Sage
would be constantly in his thoughts and his heart during
their enforced separation.

At one o'clock, just as he was about to go to bed, the
phone rang. When he picked up the receiver, he could
hear Sage on the other end of the line, hysterically crying
his name.

It took him several precious minutes to calm her down
enough to find out what had happened. When he did,
he felt his heart plummet with despair and guilt.

'Which hospital is it?' he demanded brusquely, and
when she told him he added, 'Stay there. I'll be there as
fast as I can.'

As he climbed into his own car, he prayed that matters
weren't as serious as they seemed. From what Sage had
said to him, they had gone out for a drive—perhaps Scott
had decided to explain to her that he was leaving some-

where where they could be on their own. He had no idea.

What she had told him was that they had quarrelled, that she had been angry...angry enough to distract Scott to the extent that he had failed to see the oncoming car which had run into them; a car apparently driven by a drunken driver—a now dead drunken driver.

Sage herself had hardly been hurt—scratched, bruised, and frightened out of her wits, Daniel had deduced. But Scott...Scott was in a coma and the hospital staff were asking her for the name of his next of kin.

It took Daniel less than half an hour to sort everything out. He explained to the nursing staff about Scott's father being in Australia and gave them Scott's father's telephone number and address, having discovered that Scott had luckily doodled it down on the pad beside the phone while waiting for his Australian call.

When the doctor told Sage that there was no need for her to stay and that she could go home, she practically had hysterics, crying and pleading to be allowed to stay, but the doctor remained adamant.

It was Daniel who was left with the task of half carrying and half dragging her away, of manhandling her into his BMW and then swiftly locking the doors as she tried desperately to claw at the handle and get out.

His decision to take her home to his own house instead of dropping her off at the hall of residence was based more on a reluctance to cope with any more hysterics and explanations than any carnal thoughts about proximity and propinquity.

Getting her to take the tranquilliser the doctor had handed him meant virtually forcing it down her throat, which he did as quickly and efficiently as he had once had to feed worming tablets to his puppy, holding her jaw tightly closed, and massaging her throat until he felt her swallow—and all the time she was watching him with wild green eyes blazing her bitterness and hatred.

He carried her upstairs to Scott's bedroom and dropped her body on the bed, warning her that all the doors downstairs were locked and that he had the keys—

but in the morning when he searched for her he discovered that she had gone...out of one of the downstairs windows.

After that he didn't see her again for some days even though he called regularly at the hospital to see Scott, who was still distressingly deep in his coma.

His father had flown in almost immediately on hearing about his son's accident, and when Daniel asked about Sage Scott's father told him quietly, 'I've told the doctors that I can't see her.'

'Can't see her.' Daniel wondered why 'can't' and not 'won't' but he knew better than to question the Australian.

Scott's father was a tall, still dark-haired man with green eyes and tanned skin moulded round facial bones which were sharply pared to the kind of austerity that hinted that there had been a good deal of suffering in his life. He was a remote man, Daniel recognised. A man who had suffered greatly at some time in his life. Oddly he looked as though he could possibly be a very compassionate man but he obviously had no compassion for Sage. Did he blame her for the accident? Daniel wondered.

'If you see her, please tell her also that she isn't to come and see Scott. The doctors feel it would do little good.'

If he saw her...that was hardly likely, Daniel reflected, and yet oddly that very night when he opened his front door to an unexpected caller he discovered that it was Sage.

She looked hauntingly pale and too thin, so fragile that she almost took his breath away. Her eyes had lost their fire and become flat discs of banked-down pain.

Even the wild fieriness of her hair seemed tamed somehow and subdued.

'Sage...' He stepped back to allow her to come in.

'They won't let me see Scott,' she told him, almost wringing her hands, her voice thick with suppressed tears and anguish. 'I must see him, Daniel... I must see him... I love him. He loves me...' Her voice had started to rise. Daniel caught hold of her arm and guided her into his small sitting-room, pushing her gently into a chair.

'Scott is a very sick man, Sage,' he told her quietly. 'Surely the most important thing of all is for him to get properly well? His father believes that this can be best accomplished in his own home. He's flying back to Australia and with the doctor's agreement Scott is going with him.'

'No!'

The denial was ripped from her throat, the frantic wild sound of an animal caught in a trap. It hurt his ears and savaged his senses, but he couldn't allow himself the luxury of those emotions.

'Yes, Sage,' he repeated firmly. 'And I'm afraid there's nothing you can do about it.'

'It's your fault...all your fault,' she suddenly cried out, beating at his chest with her fists. 'You wanted this to happen...you wanted to break us up.'

For a moment Daniel thought she was actually going to say that she knew that he wanted her, and he braced himself to reject her accusations even while he knew it was true. He had wanted her. Still wanted her...but never at the price of Scott's accident and this terrible grief that was now possessing her. But instead she said furiously, 'You've never liked me... I knew that right from the start—you've never thought I was right for Scott.'

'No, I haven't,' Daniel agreed truthfully. 'But that doesn't mean that I've ever tried to break you up. Scott is a man, Sage, not a boy. He makes his own decisions.'

'Not now, he doesn't... It's his father who's insisting that he must go back to Australia... If only I could see Scott. Get him to come out of his coma and respond to me.'

'You can't,' Daniel told her flatly. 'His condition is still far from stable. Life goes on, you know,' he counselled her. 'You'll see——'

'No,' she denied fiercely. 'Without Scott I have no life...without him I have nothing... I am nothing.'

Her words shocked him, but he hid both his shock and his compassion behind his next cynical question.

'You see him as your soul mate, is that it?'

'Yes...no...' Her voice sounded harsh, drugged, her eyes flat and unseeing. 'Not my soul mate,' she told him jerkily. 'He *is* my soul itself, my other half...he is a part of me and without him I cannot exist... Don't you understand?'

Daniel stared at her, curiously moved by her passionate outburst, feeling against his will a helpless compassion for her in her agony and her ignorance.

Strange, when he had always known she would be capable of intense physical passion, that he had not realised she would be capable of equally explosive emotional passion as well, but then men never wanted to meet danger head on...to heed such inner warnings.

'It's over, Sage,' he told her softly. 'And the sooner you accept that, the easier your life will be.'

'No!' she screamed at him. 'No, it isn't over. It can never be over, not while either of us lives... He loves me...I love him...'

'No, Sage,' he corrected her. 'You love yourself. You want him as a greedy child wants a new toy, and in your wanting you've almost destroyed him... It was your temper that provoked the accident, your refusal to accept that he had to return to Australia.'

She stared at him.

'I'm right, aren't I? That was how it happened. You refused to accept that he had to go and in his attempts to placate you and make you understand he lost his concentration...and almost lost his life. Let him go, Sage, before you destroy him completely.'

She had flown at him then, attacking him with her fists and then her nails, tears pouring from her eyes as she screamed her anguish and defiance, but he had held her off until finally, frightened that she might actually hurt herself, he had yanked her into his arms and bound her so tightly to him that he could actually feel the frantic race of her heart as though it were beating within his own chest.

She was so thin, so fragile...and yet her breasts still so surprisingly voluptuous that his body was suddenly intensely aware of her and aroused by her.

Battling against his own conflicting feelings—those of man the primitive ruled by his most basic hungers, and those of man the thinker, the product of millenia of civilisation who had learned to tame and control those hungers and to put other things before them—he held her off from his body, but already it was too late, already he could see the mixed emotions of fury and outrage mingling in her eyes with her recognition of his reaction to her.

'Traitor.'

Did she actually spit the word at him, or was he simply imagining it? he wondered ruefully as he held her firmly a safe distance away from his unruly flesh and spoke to her levelly and calmly. 'Sage——'

'I'm not letting him go...I love him.'

'Yes,' Daniel heard himself agreeing, 'but you're not sure that he loves you with the same intensity, are you, Sage?'

He didn't know what made him say it. Scott had never said anything to him to imply that his feelings for her were not just as strong as hers for him. True, Scott's was a different nature, calmer, less passionate, less intense, but Daniel had never doubted the strength of the younger man's feelings, and yet when Sage went limp in his arms, her face suddenly ashen, her mouth trembling with a vulnerability he had cut too deep for her to hide, he realised bleakly that his chance remark had touched a sore spot, an Achilles' heel which he had never known existed.

'He does love me. He does...'

She said it like a little girl, the rage, the passion suddenly all gone from her, leaving in its place such an open expanse of self-doubt and fear that Daniel felt his heart turn over inside his chest in compassion and an odd, inexplicable anger, directed not just at her for that vulnerability, but at all those people in her life who had undermined that magnificent pride and arrogance and taught her instead to feel pain and anguish.

'She has always felt that to her parents, especially her father, she's a poor second best,' Scott had once told him, and he had been amused and a little scornful, refusing to accept that she had ever believed any such thing, comparing the luxury of her childhood with the paucity of his own, her imagined lack of paternal love with his very real one—but now, abruptly, he wasn't so sure.

What he was sure of was that he had an overwhelming longing to take hold of her and hold on to her, to keep her safe and secure, to carry her away with him right now to his bed and keep her there until...

Lost in his own thoughts, he relaxed his hold on her just enough for her to break free and whirl round, heading for the door.

He had to let her go. Common sense told him that he couldn't keep her here by force, and yet as he watched her he felt in some odd way as though he had failed her. Failed *her*! Scott was his friend, not Sage. Scott had already made his decision to return home even before his accident.

At home he would receive the constant twenty-four-hour-a-day attention he needed if he was going to make a full recovery, if he was going to come successfully out of his coma. Sage couldn't give him that kind of attention. She didn't have that kind of rock-solid, slow, steady ability, she didn't have that kind of emotional strength. She was a child still in so many ways... A spoilt, pampered child, who had shown him tonight that coming from a wealthy protected background did not automatically protect that child from emotional starvation and hunger.

While Daniel was reliving the past, Sage too was remembering, shivering a little as she wondered if she was doomed always to lose those she loved the most.

First David, then Scott, and now her mother lay ill ... She stopped her thoughts abruptly and closed her eyes.

She loved her mother? How could she, when she knew that love was not returned?

For a moment she felt all the helpless anguish of a child; not *a* child, *the* child, the child she had once been, her sense of alienation enforced as she stood apart from the others at David's funeral, watching them as an outsider, knowing she *was* an outsider, an outcast, knowing that she wasn't wanted or needed. She had watched as her mother had bent over her father's chair, concern darkening her eyes. She had watched as Faye had drawn closer to her mother's side, she had watched as her brother's coffin was lowered into its grave, knowing that, if she walked away now, none of the other three would even notice she had gone.

It had been while she was in her last year at school, having taken her A levels, that David had died. Only that morning he had been talking to her, soothing her after her latest row with her mother. It was such a needless, wasteful, cruel death. She had often wondered how her mother had found the strength to bear it. Had David been *her* child... She shuddered, acknowledging that it was perhaps in David's death that the seeds of her own reluctance to conceive lay, her fear that she could never cope as her mother had done with the death of so dearly loved a child—and her mother had loved David, far, far more than she had ever loved her.

By one of those odd quirks of fate they had all been together when the news came. Sage had been home from school and Faye and David had been visiting them with Camilla, who had only been a baby at the time. Sage remembered the jealousy she had felt when she saw David's obvious devotion to Faye and their child.

David had had a meeting to attend, something connected with the parish council. He wouldn't be long, he had said, and then he had gone.

Less than an hour later the police had arrived to tell them that there had been an accident; that David had swerved to avoid hitting a child, who had been riding a bike out into the road without looking first, but that as he'd swerved he had lost control of the car which had crashed, killing him on impact.

They had all been in her mother's sitting-room. Her father had been having one of his rare good days. Sage remembered that she had automatically looked first at her mother and then at her father.

Her mother's expression had been calm, controlled— but her father's...

She remembered how she had got up from her chair and run to him, wanting to share his grief, wanting to hold him and be held as she gave way to her own. But as she reached him he had pushed her away with so much force that she had fallen, striking her shoulder on the edge of her mother's desk.

'Get out of here...get out!' he screamed at her. 'Oh, my God, why did it have to be David? It should have been you...it should have been you,' he had told her, and his voice had been full of rage and loathing.

It had been worse than if he had physically hit her, far, far worse. She remembered how she had fought back her tears. She had always known that he preferred David, of course, but to hear it said, to see how great the gulf between his love for David and his lack of love for her actually had been cruelly underlined...

She could remember as though it had just happened the throbbing pain in her shoulder, and the tearing, agonising pain she could feel inside.

She remembered her mother coming towards her, taking hold of her arm. She remembered how she had pulled away, white-faced and sick, as her mother had quickly bustled her out of the room.

Her mother had been still dry-eyed and calm-faced. 'Go up to your room,' she had told Sage. 'I'll deal with your father...'

She had paused as though she was about to add something but Sage hadn't let her, bursting out, 'Oh, yes, send me to my room, get rid of me...after all, you don't want me, do you, any of you? I'm not your precious David... Well, I don't want you either...any of you.

You all wish it was me who was dead and not David. Well, I don't care... I don't care...'

But she had cared, of course—she had cared terribly, achingly, devastatingly.

Later Chivers had brought her some tea. She could tell that he had been crying.

'Your mother said you was to stay up here for a while, Miss Sage,' he told her uncomfortably. 'She's sent for the doctor... Major Danvers...'

Sage had stopped listening. She didn't want to hear about her father, didn't want to know... Just as he didn't want to know about her...

Upstairs alone in her room, she had cried for her brother and for herself, and she had vowed that one day there would be someone in her life who would love her, truly love her.

The funeral had been a nightmare. Faye had collapsed completely, utterly devastated by David's death. Her father looked so ill that Sage was surprised their doctor allowed him to attend the funeral.

Only her mother had appeared unaffected, standing dry-eyed at the graveside, and then later back at the house, moving with composure among the mourners.

After they had gone, after it was all over and Faye had been put to bed, heavily sedated, and her father had shut himself up in his study, she remembered she had screamed at her mother, 'David belonged to me too, you know... He was my brother, *my* brother. And he was the only person in this house who ever gave a damn about me.'

She had told herself that she was glad she was going away to university. That she didn't care if she never saw Cottingdean again—and then six weeks after David's death her father became seriously ill and took to his bed.

His health had always been frail, but after David's death it was as though he had lost the will to go on.

Once again her mother had been composed and capable. Sage was the one who had stood outside his bedroom door with tears pouring down her face, crying out to him in her heart to ask why it was that he had never allowed her to love him, never allowed her to get close to him, that he had always rejected and disliked her. Not expecting that she would ever know the answers to those questions, ever know what it was within her that made those who should have been the closest to her turn from her. One short year after David's death, the expected happened—Edward passed away peacefully in the night.

Faye and Camilla had now been living permanently at Cottingdean. She had felt more alien and unwanted there than ever. She had been glad that she was going away to university. Cottingdean held nothing for her now. Her mother was a stranger to her; a stranger whom she neither liked nor loved, or so she had told herself then.

She got up and prowled restlessly round the room. And yet despite that she had taken Scott home here to Cottingdean... But that was because he had been curious about the house, because he had wanted to see it.

She remembered that she had deliberately chosen a weekend when she had thought her mother would be away on business, only when she and Scott got here she discovered that her mother's business trip had been completed early.

Naturally her mother had not shown either anger or surprise that she should choose to bring a visitor home when she was not there. She had welcomed Scott and quickly put him as his ease.

She had also made sure that the guest-room given him was well away from her own, Sage remembered wryly.

Scott had quickly fallen under her mother's spell. She had been jealously conscious of how well the two of them were getting on together, of how eagerly Scott responded to her mother's interest in him.

Jealous and protective of her burgeoning love, she had told her mother as little as she could about him, leaving it to Scott to explain that his father had sent him to England to get what he termed 'some polish'.

'McLaren,' her mother had repeated when Scott told her his surname, causing Scott to hesitate and explain,

'Yes...my forebears were from Scotland, I believe.'

'Yes, yes, they would have been.'

After that, or so it seemed to Sage, her mother had virtually monopolised Scott's time, so that Sage had never been able to be alone with him, and to her irritation and jealousy Scott had seemed to be quite happy with the situation, only too pleased to answer all her mother's questions about his life at home.

'Look, why don't the two of you come out and see the station for yourselves? I'll leave you the address and number,' he had suggested.

Sage had told him scornfully, 'The last place on earth Mother would want to go is an outback sheep station, isn't it, Mother?' she had challenged.

She had been jealous, she had realised later, jealous of her mother... jealous of the way she had so quickly and easily charmed Scott, Scott who was hers, hers and hers alone.

She could have sworn that her mother liked Scott, and yet she had been the one to get in touch with Scott's father, and to put in train the events which had eventually led to her and Scott being parted. She had hated her mother for that, especially when she had discovered the truth: that her mother had actually telephoned Scott's father to warn him that the relationship developing between their two offspring was one that neither of them would find advantageous.

She had thought then that it was because her mother had wanted a very different kind of marriage for her that she had interfered, and she had decided that, no matter what else she did with her life, she would never, ever marry a man chosen for her by her mother.

When she had accused her mother of deliberately setting out to break up her relationship with Scott, she had not denied it, simply saying that she believed she had acted in Sage's best interests.

'I'm a woman, not a child,' Sage had answered bitterly. 'I love him.'

'You love him now or at least you think you do,' her mother had told her quietly, but she had gone very pale, and looked unusually strained. 'But he isn't the man for you, Sage. Marriage to you would destroy him,' she had told her cruelly. 'Is that what you want? He needs someone gentler, calmer...'

'How do you know what he wants or needs?' Sage had demanded, white-faced. 'You know nothing about him!'

'And you do? Sage, as always you see only what you want to see. You need a much stronger man to make you happy.'

'To keep me under control, don't you mean? I'll never forgive you for what you've done,' she had told her. 'Never...never...and if you think I'm going to marry the oh, so suitable Jonathon——'

'Marry Jonathon,' her mother had repeated, and she had laughed then, infuriating Sage. 'My dear, if you could persuade Jonathon to marry you, you would be a very fortunate young woman indeed, but I suspect he has far too much sense for that, and that he'll find himself a dutiful, biddable wife whom his mother will boss around, poor girl.'

But Sage hadn't believed her—she knew her mother and her Machiavellian mind, or at least she had thought she had.

Her mother had been out of the country again on business when Scott had had his accident. She had obviously taken to Scott, because even in the depths of her own anguish Sage could remember how her mother had questioned her about what had happened, about Scott's chances of recovery. 'Why not ring Scott's father and ask him?' she had challenged bitterly. 'Just as you did when you rang him to get him to drag Scott home and away from me. How did you get him to do that, Mother? Did you use some of your famous charm or did you simply tell him a sheep station owner's son simply wasn't good enough for a Danvers?'

'Don't be ridiculous,' her mother had answered coolly, refusing to discuss the subject.

And yet at the same time—when Scott had gone back to Australia and she, losing the will to do anything other than lock herself away in her room in her hall of residence, huddling under the bedclothes, not eating, not sleeping, not doing anything other than longing for Scott—it had been her mother, alerted by Daniel to what was going on, who had taken her home to Cottingdean, and who had kept her there until her pride, outraged by the knowledge that her mother, her enemy was witnessing her weakness, had forced her to take control of her life again, to build for herself a mask behind which she could hide her pain.

She had gone back to university at the start of the academic year, determined to catch up on her studies and determined, too, that no one, *no one*, would ever hurt her through her vulnerability again, that never again would she allow herself to care so deeply for anyone that they could hurt her.

She had also gone back to university determined to get her Arts degree and to make herself independent from her mother, to cut herself off from her and shut her out of her life, so that never, ever again could she interfere in it the way she had done over Scott. Daniel by this time had left Alcester, and she had felt relieved that she did not have to see him again.

Sage had pushed to the far reaches of her mind her last confrontation scene with Daniel. The wounds from that encounter were still too raw for her to want to risk opening them again by any further contact with Scott's so-called 'friend'.

CHAPTER SIXTEEN

DANIEL hadn't in fact seen Sage again for some days after their last disastrous meeting and it was a telephone call from the hospital that alerted him to what she was doing.

He frowned as he listened to the message he was given, and then, picking up his jacket and his keys, headed for his car.

He felt sorry for her, and wondered a little at what manner of man Scott's father was, not to allow her these last few hours with his son.

As far as he knew he was the only one who had guessed that it was her temper that had provoked the accident; he could well understand that Lewis McLaren would want to take his son home, that he might not particularly have wanted his son and heir falling in love with an unknown English girl, but to banish her from Scott's bedside, especially when within a very short space of time he would be putting so many thousands upon thousands of miles between them anyway, seemed unnecessarily cruel.

The sister who had rung from the hospital had explained to him that Sage was positively haunting the place, that she had begged and pleaded with them to be allowed to see Scott, even though she knew he was still in a coma and unlikely to respond to her.

They had apparently had to remove her forcibly several times but even this hadn't deterred her, and now it seemed the hospital staff were becoming concerned for her health.

Knowing from his visits that he, Daniel, was one of Scott's closest friends, they were appealing to him in the hope that he would be able to make Sage see reason.

Scott's father had made it plain that Sage was not to be allowed to see his son and, since Scott could not speak for himself as yet, the older man's wishes had to be obeyed.

There had been an accident in the high street—a lorry had overturned disgorging its load. Luckily no one had been hurt, but there was a considerable delay to the traffic, causing Daniel to reflect as he waited for the congestion to clear that with the projected increase in road traffic, the majority of Britain's small towns, with their narrow streets, would encounter severe congestion problems, which would eventually result in a good deal of replanning and new roads. Good news for companies like his father's . . . good news ultimately for him as well.

Eventually the road cleared and he was able to get through but it had taken him longer to reach the hospital than he had anticipated and he half expected to discover that Sage had gone.

He went straight to the ward, where the sister, a pretty and very efficient-looking girl in her mid-twenties, gave him a warm smile and explained that Sage was in the waiting-room.

'And Scott?' Daniel asked her.

She shook her head.

'He's still in a coma...there have been occasional signs that he's starting to come out of it . . . His father's very anxious to get him home. In fact he's made arrangements for them both to leave tomorrow... He's chartered a specially equipped plane...' Her eyebrows rose. 'Nice if you can afford it.'

Acting on impulse, Daniel asked quietly, 'I don't suppose there's any chance of Sage seeing him, just for a few minutes? After all, if he's leaving so soon...'

The ward sister looked at him.

'Well, it does seem as though Mr McLaren has relented. He has said that she can have five minutes with him but that a nurse must be in attendance. Only five minutes, mind, and it might be an idea if you could accompany her.'

Thanking her, Daniel headed for the swing doors and the corridor. He found Sage sitting alone in an airless, depressing cube of a room with no windows, furnished basically with several chairs and a table heaped high with out-of-date magazines.

When he walked in she was staring blankly at the wall. His heart somersaulted and then stood still. He had never seen such a dramatic change in anyone.

All the life, all the colour seemed to have drained out of her. She had lost more weight...too much—where she had been slender she was now haggard. She raised one hand defensively to her face as she saw him and he was shocked by the thinness of her wrist. He suspected he could have circled it easily with his thumb and forefinger.

She was dressed all in black, whether deliberately or by accident he had no way of knowing, but the sombreness of her clothes added a shockingly clown-like falsity to her appearance, as though it was impossible for anyone to actually look as intensely unhappy as she so patently was. Her suffering was all the more shocking for being so unhidden; he could well imagine how others would turn away from it, frightened or angered by its intensity. In this world it was considered self-indulgent, immoral almost to allow one's feelings to show so clearly, to the discomfort of others.

She wasn't crying, but her eyes were red-rimmed, as much from lack of sleep as anything else, he suspected, and when she looked at him they were without their usual fire, without fight, without hope...without anything, he recognised.

'Sage.'

When he said her name she focused briefly on him but with so little reaction that for a moment he actually feared that her grief might have even affected her mentally.

'Daniel. What are you doing here?' Her voice was slow and heavy, apathetic and without inflection, like someone heavily tranquillised.

'The hospital rang me...they're very concerned about you. You've got to stop doing this,' he told her when there was no response, wondering angrily where her family were, her friends. Did they know what was happening to her? They must do...and if so why weren't they doing something to help her? Or did they simply not care?

He waited for her to explode with anger and frustration, to fly at him physically and verbally as she had done before, but shockingly she stayed mute, simply looking at him with vacant, uncaring eyes until he said quietly, 'It seems that Scott's father has relented and said that you can have five minutes to say goodbye to Scott and I have to stay with you... But Sage...'

She wasn't listening. She was standing up and half walking, half running towards him, her face suddenly transformed with a happiness so brilliant, so luminescent that it was almost frightening.

He caught up with her as she reached the door, his hand closing round her arm, his mind wincing with pain as he felt its thinness.

'No scenes, Sage,' he warned her, keeping hold of her. 'Scott is very sick. He's still in a coma, so he won't recognise you. You know his father is having him flown back to Australia tomorrow?'

She nodded. Her hands suddenly twisted together as she turned to him and spoke for the first time. 'It won't make any difference. I love him and he loves me...nothing can change that. Once he's well he'll come back for me, you'll see...'

Scott was in a private room, a nurse discreetly in attendance when Daniel opened the door and ushered Sage in.

He felt the shudder that went through her as she stared at the bed. Scott was still unconscious, his body connected to a vast battery of medical equipment.

A cassette recorder was playing silently in the corner, and the nurse explained briefly, 'We're playing him messages from his father...that's why he's wearing ear-plugs.'

'Scott's father said you could have five minutes with him, Sage,' he reminded her, but if she heard him she gave no indication of having done so.

All her attention was concentrated on the bed, as she leaned over Scott, the look on her face as she gently touched his arm a mixture of youthful anguish and almost maternal love.

'How is he?' she asked the nurse without looking away from Scott.

'Still very poorly,' she told her.

'Will he...will he get better?'

'It's too early to say yet. He's very strong physically, and young. We've had patients with far more stacked against them who have made remarkable recoveries.'

There was a chair beside the bed. Daniel pulled it back a little, inviting Sage to sit in it. She did so, and he noticed how much she was trembling. She reached out over the bed, smoothing the already immaculate cover, and although he didn't know why something about the awkward, tender little gesture brought a huge lump to Daniel's throat.

He wanted to take hold of her and to go on holding her, to give her all the love, all the security he knew instinctively she craved, and the reason he knew she craved it was because he recognised within Sage the same doubts, the same vulnerabilities, the same loneliness that had so often plagued him.

And yet why should he feel like this about her? They were worlds apart in every way. Her life had been completely different from his. There had been no John Ryan in her life, no bullying cousins, no taunts, no feelings of not fitting in, of being different.

And yet still he couldn't stop his thoughts from focusing on her. Her head was bowed, her hair parting to reveal the vulnerable nape of her neck. Her skin there was white and fine, the bones of her spine far too sharp beneath her skin. The radiant vivacity that had made her such a beauty had gone and yet strangely he found her almost as desirable now as he had done before, even if now his desire was muted by compassion and concern.

Now if he were to make love to her it would be with tenderness, his possession gentle and coaxing, rather than with the fierce intensity which had burned in him before.

She was crying, he realised, watching the silent glissade of tears fall on to her hands.

The nurse coughed warningly and glanced at her watch.

Daniel touched Sage lightly on her shoulder, but before he could speak she reached down and gently removed the ear-plugs from Scott's ears and before either of them could stop her she was whispering pleadingly to him, 'Scott... please, please get well... I need you so much. You mustn't leave me... I can't live without you. Scott... Scott.'

The nurse was frowning, moving closer to the bed, and, anticipating her next action, Daniel took hold of Sage, firmly pulling her back, telling her quietly as he pulled her to her feet, 'That's enough, Sage... It's time to leave now...'

As they all moved towards the door, unobserved by any of them, the still figure in the bed made a small seeking movement, a frown furrowing his forehead as though he was searching the silence.

As they left the room Sage kept her head down, trying to conceal the fact that she was still crying. Tactfully Daniel affected not to notice, looking away from her.

There was a man standing in the shadows of the corridor watching them. Daniel's mouth compressed a little as he recognised Scott's father. He was staring at Sage... What was he doing, checking to make sure she didn't overstay her allowed five minutes? He could understand the older man's pain, but he still wasn't going to allow him to vent it on Sage, although why on earth he should feel this urge to protect her he certainly had no idea. One thing he did know, and that was that she wouldn't have thanked him for it.

She looked so ill that Daniel half expected her to faint before he could get her outside and inside his car.

He had to fasten the seatbelt for her, though. She had stopped crying, but in a brief moment of forgetfulness

he looked directly into her eyes and saw such a terrible
hell of pain and anguish there that he felt as guilty as
though he had stripped the clothes from her body and
looked openly at its nakedness.

He took her back with him to his home, as he had
the night of the accident, not knowing what else to do
with her. She wasn't the suicidal type, or at least he had
never thought of her as such, but he didn't want to leave
her alone. And besides, if he kept her under his roof
where he could keep an eye on her, it would stop her
heading back to the hospital.

He would put her in Scott's room again, he decided,
as he parked his car outside the small narrow house, and
went round to open her door for her and help her out.

The apathetic lack of reaction to him disturbed him,
and once he had got her inside, even though he told
himself it was not his business and he ought not to get
involved, he rang his own doctor, and asked him to call
round.

'She's suffering very badly from shock,' the doctor told
him three hours later. 'How long did you say it was since
the accident?'

Daniel repeated what he had already told him.

'Mmm . . . well, I've given her a tranquillising shot for
now. She'll probably sleep for twenty-four hours, which
won't do her any harm. She needs to rest and eat. The
rest we can arrange—the eating . . .'

The tranquilliser the doctor had given her did its work,
and Sage was deeply asleep when the private jet Lewis
McLaren had hired took off with its passengers. Her
body, craving sleep and a chance to restore its strength,
slept well into the next day and night.

Daniel, who had been checking on her every couple
of hours, found her awake at midnight when he went
up to look at her.

'What day is it?' she asked him, ignoring all the questions he had expected her to ask, such as, what was she
doing here in his home?

Sensing the direction of her thoughts, he told her evenly, 'It's too late, Sage. He's gone...the flight left at nine this evening.'

It was perhaps cruel of him, but sooner or later she would have to accept that Scott had gone.

'I'm just going to have some supper,' he told her casually and untruthfully. 'Fancy some?'

He saw that she was starting to shake her head and continued as though he hadn't noticed, 'It's only an omelette, but I'll bring you some up, shall I?'

She had turned her face away from him and he was reasonably sure that she was crying. Repressing a sigh, he got up off the bed and went back downstairs to make an omelette he was quite sure that neither of them were going to eat.

He put half of it on a tray, poured Sage a glass of milk, and opened the door into the sitting-room where he came to an abrupt halt.

Sage was standing there in the shadows facing him, and even though the room was only illuminated by the lamp he had been using for reading there was enough light for him to see that she had pulled on his robe without fastening it and that beneath it she was naked. Her hair was wet and starting to curl wildly—tiny droplets of moisture escaped from it, to gather at the base of her throat and run down between her breasts and over her belly to become lost in the even more tangled curls between her legs.

A suffocating heat overwhelmed him, a fierce jolting surge of need that blotted out everything else but his need to discover if the shadowed areola of flesh surrounding her nipple was the delicate clear pink he had always envisaged, if her nipples themselves really were so hard that they were pushing out the fabric of his robe or if he was just imagining it. He wanted to take hold of her and show her what she did to him, to rub his face against that tormenting triangle of damp curls and breathe in the individual woman scent of her, to slowly touch her sensitive woman flesh with his tongue and delicately explore its most intimate secrets while she trembled with a need as explosive as his own and opened herself to him, whispering to him how much she wanted him to pleasure her.

All sheer fantasy, of course. He didn't know what she had come downstairs for, but it certainly wasn't because she wanted to make love with him—and yet as he put down the tray and started to speak, she slid his robe off her shoulders and came slowly to him, her eyes fixed on his face, as though it drew her like a lodestone.

'Sage . . .'

He told himself later that he had intended to hold her off . . . that he had only wanted to talk to her, but she walked into his arms and pressed her body against his, winding her own arms around him, her voice a feathery, urgent plea against his ear as she begged,

'Make love to me, Daniel . . . Please make love to me . . . I need it so much . . .'

He forgot what he had been intending to do and could remember only how many nights he had lain alone aching for her, dreaming of her coming to him like this, wanting her so much that he had scarcely been able to admit even to himself how much he desired her.

His brain became jammed with conflicting signals, any warning it might have tried to put through brutally murdered at birth by the overwhelming need of his body.

He held her, and discovered that he was trembling like a boy with his first girl, far more apprehensive and enthralled in fact than he had ever been that first time. Her body was still half cloaked in shadow. Alluring, mysterious, a small slight upwards curve of her mouth and the dark, knowing watchfulness of her eyes holding all the enticement and promise of a Lilith.

He touched her, smoothing his hands over her skin, feeling the first magical assurance that she wasn't a phantom conjured up by his imagination, that she was actually real flesh and blood, and then letting his hands drift slowly, absorbing the texture of her skin, satin-smooth and cool, still damp in places from her shower, still and quiescent beneath his hands as though waiting for him to give it life.

He purposely didn't touch her breasts, just skimming their outer curves as he took his hands upwards to cup her shoulders and then to close them round her throat, his thumbs searching for the pulse at its base as he kissed the curve of her jaw, and felt the violent churn of sensation in his stomach as he dragged his mouth towards hers.

For what seemed like a lifetime he had wondered how she would taste, how those so full lips would feel, whether those small sharp teeth would bite frantically at him in passion, but abruptly she turned her head, her body stiffening, her withdrawal startling him.

Her sex normally enjoyed the sensuous contact of mouth upon mouth, of tongues twining and entwining, of a lover's hands stroking the soft contours of their face, of his fingers tangling in their hair, and he enjoyed it too, relishing this small act of foreplay with almost as much enjoyment as he enjoyed the physical act of possession itself.

Daniel liked women and he liked making love to them, and he knew without vanity that he was a good lover; not because he deliberately strove to be—anyone could learn such mechanics and still not be able to give and take one tenth of the pleasure shared with a partner who had an instinctive delight in, and love for, his lover's very different and wholly desirable female flesh. He liked women; liked to hear their soft sighs of pleasure, liked to feel the soft satin of their flesh against his own, liked to stroke and taste every inch of them until their own arousal was as great as his; and never had he wanted that more with any woman than he wanted it with this one.

The second time she tried to turn her face from his, he stopped her, anticipating her and sliding his hand along her jaw to hold her still so that he could slowly explore the unbearable softness of her lips. They trembled when he caressed them, causing deep shudders of need to jerk through him as he fought to hold on to his self-control and deny the ferocity of his instinctive need to lay her down on the rug where they stood and stamp his possession on her so thoroughly that no other man would ever be able to overlay its memory.

Such instincts were not commensurate with his desire to be compassionate and civilised, with his need to show her tenderness and respect.

He traced the shape of her mouth with his tongue and tried to slide between their closed softness, but she wouldn't let him. She even trembled against him as though she was afraid.

He was the one feeling fear. Fear that he wouldn't be able to match the skills of her past lovers... fear that she might after all change her mind... fear that—what— that she was using him as a substitute for Scott? Scott whom he knew she loved...?

He closed his mind to the thought, whispering to her that he wanted to take her to bed and make love to her until she cried out with the pleasure of it, telling her how much he wanted her, how much she pleased him, stroking her skin with ever-increasing urgency, kissing the smooth flesh of her throat, the sharp angle of her jaw, the unbelievable delicacy of her ears.

She trembled in his arms, her eyes closed in the shadowed half-darkness that cloaked her body.

He shuddered as he looked at it, feeling his stomach twist in knots as he gazed at the soft paleness of her skin, the firm fullness of her breasts, their areolae the deep, dark pink he had envisaged, her nipples hard, swollen.

He stared to undress, almost tearing off his clothes in a feverish sweat of anxiety not to lose her, not to let her somehow slip away from him. Every inch of her was perfect... perfect...

He wanted to shape the firm roundness of her breasts with his hands, to feel her breathing quicken so that her body lifted urgently against him and with it the taut hardness of her nipples pulse as he lapped them softly with his tongue, delicately laving them with its moistness until she cried out and held his head to her, urgently begging him to suckle at them and rake them with his teeth as her passion caught fire from his.

He ignored the message from his brain that something was wrong, that she was too still, too tense, too unaroused, that she was not sharing his need. It was too sudden, too unexpected; she was not motivated by desire. Nor even by lust; the coldness of her skin reflected the coldness of her desire, and it was this inner and outer chill that was responsible for the erect stiffness of her nipples, just as it was responsible for the rash of goose-bumps he could feel beneath her skin.

He didn't want to listen to such cerebral arguments; he wanted...

He groaned out loud as he threw off the last of his clothes. In the darkness he saw her eyes flicker and felt a fierce elemental stab of male pride. His body was so different from hers, his skin tanned from his last stint on one of his father's building sites, hard and calloused still in places, his torso covered in thick, fine dark hair, his belly hard and flat where hers was soft and gently rounded, his arms roped with sinewy muscles, rough with dark hair where hers were soft and white...and too thin. His heart gave a painful jolt. Despite the voluptuousness of her breasts, the femininity of her curves, he was suddenly conscious of her fragility—his hands could easily, too easily span her waist. On an impulse he didn't try to decipher he bent his head and dropped a light kiss on the soft flesh just above her navel, and while she quivered wildly in reaction to it he picked her up and turned towards the door.

'No...' Her voice was surprisingly strong, almost harshly so, stopping him.

'It's all right,' he told her softly. 'I'm not going to hurt you. I only want to carry you upstairs. We'll be more comfortable in my bed.'

'No.' This time the denial was almost guttural. 'No, not upstairs. Here...now...'

'Now.'

He stared at her and then slowly released her as he looked round the shadowed room. Funny child—she deserved to be humoured, though...and then later, when she was less on edge, more relaxed with him, then he would take her upstairs...

He smiled to himself, anticipating the pleasure they would share, slowly leaning towards her, pushing the half dry and tangled cloud of hair back off her face and dragging his open mouth against her skin, savouring its texture and its taste. When he reached her ear he nibbled at its lobe, while his fingers stroked the delicate skin behind it.

She reacted as though she had been stung...as though no one had ever touched her like that before, tensing and wrenching back from him, crying rawly, 'No...no more of that... Now...I want you to do it now...'

Daniel stared at her, frowning. He hadn't realised she was already so aroused... In fact...

Storm signals flashed from her eyes, as he watched her.

'You do want me, don't you?' she demanded, watching him. 'Because if you don't...'

He grinned to himself. He could hardly deny wanting her, since the evidence of that wanting was throbbing achingly and very visibly for her to see.

And that was when he made his biggest mistake. Instead of listening to the small inner voice urging caution, warning him that all was not as it seemed to be—as he wished it to seem to be—he took her words at face value and caught hold of her, making it explicitly obvious to her that he did want her, and how much, by giving rein to the need which had ridden him virtually from the moment he had first set eyes on her.

He tried to tell himself that he wasn't disappointed that she didn't want the long, slow lovemaking he had been aching to give her, that she simply seemed to want...to demand the raw immediate heat of his physical presence within her body without any of the preliminaries to that possession. He even tried to tell himself that he wasn't even disappointed by her refusal to kiss him or to look at him, to touch him, that her attitude towards him did not reduce him in his own eyes to the status of a hired stud. He even tried to tell himself, as he laid her on the floor and covered her body with his own, that she wanted their coming together as much as he did himself.

It was true that he was puzzled by the tension of her body, by the way she refused to do anything to help or accommodate him, by the way he had physically to manoeuvre her legs before he could actually try to enter her, but again he was so blinded by his own need, so convinced that secretly she must perhaps always have shared it, *must* have done surely to have come to him like this now, begging...demanding that he make love to her, that the obviousness of the truth didn't hit him until he thrust powerfully into her, felt the tensing of her muscles, recognised the tightness of her body and the immediacy of its recoil, and recognised what he ought to have recognised the moment she told him, 'No more...'

She hadn't said those words because she was so eagerly ready for him, he knew in angry shock; she had said them like a child preparing herself for a nasty-tasting medicine...like an adult preparing herself to go through a necessary but unwanted ordeal. And the reason she hadn't done anything to help him hadn't been because she was playing games with him, teasing him into a greater frenzy of desire, but simply because she hadn't known what to do.

'You're a virgin...'

He hadn't realised he had said the words out loud, until she rolled back from him, drawing her knees up under her chin, hugging her arms protectively around her as she glared back at him, demanding aggressively, 'So...?'

He stared at her in shock, torn between rage and disbelief. She was a virgin. A bloody virgin...the woman he had been fantasising about for months, the woman he had stupidly imagined had all the sexual knowledge of every woman who had ever been born at her finger-tips, was so totally inexperienced...

Anger boiled up inside him. Anger against himself, anger against Scott and most of all anger against her. What the hell was she playing at? Why...?

'Don't you make love to virgins? Is that it?'

Her taunt scalded him, and he reacted immediately to it, saying acidly, 'No, I bloody well do not. For one thing, if I'm going to make love to a woman it's a *woman* I want, not a frightened little girl. A woman who can give me as much pleasure as I can give her, not a little girl who tightens up her muscles and says "don't". For another...' He paused, knowing that he was being unnecessarily brutal, wanting to call back the words, but driven by something he couldn't control, something he didn't want to call sexual frustration because to do so lowered him in his own estimation as a civilised human being.

'For another, I don't suppose you're on the Pill and I certainly wasn't about to take any precautions. Have you no sense?' He got hold of her, dragging her to her knees, practically shaking her as reaction set in and his anger overwhelmed him.

'Or was that it?' he demanded unforgivably. 'Did you hope that I might make you pregnant? What is it you want from me, Sage? A child, a substitute for Scott? Because you damn sure don't want me as a man. My God, you wouldn't even know what to do with a real man. All that noise about loving Scott...all that fuss... Why didn't he make love to you, you——?'

'Well, it wasn't because I was a virgin...'

The words were laced with acid, belying the tremble in her voice and the tears he was nearly sure he could see shining in her eyes.

Now, when it was too late, he understood what he had done and ached to call back his cruel words.

As she scrambled to her feet, he reached for her, but she evaded him, snatching up his robe and pulling it protectively around her.

'Scott did love me. He respected me. He wanted...he wanted us to wait...until our families... He *did* love me...' She practically screamed the words at him, and

Daniel, noting the past tense, hearing her terror and the panic in her voice and recognising the doubts now tormenting her, felt his heart turn over with pain and compassion.

Dear God, if only he had been able to see beyond his own need—if only he had not allowed his physical desire for her to rule him. If only he had listened, waited, questioned.

'Why did you come to me?' he asked her soberly, knowing she would know what he meant.

'Why?' The face she turned to him was contorted into a mask-like grimace of hatred and bitterness. 'Why? Do you really need to ask? I've lost Scott. He's the only one I'll ever love, and you're right about one thing—the accident was my fault. I could have killed him... Afterwards I prayed for him to be safe. I promised I'd do anything, pay a price if only he might live... I never guessed what that price might be, that that price would be Scott himself. Don't you understand?' she cried out desperately. 'I wanted to punish myself, I wanted to suffer the way I deserve to suffer. That's why I came to you, because I knew there could be no greater self-betrayal, no worse physical degradation, no more emotional humiliation and pain than giving you what I wanted to give Scott. That's why I came to you...' She started to laugh, the sound too high-pitched, grating painfully on his ears as he tried to assimilate what she was saying to him... as, through his outrage, through the blow to his pride and his maleness, he heard the hatred and the scorn she was pouring out over him. In that moment he knew that if he touched her he would probably destroy her, and because of that he stepped back from her, turning his back on her so that he wouldn't have to look into the wildness of her face and see in that wildness all the false promise of the passion he had thought they would share.

'Daniel!'

He heard her call his name and felt his lungs contract; there was so much uncertainty in her voice, so much pain, so much need, like a child confused by the violence of her own emotions crying out for comfort and reassurance, but he hardened his heart against her, keeping his back to her as he said coldly, 'Whatever it is, I don't want to hear it. I pity you, Sage. I suppose you think I should be grateful for being made a gift—no, a sacrifice of your body. But I don't wish to accept it. You can stay for the rest of the night, but first thing tomorrow I want you to leave.'

'Daniel, please——'

'No, Sage . . . whatever it is you want I can't give it to you, sexually, emotionally or any other way. You're trouble with a capital T, and if you want my opinion Scott has had a lucky escape. You'll destroy every man who ever comes anywhere near you. You're that type.'

'You wanted me . . .'

'No. I wanted the use of your body,' he told her brutally and untruthfully. 'I didn't want *you*, Sage. Now go back to bed.'

Unbelievably she did, but in the morning predictably she had gone. Not just from his house, but from the campus as well. It took him several days to discover that she had just simply locked herself away in her room, without telling anyone why, although most of those who knew her seemed to assume that it was because of Scott.

After a week of indecision he had telephoned her home. Her mother, he had learned, was on a prolonged business tour and not due back until the end of the month, but they would pass his message on as soon as Mrs Danvers returned.

He tried to alleviate his guilt by submerging himself in his work, but it lingered, and festered, and it still festered today, Daniel acknowledged, staring frowning at his empty glass. It still festered today.

CHAPTER SEVENTEEN

DANIEL had time and plenty to spare in order to prepare for his meeting with Sage and to drive down to Cottingdean, and yet he discovered that he was deliberately delaying himself, deliberately, almost, trying to make himself late... So late that Sage might grow tired of waiting for him and cancel their meeting?

The trouble was that if he'd known, if he'd had the remotest idea that she was going to be involved in this thing in any way at all, he'd have found someone else to stand in for the company; Dale Hughes for instance, the head of their PR department, or Matthew Petrie, his deputy. There had been no real reason for him to get personally involved... not really, and yet when he had seen the first outline plans for the proposed routes, when he had read the name Cottingdean, he had told himself that he was simply following sound business practice, that his reasons for driving down to Cottingdean, long before the proposed route had become public, had simply been business curiosity, nothing more.

He had been surprised to discover it so much a village still and yet at the same time so obviously thriving, a small rural backwater, and yet not so much of a backwater really since the wool produced by its mill found markets virtually all over the world, or at least in those parts of it where people were rich enough and discerning enough to appreciate the quality of cloth spun from the wool from the best of English flocks, in a combination of methods which comprised the best of both the old and the new.

For the woman who had masterminded and breathed life into this profitable industry he heard nothing but praise; for her daughter... He had been surprised how few local people knew anything about Sage, far less in most cases than he knew himself, but then in many ways London was a series of small villages whose permanent occupants soon became familiar to one another, especially when they lived as high profile a life as Sage.

It was true that the tales of her wildness, her lovers, her unpredictability had grown less over the years, just as her reputation as a gifted muralist had grown.

He had seen one of her murals last summer in the home of a friend of a friend who had a villa on a still remote part of Ibiza. He had been startled by it, stunned by its creativity, its depth and intensity—without knowing her, just from looking at her work, he would have known that here was a person who had intuition, compassion, intensity and vulnerability; and he hadn't been able to stop himself from thinking how much he would have liked to commission her to do some work for himself and how impossible it was that he should.

The most recent news in the Press was of how Sage was being pursued by some Australian Greek who had followed her as far as London. Whoever he was, he didn't seem to be part of her life now.

He often wondered how different the course of both their lives might have been if he had given in to his need that night . . . if he had gone ahead and made love to her, been her first lover...perhaps even impregnated her with his child.

His mouth twisted in self-mockery as he picked up his papers and walked out of his flat.

Then the last thing he had wanted to do was to have a child by any woman, so why should he now suddenly be able to picture so comprehensively and so disturbingly the child they might have had?

As he climbed into his car and started the engine he knew he would have to drive fast if he wasn't going to be late. If he'd known before he'd taken on this thing that he was going to have to confront Sage over it on a one-to-one basis, he'd have moved heaven and earth to ensure that he didn't have to do so. The trouble was...the trouble was that he still wanted her...

He swore suddenly, putting his foot sharply on the brake pedal, half inclined to turn back and pick up the phone and tell her the meeting was off, and yet knowing that he wasn't going to do so; that something stronger than logic and common sense was driving him.

He cursed under his breath. He was thirty-seven years old, and the thought of her still made him feel like a raw boy of seventeen. He, who was so fastidious, so aware not merely of the health dangers of sharing his life with any woman who had had a variety of sexual partners, but also of the potential emotional paucity of such a relationship, the lack of any real intimacy; he who found nothing to appeal to him in any relationship which was based merely on mutual sexual excitement and need. It was perhaps a weakness in him that when he shared his body with a woman, he wanted to share his mind...his thoughts...the small intimacies of his life as well as the large ones—and yet there had never been a woman he had ever come close to wanting to have permanently in his life. He had never even invited one of his lovers to move in with him.

One of his lovers... He grimaced wryly to himself. During recent years there had been no one; oh, he had dated a variety of women, enjoyed their company, known that if he had wished to do so he could have taken these relationships further, but sex for sex's sake had never really appealed to him.

At present there was no one in his life; Helen Ordman had made it discreetly plain that she would like to take their business relationship a stage further, but while he admired her business acumen he felt no real desire for her. Was it true that the price of success in today's high-powered and stressful world was an automatic loss of libido? He had only to think of Sage to know that it wasn't, and annoyingly he was finding that he was spending more and more time doing just that. He had been surprised to discover just how much she was prepared to involve herself in their business... Sage was essentially a loner—an individualist, someone who guarded her privacy almost ferociously. Her mother was the philanthropist of the family, and nothing he knew about Sage had ever given him to believe that she would step so willingly or so competently into her mother's shoes. The fact that she had done so disturbed him and yet why shouldn't she have changed? People did. Why shouldn't she have matured? He had himself. Why should his awareness that Sage had done so rub at him like a piece of grit against his skin? No more than irritating at first, but gradually becoming more and more acutely painful.

He had never really shed his guilt over the way he had treated her that night—never really forgiven himself for not handling the situation with more finesse, never really stopped wishing that things might have been different, never really stopped himself from feeling that he, with his greater maturity, should have been able to find a way through the thicket of emotional thorns she had thrown up around herself, and been able to lead her out of it, to set her free from the trauma of loving Scott and losing him, to establish with her enough rapport, enough trust for her to treat him at least as a friend, for her to come to him in her need. That night, when she had so clearly betrayed her hatred and loathing of him, he had been too completely thrown to react rationally, to question why she should feel such violent and intense emotions towards him, to wonder if perhaps he had been right all along and she had felt desire for him—a reluctant desire, an unwanted desire, a desire that terrified and infuriated her maybe, but a desire none the less.

It was too late now to wish he had handled things differently, and he had enough of his parents' Celtic inheritance to believe beneath the logic of education that there were perhaps some things which were decreed by fate and which no amount of human endeavour could change.

The moment he reached the motorway he put his foot down; God—and the traffic police—willing, he wasn't going to be late after all, and suddenly it was important to him that he shouldn't be.

* * *

Half-past eight; Sage was starting to panic. Not outwardly. Outwardly she had long ago learned to control
any visible sign of her inner emotions, but inside her
stomach was a turmoil of terrified, fluttering butterflies,
her muscles already tensing, closing, the strain of the
ordeal ahead beginning to break through her outer
control.

It didn't help reminding herself that this confrontation with Daniel was at her own instigation...her
hands, she discovered, were damp with the perspiration
of tension. What if Daniel refused to give in to her
threats? What good would it do anyway if he did? To
have their main contractor pull out of the deal would
cause the Government some problems in finding an
alternative, but the road would eventually still go ahead.

Eventually... If she did manage to blackmail Daniel
into pulling out of the contract then at least she would
have bought them some time. Enough time perhaps for
her mother to recover, to take charge...

If she ever recovered. Sage shivered, hugging her arms
around her body, rubbing tense fingers up and down the
goose-flesh of her upper arms.

What if her mother didn't recover? What if...? She
bit down hard on her bottom lip and started to savage
it with her teeth. Her mother *had* to get well, she had
to...and the doctors were optimistic. She was very strong,
they had said...but not yet strong enough to undergo
the necessary surgery to remove the pressure on her
brain...

Alaric Ferguson had been brutally explicit to her in
describing her mother's chances of survival. A blood clot
caused by the accident had lodged in her brain; they had
hoped to disperse the clot without surgery but this had
not proved possible... Now they had to wait until her
mother was stronger, until they need no longer sedate
her to help her body through the shock of the accident,
before they could operate to remove the clot. It was time
here that was all important, Sage had been told; a fine
balancing of time and opportunity, a judgement to be
made by the surgeon in charge. A judgement which

would mean life for her mother—or death... She shivered again, wondering if her mother could know how much she was in her thoughts, in her prayers—how much she wanted her to recover. Not just out of guilt, out of remorse or even out of love. There was a great need in her now, a great thirst to know more of this woman whom she was coming to know so well through her diaries—a great need to talk with her, to find out why she had never known her before, a great need to tell her how much she admired her, how much she wished they might have been peers and close friends, instead of being separated by the enforced chasm of their difficult relationship.

She heard a car outside and started up, hurrying into the hall, relief and a tiny unexpected stab of disappointment panicking the butterflies into fresh flight as she realised it wasn't Daniel but Faye.

'Sorry I'm so late,' Faye apologised tensely as she came in. 'It wasn't intentional...if it hadn't been for that stupid man...' She broke off and Sage focused on her, frowning as she realised that Faye looked different, that there was something almost approaching a wildness about her, that there was a vivid, strong colour burning along her cheekbones, that she looked animated and alive in a way that was totally different.

Even the way she moved had changed, Sage recognised, her eyes following the quick, almost savage movements Faye made as she paced the hall, finally whirling round to demand bitterly, 'Do I look like someone who can't control her own life, who has to be treated like a child? I'm over forty years old, dammit...'

Sage blinked, as stunned to hear Faye swear as she was to witness her rage.

Sage merely said mildly, ignoring the first part of her tirade, 'I'm glad you're back, we were worried about you.'

'There you are!' Faye exploded. 'You were worried. Why? I'm a fully functioning adult, not a child. Would you expect me to say I'd been worried about you if you came in late?'

'Perhaps if I'd disappeared for a full day without letting anyone know where I was going,' Sage told her drily, and then added, before Faye could explode a second time, 'I'm not prying, Faye. What you do with your life is your own affair, but Cam was upset. This is a very difficult time for her—her exams coming up, Mother so ill... I think she feels her whole life has been thrown into turmoil. Girls of her age expect life to go on in the same way for ever; they expect the people they love to be around for ever—and when they realise they might not be...'

'Yes. I know,' Faye agreed. 'I miss your mother too...'

'I suspect that Camilla's a little bit miffed that you didn't tell her where you were going. She said something about you and Mother taking off one Tuesday a month to some WI meeting or other.'

'And you didn't believe her,' Faye challenged. 'Is that it?'

'It isn't a matter of what I believe, it's what Camilla believes,' Sage pointed out.

'So what is it you're trying to say—that you think that your mother and I sneak off once a month to pick up a couple of men? You would think that, Sage. Well, for your information——'

'I don't want to know what you do. I don't even care what you do, Faye,' Sage told her irritably. This meeting with Daniel was getting to her. She was so on edge, so screwed up inside at the thought of seeing him, being with him. It was all so ridiculous to keep remembering now something that happened over fifteen years ago, something she had little doubt that Daniel himself had completely forgotten—at least she hoped he had.

'No... You don't care what anyone does, do you?' Faye threw back at her, her soft features suddenly almost hardening. 'You don't care about anyone or anything, do you, Sage? Not even yourself. Well, for your information, you may sleep around with every man who takes your fancy, but I don't... If I want to keep that part of my life private then perhaps it's because it's necessary that I do so, not just for my own sake but for Camilla's

as well, but that would never occur to you, would it?
Because you've never, ever put anyone else before
yourself...'

Faye broke off, her eyes suddenly swimming with tears.
Dear God, what was she doing... what was she saying?
But she had been so angry when that man, that interfering, busybodying doctor had dared to imply that—
what? That she was incapable of a simple task like
driving herself home, that she was weak and stupid?
Hadn't he after all only been underlining everything she
had been thinking about herself? Maybe, but she was
only human and resented someone else pointing out her
weaknesses as much as the next person. That was why
she had loved David so much. He had never made her
feel stupid or weak. He had never made her confront
the evil ghosts which haunted her. He had never pushed
or prodded her into doing anything she hadn't wanted
to do. And yet perhaps he should have done.
No...perhaps *she* should have done. Why should it have
been necessary for someone else to do her thinking for
her? Why couldn't she have seen for herself that her best
way to fight free of the past was to confront it, to face
up to it?

It was the diaries that were making her feel like this;
the knowledge she was gaining from them that others
had their own ghosts, their own fears and dreads, that
she was not after all alone with her burden of guilt and
hatred.

'I've finished another of the diaries. I've put it up in
your room,' Sage told her, ignoring her outburst. 'I've
also arranged for Daniel Cavanagh to come here tonight. There's something I want to discuss with him...'

'Daniel Cavanagh... Isn't he the head of the construction company building our section of the road?'
Faye looked confused. 'Is that wise? I mean...' She
shook her head. 'I'm sorry, Sage. I'm afraid I'm not
being much help to you over any of this. I'd better go
and make my peace with Camilla. Where is she?'

'She's gone out. She said something about going to
see a school friend. She asked Jenny to drive her. She

did say you wouldn't mind,' Sage added when she saw Faye frowning.

'Well, no, I suppose not . . . It's just that she knows I like to know exactly where she is and with whom. You can't be too careful these days . . .'

'She is almost eighteen,' Sage reminded her. 'You can't keep her wrapped in cotton wool for the rest of her life, Faye.'

She had never seen Faye so temperamental before, she reflected curiously as her sister-in-law gave her a tight smile and headed for the stairs. She wondered what had happened to her to provoke such an outburst, and then put Faye and her potential problems out of her mind when she heard the sound of another car crunching over the gravel.

She had purposely asked Jenny to open the door to him when Daniel did arrive, hoping that such a show of formality would add to her own power base—which was one of the reasons she had invited him to come to Cottingdean, instead of meeting him somewhere more neutral.

She certainly needed every advantage she could snatch, she admitted as she heard the opening of a car door; Daniel had a formidable reputation in the City . . . not just as an astute and shrewd businessman but also, surprisingly, as a man of honour and very high moral ethics. That had surprised her, and yet why should it? That night when he had rejected her, when he had turned his back on her and made her feel like something that had just crawled out of the gutter, she had seen that formidable will-power and moral code in action. She could have sworn that he'd wanted her, had sensed it all the time she and Scott had known him, had been so sure he would take her . . . so sure that if he did so somehow she would be able to lose herself and her anguish in the fierce heat of the mutual passion she had known they would generate. What had she wanted? To burn away her hopeless love for Scott in the fires of Daniel's desire?

The sound of the car door closing brought her abruptly back to reality. She hurried towards the study door, and yet she was unable to stop herself pausing briefly in front of the seventeenth-century giltwood mirror which had been one of her mother's many auction bargains.

This one had originally hung in the drawing-room of a house in Ireland and contained the symbolic arms of the noble family who had originally commissioned it in its frame. It was a beautiful piece of workmanship, each detail of the fruitwood frame lovingly carved, but Sage barely glanced at the frame, concentrating instead on her own perfectly made-up face, wondering what Daniel would see when he looked at her. Would he transpose on these features she could now see—the firmly bowed mouth discreetly coloured with soft rose lipstick—the trembling swollen mouth of that girl who had stood and cried out his name in mortal anguish and need?

Would he look into the veiled and exquisitely made-up green eyes and see, not the control and knowledge which coloured them now, but the need and pain of her nineteen-year-old self? Would he look at her hair and see not its carefully tamed artful sleekness but the wild disarray of curls which had tangled round her tear-stained face, as she hurled her insults at him, driven into a mad, frenzied need to hurt him the way he had hurt her?

It had been bad enough to live with the knowledge that Scott was not driven by the same wild hunger to consummate their love that drove her; she had told herself that Scott was right, that in saying that he wanted to wait he was saying only how much he loved and respected her, that in saying that they must establish their relationship with their parents before becoming physical lovers he was showing only the concern that made her love him so much... but when Daniel had rejected her, Daniel, whom she had often and scornfully witnessed watching her with hot eyes whose message had needed no translation, when Daniel had removed himself from her and told her explicitly and brutally that he didn't want her, then she had suffered in a way she had never suffered before. Then she had endured her first painful doubt about herself and her sexuality, about her entire psyche as a female being... If she was not desired and

desirable, then why was she suffering this pulsing, aching
need to be part of another human being, why was she
forced to undergo this humiliating surge of physical
awareness, of physical wanting?

What was she, then—a woman without sexuality,
without true femininity, without the ability to arouse and
be aroused in turn?

Outside, their visitor rapped on the ancient knocker.
Swiftly Sage turned away from the mirror and hurried
into the study, quickly checking the room to ensure that
the stage was set as she wished it to be.

Jenny had been in earlier and lit the fire, giving the
room an air of warmth and intimacy which she hoped
would deceive Daniel into relaxing his guard, into making
him feel welcome and wanted . . .

A silver tray holding a bottle of sherry and some crystal
glasses winked in the firelight. The sherry had come from
the small stock laid down by her great-grandfather, and
which had mercifully escaped the attention of Kit. The
glasses were Waterford and antique, the silver tray merely
plated and of no particular material worth at all, but it
had been presented to her mother by the children from
the local junior school, which she had fought to keep
open and operational, donating several very large sums
of money both personally and via the mill to ensure that
its facilities were among the most modern in the country.

This tray had been the children's way of thanking their
benefactress. It had her mother's name engraved on it
and the date of its presentation, and Sage, who had often
wondered cynically why her mother, who loved and
needed to have things of beauty and value about her,
seemed to cherish it so assiduously, now felt she knew
exactly why. That knowledge was humbling and
painful . . . like all knowledge gained through hard work
and endeavour.

She heard footsteps in the hall outside . . .
voices . . . Jenny's bright and cheerful, Daniel's deeper,
muted and very male.

She felt her stomach muscles tense in protest as Jenny
knocked on the study door, and discovered to her chagrin

as it opened that she was actually curling her toes in her shoes like a terrified child.

That was not the impression she wanted to give at all. She flicked a glance downwards, frowning, removing a small piece of fluff from her immaculately tailored suit. It was an outfit she thoroughly detested; she normally kept it for clients or meetings she didn't particularly like because she knew it gave her a polished, sophisticated image. The short, straight skirt subtly emphasised her sexuality, the long double-breasted jacket adding a sharper, disconcerting touch of hard-edged masculinity.

The fabric was a fine woollen Prince of Wales check, which she had been cynically amused to discover had been woven here at her mother's mills.

Beneath it she was wearing a tailored off-white silk shirt, and beneath that ... beneath that she was wearing the equally plain and even more expensive silk underwear that was one of her few material indulgences. She bought it from Rigby and Peller in London, but over it when she was working—which was most of the time—she normally wore jeans and an oversized man's shirt. When she wasn't working she wore virtually the same thing, except when she was attending the odd and unwanted formal "do" or when she was coming down here to visit her mother, who expected certain standards to be observed.

Previously Sage had always thought her insistence on these standards petty-minded and yet another indication of her mother's refusal to move with the times, but now, after reading her diaries, she saw things differently, realised how difficult it might be for a woman raised as her mother had been raised, married so young to a man like her father, a woman who had known such financial and material hardships, to let herself go and dress in the casual classless uniform of which Sage herself was so fond.

If she in turn ever produced a daughter, would she find it as difficult to understand her—would she in turn not be able to bridge the chasms between them?

A daughter... Strange that when she had not thought of herself in the context of motherhood for so long, when she had not allowed to think of herself in that context since losing Scott, she should think of it now, no matter how obliquely.

She had told herself that she was more than ready for her confrontation with Daniel, that the physical reality of him held no traumas or fears for her, that once over the shock of seeing him walk into the hall that night she was finally free of the past... but as he walked into her mother's study she knew that it wasn't true.

Why, when she was a relatively tall woman herself, did the sheer physical presence of him make her feel so breathless and nervous? He was tall, but not overly so, broad without the almost ape-like torso of so many large men, which she personally found repellent rather than attractive.

As he came towards her she looked for signs of grey in the thick darkness of his hair, and, finding none, wondered idly if he had it tinted before dismissing the notion as totally implausible. Daniel simply wasn't that kind of man.

Even now, with his hair expensively cut and shaped, his nails well-manicured and buffed, his hands and wrists were still sinewy and brown as though he still spent long hours physically working alongside his men. She remembered how much Scott had admired him for that, cataloguing his virtues for her, when she had sneered at her beloved's new friend, claiming that she didn't like him.

Scott... What was he doing now? Did he ever think about her? She knew that he was married... Someone, she didn't know who, since the magazine had arrived anonymously, had taken the trouble to send her a copy of an Australian magazine describing his marriage to the daughter of a successful entrepreneur as the 'Wedding of the Year'.

That had been six years ago, and certainly he had looked happy enough. The letters she had sent to him in the first frantic throes of her grief had all been returned to her unopened. Her telephone calls remained unanswered. Only once had she heard from Scott's father, a brief note telling her that Scott was recovering and that he didn't want to hear from her again.

The years between Scott's accident and his marriage were ones she preferred not to remember now. Years in which she had drunk deep of the rich, heady wine of life, and had sometimes found that such drinking had brought her a miserable sickness of the soul which refused to go away.

Sex had been the panacea she had used, or tried to use, to blot out the past—until the morning she had woken up and realised that she would far rather be sleeping alone than with the man beside her . . . that sex, like any other crutch, worked only as long as you allowed yourself to believe that it would, and that in the end it was far better to face up to the harsh realities of life and the pain they brought without any crutches at all; that sex on its own, while physically pleasurable, was emotionally barren, and, ultimately, that it was something she did as an act of destruction against herself, masking that fact in the illusion that she was doing it simply for its physical pleasure.

It had taken many solitary hours of painful self-analysis for her to realise this, to realise that what she was doing was punishing herself, hurting herself, destroying herself.

That had been over six years ago, and yet still the gossip columns accredited her with an ever-changing list of lovers, while in fact . . . while in fact there had been none for two years, and even before that . . . even before that there had been far less than the world seemed to assume.

But those men that there had been had wanted her, some of them almost to the point of insanity . . . Unlike this man, she reflected, watching as Daniel came towards her.

He hadn't really changed; only matured, grown harder, shrewder. The assessing grey eyes were still the same, seeing far more than one wanted them to see, the handshake just as determinedly firm, the mouth still discon-

certingly passionate, even when it was smiling with the
cool, watchful smile he was giving her.

'Daniel... It was good of you to come at such short
notice.'

She smiled back at him, the distant, professional smile
she used to warn off those clients who dared to presume
that she was available as a woman as well as a professional muralist.

'As I recall, you didn't give me much option.'

His voice had changed, deepened, steadied, become
more measured... perhaps like the man himself?

He was looking, Sage noticed, at her mother's desk.

'Good piece,' he commented, eyeing it thoughtfully.

'I believe so, although I'm afraid I'm not very knowledgeable about antiques. My mother picked it up at a
sale in Ireland. She was fortunate enough to have the
wisdom to pick up quite a lot of old stuff that way in
the fifties when no one wanted to be seen dead with anything over six months old, and a lot of old houses were
being pulled down.'

Daniel smiled to himself at the way she described what
were no doubt priceless antiques as 'a lot of old stuff'.
He had initially been slightly taken aback when he was
shown into this room and discovered Sage standing there,
dressed like the very toughest type of American female
executive, or, at least, her own very feminised and unique
version of that.

He wondered obliquely if she had chosen the silk shirt
deliberately because of the way it emphasised her breasts,
and then dismissed the idea as unfair.

As well as he had known her—and he had considered
he had known her well in the old days, despite that final
débâcle—he could never have accused her of being deliberately sexually provocative. She had never had any
need.

He wondered if it was true, as he had heard recently
on the grapevine, that she had become virtually celibate.
Quite a turn-around after the wild years of changing her
lovers almost as frequently as she changed her clothes,

if it was true, but then she had always had that rather unexpected core of inner purity about her.

He remembered how she had once rounded on Scott when he had idly suggested trying some of the hallucinatory drugs so fashionable among some of the undergraduate set... How she had heatedly and graphically described to him the potential hazards of such a course. He personally hadn't done drugs in those days, and had never felt the need to since, but it had struck him quite forcibly at the time that she could potentially become a woman of strong character and resolve...that once her mind was set to a course no amount of peer pressure or any other kind of pressure was likely to change it. And if she had become celibate, well, she had certainly been running well ahead of the field.

'You said there was something you wanted to discuss with me,' Daniel reminded her as Sage waved him into a chair. 'Something too urgent to wait.'

'Yes. I've asked Jenny to bring us some tea, although if you'd prefer coffee...'

In the old days he had always drunk coffee, only coffee, and now, listening to her dulcet offer, looking into her guarded green eyes, he smiled an equally crocodile smile and shook his head.

'Tea's fine. Like everyone else, I've probably become over-diet-conscious these days. I found that the threat of suffering a bout of caffeine poisoning effectively had me switching to tea.'

As Sage turned her back on him he heard her drawling mockingly, 'My God, how the mighty are fallen with a vengeance. Is this really the hard man of the Welsh hills, afraid to drink a cup of coffee in case it over-excites his adrenalin flow?'

Daniel refused to rise to the bait, simply saying with false gentleness, 'Oh, I think we're all far more health-conscious these days, don't you?'

If she picked up the underlying taunt, it didn't show. The colour which had once come so swiftly and betrayingly to her pale skin had somehow become controlled over the years, only the faintest glimmer of something that could have either been anger or amusement glinting momentarily in the green eyes as she turned back to him.

'I expect you know that as far as the committee is concerned I've had to step into my mother's shoes at rather short notice,' she told him, completely changing the subject. 'Initially I didn't have much opportunity to do any research——'

'No? Which reminds me, how is your mother?'

He hid his smile as her dark eyebrows rose in aloof surprise.

'Holding her own,' Sage told him dismissively, her tone implying that he had no right, no right at all to dare to assume such familiarity with her family. Once, even after knowing that he was Robert's son and not John Ryan's, the snub would have angered him, brushing too roughly over very sensitive areas of his psyche, but now he had both the maturity and the wit to smile inwardly at it.

His placid amusement niggled at Sage; for a moment she forgot that he was her adversary and dangerous and reacted to his infuriating male arrogance in much the same way she might have reacted once to David, challenging him angrily, 'I didn't realise you knew my mother.'

The moment the words were said she regretted them; of course he didn't know her mother, and in underlining that fact she was behaving not as the woman of sophistication and assurance she wanted him to see but as the child they both knew she had once been.

However, to her astonishment, instead of acknowledging the truth of her remark he said, 'Well, I can't claim to know her. I suspect very few people can do that—on the one occasion we did meet she struck me as a very complex lady indeed.'

Sage felt her mouth start to drop open. Before she could close it she saw that Daniel was looking at her and smiling.

'Catching flies, Sage?' he teased her.

Angrily she snapped her lips together.

'I met your mother when news of the motorway first became public. She attended the initial open meeting— I was there as well.'

What he didn't tell her was that her mother had deliberately sought him out, not because of his role as chairman of the company which would be constructing their section of the motorway, but because she had recognised his name, recognised it and remembered it as belonging, as she explained to him, to the young man who had telephoned several times asking for news as to Sage's health and well-being in those long dark months after Sage had lost Scott.

They had had a long talk together, he and Sage's mother, and afterwards he felt he had come closer to understanding much about Sage that had puzzled him before.

Angry with herself, Sage turned away from him. Why on earth hadn't she thought of that, that he might have met her mother in her capacity as chairperson of the local committee? Why was she allowing her thoughts to drift back into the past, and on to a personal level, the kind of personal level which meant she was digging pits for her own unwary feet?

'Yes... I'm afraid I'd forgotten what an important person you are these days,' she responded tartly. 'Chairman of a public company...and managing director of a small subsidiary one.'

'Mm...' Daniel agreed, not sure where her conversation was leading, but convinced suddenly that she was about to get to the crux of why she had insisted on this meeting.

'You don't deny, then, that you are the managing director of Hever Homes?' Sage pressed.

Daniel stared at her and then shrugged his shoulders. 'Is there any reason why I should?'

'I don't know,' Sage told him smoothly...as smooth as a snake before it strikes, Daniel reflected, watching her, fascinated by the way her moods were reflected in the green depths of her eyes. Here was a woman who, no matter how hard she tried, would never be able to totally disguise her feelings…at least not with those who knew her.

Sharply and uncomfortably it struck him that he knew her far too intimately and in far too much detail for someone who had supposedly put all thought of her out of his life fifteen years ago. He also wondered why on earth it was, when he knew damn well that she had had countless numbers of lovers, that she should have such an air of fragility and vulnerability. He hadn't missed the way, when he had first walked into the room, she had backed off from him. Not in the way of someone arrogantly infuriated that another should dare to infiltrate their personal space, but like someone threatened and made nervous by the close proximity of another human being of the opposite sex.

That had intrigued and puzzled him, especially when it had been done so quickly and so instinctively that it had been completely free of any artifice.

She was a bundle of contradictions, a child wearing the mask of a sophisticate. A wanton who loved sex for sex's sake according to rumour, and yet at the same time a woman who stepped back out of reach of a man's touch with the immediacy of a timid virgin. And he knew she wasn't that. Had she thought of Scott that first time, ached for Scott with all of that intensely passionate nature of hers? Had she gone home to her solitary bed and lain there imagining, pretending that the man who had taken her maidenhead had been her precious and too dearly loved Scott?

They were interrupted briefly when Jenny came in with the tea tray, and then quickly withdrew.

Sage poured his tea with the same stylish grace with which she did everything, and yet there was also a hesitancy about her movements, a momentary clumsiness almost that made him reach out instinctively to steady the hand that held the teapot.

The moment his fingers closed on her wrist he felt their tension. His thumb had accidentally rested against the pulse in her wrist and now it lingered there, feeling its too fast beat, as she demanded breathlessly, 'Don't touch me!'

Just for a moment he looked steadily at her and saw in her eyes what she was too proud to try to conceal—that she remembered as faultlessly as he did himself a time when she had asked him for just the opposite.

He released her wrist slowly, knowing that long after he had left her the scent of her would still be clinging to his skin from that brief touch.

'What is it you wanted to say to me, Sage?'

'It's this,' she told him, putting down the teapot, not trusting herself to pick up the cup and hand it to him, but instead indicating to him which cup was his and forcing herself to try to appear in control of a situation which was fast escalating into something way, way beyond that control.

'I happen to have found out that you, in the name of your company Hever Homes, have bought the Old Hall and its ten acres of land, no doubt intending to develop that land and turn it into a shoddy neo-Georgian housing estate, or some such thing,' she told him scornfully, 'and in the process of so doing making a very substantial profit for yourself. You bought that land before the news of the planned route for the new motorway became public knowledge. You therefore bought it with privileged information, didn't you? I wonder how it would look in the papers if it became known that a chairman who, as the Press are so fond of telling us, prides himself on his honesty and his moral strength should have used such privileged information for his own gain...and in fact should have bought that land and the house standing on it almost by fraud—by telling its previous owner that he would keep the house intact and allow nothing to destroy it.'

Daniel stared at her, sipped his tea thoughtfully and then put down his cup and saucer, while Sage held her breath, waiting for him to retaliate, to lose his temper, to throw her accusations back in her face.

Instead he simply said calmly, 'You have been busy, haven't you? And if I don't agree to...? What is it exactly you want me to do, Sage?'

Now it was her turn to stare. She had expected more from him. Rage, sarcasm, contempt for the tactics she had used. Anything other than this cool calm.

It took her several minutes to realise that he was waiting for her to speak. When she did she discovered that the pitch of her voice was slightly husky and uncertain...that she sounded more like someone suing for favours than a victor stating terms to the vanquished.

'I want you...or rather Cavanagh Construction, to pull out of the motorway contract.'

Even now he remained calm. 'To what purpose? I mean, is this a personal vendetta, payment for past mistakes...' he paused and watched her '...or does it have some other more altruistic purpose?'

For the first time that evening he saw the scarlet colour run up under her skin. He almost felt sorry for her as he watched her and saw her change before his eyes from capable businesswoman to insecure girl.

She was thirty-four years old and her skin was still as fine and fair as it had been at nineteen. He badly wanted to reach out and touch it, to see if it felt as smooth and warm, to see if it tasted—if she tasted—the way he still imagined she would. He closed his eyes and immediately wished he hadn't as he was visited by fifteen-year-old visions of her body unclothed, of her arms held out towards him.

'How dare you suggest there is anything personal in this? Do you really think I'm stupid enough to harbour grudges, or even that what happened between us is so important to me any more? It's the road I'm concerned with here, Daniel, and it wouldn't matter a damn to me whether I knew you or not. In fact I'd prefer it if you were a stranger to me. I may not be my mother—I don't have her skills, her gifts—but I damn well will do anything I can to carry on her work.

'When I first came back I told myself it was stupid to make such a fuss about a road. What did it matter where it went? It had to go somewhere—someone's back garden had to be a little spoilt, someone's fields had to be sacrificed. Why not the villagers', here? But then I saw what it was really going to do, learned how people really felt about it.

'This isn't a dead dormitory village filled with migrants from London, weekend country-dwellers...it's a working village with not just a past but a future as well, a future that the people here want for their children and their children's children; and they don't want their lives cut in half by a motorway that could easily be rerouted to go right round their homes instead of straight through the middle of them.

'My mother must have had some plan of action in mind. She was in London the day of the accident. Who knows whom she might have been going to see? She had many important contacts... I have to buy time, time for her to get better, to take over. Time—that's the only thing I can do here for her, and the only way I can buy that time is through you. It's down to you. Withdraw from the contract and I'll keep quiet about the land.' Her lips curled. 'Oh, that doesn't mean I approve of what you're doing—I don't, I think it's despicable.'

She came to a full stop, disgusted to find that her body was trembling as well as her voice.

During her tirade she had got up and started pacing the room.

Now Daniel stared at her. She could read nothing in his face...see nothing but cool indifference in the hard implacability of his eyes.

'You intend to blackmail me into dropping out of the contract, is that it?' he asked her coolly.

Blackmail. The sound of the word made her squirm inwardly, made her feel guilty, unclean somehow.

'*You* can call it blackmail if you wish,' she told him haughtily. 'I call it using whatever advantages I can. After all, I'm not the one who promised a sick old lady that I'd take care of her family home, that I'd restore it and live in it.'

'No... No, you aren't, are you?' Daniel said heavily, standing up so abruptly that his movement startled her.

He was coming towards her and instinctively she backed off, until she saw the way he smiled at her reaction.

Damn the man. What did he think he was doing? She was no frail old lady to be intimidated and bullied.

'Well?' she demanded aggressively.

'I need time to think this over...'

Sage frowned. This was a reaction she hadn't expected. She had anticipated an immediate yes or no, a fierce rage of temper, some brutal accusation—perhaps even a moment's physical violence, or at least the threat of it, but not this cool, unreadable demand for time, and instinctively she suspected it, watching him warily.

'How long?'

'Two days. I'll give you your answer in two days' time.'

She wanted to argue, to press him for an immediate decision, but something held her back, an instinct that she held on to, silently nodding in bitter acceptance of his terms, knowing as she did so that in some sinister way he had subtly managed to wrench control of the situation away from her and in to his own hands.

Although she badly longed for the arrogance to summon Jenny to escort him to the front door, she knew she just could not do it. For one thing she wouldn't have put it past him to have simply walked out without waiting for Jenny to appear; for another... for another it went against everything her mother had taught her, and even in this instance those were not teachings she could ignore.

And so, feeling foolish and oddly vulnerable, she walked with him to the front door and then opened it for him, saying curtly, 'Two days, Daniel. That's all. After that I go to the Press.'

'Two days...' As he stood on the steps he was standing below her, his eyes directly level with hers. Just before he turned away from her he asked conversationally, 'By the way, do you ever hear anything from Scott these days? I have to go to Australia on business later this year—I thought I might look him up. We still exchange the odd Christmas card . . . he named his eldest son after me . . .'

Sage felt the breath leak from her lungs in small excruciatingly painful spurts, like blood from a fatal wound.

As he turned and walked away from her into the darkness, she stood where she was and prayed that he wouldn't turn round and see the tears burning like acid in her eyes.

Scott . . . Scott . . . Even now part of her still mourned him, still ached for him, still refused to accept that he was gone from her. She no longer desired him, had stopped desiring him many, many years ago—that night in Daniel's room, in actual fact—but she hadn't stopped needing him. Hadn't stopped feeling that losing him had been like losing part of herself . . . that without him in some way she was physically incomplete.

His loss was an ever-open wound that would never heal . . . She had kept that fact a secret from everyone who knew her, and yet here was a man who didn't know her at all, and yet at the same time who knew her so well. Who read her so intimately that he had with a few casual words shown her just how vulnerable she was to him, just how few her secrets from him were. She trembled as she went inside, wondering just what else she might have betrayed to him. Just what other secrets he might have discerned. Just what other vulnerabilities she might have accidentally and dangerously laid bare to him.

CHAPTER EIGHTEEN

SAGE woke up abruptly. Traces of her nightmare still clung to her mind like sticky veilings of mist, darkening her perceptions, even while her conscious mind acknowledged reality.

She had been dreaming about her childhood; about her father... about her longing to get close to him, to be accepted and loved by him in the same way that David was accepted and loved.

The incoherent, blind jealousy and rage she had felt so strongly as a child, and which through her mother's strict control of her she had never been allowed to voice, had known no such barriers in her sleep, and yet there had been none of the satisfaction, the relief there should have been in giving vent to it; rather a sickening awareness as she stood there looking into her father's aloof, withdrawn face that she had now added contempt to his dislike and disapproval of her.

Why hadn't he loved her as he had David? Was it because she was a girl? Once she had thought so, had clung to that belief because it was far easier to be rejected for her sex than for a specific lack of something in her personal make-up.

She touched her face, not surprised to discover it was wet with tears, closing her eyes momentarily as she fought to break free of the weight of the nightmare's misery, as she fought to ignore that shocking moment of clarity when she had looked into her father's face and seen all his dislike of her laid bare in it, and then shockingly his features had melted into the shadows and somehow rearranged themselves, so that it wasn't her father looking at her with such resentment and contempt, but Daniel.

Daniel... What was she going to do if he actually refused her demand? Would she expose him to the Press—could she? He deserved it for what he was doing. She shivered, hugging her knees. Even if he did agree, even if he did withdraw from the contract, he would soon be replaced. She couldn't halt the construction of the new road for ever. Would the time she was buying be sufficient to allow her mother to recover and take over?

She pushed her hand into the heavy mass of her hair. Her body felt drained of all physical energy, while her mind conversely was almost hyperactive, her thoughts feverishly intense and confused.

She didn't need a psychiatrist to tell her that her nightmare had been brought on by her own doubts about what she was doing, her own insecurities, her own fears. What she didn't understand was why Daniel Cavanagh should have become the focus for those fears. Or was it more that she didn't want to understand?

He had always been a powerfully male man, the kind of man she had automatically shunned when she was younger, sensing the danger within herself of any responsiveness to his brand of sexuality. His was the kind of maleness which would mean that he would automatically and instinctively seek to subjugate a woman to his sexual charisma, and for some reason she had sensed even in those days that she was particularly vulnerable to that kind of intense relationship, that something within her almost wanted to be absorbed and swamped by the sexual power she sensed within him, that some part of her had wanted simply to sink herself into its potency, to abandon independence, self-will: everything she had fought all her life to have.

She had been like an animal fascinated by the danger of fire, wanting its heat and light and yet knowing that to allow herself to get too close could destroy her—and yet still she had lingered within sight of the flames, resenting their power over her, hating herself and hating him, because, despite the strength of her love for Scott— a kind of love which had a clean, sharp purity about it, a simplistic, wholesome innocence—she had still been conscious of the darker side of her nature, had known it was slowly gathering force inside her, had known that it responded to everything that was male in Daniel in a way that no part of her had ever responded to Scott . . . Had known that Daniel had the ability to reach out and touch that innermost part of her that she kept hidden and locked away not only from others but from herself as well.

In those days she had feared that deep core of sensuality; had compared it to her mother's icy purity, to David and Faye's idyllically romantic relationship, had felt the deep yawning gap that existed between the emotions she perceived in them and those she knew herself to be so unwantedly capable of feeling, and had angrily repudiated her sensuality, seeing it as the whole centre of her flawed personality, sensing with burgeoning maturity that still clung too much to childhood to allow to her to assess it either accurately or with detachment that it represented danger to her, that it exposed her to vulnerability and to emotional and physical abuse. She had felt she was not as the other members of her family; that those deep, dark tides that moved within her were almost an ancient and destructive curse which she must learn to control and deny, so that the moment she had looked at Daniel and felt them rise inside her in a wild, fierce rip-tide of responsiveness to him, she had hated him with all the intense passion of her still untamed nature.

Someone not knowing her as well as she knew herself would undoubtedly wonder why after being repudiated by Daniel she should have flung herself headlong into what appeared to be a series of intensely physical affairs.

The reason was that those men with whom she had enjoyed the physical expression of her deeply sensual nature had not had the power to touch the equally intense emotional core of her.

Physically she had desired them, had found their love-making pleasurable, had even with some found them intellectually stimulating, but always, always she had

taken care never to become involved with anyone to
whom she might become vulnerable emotionally.

The lessons of her life had been hard learned. None
of those whom she had loved had ever returned the
intensity of that love—all of them had seen the flaws in
her and rejected her because of them: her father, her
mother, Scott. She was safer by far allowing herself only
the physical, sexual expression of that intensity, and now
even the pleasure of that had palled. Like a child sated
on too many sweet things, she had found herself turning
away from those pleasures, abandoning their reckless
pursuit, finding a longer lasting pleasure and satisfaction in her work than she had ever found in the arms
of a lover.

Now when she looked back she viewed the woman she
had been with distant amusement. For the first time in
her life she had begun to feel at ease with herself, to
accept herself as a whole person, flaws and all, to
acknowledge that she could never be her mother, that
she could only be herself...to accept herself. As she
watched the companions of her early twenties marry and
settle down to produce families she remained aloof from
their—to her—lemming-like desire to fulfil their
hormonal destiny. She was a loner; she liked it that way,
she was content with her life, or at least as content as
any human being could expect to be. She was well past
the age when she had believed that the only real value
of a human life came from sharing that life with a twin
soul; had long since abandoned the restless searching of
her growing years for that part of herself she had always
felt was missing, that cooling sanity of mind to still the
heated frenzy that was her own emotional burden. In
Scott she had believed she had found that person, had
believed it so intensely and so passionately that to lose
him had been like losing a part of herself.

She had long since accepted that had they married she
would ultimately have destroyed him, that in all the
wrong ways she was the stronger of the two, and yet
those months she had spent with him had had such a

softening effect on her, had made her feel so different about herself...

Daniel Cavanagh... Even now she had not forgotten that final collision between them. That night when she had gone to him in an agony of need and despair, when she had deliberately blinded herself to everything she knew both about herself and him, when she had...

Stop it, she told herself fiercely. Stop it... Hadn't she writhed for long enough on the acid fires of self-hatred and contempt? So Daniel had rejected her. She ought to be thankful that he had. If they had become lovers...

Against the darkness of her mind, she had a moment's brilliant awareness of how many dangerous memories were still stored in the sensors of her body, of how she could still conjure up so clearly the sensation of those long-fingered hands touching her skin, of how the shocking thrill of that contact had run along her nerve-endings, drawing tight the pulsing flesh of her nipples, spiralling an aching, restless heat through her belly, making her want to reach out and touch him in turn, not gently, or virginally, but with hunger and need, with all the deep yearning heat that boiled inside her.

Yes, she ought to have been grateful that he rejected her... To have given in to that need would ultimately have destroyed her, and yet the shadows cast by his rejection still darkened certain areas of her mind, still lay like bruises against her pride. There were still nights when she woke up, her body aching and her mind confused, tears on her face, heat under her skin, aware that somewhere in her dreams she had been pursuing the touch of hands so much needed by her body, so intensely desired by her emotions that she was destined to pursue it ceaselessly throughout eternity and beyond. And then reality would sweep away the darkness of her dreams just as she banished what she considered to be an illogical weakness. She hadn't thought about Daniel in years now, not since she had finally grown up and accepted that she was more than capable of being her own person, that she could survive alone, that she had more strength, more will-power, more pride than she had ever allowed herself to admit.

She didn't need Daniel Cavanagh in her life.

So why was she deliberately seeking him out? She wasn't . . . At least not for any personal reasons. She was simply using him because he was there. That was all there was to it.

She moved restlessly, pushing aside the bedclothes, and swinging long slender legs to the floor. It was time to get up and stop dwelling on the past. She had far more immediate and important things on which to focus her mind.

When she got downstairs Faye and Camilla seemed to be arguing. She paused on the threshold of the breakfast-room, frowning as she listened to them.

Camilla's voice was indignant and angry, Faye's sharper than usual.

'I'm sorry, Camilla, but I don't want you to go. For one thing, you've got your A levels coming up...'

'And one evening off from studying is going to make the difference between passing and failing?' Camilla retorted indignantly. 'Come off it. You don't want me to go because you don't want me to enjoy myself.'

'Camilla, that isn't true,' Faye protested. 'Of course I do——'

'No, you don't. Otherwise you'd let me go. Everyone else is——'

'Everyone?' Faye asked her wryly. 'I thought you said you were going in a minibus?'

Sage saw her niece flush angrily. 'Well, almost everyone. Look, I don't see why you don't want me to go.'

'Don't you? You say you're going to a party, but you don't seem to have any real idea of where it's being held. You say you're going with friends from school, and that one of their boyfriends will be driving this minibus, and yet you don't seem able to give me any of their names. I'm sorry, Camilla, but I don't feel that I can allow you to take off with a crowd of young people I don't know for a destination you don't seem able to give me to attend a party. You must have seen for yourself the dangers of attending these Acid House affairs and——'

'This isn't anything like that,' Camilla protested. 'Honestly, Mother, do you really think I'm so stupid? And anyway, why should my generation take the blame for something started by yours? It was all right for you when you were young. Everyone knows what the sixties were like. Drugs...sex... Anything went, and what do *we* get? Everyone lecturing us about drugs and promiscuity.'

Over Camilla's head Faye gave Sage a helpless, pleading look.

Coming to her rescue, Sage said quietly, 'Your mother's right, Cam. It's sheer irresponsibility these days to take off anywhere with people you don't know properly—and you're right as well. Our generation does have a lot to answer for. Recklessly we thought we could break all the rules, and now it's your generation that's paying the price for our so-called pleasure. I can understand that you want a break from your studying, though,' she added calmly, sitting down and pretending not to be aware of Camilla's sullen pouting face.

None of them was the same person she had been before her mother's accident, Sage reflected inwardly. All of them had changed and were still changing, Camilla perhaps most of all, because in so many ways she had been the closest to her mother. Underlying her present recalcitrance there ran, Sage suspected, a frighteningly fast-flowing flood of fear. Camilla was at that very vulnerable age when to lose someone she loved and relied on could have far-reaching consequences that would remain with her for the rest of her life.

She personally had never heard mother and daughter exchange a cross word before and had often marvelled a little enviously at the harmony that existed between them. Now with her mother's accident that harmony had vanished, and Faye, like Camilla and herself, had changed. Sage had never seen her so on edge, so...so human—as though the fine bubble which had always seemed to protect her from reality had finally burst, leaving her exposed to the rough abrasions of real life.

She even looked different, Sage reflected, studying her. There was more colour in her face, more fire in her eyes, and an unmistakable air of tension about her movements.

'Oh, I might know you'd side with Ma,' Camilla expostulated, and then added bitterly, 'If Gran were here, she'd understand—— '

'Don't be ridiculous, Camilla,' Faye interrupted her crossly. 'You know quite well that your grandmother would no more have sanctioned this party than I would. Please be sensible. You've got your exams to think about.'

'Exams, exams... Is that all you think about? Is that all I mean to you? A set of A level passes you can brag about to your friends? Only I forgot—you don't have any friends, do you? But I'm not like you, Mother, I can't spend the rest of my life shut off from everyone else. I want to live. I'm sick of studying, sick of doing what I'm told. I'm almost eighteen. I'm not a child any longer—— '

'Then stop behaving like one.'

Sage sighed under her breath. Couldn't Faye see that all she was doing was alienating Camilla even more? Couldn't she see that the underlying cause of her rebellion was probably her fear of losing her grandmother? That this bid for independence, this furious teenage anger, was probably sparked off by that fear?

Sage flinched as Camilla stood up abruptly, pushed her chair back, tears thickening her voice as she claimed, 'I might have known you wouldn't understand. Well, whatever you say, I'm not a child. I have a right to choose what I want to do with my life, not to have you make those decisions for me.'

'Camilla, come back here.'

Faye stood up too, angry spots of colour burning along her cheekbones as she stared in disbelief at Camilla's retreating back.

'Let her go,' Sage counselled.

'I can't understand what's got into her. She's always been so sensible...'

She saw the way Sage looked at her as she asked drily, 'Isn't that rather dangerous? Sensible behaviour from a teenager... a sign perhaps of hidden unrest and turmoil beneath the surface?'

'You mean that you think that Camilla's been deliberately repressed?'

'No... What I mean is that Camilla is reacting fairly predictably. She's young and she's frightened. Alongside yourself, the one person she can normally rely on to listen to her and to guide her, the one person she has always felt she can rely on, has suddenly become frighteningly vulnerable herself. Right at this moment, she's probably lying on her bed, crying her eyes out, wondering why on earth she feels so furious with Mother for having this accident and feeling guilty because she does feel angry. Is this party really out of the question? It might do her good to relax, let her hair down a bit...'

'Absolutely. For one thing she can't or won't tell me who's organising it or where it is. All she will say very vaguely is that a crowd of girls from school are going, and some boys that they know.'

'Mm... it does sound rather suspect. How about organising a rival distraction? A sort of pre-exam fling... There's plenty of space here and I'm sure Jenny would be only too pleased to help out with the food et cetera. It might even be an idea to get Camilla and her friends to do the catering themselves. Give her something other than Mother and her exams to occupy her mind...'

'You mean let her have a party here... now, with Liz still desperately ill and——'

The shocked disgust in Faye's voice irritated Sage.

'For goodness' sake,' she broke in cynically, 'what difference is it going to make to Mother? All I'm suggesting is using a healthy diversionary tactic to prevent Camilla from going into a headlong rebellion which could result in something far more dangerous than sulks and a bout of tears.'

Faye went pale. 'You aren't suggesting that she'd defy me and go to this affair behind my back?'

Was Faye really so naïve? Sage wondered grimly. Couldn't she see that by her refusal to find some middle road that she and Camilla could travel together she was virtually alienating her altogether, and that Camilla might see her refusal to accept that she was almost adult and that she had a right to govern her own life, at least in part, as the kind of challenge no right-minded teenager could ignore?

'But she's never done anything like this,' Faye protested, genuinely shocked and disturbed. 'She's always been so well-behaved...'

When Sage remained silent she frowned. 'You think I'm being unreasonable and unfair, don't you?' she said bitterly into the silence. 'Can't you see that all I want to do is protect her? To keep her safe to make sure...'

She broke off, but not before Sage had heard the fierce passion in her voice.

'I'm not trying to criticise, Faye,' she said quietly. 'God knows in your shoes I'd have made every mistake in the book, and I can understand how you feel, but you can't protect her all the time... not without making her so vulnerable that the moment she's exposed to reality she'll be in mortal danger, like a child kept in a totally germ-free environment who is so vulnerable to infection that it could die from a common cold.

'It's only natural that a girl of her age should want to go out and have fun. I'm simply suggesting that if you allow her to have some measure of that fun here in the relative safety of her own home she'd be less at risk than if she did defy you and go off to this party, which I agree with you sounds very suspect indeed.'

'A bit like saying that it's all right for a child to play with matches as long as there's someone around with a fire extinguisher,' Faye suggested sarcastically.

Sage refused to rise to the bait, saying only, 'Something like that, yes. With any luck she'll burn her fingers and nothing else and the shock of that small pain will ensure that she doesn't run the risk of a much bigger and possibly fatal one.'

'I'm not listening to any more of this——' Faye began, her mouth tightening, making her look oddly like her daughter. She stopped as the phone rang imperiously.

Sage, who was closest to the receiver, reached for it, her muscles tensing as she heard a female voice saying crisply that Dr Ferguson wanted to speak with her.

She had to wait several seconds before she was put through; something which would normally have irritated her immeasurably, but on this occasion she found she was holding her breath, mentally praying, Dear God, please let her be all right. Please...please...

'Miss Danvers, I wanted to have a word with you about your mother.'

How on earth did he always manage to sound so exhausted and clinically distant at the same time? Sage wondered as she tightened her grip on the receiver.

'She's holding her own very nicely now, and we think her condition has stabilised enough for us to go ahead and operate...'

Sage tried to speak and found she couldn't. Her mouth had gone dry, her throat muscles locking against the spasm of fear that wrenched through her.

'When?' was all she could croak into the heart-numbing silence. She found herself wishing desperately she could see him. If she could she was sure that by looking into his eyes she would know whether or not he expected her mother to survive, whether he was simply talking about an operation for form's sake, knowing how limited were its chances of success, or whether he really believed her mother had a fighting chance.

'The day after tomorrow.'

Two days... Two days, that was all. After that...

'I... We... Can we see her first? Today?'

'Not today—we've only just got her stabilised. She is conscious though, and the excitement and anxiety of having visitors could destabilise her too easily. You can see her before we operate. I'll get my secretary to get in touch with you and let you know when...'

Sage was just about to hang up when he asked her in a totally different voice, almost as though the question was being dragged from him against his will, 'Your sister-in-law got home safely, did she?'

Sage just stared across the table. Faye must have been able to hear what he was saying because her face, which had been pale and set, suddenly burned with the hot colour that crawled up under her skin.

'Yes... yes, she did,' Sage told him, not taking her eyes off Faye. 'Would you like to have a word with her?'

Faye was making frantic dismissive signals to her, anger sparkling in her eyes.

The faint hesitancy had gone completely from his voice as he denied curtly, 'No, that won't be necessary. Goodbye, Miss Danvers.'

Sage stared at her sister-in-law as she replaced the receiver, waiting for Faye to say something, to make some comment, but to her surprise Faye stood up awkwardly and said only, 'So they're going to go ahead and operate... Oh, my God, I hope they know what they're doing...'

'So do I,' Sage agreed. In the desk drawer there were still several unread diaries, and suddenly she had a fierce urge to read them now, as though there was a compelling need to do so before her mother's operation.

There was plenty of time, she told herself... She could read them tonight while she waited for Daniel Cavanagh to let her know his decision—perhaps he might call today, instead of tomorrow.

Daniel Cavanagh... Odd how she had never realised he had met her mother, but then why should she? She and Liz had not exactly been close confidantes over the years. Enmity rather than love had been the strongest emotion between them. On her part at least... The coldness her mother had always shown her, which had so distressed her during the years of her growing-up, repelled and angered her once she was adult, and yet the Liz she was coming to know so well through the diaries was the exact opposite of the woman she had always believed her mother to be. There was no coldness in that woman; no lack of compassion, of emotion—far from it... So why had she reacted so differently to her? She had heard of some women rejecting a particular child. Was that what had happened to her? Had her mother rejected her for some reason—was that why she had held her so much at a distance?

As an adult she had tried to analyse why her mother had always been so distant from her, and had ended up persuading herself that it was simply a matter of two personalities that would always clash rather than meld. It could not be that she was the result of an unwanted pregnancy; the mere fact that her mother had gone through what surely, to a woman of her temperament, must have been a comparatively difficult and embarrassing set of procedures to even conceive her had to prove that she had been wanted.

She wondered whose had been the decision to initiate that conception. There was such a large gap between herself and David that she could not have been wanted as a companion for an only child.

For her mother to have even contemplated conception by artificial insemination could only point to a deeply felt need for a second child in its own right. Had it been perhaps that she had wanted another boy?

What was the point in asking herself these questions now? Maybe the diaries would give her the answers. All she could know was that surely both her parents must have wanted a second child to have agreed to the procedures necessary to produce her. She had long ago come to accept that her father most probably had rejected her because it was not his seed which had given her life...another man had supplied that all-important spark, even if anonymously and totally distantly, without any physical contact between himself and her mother.

It seemed ironic to her that she, with her wild, hot-headed temperament, should be the product of something as cold and clinical as conception via the instrument of modern technical science.

Jenny came in while she was absorbed in her own thoughts, her eyebrows lifting when she saw she was alone.

'No one else hungry?' Jenny questioned, eyeing both Faye's and Camilla's clean plates.

'They had a row,' Sage told her. 'We've had some news about Mother. They're going to operate in two days. It will be very much touch and go. They're going to let us see her beforehand...'

She was surprised when Jenny reached out and hugged her. Women rarely touched her. She had an aloofness about her which, married to her elegance and sexuality, made her own sex unnecessarily wary with her, and now, with Jenny's plump arms around her, she felt an unexpected urge to give in to a surprisingly childish reaction to her comfort by bursting into tears.

'It will be all right, Sage, love. You'll see. Your mother's too strong to give up...'

'I hope so, Jenny, I hope so... Look, I'm going out for half an hour or so. If anyone should ring...' She paused, wondering if Daniel would ring while she was out, suspecting that he might deliberately wait until his forty-eight hours were up before making any attempt to get in touch with her.

'Tell them... Oh, just tell them I've gone out.'

She took the Porsche, driving into the village where she stopped at the post office to buy herself a paper. The small shop-cum-post office was packed. Everyone seemed to know about her mother and wanted to commiserate with her. They also all seemed to have strong and voluble views on the new road, which they also wanted to communicate to her, so that it was almost an hour before she was free to escape.

A restless gnawing urgency, reminiscent of the worst of her teenage moods, seemed to have overtaken her; she didn't want to go back to the house and Camilla and Faye's squabble, and yet she didn't want to be too far away either. Why? In case Daniel suddenly unexpectedly arrived? And what if he did? It wouldn't mean anything other than that he had come to a decision. You didn't blackmail a man like Daniel and suddenly miraculously transform his dislike and contempt both for you and for his own physical desire for you into respect and . . . And what? What was it she wanted from him?

Nothing, she told herself savagely, climbing into the Porsche and jerkily starting the engine. She didn't want anything from him.

Not even the satisfaction of wiping away the memory of how he had rejected her—not even the satisfaction of supplanting it with another and far more satisfactory reaction. Her body tensed, a wild pulse suddenly throbbing at the base of her throat, her skin tight with heat and shock. Why, why, why did the thought of Daniel finding her desirable...wanting her...being aroused by her have such an immediate and erotic effect on her own senses?

Cynically she answered her own question. If you don't know the answer to that one by now, my girl, then you haven't learned much over the years.

She knew the answer all right, but she didn't want to confront the reasons behind it.

Forget Daniel Cavanagh, she warned herself, and yet she still drove north of the village instead of south, still turned the car down the lane that led to the land Daniel had bought, still parked it there, a showy scarlet monstrosity that suddenly had lost its appeal for her.

What was she trying to prove with it? That she could afford to buy it, that she could drive as well as any man, that she liked danger and excitement—was she really still so immature? She eyed the car with disfavour as she clambered out of it and mentally made herself a promise to replace it. What with, though? Perhaps an Aston Martin. She chuckled to herself at the improbability of her ever being able to afford such a luxury, and she was still smiling as she climbed over the stile and down on to the overgrown path that led to the Old Hall.

Derelict now, it had gates to its drives which were padlocked and bolted. Agnes Hazelby, its last occupant, had lived in it in a state of eccentric stubbornness, refusing to admit that the place was falling down around her.

From the top of the slight hill where she was standing,
she had an uninterrupted view of the house. Larger at
one stage than Cottingdean, the oldest section had been
built at the same time, with a wing being added on by
a Georgian owner and another by his Victorian successor.

The Victorian wing had been destroyed by fire; the
ancient lathe and plaster mid-section was still standing—
just—while the Georgian wing, cursed with the inheritance of sound building principles being sacrificed for
outward show, had massive cracks in its walls and was
very obviously subsiding beneath the weight of its top-
heavy structure on insubstantial foundations.

And yet there was an odd raffish charm about it, a
compelling, almost laughable arrogance that demanded
recognition and respect.

She was not surprised that Agnes had stipulated that
whoever bought the land must not tear down the house,
and yet what use was the land to Daniel if he didn't?
The type of people who would buy his expensive, modern
executive houses would never tolerate an eyesore like the
Old Hall on their doorsteps.

It surprised her that she should feel such sharp and
searing pain in the knowledge that he had lied and
cheated. She ought to be glad...

Slowly she made her way down the path, not really
knowing what she was doing here, why she was bothering, what she hoped to find... or why she should even
need to think there might be something to find.

The closer she came to the house, the more obvious
its decay became. Distance had lent a veil to its dereliction and she was almost glad when she eventually
reached the valley bottom, and the garden wall, with its
enshrouding band of tangled overgrown trees and shrubs,
hiding everything bar the chimneys from view.

As a child she had been fascinated by this house,
something about its derelict and overgrown mystery
appealing to her in a way which her own immaculate
home never had.

Perhaps she was more like her mother than she had
known, she realised. She had seen from the diaries how

much a part of her mother had enjoyed the challenge of taking Cottingdean and making it into something that was almost purely her own. Her mother was a builder, she recognised; a creator who enjoyed the challenge of taking the most basic raw materials of life and constructing something for the future from them. Take the way she had seen the potential of the sheep and developed the mill into the prosperous business it was today.

Only someone with vision could have done that. She too, she saw now, had her own share of that vision, her own specific talents . . . not her mother's talents but her own. So why, when she had come to know herself so well, when she had struggled to come to terms with all that she was and all that she was not, why, when she had told herself that she must accept herself the way she was—that she must like and respect herself before she could expect others to follow suit, that she must find a way of living that allowed her to dwell in harmony and peace with herself—was there still a small part of her that was the child crying and kicking at her father's door, demanding to be allowed in to his presence . . . demanding to be given his love?

Was it something within her that made it impossible for her to be loved in the way she had once craved? Or was it simply that she had asked too much, wanted too much . . . that such an intensity of emotion was bound to repel anyone at whom it was directed?

Whatever the case, she had long ago learned to repress and restrain the intensity. After losing Scott she had turned her back on the deeply emotional side of her nature and concentrated on the physical, but all too quickly the efficacy of that pleasure had waned, forcing her to acknowledge that for her there could never be a safe middle road; that she must either opt for physical and emotional celibacy, holding herself aloof and distant from all but the most casual of emotional relationships, or she must commit herself totally and wholly to the fulfilment of the intensity of her need to love so completely and utterly. She had learned enough from her

relationship with Scott to be aware of how dangerous
that kind of commitment would be.

She found a gate in the wall and pushed it open. The
wood was rotting and split, the garden beyond it a wild
tangle of overgrown shrubs, knee-high nettles and weeds.

The garden lay under an almost magical veil of for-
gottenness, like Sleeping Beauty's castle. She smiled bitterly to herself as she fought her way through the
undergrowth and along the narrow path.

Daniel was no prince to awaken the house to life with
loving tenderness. Rather he was its destroyer.

Beyond the trees and shrubs lay what might once have
been immaculate lawns but which now resembled an
overgrown meadow, the long grass interspersed with wild
flowers and weeds.

The grass was damp, soaking through her jeans, but
she had come too far to go back now. Her arms were
scratched from the brambles, stung by the nettles, and
her normally sleek hair had been caught by so many
overhanging branches that she lost her patience and
angrily twisted it into an untidy ponytail with a piece of
string she had found in the pocket of her jeans.

She had approached the house from the side, where
the full dereliction of the ruined Victorian wing with its
sprawl of weed-cloaked remains and blackened timbers
yawned eerily out of the thin whispers of the morning
mist.

It was said in the village that, after the fire, those who
had come originally to help put it out returned later,
pushing whatever carts they could find to remove the
best of the undamaged bricks, and that several cottages
in the village had sprouted sudden additions.

The sight of the derelict, shattered building always
saddened Sage and she hurried past it quickly, turning
her face away as she rounded the corner of the building,
and walked into the enclosed courtyard to the rear of
the house.

Weeds had sprung up between the cobbles of the yard,
windows yawned emptily from both the out-buildings
and the house itself.

Someone had placed a large and very efficient padlock on the heavy wooden back door. Sage studied it for a moment and then shrugged her shoulders. Quite why she wanted to go inside the house she really had no idea. Something had driven her here this morning—some instinct, some need, and she did not intend to be balked of that need by Daniel Cavanagh's padlocks.

It was a simple matter for her to clamber up to one of the yawning windows; less simple perhaps to slide her body through its narrow aperture, but with some wriggling she did manage it, grimacing a little at the dust marks on her jeans from the stone lintel as she scrambled down on to the uneven stone floor of one of the sculleries.

The house smelled of damp and decay. An old chair, gaping holes in its worn cover, the stuffing spilling from them, added to the air of desolation. As she walked across the floor, Sage closed her ears to the soft scufflings and squeaks that rustled around her.

In Agnes's day she had visited the house quite often. Her mother had kept a neighbourly eye on the older woman, and Sage had been fascinated enough by the house and its occupant to relish these visits.

In those days Agnes had lived mainly in one bedroom, the kitchen and a small sitting-room. The rest of the house had even then been falling into a state of disrepair, what furniture there was in the other rooms enshrouded with white linen covers, which had been referred to as 'hollands' and which, her mother had explained to Sage, was an old-fashioned term for the covers used to protect the furniture in large houses when its occupants were away.

To Sage they had always been reminiscent of shrouds; white and ghostly and somehow filled with sadness.

Now, as she walked through the sculleries and pantries, and then the kitchen, she saw that most of the furniture had gone.

No doubt Daniel with his orderly mind wanted the house cleared before he finally dealt it its death blow.

The Tudor section of the house had a small narrow hallway with a flight of equally narrow stairs, which Agnes had always referred to as the servants' stairs. The main hallway was in the Georgian wing of the building, a pretty oval room, with a delicate marble and wrought-iron staircase that seemed to float upwards through all four storeys of the building. Sage remembered how amazed and enthralled she had been as a child to look up the entire height of the building and to see a painting on its ceiling enclosed in a delicate oval plaster frame— a mural depicting what her mother had explained to her was meant to represent the Greek god Zeus peering down towards the earth through dark thunder-clouds.

As she picked her way through rooms thick with cobwebs and dust, filled with stale damp air, trying not to look at the betraying stains on the walls and ceilings, trying not to notice rotting panelling and damaged stucco, she wondered if the mural was still there.

It was... True, the once magnificently storm-laden clouds had now turned a uniform leaden grey, the paint flaking off in places. True, Zeus's once proud features had become obscured and faded. True, since she had first set eyes on this mural she had visited Italy and seen the magnificence of Michelangelo's breathtaking Sistine Chapel. But perhaps your first awareness of something that was to motivate your whole life was like your first lover... Something you never forgot, something you always remembered with affection and tenderness, something you cherished in your heart with loyalty and love.

She might cherish her awed reaction to her first realisation that someone, a person had actually painted Zeus and his clouds on the ceiling, but she certainly did not cherish any memories of her first lover. Not in the way she would have done if Daniel...

She tensed immediately like someone trying to clamp down on intense physical agony, the ceiling blurring as she fought against what she was feeling.

She started to climb the stairs, trying to concentrate on her physical movements to blot out the enormity of her thoughts.

At first-floor height, a narrow oval gallery encircled the hallway. A corridor led off it to the bedrooms, its style repeated on the second floor. Sage paused at first-floor level, noticing how much of the balustrading was missing...how dangerous and uneven the floorboards were. Plaster and dust covered the floor, and no matter how carefully she placed her feet every time she moved she sent up choking clouds of dust. The closer she got to the mural, the more she was aware of its destruction. Paint was peeling away from the plaster in thin soft sheets. Daniel would need to do nothing to destroy Zeus—time and neglect had already done his work for him.

She felt tears sting her eyes. Suddenly all she wanted to do was to escape from the house and its forlornness.

She turned on her heel and started back down the stairs, coming to an abrupt halt near the bottom, the breath hissing out of her lungs, as she saw Daniel Cavanagh standing below her in the hall watching her.

'What are you doing here?' she demanded aggressively, masking her own shock.

He looked up at her and then said with deceptive calm, 'Well, I'm not trespassing.'

Sage stared at him, felt herself flush as guiltily as a schoolgirl, saw him come towards her, and, without knowing why, took an instinctive step backwards, losing her balance as she stepped on to a piece of fallen plaster.

She heard Daniel call out sharply and warningly. As she stumbled she reached for the balustrade, only she missed it and with nothing to hold on to...nothing to stop her fall, she plummeted through space and down towards the marble floor.

She heard herself cry out, closing her eyes automatically, tensing her body for its impact with the floor, but instead she felt hard fingers grab hold of her, heard the savage rush of breath that left Daniel's chest as he caught hold of her, heard him curse with what was left of that breath as he dragged her free of the plaster and debris which were showering down around them.

'You little fool, couldn't you see those stairs weren't safe?' Daniel was shouting in her ear.

The shock of her near accident had made her light-headed. 'Is that what you're going to claim when you raze it to the ground?' she flung at him.

She then gasped as he literally lifted her off her feet and shook her, saying angrily, 'You stupid woman, don't you understand? You could have been killed.'

She already knew that, and her stomach was still twisting nauseously with that knowledge, and yet she still fought it and him, saying mockingly, 'So what? It would have let you off the hook, wouldn't it? Pity you didn't think about that before rushing in to play Sir Galahad.'

'My God.'

She could feel the bite of his fingers into her skin, even through the protection of her sweater, wincing at their crushing strength. She felt faint and sick and more vulnerable then she could remember feeling in a long time.

There was something sticky and hot on her face, and as she raised her hand to touch it her fingers came away stained with blood.

'It's all right,' Daniel told her roughly, one hand leaving her arm to push her fingers away. 'It's only a scratch.'

She jerked back from him as he reached out to touch her skin, her eyes reminding him in their ferocity of an eagle's. There was dust on her skin, and with her hair tied up in that ponytail she looked as young as she had done the first time he had seen her. Emotions he had thought he had long ago taught himself not to feel boiled up inside him. She could have been killed, could have been lying there on the floor under that crushing burden of wood, plaster and metal, her face as white as it had been the night she had come to him and...

Sage didn't like being so close to him. It stirred up too many memories. She was having to fight too hard to stop herself from simply letting go and leaning into him...on to him... From...

'You've always got to fight, haven't you, Sage?' she heard him challenging her. 'You've always got to prove how tough you are. How independent, how invulnerable, and how you enjoy it... You just love putting us down, don't you? Do you know what they call you behind your back, when they've finally managed to crawl out of your bed? They say that for all your sexual skill, for all your experience and your inventiveness, at heart you're a real balls-breaker, and as destructive as hell.'

She went white and then red, not knowing why she should feel this raging, searing pain, not knowing why she should care what he thought of her, not knowing why she felt this helpless, crippling, endless pain, only knowing that she had to hurt him back, to kick out at him...to retaliate and wound him as cruelly as he had done her.

She tried to break free of his hold and, when he wouldn't let her go, said bitterly, 'Then it's just as well that you turned me down all those years ago, isn't it? Trust a man like you to protect his precious machismo...'

'A man like me.' He was furious with her and showing it. 'You don't know the first thing about me,' he told her.

'And you don't know the first thing about me,' she flung back.

'Oh, no? I know you want this.'

She had been kissed before in anger, had even deliberately incited that kind of anger, enjoying the sexual power it gave her, but suddenly and painfully this was different, her mind and body wiped clear of the memories which should have given her the experience to cope with what was happening to her. She couldn't move in his arms, felt frighteningly helpless beneath his mouth, unable to reject its bruising pressure, so that her lips were as vulnerable and defenceless as though the only kisses they had previously known had been those free from any kind of sexual intimacy. Her body felt curiously stiff, locked in a strange paralysis, which she recognised as stemming from intense shock. The shock of her near accident, the shock of Daniel's presence...and most of all the shock of this brutal, punishing kiss that wiped away all the years that lay between them, transporting her instantly back to another time, another place, another occasion when she would have welcomed the ferocity of that angry male mouth.

Suddenly she broke free of her paralysis, biting angrily at his mouth as she fought its dominance, but to her shock he retaliated equally violently, his teeth savaging her bottom lip so that she could taste the hot salt of her own blood.

She made a helpless, angry sound and touched the wound with her tongue, only to have it pushed out of the way by his as he quickly explored the small wound and then explored it again, far more slowly, stroking the violently sensitive flesh.

It was such a brief touch, such a stupid weakness...such an implausible cause of the heat that exploded so violently inside her, taking her so completely off guard that she had no way of protecting herself against it, could only stare at him with angry, betrayed eyes as she felt the rolling heat burn through her body. Helpless to stop the sudden fierce tightening of her nipples, the brief flaring of longing that darkened her eyes, the small betraying sound she tried to stifle in her throat. All of these were nothing compared with the reckless racking agony of need that pulsed so sharply through her lower body, enforcing on her too-intelligent mind the knowledge that if he chose to, right here and now, without the softening veils of shared liking, humour or respect, without any of the trappings of civilisation and sophistication, without the excuse of senses blurred by a good wine, soft light and sensual music, without even the comfort of her own bed, without any of the fastidious trimmings she normally considered an essential ingredient of any kind of sexual intimacy—clean linen sheets, the amusement and assurance of knowing how much her partner desired her, of how much she could tease and torment him—without even the most simple and basic precautions against pregnancy, she would eagerly, hungrily, wantonly have allowed Daniel to bring the explosive violence between them to its natural conclusion, in an act of possession as immediate and violent as the need it had aroused within her.

It was a knowledge that nauseated and horrified her. Whatever else she might have been, she had never, never descended to those depths, to that kind of personal degradation... She had never wanted a man like this...never felt this savage raw hunger for another human being to such an extent that it transcended every single one of her most deeply held and most private tenets of self-respect and pride...

As she stared into his face she had a second's horrifying awareness that Daniel knew exactly what she was feeling, just as intimately as she did herself; she saw the knowledge in his eyes and was sickened by the realisation of it, shocked back to a burning, bitter reality that had her tearing herself out of his arms, at the same time as he said thickly, 'No, Sage, don't...'

He was standing between her and the door, and she could see no way of effecting the escape she so desperately craved. No way of salving her pride by ignoring what had happened, by lying or pretence...

There was nothing for her to do but face him. She did it as bravely as she could, knowing there was no point in concealment, in the fiction of a deceit which would convince neither of them, and only leave her feeling worse than she already did.

Head held high, she asked bitingly, her voice low with self-revulsion, 'Don't what, Daniel? Don't lust after you like a bitch on heat?'

She saw the bones in his face tighten as his jaw clenched and she laughed bitterly. 'You're quite right. It's obscene, isn't it? Disgusting—the very last thing you want, and the very last thing I want as well. You needn't worry—these days I do have some small measure of self-control.'

She gave him a glitteringly painful smile that made him wince and ache inside. 'Don't ask me why I want you—I don't know the answer. Perhaps it's the old story of the one who got away.' She was back in control of herself now, her voice strong and self-mocking, the whiteness dying out of her skin, the shock leaving the green eyes remote and wary, as though she was looking not at him, but beyond him.

Determinedly she walked towards him, intending to leave, but he checked her, standing in her way, 'Sage, we——'

'There is no "we",' she told him sharply. 'There never has been and there never will be.'

'You want me.'

She looked at him, her eyes a bitter hell of rage and impotence. 'Yes,' she agreed shakily. 'But I want my self-respect more. Gaining it has been a long, hard fight for me, Daniel. I don't need any man to have sex with me out of pity or curiosity... and if you were thinking of using my... my vulnerability towards you in order to bribe me into conveniently forgetting about your involvement with this place...'

She'd gone too far. She saw it in his eyes, felt the fierce burn of his anger, suddenly gone out of control.

Panic clawed at her, an entirely female panic born of instincts given to the feminine sex at the very beginning of time. She tried to push past him, forgetting all that her life had taught her, but instead of standing to one side he caught hold of her, half lifting her off her feet as he almost slammed her back against the wall, imprisoning her there with the weight of his body, while his fingers closed round her wrists, restraining her flaying arms.

As his mouth touched hers, she heard him saying fiercely, 'I should have done this years ago. God knows if I had...'

The words stopped, dying beneath the pressure of a kiss she tried to tell herself that neither her body nor her soul had hungered for for nearly a half of her whole lifetime. Memories she had thought long forgotten stirred, giving birth to an aching need, and with that need came her old fear, her old dread that this man above all others possessed something that was so dangerous to her that even to allow herself to acknowledge its presence was to fatally weaken her own defences.

She fought against herself and him with every ounce of self-control she had, but he knew her vulnerability now, knew it and used it against her, refusing to accept the closed hard line of her mouth, the rigid, defensively tight muscles of her body, letting his full weight rest tormentingly against her, keeping her arms at her sides, while he moved against her with such deliberate sensuality that her soul cried out inside her in silent anguished need and her flesh ached as though it had been pummelled by a thousand tormenting fists.

As he felt the response stir inside her, and suffered his own helpless, overwhelming reaction to it, he lifted his mouth from hers, briefly relaxing the pressure that imprisoned her, wanting to find the words to soften the bitterness in her eyes, to tell her that she wasn't alone in either her anguish or her need, but that brief moment of relaxation was all she needed to break his hold on her, and to push past him, almost running towards the door.

He could have stopped her... could have caught up with her and taken her back in his arms, but he had never forced a woman to make love with him in his life, and the revulsion he felt at the thought of doing so now checked him.

CHAPTER NINETEEN

SAGE didn't stop running until she had reached the sanctuary of her car.

Once there, she turned the key in the ignition and locked the doors, but she was shaking far too much to drive. Her body was hot with sweat and fear. She wiped her trembling hands on her jeans, grimacing as she did so. She was appalled by her own self-betrayal, her almost total loss of self-control. She wasn't nineteen any more, for God's sake, she told herself angrily as she set the car in motion at last. What on earth had made her go overboard like that? She had enough experience of her own sexual needs and those of the majority of the heterosexual male sex to have been able to avoid that disastrous conclusion to her run-in with Daniel.

It was no use telling herself that it was the shock of seeing him so unexpectedly—it was no use telling herself anything other than the truth, and since that truth was something she didn't have the strength to face up to right now, the best thing she could do was to blot it out of her mind. It wasn't as though she didn't have anything else to think about... She smiled cynically to herself, wondering how her mother would have reacted in similar circumstances...

Would she have retained her ladylike self-control, her calm self-assurance? Would she...?

Angrily she pressed down harder on the accelerator, trying to use the car's swift responsive surge of power to drown out what she was thinking. She would find some escape from her thoughts by pulling up the opportunistic weeds in her mother's garden for the rest of the day. She needed some physical activity to keep her mind away from Daniel.

* * *

The next morning she came downstairs to find Faye pacing the hall, her normally almost too bland sweetness of expression marred by a deep frown.

Suppressing a faint sigh, not really wanting to hear any more about her problems with Camilla, Sage stopped to ask, 'Is anything wrong?'

'Yes... No... I've got to go out. Camilla's gone down to the stables. Will you tell her when she comes back?'

She was heading for the stairs before Sage could say anything, moving so quickly and tensely that Sage stared after her curiously.

What on earth was the matter with Faye? Her behaviour these last few days had been so out of character, but, come to think of it, that same charge could be laid against all of them recently...

Without her mother's presence in their lives, all of them seemed to be—to be what? Changing—or simply exhibiting certain aspects of their characters under the stress of her mother's accident?

Almost without knowing she was doing so, Sage found she was walking towards the study and opening its door, breathing deeply and exhaling the tension from her body, almost as though she found the room a haven of some kind.

Her glance focused automatically on her mother's desk, and she knew without having to question her own actions that the thought of losing herself, of separating herself from the present and her own problems in the past and the gradual unrolling of her mother's life, was the panacea she sought to distance herself from the events of yesterday.

In reading the diaries she could blot out her own problems... her own memories... her own pain.

Muted sounds reached her from the rest of the house. Somewhere Jenny was vacuuming... Faye was no doubt preparing herself for wherever it was she was going, but these activities were as distant from her as though they were taking place on a different planet.

She settled herself behind the desk and unlocked the drawer containing the diaries, searching through them until she found the right one.

As she turned the pages almost feverishly, she admitted to herself that now her need to discover more about this stranger who was her mother was almost overwhelmed by her urgent desire to lose herself somewhere where she could escape mentally from yesterday morning's débâcle with Daniel.

Daniel. She shuddered involuntarily, her senses flooded by her memories of the scent and feel of him. Under her fierce self-anger, her outrage, her fury, and just as strong as her sense of self-loathing was her awareness that some part of her must have always known of this vulnerability lying within her like a trap set long ago and that part of her had accepted what had happened with a sense of inevitability that had left her with no resources with which to fight against her emotions.

For years she had never given him a thought, would if asked have claimed that she could barely remember the man, and it hurt her very sharply that she, who had always demanded of herself far more honesty than she had ever asked from others, should be confronted by the knowledge that she had practised on herself the most dangerous and foolish of all self-deceits.

The open pages of the diary swam in front of her, and she focused fiercely on them, almost as though they were an actual physical escape route and if her will-power were strong enough she could actually force herself out of the present and on to those pages. Nothing could ever totally banish from her mind the memory of her surprise meeting with Daniel but perhaps for a time at least she could find enough surcease from her thoughts to allow herself a little much needed peace of mind.

She frowned fiercely as she read the first few words.

'*Today, young Vic left us* on the start of his long journey to Australia. I drove him to Southampton. Edward did not want to come with us. He finds travelling even small distances in the car these days too painful. Don't ask me how he managed it, but Chivers managed to find enough petrol from somewhere for us to make the journey. Quite what we'd do without him I have no idea. He's wonderful with Edward, who has found this cold, wet summer a trial. The damp gets into his bones and makes his amputations ache. Ian Holmes does the best he can, but, as he has explained to me, once he starts prescribing morphine for Edward, which is the only thing which can totally alleviate his pain, there is a very strong possibility that Edward will become so totally dependent on the drug that he will not be able to live without it. Chivers tells me that cod-liver oil is marvellously good for all forms of rheumatism, and so somehow or other he has persuaded Edward to have two large tablespoons of the filthy stuff every morning.

'Ian Holmes has mentioned that having the house centrally heated would be a benefit to Edward, and that maybe we ought to consider approaching the Ministry, to see if something might not be done about relaxing the rules a little in view of the fact that Edward is a casualty of the war, but, even if we could get permission to purchase the materials we need for such a task, at the moment I doubt if we could afford it.

'We do the best we can, Chivers and I between us, making sure that both Edward's bedroom and the library always have a good fire.

'Chivers has managed to find us two men who now work here full time... One of them, Dan Holcombe, is actually a fully trained carpenter and he is proving a marvellous help in repairing and restoring the house. The other, Sam Oldfield, is a little bit slow mentally, but strong enough to do all manner of jobs which were outside Chivers's and my own capabilities. He is wonderfully gentle and adores David. His mother is widowed and lives in the village so that Sam is able to walk from there to work and home again each day, while Dan Holcombe is living in the small flat above the stables which he has somehow or other made habitable for himself. He is a very quiet man in his late fifties with a pronounced London accent. He says very little about himself and I suspect that there is some sad tragedy in his life.

'It seems that his family were killed during the Blitz and that after his discharge from the Army he could not bring himself to return to London and his old life...'

Liz hesitated before putting down her pen. For the first time since she had started writing her diaries, she had found it difficult to commit her thoughts to paper. She read what she had written and then read it again with shadows in her eyes. Her fingers touched the smooth page, trembling a little as she traced the words, *'Today, young Vic left us...'*

Was it really only this morning that they had got into the car with her driving, Vic sitting a little nervously in the passenger seat in his new suit, his hand reaching out anxiously every now and again to touch the wallet where he was keeping his tickets and other papers?

Both of them were silent during the drive, but it was a good silence, between two companions who were comfortable with one another. Every now and again one or other of them would break it, Vic normally to warn her of some danger to the flock ... some disease or parasite which he might not already have mentioned to her.

It had been Ian Holmes who had taught her to drive, at Edward's insistence, and this was Ian's old car.

She had thought at first that a car was a luxury they did not need, and that besides with petrol rationing they would hardly ever be able to use it. Even though it was second-hand, it would still take the last of Aunt Vi's money, after the ram had been bought, but Edward farsightedly had pointed out that they would not always have rationing and that in the brave new world everyone was talking about the ability to drive and it could well become a necessity rather than a luxury.

Much to her surprise, she had discovered that she quite enjoyed driving.

They had set off just before dawn, since young Vic's boat was due to leave Southampton at four in the afternoon, which meant that he had to be ready to embark at noon. She had sensed that Edward would have

preferred her not to drive Vic to the boat but to let him
make his own way there. She knew that Edward resented
Vic, that he was jealous of him. She knew in fact that
Edward bitterly resented her spending time with any
other men, with the exception of Ian. He was becoming
increasingly morose, increasingly possessive, yet when
she felt impatient with him, she forced herself to remember how much she owed him and how painfully he
suffered physically and emotionally from his wounds.

Contrarily, after a poor summer which had left her
garden bedraggled and her larder without its normal store
of fruits and jams, the last few days of September had
been warm and benign.

They reached Southampton in good time and made
their way to the docks. They had to stop several times
to make enquiries as to where they could find Vic's vessel.

'Emigrating?' one man asked them, obviously mistaking them for a married couple. 'Can't say as I blame
you... There's not a lot left for the ordinary man in
this country these days. At least that's what it seems
like. You go off to fight for your country and what
happens when you get back? Like as not your wife's
gone off with some Yank, or they've got someone
else... someone who never lifted a finger to protect this
country when it needed it, sitting snugly in your old
job...'

There was a lot of unrest in the country, Liz acknowledged as they thanked him for his direction and she drove
cautiously into the open dock yard.

People were no longer content to be told what was
good for them and how they should live. The war had
changed things, many of them for ever.

The number of large vessels tied up along the dockside
surprised her, as did the number of people milling
around, families with small children saying tearful
farewells...

She had read in the papers and heard on the wireless
news that many people were emigrating, making new
lives for themselves in Commonwealth countries such as
Canada and Australia and New Zealand, but to see so

many people surrounded by their belongings, obviously on the point of leaving their homeland for ever, made her feel suddenly very insecure and emotional.

She tried to imagine how she might feel if she was leaving England for ever... leaving Cottingdean, which had come to mean so much to her, and she gave a tiny shiver.

Was it wrong to love a house so much? To feel so at one with it that it was almost as though in some way she and the house were indivisible, as though it was her spiritual home? Normally pragmatic, she chided herself for the foolishness of her thoughts. Cottingdean was, after all, only a house—a very beautiful and precious house, but only a house. David, Edward... they were what was really important.

Since they had arrived in good time, she suggested to Vic that they look for somewhere to have a quick meal. He demurred at first, but gave way beneath her insistence.

They drove into Southampton itself, parking the car along with some others on a half-cleared bomb site.

It amazed her to see how much building work was going on in the city, and she paused to gaze enviously at the industry of half a dozen men working on the foundations of a new building, wishing momentarily she might have their energy and expertise for just long enough to repair a little more of the crumbling fabric of Cottingdean.

They had a quick lunch at a Joe Lyons, where Vic insisted on paying the bill, and she tactfully let him.

There had always been a bond between them since David's birth, and, although he was her senior by a couple of years, in many ways to Liz it was as though he was the younger brother she had never had.

He was an inarticulate man, with little to say for himself, but one only had to watch him with his flock to sense his tenderness and compassion.

Liz knew she could trust him absolutely with the task she had set him, but she still felt a little guilty at separating him from all that he knew... at sending him out into a world with which he was totally unfamiliar. She also felt, she discovered, as they headed back to the docks, in some small way envious and resentful of his freedom.

Much as she adored David, much as she loved Cottingdean, much as she was grateful to Edward, there were times when she ached for the freedom to just be herself... to escape from her responsibilities—and then she would remind herself that it was those responsibilities, and in particular Edward, which had enabled her to live as she did... that without Edward her life and David's too would have been very different indeed...and she would be overwhelmed by a fierce tide of guilt and pain and would push her rebellious thoughts to the back of her mind, forcing herself to lose them in a sudden exhausting burst of hard physical work that would drive everything else but the knowledge that all her time, all her energy, and much of her love was needed if she was ever to come anyway near fulfilling her self-imposed task of bringing Cottingdean back to life.

Between them she and Chivers had already achieved a great deal, or, as Ian Holmes was inclined to say wryly, 'had worked miracles'... Certainly, when David had been born, she could never have envisaged a time when she would not only have her large vegetable and fruit gardens productive and under orderly control, but that also she would have gone a long way to restoring the gardens' long double herbaceous border to something of its original beauty... Here she had been helped enormously by Sam, who, despite his handicap, seemed to have a natural affinity for anything that grew, as well as a knowledge about plants which constantly amazed her.

It was Sam who from here and there produced the cuttings and plants which were beginning to fill the empty spaces in the border... it was Sam who had spent long back-breaking hours cleaning away the weeds and thick thorny briars, so that today when she had returned home she would be able to spend a precious solitary hour in her gardens, admiring all that they had done, absorbing its peace and tranquillity.

Between them Chivers and Dan had set to work inside the house, using whatever materials they could 'find' to repair the worst of the havoc. The roof no longer leaked, the kitchen range produced hot water, the damp patches had begun to disappear from the walls, and Dan had proved unexpectedly inventive in managing to do a great deal to repair the old plaster ceilings so that little by little the house was gradually coming to life again.

She could tell that young Vic was nervous as they parked the car and walked along the dock. She slipped her arm through his, squeezing it reassuringly in a sisterly fashion, while a tiny corner of her mind had a second's shocking awareness of how very different his body felt from David's soft baby flesh, and Edward's wasted, damaged frame. Just for a moment she remembered Kit... Something that happened rarely these days. After all, there was nothing about him that she wanted to remember, but just for a brief, searingly painful breath of time she had felt, in touching young Vic's muscled, male body, a *frisson* of memory... of sensation... of how it had felt to be young and in love...to desire a man, to...

Quickly releasing him, she turned her head away, looking out to sea. These were foolish thoughts for a woman of her age and in her situation. Very foolish thoughts. Especially when she had not in fact enjoyed Kit's physical possession of her.

When the passengers were finally allowed to board, Liz went on board with Vic. He was sharing his small cabin with another man travelling alone, and once Vic had stowed away his things in the cabin's minute storage space they went back up on deck, both of them silent, both of them engaged with their own private thoughts.

Vic broke the silence first, turning to her to say anxiously, 'Tom Hudson is a good farmer, but it won't be like he's looking after his own...'

'I know that, Vic,' Liz assured him gently. 'Don't worry. I'll make sure the flock is properly cared for.'

The intercom crackled into life, announcing that it was time for all those who weren't sailing to disembark. Vic walked with her to the gangway, and then, once there, just as she was about to turn to him and wish him good luck with his mission, to her astonishment he took hold of her, gripping her almost too tightly as he gave her a clumsy but hardly fraternal kiss.

Almost instantly he released her, his face red, avoiding her eyes as he made a stumbling apology, but the shock of that unexpected embrace, of the sensation of a male mouth moving against her own, however lacking in experience its touch might have been, awakened so many memories that for a moment she couldn't speak. Had he somehow subconsciously read her mind earlier—had she however unintentionally somehow given him the impression that she wanted...? She swallowed, angry with herself, fighting to take control of the situation as she gave him what she hoped was a reassuring smile and said briskly, 'This is a very emotional time for you, Vic, leaving England for the first time.'

'Yes.'

His assent was muffled as he turned away from her. He was embarrassed, she knew, suddenly awkward with her. She couldn't let him leave like this...not when she owed him so much—David's life and possibly her own.

She reached out and touched him, trying to convey both comfort and understanding as she felt his forearm muscles bunch under her fingertips.

'I'm going to miss you, Vic,' she told him softly. 'But it would be selfish of me to keep you at Cottingdean, especially when we need that ram so badly. Who knows?' she added with false brightness. 'You might even bring a pretty Australian bride back with you as well as one of Woolonga's prize rams!'

He was smiling back at her now, valiantly trying to match her distancing conversation as he told her drily, 'A ram's of more use to me right now than a wife...' He hesitated and looked at her, and the look in his eyes made her look sharply away, her stomach muscles quivering in silent tension. She had seen that look in a man's eyes once before. Then she had mistaken it for love... Young Vic could not love her, must not love her... If he did she would have to send him away and they needed him too much, Cottingdean needed him too much. And besides...

She closed her eyes, trying not to imagine how sweet it would be to go up to him and lean against him, to let him take her in his arms and to whisper to her that there was no reason why both of them should not go in search of their golden fleece... That this could be their special private time... That...

That what? That they could be lovers? she demanded bitterly of herself. Hadn't she learned anything, anything at all from the past?

She was a married woman with an ailing husband and a young child... A married woman, moreover, who had willingly chosen celibacy.

And yet as she looked at Vic standing there, remembering how tenderly he had cared for her during David's birth, remembering how gentle his hands were, how caring his touch, there was so much she wanted to say to him that the words burned in her throat. So much she wanted to say and yet could not say, because she knew in her heart of hearts that, much as she liked him, much as she needed his strength and companionship, she did not love him. That to allow him to think otherwise would be to cheat not only Edward and David but Vic himself as well; and so, even though it tore at her heart to do so, she stretched out her hand to him, forcing her lips to curve into what she hoped looked like a smile, and, shaking his hand, said as brightly as she could, 'I'd better go. *Bon voyage*, Vic...and remember, we're counting on you to bring back that ram. I've got very big plans for our new flock...'

He laughed then, even though the laughter sounded slightly forced.

They had talked, the two of them, or rather she had talked and he had listened, as her enthusiasm had caught fire and she had told him of how ultimately she would like to revive the old tradition of weaving wool cloth locally from the Cottingdean flock ... of bringing back to life the old mill which belonged to the Cottingdean estate, and which now lay empty and neglected, the water wheel which had once powered its machine rotting in its weed-choked mill pond.

'Goodbye, Vic,' she whispered to him, her voice suddenly deserting her as she leaned up and kissed him briefly on the cheek, and then, without daring to look back, she turned and hurried to join the others leaving the ship.

She didn't stay to watch it weigh anchor, getting back into her car and setting off back to Cottingdean, forcing herself as she drove homewards to concentrate not on what she had left behind but on what lay ahead of her. That was where her life lay... In Cottingdean with her son... with her husband... with her responsibilities to them.

So she analysed the situation, defusing it until she was sure she had made it quite safe... Until she was sure she could return to her home and her family with her heart and mind clear of any stain of guilt.

As she drove through one small village she had to stop to allow a small procession of people to cross the road. They were carrying an enormous heavily carved oak chest and as she watched them it suddenly struck her that the chest would be ideal for Cottingdean's empty hall.

On an impulse she couldn't define she stopped the car and parked it, hurrying after the slow-moving procession, and then stopping them to enquire breathlessly what they were doing with the chest.

'Throwing it out,' one of the men told her grimly. 'Been cluttering up our front room since my old mother moved in with us, it has, and now that she's gone the wife says it can go too.'

It was old ... very old, worn in places, and very dirty, and yet beneath that she could see the potential beauty of the wood, could almost feel how much it called out for care and attention.

'I'll buy it from you,' she told him impulsively, not allowing herself time to think, to hesitate. 'I'll give you five pounds for it,' she added quickly. 'Six if you can secure it on the roof of the car...'

It was plain that he thought she was crazed. He eyed her uncertainly, saying dourly, 'Firewood, that's all he's good for... Still, if you're sure you wants 'im... I don't want no husband coming down here and making us take 'im back...'

'No, no, he won't do that,' Liz assured him, quickly producing six pounds from her purse and thinking how fortunate it was that Edward had made her take some extra money just in case she should decide not to make the return journey until the morning.

It took the men a good hour to secure the chest to her satisfaction, but at last it was done, the money handed over, and she was on her way home.

A feeling of well-being and excitement had replaced her earlier *malaise* and, although she didn't know it, she had just begun what was to be a lifelong love-affair with antique furniture. There would be occasions when she would find and buy far more valuable pieces than this ancient oak chest, but there would never be a time when the thrill of finding them would exceed the sweet pleasure she felt now, as she drove slowly and proudly along the empty English lanes, humming contentedly under her breath, while the chest rocked precariously on the car's roof.

The six months of Vic's absence were very busy ones; there were the inevitable problems with the flock, and David was growing quickly, a placid, endearing child with such a quality of sweetness about him that sometimes he made Liz catch her breath in wonder. There was nothing of his father in him... none of Kit's cruelty or vice. He was his own person.

Vic wrote to them that the owner of Woolonga's prize rams was being stubborn about selling them one of his beasts, and Liz formed the impression that the Australian was tough and uncompromising, with little room in his life for sentiment or emotion.

From Vic's letters she gained the impression that he had fallen a little under the Australian's influence, and she began to worry about whether, once he returned, Vic would ever be content to settle for their quiet unexciting life. Vic was a young man—just as she was a young woman, a rebellious inner voice reminded her. It was a voice she didn't want to hear...a voice she could not afford to hear.

They had a hard winter, but somehow or other between them they managed to keep the flock's losses to a minimum. Liz lost count of the number of nights she sat up with a birthing ewe, grimly determined to honour the trust Vic had placed in her, reminding herself over and over again of the night David was born.

The kitchen seemed full of orphaned lambs. She watched David with them, surprised and moved by his tenderness towards them. He was a child who seemed instinctively to sense the suffering of others and feel compassion for it. She wondered sometimes if it was a good thing that he spent as much time as he did with Edward...if she ought not to be encouraging him to become more boisterous and adventurous like the village boys—but they enjoyed one another's company so deeply, communicating without any need for words.

Chivers had abandoned his care of Edward to help her with the sheep, and just when she thought that winter would never be over, that spring would never come, the snow started to melt; crocuses blossomed in sheltered patches of the garden, and then best of all they had a letter from Vic saying that he was on his way home and that he was bringing with him their much-needed new ram.

There was nothing in his letter to say how he had managed to persuade the Australian to part with this beast, but Liz was too overjoyed by the news to worry about how such a miracle had been achieved.

Vic himself arrived within weeks of his letter...a sun-burned, broader, different Vic, whose eyes seemed to look far beyond the enclosed horizons of their own hills, a Vic who took her to one side and told her quietly that he had brought more than the new ram home with him.

'It was you who put the idea in my head,' he told her quietly, and the sensation of knowledge and loss that touched her as he looked at her made her throat close up in anguish.

'You've found yourself a wife,' she said simply.

'Yes. She's the daughter of Woolonga's foreman. The thing is...the thing is, she's lived all her life out there in the outback and it's a strange thing...a magic place almost. It gets a hold of you. I felt it myself... She wanted to come over here, to see what England looks like.' He smiled briefly and painfully. 'But once we've got the ram settled in and I've found you a new shepherd, I reckon we'll be going back to Woolonga...'

Woolonga... Woolonga... The name tasted bitter in her mouth and as she raised her eyes to Vic's she now saw in his all that he was not saying to her...all that he could not say to her.

'Who knows?' she had said brightly. 'You might even bring a pretty Australian bride back with you...'

But she had not meant it...had never meant to drive him from her and from Cottingdean. They both needed him too much to lose him.

The knowledge was like a knife twisting inside her, a double-edged pain that came from knowing how much she would miss him and from acknowledging her own selfishness. She had no right to expect him to stay when she knew she could offer him nothing... Or at least when she could not offer him what he would find with his new wife.

She had no right to even think of feeling what she was feeling, no right at all.

She met his wife a couple of days later. Beth was a small dark-haired girl with deeply tanned skin and vivid blue eyes. Her manner towards Liz was both curious and slightly aggressive, and Liz acknowledged with a sinking heart that the two of them could never have forged an easy relationship. Whether because she felt that Liz was somehow a threat to her own relationship with Vic, or whether it was simply that, as a girl brought up in a land which did not acknowledge any class barriers, she refused to treat Liz and Edward with the old-fashioned deference given to them by Vic himself, Liz had no way of knowing... All she did know was that, much as it made her own heart ache, Vic's decision to make a new life for himself in Australia was probably the wisest one for all concerned.

True to his word, though, he refused to leave until he had found them a new shepherd he considered worthy of the task. This took over three months, during which time Liz became heartily sick of hearing from Beth the words, 'At the homestead,' and 'Woolonga.' Both the sheep station and its owner, or so it seemed, were larger than life, and certainly far more imposing than anything Cottingdean had to offer. It was ridiculous to feel this resentment of a place she had never seen, to feel that every time Beth boasted about Woolonga she was challenging Liz to deny that Cottingdean was inferior to it in every way, but that was what Liz did feel.

She was astonished to hear herself saying crossly to Edward one evening, 'I shall be glad when young Vic and Beth leave... I'm getting quite sick of hearing the name Woolonga.'

'Beth is homesick,' Edward pointed out mildly. 'That does tend to make people defensive. I'll admit, though, she is a trifle abrasive in her defence of all things Australian. I suppose part of her is afraid that Vic will change his mind and stay on here.'

'Oh, he won't do that,' Liz denied flatly. She could sense that Edward was watching her and remembered that Edward had always been slightly antagonistic towards the young shepherd ever since he had been the one to deliver David, and so, even though it hurt her to do so, she added as carelessly as she could, 'And perhaps it's a good thing that he's going... There's no real future here at Cottingdean for him. This new shepherd is older, more likely to stay with us—and from all that Vic says he's already settling in well with the flock.'

'Mm... Well, I hope you're not going to be disappointed with all this money you've laid out on this new ram. I applaud your determination to build up the flock, but it's meat this country needs, not wool...'

'At the moment it's meat,' Liz agreed, 'but I'm looking to the future, to a time when goods aren't rationed...when people want and can have a wider range of things. This country's starved of good-quality cloth. Few companies make it any more, but there's going to come a time when there will be a demand for it.'

'And *you're* going to provide it?' Edward asked. 'My dear, I don't want to spoil your dreams... Once, a long time ago, it's true that Cottingdean flocks produced fine-quality wool, and wove it into cloth in our own mill, but those days are gone... The mill is fit for nothing other than knocking down, there's no machinery, no labour force, nothing... and we certainly don't have the money to pay for either. We can barely keep a roof above our heads...'

'It will all come in time,' Liz protested stubbornly. 'You'll see. This country needs new industry, people need what we could produce. We will find a way.'

She heard Edward sigh, saw the way his mouth pursed with rejection, and felt an intense build-up of frustration inside her. She had so many plans, so many hopes... and so little of anything else. Couldn't he see how much she *needed* to believe in what she was doing? Couldn't he see how much she needed this dream? After all, what else had she to occupy her mind? David wasn't a baby any more and already scarcely seemed to need her... He was such a self-possessed child... Edward was turning more and more to Chivers for the physical help he needed and Ian Holmes and the vicar for mental stimulation. She needed something in her life, something to work for, something to challenge her... something in which she could pour those energies which sometimes tormented her so restlessly.

She was a young woman with all her life stretching out ahead of her. What had happened with young Vic had opened her mind to the pitfalls that could confront her, the dangers she could fall prey to if she wasn't careful, if she didn't have something else to occupy her thoughts, her time. It wasn't enough any longer to work herself so physically hard that she fell into bed exhausted every night, and, besides, they were getting to the stage where they had done as much to the house as they could by themselves. What still needed to be done needed expert hands. She *needed* this dream of building from the ashes of the past a new, strong future for the house and its lands. Sheep had been Cottingdean's wealth before and sheep could be its wealth again. And if she no longer had anyone to share that dream with her, if she had to pursue it on her own, well, then, she would do so, she decided stubbornly.

It *could* be done. She knew it could be done, she knew that one day there would be a market, a demand for all that her mill could produce, and when that demand came she wanted to be ready for it... She *would* be ready for it.

This time when she said goodbye to Vic she didn't say goodbye to him alone. He and Beth had a semi-formal send-off from Cottingdean; Liz had organised a farewell party for him, inviting almost everyone in the neighbourhood.

She and Edward had no money with which to buy them an expensive gift, but instead she had carefully selected from two of the house's dusty cupboards a pretty Wedgwood tea service in delicate bone china.

She saw Beth eye it disparagingly, and then watched Vic handling the fragile cups in his large hands, his touch so gentle and familiar that she felt a deep inner pain. She tried not to think how different things might have been, if... If what? If she hadn't been married to Edward? But she was married to Edward and she ought to be damn grateful for that fact. Even in the village there were girls without fathers for their children, some of them widowed by the war, others...

Others were the result of wartime affairs, fatherless and condemned for it. She would have hated that fate for David...

When it finally came time for her to say goodbye to Vic, he avoided looking at her and, even though she knew that what he was doing was probably for the best, watching him go hurt her. She wished him well with deep sincerity, and yet she knew that her own life would be the poorer for his going.

As though he sensed what she was feeling, David came over to her side and slipped his hand into hers. His flesh felt soft and warm, when what she really yearned for was a stronger, harder grip... A man's grip, and not a child's. She blinked back tears which she told herself were stupid and self-indulgent. It was the future she must look to and not the past. The future... And what after all did she want with a man like Vic, a man who would ultimately demand of her the sexual intimacy her relationship with Kit had shown her she was not capable of sustaining? And yet there were nights—long, wearying nights when she lay awake tormented by the ache of her body, by the beginnings of a need she could neither understand nor explain. A need that confused and shamed her.

CHAPTER TWENTY

As SHE reached for the next diary, Sage reflected wryly to herself that she was discovering in her mother an unexpected and no doubt accidental gift for drama.

All through this last section of the diaries she had been conscious of a growing sense of urgency, a feeling that her mother's life was slowly reaching some kind of climactic turning point. Or was it simply that her impatience, her sense of sharp tension and awareness sprang from other influences; influences outside the diaries?

The fact was that while she was reading about her mother's past Liz herself was fighting for her future; the fact was that her own life seemed to be reaching some kind of turning point ... Or was it simply that in her desperation to lose herself, to escape from her own thoughts, her own problems, she was investing the diaries with a sense of mystery, of secrecy almost, that they really did not possess ...?

Or was it perhaps that having at last seen her mother through the eyes of an adult and not of a child, she was suddenly and sympathetically aware that her mother was a woman, with emotions and needs which could hardly have been fulfilled by her relationship with Edward?

As she picked up the next diary she frowned over the dates written inside it, just inside the cover. It was obvious that the contents of this diary spanned virtually an entire decade of her mother's life.

The decade which would have included the year of her own conception, she recognised, her heart suddenly thumping fiercely, heavily.

She had never had the kind of relationship with her mother which had allowed her to ask what had prompted her, a woman with a son of ten, a husband whose health was declining, a place like Cottingdean to run and a very new and fragile business barely off the ground, to go to such lengths to conceive and give birth to a child which she then seemed to spend a great deal of time holding at a distance.

Previously, aside from the fact that she and her mother were just two people with temperaments which did not jell, Sage had also believed that her mother was one of those women who simply did not have the facility or the desire to express their emotions freely, and yet she had realised very early on in reading the diaries just how wrong she was. So why had she always been held at such a distance?

She had a momentary and vivid memory of running into the house as a child and running into her mother's arms, or at least trying to do so. Liz had been in the study with Edward, and Sage could picture so clearly the look of displeasure, of resentment, on her father's face as she burst into the room...the quick, almost angry way in which her mother fended her off and bundled her out, the feeling even as a child of being an outsider...of being unwanted.

If it hadn't been for David, for his love... She smiled sadly to herself, remembering how much she had longed to emulate her older brother... How much she had ached to have his calm gentle temperament, his way of turning aside anger with the sweetness of his smile. She had been adult herself before discovering how rare people like David were. She could understand how much Faye must miss him as a human being. She still did herself... In those wild years after losing Scott, David would have been the person she could have turned to for counsel. In David alone she would have felt able to confide, to admit how very betrayed she had felt by Scott's defection. But David hadn't been there for her. David could never be there for her again, because he had died. She had no outlet for her hurt and, instead of turning her anger against Scott and against his father, she had found that she had, for some obscure reason, turned it against Daniel Cavanagh, perhaps because she had felt that in doing so she was leaving the door open for Scott to change his mind and come back into her life... perhaps because she had felt in some subconscious way that only Daniel was strong enough, secure enough in himself to accept her anger.

Certainly she knew logically that it wasn't his fault that Scott's father had insisted on taking him home, nor that Scott had never once attempted to get in touch with her.

What she had not been able to tell anyone, though, was the confusion and self-disgust caused by her own sexual responsiveness to Daniel. Nor had she confided in anyone how Daniel had rejected her... Why? She paused, frowning a little.

Was it because she had been ashamed of those feelings, or of her behaviour...or was it because she had felt even *David,* even had he been alive, might not have been able to understand... Much as she had loved her brother, she had always known instinctively that he did not share her deep-running, silent vein of sensuality; that for David, sex was not a human appetite, but a gift of God sanctified by the procreation of children...that David did not possess the sharp curiosity about others, about their motivations, about all that was hidden and secret in their lives in the way that she did... That David preferred not to look too closely into the dark places of the human soul, whereas she often surprised in herself a thirst to know and understand what motivated others, not just sexually but emotionally as well.

Yes, she had loved David... She missed his gentle presence in her life even now, his calming presence, but it surprised her a little that Faye as a woman—a mature and very attractive woman now—had never looked back towards her relationship with David, and perhaps realised that sexually it might not have withstood the pressures of her own growing maturity and needs. Faye was not a cold woman; rather she was an almost totally un-awakened one, Sage recognised, and, knowing what she now knew about her own mother, she suspected that Liz must know this as well. Was that why she had always been so protective towards Faye? Not because she loved her more than she did her own daughter, not because she approved of Faye's reticence and modesty and wanted to hold them up as an example to her own erring child, but because she had long ago sensed in Faye the need and vulnerability, the fear that Sage herself, to her shame, was only just beginning to recognise?

Why had she never noticed before the way Faye flinched away from men? Why had she never noticed the tension in her eyes and her body whenever she was in unfamiliar male company? That fear hadn't been put there by David, Sage was sure, but it might explain why Faye had married him, and why she had stayed so fiercely, determinedly under Liz's protective wing after his death. It was only now, with her mother removed from them, that Sage was beginning to see the real emotions that Faye had always cloaked beneath her air of remote calm. To see them and realise the danger of the strain her sister-in-law was placing upon herself.

Tonight, when Faye came in, she would talk to her, she decided firmly. She would find out what was wrong. She would encourage Faye to confide in her...

As an escape route from her own problems, or because she genuinely cared?

Of course she cared... She had always cared about her family, more than she had ever allowed even herself to know. As a child she had lived under the constant shadow of her father's dislike of her and her mother's coldness towards her... Unlike others in a similar position, she had not spent her adult life seeking male approval—instead she had taken the opposite stance. She had punished men... rejected them for her father's rejection of her, she recognised grimly. And most of them had let her... Most of them, but not Daniel... Never Daniel...

Daniel, Daniel... her thoughts were locked in a circle that always ended up at the same point. Daniel Cavanagh... Would he ring her, or would he simply ignore her ultimatum? If he did...

She found that she was shaking. She took a deep breath and then another, quickly turning the pages of the new diary. She didn't want to think about that morning. She didn't want to get caught up in the folly of remembering, or recalling, of allowing her body...her femininity to hold sway over logic and intelligence.

She read swiftly, quickly absorbing the brief, dry facts noted down in the diary's early pages; the new ram had proved a great success, his progeny developing the valuable fleeces her mother had sought, and if she sensed the pathos behind the curt inscription, 'Heard from young Vic today. Beth is pregnant,' Sage did not allow herself to dwell on it, or to feel pity, knowing that self-pity was the very last thing her mother would have indulged in.

It was a diary of brief entries, even briefer the winter Edward was severely ill with influenza and had to go into hospital. That spring was a productive one for lambs and Liz wrote that she was thinking of buying another ram.

She had been looking into the feasibility of reopening the mill and weaving their own wool. At present she was selling the fleeces to a small concern just inside the Scottish border. She had been in touch with the mill's owners and had arranged to visit them. She had also been making tentative enquiries to see what if any government help she could get with her new venture.

People were gradually recovering from the dark years of the war... gradually beginning to think in terms of the years ahead and not merely the weeks. Those people who had lived through it, who had experienced its horrors, who had known what it meant to live constantly with the threat of death, were promising themselves that for their children things would be different.

There was a new mood spreading over the land—a new purposefulness, a sense of determination that things must change for the better, that no one could live through what had been lived through, could endure what had been endured and not emerge from such a holocaust without undergoing some kind of rebirth. Coupled with this awareness was a desire to make sure the next generation, those children conceived at a time of great darkness and despair, should throughout their lives know only happiness and light, and so a mother who had perhaps throughout the war years only possessed poor quality cheap clothes now hungered, even if only subconsciously, for better things, not for herself but for her child.

The market was there for the cloth her sheep could produce, Liz knew it, and she was determined to be ready to cater for it.

The opposition to her plans was such that another person, a weaker person, would have given up, given in to the pressure, albeit a gentle caring pressure, which was being subtly placed on her.

Edward had begun to retreat into a distant silence whenever she tried to discuss her plans with him...the kind of silence often used by a spoilt child to punish a caring adult, Liz recognized uneasily.

Edward's health was a constant source of concern to her. He would never be strong, always need care and cosseting, and this latest bout of influenza had left him even frailer than before, and not just physically but emotionally...more inclined to cling and demand, more inclined to sulk and lapse into aggrieved silences when he felt he was not getting enough of her attention.

It was just as well that David was such an easy child... Almost too easy, she sometimes felt, contrasting his behaviour with that of other boys his age.

When she had confided her concern to Ian Holmes, he had quickly assured her that David was perfectly healthy, adding gently, 'He is quiet, I know, but it is a happy quietness, I think, not a discontented one.'

'But he spends so much time alone...'

'Again, he's happy solitary, although that's bound to change once he's off at school.'

This was another small bone of contention between Edward and herself, Liz reflected. Edward wanted to send David to the small public school he had attended, but she was concerned that seven was far too young to send a child away from home. Here again it seemed that almost everyone else totally opposed her view. The vicar's wife said sympathetically that she had hated sending her two away, but that boys really did need the discipline of a good school. Edward had told her that it was at school that David would make the contacts, the friends which would establish his position in adult life, and, although nothing else was said, for the first time she felt as though Edward was subtly reminding her of the fact that her own birth had been into a far different way of life from his.

The last thing on her mind when she had married Edward had been any idea of elevating herself socially, but she was not a fool, and even now in these post-war days deference was still paid to people with the right accents...the right backgrounds... They could just afford to pay the fees, but Liz knew she would have to make some savings in their household expenditure.

When challenged, she was forced to agree that of course she wanted the best for David. David himself, when she discussed it with him, seemed quite happy with the idea of going away to school. He was a pragmatic, sunny-natured child, who gently reassured her that he would not be lonely or unhappy... Much as though she were the child, she thought wryly.

For all that she had achieved at Cottingdean, for all the work she had done, it irritated her at times that she should still be subtly so much under the domination of the men in her life.

Edward had made it plain to her that he thoroughly disapproved of the idea of her reopening the mill. It wasn't fitting, especially not for a woman, he had told her, but something in her rebelled. She owed him so much, everything really, and she had repaid him as best she could. She had a lovely son, a home which she was coming to cherish and love, and if they were not well off financially, well, at least they were better off than many. The vegetable garden was productive enough to make sure that they were never without fresh fruit and vegetables; they kept enough livestock for their own needs, hens for their eggs, and with careful management they were actually able to live well within Edward's pension and the money coming in from the rich arable fields they let out.

It was true that the process of refurbishing the house was a slow one, but Liz had a good eye for a bargain, and since that unscheduled stop on the way back from Southampton she had spent many a happy hour rummaging through the sale rooms and attending country house sales.

The latest one had provided the very handsome brocade curtains which now covered the drawing-room windows. She had bought them for next to nothing, and had brought them home and cut them down to size for their own drawing-room, which was much smaller than the crumbling double-height ballroom they had originally been made for.

The success of their subtle colouring and the richness of the fabric, which she suspected had originally been woven when Victoria was on the throne, and which far surpassed anything she could have bought even if she had had the wherewithal to do so, had made her consider repainting the drawing-room in its entirety.

The original paint had faded to a dirty indeterminate colour, but the library—now with the books carefully placed on the shelves which had received the loving attention of Chivers's linseed oil and then some homemade beeswax polish—had yielded a set of original design details for the drawing-room, from which she had discovered that the walls had originally been painted a soft yellowy green which she suspected would have gone beautifully with her gold brocade curtains.

White distemper could be obtained, Chivers had informed her judiciously, but as for staining it . . .

Undeterred, she had been experimenting with various vegetable dyes, keeping to herself the fact that already, in her own secret plans, she was looking ahead to the day when such knowledge would not just enable her to find an economical way of dyeing distemper. What she had in mind were the subtle colours of some of Lady Jeveson's hand-me-downs; the soft muted tones of her

Scottish tweeds, which had none of the harshness of modern wools.

Liz had a very clear idea of what she wanted from her mills. The best and only the best would be good enough to carry the Cottingdean label.

At one of her house sales she had been standing next to a party of American tourists and their conversation had been illuminating. These people had quite obviously been very wealthy and very discerning. They had been on an antique-buying trip, and had snatched a very pretty *bonheur du jour* from right under her nose at a price that made her sigh with slight envy. These were the people who would one day buy her wools...

Let the others tease her, and gently mock her dreams...she knew that one day she would be proved right. She knew, but being Liz she held her peace and smiled pacifyingly while making her plans. She didn't want to antagonise Edward to the extent that he refused outright to allow her to continue. The mill was, after all, his property and not hers, and besides, she had genuinely come to like him...to want to make his painful life as easy as possible.

She would have been surprised had she known how many people who knew them marvelled at her patience with him, and not just her patience, but her obvious devotion. Especially Ian Holmes.

As he regularly remarked to his wife, it was no life for a young woman... He knew of course that David was not Edward's son, and initially in the early days of their return to Cottingdean he had half expected that eventually nature would take its course and that she would take a lover. He would not have blamed her if she had. She was a beautiful woman, not just physically but mentally as well, and in the end it was Ian who persuaded Edward to allow her to go ahead with her plans, simply by pointing out to him that a young healthy woman needed a natural outlet for her energies, needed something on which to hook her dreams, needed something to plan for.

Edward had given him a sharply suspicious glance and for the first time in their long friendship had treated him with the same almost childish silence which Ian had so often helplessly watched him use against Liz. But at heart Edward was a fair man, a caring man, and if it was his love for Liz, his insecurity, his fear that a woman like her must surely one day grow bored with him, must surely one day leave him, that made him sometimes unkind to her, he was honest enough to admit that his doubts were self-inflicted and that no man had a more devoted wife than he.

And so, reluctantly, he agreed that maybe—some time in the future, finances permitting—they could consider reopening the mill.

Finances permitting. Liz kept her thoughts to herself. She had her own plans for raising that much needed money. Following upon Vic's advice to her before he left for Australia, she and the new shepherd had been diligently and selectively cross-breeding their stock with the purpose of producing prize-winning rams, not to sire flocks for wool which their own flocks would produce, but to capitalise on the sudden demand for lambs for meat.

Just as the war had bred in people a hunger for a new richness, a new luxury, so it had also bred in them a different kind of hunger—a hunger for food, for a diet that was not pared down to absolute necessities, a diet that tempted the taste-buds and the eye. Farmers all over the country were busy raising stock to meet these new demands, and Liz with her far-seeing intelligence was steadfastly working towards her own goals.

Edward had been angrily opposed to it when she had first mooted the idea of showing their young tups at some of the local county fairs. She could almost see his aristocratic nose quiver a little in disgust, and she had had to subtly remind him that there was a great English tradition to support farming as a suitably gentrified pursuit.

Reluctantly he had given way, and so, slowly, carefully, never overreaching themselves, Liz and her shepherd had begun to make a name for themselves and for their rams.

So much so that at Smithfield this last year they had taken the Best of Breed award for one of their tups, and it was his male progeny which, when sold, would start to produce for her the capital she needed to start work on renovating the mills.

Secretly, she had already been round it many times, trying to see, not its dilapidation, but its advantages.

If she was honest its only real advantage was that it was slap bang in the middle of the village, and in an area where work was hard to come by. For that reason and that alone, her plans might just find favour with those in authority. Men who fought for their country did not take kindly to being without jobs, without money... Anyone who could guarantee to provide work, especially in such a rural area, was already in an advantageous position.

Ian Holmes was on his way to visit Edward, not a social visit this time but a professional one. Several times a year he examined Edward and tried to talk to him about his condition, but Edward wasn't the kind of man who found it easy to confide in others, and he tended to become brusque and withdrawn on these occasions, no matter how tactful Ian tried to be.

At least he had been successful in persuading Edward to look more favourably on Liz's new business venture. It had been at his suggestion that Edward had on Liz's behalf approached some of his contacts among the local county fraternity, including the Lord Lieutenant, a hard-hunting man and a good landlord, with considerable influence at Whitehall.

Liz was beginning to know how to play the game. Officially, now, the mill was Edward's idea—she was simply his mouthpiece, putting forward his views, since his own poor health made it difficult for him to attend long, wearying meetings.

It was through the Lord Lieutenant that Liz had managed to obtain an introduction to a small private merchant bank looking for new investments. Ian admired her and sincerely hoped that the mill would succeed. She needed something in her life after all, poor girl. David was now away at school, and as for Edward...

He frowned to himself as he drove up to the house. Edward's increasingly frequent bouts of depression were beginning to worry him, all the more so because the other man refused to admit that they existed.

Ian had tried to suggest to him on several occasions that it might be a good idea, both from his own point of view and from Liz's, for him to spend a week or so in one of the new private convalescent homes being organised for men like himself, men who had been grievously injured by the war, but he had refused point-blank to even consider it.

The strain of looking after him was beginning to tell on Liz; it couldn't be very easy for her, after all, a young, healthy and very beautiful woman married to a man like Edward. Liz was always remarkably patient and gentle with him, but he had been there on several occasions when Edward's behaviour towards her had made him long to intervene and to point out to the other man that his jealousy had no foundation whatsoever.

Poor Liz. He wouldn't have blamed her if she *had* taken a lover.

Liz was out on business to do with the mill, Chivers told him when he admitted him. For once Chivers seemed to have lost something of his normal calm. He looked disturbed and unhappy, and just before he showed Ian into the library, he asked hesitantly, 'If I could have a word with you, sir...?'

His formality, as much as his request, made Ian frown. 'Yes, of course you can, Chivers,' he responded immediately. 'What's the problem?'

In reality he ought perhaps to have told Chivers to make an appointment and come down to the surgery, but Ian knew quite well that many of his patients found the surgery atmosphere intimidating and preferred to confide their problems somewhere where they felt more relaxed and secure.

'Well, it's the Major, sir,' Chivers told him unhappily, surprising him. He had assumed that Chivers wanted to discuss a more personal problem with him.

'Yes?' he encouraged calmly.

'Well, you know how he has these moods, sir? Can't blame him for that. The pain he suffers is something chronic. No one can blame him for that, but recently... Well...' Chivers paused. 'I don't rightly know as I should be the one to tell you this, sir, but someone has to, and madam, well, she'll never say a word, and like I've tried to say to the Major myself, it isn't right...'

Ian tensed, and questioned, '*What* isn't right, Chivers?' But his heart was sinking and he suspected that he already knew the answer.

'Well, it's the Major, sir... Gets in a proper paddy sometimes, as you know. Says things we all know he doesn't really mean... After all, it's hard on a man in his position... And madam...well, she's like a saint with him. Always gives him a sunny smile and coaxes him out of it, cosseting him, telling him there's nothing for him to worry about. But recently...' He hesitated and said anxiously, 'I hope you don't think I'm speaking out of turn, sir. Gossip never has been and never will be something I've ever lowered myself to, but when it comes to standing by and watching...' His mouth compressed for a moment as he struggled to find the words to express himself.

Patiently Ian waited, not wanting to put words into his mouth.

'The thing is, sir, that recently the Major's temper, well, it's got a lot worse... Some of the things he says to madam, they're things no lady should hear, but she says it's all on account of his pain and not to pay any mind to it... But the other week she was late getting back from some meeting or other. She took the Major's supper up to him. I could hear him raging at her, and so too could Master David...' His mouth compressed again.

'I thought I'd better go and see if she needed any help... Sometimes when he's really bad he tries to get out of his chair... and she's always afraid that he might fall and hurt himself even more. Anyway, as I opened the door I could see what I thought was madam leaning over his chair. He was holding on to her... Or at least that's what I thought, and then I realised...' He swallowed hard and then looked directly at the doctor.

'Then I realised that he was hurting her, sir... That he had his hands round her throat, and I'll be honest with you, for a moment I thought... But then he saw me and he let go of her...

'Madam, she made me promise not to say anything about it... Said that he had forgotten himself for a moment. But the next morning her throat was all bruised and she had to wear a scarf for almost a week. And there have been other things... It's not that he's a violent man by nature, sir, and madam would be the first person to say as much, but he gets so cruelly jealous of her... And I was wondering, well, if there wasn't something you could do, sir, something you could say to him perhaps.' He stopped and then said uncomfortably, 'I hope you don't think I've spoken out of turn, sir, but like I said, Mrs Danvers said it was nothing and made light of it, but...'

'You did the right thing in telling me, Chivers,' Ian reassured him. 'As you so rightly said, poor Edward suffers a great deal from the pain of his amputations. I'll talk to him... There are several new drugs coming on to the market soon, and perhaps a brief spell away from here...'

'It would kill him if he were to lose madam,' Chivers told Ian sadly. 'She's a wonderful wife to him. Like I said, she's a saint with him...'

But Liz was also a normal, healthy young woman not yet thirty, Ian added mentally to himself as he opened the library door, and if Edward wasn't careful his own black moods, his own violence towards her, could precipitate the very thing that terrified him so much. Of course he was afraid of losing her, of course he was jealous.

As Ian had expected, Edward was very antagonistic towards his suggestion that perhaps it was time to review his situation and that maybe a short spell away from home might be a good idea.

He moved violently in his chair, his fists clenching and unclenching in his aggression, and watching him Ian could well believe that he was, as Chivers had suggested, being violent towards Liz.

In the circumstances it was perhaps a foreseeable outcome of their relationship, but in Ian's view that did not excuse it. He had no wish to expose Liz to further violence by directly confronting Edward, but everything about Edward's attitude only confirmed what Chivers had already told him.

Perhaps the best thing, he decided when he was forced to acknowledge that he wasn't making any progress at all with Edward—who flatly denied that either his pain or his jealousy were beginning to get out of hand—was for him to talk with Liz.

'Why are you asking all these questions anyway?' Edward attacked. 'Liz been talking to you, has she, complaining? That damned mill, that's all she cares about these days...'

As the aggression left him he was rapidly descending into a mood of maudlin self-pity, Ian recognised.

'You know that's not true, Edward...and, no, Liz hasn't said anything to me. The reason I asked if you were finding it difficult coping with the pain is that it's a well-known medical fact that, no matter how good a drug might be, after a while the human body becomes used to it, that its efficiency is decreased. There are new drugs coming on to the market, and, as I've said before, a spell away from here——'

'No. No. I'm not leaving here until they carry me out in my coffin,' Edward told him fiercely. 'This is my home and this is where I intend to stay.'

'But remember, Edward,' Ian cautioned him quietly, 'the only reason you *can* stay here is because Liz is so devoted to you...'

He saw with pity the way the other man flushed and tensed. It was perhaps unkind of him to remind him of his dependence, but the words still had to be said.

'Look, why don't I leave you to think over our discussion?' Ian suggested, getting up.

'Nothing to think about,' Edward told him angrily.

Ian was halfway across the hall when Liz came in through the front door. She looked tired and drawn, but the moment she saw him her face was illuminated by a warm smile.

'Ian, how nice... I thought I might have missed you. How is Edward?' she queried anxiously. 'He's been in such a lot of pain recently. I'm worried about him...'

It gave him the opening he needed, and, walking up to her, he said quietly, 'Yes. I know... Look, I'd like to have a little talk with you. Do you have the time now?'

Given the opportunity to prepare herself Liz suspected later that she would have been more on her guard—as it was, she had no suspicion of what was to come until they were both seated in her sitting-room.

'I'm very concerned about Edward,' he began without preamble, and then, seeing the question darkening her eyes, quickly reassured her, 'No... not physically—in many ways he's in much better shape than anyone could have originally predicted, and that's down to you, Liz... No, it's his emotional state that concerns me. There's no doubt that the pain he suffers from his amputations is having a detrimental effect on him. I've suggested to him that we try a different drug, but what concerns me now is his attitude towards you, Liz.'

He saw the way she tensed and said gently, 'You're a very special young woman, Liz. What you've achieved here, what you've done for Edward, these are magnificent, wonderful achievements, but you are after all a normal young woman, with a normal young woman's natural appetites, and Edward——'

'If you're asking me if I've been unfaithful to Edward, then the answer is no,' Liz told him jerkily, her face flushing but her eyes determined as she looked directly at him and told him frankly, 'I'm not a very sexual

woman, Ian. I discovered that years ago with
Kit...David's father. He was my first...my only lover...'
She bit her lip. 'I knew what I was taking on when I
married Edward, and I did so willingly. I've *never* been
unfaithful to Edward and I don't intend to be. I don't
need or want a lover...' She saw his face—the compassion and the pity in it—and pressed on desperately.
'It's very difficult for me to talk to you like this. No one
likes admitting their failings, their inadequacies, do they?
But, believe me, I know...as far as sex is concerned...
Well, I just don't seem to have the...ability to
respond——'

All the things he had heard about Kit Danvers, and
his knowledge of Liz herself, made Ian frown. He was
a doctor very much ahead of his time; a man who
genuinely liked and admired the female sex, and who in
addition had a great deal of respect and affection for
Liz herself, and he interrupted her and said gently, 'When
you talk about failings and inadequacies, it seems to me
that *you* are shouldering the blame which rightly belongs
to another.'

When she looked blankly at him, he added, 'I know
from what you've told me about your life with your aunt
that she was an extremely repressive and cold woman;
something like that is bound to have had an effect on
you, especially during your teenage years. You were how
old when David was conceived, eighteen?'

'Seventeen,' she told him hesitantly, a small frown
puckering her forehead.

Seventeen... He sighed to himself. Still a child, and
Kit Danvers had been what? Late twenties, at least. Old
enough and surely experienced enough to have led her
gently and caringly towards the discovery of her own
sexuality. But then if all that he had heard about the
man was true, he had been undoubtedly one of those
men who took their pleasure greedily and uncaringly,
and certainly without any consideration for the emotions
and feelings of his partner.

'Those inadequacies of which you speak belong more
properly on Kit's shoulders,' Ian told her firmly. 'He

was a good deal older than you, and certainly a good deal more experienced...'

Liz moved uncertainly in her chair, and then said honestly, 'I don't think it would be fair to blame Kit... After all, in the years since... Well, I've never...' She broke off, flushing a little. It was hard for her to discuss something so personal even with a doctor she knew as well as she knew Ian.

'You've never what?' he probed. 'Never experienced desire? Never...?'

She flushed again, wondering if he could possibly know of those nights she had woken up aching, tense, aware of a need buried deep inside her.

'I've never wanted to have a sexual relationship with anyone,' she insisted huskily.

'You mean you've never *allowed* yourself to want to have a sexual relationship with anyone,' Ian corrected her shrewdly. 'Which is a very different thing indeed. I don't want to embarrass or upset you, Liz...it's just that I'm concerned about the way Edward seems to be directing his frustration and bitterness towards you. Oh, I know it's a natural enough reaction, but when it comes to actual physical violence...'

He saw from her tension that Chivers had not exaggerated. 'That sort of thing can't be allowed to happen, Liz...'

'He gets so jealous... I don't really understand—I've never...'

She swallowed and Ian told her compassionately, 'He *loves* you, my dear; he has all the normal sexual feelings of any man deeply in love, but he cannot physically express them and of course he's afraid that some other man more able than he will take his place as your lover...'

Her face had drained of colour. 'But that's... that's——'

'That's how men are,' Ian told her drily. 'It's a gut-deep atavistic thing, something beyond logic and reason—we're all of us capable of jealousy where our chosen mates are concerned, but I'm afraid that in Edward's case his natural jealousy is getting out of hand.

I think a short spell away from here would give you both a much-needed break——'

'He'd never agree to that,' Liz interrupted him.

'No. . . it seems not, but unless we can find a way of getting him to confront his jealousy and admit that his behaviour is becoming irrational. . . Well, I'm afraid that his violence . . . and he is violent at times, we both know that . . .' Ian sighed, then continued, 'You can't be happy in this marriage, Liz. You . . .'

'I'm Edward's *wife*,' she retorted stiffly. 'I owe him so much, Ian, more than you can possibly know. If I left him . . .'

'If you left him *his* world would come to an end, but what about your world, Liz, what about *you*? I suspect that you've spent so much of your life putting the needs of others before your own that you're in danger of forgetting that you do have those needs.'

'What are you suggesting? That I leave him and take a lover?' She gave him a bitter look. 'How could I do that? Even if I wanted to, I couldn't. I have David to consider, and Edward himself. . . He can't help it, you know. . . These black moods of his leave him so frightened and broken, poor man. He doesn't really mean the things he says and does. . .' She broke off, biting her lip. 'He needs me, Ian, and for as long as he does need me I intend to be here for him.'

'Very well. But remember *I'm* always here if *you* need me. . . and I still intend to try to persuade him to give you both a break by going into a convalescent home for a week or so.'

As Ian drove away he wondered if he had after all done more harm than good. Would it perhaps not have been kinder to have left her in ignorance, believing that her sexuality was warped and stunted, rather than that she was the victim of a man too selfish, too uncaring to have allowed her to discover it slowly, and to have helped her to nourish and develop it? After all, at seventeen her body had barely even finished growing, never mind her emotions and her mind.

For a long time after Ian had gone Liz stood staring out into the garden. Could what he had said about Kit possibly be true...?

But even if it was, what did it matter now? She was committed to Edward and she intended to remain committed to him. She loved him... not perhaps as a man, and certainly not as a lover, but she cared about him none the less and it distressed her that Ian had guessed how violent he had become and how he was abusing her, because she knew how much Edward himself in his rational, gentle moments shrank from the knowledge of what his black moods of depression and violence were doing to their relationship.

Sensitive, caring Edward, who would never willingly hurt anyone... but, like all human beings, there was a darker side to his nature, a darker side which pain and mental despair were beginning to bring to the fore. Sighing to herself, she walked to the door. Edward would be wondering where she was.

For a while after Ian's visit things improved. Edward's black moods eased a little, and Liz found it easier to talk to him about her plans for the mill without him losing his temper and accusing her of caring more about it than she did about him and David. She pushed to the back of her mind Ian's gentle comments about her sexuality. After all, what was the point in dwelling on them?

Work started on the renovation of the mill. Liz no longer read her trade journals in secret, but discussed their contents with Edward, brightly ignoring his sulkiness, trying to get him to take some interest in what she was doing, scrupulously including him in each and every small stage of progress.

A manager would have to be found for the mill, a man with the experience to take charge of and train a raw workforce, and a man who understood what it was she wanted to achieve.

The best place to find such a man was surely either in the mill towns of Lancashire or the Scottish borders, and so after consultation with Edward, who was reluctantly beginning to accept the presence of the mill as a reality in their lives, and after discussion with her backers—the merchant bank—advertisements were placed in suitable local papers.

The number of replies she received in response brought a fresh deluge of doubts from Edward. The textile industry was in the doldrums if not a decline, cloth was being produced far more cheaply abroad, and, if that was the case, then how on earth could she ever expect to sell the high-priced wool she was so intent on weaving?

'We'll sell it abroad. America . . . places where they do have the money and the desire to buy the best . . .'

Edward stared at her in stunned silence. What had happened to the timid, terrified child he had married? The child who had been so dependent on him, who had needed him . . . Now he was the one who needed her and that chafed his sore skin, leaving weeping open sores that refused to heal.

The history of the factory and its success was so well known to her, not through her mother, but through those who worked for her and had been there at its inception, that Sage, who could recite its story almost as a litany, had found that she was skipping paragraphs and half-pages in her anxiety to reach the year of her own conception.

So far, she had discovered nothing at all to make her feel that her mother, a woman with one child at boarding-school, a husband in declining health and a shaky new business to run, could possibly have wanted a second child with the single-minded determination she must surely have felt to have allowed herself to be used virtually as a human guinea pig. Because in those days conception via artificial insemination had been a very advanced and extremely rare process, so much so that surely only a woman with a very deep-seated need to have a child would have gone to the lengths of undergoing it?

She had just finished reading a couple of paragraphs describing David's summer holiday and the progress he was making at school when the phone rang sharply.

Panic thrilled through her immediately. She knew even before she picked up the receiver that Daniel would be on the other end of the line, and yet even so when she heard his voice shock paralysed her vocal cords... Shock and resentment. How could he sound so calm, so...so unconcerned, when her whole nervous system, never mind her emotions, were still in chaos from their encounter at the Old Hall?

She forced herself to focus on what he was saying and not on the effect the cadences of his voice were having on her body, cutting through his polite enquiries as to her mother's condition with a ruthlessness born of self-preservation. 'Your decision, Daniel,' she prompted him.

There was a small pause and her heartbeat accelerated to what felt like twice its normal rate, pumping adrenalin through her veins as her brain responded to her emotional panic.

'I'm afraid I still haven't been able to make one. I need more time... at least another forty-eight hours...'

Another forty-eight hours... by then her mother's operation would be over. By then... By then it might not matter any more which decision he made. Without her mother she doubted that there would be any campaign, any strong enough opposition to the new road.

'Sage, are you still there?'

That couldn't be concern she could hear roughening his voice and so she clamped down on her own weakness, saying grittily, 'Yes, I'm still here. I wasn't making an idle threat, you know, Daniel.'

'I never thought you were. You forget I know you, Sage.'

She stiffened, wanting to reject his claim but knowing that she couldn't. Instead she had to content herself with saying icily, 'You mean you *knew* me, Daniel, but that was a long time ago.'

He didn't respond, simply saying evenly, 'Forty-eight hours, Sage, and then I'll be in touch with my decision. I'm not in this alone, you know. I have a board to consider, to——'

'Very well,' Sage agreed impatiently. 'Forty-eight hours, Daniel.'

As she replaced the receiver she wondered if she had been wise in giving way to him, if she had not perhaps lost the advantage her surprise attack on him had given her.

In his office Daniel replaced his own receiver. She had given way much faster than he had anticipated. Ruefully he acknowledged to himself that the speed with which she had acceded to his request had left him feeling somehow cheated, as though in some way he had been looking forward to a confrontation between them, to engaging her in a longer conversation.

His own weakness was like a spectre haunting him. Yesterday... But what was the use in thinking about that? She had made it more than plain how she viewed the explosive sexual chemistry which existed between them, and in all honesty he couldn't blame her for her reactions.

In her shoes he would have felt the same way, would have resented the ferocity of his sexual need pared down to its barest elements as it was without the softening, cloaking tenderness of any emotional bonding between them. On her part, at least.

As to his own feelings... He smiled grimly to himself. He had no doubts at all about the way she would react if he was ever idiotic enough to betray the truth to her. He had heard how she had treated those men foolhardy enough to admit that they loved her. And he had no intention of joining that particular little band of martyrs. Loving her was something the years had accustomed him to, a painful condition he would rather be without, but something which very aptly fitted the old saying, 'What can't be cured must be endured.' Like a sufferer from rheumatism, he found that there were days when the pain was more intrusive and less easy to cope with, and days when the ache of loving her threatened to overwhelm everything else. But he had learned to live with it, even if the learning process had been hard and painful.

Forty-eight hours. If the rumour he had heard this morning was true then, potentially, well before he was

due to give Sage her answer her threat against him would
no longer be tenable.

He loved her, of course, but with an intensity that
went way, way beyond the immediacy of satisfying a mere
sexual need. How many years ago was it now that he
had first recognised that it wasn't just lust he felt for her
but love as well? When had he first known that? When
Scott was in hospital? Or had it even started to happen
before then? Right from the first moment he had seen
her, for instance?

But despite his own personal problems he still had a
corporation to run, and he wasn't a teenager to sit helplessly dreaming of a woman he would probably never
be able to have in his life in all the ways that he wanted
her.

Idiotic to think that while he was speaking to her on
the phone he had actually been visualising the children
they could have together.

Shaking his head over his own folly, he turned his attention to the papers in front of him.

It was almost an hour after she had finished speaking
to Daniel before Sage was able to concentrate fully on
the diaries again. During that time she had used the
excuse of wanting a cup of coffee to pace restlessly in
the kitchen, and then in the study, her emotions in a
turmoil. What was happening to her? Why was she allowing herself to react like this? She was behaving
like...like...

Like a woman in love.

Impossible... She gave a deep shudder, closing her
eyes while she fought to deny the wretched betrayal of
her own thoughts.

A woman in love... Ridiculous. Lust...that was all
she felt for Daniel. Lust... That was all she had ever
allowed herself to feel for any man since...

Restlessly she sat down and picked up the diary, and
started to read.

                    *   *   *

The summer had been a good one for them. They were getting a good name as providers of first-class rams, and under the new manager's skilled tutelage the mill was slowly beginning to produce woollen cloth of the quality Liz had wanted.

David was doing well at school, and although it worried Liz at times that he was such a solitary, quiet child, he seemed more than content. Even Edward's health seemed to have improved a little, although his possessiveness was putting an increasing strain on her. Ian Holmes had got him on a pain-killer which seemed to ease the discomfort more effectively than the others, and Edward had even taken to spending fine afternoons seated in the garden. As a consequence of the fresh air and sunshine his skin had lost its sick-room pallor and Liz knew that she was gradually allowing herself to relax from a mental and physical tension which had become such a familiar part of her life that at its first slackening she had wondered a little fearfully what was happening to her.

It was wonderful not to have to watch every word she spoke to Edward . . . not to have to gauge his reaction to everything she wanted to do, in order to avoid any kind of upset with him. About the mill she had his confidence, but she knew the thought of other men still plagued him.

Now that the mill was beginning to be successful, albeit in a very small way, all those who had been her detractors when she had first mooted the idea were now full of enthusiasm and praise.

It was several years now since she had first got Edward's reluctant agreement to go ahead with her plans, and next year, although Edward did not yet know it, she planned to make her first assault on the all-important American market.

She had been doing her research carefully and quietly, making sure of her facts before she presented them to Edward. What she needed was a representative— someone who knew the American way of doing business, someone she could trust, someone who had the same

belief in their product as she did herself. She sighed to
herself as she dead-headed the roses... What she really
needed was to be able to travel to America herself, but
that was out of the question.

It was with a feeling of calm and contentment that
she set out to take David back to school at the end of
the long summer holidays...a feeling that for the time
being at least her trials and hardships were behind her.
She could now even read Vic's rare letters without that
painful pang of 'might have been's, without that secret
sensation of loss, of envy almost of his wife, of faint
yearnings for what might have been in different
circumstances.

When Sheila Holmes remarked to her husband that
Liz was making a wonderful success of her new venture,
Ian agreed and added wryly that it was marvellous what
the human sex drive could achieve when it had no natural
outlet for its energies.

He liked Liz and he admired her, but he couldn't help
thinking almost chauvinistically that it was a pity that
such a woman did not have a more natural outlet for
her sexuality.

Liz took her time driving David back to school, enjoying these rare hours alone with her son. They stopped
for lunch in a comfortable hotel on the river, and after
she had left him she was surprised to find that she had
to stop the car to blow her nose and rid her eyes of the
tears that suddenly filled them. She did not consider
herself to be a particularly maternal woman. She loved
David, but then he was an easy child to love; everyone
loved him. Certainly she no longer—as she had done
when she'd first realised she was pregnant—loved him
fiercely and intensely simply because he was his father's
child.

All that was left of her youthful adoration for Kit was
dislike and relief that he was gone from their lives. If
anything David was closer to Edward than to herself,
perhaps because of his schooling or perhaps simply because they were both male and of the same blood.

It pleased her to see them together and to know that Edward felt no resentment of David because of his birth... to see how much he loved him.

They were enjoying a brief Indian summer, and in the rush this morning to make sure that they set off in good time she had left her hair down instead of putting it up in the neat knot she had begun to favour since the mill reopened. She felt that it lent her authority... made her seem more businesslike. Edward didn't like it and had told her so.

Knowing how important these things were to the male pride, she was wearing a new dress; a Vogue pattern copied from this season's Paris couture fashions. It had a fitted bodice with cap sleeves and a V neck, the skirt semi-circular, emphasising the narrowness of her waist. She had made it herself, choosing a crisp cotton piqué fabric in yellow and white.

For those rare formal occasions when she needed to dress up she had bought herself a fashionable white coolie hat in the same cotton and, extravagantly, a pair of formal elbow-length white gloves. She wasn't wearing these today, but she had worn the whole ensemble for David's parents' day and she had been told admiringly by one of her son's fellow pupils that she looked 'absolutely smashing'.

She smiled to herself. It was indicative of her whole way of life that she should still be cherishing the idle compliment of a schoolboy, but then what good would men's compliments be to her? She was Edward's wife, David's mother... She had led a full, busy life and had been more than lucky with the way things had turned out for her. If the price she had to pay for that luck was the suppression of herself as a woman, then it was a small price to pay. In truth, whenever she was confronted by a sexually aggressive male, which thankfully was extremely rare, she felt an immediate revulsion... a fear almost, plus a far too vivid memory of Kit's possession of her.

No... There might be times when she saw a couple embracing, when she witnessed a tender look being exchanged between two lovers, when she felt an aching emptiness inside herself, but she did not allow herself to dwell on these feelings. What was the point?

Edward needed her... David needed them, far, far more than she needed any brief, senseless moment of pleasure with an unknown man.

As she drove through the village, the warmth of the September day was settling into late afternoon like a golden cloak of beneficence.

She noticed as she drove that the blackberries were ripening fast, black and luscious, and regretted that the fact that she was wearing her one and only good dress meant that she dared not stop to pick some. With some of the early apples they would make a lovely apple and blackberry crumble for Edward's supper.

She was halfway down the drive and in sight of the house when she saw the unfamiliar car parked outside. A new Ford, with bright, shiny paintwork that made her old Morris look even more tired and shabby than it already was.

She frowned as she saw it, wondering to whom it belonged. They so rarely had unheralded visitors that the sight of the car caused a faint *frisson* of apprehension to run through her.

Quite without knowing why she entered the house through the front door instead of the kitchen, knowing that their visitor could only be with Edward.

As she approached the open library door she could hear male voices, Edward's tired and slightly strained, the other vigorously male and yet quiet in tone, with an accent she initially found hard to place.

As she walked into the library she saw that Edward was looking tired, his thin frame and grey hair in stark contrast to the powerful whipcord build of the man with him.

Vivid green eyes studied her as she walked towards them, not as a man studies a woman, she recognised, but in a distant, remote way, an indifferent way almost.

'Darling, this is Lewis McLaren,' Edward told her. 'He's over here from Australia and he thought he'd call on us and see how his ram is doing.'

Lewis McLaren...Vic's Australian boss...owner of Woolonga, who had first bred the wonderful ram which was providing her with her valuable fleeces of top quality wool.

'Mr McLaren.' She looked uncertainly at him, her eyes guarded, unfriendly almost. Once that would have made him curious about her. Once... His intellect registered the fact that she was an extremely beautiful woman, his brain acknowledging his surprise at this fact.

He had heard about her, of course, from Vic, and from Beth; had registered Beth's dislike and resentment of her, and Vic's silence. He had heard too about Edward Danvers, and had been prepared to find him an invalid. An invalid—but he was still a man with a wife and a son.

His mouth twisted bitterly, and Liz, noting it, stiffened, wondering what it was she had done to cause the grimness in his eyes. He had extended his hand towards her, more out of politeness than anything else, she was sure. She touched it briefly, reluctantly almost, tensing as she felt its calloused hardness. A shock of sensation seemed to run through her, a sharp poignant awareness of his maleness, his healthiness in contrast to Edward's infirmity, but immediately she pushed the comparison away from her.

She was tired and on edge, that was all. Tired of having to tread so soft-footedly around Edward's increasing moods of depression and violence.

'You got David safely back, then,' Edward was asking her, and without waiting for a reply he turned to their visitor and told him proudly, 'David is our son. A fine boy...'

His love for David, his pride in him touched her heart as always, reminding her of how much she had to thank him for.

'Do you have a family, Mr McLaren?' Edward enquired.

'No... No, I don't.'

The words were bitter, savage, accompanied by a grim flexing of his mouth, a betraying pulse of the muscle in his jaw.

Liz frowned. She was sure she could remember Beth and Vic mentioning in one of their recent letters that the owner of Woolonga was married and that his wife was expecting a child, but it was obvious from his expression that his private life just wasn't something that Lewis McLaren wanted to discuss with them.

Tactfully she changed the subject, taking great care to keep a formal distance between herself and their visitor.

It wasn't very difficult. He was polite to her, but she had the feeling that he was not really seeing her as a woman at all.

She was relieved about that. She was finding it increasingly difficult to cope with Edward's jealousy.

Only the previous week he had lost his temper with her, accusing her of growing tired of him, of their marriage. Increasingly these days, whenever these black moods overtook him, he would rage furiously against his fate until he was too exhausted to continue, and then he would break down in tears and weep as helplessly as a child, clinging to her, begging her never to leave him.

These scenes were slowly taking their toll of her, and heaven alone knew what they must be doing to Edward himself.

Sage put down the diary, staring blankly into space. Lewis McLaren! But he was Scott's father. It had never ever occurred to her that her mother might actually know him. But then, why on earth should it? They lived thousands of miles apart. She had known, of course, that her mother had obtained her first ram from Australia, but even in her earlier reading of the diary she had never connected Woolonga with Scott, never realised it was Scott's home. He had always referred to it simply as 'the homestead'.

And yet her mother had never said a word to her about knowing him, not even when she had taken Scott home and introduced him to her. The shock of it was making her heart beat faster, reminding her of old pains, old betrayals.

It was like turning a familiar corner and, instead of seeing a well-known and recognised view, discovering that everything had changed, had become distorted and in some way alien.

'Sage, Sage! Oh, thank goodness you're here. Can you come...? Ma's just come back and she's in the most terrible state...'

Sage frowned, focusing reluctantly on Camilla as her niece rushed up to her, her face flushed, her eyes bright with tears of fear and shock.

What was Camilla saying? Something about her mother—about Faye. Automatically Sage got up.

'She came in and rushed straight upstairs. She was crying, really crying, and she never cries, not like that.' Panic was sharpening Camilla's voice.

'Sage, you've got to do something...'

Do something... What could she do? Had her mother been here, she would have known what to do, she would have... But she wasn't here, Sage recognised dully. And she was. She was...

She stroked Camilla's hair as she stood up, smoothing the tangled curls, surprised by the odd shaft of emotion she felt as she stroked its youthful softness; a nostalgic sensation that was half pain and half wry self-knowledge—for a briefly betraying moment she had recognised that if Daniel had made love to her all those years ago she too might now have a child...his child.

All her adult life she had sworn that children were not for her; that she had neither the inclination nor the need to fulfil woman's most basic and to her most unfulfilling role; and yet here she was experiencing physical regret that she had not had a child by a man who had never fully been her lover. Simple biology...or something more?

'Come on,' Camilla urged her. 'Please hurry... I'm so afraid... I've never seen her like this before. Everything's changed,' Camilla told her passionately, angrily

almost as though unable to accept that fate had dared
to alter a single aspect of her life. 'Since Gran's accident
nothing's been the same... Nothing feels right any
more...'

For all her burgeoning maturity, she was still so much
the cherished, cosseted, protected child, Sage reflected
as she followed her out of the room.

Faye in tears... Faye behaving in a way that was more
evocative of her own emotional bravura in those early
days of rebellion and resentment against her mother than
the kind of thing one expected from calm, controlled
Faye, and as she hurried upstairs some of Camilla's apprehension communicated itself to her.

Faye's bedroom door was closed and she knocked on
it, saying quietly to Camilla, 'I think it might be a good
idea if you went downstairs and asked Jenny if she could
make us all some tea...'

'You mean you think it would be a good idea if I disappeared for a while?' Camilla contradicted her
shrewdly.

'Perhaps... If your mother is as upset as you say...'

'You mean she might not want me to know what's
upset her?'

Sage nodded and waited until her niece had gone to
push open Faye's door.

Her sister-in-law was sitting on her bed, her head in
her hands, her whole body heaving with the violence of
her silent racking tears.

Instinctively Sage dropped to her knees in front of
her, placing her hands on her shoulders, shaking her
gently as she asked, 'Faye... My dear, what is it? What's
wrong?'

Faye raised her head and stared at her, her eyes so
wild, so feral that for one heart-stopping moment Sage
almost feared that she had actually gone beyond any
form of reason, but then she focused on her, the wildness
abating a little.

'What's wrong?' Her voice was sharp, bordering on
hysteria—she was plainly fighting for self-control. 'Oh,
nothing much...nothing at all... I've just spent the

afternoon watching my mother die, that's all... Nothing really... Nothing's wrong—how could there be? After all, it's what I've been waiting for for the last twenty-five years or more... I should be laughing, not crying, shouldn't I? She's dead...and at last I'm free... Oh, God, Sage... I don't know why I'm behaving like this. I don't recognise myself any more... Perhaps I'm more like her than I ever thought... Perhaps I'm going mad too... Oh, God...'

'Faye, stop it. And listen to me... You've had a bad shock, but it might help if you tell me about it...'

'Tell you about it?' Her mouth twisted. 'If you only knew how often I've wanted to do that—to tell the world about it, to cry out to it everything that I feel, to tell people that it wasn't my fault, that I wasn't to blame, that I didn't know...'

She was crying again, dry, racking sobs that made Sage's own chest feel sore. 'It's all right, Faye... It's all right. It's over now...'

Unwittingly she had found the right words, because Faye muttered rawly, 'Yes...it's all over now... Thank God. I'm all right really—this is just a reaction, shock, I suppose... I've been waiting for her to die for so long, and yet somehow I never really believed that she would, or that I'd feel such...such pain...'

Her eyes were focusing not on Sage, but into the distance, as though she could see events unfolding beyond the confines of the room.

'You think you know what it's like to hate your mother, don't you?' she asked Sage bitterly. 'But you don't, you don't... You think your mother destroyed your life, but that was nothing... *Nothing*...

'Do you know what my mother did to me? *Do* you?' she demanded savagely, her fingers locking round Sage's wrist, her nails pressing painfully into her skin. 'Do you know what my mother did to me? She let my stepfather rape me... She let him abuse me and destroy me and she stood by and did nothing...'

Sage couldn't speak, couldn't think beyond thanking God that she had had the foresight to send Camilla downstairs.

'You're shocked, disgusted... You're wondering if I'm lying... exaggerating... You're probably even wondering if I encouraged him, wanted him——'

'No,' Sage assured her. 'No, Faye, I believe you...'

And she did... Automatically, instinctively she felt as though a key had suddenly turned in a locked door, exposing to her horrified gaze a view so tortured, so filled with pain and misery that, like Pandora, she wished she had never turned the key. But it was too late for that now... Faye obviously needed the catharsis of talking, of describing all that she had suffered, and since she was the only person here who could listen, listen she must.

In a voice more like her mother's than she herself knew she suggested softly, 'Why don't you tell me all about it, Faye? Why don't you start at the beginning, and tell me everything?'

CHAPTER TWENTY-ONE

FAYE took a deep breath and then another. Ever since she had received that phone call early this morning to tell her that her mother was seriously ill and not expected to live she had been trying to fight against her emotions. Not the normal emotions of a child, even an adult child, learning that she was about to lose her only parent, but emotions that made Faye shrink from herself, because they were ugly: anger, fear, relief, resentment that she was actually experiencing all this...that through her mother's lack of care for her she had been forced to suffer the guilt of not being able to love her. How often during the night had she woken, shivering and sweating, fighting to break free of the nightmare that engulfed her...the nightmare that had always taken the same course? The slow opening of her bedroom door, the shadowy unseen and yet so terrifyingly familiar figure coming closer and closer to her bed...smiling at her, the hated dreadful smile of a torturer, of someone who enjoyed inflicting pain and degradation.

She had tried to scream, to escape...but every time she reached the door she found it barred. Not by him, but by her...her mother.

How often had she woken David with that nightmare, with her fear, finding comfort in the warm, tender hold of his arms? David, who in some ways had been both the mother and the father she had never known... David, who had been her protector, who had surrounded her with the deep but sexless love she had craved so much from her mother and yet never received.

The lack of passion in their marriage had been their secret...hers and David's. Something she had not even shared with Liz. He had loved her, he had told her that and she had known it was true. But he did not have the

desire that motivated other men, he had said it was as
though that motivating force had somehow been
excluded from his make-up.

Neither of them had felt its loss. She had been happy
with him and he with her. She had given him a child and
would have given him more had they had the time fate
had not allowed them.

He had told her before they married that he wanted
children. Children were important to him, he had told
her, far more important than sex. They had been lucky
to find one another, but then she had lost him. Another
punishment...

'Faye.'

She focused briefly on Sage's face, noting absently
that these last days had changed her sister-in-law in some
indefinable way... had wiped away the taut mask which
had begun to harden her features and had left her face
somehow younger and more vulnerable.

She had always deliberately held Sage at a distance.
How could she, a woman so obviously sexually orien-
tated and experienced, ever understand her own dark
fears? And yet now somehow she sensed that in Sage
she would find the one confidante who would not make
judgements, whom it would be impossible to shock...or
would it? She smiled grimly to herself, even now almost
unable to believe what she had actually done.

'My mother's dead.'

She said it unemotionally this time, wearily, tasting
the words and finding as she had already suspected that
they had no meaning for her, no flavour... that in her
mother's death there was for her no joy, no release,
nothing other than a vast melancholic sea of pity, not
for herself but for the woman who in her own way had
surely endured just as much, and maybe even more than
she had done herself.

'Look, if you'd rather not talk... I've sent Cam for
some tea...'

'No.' Faye reached out and touched Sage's arm. 'I do
want to talk—I need to talk.'

She started speaking, slowly at first, anxious to find the words...the phrases that would lay bare the stark reality of what had happened to her, knowing with distaste that the last thing she wanted to do was to shroud what had happened to her in drama, not realising that, as Sage stiffened with shock and disgust at what she was hearing, the very fact that Faye was paring her past down to its bones made what she was saying all the more horrendous and appalling.

They were interrupted once when Camilla arrived with the tea.

Sage took the tray from her, reassuring her that Faye was no longer hysterical, watching half enviously as mother and daughter embraced and then Faye said firmly, 'I think you ought to be doing your homework. You've still got those exams ahead of you, you know...'

'Homework...exams... I'm tired of them,' Camilla protested, but Sage could see that she was reassured by her mother's calm and placid manner.

She hesitated a moment in the doorway, but Faye clapped her hands and said quietly, 'Homework, please, Cam. After all, after Liz has had her operation we'll be spending a lot of time at the hospital.'

'Do you think Gran will be all right? I mean...'

'We don't know, Cam. What we do know is that she has a very strong constitution and that she's in the best possible hands,' Faye told her, and once again Sage reflected how wise Faye was in not giving her daughter any false promises, any false hopes, in treating her as the adult she was starting to become without burdening her too much with the reality of Liz's chances of recovery.

After Camilla had reluctantly closed the door behind her, both women were silent for a moment while Sage automatically poured the tea.

She was handing Faye her cup when the other suddenly laughed shakily.

'What is it?' Sage asked her anxiously, fearing another outburst of hysteria.

'Nothing. It's just that for a moment you were so like Liz—you poured the tea without spilling a single drop...'

Sage stared down at the pristine white tray cloth, frowning a little as she searched for the familiar stains which were the normal result of any attempt on her part to wield the heavy antique silver teapot which her mother always insisted on using for afternoon tea.

'Heavens, so I have...' She smiled too, and then her smile quickly changed, her eyes sombre and vulnerable, so that Faye immediately read her mind.

'Don't,' she chided quietly, putting her hand over Sage's. 'It isn't an omen, a sign that...that things won't go well for Liz. She will be all right. Don't ask me how I know it...I just have this feeling...' She flushed and looked uncomfortable before adding huskily, 'It may sound strange, but today in some way I've felt so close to David. Almost as though he's here with us, but just in another room, if you can understand that...I felt it this morning, when...when I was with...with her, and then again afterwards...'

'You still miss him, don't you?'

'Don't you? He was such a unique person—so very special.'

'Yes,' Sage agreed. So much that she had never understood before about the relationship between her sister-in-law and her brother was now becoming clear to her. She thought she had suffered, had known pain, but her pain was nothing when compared with Faye's... Nothing.

They talked for a long time. Faye held nothing back, her hands twisting frantically together when she explained how much she had resented her mother. How much she had dreaded going to see her.

'Then why did you?' Sage asked her. 'In your ___'

'___d to. It was a compulsion, a bargain I had made ___ gods, if you like. I can't explain...I only know it was something I had to do. A bargain I had made with fate—payment for the good things in my life.

'You see, when I married David I refused to let her come to the wedding. I refused to have anything to do with her, in fact, and then after he was killed...' She gave a tiny shudder, and Sage squeezed her hand sympathetically, understanding all too well what she was struggling to say.

She marvelled that Faye had been able to endure, to survive what she had survived, knowing humblingly that in the same circumstances she could never have done so; that her too highly tuned nervous system would have snapped under such an enormous strain. No words she could think of were adequate enough to convey to Faye all that she herself was feeling. She could feel tears of sympathy and rage sting her eyes as she contemplated all that her sister-in-law had had to endure.

Now she could understand Faye's marriage with David...and she could understand something else as well. 'My mother knew, about...about what happened to you?'

'Yes,' Faye said simply. 'I was living here when they wrote to me to tell me that my mother had become ill, that she had had a nervous breakdown of sorts. Your mother came home and found me in the most dreadful state... I confided in her. She was wonderful...not critical in any way.'

'*Critical*...' Sage stared at her. 'Critical of you, do you mean? Faye, how could anyone criticise you?'

'Quite easily,' Faye assured her sombrely, shadows chasing across her eyes as she remembered her time at university. 'Sometimes I even wonder if it was all my fault, if I didn't somehow subconsciously invite——'

She stopped as Sage shook her head and said fiercely, 'Don't you *dare* say that—don't you even dare think it. You were six years old, Faye...a child...a *baby*... My God, when I think of what you must have endured... How could your mother, how could any woman allow that to happen to a child...?'

Sage broke off. 'I'm sorry. I shouldn't have said that.'

'I'm glad you did. You know, for a moment then you sounded quite frighteningly maternal...'

Sage closed her eyes. Faye wasn't to know that she had suddenly had a mental picture of a child in Daniel's image, with Daniel's features softened into female form—his child, her child...and that the thought of that child suffering in that way made her want to clench her hands and tear at the flesh of the people who had made her suffer until they were screaming in agony...begging for release...begging for death.

The ferocity of her own emotions frightened her. She had never envisaged herself feeling so violently protective towards a child, had never envisaged herself as a maternal woman, and yet this was not the first time recently that her imagination had created for her the child that nature had never allowed her to conceive.

A small voice whispered that it wasn't too late...that Daniel was not sexually indifferent to her, even if his desire was spawned by anger and lust rather than tenderness and love. She could still have his child...she could still steal that most precious of all gifts from him.

It shook her that she, who had always tried to be so honest with herself and with others, should so easily be able to envisage herself acting with such guile and deceit. But she could not do it...would not do it. It wouldn't be fair to the child, the child who would one day want to know who had fathered him or her, who would one day look at her with Daniel's eyes holding all of Daniel's dislike and disgust...

She shuddered again, causing Faye to say anxiously, 'I'm sorry, I've shocked you. I——'

'No, no, you haven't shocked me. I just wish that I'd known sooner, that I'd realised...'

'It wouldn't have made any difference—telling people wasn't any help... I discovered that with David. Oh, for a while it eased the torment, the anguish, but it never made it go away. I loved David. He gave me the happiest years of my life and he gave me Camilla, but sexually...' She hung her head, and Sage's heart ached for her. How could a man be allowed to do this to a child? Destroying her so completely that the woman within her would never be fully allowed to mature, that she would always have her right to her own sexuality shadowed by the crime perpetrated against her.

'David loved you. Sex wasn't important to him... You know, I often used to think that he ought to have been a Jesuit, a priest...'

'Yes, I think he thought the same thing himself. He loved young people, he loved teaching them and guiding them, but he was too honest to enter the church when by his own admission he felt no religious call to do so. He always felt that he could not believe strongly enough to be able to do God justice...at least that was what he told me, and then of course I think he wanted children for Cottingdean, for Edward. He knew how much that meant to Edward...' She broke off as she saw Sage's face, making soft sounds of distress in her throat.

'Oh, Sage, I am sorry. I didn't mean to hurt you... Of course you could have married and had children...in fact I'm sure one day you will, but...'

'My children could never have come anywhere near meaning as much to my father as David's,' Sage supplied heavily for her, waving aside Faye's anguished protest.

'Let's not lie to one another, Faye. You've been honest with me—let me be equally honest with you. My father never loved me, not the way he loved David—not even the way he loved you. As a child I fought desperately hard to make him notice me...all I succeeded in doing was making him dislike me even more. I can never really understand why my mother had me.'

'She loves you, Sage.'

Sage gave her a wry smile. 'Does she?'

'Yes,' Faye told her firmly, surprising her by adding thoughtfully, 'In fact I've always wondered if secretly she didn't love you even more than she did David.'

Sage lifted her eyebrows and gave Faye a glinting, mocking smile so hard-edged with self-dislike that it made Faye wince for her.

'Now I *know* you're imagining things. David's death killed my father. They both loved him far more than they loved me...and why not? He was far more worthy of being loved.'

'Yes...I often used to think that he was almost saint-like, so far above me in his attitudes to others that I used to despair...'

'I've often wondered why you never re-married...now I do know,' Sage told her quietly. 'You're such a beautiful woman.'

Faye made a sound of embarrassed denial deep in her throat, but Sage insisted, 'Yes, you are...and I'm not the only one to think so. Mother's specialist definitely has a soft spot for you.'

'Alaric Ferguson?'

If Faye was aware of how much she had given away in using his Christian name she didn't betray it.

'He's a very attractive man,' Sage told her. 'Very attractive, and rather sexy as well.'

'You forget...sexy men...'

'God, Faye, I'm sorry...'

Faye shook her head. 'It's all right. As a matter of fact...' She gave Sage a thoughtful look and then said quickly, 'I don't know what you're going to think of me for telling you this, but today, after...well, after she had gone... I felt so different, so...cleansed in some way. You see, before she died, she was lucid for just a very short period of time. I was sitting with her, holding her hand... They'd taken her to hospital when they first realised what was wrong. She'd had a heart attack during the night, a massive one which hadn't killed her...not quite. Anyway, she opened her eyes and looked right at me and then she said my name... That's the first time she's done that for years...and as I looked at her, such a look of misery and regret, such a look of desperate pleading came into her eyes that I knew she knew, that she was remembering...that she was asking me...'

'For forgiveness,' Sage supplied as Faye's voice broke.

'Yes...yes...for forgiveness, and, well, it was as though for a moment David was there beside me, guiding me, telling me that I must choose, that I could pay lip-service to her silent plea... that I could say I forgave her, speak the words, but withhold my true forgiveness from her, keep my heart locked against her, or I could open my heart to her as an adult, a woman, and take from her the huge burden of her suffering so that she could go from this life in peace. The choice was mine... and mine alone.

'I can't describe the feeling to you... David *was* there, but there was no pressure from him, no instruction as to what I should do. I looked at her, and it was as though she knew, and suddenly the entire room seemed to be filled with some kind of light... It seemed to fill me as well... I actually felt almost euphoric, as though a burden had been lifted from me, and I swear as she looked at me that she knew without my having to say it that I had forgiven her...

'She died moments later...'

Sage discovered that her eyes were wet with tears. Without even thinking about what she was doing, she opened her arms and they embraced, hugging one another, gently rocking together as they communicated in mutual female understanding.

'And that's not all,' Faye told her shakily when they had disengaged themselves.

She couldn't quite meet Sage's eyes.

'I'm sure this will shock you—it certainly shocks me... but I've got to tell you, because although it was really quite dreadful, in a way it was the most wonderful, magical thing that's ever happened to me.

'After my mother died, I just walked out of the hospital and kept on walking, for miles and miles... I ended up on the beach, watching the tide... feeling its ebb and flow like a tide inside my body.

'There was a man there—not young, not old, a very ordinary kind of nondescript man playing with his dog. He must have thought I looked suicidal or something because he came up to me after a while and asked me if I was all right.

'I told him that I was, but—I don't know why—I started to cry.

'He insisted on staying with me, talking to me... I told him my mother had just died. He had a flask of coffee with him and he poured me a cup. He said he knew what it was like, that his wife had died of cancer earlier in the year... He told me that they had no children and that the dog had been hers. He lived in Fellingham—he was a teacher, he told me. He asked me if I'd like to go back to his house with him. Not for any kind of sexual reason, I swear. He was simply being kind. He knew what it was like, you see, the shock of death, the void it leaves, the feeling of instability and insecurity.

'Because I wasn't ready to come back here I went with him.

'It was a nice house, small and well kept; there were photographs of his wife in the sitting-room—and although the house was immaculate I could tell it was empty in some way.

'He told me that since her death he'd moved out of their bedroom because he couldn't endure sleeping in their bed on his own... I don't know what came over me, Sage, I really don't... But I looked at him, and without even knowing I was going to say it I suddenly heard myself asking him if he'd like to make love with me...'

Her face went pink, her eyes darkening. 'I shouldn't be telling you any of this. It's——'

'You should be telling me,' Sage contradicted gently, 'and I'm not shocked. How did he respond? Did he make love to you?'

'Well, yes...yes...he did... I think he was rather taken aback at first... I didn't tell him anything, not about myself, not about David, but it was as though in some way he understood that it wasn't simply a matter of a bored housewife looking for a sexual adventure... It was as though in some way he had been sent to me, if you know what I mean...' She gave Sage a defiant, shame-faced look. 'I suppose you think I'm making that up just to excuse myself?'

'No. No. I don't... You're not promiscuous, Faye. You don't need to tell me that.'

'No...sexually I must be the most inexperienced forty-one-year-old there is—or at least I was...'

Again a blush tinged her skin. 'Well, I don't know very much about men. As I've said, he was very ordinary—the kind of man you'd never really pay much attention to, and I certainly don't have the experience to make comparisons, judgements, but...' She broke off, her blush deepening.

'It was good?' Sage guessed delightedly.

'Good?' Faye grinned at her. 'It was...it was wonderful. I'd never dreamed...never known...never imagined...'

Wisely Sage said nothing to her about the heightening effects strong emotion could have on a woman's sexual responsiveness, nothing about the fact that Faye had already inadvertently told her that she was in a state of euphoria, and said gently, instead, 'I'm glad for you, Faye. Will you be seeing him again?'

Instantly Faye looked shocked. 'Oh, no...it was nothing like that. We both said, both agreed... He said it was the first time since...since his wife. Oh, but, Sage, he was so tender, so caring, so...so knowing somehow of everything I needed. He made me feel... He made me feel like a woman. For the first time in my life I realised what sexual desire was like. It was as though something clicked into place. As though a missing piece of me was suddenly there. I wanted to laugh and cry at the same time, I wanted...

'When he touched my breasts, kissed them...instead of feeling revulsion and horror I felt pleasure, joy. Instead of only wanting him to touch me in the darkness, I felt proud of my body. I wanted him to see it. I wanted...' she shook her head '...I wanted so many things I'd never even wanted to think about, never mind experience. I didn't feel at all as though I was betraying David, as though I was doing something dirty or wrong. It didn't matter that he was a stranger, that I didn't love him or he me. It was as though...as though for both

of us it was a true celebration of life. Yes, that was it—
it was as though after years of deprivation, of hunger,
I had been given a banquet filled with things to tempt
and please me...as though I was being given a gift de-
vised especially for me.'

'A gift that might perhaps have consequences,' Sage
pressed gently.

Faye frowned and then shook her head. 'A child?
No... He had already told me that he was infertile—
that was why they had no family. He had a low sperm-
count.' Now that she had started talking, confiding, she
was finding it impossible to stop.

'The things he did for me,' she said breathlessly, her
eyes glowing like a child discovering Christmas for the
first time. 'The things I did for him...'

Sage laughed. Sex held no embarrassments or surprises for her. She felt no disgust, no shock, only pleasure
and happiness for Faye and a little gentle amusement at
her sister-in-law's new-found enthusiasm—plus, if she
was honest, more than a small amount of envy. Not of
Faye's lover, but of her joy, her innocence. They made
her feel jaded, used, regretful that the kind of joy
radiating from Faye was something she had never known
or ever would know. No matter what Faye did, she would
always have that look of awed innocence about her, that
sweetly feminine aura of mystery so very different from
her own potent sexual allure.

'Tell me about them,' she invited, sensing that that
was exactly what Faye wanted to do...that she wanted
to relive what had happened and that in telling her about
it she could do so. It was no sordid or voyeuristic impulse that made her invite Faye's confidences. After all,
Faye could hardly tell her anything she had not already
experienced for herself. No, it was simply that she wanted
to reach out and help her, to give her something...to
make this special time even more special for her.

'Well, once he had got over his shock, he looked at
me and said quietly, ''I didn't bring you here to have
sex with you, you know, but if you're sure...''

'I told him that I was. We went upstairs... I don't know what I expected, really, I just knew it was something I had to do. When we were in the bedroom he put his arms round me and started to kiss me. I hadn't expected that...

'It was nice. He was very gentle... very slow. He told me how lovely I was, how happy I was making him, and then he started to undress me... I'd thought I'd have to take off my own clothes and his but he wouldn't let me. It was as though in some way he knew. I felt so safe with him, Sage, so free, so completely myself. I knew it was something I was doing for myself and not for him, and that made me feel very strong, very powerful.'

Sage dipped her head, smiling wryly to herself. How well she had once known that feeling. But not with Daniel. Never with Daniel... With him she had felt vulnerable, afraid, weak.

'When he touched my breasts, well, it felt... Oh, I don't know... I just wanted him to go on stroking me. We were on the bed then, lying down... He kissed my throat and then my breasts, first one and then the other, so slowly that it was like being lapped in warm water.

'And then suddenly, so quickly that I hardly knew what was happening, I wanted him to be less gentle with me, to...' She broke off, flushing, avoiding Sage's eyes.

'I know what you mean,' Sage told her easily. 'It's a strange feeling, isn't it—but a pretty nice one?' she added with a grin.

Faye gave her a relieved look.

'Yes...yes...and he seemed to realise how I felt, what I wanted because he... Oh, Sage, he made me ache so much inside. I'd never realised, never felt... It was as though I could almost feel something inside me softening and opening... Before—with David—well, he was always gentle, but it was always uncomfortable, never really easy, if you know what I mean, but when *he* touched me, just with his fingers at first, it was as though he'd touched a secret lock...'

She sounded so amazed, so wondering that Sage had to smile. Privately she had already decided that Faye's

stranger sounded a very accomplished lover indeed and
had quite obviously known how to arouse a woman, but
she kept these thoughts to herself. If Faye wanted or
needed to believe that his touch had been invested with
a special magic, then so be it. She for one didn't want
to do a single thing that would cast the lightest shadow
over Faye's joy.

'And...And he didn't just touch me...' Faye told
her breathlessly. 'He...' She broke off, her face suddenly red, her breathing accelerated as she twisted restlessly on the bed.

'Oral sex can be pretty special,' Sage supplied matter-
of-factly for her.

Faye gave her a thankful half-relieved, half-triumphant
look, her eyes suddenly shy, her mouth quivering a little
as it curled up at the corners with remembered pleasure.

'Sage, it felt so good. I had no idea... I just wanted
it to go on and on, but then when it did, suddenly...suddenly it wasn't enough and I wanted...' She
gave a tiny shudder, closing her eyes as she whispered
huskily, 'For the first time in my life, the very first time,
I realised what it was that makes sex so important,
so...so powerful. I couldn't believe what was happening...couldn't believe that I could actually feel like
that, could actually feel such pleasure...

'And afterwards, oh, Sage, he made love to me all
over again, only this time he showed me how to please
him, to give him the same pleasure he had given me,
and when it happened again...' She shuddered again.

'When I left we both knew that we'd never meet again,
that it would never happen again. It was as though we
were fated to meet—as though...' She swallowed
nervously and huskily.

'Don't laugh at me or judge me. I'm not trying to
make excuses for myself, but when I left him I felt as
though it was David's way of rewarding me for forgiving
my mother.'

Or nature's way of reacting to the removal of a burden
which must have been an intolerable weight for far too
many years? Sage wondered wisely, but she kept this

thought to herself. Who was she to question what was obviously for Faye a deeply held belief? And the last thing she wanted to do was to mar her sister-in-law's release from the kind of bondage that made Sage feel sick with disgust and hatred for the man who had degraded and hurt her, imposing it on her.

'You aren't shocked, disgusted...?'

'On the contrary, I think I'm rather envious,' Sage told her wryly. 'You didn't happen to make a note of this wonderman's address, did you?' she asked mischievously.

Faye gave her a round-eyed look and then, realising that Sage was trying to lighten the emotional mood, laughed herself and shook her head. 'No...nor do I intend to make a habit of having sex with strangers...'

'I'm very pleased to hear it,' Sage told her drily. 'After all, if it's sex you want, as I've already said, I suspect Mother's very dishy surgeon would be only too pleased to partner you... In fact, I suspect he's more than half in love with you already. He certainly seemed most concerned about you when he rang here.'

'Oh, he saw me in Fellingham the last time I visited my mother in the home. He tried to question me, to talk to me, but I was in such a state that I was rather unpleasant to him, poor man...'

'Mmm...well, I'm sure he'd be only too pleased to allow you to make amends for it, if you wanted to.'

She said it half expecting to hear the embarrassed, stiff repudiation she would have heard from the old Faye, but to her surprise and amusement instead Faye seemed to be digesting her comment rather thoughtfully.

'He seemed quite nice,' she said eventually.

'Very nice,' Sage agreed, straight-faced.

'Oh, Sage, we oughtn't to be thinking like this...not with Liz...' She broke off, shaking her head. 'I feel so confused about everything at the moment...'

'I'm not surprised,' Sage acknowledged. 'And as for Mother, I'm sure she'd be the first to tell you that doing the right thing for yourself is far more important than paying lip-service to convention. She knows you love her,

Faye—she knows how much you care. The fact that you
and I are sitting here laughing doesn't mean that both
of us aren't thinking about her, aren't willing her to
survive, and to suggest that she might think it is an insult
to her...'

Sage saw the curious look Faye gave her and turned
her head away defensively and then explained huskily,
'It's the diaries. They're making me see her in so many
different ways—as...as a woman rather than as a mother,
if you know what I mean...' She hesitated, groping for
the right words to explain her own confusion in the discovery that her mother, the woman she had always
privately thought of as cold and withdrawn, was in fact
the very opposite. *Why* had she misjudged her so badly?
Was it because of their relationship, or was it because
her mother had deliberately fostered that belief? If so,
why? Why had she wanted to drive a wedge between
them, to ensure almost from her childhood that they
would never be close?

'You know, I never realised that my mother had
actually met Lewis McLaren before Scott and I knew
one another.'

'Lewis McLaren?' Faye repeated, puzzled. 'Oh, you
mean your Scott's father?'

'She never said a word about knowing him when I
brought Scott home that weekend.'

'Perhaps she'd forgotten,' Faye suggested practically.
'After all, she meets so many people. Where did she meet
him? At a dinner somewhere?'

'No... Nothing like that,' Sage told her slowly. 'He
came here to the house... It was before I was born. I'd
never realised before, but Woolonga, where the ram came
from, where young Vic went to work, actually belonged
to Scott's father. Scott never mentioned the station by
its name, and in her diaries Mother never mentioned
Scott's father's name... At least not until now.'

'Perhaps she didn't know it before she met him.' Faye
was looking puzzled, as though she couldn't understand
why Sage was so concerned about something so minor,
but Sage was beginning to know her mother very well.

Just those few words, describing her surprise at discovering Lewis McLaren with Edward, had given away so much. Lewis McLaren had not simply been another visitor; he had been someone whom her mother had reacted to in a very intense and intimate way.

Suddenly she was impatient to get back to the diaries. She glanced at Faye and saw that she was back in control of herself. Pausing for a moment, she suggested quietly to her sister-in-law, 'You know, it might be an idea to tell Camilla what you've told me. Not about this afternoon, but about the other...your childhood. She's feeling very shut out at the moment...very much alone and afraid. To know that you trust her, that you feel she's mature enough to share that kind of pain with you will be something she'll remember all her life. Don't shut her out, Faye. Don't make her feel that you don't care, that you don't think her mature or value her.'

'Of course I care, but I want to protect her... I——'

'She's not a little girl any more. She's almost a woman. Let her into your life... Let her grow up, Faye. She's at a very critical age.'

'I can't tell her now, not when she's so worried about Liz.'

'You're wrong. I think you *should* tell her now. It's what she needs—something else to focus on. It's probably what we all need right now... I'm going to ring the hospital later, just to check that they're going ahead.'

'But Alaric said he would let us know if the operation had to be rescheduled.'

'Yes. I know...but I just want to check. They said there was no point in us trying to see her tomorrow. Look, I know it sounds terrible, but would you mind if I skipped dinner tonight? I'm almost through this present diary, and I'd like to finish it.'

'No, you go ahead. I've got a lot of catching up to do on them, I'm afraid—I've been putting off reading them because of David... I was afraid it might bring it all back. The accident, his death, your father's collapse.'

'David always was his favourite,' Sage said unemotionally. 'I don't think he had the will to go on after
he died.'

'No...' Faye agreed.

She watched as Sage left the room, half envying her
graceful, elegant prowl, wondering if Sage herself knew
how much these last weeks had changed her, how much
she had softened, losing that hard edge which Faye had
always found so intimidating. Watching her now, for
instance, Faye had the impression that there was almost
something vulnerable about her.

She frowned, checking the impulse to ask her if there
was anything wrong.

Talk to Camilla, Sage had suggested. Confide in her.
Perhaps she should... It wouldn't be easy. She had spent
so long protecting Camilla from the past, dreading its
darkness reaching out to touch her, that the very idea
of telling her about it now made her stomach churn
nervously. And yet Sage was right; a rift was developing
between them. Camilla alternated at times between
sulkiness and outright hostility. She had even started to
accuse her of not caring about her.

As she stood up, she winced a little, a tiny thrill of
awareness racing through her veins as her body reminded
her of the way she had spent the afternoon.

Even now there was no regret, no remorse, no guilt,
only a delicious sense of smug completeness. A feminine
joy and secrecy, and the firm knowledge that she had
finally detached herself from the past. She would never
forget it ... never try to bury it or hide from it, but she
was at long last free of its power to cripple and hurt her.

This afternoon she had responded sexually to a man
as she had thought she would never be able to respond.
She was suddenly, miraculously aware of the fact that
she was a sexually functioning woman and that she still
had a large part of her life ahead of her. She would never
be promiscuous—that held no appeal for her—but she
knew now that it was possible for her to feel sexual desire,

to enjoy a physical relationship with a man. Quickly, before she could lose her courage, she went in search of Camilla.

CHAPTER TWENTY-TWO

As ANXIOUS as she had been to get back to the study, to the diary, once she was there Sage experienced an unfamiliar reluctance to pick it up and start reading. It wasn't so much that she felt that in doing so she was invading into her mother's privacy—after all, it was at Liz's insistence that these diaries were being read. It was more—more...more what? Apprehension on her own behalf? Why? What was it she was frightened of discovering? That her mother didn't love her, had never really wanted her? She frowned as she dismissed the lack of logic of such thoughts. How could her mother not have wanted her, when she had deliberately brought about her conception and birth?

Maybe the person she had turned out to be had been a disappointment to both her parents, but originally they could not have known that; they must have actually wanted her.

She stared down at the desk, at the diary, feeling a shiver of tension zip along her nerves. She reached out for the diary and then stopped, paced the room for several seconds and then, telling herself that she was being ridiculous, she went and sat down, firmly picking up the diary and started to read where she had left off.

Lewis McLaren was conscious of the tension which had come into the room with Liz, and made him look at her rather more closely.

For such a beautiful woman she was curiously unsure of herself, oddly vulnerable in some way, and he hadn't missed the anxious, almost appealing look she had given Edward, but appealing for what?

His own unexpected curiosity about her made him tense a little.

It had been his doctor who had suggested he take this trip, pointing out to him that he needed to distance himself a little from what had happened . . . to get away.

And so he had come to England, and it had been Vic who had suggested rather diffidently that he might like to call at Cottingdean to see the flock there and the breeding stock.

He had known from the timbre of the other man's voice how much he still missed his home and he had wondered why Vic had chosen to put so many miles between himself and a place he obviously loved.

Beth hadn't been very impressed with England, nor with the Danverses. From her comments about Liz Danvers he had expected to meet an older, harder woman, not this hesitant, almost nervous girl—because it seemed to him that she was little more than a girl really.

His own curiosity about her made him wonder if perhaps Ralph Forbes, his doctor, had been right after all. That in order to start the healing process he had needed to get away from the station.

The trouble was that he hadn't been sure if he did want that process to start. What was the point? The loss of his wife, his child—they were things he would never be able to forget, especially when . . .

He realised that Edward was saying something to him, questioning him about the length of time he expected to stay in the area. There was hostility in the older man's voice, and it made him frown.

Initially, or so it had seemed, Edward Danvers had welcomed him quite warmly—now suddenly everything had changed. And everything had changed from the moment his wife had walked into the room.

An older and obviously disabled man and a much younger and very beautiful woman. On the surface it was easy to see why Edward Danvers might be jealously protective of his wife, his marriage. But the couple had been married for quite some time; they had a son, and even Beth had not been able to fault Liz Danvers's devotion to her husband.

Later he couldn't quite understand what had prompted him to say easily, 'Oh, quite some time, I think. There are several people I want to look up around these parts, and Vic told me that this would make a good base from which to explore the area. The pub in the village is letting me have a room. It's clean and comfortable.' It had been his intention only to stay overnight in the village, and to make this one brief call here at Cottingdean to pass on to the Danverses Vic's messages.

It was true, though, that Vic had told him that the village would make a good base for him to look around at the countryside, and he suspected that the landlord of the pub would be quite willing to allow him to keep his room.

But why should he want to?

Perhaps because for the first time since Elaine and Alistair's deaths his thoughts were actually focusing on someone other than them.

He still wasn't sure if it was her beauty or her obvious apprehension which had first drawn his attention to Liz Danvers; he only knew that once he had started to study her, to wonder about her, he was finding it impossible to drag either his gaze or his thoughts from her.

'I was also hoping it might be possible to see something of your flock while I'm here,' he continued, addressing himself to Edward, even though he knew full well that it was his wife who was responsible for the development of the flock and the breeding programme for which his ram had been purchased.

Edward moved restlessly in his chair.

'Oh, the flock... That's Liz's province,' he told him abruptly. 'Although I doubt if she'll have time to spare from her precious mill to take you out to see the sheep.'

'We rent summer pastures for them,' Liz intervened quickly. 'Land higher up than Cottingdean's. It's several miles away...'

'There's no need for me to put either of you to any trouble,' he told them easily. 'If you could just give me directions, and perhaps a letter of introduction to your shepherd.'

'Yes...yes, of course,' Liz agreed. 'If you'll excuse me, I'll go and do it now.'

Lewis was surprised to discover how great an effort of will it took for him not to watch her leave. Edward Danvers watched her, though, his gaze brooding and possessive.

She wasn't gone long, returning within minutes with a note addressed to her shepherd which she handed to him and a neatly written list of directions as to how he could find the pasture.

Edward's reference to the mill had increased his curiosity about Liz, but he sensed that any questions would not be welcomed by either husband or wife.

They were an odd couple, he reflected as he drove away, and not just because of the disparity in their ages. There had been a tension between them, a fear in Liz Danvers's eyes which contrasted with the picture of domestic harmony and devotion which Vic had drawn for him.

'David's getting so grown up now,' Liz commented brightly to Edward when their visitor was gone.

She was conscious of a sick tension in the pit of her stomach, a combination of anger and anxiety, and helpless pity for her husband. She had seen the way he had been looking at Lewis McLaren, knew what was coming even before Edward burst out furiously, 'What's going on between you and McLaren, Liz? And don't lie to me, don't try to deny it. I saw the way he was looking at you... Where did you meet him? What's he—'

'Edward, please...' She was close to tears, as always unnerved by his illogical rage. 'I've never met Mr McLaren before today. You *heard* him. He's the owner of Woolonga... He merely called out of politeness.'

'You're lying to me,' Edward told her harshly. 'I'm not a fool, Liz. I can see what's going on. You're having an affair with him, aren't you? You're...'

He was working himself up into a rage which she knew from experience would lead to a violent explosion of temper. Inwardly all she wanted to do was to open the library door and escape, but her pride, and her compassion for the real Edward, not this Edward who was screaming abuse and accusations at her, an Edward who had become warped by his suffering, made her stay.

She longed to open the door and to call out to Chivers for help, but to do so would be to admit that she could no longer control the situation...that she could no longer deal with Edward's growing hostility and violence.

She had learned now to keep as much physical distance between them as she could when Edward was in one of these moods. Moods which were becoming increasingly common, moods which could be sparked off by the smallest thing, although this was the first time he had actually accused her of having an affair with a specific man.

'Edward, please,' she tried to reason, forcing herself to keep calm. 'Please listen to me. Mr McLaren means nothing to me...he's a stranger.'

'A stranger? Then why is he staying in the village? Why did he come here? What was in that note you handed him—what had you written there?'

'Edward, you *know* what was in it—it was just a note to the shepherd explaining who Mr McLaren is——'

'You're lying, damn you!'

She winced as he screamed the words at her and then turned to his desk, sending the chess set standing on it flying. He had a considerable amount of strength in his arms, and the noise of the pieces scattering all around the room seemed violently loud.

It was certainly loud enough to reach Chivers's ears, because he came hurrying into the room, giving her an anxious, uncertain look.

'Who the devil sent for you?' Edward demanded, glaring at him. 'Get out of here, damn you!'

Liz gave him an imploring look, wanting him to go. She hated others seeing Edward like this. It hurt her for him and for herself, even when it was someone as close to them and as understanding as Chivers. Increasingly it was getting very difficult to prevent David from seeing what was happening. He had such a good relationship with Edward, and she didn't want anything to prejudice it. A boy should respect and admire his father, it was only right and natural, and, to David, Edward *was* his father. Certainly he had been a far better father to him than Kit would ever have been. Edward almost worshipped David... For the first time she was glad that David was away at school.

'There's a phone call for you, madam,' Chivers was saying woodenly. A phone call... They had been having some problems at the mill with one of the machines and the call was probably about that. She looked apprehensively at Edward, knowing how much in these moods he resented her involvement with the mill, but he wasn't looking at her any more—he was staring blankly at the scattered chess pieces, almost as though he had no idea how they had got on the floor.

Chivers was already starting to pick them up. The storm had passed... for the moment at least, Liz recognised tiredly. Later would come the remorse, the tears, the pleas to be released from his earthly torment, his anguish and fear of losing her, all of which in their way were even harder to bear than his unwarranted accusations and his loss of temper.

Perhaps Ian was right. Perhaps it *would* do them both good if Edward could be persuaded to go to one of the convalescent places for a little while, but how would she persuade him to go? He would immediately assume the worst. He would feel frightened, betrayed, deserted... and much as she felt the need for a small oasis of calm and peace, she couldn't take it at the expense of Edward's peace of mind.

When she picked up the telephone receiver in the study, there was no one on the other end of the line. When she mentioned this later to Chivers he merely said quietly, 'Wasn't there? They must have hung up, then, madam.' She suspected that he had deliberately invented the call in order to help her.

She sighed to herself. Her head ached and there was an uncomfortable gritting sensation at the back of her eyes. An hour or so spent working in her garden would ease her tension. No one would disturb her there.

Only she was wrong in that assumption. Someone did disturb her—someone who had no right to be in her thoughts at all. And that someone was Lewis McLaren.

She stopped weeding, her body suddenly trembling. What was the matter with her? She had no right to be thinking of Lewis McLaren, no right at all, and even less to be comparing him with Edward.

And yet she couldn't help recalling how when he had touched her hand her whole body had reacted as violently as though it had come in contact with high-voltage electricity. Why?

Stop it, she warned herself, you're imagining things. Just because Edward has invented some fantasy affair between the two of you, it doesn't mean that...

Her body tensed abruptly and then she started to shake. She *couldn't* be thinking those kind of thoughts, couldn't be having those kind of feelings, not about a man she had only just met, a man she had known for only a handful of minutes—a man who, moreover, was married...

Married... she sat back on her heels, wondering why her vision had suddenly clouded and then discovered that she was actually crying.

Married... she was sure that Lewis McLaren's wife didn't sleep alone, that *she* didn't carry the burden of both doubting and fearing her own sexuality, that *she* knew what it was to share physical pleasure with a man, that *she*...

Oh, God... what was happening to her? What was she doing? What was she thinking? And, besides, if the McLarens had such a perfect marriage, why wasn't she with him? Perhaps she was—perhaps she had simply not chosen to visit Cottingdean. If that was the case...

How much better it would have been if she had. Edward would have had nothing then on which to base his totally fictitious accusations, and she... she would what? Not have felt that extraordinary and disturbing *frisson* of sensation when he touched her, that deep and vividly clear mental image of him as a man... a lover. She was crying in earnest now, tears pouring down her face. She had to stop this, and the only way to do it was through work, more and more work, until she was too exhausted to be able to remember that a man called Lewis McLaren even existed, never mind to indulge in such pointless and dangerous fantasies about him.

For three days she almost succeeded, but it wasn't easy. Lewis McLaren was a stranger in a very small village, and quite naturally his presence there caused a good deal of interest and curiosity. It was known that he intended to spend some time in the area, and from the comments she overheard it was obvious to Liz that he had the village's approval.

He had not returned to the house. She told herself that she was glad, but when she woke up in the night, her body tense, her skin slick with sweat, and an ache deep inside her that could only confirm the eroticism of dreams she would much rather have not remembered, it was hard not to give in to the temptation to let the shadowy man who partnered her in her dreams take on the form and features of the real man she knew him to be.

In her weak moments she told herself that it did no harm, that her dreams, her fantasies were hers and hers alone and yet she was still tormented by guilt, by her fear of the emotions and needs her dreams unleashed. Despairingly she longed to return to that time when she had not known the depths and heights of her own sexuality, when she had firmly believed that it did not exist.

She tried to tell herself that she was like a foolish girl daydreaming over a film star, she tried to lose herself in her work—but, while that might keep her thoughts at bay during the day, it only seemed to unleash them to torment her even more intensely at night. What was wrong with her, she asked herself dejectedly, why was she developing these foolish thoughts, this dangerous obsession for a man she had only seen once?

Five days after her brief meeting with Lewis McLaren she woke up and remembered that it was the day of her bi-monthly visit to see the flock and the shepherd. She dressed sensibly for this exercise in an old tweed skirt and jumper, putting a pair of brogues on her feet, and taking with her a warm tweed jacket. The forecast was for rain later on in the day and it was far from warm.

Since his outburst over Lewis McLaren, Edward had been very quiet and subdued. Liz was becoming used to these mood swings now: the fierce outbursts of temper, followed by remorse, followed by a period of apathy.

As she kissed Edward goodbye she found herself hoping that it wouldn't be too long before Ian was able to prescribe for him one of the new drugs he had mentioned, if they could only get Edward to agree to take them.

It wasn't a long drive up into the downs where the sheep had their summer pasture and normally it was one which she enjoyed. The narrow country lanes were virtually free of other traffic, and the rich contrast provided by the different fields of crops never failed to entrance her, just as she was always fascinated by the way the sunlight and shadow moved over the hills as clouds raced across the sun.

There was something about this land, about its time-lessness, about its peace that made her vividly aware of how many many others before her must have watched as she was watching and marvelled at the power and strength of nature ... and how many would do so in time to come. It was like being part of an unbreakable chain, an awareness of how infinitesimal her link in that chain was; from her it would pass to David and from him to his children and to theirs after him. She had so much to be grateful for; it was wrong of her to yearn for something she could never have, something she had no right to have.

It wasn't possible to drive out to where the flock were grazing. She had to park her car beside the field gate and get out and walk the final mile or so, but it was a task she didn't mind. Tying a scarf over her hair, and pulling on her jacket, she set off. The wind had momentarily blown the sky clean of clouds and the sun shone warmly.

High above the land a kestrel hovered . . . watching, waiting. She paused to watch him swoop downwards into a cornfield and pitied the tiny creature who was his victim even while she admired the control and grace of his swoop and the power which took him up again to hang motionless in watchful prey.

Before turning to resume her climb, she looked behind her the way she had come and saw that someone else was coming up the hill towards her, his head bare, his dark hair tousled by the wind.

She knew who it was from the clenching of her stomach muscles, the instant recognition of her soul and her heart, even before he called out her name and she recognised the distinctive Australian accent.

Common sense told her that the worst thing she could do was to wait for him, and yet that was exactly what she did do, caught as helplessly in the snare of her own feelings as the small creature had been in the talons of the kestrel.

'What a coincidence,' Lewis smiled as he caught up with her, although in point of fact it was no coincidence at all. This was his second visit to the summer pastures. It had been on his first visit, during his conversation with the shepherd, that he had discovered Liz was due to visit them later in the week.

He had warned himself that what he was doing was folly, that curiosity was one thing, that something to take his mind off Elaine and Alistair could only be of benefit to him, and yet his instincts, his senses warned him that it was far more than idle curiosity that stirred his interest in Liz Danvers. Far, far more.

This morning she looked younger than ever. He knew her age—five years younger than his own—but today she looked as though a whole decade could quite easily have separated them, and as he drew close to her he marvelled at the clear perfection of her skin, its softness, its paleness, so different from the sun-browned skins of his own countrywomen . . . How Elaine had bewailed the harshness of the outback sun, claiming that it was making her old before her time. She had hated the outback, hated Woolonga, hated him sometimes...or so she had claimed. The pity of it was that he hadn't listened to her, hadn't realised—if he had then perhaps both she and his son would still be alive today.

Don't blame yourself, Ralph had told him. Don't descend into the depths of self-pity and guilt—it won't bring them back. Accept that Elaine was a very highly strung woman, whose outlook on life, whose mental strength, had become seriously undermined by the birth of their child. Sometimes it happened like that. He could not, must not blame himself for what had happened. But how could he not do so?

She had never wanted to marry him. She had told him as much, but they had really had no choice in the matter. It had all been arranged for them by their respective fathers, both of them indomitable men used to having their every word obeyed, used to the power and control that came from owning thousands upon thousands of acres of land and from running on that land thousands of head of sheep. Both men had been autocrats, both used to ruling their own private worlds as they saw fit. And they saw fit to unite their vast tracts of land in the marriage of their son and daughter.

Perhaps if they hadn't both been killed in the same plane accident, a plane flown by his father... Elaine had adored her own father, had come close to worshipping him in fact. After his death she had become very withdrawn; she had blamed Lewis's father for what had happened and, through him, Lewis himself.

It had been shortly after the news of the accident had been brought to them that she had miscarried their first child.

After that she hadn't let him touch her for almost three years. He had tried everything, wondering if she realised that he now had as little appetite for their marriage as she had herself, but they were married, divorce was out of the question, and they had to have a child, an heir for Woolonga. In the end he had been forced to take matters into his own hands. Even now, he shuddered when he thought of the way he had deliberately got her drunk, and then carried her virtually comatose to bed, undressing her and then entering her unresponsive, flaccid body, summoning every ounce of will-power he'd had in order to do so.

Afterwards she had rounded on him with a stream of profanities as she'd cursed him for the death of his father and for the death of her child.

He had wanted to tell her that it wasn't his fault, that he mourned their child as much as she, but he knew already that he would be wasting his time, that something in her had turned away from him and inwards.

Sometimes the outback affected women like that. It was a demanding land, a man's land, cruel to those women who dared to brave its harshness. It took a woman of great strength, great fortitude and endurance—a woman with a great love for her man—to withstand its cruelties.

Elaine had not been like that. She had been weak and vulnerable and it had given him no satisfaction to have compelled her to resume their physical relationship. He had hoped that perhaps another child would help her to overcome her grief, her almost obsessive clinging to the past and her father's death, and when they had discovered that she *was* pregnant it had seemed as though his hopes were answered.

Certainly she had prepared for the baby's birth with a vigour, an enthusiasm that had lightened his anxiety for her. Their marriage could never be the kind of relationship he had once idealistically hoped for, and if he could not love her with passion and delight then he could at least cherish her and honour her both as his wife and the mother of his children.

The outback life was a harsh one, with scant time for introspection or idleness, and certainly he had never been tempted to break his marriage vows even if he had had the opportunity to do so. He had married Elaine thinking he was doing the right thing, for Woolonga, for himself and for her. His father had hinted to him that she would welcome the marriage, that she was in love with him, and he had only discovered after they were married that this was not true, that she had married him in obedience to her own father, and that if she loved any man it was him and not her new husband.

It was nervousness and nothing more, a fear of her own feelings, a fear of somehow revealing them, that made Liz ask as he caught up with her, 'Have you come to England without your wife, Mr McLaren? Doesn't she mind? I——'

'My wife is dead,' Lewis told her abruptly, and then, seeing her face, apologised, 'I'm sorry. I was abrupt...'

'*You're* sorry.' Liz turned a white, strained face towards the hills, unable to bring herself to look directly at him. 'I'm the one who should apologise,' she said huskily. 'I had no idea... Vic mentioned in his letters that you were married. He never...'

Was that why he had come to England—to try and forget? He must have loved her very much. What had she been like? Tall, and sun-bronzed with a wild mane of hair...?

'I didn't love her. I never loved her... I should never have married her.'

The quiet, slow words ran through her like a shock. When she looked at him he was standing motionless, his profile carved against the blue arc of the sky. She hadn't realised until now how tall he was... but then she hadn't stood so close to him the last time they had met.

Silly, trivial thoughts passed through her head, like how well the tweed jacket he was wearing fitted him, and how very male he looked, how full of life and vitality. She liked the way his hair grew on his scalp and against the tanned, taut column of his throat...

'She killed herself... took her own life and the life of our child...'

Again his voice was quiet and slow, the words enunciated carefully as though they were unfamiliar to him, as though he had never said them before, and she knew instinctively that he had not... that she was the first person to whom he had unburdened himself, to whom he had talked of the terrible tragedy which had blighted his life.

'I blame myself...' He wasn't looking at her now. 'I should have seen, should have known...'

Steadily Liz sat down on the grass and patted the earth beside her, inviting him to join her as she asked softly, 'Tell me about her...'

Once, the old Liz, the Liz with whom she was familiar, would have shrunk from making such an invitation, from prying into the life of another human being, from witnessing his anguish and pain, but suddenly she was a new Liz, a different Liz, a Liz who saw beyond her own fears and needs and who reached out instinctively to offer him the succour she knew he wanted.

He sat down beside her and started to talk, slowly, hesitantly at first, leaving nothing out, looking directly into her eyes now and again as he told her of his guilt for his unwitting neglect of his wife, his complacency in believing that she was content, his culpability in assuming he had the right to decide what was best for her.

'I thought when Alistair was conceived that she was happy. She seemed to be... She was anxious, of course, during her pregnancy—we all were, after her earlier miscarriage. I wanted her to have the best medical care, and so, three months before Alistair was due, I flew her down to Melbourne. She had an aunt there, and I visited her as often as I could. She seemed to thrive in the city—she seemed to be so happy. I thought...' He swallowed.

'She had a long and difficult labour, but once Alistair was born... She seemed to worship him. I felt quite jealous at times—she would barely let me near him...

'When Alistair was a month old I took them both home to Woolonga. At first everything seemed all right, but then gradually Elaine seemed to become more and more depressed. I wanted her to consult our doctor but she wouldn't. She said she missed Melbourne, so I promised her that we'd go there for Christmas, but when Alistair was six weeks old and I was out mustering, she picked him up and carried him out to the creek. We'd dammed it to make a pool that we used for bathing before we had a proper pool installed.

'We think she must have just walked right into it holding the baby, because when we found them they were still together...' His voice broke, and Liz felt her eyes sting with sympathetic, helpless tears.

'She'd left me a note, saying that since I'd stolen her child and killed it she was now stealing and killing mine...'

She could hear the tears in his voice and moved instinctively towards him, putting her arms around him as naturally as though she had been doing it all her life, cradling him to her while he wept, knowing that somehow or other fate had decreed for both of them this meeting place in their lives, this coming together and bonding, and that no matter how hard she had tried she would have been powerless to avoid it.

It was as though somewhere inside her a missing piece had suddenly slid into place, setting in motion the eternal, soundless music to which the whole universe moved...as though she had found a half of herself which had previously been lost, as though for the first time in her life she was truly complete.

She had known love before: the love of a child for her parents and her family, the love of a mother for her child—she had even thought she had known love for Kit, however unwise and foolish that love had been—but as she held Lewis to her and shared the outpouring of his grief and guilt for the deaths of his wife and child, as she listened to his words of contrition, pain and anger, she knew that she had never truly known before what love was.

But, even in the moment when she acknowledged that somehow, somewhere, by some alchemy she could not begin to understand, fate had brought her face to face with this very special man, she also knew that they could not be together. Her course through life was already set. She had commitments, had made promises she could not break, had loyalties, responsibilities, duties, all of which weighed far heavier in the scales of life and conscience than her love for Lewis.

When Lewis raised his head and looked at her, the look he gave her only confirmed what she already knew.

'How has this happened?' he asked her tenderly. 'How have we managed to find one another like this? Oh, my love, when I think how easily we might not have met...'

'Perhaps it would have been better if we had not,' Liz told him quietly.

For a moment he was very still.

'You can't mean that, and don't try to tell me that you don't feel it too... That you don't *know*, as I know...'

She had to stop him. To allow him to go on would only add to the pain they were both going to suffer.

'I'm married,' she reminded him huskily. 'I have a husband...a son...'

'You're mine,' Lewis contradicted her flatly. 'You're mine, Liz, now and throughout eternity. I think I knew it the first time I saw you... Why do you think I've been hanging around here? Trying to tell myself I'm acting like a fool, and yet knowing nothing on this earth could make me leave. I *knew* you'd be here today. Your shepherd told me.

'Oh, God, Liz, after everything that's happened, everything that my life has been, I still can't believe I've been lucky enough to find you. Don't try to send me away, because I won't go, and don't try to tell me that you love Edward either,' he challenged her flatly, 'because I won't believe you. Not now!'

'But I *do* love him,' Liz told him sadly. And it was true. She did love Edward, not as she might love a man, not in the way she now knew that a woman *did* love the one man who was her chosen mate, out of instinct and desire. No, her love for Edward was a love born of necessity, both his and her own. He had helped her when she needed help and she would never allow herself to forget that.

'Liz, please.'

She turned her head automatically, unable to resist the plea in his voice.

Because they were still sitting down on the grass the disparity in their heights was not as noticeable, so that when she looked at him her gaze could easily meet the steady green regard of his.

The flesh round his eyes burned from long hours in the hot outback sunshine, was fanned with small lines, the jut of his cheekbones hard and planed.

The hand he lifted to cover hers was tanned and calloused, enveloping hers completely. He had removed his jacket and pushed up the sleeves of his shirt and her stomach clenched on a dangerous ache of need as she looked at the muscled hardness of his forearm and knew without knowing how she came by the knowledge that to be held by those arms, to be caressed by his hands, to be a part of his body, would touch her so completely and so wholly that if once she allowed him to love her she would never want to send him away.

And yet even as she held up her hand in a mute appeal to him to stop what they had started now, before it went any further, she couldn't help focusing on his mouth, watching the movement of his lips as he formed words her outer ear didn't hear, because all her senses were absorbed in taking into herself as much of the essence of him as she could so that it could be stored deep within her memory, a panacea for the days, the months, the years ahead when those memories of him would be all she had to sustain her.

'Liz, my darling one... Don't deny our love.'

She heard the words, felt their agony, their desire, felt her heart seize in unbearable pain and her eyes fill with tears as his hands lifted to her shoulders and held her, so gently, so lightly that she could quite easily have broken away, could quite easily have avoided the downward descent of his mouth. And yet for some reason she had no will to move.

When he kissed her it was with tenderness and joy, like a man worshipping at a shrine he had long believed denied to him. Beneath his her mouth yielded helplessly to her need. The kiss deepened, his arms enfolding her so that she was wrapped in tenderness and love.

It would be the easiest thing now to open the doors to the physical urgency of their love, to give herself to him here on the downs beneath the clean wind-washed sky...

No, not the easiest thing...the most necessary, precious and right thing; but even as her rebellious heart demanded to know why she should not after all have this brief time of happiness, of love, her conscience, her upbringing, her deep and strong sense of loyalty were already closing the door on her need. She might not be able to deny the love in her heart—that was impossible—but she couldn't betray Edward, David and all that their lives together were: each month and year, carefully built and nurtured, so that she had believed she had built their marriage into something strong and sturdy enough to withstand even the most violent of storms. No, she couldn't do that...

Not even for this wonderful, special man, whom she knew now she would love beyond life and time.

As she eased herself away from him, she touched his face lingeringly, her emotions showing plainly in her eyes as she told him quietly, 'I can't, Lewis. I can't betray Edward...'

He looked at her for a long time, still holding her, so that she could feel their pulses beating in unison, as though their bodies were already one.

'No,' he said despairingly. 'But can you betray our love? And if you stay with him that is what you will be doing. Leave him, Liz, come back to Australia with me...'

'I can't——'

'If you're thinking of your son, of David—he will come too.'

She shook her head. 'Edward would never let me take him, and I can't leave them, Lewis. Either of them. They need me...'

'*I* need you,' he told her. '*I* need you, Liz. Oh, God...you don't know how much I need you.'

She felt tears sting her eyes... How could she deny him, when his need, his love were her own? But she had to. She had no choice. She had chosen her path when she married Edward and she must stick to it.

'I must go,' she told him quietly, standing up. 'The shepherd will be wondering where I am. Please don't come with me, Lewis...'

'I'm not giving up,' he told her fiercely. 'I'll never give up, Liz. Never.'

As she climbed the rest of the hill she didn't dare turn around. Not even when she heard the sound of a car engine firing, and knew that he had gone.

It was only when she reached the top of the hill that she realised she was crying.

CHAPTER TWENTY-THREE

'ARE YOU all right, Liz?'

She forced herself to smile at Colin Hedley, her mill manager. The two of them had spent the morning going over the accounts, and this afternoon she had a meeting with a buyer from one of the larger London stores. She hadn't slept through one night for the last three weeks. Since the day she had met Lewis McLaren out on the hill.

He was still staying in the village. She hadn't seen him. He had called at the house a couple of times, but she had given Chivers instructions that she didn't want to see him. Didn't want to see him? A wan smile crossed her face. If only that were true.

She might have banished him physically from her presence, but his image was with her constantly. During the day when she tried to work herself hard enough to ensure that she slept at night, and during the night when she was almost afraid to fall asleep because of the intensity of her dreams of him.

She had lost weight, there were shadows under her eyes and it was no wonder that Colin Hedley was frowning at her, worried.

She gave him an abstracted smile.

'Yes, Colin, I'm fine,' she lied. 'Just a bit tired.'

'Look, why don't I see the buyer for you?' he suggested.

She was about to refuse when she had a sudden mental image of her garden, a sudden fierce thirst for the comfort of her long herbaceous borders where the mingled colours of her plants would rest coolly on her sore eyes. Eyes that were sore from the tears she cried at night when she was restlessly asleep. She wanted to feel the cool moistness of the earth in her hands; to have her faith, her belief that what she was doing was worthwhile and right reinforced. An hour or so working in her garden would soothe and calm her nerves in much the same way as its cool, healing colours would soothe her tired eyes, and who knew, perhaps if she worked hard enough, breathed in enough healthy fresh air, she might even be able to sleep properly and not be tormented by her dreams of Lewis?

Woolonga ... She could see it so clearly in her mind's eye, and had not realised until now how treacherously her brain had stored up from Vic's letters so many details of the sheep station and the homestead itself. It would be a harsh environment and certainly not one that would welcome the soft pastel colours of her English flowers with their thirst for the cool rain and gentle sun of an English summer, but she could have a garden there none the less; she could ...

Stop it, she told herself fiercely as she turned to Colin Hedley and thanked him, agreeing with his suggestion. The buyer was one who had visited the mill before, and who was merely coming to place a repeat order. The store which he represented had been pleased with the cloth they supplied. She herself had paid a discreet visit to its drapery department on her last visit to London and had been pleased to see how advantageously it was displayed and how well it was selling.

As she had so correctly foreseen, there was a growing need, a growing desire for softness and luxury, so that her soft-hued tweeds, despite their cost, were outselling their duller, harsher competitors.

It was a relief to get back into her car and drive through the leafy lanes to Cottingdean.

The house drowsed in the sunshine, slumbering beneath the weight of its venerable years. As always when she came back to it she was conscious of a deep sense of peace, of continuity, of being part of the magical chain that linked generation to generation.

Here was a different kind of completeness from that she had experienced with Lewis. Their completeness had been that of two people designed by nature to be together—here her completeness came from the knowledge that she was a very small but very necessary part in the huge mosaic that was humanity.

She parked the car and walked round the side of the house so that she could walk through the kitchen garden and along the double border. Lavender lined the footpath that led to the kitchen garden, her progress wafting its scent around her, her tweed skirt, made from a Vogue pattern in tweed woven at the mill, of the same soft-hued shade as the plant so that she blended perfectly into her surroundings. The skirt was a copy of the latest Dior line, pencil-slim with a flirty back pleat. She had thought it rather sophisticated for her lifestyle but the vicar's wife had persuaded her to make it, claiming that in her position as proprietor of the mill she needed to show visiting buyers just how well the fabric made up.

She had allowed herself to be persuaded, although she still felt guilty over the added extravagance of the court shoes she had bought in Bath to go with her new outfit.

As she approached the house, she wondered if Edward would have had his lunch. His appetite had diminished recently, and his temper had become alarmingly short. She felt her stomach muscles bunch and tense.

She knew the signs now, knew quite well that his almost childish sulks would lead eventually to one of his violent outbursts.

Ian had told her quite firmly that she was not to put up with them; that if they continued, for her sake if not for his own, Edward would have to submit to some kind of restraining treatment.

'He can't help it, Ian,' she had told the doctor. 'He doesn't mean any harm.'

'Not afterwards,' Ian had agreed shortly. 'But he's a very strong man, Liz, far stronger than you.'

She knew it was true; the muscles in Edward's arms had of necessity become extremely powerful, and the last time he had grabbed hold of her during one of his jealous rages she had indeed felt very afraid, and the bruises his hands had left on her skin had taken over a week to fade.

She frowned as she approached the house, the breeze rustling her crêpe de Chine blouse, so that the fabric pressed lovingly against her breasts as she leaned forward to touch the petals of a newly opened rose.

From the library window Edward watched her jealously. She looked so young, so beautiful, with the breeze moulding the soft cloth to her body. So desirable... He felt the familiar burn of helpless frustrated desire sear through him and cursed under his breath. If fate had seen fit to destroy his manhood, to take from him the physical ability to express his desire for her, then why could it not also have taken away the mental and emotional capacity to feel that desire?

He watched her with bitter, brooding eyes. There was a pain in his head, where a great vein throbbed. He touched it with his hand and felt the pulsing throb right down through his body. It had rained during the night, and despite all Liz's attempts to keep his rooms dry and warm his sensitive flesh felt the aching bite of the rheumatism that tormented him.

With all the too keen perception of a jealous lover he sensed that Liz had changed, that his relationship with her was somehow threatened; that she was slipping away from him.

As he watched her progress through the garden and saw the way she stopped to inspect and admire her flowers, the very way she looked and touched them so expressive of the love she felt for them that he was actually jealous of the attention she gave them, hating them almost for the way they took up her time and her care, time and care which ought to have been given to him. He hated those hours when she was out of the house, gone beyond the control of his jealous demands, gone where she could meet other people... other men.

As Liz straightened up from what she was doing she glanced towards the house, tension gripping her body as she saw Edward watching her.

From this distance it wasn't possible for her to see his expression, but she could tell simply from the way he held his body that he was angry.

She had a moment's cowardly desire to turn her back on him...not to go into the house at all, but to hide herself away in the garden where it was impossible for him to come after her.

Her own thoughts made her grimace in distaste. It wasn't Edward's fault. She must never forget that he was in constant pain or how he had suffered...

Or how much he loved her... A love which she didn't want, a treacherous voice whispered. A love which threatened to suffocate and destroy her...but she banished these thoughts, refusing to give in to the temptation to listen to them.

The forecast was good. She would go in and persuade Edward to sit in the garden. He could sit in his chair in the shelter of the long border while she did some weeding.

Not even to herself would she admit how much she would have preferred to work there alone, and that in deciding to have Edward with her she was in reality giving herself a penance.

Once inside the house, she didn't pause to admire the way the sunlight picked out the mellow richness of the restored panelling, nor to let her fingers stroke gently down the rich pattern of the damask curtains, all small pleasures which normally brought so much simple joy to her day.

Sometimes, on her way through the house, she would find herself standing for minutes at a time admiring the workmanship in a Persian rug she had rescued from one of her bargain-hunting expeditions at country house sales, which had then been carried home and lavished with affection and care until it was cleaned and restored to its original beauty.

Slowly she was filling the house with beautiful things, bought not because she had a shrewd eye for a bargain and not even because Cottingdean was a large house which needed a large amount of furniture no matter what it looked like, but simply because a certain piece, a certain painting, a certain fabric, would catch her eye, its beauty calling out to her so that she just could not resist it.

Had anyone told her that she had the natural eye of the true collector, that her bargains would one day be worth many, many times what she had paid for them, she would not have been impressed. She had bought them because she had fallen in love with them and that was how she cherished them, as much-loved friends, just as she loved and cherished her garden and its plants, the flock and its sheep, and all those human lives that fell within the domain of her care.

She paused outside the library door and then opened it; Edward was now positioned behind his desk. He didn't look up as she walked in and her heart sank, but, ignoring the obvious signs that he was not in a good mood, she chatted cheerfully to him, coaxing him out into the garden.

Leaving him in a warm, sheltered spot, she then went upstairs to shower and change, cursing under her breath as the water in her bathroom refused to run hot.

One day Cottingdean's antiquated hot water system was going to have to be replaced. She closed her eyes, not wanting to think about how much it would cost or where the money was going to come from.

If the mill was successful.

She dressed quickly in an old skirt and blouse and then hurried back outside, collecting her trug and her tools on the way.

Edward was where she had left him. He ignored her while she adjusted his chair so that he could get the full benefit of the sun, but while she worked in the border, gently removing the clinging, throttling weeds from around the base of her plants, she was conscious of his brooding presence, his anger and jealousy, and she wished whole-heartedly that she had left him inside so that she could enjoy the peace of the garden unhindered by the souring atmosphere created by his mood.

'That Australian's still in the village, then.'

She tensed as he spoke, glad that her back was to him as she felt the guilty heat of the colour running up under her skin.

'Yes,' she agreed, keeping her voice as expressionless as possible.

'He's been here looking for you,' Edward told her.

Liz held her breath. She knew that Lewis had been to the house on a couple of occasions but on both of them she had told Chivers to tell him she wasn't available. Even so, something in Edward's voice sent a shiver of presentiment running down her spine. Or was it simply her own guilt that was making her so presciently aware of Edward's antagonism towards him?

It was just as well she had told Lewis there was no future for them, she thought tiredly. She certainly wasn't cut out for a life of deceit, for lies. Leave Edward, he had said to her. Leave him . . . leave him . . . How could she? How could she leave a man who was so vulnerable, so dependent on her, a man who had after all done her no wrong?

And what about David? David who loved Edward as Edward loved him . . . How could she destroy David's security, his home?

'He wants you,' Edward said challengingly from behind her, causing her to turn round abruptly.

'No . . . no, that's not true,' she denied.

'He wants you,' Edward persisted, ignoring her. 'And you want him. And why shouldn't you, after all? He's a whole man, able to give you what I never can, but you're my wife, Liz . . .'

Guilt, compassion and her deep inbuilt dislike of seeing anyone suffer either emotionally or physically took her from the border to the side of Edward's chair, her hand going out to touch his arm comfortingly.

'I'm not letting him have you,' he told her. 'Him or anyone else . . .'

The vein in his temple was throbbing ominously, and Liz recognised despairingly that he was in the grip of one of his black moods.

She tried to soothe him, to reassure him, but he refused to listen to her, making such wild and impossible accusations about relationships he imagined she had had with other men, and using such obscene words to describe her that for a moment she felt too sickened, too shocked to do anything other than stand in stunned silence.

But then she forced herself to step outside her own humiliation and shame that he should harbour such thoughts about her, such appalling, shockingly untrue thoughts, and to calm him down, but it was already too late. As she put her hands on his arms, gently trying to restrain him, he fastened his hands around her throat with such strength and power that she couldn't break free.

'I'll kill you before I'll let him have you, Liz... Oh, they'll hang me for it, I don't doubt, but why should I care? What is there left in this life for me other than to rot away inside the prison of my own flesh? I can't be a man ever again, not the kind of man you could love or desire. Not a man like the men you take to your bed in place of me... Who are they, Liz? Tell me their names, tell me, damn you...'

He was shaking her, his fingers pressed against her windpipe so that even if she had wanted to speak it would have been impossible.

A red mist filled her vision, darkening the world around her, so that she felt as though it were covered in blood.

From a distance she could hear Edward's voice, loud and angry. Her chest felt tight, so tight that she couldn't breathe... There was an unbearable pain... She could feel her consciousness receding in ebbing waves despite her attempts to hang on to it.

She was going to die, she recognised floatingly. She was going to die but somehow it didn't matter because if she was dead she would be free of this awful pain, of this inability to breathe.

And then, just as the red mist turned black, she heard Lewis calling her name, the sound of feet running along the gravel path, and then blessedly, unbelievably, Edward's fingers were wrenched away from her throat. She collapsed on to the path, dragging air into her tortured lungs while above her Lewis was demanding fiercely, 'Chivers, get the doctor... Now, man! Hurry! I ought to kill you for this,' he told Edward bitterly.

She tried to struggle to her feet, to speak ... to tell him that it wasn't Edward's fault, that he wasn't responsible, but the words wouldn't come.

In the distance she could hear someone crying and thought that the tears were her own until she realised it was Edward who sobbed as helplessly as a child, and as always her fear subsided overtaken by her pity and her guilt. Poor Edward—it wasn't his fault.

She closed her eyes. She felt so tired. Too tired to do anything other than lie here on the path.

She was still lying there semi-conscious when Chivers came hurrying back, panting for breath as he told Lewis, 'The doctor's on his way... I'd better get the Major inside,' he added gruffly, avoiding looking at Lewis's set face.

'Yes, get him inside,' Lewis agreed curtly. The sound of Edward's sobs, the sight of him cringing in his chair like a whipped child, the knowledge that the man was not really responsible for what he had done, did nothing to soften his anger against him.

If he hadn't arrived when he had...if he hadn't decided to ignore Liz's dictate that she did not want to see him again, Edward would have killed her, he was sure of it. As it was...

He dropped to the path beside her, gently taking her body in his arms and holding her to him, while he whispered her name over and over again, tenderly kissing the bruise marks already purpling her throat.

Dear God, she would have to leave Edward now. The man was insane—he had to be... To have attacked her like that.

When Ian Holmes arrived at the house, an ashen-faced Chivers explained to him what had happened.

'If Mr McLaren hadn't arrived when he did I don't know what would have happened,' he told Ian. 'I was just showing him out into the garden. We both saw what was happening...' He shuddered and Ian patted him gently on the back.

'How is Edward now?' he asked him.

Chivers looked uncomfortably at him.

'The way he always is after one of his attacks, sir...
I've given him two of those special sleeping tablets of
his and put him to bed. He should sleep like a baby for
a good twelve hours now. Always does after...well,
afterwards...'

'Right. Where's Liz?'

'She's still out in the garden. Fainted, she had...'

He stopped speaking as Ian walked past him, hurrying
out into the garden.

He hoped that all she had done was faint, Ian thought
worriedly. From Chivers's description of the way Edward
had been gripping Liz's throat, it was a mercy she was
actually still alive.

When Liz opened her eyes she was in Lewis's arms. He
was gazing down at her, and as she looked hazily back
at him she thought that heaven itself must be like this,
must feel like this—a protective haven which she never
wanted to leave...but as awareness returned fully to her
she knew that no matter how much she might ache to
stay here, protected from the world by the warmth and
strength of his arms, she could not do so.

She heard footsteps on the gravel and pushed herself
away from him.

'Liz, my dear, are you all right?'

Ian was kneeling on the path beside her, Lewis answering for her as he said bitingly, 'Of course she's not
damned well all right. That...that...that idiot damn
near killed her.'

'I'm fine, Ian,' Liz told him, smiling shakily at him.

'She's not fine at all,' Lewis contradicted flatly. 'Look
at her, man, look at what he's done to her. Another
minute——'

'It was an accident,' Liz protested. 'Edward didn't
mean...' She looked appealingly at Ian but he was
shaking his head.

'I'm sorry, my dear. I know you only want to protect
him, but for his own good I'm afraid we must get him

into hospital. These moods of his...' He shook his head. 'If Mr McLaren hadn't arrived so fortuitously——'

'He'd have killed her,' Lewis supplied for him.

'No...that's not true,' Liz protested.

'I'm sorry, Liz, but you *must* see we can't allow you to take any more risks. I know how Edward feels about taking stronger drugs, but I'm afraid I'm now going to have to insist that he at least undergoes trials to see if they could help him, and the best place for that is in the controlled atmosphere of a hospital. Don't worry about him. You'll be able to visit him as often as you wish.'

'He'll be so afraid,' Liz protested.

'He's a grown man, my dear,' Ian told her quietly, 'not a child, and think... At the moment his anger, his bitterness is focused on *you*, but what if it happened that he started to focus it on someone else? Chivers, or David—or even a stranger? You might have the right to take risks with your own life, but if Edward should injure someone else—kill them, even—how would you then feel?'

He hated having to be so cruel to her, but it was necessary, and he could see that the words had hit home from the whiteness of her face.

'You shouldn't be with me,' Liz told him shakily. 'You should be with Edward, he needs you more.'

'Chivers has very wisely given Edward a couple of strong sleeping tablets. Now, let's get you upstairs where I can examine you properly. If Mr McLaren could carry you...?'

'No.' The sharpness of the way she said it made Ian frown and hesitate. 'No, it's all right. I can walk,' Liz told them both.

She could, but only just, and she had to lean on Lewis more than once on her way upstairs to her room.

Once she was there, Ian tactfully but firmly banished Lewis while he examined her.

Afterwards he sat down on her bed and told her quietly, 'You are very, very lucky to be alive. And Edward is very, very lucky that it's only hospital he's going to right now and not prison.'

'Lucky... I don't feel it, not with my throat so sore that I can hardly speak,' Liz told him ruefully, trying to make light of what had happened.

'Yes, it will be sore,' Ian agreed. 'Liz, you do understand, don't you, that it is imperative now that we get Edward into hospital? As his doctor I have to insist, in fact, that we make immediate arrangements. If I could use your telephone...?'

'But what can you do for him there that can't be done at home?' Liz protested.

'Many things. For instance we can monitor his responses to the drug tests much more closely, in much more controlled conditions. It *is* necessary, Liz, and I'm afraid on this occasion you must accept my judgement on that. You must see that if I don't do something now and at some later stage Edward attacks you again, or someone else, I would virtually be to blame... I don't want your death on my conscience.

'Now, you try to get some rest. I'm going downstairs to ring the hospital and organise a bed for Edward. I'll go with him and see him settled in, and I promise you that just as soon as he wakes up I'll be there to explain to him what's happening.'

He saw that she was trying to speak and shook his head.

'No. You must rest that throat of yours, and anyway I know what you're going to say. *You* want to be there. Well, for once Edward is going to have to do without you, and I promise you when you wake up tomorrow morning that throat of yours is going to be so stiff and sore that you'll be glad I'm insisting on your staying in bed. In fact, if necessary, I'll tell Chivers he has to lock you in here and remove the key,' he warned her, smiling at her as he got up and walked over to the door.

Downstairs he found Lewis pacing the library floor waiting for him. 'What's happening? How is she?' he burst out as Ian walked in.

'Her throat is very badly bruised and she's shocked, of course, but there doesn't seem to be any permanent damage.'

'No permanent damage...' He wheeled and stared blindly out of the window, his voice shaking as he demanded, 'Do you know what he was trying to do to her? He was trying to *kill* her.'

'Yes. Yes, I do know,' Ian agreed quietly.

There was another silence and still Lewis couldn't bring himself to turn round and look at the other man in case he read his feelings in his eyes; for Liz's sake he couldn't allow those feelings to be seen, no matter how much he might want to stand on the highest hill he could find and shout his love for her to the world.

'Then why in God's name does she stay with him? *Why?*'

He couldn't keep the words back nor the pain out of his voice. Ian watched him for a moment and asked him quietly, 'How much do you know about them...about Liz herself and her relationship with Edward?'

He could see Lewis's back stiffening.

'In many ways I agree with you, but I know Liz. She'll never leave him.'

'But why? *Why?*'

'Because he needs her,' Ian told him gently.

'Does he? It didn't look like it when I saw him today—he was trying to kill her.'

'Yes, I know. Look, come and sit down and I'll try to explain.'

Unwillingly Lewis did as he asked. He still hadn't got over the shock of discovering Edward with his hands wrapped round Liz's throat, his eyes bulging with maniacal hatred as he tried to squeeze the life out of her.

'Edward loves Liz. He's also paranoically jealous of her—and of any man she comes into contact with,' he added warningly. 'He's obsessed with the fear that he's going to lose her, a fear that's exacerbated by the frustration of the desire he feels for her but can never physically express. He is mortally afraid of losing her to another man, a man who could be a husband and a lover to her in all the ways that he cannot.'

Slowly Lewis stared at Ian, the colour receding from his skin as he said, 'But they have a child—a son...'

The pain in his voice made Ian wince. Perhaps he had
said too much, but it was too late for him to stop now.
'*Liz* has a son,' he corrected him. 'I shouldn't be telling
you any of this and I don't know really why I am, except
that I happen to think a great deal of Liz and I just
wish...' He stopped and sighed. Quite what he wished
for Liz he wasn't sure. That she could find fulfilment
as a woman; that she could be relieved of believing that
the burden of a lack of sexual responsiveness to Kit
Danvers was hers when he was pretty sure it belonged
on Kit's own shoulders... So what was he trying to do?
Push Liz into the arms of this man who so plainly wanted
her?

'It isn't my place to tell you any more,' he said slowly.
'I'm going to ring the hospital now and arrange for an
ambulance to come and collect Edward. I want him to
go into hospital for a few days so that we can run some
tests on him with a new drug that I'm hoping we'll be
able to use to control these violent depressions he's been
getting. It isn't easy for him either, you know,' he told
Lewis. 'He *loves* her.'

'He would have killed her,' Lewis told him tiredly,
repeating, as though he could hardly believe it himself,
'He would have *killed* her.'

'But fortunately he didn't,' Ian returned. 'I've given
Chivers instructions to make a cup of tea into which he's
going to slip a sleeping powder. If I know Liz she'll refuse
to take anything I prescribe, but she needs to sleep, to
give her body time to heal.'

While Ian was making arrangements for the ambulance to come and collect Edward, Lewis walked out into
the garden, his footsteps automatically taking him to the
beginning of the walk between the double borders. At
the top of it he stopped and stared down it, his throat
going dry with tension and fear as he remembered how
he had stood there and seen Liz—his Liz—and that fiend
of a husband of hers with his hands round her throat...

He started to shake; to feel sick with rage and love.
The stones on the path were scattered unevenly where
she had fallen. If he had only been seconds later... Was

this fate's way of punishing him? First his wife and his child, now Liz... What had he ever done to warrant such pain? He had married Elaine in good faith, believing it was what she wanted, believing they would be happy together. He had intended to make her a good and faithful husband, a good father to their children even if he had not loved her, at least not as a woman... Had there been signs he had missed, warnings he should have picked up but which he had been too busy running the station to notice? Had she made silent cries for help which he had ignored? How many times had he asked himself these questions? How many times during the dark, lonely hours of the night had he longed to turn back time, to save her and their child?

When he had come to England there had been no purpose to his life, only a vast, wasting emptiness. And then he had met Liz and everything had changed.

'I can't,' she had told him. 'I can't leave Edward.' But surely now...?

From the garden he paused and looked back at the house, picturing her lying in her bed. She had felt so light when he had caught her to him, so small and fragile.

He turned back towards the house and started to walk and then to run. He met Ian Holmes just as the latter stepped out of the french windows.

'The ambulance will be here shortly. Chivers informs me that Liz is asleep. You're staying in the village, I believe...'

'I was,' Lewis told him, adding, 'Until Liz is fully recovered I shall be staying here...'

'Yes...'

They looked at one another for a long time and it was Ian who looked away first.

A vehicle was approaching the house. When he saw it was the ambulance, Ian excused himself, leaving Lewis to watch him walking away.

CHAPTER TWENTY-FOUR

LIZ woke up abruptly, conscious with the odd clarity that came in the heartbeat of space between sleeping and waking that something was wrong, that the light coming in through her closed curtains was not the light of early morning—and then she saw the motionless figure seated in the chair.

'Edward.'

As she said his name she was aware of a feeling of coldness and fear, a sense of despair and panic.

'It isn't Edward, Liz, it's me, Lewis.'

The relief, the joy—the immediate reversal of all her earlier emotions as Lewis's voice transmuted them from the darkness of fear and pain into the shining gold of exaltation and delight—made her shiver with the knowledge of how dangerous her emotions were, how impermissible and wrong.

'Edward's in hospital,' Lewis told her, getting up and coming over to the bed, quickly adding, 'It's all right. There's nothing wrong with him. But your doctor... He seemed to think that it was the best place for him right now. Personally,' Lewis told her grimly, 'I should have thought prison...'

He saw the small anguished movement of her body beneath the sheets and stopped before telling her emotionally, 'My God, Liz, he could have killed you, *would* have——'

'No,' she denied immediately. 'No. He didn't mean——'

'Didn't he?' Lewis interrupted her. 'When I arrived...' He stopped and then demanded passionately, 'Why do you stay married to him, Liz? He's no husband for you... Why *did* you marry him in the first place?

And don't tell me you love him. I saw your face just now when you woke up and thought I was him.'

Liz winced, her face going paler.

Her throat was almost too sore for her to speak. It felt swollen and raw inside. She felt weaker than she had ever felt in her life. She could feel the tears burning at the back of her eyes and knew that there was nothing she wanted more than to reach out to this man who watched her with such angry, hungry eyes and to tell him how much she loved him, to beg him to take hold of her and to go on holding her, to keep her safe not just from Edward, but from all her own fears as well.

But if she did that... She shuddered, knowing the burden of guilt they would both have to carry if she allowed herself to give way to her vulnerability.

He was right to criticise her... to condemn her. It was *her* fault that Edward had attacked her. It was her fault because she had never realised, never known until it was too late how much Edward loved her, and how dangerous that love would become without any natural outlet, how it would turn in upon itself and slowly poison their whole relationship.

'I'm sorry,' she heard Lewis apologise huskily. 'I had no right... I'm behaving as badly as Edward—worse...'

'No,' Liz contradicted him tiredly, 'I shouldn't have married him, but you see...'

Suddenly she wanted to talk to him, to unburden herself to him, to explain to him why she had acted as she had.

She told him as quickly and as briefly as she could, skimming over the emotional poverty of her life with her aunt, and the deliberate cruelty with which Kit had treated her.

'It's too easy to make excuses for myself now, but if I had known how Edward really felt——'

'How could you have known?' Lewis interrupted her tenderly. 'You were just a child.'

Liz gave him a wry smile. 'Hardly... I was seventeen, more than old enough to——'

'As I said, you were just a child,' Lewis told her grimly. He was fighting to control his anger... against Edward and against his cousin.

'And this Kit, David's father... You still love him, still want him.'

Like lovers throughout eternity, he couldn't quite keep the jealousy out of his voice, but the tiny shudder that went through her still body, the look in her eyes, at once so haunted and so anguished, immediately reassured him.

'No,' Liz told him honestly. 'Nor have I wanted anyone else since. I've been content in my marriage to Edward...'

Liar, an inner voice taunted her. You might have been content once but you aren't now.

She shivered beneath the bedclothes. It was true. She wasn't content any longer, hadn't been since...

'Content.' Lewis looked grimly at her. 'Are you, Liz? Are you really content to live with a man who might quite easily murder you, a man...?'

She didn't want to be reminded of Edward's attack on her. She moved jerkily, covering her face with her hands while her body trembled violently as it remembered the frightening sense of helplessness and fear which had overwhelmed her when she realised she couldn't break free of Edward's hold.

'Oh, God, Liz, my darling... Don't, please! Don't.'

She hadn't seen him move, hadn't been aware of anything other than the shock of her remembered fear, until she felt the bed depress beneath Lewis's weight and looked up to find he was reaching down to her, taking her into his arms, holding her, cradling her, whispering to her all the soft sweet words of love for which her lonely heart had so dangerously yearned.

While he kissed her face and stroked her hair, she told herself frantically that she must stop him, that she must not allow this to go any further, but there was so much sweetness, so much warmth, so much love in the way he held and touched her that her starved senses refused to listen to the warning urgings of her brain.

Instead of telling him that he must leave, that to stay here with her now was to promote a situation which could only ultimately increase her pain, she found herself telling him more about her marriage, about her unhappiness in her brief affair with Kit, about her son, and even, self-betrayingly, and oh, so hesitantly, she actually found she was confiding to him her awareness of her own lack of any strong sense of sexuality.

'If you're telling me that because you think it will put me off, you're wasting your time,' Lewis told her gravely. 'It's you I want, my darling. You...'

As he spoke he smoothed the hair back off her face and looked down into her eyes. 'Leave him, Liz,' he begged her huskily. 'Leave him now and let me take care of you...'

Just for one wild, crazy moment she wavered, telling herself that she had the right surely to snatch at this precious, undreamed-of happiness...that she and Lewis loved one another and that their love must be allowed to live and grow...that whatever she had to sacrifice to be with him must be worthwhile...and then sanity took over and she realised how impossible it was for her to do what she was contemplating.

'I can't,' she told him. 'Please try to under-stand——'

'I understand that I love you,' Lewis interrupted her savagely. 'And that you love me... Don't try to deny it. I've seen it in your eyes, felt it in the way your heart beats when I touch you. We were meant to be together, Liz. To try to prevent that from happening would be the sin, staying with Edward when you don't love him—those would be sins...not leaving him to come to me...'

She closed her eyes, her heart and her body both filled with unbearable pain.

She wanted to give in, to say yes, to throw everything else aside and simply go with him. Perhaps if she had still been a girl of seventeen she might have been able to do so, but she wasn't that girl any more. She was a woman; a woman, moreover, who was a whole decade older...and wiser.

As she looked at him, she felt the pain inside her grow, and knew with certainty that she would love him for the rest of her life. She touched his downbent head gently, blinking back her tears as she asked herself why fate had been cruel enough to send him into her life when it knew that there was no place for him there.

'I can't leave Edward,' she told him.

He looked up, about to argue with her, about to remind her that Edward, her precious husband, had almost killed her, and as he looked at her throat and saw the bruises darkening the skin, and then into her eyes where he could see her anguish and despair, he cursed himself for his selfishness, and said quietly, 'Right now what you need more than anything else is to rest. Your doctor has left a sleeping drug...'

Immediately she shook her head.

'Right now all I really want is a cup of warm milk,' she told him huskily. She knew she should ask him to leave...tell him to leave if necessary. After all, there was no real need for him to stay. She had Chivers and by tomorrow she would be back to her normal self, fully able to get up and take control of her life again. She would have things to do, as well. She would have to get in touch with Ian, and arrange to go and see Edward...

Edward... She could feel her mind fighting to get away from even thinking about her husband, her body clenching with fear and misery at the mere thought of being with him, and yet what else could she do? How could she leave him now when his need of her would be so great? It wasn't a matter of being concerned about what others might think—it was what she would think of herself if she abandoned him now, turned her back on him now...

'I'll go downstairs for that milk,' Lewis told her softly. 'Don't you dare move from this bed, and that's not coming from me, it's coming from that doctor of yours.'

As he stood up she turned her head, revealing more swollen, dark bruises along her throat.

A feeling of such pain and rage welled up inside him that he knew that if Edward were there in the room with them, despite his infirmities he would probably have slowly strangled him. How could he have done this to her, hurt her like this...?

Almost without realising what he was doing he reached out and gently traced the dark marks with his fingertips, and then, when she shuddered and closed her eyes, he bent his head and tenderly pressed his lips to each individual bruise. When she trembled, he released her and stood up, watching her for a moment before saying quietly, 'I'd better go down and heat that milk.'

After he'd gone Liz told herself that just as soon as he came back she'd tell him that he must leave, but her fingers strayed to her throat, touching the bruises he had kissed, and her body quivered with sensations that drowned out logic and common sense.

There were so many things she ought to be doing. It was foolish of her to stay here like this in bed when she ought to be up, and yet her body felt so drained, so weak and exhausted. She closed her eyes, telling herself that she would just rest until she had had her milk and that then she would get up and ask Lewis to leave, but when he eventually arrived with the milk he had heated for her she was fast asleep.

He watched her for a moment and then put down the tray. Somehow there had to be a way of convincing her that there was no debt she owed Edward. Somehow... and he would find it, because when he left England to return home he was taking her and David with him and nothing was going to stop him. Nothing.

Liz was dreaming. In her dream she was in her garden, the sun was shining and she was warm and relaxed, and then suddenly a shadow started to creep over the sun, obliterating the light. She looked up towards it, her happiness giving way to fear as she saw that the shadow was that of Edward, her husband, who was coming towards her with such a look of hatred in his eyes that she cried out to him not to come any closer, but he wouldn't stop, he was reaching out towards her and she couldn't move, even though she knew that once he took hold of her he would hurt her, kill her even... Already she could almost feel the bite of those hard fingers against her skin, already she could almost feel their pressure on her throat, already...

Lewis had fallen asleep in the chair. Her first low cry of fear woke him, so that he was already stumbling stiffly towards the bed as she started to cry, smothering the high, frantic sound against his own body as he took hold of her and half lifted and half dragged her from the bedclothes and into his arms, soothing her, rocking her in his embrace as he held her to him with one arm, and pressed her face against his shoulder with the hand of the other, his fingers splayed out beneath her hair as he cradled her head and whispered soft, reassuring words in her ear.

The relief of discovering that she had been having a nightmare and that Edward was not actually there over-whelmed any instincts of caution and restraint which might have urged her to think beyond the present to the future.

As she trembled in Lewis's arms and felt the tender comfort of his lips caressing first her temple and then her cheek, she turned towards him.

'Liz.'

She felt the emotion in his voice, deep within her body. She shouldn't be doing this... Shouldn't be here with him like this... But already it was too late, already he was kissing her, caressing her mouth with his so that her lips parted helplessly beneath the pressure of his.

For a long time he did nothing more than kiss her, but they were kisses unlike any she had ever known, kisses which she hadn't even realised could exist, kisses which were a whole world of intimacy in themselves. Kisses which turned her bones to water, and her senses to a mindless confusion of delight while she responded to them as helplessly and innocently as though he were her first lover. Which in reality he was.

There was no rush, no hurry, no impatience in the way he touched her, and then watched her as he saw the wonder of what was happening to her reflected in her eyes.

He undressed her carefully and tenderly, kissing the soft flesh of her throat, each swollen bruise, and then the pulse that was beating so frantically fast at its base.

The room was in darkness, her body cloaked in shadows so that he had to learn her by touch and not by sight.

He felt her tension when he touched her naked skin, and the intensity of his own anger and compassion held him motionless.

'There's nothing to be afraid of,' he told her rawly. 'I'm not going to hurt you.'

'I know,' Liz told him. Her throat was so sore that to speak was an effort. 'I'm not afraid of that ... just of disappointing you.'

It had cost her so much to make the admission. She closed her eyes, half afraid to look at him. She shouldn't be doing this ... shouldn't be here with him like this. She was Edward's wife ... Edward's, and yet she knew that if Lewis left her now she would die from the pain of it.

'You couldn't disappoint me,' Lewis told her, swallowing back his compassion, his anger against the man who had made her feel that *she* was responsible for *his* inadequacy.

'I love you,' he told her. 'And you love me, and nothing, nothing is more important than that ...'

He loved her ... She loved him ... These were forbidden words, forbidden emotions, and yet, as he removed his own clothes, and she felt the heat of him, felt the scent of him enveloping her, she reached up to him, watching him with tentative anxious eyes.

'It's all right,' he told her softly. 'Everything's going to be all right.'

And then he was holding her so that they were lying body to body and she recognised in wonder and bemusement how much her flesh had yearned for this tactile mating with his, how much her skin welcomed the heavy warmth of his body, its muscled hardness, its weight and its power. Every tiny movement he made against her created such an erotic friction that she could hardly believe she was actually experiencing such sensations.

Her need to reach out and touch him, to stroke her fingertips over his skin, to taste its warmth and maleness, to explore its alien contours, was so strong and so unexpected that she made a small sound of protest against it in her throat.

'What is it—what's wrong?' Lewis asked her anxiously.

'I want to touch you. To feel, to know...' She could hear the confusion and bewilderment in her voice and knew that Lewis could hear it too.

'I hadn't realised. I didn't know...'

She heard Lewis saying huskily, 'Give me your hands,' and almost like a child she obediently did so, shivering with pleasure when he placed them against his skin and told her, 'I'm yours, Liz. You can touch me however and wherever you wish. If my heart doesn't have any secrets from you, why should my body?'

He was touching her as he spoke, his hands caressing her shoulders and then her breasts, his touch so tender, so full of love that it was impossible for her not to respond, not to arch her body and to press herself closer to him. The sound he stifled in his throat made her tense a little as her body recognised his arousal and shied away from it, remembering Kit's possession of her. But Lewis wasn't Kit. Lewis's touch wasn't Kit's. Lewis's loving wasn't Kit's lust and long before his mouth had touched the sensitive flesh of her nipples her stomach had turned fluid with longing and need and her body was twisting recklessly, pleadingly against his, while her hands moved yearningly over his body, seeking to convey to him how much she needed him.

When he did draw the tender, sensitive hardness of her nipple into his mouth to stroke it with his tongue and then suckle on it, her body arched convulsively beneath his hands, her soft cries of pleasure inciting him to bite passionately on the swollen flesh as she was pressing eagerly against him, as her whole body moved against his in a rhythmic eroticism of which she was completely unaware.

As he struggled to control his own desire, Lewis marvelled that she could ever have believed herself to be lacking in sexuality. Her body, innocent and untutored in terms of experience, possessed an awareness and instinct that had caused him to become so intensely aroused that he wanted to devour her inch by inch, to touch and taste every silky particle of skin, to possess her so completely that her body would never forget him.

When he finally released her she lay in his arms, shuddering from head to foot, her nipples gleaming damply in the shadowy light, so sensitive now that merely to feel his breath against them caused her to moan his name in protest and reach out blindly for him.

But as though she had actually said the words, made the plea that was pulsing so fiercely through her body, he said thickly, 'No, not yet, my darling... Just be patient, and I promise you...' He was kissing her stomach, his mouth open and moist as he dragged it over her flesh. His hands held her thighs, moving her, lifting her, her senses so overwhelmed and bemused, so hungry for his total possession that she had no awareness of what he intended to do until she felt the warmth of his breath against the most intimate part of her body.

She tensed immediately, but still had no awareness of what he intended to do; her own experience fell very far short of such intimacy, so that the sensation of his tongue moving, stroking firmly and deliberately against her body was doubly shocking. Shocking because beneath that first sensation of reaction and withdrawal lay a far different and more compelling feeling; a need not merely to lie tensely and still and force herself to accept what he was doing to her, but rather a need to move with voluptuous encouragement, to incite and invite the deeper penetration of her flesh, to have his mouth caressing her now as he had done before when he had drawn first one and then the other nipple into his moist heat, when he had first sucked and then bitten so erotically on her flesh.

She started to cry out in denial of her own feelings, and then discovered that she was crying out instead because Lewis had put her unspoken wishes into practice and because the sensation he was causing within her body both excited and terrified her, so that she both wanted to beg him to stop and at the same time to plead with him never, ever to cease what he was doing to her.

As she struggled to hold on to reason her body defied her, the sensation building up inside her, driving her, possessing her, obliterating everything else.

The unbearable tension within her body, the intensity of her physical need, were things she could barely comprehend, crying out to Lewis that they were something she just could not endure, even as the fine-drawn threads of desire snapped, setting her free to fly beyond the barriers of mortality, and then to float there lapped in the warm, soft darkness of completion.

Her body was trembling with reaction and shock when Lewis took her in his arms, tenderly stroking her skin, whispering words of praise and love to her.

'But you didn't . . . we didn't . . .'

'We will,' he told her gently. 'When you're ready.'

When she was ready... He was turning her in his arms, curving her into the warmth of his body, and as she felt its male arousal a tiny *frisson* of responsive sensation danced through her.

'When you're ready,' Lewis had said.

She looked at him and said huskily, 'I think . . . I think I shall be ready very soon. In fact I think...' She stopped abruptly as he started to kiss her and she discovered that that earlier tiny *frisson* of sensation had become much stronger, so much stronger in fact that she was already moving eagerly against him, wanting him, needing him, inviting him . . .

This time she knew what to expect; this time, her body, tutored by his tenderness and love, meshed rhythmically with his so that the sensation building inside her was something reinforced and shared with the growing urgency of his body's movements within her.

The sensation was the same but different, deeper, so that her whole body seemed to sigh with pleasure and open to him as though it wanted to draw him within it so deeply and intimately that her flesh would have the memory of him imprinted within it long, long after he had gone.

Later, when she had cried out her love to him and their bodies were at peace, he turned to her, tensing when he saw the tears glittering in her eyes.

'I'm sorry. I'm sorry,' he whispered, holding her, anguish making his voice harsh. 'If I hurt you——'

'You didn't,' she assured him. 'It's just . . . just that I never knew it could be like that . . . Once as a girl I thought, believed . . . but then Kit, David's father——'

She stopped as he took hold of her hand and kissed the pulse that beat in her wrist and then slowly and tenderly kissed each finger.

'It was the same for me,' he told her. 'That's the difference that love makes. It transforms the base metal of our desire into the pure brilliance of gold; takes us from our mortal plane to one that's higher.'

They made love again, slowly, lingeringly, and this time Liz took the initiative, caressing him as intimately as he had done her, tentatively at first and then more surely when she saw how much she was pleasing him.

She woke up early, well before dawn, turning to study his sleeping form in the shadows of her room, taking each memory to her to cherish, knowing they would be all she could keep of him, knowing she could not allow it to continue no matter how much her heart might cry out that it needed him, that it would die without him.

She woke up again just after dawn to find herself held securely in his arms. He was already awake watching her.

'I love you,' he told her, kissing her tenderly. 'I love you more than I believed I would ever love anyone. You're mine, Liz, and when I go back to Woolonga you and David are coming with me.'

She tensed in his arms, 'I can't——'

'You can and you shall,' he contradicted her, telling her, 'You can't stay with Edward now. Not after what he tried to do to you. No one would expect it.' He just managed to stop himself saying what was in his heart, and that was that Edward was either criminally or emotionally insane and that, that being the case, he should be locked away for his own good as well as that of the rest of humanity.

'The man's dangerous, Liz,' he told her. 'He could have killed you. No court would oppose granting you a divorce once they knew what he'd tried to do.'

A divorce... The word chilled her, shocking her back to reality.

'I'll have to go and see him. I can't just leave him there...'

She felt so confused, so unsure of herself—her heart, her body, her senses all urged her to do what Lewis was suggesting. Edward had changed—yesterday he had really frightened her. She had looked into his eyes and seen that he did actually want to kill her. But she was his wife. His wife...

And Lewis was her lover!

'I'm not letting you stay with him, Liz,' Lewis told her later as he gathered up his clothes. 'You love *me*.'

It was true, she acknowledged when Lewis had gone to the bathroom. She did love him, she wanted to be with him more than anything else in the world, and yet the thought of Edward and what would happen to him if she divorced him haunted her.

Lewis wanted her to stay in bed, at least until Ian Holmes had been to see her, but she refused, insisting on getting up.

The bruises round her throat looked even worse this morning. Her throat itself was still sore, raw and painful inside, so that she couldn't eat, and could in fact barely swallow the coffee Chivers brought them. Did he suspect that Lewis had done more than keep watchful vigil beside her bed last night? Liz wondered. She felt guilty in testing Chivers's loyalty to Edward.

Ian arrived just as they were finishing breakfast. As he greeted her Liz wondered if what had happened was visible to him in her eyes. She now felt no sense of guilt in physically loving Lewis. Her body was, after all, her own, as was her love.

Maybe, but her fidelity, her duty as a wife...those belonged to Edward. She bit her lip, no longer wanting to listen to her own conscience.

'How...how is Edward?' she asked Ian nervously.

'Heavily sedated and full of remorse... He's been asking for you,' he told her gently.

'Why?' Lewis intervened bitterly. 'So that he can have another go at murdering her? Look at her...look at her throat, man. Look at what he's already done to her.'

'I'm sorry, Liz. I should have asked you how you're feeling,' Ian apologised, ignoring Lewis's bitter comments.

'I'm fine. My throat's a bit sore, but Edward... How is he, really, Ian? Does he——?'

'Physically he's fine, but mentally... Well, you know how he feels about being away from here. He wants to see you, Liz... He needs to see you, really. You needn't be afraid... I'll be with you, and as I said he is very heavily sedated...'

She was biting down hard on her bottom lip, wanting to tell him that she couldn't bear the thought of ever seeing Edward again, that she wanted to shut him completely out of her mind, that she wanted to turn her back on him and walk away from the shadows of her life with him so that she could live in the sunshine and warmth of Lewis's love, but she knew that the words could not be said, that if nothing else she at least owed it to Edward to go and see him. And besides she was concerned about him, despite what he had done to her.

At her side Lewis made a small movement towards her. She could feel his concern, his love reaching out to enfold and protect her.

Lewis was a gentle man, a tender, caring man; she had known that when he'd told her about his dead wife and child, and had had that knowledge reinforced last night when he'd made love to her. With Lewis she would be loved and protected, cherished and adored, with Lewis she would be truly fulfilled as a woman, for the first time in her life. Didn't she have the right as a human being to reach out and take what Lewis, what life was offering her? Why would fate have sent him into her life in the first place if it only intended to part them again?

Ian was still waiting for her response. She looked at him as bravely as she could and saw from his eyes that he had guessed what the situation was between Lewis and herself. There was compassion and understanding in the way he was watching her, but there was sadness as well.

'I will go and see Edward,' she said quietly, ignoring Lewis's barely checked protest.

'If you'd like me to come with you——' Ian began, but she shook her head firmly.

'No, Ian. Thank you, but it's all right.'

'You've no need to be afraid of him now,' Ian reassured her. 'I know what happened yesterday must have terrified you.'

'I'm not afraid,' Liz told him. 'I know that when Edward has these . . . these attacks he isn't really responsible.' She bit down hard on her bottom lip. 'What will happen to him, Ian? Will he . . . ?'

'If the drug therapy works and he agrees to keep it up, it should ensure that his outbreaks of rage are controlled. Of course, no one can take strong drugs over an extended period of time without suffering some adverse effects. It will mean that he's in a state of almost constant semi-sedation, and it's too early yet to say quite what effect that will ultimately have on him. Once he's back home . . . Well, we shall just have to monitor the situation very carefully. What we do know, though, is that those patients—admittedly patients with far more severe behavioural problems than Edward—who have already been on the drug for some time suffer a tremendous drop in motivation, but we are talking here about patients who for one reason or another are institutionalised.'

Liz shuddered, far too clearly able to see the picture he was drawing for her.

When Ian had gone she turned to Lewis with tears in her eyes. Silently he took her in his arms, comforting her.

'Liz, Liz, I know how you must feel,' he told her rawly. 'But you can't allow your natural pity for Edward to ruin our lives. If you stayed with him you'd virtually only be performing the duties that a trained nurse could perform far better. Can't you see, my darling, he's going to need constant care, constant watching? I know right now it might seem cruel——'

'I know what you're trying to say,' Liz interrupted him. 'But I can't...I can't just turn my back on him...I owe him so much.'

'You owe him *nothing*,' Lewis interrupted her. 'Look, if you must go and see him at least let me come with you.'

Liz shook her head. This was something she had to do on her own... Last night, held safely in Lewis's arms, anything had seemed possible, but today, this morning... She shivered slightly.

'I'd better go down to the village,' Lewis told her. 'They'll be wondering where on earth I am.'

Liz gave him a drawn smile.

'I'd like to move in here with you,' Lewis continued. 'But in the circumstances... Last night was something very special, but while you're Edward's wife, while you're still committed to him, even if it is only legally... Well, I don't want to tempt fate by being pompous and saying that it's against my principles to make love to another man's wife. I think last night showed us both how fragile my self-control is when it comes to you...' He smiled at the way her skin took colour, touching her face lightly with his fingertips, and then less lightly, passion darkening his eyes as he caught the betraying sound of her quickened breathing.

'I'm not saying this because of any hypocritical desire to pay lip-service to convention—there's nothing I'd like more than to tell the whole world that we're in love— but while you're Edward's wife...'

'I know...' Liz agreed shakily. 'I feel the same way...'

'So we're agreed, then?' Lewis continued. 'Until the divorce is set in motion, and you're free to leave Edward, we'll have to try to make sure that we don't spend too much time alone.'

'That shouldn't be difficult,' Liz told him wryly. 'What with the mill to run and visiting Edward...' She broke off as she saw his face, touching his sleeve pleadingly. 'Lewis, you do understand, don't you? I *must* go and see him...'

'Yes. I understand,' Lewis agreed gravely. 'I just wish you'd let me come with you. You've got such a tender heart, my love. I'm afraid... I'm so afraid that he'll find some way of keeping you...'

Liz closed her eyes, resting her head on his shoulder. What could she say? That she was mortally afraid of that as well?

Two hours later, as she followed the nurse into Edward's private room, she was thinking of Lewis, wishing that she *had* allowed him to come with her after all.

Edward was in bed. He turned his head as she walked into the room, his expression so listless and dulled that a wave of compassion swept over her. Behind the dullness she could see in his eyes the same pleading, agonised expression she had seen in the eyes of a stray dog she had found starving as it scavenged for food around the mill.

That dog was now housed in its own kennel at the mill, fed regularly and petted by her workers.

'Liz... Liz...'

Edward struggled to sit up when he saw her, reaching out to her with eager hands, his whole expression transformed to one of joy and relief.

'Liz, I want to come home... I don't like it here...' Momentarily the joy faded from his eyes. He looked confused and uncertain, like a child almost, and her heart sank, loaded down by an unbearable and unwanted weight of compassion and pity.

'Don't let them keep me here, Liz. Tell them that I'm going home... They don't understand...'

He was starting to tremble. There were tears in his eyes. They started to roll down his face as he pleaded with her to take him home.

A terrible feeling of sickness and despair swept over her. At her side the nurse was clucking professionally and advancing towards Edward, saying firmly, 'Now, come along. This won't do, will it? Poor Mrs Danvers is going to think we're mistreating you if you carry on like this.'

She turned to Liz and told her quietly, 'It does sometimes affect them like this. It can be a while before we can get the exact dosage of the drug properly adjusted. It can have a depressive effect on the nervous system.'

'A depressive effect?' Liz queried uncertainly, horrible visions of Edward growing distraught and perhaps even trying to take his own life filling her mind.

'It can do,' the nurse agreed.

As she looked at Edward, as she listened to him, Liz knew that there was no way she could tell him now that she intended to leave him. Just for one cowardly moment she wished it were possible for her to simply walk out of the hospital and out of his life forever, to collect David from school, and for both of them to walk away from Cottingdean and make a new life for themselves with Lewis.

But that was impossible.

As she drove back to Cottingdean she wondered how Lewis was going to react when she told him that she hadn't been able to tell Edward that their marriage was over.

At first he was angry, but then, when he could see how upset she was, he groaned and took her in his arms, telling her how much he loved her, how much he wanted her, and how he hated to see her so upset.

'Give me time,' she begged him.

'My darling, I don't want to hurt you, but, can't you see, it isn't going to get any easier? A clean break now...'

'I can't do it,' she told him painfully. 'I just can't... Oh, Lewis, if you'd seen him today...'

She started to cry. Lewis took her in his arms, wishing he could share her compassion for this man whom he only saw as vicious and dangerous.

* * *

Ian had announced that Edward would be in hospital for a full week.

Every day Liz visited him and every day he begged and pleaded with her to be allowed home, his distress so great that on each occasion she came away knowing it was impossible for her to even think of leaving him while his emotional and mental condition was so unstable.

Lewis had gone from being patient and understanding to demanding to know if it was him she loved after all.

Liz could understand his feelings, and his fears; she tried to reassure him, but all she succeeded in doing was increasing his resentment against Edward.

'*I* love you, Liz, and *I* want you as my wife. If *you* loved *me* in the same way you'd leave Edward. No matter how painful it might be.'

'Just as you would have left your wife in the same situation?' Liz challenged quietly.

'Yes. Of course I would...' he began and then stopped, telling her abruptly, 'It's no use, is it? We're just going round and round in circles. Edward comes home tomorrow. I hate myself for doing this to you, Liz, but I don't have any alternative. Either you tell him that you're leaving then, or...' He hesitated and then looked at her and said flatly, 'Or I'll have no alternative but to assume that, no matter how much you might *say* you love me, that love isn't strong enough or compelling enough to make you want to be with me no matter what the cost.'

'Oh, Lewis... Please don't... Can't you *see* it isn't the cost in terms of my own guilt or pain? It's Edward——'

'Edward, Edward, always Edward. What about us, Liz? What about me? Don't you think *I'm* suffering, hurting? Don't you think *I'm* terrified of losing you?

'I'm giving you twenty-four hours, Liz. Twenty-four hours in which to decide whether it's me you want or him.'

For a long, long time after he had gone she sat motionless in her sitting-room, staring into space, unable to see anything other than his face and the pain in his eyes. Why was she even hesitating? She *loved* him. She wanted to be with him more than anything else on earth. But then there was Edward... Edward who looked at her with such helpless and pleading eyes... Edward who cried her name every time she walked away from him, Edward who was coming home tomorrow.

She hardly slept, her vivid, painful nightmares of emotional anxiety and unhappiness draining her small store of energy so that in the morning she was heavy-eyed and exhausted.

In the garden she picked some fresh flowers and then took them inside. The phone rang while she was arranging them and her heart leapt, her fingers trembling as she went to answer it. It wasn't Lewis, though, and as she replied automatically to the caller's concerned enquiries about Edward's progress she felt the ache in her heart intensify. She wanted to be with Lewis so much; would give up anything, everything, to be with him, but she was not free to do so... she was not free to make others suffer so that she could be happy.

When the ambulance arrived and the men helped Edward out and into his chair, she was appalled to see how gaunt he had become, how much weight he had lost.

Chivers was giving the men instructions as to where he was to be taken. For a moment she stood outside the small group, her heart and body gripped by iron bands of pain, and then she saw that Edward was looking at her and she forced herself to smile and step forwards.

As she reached his chair he took hold of her hand, gripping it almost painfully.

'Don't let them take me away again, Liz, will you?' he begged her as he was wheeled inside.

The change in him shocked and upset her. In the week he had been away he had changed, or so it seemed, from a man to a dependent child.

Was the change caused purely by his medication or did it go deeper? She shivered as she followed him indoors. Twenty-four hours, Lewis had said. Twenty-four hours.

It was while she was settling Edward in bed, and Chivers was downstairs making a pot of tea, that Edward took hold of her hand and said huskily, 'Ian told me about...about what I did to you, Liz. I didn't mean to hurt you...' He started to shake, tears filling his eyes. 'Don't ever leave me...'

She couldn't speak. Her own emotions were too raw...too painful. When Chivers came in with the tea she escaped to her own room to fling herself down full-length on her bed and to wish there were some way she could just close her eyes and make all the problems disappear.

An hour later Chivers came to find her, his face creased in worried lines of concern.

'It's the Major,' he told her anxiously. 'I don't think he's very well...'

'Not well...? What...?'

'He seems to have some kind of fever,' Chivers told her.

Quickly she hurried into Edward's room. He was flushed and feverish, his eyes too bright in his over-heated face.

'I think we'd better send for Ian,' Liz told Chivers quietly.

When Ian came he examined Edward and then announced gravely that he suspected that Edward might have succumbed to a gastro-enteritis infection.

'It started in the maternity ward,' Ian explained to them. 'Normally an adult of Edward's age would be strong enough to fight it off, but in Edward's case...'

He looked so grim that Liz knew immediately that he was extremely concerned.

While he was talking to her the phone rang and she knew it would be Lewis wanting to know if she had spoken yet to Edward.

Her twenty-four hours were not yet up but she couldn't bring herself to speak to Lewis and explain what had happened, not with someone else listening, and so she let the phone ring unanswered.

'Edward is going to need constant nursing,' Ian warned her. 'If you like I could arrange for someone...'

Liz shook her head.

'No, I think Chivers and I can manage between us, and Edward is upset enough as it is...'

'Yes,' Ian agreed. 'Unfortunately it was necessary to keep him hospitalised in order to stabilise his condition and his medication, but I agree with you that it has had a severe effect upon him.'

Throughout the night Liz and Chivers took it in turn to minister to Edward. There was no doubt that he was gravely ill. At times he was almost delirious, and, as at last the cold grey dawn broke, Liz watched exhaustedly as he drifted into an uneasy sleep and acknowledged the painful truth.

No matter how much she might want to do so she could not leave him, or at least if she did... If she did she would feel so guilty that it would affect her whole relationship with Lewis, possibly destroying it, certainly souring it. She could feel tears stinging the back of her throat, still sore from its bruising at Edward's hands. The outward marks of the bruises had almost faded now. Ian had assured her that just so long as Edward continued to take his medicine there would be no further repetition of his violent attack. If only he were stronger, fitter—if only she could leave him with a clear conscience. If only he were not so dependent on her.

If she left...if she left he could not stay on at Cottingdean alone, which would mean that he would have to go into some sort of institution, and she already knew what would happen then. It would kill him... And she would have been the one to sign his death warrant. And why? So that she could be with Lewis.

She couldn't do it.

Wearily she got up. Was Lewis asleep in his bed at the pub or was he laying awake thinking about her, wanting her?

She would have to go and see him.

* * *

She rang him and arranged to meet him outside the village where it was quiet and no one was likely to see them. It had, fittingly, after so much fine weather, started to rain, and a soft grey mist hung over the landscape.

His car was already parked on the lonely cart track when she arrived. Lewis was standing beside it, his body tense.

As she got out of her own car and hurried towards him he came to meet her, demanding tersely, 'Well, have you told him?'

She shook her head, and then said huskily, 'I can't, Lewis. He isn't well... Ian says——'

'I don't give a damn what Holmes says,' Lewis interrupted her angrily. 'What am I supposed to do, Liz—keep on hanging around until Holmes decides he *is* well enough for you to tell him? How long will that take? A week...a month...a year...ten years?'

His bitterness, his sarcasm hurt her, but it was no less than she had expected. 'No... No, I don't expect you to do that.' She took a deep breath and then faced him, saying quickly, 'It's over, Lewis. I can't... I can't leave Edward... I know that now... No matter how much I...I love you...I can't leave him.'

She saw from his face how much she had shocked him. For a moment he was silent as he tried to take in what she was saying and then he said savagely, 'You mean you *won't* leave him... *Why?* Tell me that, Liz—why?'

'He needs me,' she told him shakily.

'*He* needs you... what about me, damn you?' He had taken hold of her and was virtually shaking her. 'Don't you think *I* need you?'

She could feel the tears burning behind her eyes. Another minute and she would break down completely and she must not do that...

'Not in the same way,' she told him quietly. 'Lewis, don't you see if I leave Edward now it will be on my conscience for the rest of my life? It would spoil our love, come between us... I *can't* let that happen. You deserve a woman who can give herself to you completely and wholeheartedly, and I don't think I could live with the burden of what I'd done...'

'And yet you have no compunction whatsoever about hurting *me*,' he told her flatly. 'Don't *I* matter at all to you, Liz? Don't you care about *me*?'

Of course I care. The words were on the tip of her tongue but she forced them back. What use was there in saying them, in prolonging their mutual agony?

'What do you want me to do? Hang on here begging for the favour of the odd stolen hours of your company like a dog existing on scraps? I can't do that, Liz. It must be all or nothing...'

'And I can't leave Edward,' she reiterated. She was feeling sick and light-headed. If he took her in his arms now...held her...kissed her... She fought against her desire that he would do exactly that, that he might pick her up and carry her off, physically abducting her, physically taking the decision out of her hands, even while she knew it was impossible.

'So you've chosen him... He means more to you than me,' Lewis accused her heavily. 'It was all a lie, was it? You even love Cottingdean more than me. Our love was just a game...'

She wanted to deny what he was saying, but her love for him guided her, telling her that it would be easier for him if she let him go in anger rather than in love; that he would need that anger to sustain him in the days ahead; that it would be weak and selfish of her to try to tie him to her with her love when she knew that love was something she had to banish from her life.

'Maybe it was,' she agreed lightly, fighting to hide from him how much pain the words cost her.

The look he gave her almost destroyed her.

'Do you really mean that?' he demanded harshly, releasing her and stepping back from her as though suddenly he found her contaminated.

'Was that all it was all the time? Just a game, a diversion? *Did* you ever intend to leave him, or were you simply playing out some fantasy? A cruel fantasy, since I actually thought...'

She kept silent, letting him throw all the bitter, hurtful words at her, letting him savage and destroy her, letting him have the outlet he so badly needed, knowing that it was the only gift she could give him, the only panacea he would have.

As he finally turned away from her he said cruelly, 'Well, all I hope is that someone will some day come in to your life who'll destroy it in the way you've destroyed mine, and you with it . . . Do you know something, Liz?' He turned to look at her, his eyes cold and bitter. 'I almost feel sorry for that husband of yours . . . I certainly wish him luck, because he's going to need it . . .'

She stood where she was until the dust from his car tyres had died down, and the mist had swallowed it up, obliterating it from her view.

Even then she didn't cry. Instead she turned and walked stiffly back to her car, driving it slowly and carefully back the way she had come.

Inside she felt as though she were being torn apart, but no one else must guess what was happening to her . . . no one else must know her pain.

This was something she had to endure by herself, something she had to live through alone. She had done the right thing. The only thing . . . Now all that remained was for her to convince herself that this was so.

Later she suspected that if it hadn't been for Edward's illness keeping her so physically busy she would have weakened and gone in search of Lewis, begging him to wait, to give her more time, but by the time Edward was well enough to be left for more than half an hour at a time she discovered that Lewis had left, and that no one seemed to know where he had gone.

Several weeks of nursing Edward constantly while mourning for Lewis was beginning to take its toll of her health. She often felt sick and put it down to nerves until she suddenly realised just what her queasiness might portend. It was too late for her to change her mind about Lewis now, though, she reflected unhappily.

Even if she could bring herself to leave Edward and to shoulder the emotional burden of guilt that doing so would bring, how could she ever be sure that Lewis believed she had come to him out of love and not simply because she was carrying his child? No... it was too late now to change her mind. And as for the child she suspected she carried...

She placed her hand over her stomach, trying to suppress the deep, wrenching pain that tore at her heart. It should never have been conceived and could not be allowed to be born. And yet... and yet... She shivered with emotion, knowing how much she wanted to have his child, Lewis's child, and yet at the same time acknowledging that this must be her punishment for what she had done: that she must sacrifice not just her need, but also her child. A week went by and then another.

She devoted herself to looking after Edward. He clung to her emotionally like a dependent child, and was so full of remorse for the way he had attacked her, constantly begging her to promise him that she would never leave him as though in some way he sensed how close she had come to doing so.

She was losing weight, growing too thin and fine-drawn, as the physical effort of looking after Edward combined with the emotional pain she was suffering took its toll of her, and she had still done nothing to terminate her pregnancy even though she knew she must.

But how? Abortions were illegal and could only be procured with considerable danger.

Ian Holmes had seen how thin and pale she had become and was concerned about her. And yet as her health deteriorated, Edward's improved; he was almost back to being his old self again, albeit with the aid of the drug which successfully seemed to keep at bay his earlier violent changes of mood. Physically he was as strong as he had ever been, Ian told her when he complimented her on her devotion to him. As he had already said to Edward himself, without Liz to care for him it was doubtful that he could have pulled through the illness which had devastated him. He was lucky to have a wife like Liz, Ian told him. Very lucky. Edward agreed with him. He was a fortunate man.

When Ian called to check up on Edward one morning and discovered Liz on his way out, on her hands and knees, frantically tearing up the weeds in one of the long borders, while her body shook with the tears that poured down her face, he knelt down beside her and put his hands on her shoulders, gently turning her towards him.

He had seen the almost haunted way she had devoted herself to Edward, and had drawn his own conclusions. It had been obvious how Lewis McLaren felt about her, and she about him, and he could only pity them both from the depths of his heart.

'Liz, my poor girl,' he said now. 'What is it? What's wrong?'

He thought he already knew the answer. She loved a man she was not free to marry and so had sent him away, but when she turned to him and said wretchedly, 'I'm pregnant,' he couldn't quite keep the shock from his face.

'I know,' Liz agreed. 'I should never have allowed it to happen...'

Ian struggled for a moment and then asked her uncomfortably, 'McLaren... Does he...does he know?'

Liz shook her head. 'No...and I don't intend to tell him... This is my problem, Ian. Mine. Oh, God. I know what I have to do, but doing it...' She shivered. 'Lewis wanted me to leave Edward. Begged me to leave him, in fact, but I couldn't do it. I couldn't have lived with myself if...'

'And Edward couldn't have lived here without you,' Ian put in sombrely. 'At least not here at Cottingdean, and an institution...'

'Yes, I know. I wanted to go with Lewis,' she went on painfully, 'I wanted to take my happiness...but in the end I had to send him away, let him believe that I didn't care... I thought then that that was the hardest thing I'd ever have to do, that no matter what pain the rest of my life might hold it would never be greater, sharper, more agonising than the pain of losing him.' Tears were pouring down her face, her normal reserve vanishing, swept away by the force of her emotion, her need . . . 'I should have realised then.' She turned to Ian.

'Ian, I'm going to have an abortion. There's no other way. I don't want to do it, God knows, but what alternative do I have? I know I shouldn't ask you, but could you . . . would you . . . ? You're a doctor—you must know of someone who could do it . . . safely . . .'

For a moment Ian couldn't speak, he was so consumed with pity and compassion for her. She had suffered so much, given up so much . . . but as to what she was asking him . . .

'Are you insane?' he demanded. 'An *abortion*! Not only is it illegal, but my God, Liz, do you realise how many women lose their lives every year by going to those people? They're untrained, unsanitary, they butcher the women and maim their unborn children; why in the name of God do women go to them . . . ?'

'Because they don't have any alternative . . . because they're desperate,' Liz told him grimly. 'As long as our society continues to treat women who conceive illegitimate children as solely responsible for their plight . . . just as long as it continues to humiliate and condemn them, women will continue to resort to the services of backstreet abortionists . . . They have no option . . . Edward has already accepted David as his; I cannot——'

'Do you want this child?' Ian asked her softly.

Slowly she nodded her head. 'More than I can possibly tell you. It will be all I'll ever have of its father . . .'

Her simple words betrayed so much.

Ian Holmes ached with pity for her.

'Let me speak to Edward?' he suggested, but she denied him immediately.

'No, Edward must never know. He has already suffered enough . . . Promise me you won't mention this to him.'

When he gave her his promise Ian told himself that in already knowing that he was going to break it he was doing the only thing he could.

The thought of Liz offering herself to death or maiming at the hands of some unqualified butcher

sickened him, and yet his own hands were tied... There
was nothing he could do to help her... nothing at all...

'Just don't do anything until I've had a chance to think
things over,' he asked. 'To make enquiries... Give me
a week.'

It galled him to lie to her... to deceive her... but he
had no alternative.

He didn't waste any time in talking to Edward. As
luck would have it, Liz had been invited to a reception
in Bath being held for local industrialists by the Ministry,
who were anxious to encourage new development.

He found Edward alone in the library. Although
stronger physically, he looked pale and drawn—his skin
was beginning to develop the unhealthy greyness of
someone who spent too much time out of the sun. He
had aged dramatically; become an old man almost overnight, or so it seemed.

Ian didn't waste any time, telling him quickly what he
had come to tell him and then letting him absorb the
shock of it.

'Did Liz ask you to tell me this?' he wanted to know
after some painful minutes had passed.

Ian shook his head.

'No, she begged me to say nothing. In point of fact
she only told me because... well, because she wanted
me to recommend an abortionist to her...'

He saw the way Edward absorbed his words, and his
hopes grew. 'I asked her...about the father, the man...'
he continued brusquely. 'She told me...she told me that
there was no way she would leave you... That her place
was here with you and with David...'

No need to say that it was his, Edward's need that
kept her tethered to him...

'Think carefully, Edward,' Ian warned him. 'To bring
yourself to accept another man's child as your own, to
bring up that child in the knowledge that another man
has fathered it on your wife...that's a great deal to expect
of any man, and only a very brave man could do so. Liz
herself would not ask it of you, but my oath as a doctor
forbids me to give her the information she requires...
If she does go ahead with her plans to abort this child

it could result not just in the child's death but also in her own... However, I would counsel any man against taking on the burden of another's child unless—*unless* he can find it in his heart to truly love that child...and its mother...'

Liz...pregnant...Liz making love with another man...Liz bearing another man's child... Jealousy raged through Edward, tearing at his flesh, his heart, his soul. For one black moment he actually wished that Ian had not told him this, that Liz had simply gone ahead...better for her to lose her life than... *No!* The cry was wrung from him in agonised silence... To lose her, and in such a way... And could he really blame her? She was a young and beautiful woman—a woman who had given him so much, who had turned his whole life around... A woman whom he himself had almost killed. He remembered her visit to the hospital and how he had begged her, pleaded with her to take him home. Not to leave him. He remembered too how she had looked at him then and the despair in her eyes and he knew—knew that she had come that day to tell him that their marriage was over. She had sacrificed so much for him—couldn't he sacrifice his pride for her?

Wasn't he man enough to allow her this small fall from grace? And if he didn't, what were the alternatives? He tried to envisage life without her and instantly it was as though a shadow had come over his world. And yet she had betrayed him with another man. His male pride, so sorely tested by all that he had endured, rose up inside him in anguished outrage.

'I'll leave you to think things over,' Ian Holmes told him gently, standing up.

He was praying that he had done the right thing. He knew Liz well enough to know that if he hadn't caught her in a moment of weakness she would never have told him about the pregnancy. He also suspected that the man involved meant far more to her than she was allowing him to know.

Edward was a lucky man; how many other women in the same circumstances would have put his needs before their own desires? He acquitted Liz of any desire to maintain the marriage because of Cottingdean or any other kind of material advantages, but he had sensed how desperately she wanted to keep her child. He hoped that Edward would find the generosity to allow her to do so... David was not, after all, his either, and it was plain to everyone that he adored the boy...

Just as he was about to leave the room Edward called out to him in a low voice, 'If... if Liz kept this child... I don't want the whole world and his wife to know that my wife has made me a cuckold,' he told Ian bitterly.

Ian had been giving the matter a great deal of thought.

'There is a radical new method of allowing women to conceive that does not involve sexual intercourse.' Quickly he explained the research being undertaken into human artificial insemination. 'We could let it be known that both you and Liz had taken the decision to have another child... And how that child was supposedly conceived...'

'I would have to be sure that Liz had given up this... this man...' Edward muttered.

Inclining his head gravely, Ian said quietly, 'I think the fact that she is still here with you tells its own story, don't you? Liz is not a woman to involve herself in some cheap, sordid affair... nor to enter into it lightly...'

Sensing that he had said enough, he took his leave of Edward. He must be getting old, he reflected tiredly as he drove home. He was beginning to feel the burden of his patients' woes... Edward was not the easiest of men to deal with, and he admired Liz for all that she had done for him. Half of him was inclined to tell her that she must not sacrifice herself any more, that if this man meant as much to her as he suspected he did... But without her he doubted that Edward would survive more than a handful of months. He could not live alone— even with Chivers's help, as there would be little money. He would have to enter an institution...

He was not God. He could not order people's lives, but he could not help offering up a prayer that if there was a God he would find from somewhere the compassion to gently urge Edward to ignore the demands of his pride and think not of how Liz had betrayed him, but of all the kindness and love she had given him over the years, and would, Ian suspected, continue to give him at the cost of her own fulfilment and true happiness.

Duty... It was an old-fashioned word in this brash new modern world, and yet he suspected that Liz was one of those people whose conscience would always incline her to put the needs of others, her duty and responsibility towards them, before her own needs and desires.

He had asked Liz to give him a week before doing anything irrevocable and he prayed that she would not break her promise to him as he had done his to her.

Liz didn't. However much she knew that she had no alternative, that no matter how much she longed to be able to keep the child Lewis had given her she could not do so, a stay of execution was still welcome.

The thought of changing her mind, of leaving Edward and going with Lewis was one she had forbidden herself even to contemplate.

David, Edward, Cottingdean, the mill—all of them had claims on her that far outweighed her own selfish desire to be with Lewis.

And yet when the letter came from him begging her to change her mind, pleading with her to leave Edward and go to Australia with him, imploring her to forgive him for so stupidly accusing her of wanting Cottingdean and all that it could offer more than his love, she was so sorely tempted, so desperately, dangerously impelled to change her mind that she had to sit down and write back to him immediately, forbidding him to get in touch with her again, telling him brutally and untruthfully that while she had enjoyed their brief fling that was all it had been to her, and that she had never had any intentions of leaving Edward or giving up Cottingdean.

It was a cruel, callous letter. Necessarily so. If she once allowed him to suspect how much she still loved him he would never give up... he would waste his life wanting her, and, since she already knew she could not go to him, then she must set him free to find happiness with someone else.

And yet if she did leave Edward, if she did go with him...she could keep their child...

Instinctively she placed her hand over her stomach, staring down at the letter she had just finished, and then, before she could change her mind, she sealed it in an envelope and addressed it.

She posted it after lunch, passing Ian on his way to see Edward as she did so.

Edward had summoned him by telephone, telling him that he had made his decision.

Ian found him in the library, looking gaunt and withdrawn, and his heart dropped. Edward had about him the look of an executioner...

'Ian... Good of you to come so promptly,' he said formally. 'Chivers is just making us some tea...'

Ian's jaw ached with the effort it took to respond to Edward's civilities.

It was fifteen minutes before the tea arrived, was poured, and Chivers had left them.

'I've made my decision,' Edward told him abruptly. 'I've decided that she can keep the child... But...But she must give me her solemn promise that she will never see him—her lover—again... I don't wish to know who he is... I don't wish to discuss the matter with her at all. I shall leave it to you to act as an intermediary between us to convey to her my decision... I'm afraid it's something I feel I just cannot discuss with her myself. The child will be brought up as David has been as my son or daughter, but shall of course be excluded from inheriting Cottingdean... The estate will in due course be passed to David, who does, after all, have Danvers blood... This...this child is not a Danvers.' There was a distaste and dislike in his voice every time he referred to the baby and Ian felt his initial relief start to drain from him... Would Edward punish the as yet unborn child for Liz's fall from grace? Would Liz be willing to accept the terms he was laying down?

'With your assistance we can let it be known as you suggested that Liz and I made a decision for Liz to undergo this new method of conception...'

'You're a very brave man, Edward, and a very compassionate one,' Ian told him, standing up. 'I know you'll never regret having made such a decision. But remember Liz.' He wanted to remind him that Liz also would be making sacrifices, had already in fact made them, but he was too wary of antagonising Edward and of giving him an excuse to rescind a decision which he suspected was not being made wholeheartedly.

'I'll convey your wishes to Liz, of course,' he added formally. 'I've just passed her in the village, so if you don't mind I'll wait for her to return.'

'She knows you've approached me?' Edward demanded suspiciously.

Ian shook his head.

'No, she doesn't. She believes I'm making enquiries into finding someone to abort her child.'

When Liz returned he knew immediately that something had distressed her. She gazed at him through heavy-lidded, pain-filled eyes, so obviously unable to concentrate fully on what he had to say to her that he led her gently into the garden and made her sit down on a sheltered stone seat.

'I've told Edward about your pregnancy,' he told her without preamble.

If she was shocked it barely showed. Only the widening of her agonised eyes reflected her awareness of having heard him.

'He has agreed that you may keep the child.'

Now he did have her attention. She was staring at him, her eyes dilating.

'There are certain conditions, though; primarily that you will agree never to see the child's father or in any way meet him again, and secondly that the child will be excluded from inheriting any part of Cottingdean.

'It isn't too late, you know, Liz... You could leave him...'

She shook her head and spoke for the first time. 'No. No, I couldn't... It would be like signing his death warrant... I couldn't have that on my conscience.'

Ian didn't deny it. They both knew that what she said was true but nevertheless he pointed out gently, 'But you were prepared to institute the death of your child.'

She went white and then grey, her whole body trembling as she whispered, 'What alternative did I have?' And then in anguish, 'Will Edward really allow me to keep my baby?'

For the first time since he had known her she sounded young and insecure.

'Yes,' Ian confirmed but added warningly, 'He isn't happy with the situation and I dare say there will be times when he wishes he had not done so, when he will make you feel very uncomfortable. He loves you, Liz...in the way that a man does love a woman he desires, and he's very, very jealous, all the more so because fate has seen fit to destroy his ability to make love to you himself, to father his own children on you. Unfortunately removing the physical ability to have sex does not necessarily remove the emotional desire for it at the same time.

'It won't be easy for you, that's why I'm cautioning you now to think carefully—and then there's the child. He may take his resentment out on him or her,' he warned her. 'You do understand,' he told her gently, 'that to the world the child will have to appear to be fathered by Edward, that his pride wouldn't allow anything else?'

'But that's impossible.'

'Not necessarily. There is a way, a process, familiar enough to you I'm sure from your work with your stock...'

When he explained it to her she frowned and then smiled faintly. 'You think people will believe it?'

'Why not? It isn't unheard of for couples to want more than one child. Handled properly and openly...a little discreet information dropped that the process is still so chancy that no one wanted to say anything until the pregnancy was properly established... It's down to you, really, Liz. Down to how you behave. This child when it arrives can be yours and your lover's, or it can be yours and Edward's... It all depends on you.

'Oh, and by the way—I wouldn't say anything to Edward about it yet.'

In the end Liz was five months pregnant before Edward made any reference to her condition. They were having dinner with the Lord Lieutenant and his wife. The former had been praising Liz for the work she was doing at the mill, and then his wife leaned across to congratulate her on the coming birth.

'Yes,' Edward responded for her. 'We're both very pleased that things have worked out so well, aren't we, darling?' He took hold of her hand and squeezed it firmly, giving her one of his rare, warm smiles. 'Of course the procedure is a bit chancy, so we've kept our plans very much to ourselves...'

'I think it's wonderful,' Lady Susan enthused. 'One child never makes a family, does it? I expect you're hoping for a girl this time?'

'I don't think either of us mind just so long as the baby's healthy,' Liz said quietly.

Edward was still taking his medication. On the surface he appeared to be better, but there were still moments when she sensed the helpless impotent rage building up inside him. Times when she feared not so much for herself but for her unborn and vulnerable child. But then his mood would change and he would become tearful, repentant, dependent and helpless, reminding her of how much he needed her.

David was home from school for the Easter vacation. He had been told about the pregnancy and seemed genuinely happy at the thought of having a younger sibling.

This time, when she could have afforded to spend a little more recklessly on preparing for the new arrival, Liz was careful to keep her preparations to a minimum. Her condition was something that was rarely mentioned between Edward and herself. He had withdrawn from her quite pointedly during the early months of her pregnancy, but now he seemed to be opening up to her again, although she knew instinctively that he would never feel for this child the love he felt for David.

Which meant that she would never be able to show it more love than she did her son. Edward would be watching jealously to see that this new baby received no special favours...no special marks of maternal adoration.

She placed her hand on her stomach. The baby was due towards the end of July, but already she was quite large. Far larger, she was sure, than she had been when she was carrying David.

Her pains started on the thirtieth of July during the early hours of the morning. On Ian Holmes's advice she had elected to have the baby at home, and as soon as she realised how swift and sharp her pains were she rang through to him, and to the local midwife.

They arrived within minutes of one another, just in time to realise that the birth was going to take place very quickly indeed.

'That's the trouble with second babies,' the midwife chuckled, 'they're always in such a rush... It all comes from trying to catch up with their older brothers and sisters.'

As she chatted she was giving Liz instructions; a plump, motherly woman, she had an air of serenity and experience about her that would have calmed the most nervous of mothers-to-be, Liz reflected, dutifully following her commands.

'Just one more push, now... Come along, my lovely... Oh, yes, here she is...a beautiful baby girl, and she's got the most wonderful head of hair... Here you are!' She beamed, gently wiping clean the newborn infant, and handing her to Liz just as she opened her mouth and gave her first outraged cry.

Liz was still laughing gently at her new daughter when she suddenly felt another sharp, searing pain explode inside her.

She tensed so much that the baby cried out in her grasp and the midwife, who had turned away, turned sharply back, and then exclaimed, 'Oh, my goodness... I do believe...'

Quickly removing the baby from Liz's grasp and placing her expertly in the waiting crib, she said urgently to Liz, 'Better hang on a second, my dear... I think we're going to have another new arrival...'

'Another?' Liz stared at her and then gasped as she felt the resurgence of pain engulf her.

'Well, now, aren't you a lucky girl?' the midwife was saying beamingly. 'Twins, and a boy and a girl, although your young man's a bit on the small side. Never mind— boys often are smaller at birth. I suppose we shouldn't be surprised. Your stomach was quite a size. Well, your husband is going to be surprised, isn't he? I'll just clean you up a bit and then he can come in and see you——'

'No...' Her denial was sharp and instinctive. She wanted, needed this special time alone with her babies, so that she could share with them, if only mentally, a special communion which by rights should have in- cluded their father. Two babies, two special gifts—she felt her heart melt and overflow with love as she looked down into their faces. Her breath caught in her throat as she looked a second time at her newborn daughter. Now in these hours just after the birth she could see so clearly in her face the image of Lewis. She felt tears well in her eyes as she hugged them both to her, whispering weepily to them, 'So precious... You're both so very very precious.'

Edward insisted on posting an announcement in *The Times*, even though for some reason Liz would have pre- ferred him not to do so.

They had decided to call the twins Nicholas and Sage, although Edward had baulked a little at this rather unusual name for his 'daughter'.

Liz had insisted. It had been the name of Lewis's grandmother, he'd told her in passing once, and even though she knew she was being ridiculously, danger- ously sentimental she hadn't been able to resist the impulse, the need almost to give at least one of her children something of its father.

She had promised Edward that neither twin would ever know the truth about their parentage. Just as she had promised she would never again meet with Lewis himself.

Edward had eventually asked the name of her lover and Liz had told him, and since then the subject had been closed between them.

She wondered where Lewis was now... Back in Australia, of course.

In the early days after the birth, when she felt weak and emotional, she couldn't help wondering if he ever thought of her, of how different things might have been, if... So many ifs... Ifs she must not allow herself to contemplate even in the privacy of her own thoughts.

Only Lewis McLaren wasn't in Australia. He was in London, growing bitter and disillusioned as he dwelt on the pain of loving a woman who had said she loved him in return but who had lied. And then, by one of those chances of which fate was so fond, one morning when he was staying with friends, he happened to see the announcement in *The Times*, heralding the arrival of Major Edward Danvers's son and daughter.

He knew instantly, of course. Knew and could hardly believe the enormity of the deceit which had been practised against him.

His child, his children—claimed by another man... His children...his children...

Without even thinking of what he was doing he hired a car and drove straight down to Cottingdean.

The twins were three weeks old... Edward had been suffering from a slight inflammation on his lungs, and Ian had insisted on him going to the local hospital where he could be X-rayed.

Liz went with him. Edward was her husband and she suspected that from now on he would be watching her jealously to see that she did not favour the twins, did not give them more attention than she gave him or David, and so, despite the fact that she was still not fully recovered from the birth, and that she was feeding the twins herself, she ignored Edward's half-hearted objections that her place was with the twins and drove him to the hospital.

The wife of one of the mill workers, Mrs Palmer, had offered to take charge of the babies in Liz's absence. She was a cheerfully jolly woman with children and grandchildren of her own, and she often helped out at Cottingdean when they had visitors. When Lewis arrived on the doorstep she welcomed him in. She remembered him from his previous visit and had rather a soft spot for him. A good-looking man, and pleasant with it.

When he asked to see the twins, she thought it a bit odd; men weren't generally interested in babies, but then he had probably heard how they had been conceived and was curious about them, so she took him up to the airy, warm nursery, and then excused herself for a few minutes to go downstairs and see if she could find Chivers and get him to make their visitor a pot of tea.

Left alone with his children, Lewis stared at them. The girl was alert, bright-eyed, noisy; the boy... The boy was quieter, more solemn... The boy—his son... his child... Without knowing it he had picked Nicholas out of his crib and was holding him. The girl started to cry as though she resented the attention he was giving her brother. Soon the woman would be back—but these were his children. This was his son... The son who by rights should be brought up on Woolonga, should be brought up to inherit... These would be his only children, his only son, because he had made up his mind that he would never marry again now...

The decision to walk downstairs, outside and get into his car still holding the baby was not one he made consciously, but somehow or other it was done... Somehow or other he was on his way back to London, driving not back to his friends, but to the airport, where he booked himself a seat on the first flight home... A flight which was due to leave within the hour. How fortunate that he had had his dead son included on his passport—it made it all seem all the more the right thing to do somehow.

He had lost one child already—he wasn't going to lose another. He might not be able to have Liz but at least he had their child—one of their children. He felt a moment's anger with himself that he hadn't taken them both, but it was too late now. He could not go back.

A father returning home with his child... Poor man, he looked so haggard, thought the girl at the check-in desk. What had happened to his wife? Even in these modern days a woman could still die in childbirth...

She shivered a little.

When Mrs Palmer found Nicholas missing, she panicked and, instead of summoning help, ran all over the house, as though expecting to find the baby had somehow got up and walked into another room, so that it was several hours before his disappearance was officially reported to the authorities... not until Liz and Edward had returned from the hospital, in fact, to find the whole house in turmoil.

She knew of course... the moment Mrs Palmer mentioned Lewis's visit she knew... He had taken her child—their child...

She raised stricken eyes to Edward's face.

'Don't worry,' he told her. 'We'll get him back!'

But how could she not worry? How could they get him back?

The authorities had to be told, and legally it was confirmed to them that, since she had not yet registered the twins' birth, and since the man was after all their father, there was little that could be done to regain the boy twin, without the whole affair receiving a lot of unpleasant publicity.

Lewis himself wrote to her, telling her that he intended to keep his son and warning her that if she made any attempt to get him back he would make the whole affair public.

Deep in her heart Liz sensed that Edward was almost glad, although she knew he would never admit it. He probably wished that Lewis had taken both children, she realised bitterly. And Joan Palmer, overwhelmed by guilt, was only too glad when it was suggested that she and her husband, who was near retiring age, might like to return to the North of England to be near their married daughter. Derek Palmer was given a generous pension and it was generally made known in the village that the male twin Liz had given birth to had never been very strong and he had suffered a seizure and died.

The fact that Liz lost so much weight, became so withdrawn and clung so possessively to her one remaining child all reinforced this news, and it very quickly became understood that Liz could not bear to have the baby's name mentioned nor his death discussed. It was a closed subject, which no one dared to raise even to express sympathy to her.

Liz herself was inconsolable, stricken with grief and guilt, to the point where Ian Holmes began to fear for her sanity.

She clung so possessively to Sage that he had to tell her that if she wasn't careful she would destroy everything she had worked so hard for... that her protectiveness towards her daughter would alienate Edward so completely that he would very quickly begin to resent and even hate the child.

Liz saw the wisdom of what she was being told. Already she had noticed the way Edward turned away from the baby, the distant dislike in his eyes whenever she cried, the way he refused to touch her, hold her... The way he rejected her—and suddenly she was very afraid for her, deeply afraid. She began to subtly ensure that Sage was never left alone with Edward, to watch her baby with anxious protective eyes, remembering how Edward had attacked and hurt her.

What kind of home was she going to grow up in, what kind of atmosphere? What had she done...?

'Oh, please forgive me, my darling,' she whispered over her crib, her voice thick with tears. 'I wanted you so much and I've been so selfish... Better perhaps that your father had taken you both—and yet I could not have borne to let you go... Not you... You're so like him, so much a part of him...' Not to anyone would she admit that of the two it had always been this child, this twin who had been closer to her heart...closer to her by far than David. Not just because she had been born before her brother, but because she had looked into her newborn face and seen in it Lewis's. Sometimes she felt she could not bear the weight of her love for her, her adoration almost. She was terrified of showing it, though, in case it antagonised Edward even more. Sage would always be her favourite child, her most loved child. She couldn't help it, couldn't deny it and yet she must never allow anyone else to know it, not even the child herself, because if she did...if she did...

She was so afraid now after losing Nicholas—mortally afraid that somehow if she allowed anyone, anyone at all to know how precious Sage was to her, she would in some way be imperilling her child's happiness.

Already Edward resented her, disliked her. David—well, David loved everyone... But if Edward should turn publicly against her, if Edward should publicly reject her, if Edward should change his mind and make it known that Sage wasn't his...

She started to shake with fear, with anguish. No, she couldn't allow it to happen. If Edward did that she would leave him, take David and her precious baby and make a new life somewhere for them all. Nothing, no one, was more important to her than this baby, Lewis's baby. She was more important to her than life itself... She would do everything in her power to protect her, even if that meant denying herself the bitter-sweet right of showing the world how very precious she was to her.

That night Edward said resentfully, 'That child was crying all night again. I think you should get someone else to take care of her. She's taking up too much of your time.'

She was already half prepared for it. Hiding her anger and fear, her pain, she kept her head bowed over her plate and said levelly, 'If you think that's best, Edward...'

'I do,' he told her curtly.

* * *

As she finished reading the page Sage discovered that she was weeping.

'Oh, my God, oh, my God...' she repeated the words, mindlessly burying her head in her hands as she let the tears come... All these years and she hadn't known, hadn't realised... All these years when her mother had protected her, cared for her, loved her... all these years when she had carried the burden of her own knowledge...

Even after Edward's death, when she could have told her... could have acquitted herself.

She picked up the diary and raced towards the door, flinging it open and crying, 'Faye! Faye!'

CHAPTER TWENTY-FIVE

SAGE prowled the room restlessly, pausing every now and then to see how much more Faye had to read.

When her sister-in-law had come hurrying in, in answer to her frantic call, she had been too emotionally overwhelmed to do much more than thrust the diary at her and demand chokily, 'Here...read this last section... Quickly, Faye, please...'

Now, as Faye turned the last page and put down the diary, they stared at one another in silence.

'You never knew, never had any idea?' Faye asked slowly.

Sage shook her head. 'No... Did you?'

Faye sighed. 'No...no, I didn't... What an awful burden for your mother to have to carry. And when I think how selfishly I added my own burdens to hers. No wonder your father...' She caught herself up and added, 'Edward was so devastated when David was killed.'

'Yes,' Sage agreed sadly. 'I can understand everything so much better now. My mother dared not show me too much love in case my... in case Edward resented it. And then, just when she must have been thinking she could start to relax, just when I was almost adult, I had to go and fall in love with my own brother... My twin brother...' Sage closed her eyes. 'No wonder I always felt so close to him... I wonder if he knows, if he...Lewis McLaren...'

She couldn't bring herself to refer to him as her father. That knowledge was too new, too sharply painful. That time when she had gone to see Scott... He must have known then, *must* have known, and yet he had made no attempt to see her.

'We'll have to tell him,' Faye told her briskly. 'He has a right to know.'

Sage stared at her. 'But he might not *want* to know. He could have married someone else.'

Faye frowned and then said softly, 'Not Lewis, Sage. I meant Scott. *He* has a right to know about your mother's condition. As much right as either of us.'

Sage tensed, her eyes widening slightly, the pupils suddenly enormous, giving her an unfamiliar air of vulnerability.

'Yes. Yes. You're right,' she agreed shakily. 'Of course he has a right ... She's his mother too. Oh, my God ... Faye ... It's such a shock ... I can't believe ... God, what she must have gone through when I brought Scott home that time and she realised ...'

Looking at the downbent russet head, Faye wondered if Sage realised how betraying it was that her concern, her compassion was all for her mother and not for herself.

'I think perhaps Scott does know,' Faye told her thoughtfully. 'Perhaps it was only by telling him that Lewis McLaren could ensure that he made no attempts to get in touch with you.'

'Maybe, I don't know. I don't feel as though I know anything any more. All these years when I thought she didn't care, didn't really want me, didn't love me as she did David, when all the time ...'

'All the time *you* were the child she treasured,' Faye finished for her. 'That must have been so dreadful for her ... wanting to show you how much she cared and yet at the same time being forced to protect you from Edward's jealousy. Having to keep her love for you hidden for your own sake. It comes across so clearly from her diaries how terrified she was in those early years that Edward would change his mind about allowing her to keep you.'

'Yes,' Sage agreed in a low voice, 'and I didn't help matters either, did I? Do you really think we should tell Scott?' she asked Faye.

'Yes ... But I'm not sure how we're going to do it ... A letter, I suppose.'

'Or a telephone call,' Sage suggested.

'Yes, even better, but we don't have the number.'

There was a small silence and then Sage said huskily, 'I have the number!'

'Do you still love him?' Faye asked her compassionately, sensitively aware of all that the words cloaked.

Sage shook her head. 'Not in the way you mean—as a potential lover—but the memory of him still causes me pain. I've...' she hesitated, groping for the right words '...I've missed him, felt as though I've been missing a part of myself. I've always put that down to the fact that I had such a bad relationship with my...with Edward, that his rejection followed by Scott's was responsible for the fact that I've been left with this residue of aloneness, of loss. After reading Mother's diaries, I wonder if there isn't a different and more simple explanation—if it's just that a part of me subconsciously recognised the blood bond we shared, and that it's because we're twins that I've been so aware of a sense of loss. And yet I never knew. No one ever said.'

'Yes, your mother writes in her diary that it was decided to announce that Scott—Nicholas, as she'd called him, Lewis McLaren understandably must have renamed him—that Scott had died, and that because she couldn't endure to be reminded of his death the subject simply wasn't to be mentioned.'

'And it hasn't been. When you think of how easily I could have found out, if not that Scott was my twin then at least that there had been another child...all these years and I never knew.'

Faye shrugged. 'Well, I suppose most people must have assumed that you did know and that, like your mother, you didn't want to be reminded of the subject.'

'Chivers would have known, of course, but he was loyal to both of my parents and wouldn't have discussed family matters with me. I was too immature anyway, and he died, peacefully, I understand, when I was twenty-three. Well, I'll go upstairs and get that number. I hope that Scott *does* know, otherwise all this is going to come as a terrible shock to him.'

She paused, looking hesitant and uncertain. 'Do you think——?'

'I think your mother needs all the help she can get to pull through this operation... And I think that when she comes round and finds you and Scott both there...'

'Yes,' Sage agreed shakily. 'Yes, you're right...'

She found the number in the old address book she had kept without really knowing why she should give in to such sentimentality. As she looked at it, she remembered the last time she had used it and been told that Mr Scott McLaren wasn't accepting calls from her.

How that had hurt. She closed her eyes, remembering, shivering a little as she reflected on how close she had been to disaster. Thank goodness she and Scott had never been lovers. Even unknowingly, to have made love with her own brother, her twin, would have caused her such deep inner revulsion that she didn't think she could have borne such hurt...not even now with so many years to distance her from it... Something else for which she had to thank her mother's vigilance...and Lewis McLaren's—her father!

For the first time she wondered what his reaction must have been when he had heard from her mother after all those years. Heard from her to learn that his son and her daughter...their children were on the brink of becoming lovers.

Another shiver chilled her skin. She could feel the sharp pain in her throat which heralded tears. This was not the time to start crying. There was too much to be done.

She hurried downstairs with her address book and handed it to Faye.

'I'm afraid *you're* going to have to make the call,' she told her sister-in-law. 'I don't think——'

She broke off as Camilla suddenly came into the room, and then stopped as though she had come up against some physical barrier. Sage smiled grimly to herself. The emotions let loose in this room in the last hour were strong enough to permeate the atmosphere for days. It was no wonder that Camilla was looking so apprehensive, so fearful...

'What is it?' she demanded sharply. 'Is it Gran, has something——?'

'No, no, it's nothing,' Faye reassured her. 'Why don't you go upstairs and get changed and——?'

'No...' Sage interrupted huskily. 'No, I think we should tell her. I'm beginning to think there have been too many secrets in this family. All of them for the best of motives but——'

'Tell me what?' Camilla demanded, plainly bewildered.

Quickly, and as detachedly as she could, Sage explained to her what she had discovered.

'You have a twin brother?' Camilla stared at her and then flopped down into one of the chairs. 'Goodness... Does he know? What's he like? I——'

'No questions, please, Camilla,' Faye interrupted firmly. 'Sage has had rather a shock, and the last thing she wants right now is to be pestered by you. I'll make that call now, shall I?' she asked Sage.

Shakily Sage nodded her head, while Camilla begged urgently, 'What call, Ma... will someone *please* tell me what's going on? I——'

'Don't be so impatient, Cam... We'll use this phone, shall we, Sage?' Faye appealed. 'It seems more appropriate somehow to make the call here from Liz's own personal room.'

'Yes,' Sage agreed, smiling at her. 'Yes—this phone.'

Half of her wanted desperately to be the one to make the call, the other half...the other half wanted to get up and run as fast and as far from this room as she could do. She was quite frankly terrified of what Scott's reaction was going to be. What if he didn't know—what if he didn't *want* to know? And what about his father...her father?

She turned her back while Faye made the call, her mouth suddenly going dry, while sickness churned acidly through her stomach. She heard Faye clearing her throat as though she too was nervous, and then she heard her sister-in-law asking firmly, 'Yes... I'd like to speak with Mr Scott McLaren, please. My name's Faye Danvers—I doubt if that will mean anything to him... Yes... yes, I'll hold.'

Covering the mouthpiece, she turned to Sage and said quickly, 'The housekeeper's gone to find him, she said she thought he was in the office.'

'Mmm... From what Scott told me the homestead, as they call it, is a vast complex of buildings.'

She stopped speaking as Faye suddenly frowned and removed her hand from the receiver. As clearly as though she had been holding the phone herself, Sage heard a crisp, mature male voice saying, 'McLaren speaking.'

McLaren. Not Scott. She was sure of that, and so it seemed was Faye.

'Mr Lewis McLaren...?' she heard Faye saying hesitantly. 'I actually wished to speak with Scott McLaren.'

There was a small pause, and then to her shock Sage heard Faye saying huskily, 'Mr McLaren, you don't know me, but I'm sure you recognise my surname. My mother-in-law is Liz Danvers. Liz was knocked down and injured in a traffic accident some time ago. She's in hospital at the moment awaiting surgery.'

Faye hesitated, and then her voice softened as she said reassuringly, 'No... no... she is holding her own, but the operation is a major one. For a while after the accident Liz was conscious, and she instructed us—that is myself, and Sage, her daughter—to read the diaries which she had kept ever since she was a teenager. To cut a long story short, Mr McLaren, Sage and I have just discovered, that... that Scott and Sage are twins. We thought... that is to say *I* thought, that if Scott is aware that Liz is his mother that he would want to know...

'Yes... yes, the surgeon has assured us that Liz is well enough to undergo the operation. They've been keeping her heavily sedated while they waited to see if the blood clot would disperse of its own accord...

'Which hospital? Well, it's St Giles's in London. Yes, it has a very good reputation. Both Sage and I have every confidence in the surgeon. The operation? We... well, it's scheduled for tomorrow... Delay it for another twenty-four hours? Well, I don't think——'

She frowned suddenly, holding the receiver away from her ear, and said to Sage, 'He wants to speak with you.'

With *her*... Sage found suddenly that she was frozen where she stood, unable to move, unable to speak... literally petrified.

It took Camilla's gentle push to urge her towards the receiver. She took it from Faye like someone in a trance, lifting it slowly to her ear, her eyes dark, the pupils dilated, her skin devoid of colour, her breathing erratic and tense.

As she pressed the receiver to her ear she heard the unfamiliar male voice demanding, 'Sage, are you there?'

'Yes, I'm here.' Her voice was a croak, a husky, uncertain thread of sound she barely recognised.

'This is Lewis McLaren here.' There was a pause, and then the harsh, emotional admission she had never thought to hear. 'Your father... Your brother and I will be on the first flight we can get—you are not to let them operate until we get there... Do you understand that, Sage? They *must* wait until we're there... God, Liz... I can't believe it... Sage, are you listening to me?'

'Yes... yes, I'm listening. How long?'

'Twenty-four hours at most... That's all. We'll fly out to the coast today, and pick up a flight to London——'

'You're both coming?' Sage interrupted him, suddenly finding her voice.

There was a small pause, and then his voice roughened, deepened as he confirmed huskily, 'We'll both be there.'

And suddenly, achingly, Sage realised that here was a man who had loved her mother very much indeed, who perhaps, despite the way they had parted, did still love her. Perhaps, she reflected wryly, she was far more her father's child than she had ever realised in the days when she had believed Edward to be her father.

As though Lewis McLaren too was aware of the emotion of the moment he said softly, 'Don't worry, Sage. We'll be there in time. You just make sure they don't operate for another twenty-four hours. I want to see this surgeon. I want to make sure your mother's in the best possible hands...'

The old Sage, the old Sage she had been before she had set out on her journey through her mother's past, would have objected to his high-handedness... to his assumption that she and Faye were not capable of ensuring that her mother receive the best possible medical attention, but now she had discovered within herself her mother's gift of looking beneath the surface, of seeking the truth behind people's reactions, and she sensed clearly that Lewis McLaren was shocked, concerned—she could almost feel his desperation, his need to be with her mother, and so she simply said pacifyingly, 'I'll speak to the surgeon, but I doubt that he'll be very pleased.'

She paused and then was unable to stop herself asking in a low voice, 'Scott... Is he... is he happy?'

There was a small pause and then her father responded roughly, 'Yes, yes, he's very happy. Married with two fine boys, but I had to tell him the truth first. Had to explain to him just why it was impossible for you and him.'

'Yes, I...'

'I'm sorry... but your mother and I, well, we... with Edward... we had to do what was best for both of you.'

He paused and then said, 'As soon as we get to London I'll ring you. Where will you be?'

'Here, most probably, at the house.' She gave him the number.

She was just about to replace the receiver when he said urgently, 'I've never stopped loving her, you know. There hasn't been a day since she sent me away when I haven't thought about her. Or about you. I wanted you all... but she couldn't leave him, wouldn't leave him. He was more important than me.'

'You're wrong,' Sage told him huskily. 'It wasn't like that. She... She felt she had a duty... that she owed Edward——'

'Owed him what? The rest of her life... our happiness... my children?'

She could hear the bitterness in the words, the loss, and her throat closed up. Oh, yes, she was her father's daughter... and how her mother must have recognised that and been hurt by it, over and over again through the years.

When she replaced the receiver tears were pouring down her face. Wordlessly Faye held out her arms to her and she went into them.

Camilla too came and placed her arms around them and they stayed like that in silent female communion for several minutes.

It was Sage who broke away first, saying, 'We'll have to get in touch with the hospital... delay the operation... I think we'll have to explain the reason why. Would you do that, Faye? I don't think...'

'Yes... yes, I will. Look, why don't you go upstairs and lie down for an hour? You've had a shock.'

'No... no. I'll stay here... keep myself occupied answering some of the letters that keep arriving. I knew that Mother had a wide field of acquaintances, but I can't get over how many people she knows.'

'She's very popular, very well loved...' Faye agreed.

'Mmm... I wonder if she ever allowed herself to think of what she gave up when she refused to go with my father.'

'Being Liz, I expect she did... No woman could not do so, could she?'

'Not really,' Sage agreed. 'Not really.'

As Faye had anticipated, Alaric Ferguson was at first incredulously disbelieving and then furiously angry when she calmly announced that they wanted Liz's operation to be delayed for twenty-four hours.

What she hadn't anticipated was how amused she was, and even in some delicate feminine way aroused, by her own realisation that part of the reason he was so annoyed was because he could not quite detach himself from his own awareness of her which in turn heightened both his irritation and reaction.

Eventually she relented and explained the situation to him. Reluctantly he accepted that under the circumstances the operation could be delayed, but Faye sensed that he had disliked her putting him at a disadvantage.

As she replaced the receiver she realised with a small sense of shock that for the first time in her life she was tasting the kind of sexual power that most of her sex took as a matter of course.

Sage had said that Alaric Ferguson was attracted to her, and she realised that she was curious enough about him to be flattered by that thought.

Daniel frowned as he looked at his silent telephone. The call he had been waiting for had still not come through and he had been hoping that it would before he had to speak to Sage and respond to her ultimatum. In fact that was why he had delayed her original deadline.

He marvelled a little at himself that he was foolish enough to believe that giving her the news would influence her attitude towards him—soften her antagonism, make it easier for them to communicate, to... To what? Become lovers... But it wasn't just her body in his bed that he wanted. Had that been the case...

Admit it, he derided himself, you're practically obsessed with the woman and you always have been right from the start. You don't just want her, you *love* her...

The telephone rang and he reached for the receiver. It was the call he had been waiting for. As he replaced the receiver he thought that Helen had been worth cultivating, even though at times he had found annoying her possessiveness, her unsubtle determination to turn what was really little more than a business acquaintanceship into something much more personal.

At times he had felt quite sorry for her. She was an attractive woman with a good career, but she was one of those women who thought that her looks and her sexuality entitled her to preferential treatment in life.

She was looking for a rich husband, or a rich lover, and her way of going about her hunting repelled him. He couldn't help contrasting her attitude with Sage's. Sage who was so independent, so proud, so reserved...or who had been until she had broken down in front of him and told him...

He felt his stomach muscles tense as awareness wrenched through him. He had been a fool not to take advantage of that weakness. Not to... Not to what...fling her to the floor and possess her? That wasn't the way he wanted it to be between them. He wanted her...of course he did, but he wanted more than her sexual compliance...her reluctant and angry admission that she desired him. He didn't want to master her, to dominate her, to use her own need against her, he didn't want to subjugate her in any way at all. He wanted her to come to him freely, proudly, lovingly. He wanted the moon, he told himself wryly. He was never going to get her to hand her heart to him on a plate, but he couldn't prevent his mind from dreaming.

As he drove towards Cottingdean he wondered how Sage would react to his news. She wouldn't be expecting to see him as his extended deadline was not yet up and she would probably anticipate that he would telephone. She would already be tense; even more so because of her mother's serious condition. He made a silent prayer that all would be well. He liked and admired Liz Danvers. Had found her a charming and sincere woman and had marvelled a little that she should have produced this volatile, quicksilver Sage.

The drive took longer than he had expected. When he reached the house it was quiet, although lights seemed to blaze from every one of its windows. He wondered if perhaps Liz Danvers...

His body tensed as he looked up towards the upper storey. He wondered which window was Sage's... He even wondered how she had furnished that room, and then laughed at himself for acting like a boy daydreaming over some unreachable idol. He parked his car and got out.

When he rang the doorbell, the door was answered by Faye. He asked for Sage and Faye frowned at him. Sage was still in her mother's study—the last time Faye had looked in on her, she had been curled up in a chair like a small child, fast asleep, and Faye hadn't the heart to wake her.

She had taken Sage's advice and talked with Camilla about her own past. Her daughter's reaction, her shock and her anger, her immediate love and warmth... her maturity and compassion had taught Faye a great deal about her daughter and even more about herself. This child she had given birth to, had loved and protected, was now almost an adult. She realised that she had tended to forget at times that Camilla was David's daughter as well as her own; that she had inherited in full measure her father's wonderful clear-sighted vision, his compassion, his depth of understanding.

'I'm afraid Sage isn't seeing anyone at the moment,' she told their visitor, but he ignored her, firmly stepping past her so that she had no option but to let him in and close the door behind him.

'She'll see me,' Daniel assured her. 'She's expecting me...'

Was she? Sage had said nothing to her. Faye glanced helplessly and betrayingly towards the study door, and Daniel took advantage of her hesitation to walk towards the door, saying coolly, 'She's in here, is she? Don't worry, I'll announce myself...'

'You can't go in there...' Faye started to protest, but it was already too late. He was opening the door and going inside.

Sage was lying curled up in one of the chairs, one hand under her face. She had been crying and he could see the oddly touching traces of mascara on her skin. She looked like a child, he reflected, watching her, but she wasn't a child, and just the sight of her made his heart contract and his body go weak.

The room was half in shadow, illuminated by the fire and a single lamp on the desk behind her.

As he walked towards her he saw some photographs lying on her lap. Some of them had spilled down on to the floor and he bent automatically to pick them up, tensing when he recognised Scott's youthful features smiling back at him.

A mixture of pain, anger, and resentment churned through his stomach. He had a momentary impulse to pick up the photographs and hurl them into the fire. Was it never going to end...was she never going to forget, to stop looking into the past and face the future? He was jealous, he recognised. Jealous of Scott. Jealous of her love for him. So searingly jealous in fact that he wanted to destroy if not the man then at least his celluloid image.

As he bent over her she moved and frowned, her eyes slowly flickering open. For a moment she looked at him without pretence or defences, and what he read in them made him ache to reach out to her, to take hold of her, but already her expression was changing, becoming distant...veiled...antagonistic. She swung her feet to the floor and tried to stand up, but he was standing in her way.

'Daniel!' she demanded huskily. 'What are you doing here? Who let you in?'

'I came in answer to your ultimatum,' he told her curtly. 'Remember it? Or were you too busy wallowing in self-pity reliving the past? My God, Sage... What's *wrong* with you? You're an adult woman, not a girl. You...'

Muddled with sleep and emotion, it was several seconds before Sage realised what he meant. He had picked up her photographs and now he threw them down on the desk in a gesture of disgust. Impulsively she caught hold of his sleeve so that he turned to face her.

'Daniel, you don't understand... Scott is——'

'Oh, I understand all right,' he interrupted her roughly. 'I understand... And to think...'

His face grew bitter...hard...his expression chilling her.

'There was a time when I thought that you and I could have a future together, that maybe...just maybe you'd come to your senses and realise... You want me and I certainly damn well want you...and I promise you this, in *my* bed you'd have found a hell of a lot more pleasure than any other man has ever shown you...'

He stopped and cursed himself under his breath as he saw her expression—he was going about this in completely the wrong way. He knew her well enough to realise how she was going to react to that kind of announcement and he couldn't really blame her, but he had been so shocked, so angry, so bitterly hurt to discover her crying over Scott—it had been like a blow delivered right against his heart. He *knew* that he could never endure wondering how often she was thinking about Scott, how often she was wanting him, aching for him, even though he also knew that if only she would admit it the emotions they generated for one another between them were far more powerful than anything she had ever felt for Scott McLaren. But she wouldn't admit it, and suddenly the thought of forcing her to do so was like a bad taste in his mouth.

Groggy with sleep, Sage stared at him. He was jealous... jealous of Scott, she recognised, with a surge of emotion so intense and so betraying that she almost reached out to him and took hold of him. Just in time she stopped herself and said instead, 'Daniel, you don't understand——'

'Like hell,' he interrupted her furiously. 'I understand well enough—and to think I came here tonight hoping, wanting... Well, I might as well tell you, since that's why I'm here... You're off the hook, Sage, your precious village is safe... they've rerouted the road.'

She stared at him. 'They've *what*? But they *can't* have done. Not at this stage.'

'It was always on the cards,' Daniel told her brusquely. 'But you were so determined to win out against *me*, to put one over on *me*, that you never seemed to realise it. You shouldn't take things so personally,' he told her acidly.

'Daniel, I...'

There was so much she wanted to explain to him. So much she wanted to share with him. The words trembled on the tip of her tongue—just one sign of encouragement from him and they would have come tumbling out... but instead he turned his back on her and said grimly, 'Well, I'll be on my way. I apologise for interrupting your wallow in self-pity. Shame that Scott isn't here to witness it, isn't it? Goodbye, Sage!'

Somehow the way he said it made her body tense as it recognised something her heart didn't want to know. He was walking out on her. There would be no other time, no second chance...but before she could stop him, before she could say anything, Faye came in, saying quickly, 'Everything's arranged, Sage, they're putting off the operation for another twenty-four hours...'

Daniel was already in the hall—another moment and he would be gone. She tried to follow him, but her feet were numb, she couldn't move and as she tried to stumble after him she heard the front door opening and closing.

She reached it just as his car started to move down the drive. She turned and, as Faye looked into her face, her sister-in-law demanded, appalled, 'Sage, what is it...what's wrong?'

'Nothing,' Sage lied bleakly. 'Nothing at all.'

CHAPTER TWENTY-SIX

'I CAN'T believe it, Scott... even now. And to think all these years you've known and you've never——'

'I *couldn't* tell you,' Scott interrupted. 'I promised Dad I wouldn't and, remember, Sage, for all I knew your mother... our mother... might have told you and you might not have wanted to get in touch. When Dad told me you'd been on the phone...'

'My brother...' Sage repeated softly. 'My twin. That's why I always felt so close to you. So——'

'It's been the same for me,' Scott assured her. 'Better in some ways because I knew—worse because knowing made me want to be with you, to share it with you——'

'And you're a father—two boys... my nephews...' she suddenly realised with laughter that was closer to tears.

They were all at Cottingdean. Scott and Lewis had arrived last night, and from the moment of his arrival Lewis had taken charge of them all, in a way that made Sage realise all too well how easily her mother would have fallen in love with him.

He was so alive... so very vigorous and male, even now... he must have been such a contrast to Edward, Edward who, even as a child, Sage had recognised as being someone who needed constant care, constant cherishing.

How painful it must have been for her mother to love Lewis and yet know that she could not leave Edward. She *knew* how painful it had been, how much she had longed to go with Lewis, to... She must make sure that he had an opportunity to read the last diary at least, before he left for the hospital—to understand... Alaric Ferguson had told them that there was little point in their

571

being at the hospital during the operation, but Lewis
had ignored this advice and was insisting that he was
going to be there, and seeing the anxiety, the fear in his
eyes, Sage hadn't had the heart to demand that they all
share that vigil with him.

She sensed that he wanted to be alone with her
mother...that he needed to be there with her.

He was her father, she his daughter, although they
were both still a little wary of that relationship, a little
hesitant...both of them remembering the past.

Three hours before the operation was scheduled to take
place, Lewis McLaren left for the London hospital. Sage
watched him go with mingled feelings. The hours passed
slowly and for comfort she sought out Scott who came
to stand close beside her, his arms around her. She felt
so at ease with him...so relaxed. It surprised her how
easily she had accepted their relationship, how complete
it made her feel...how right. Knowing the truth high-
lighted the difference between how she felt about Scott
and how she felt about Daniel.

Even in the past she had desired Daniel...had loved
him, probably, but had not been able to recognise that
fact, her perceptions clouded by the intensity of her involvement with Scott.

She told Scott as much, laughing at his astonishment.
'You *love Daniel Cavanagh*! We still keep in touch, you
know. He's a fine guy, but the two of you...'

'Oh, he doesn't love me,' Sage assured him wryly.
'Although——'

'Although what?'

'Although he wants me,' she told Scott mischievously,
and was amused by the sternness of his expression.

'Friend or not, if he thinks I'm going to stand by and
let him sleep with my sister——'

Sage laughed at his outrage.

'I'm a grown woman, Scott,' she reminded him gently.
'Not a child. But you're right. The way I feel about
Daniel is too powerful to allow me to have a relationship
with him that's only sexual. It would be too painful, too
potentially humiliating for me when it was over. I don't

think I'd be able to trust myself to take my rejection gracefully...I never was very good at accepting rejection,' she added wryly.

Scott hugged her. 'When I knew the truth, you'll never know how much I wanted to share it with you, but Dad told me he'd given your mother his word that you wouldn't be told. It seems that she felt that even if you were told you wouldn't believe it, that you'd think she was lying to you to keep us apart—and there was still Edward...'

'Yes,' Sage agreed quietly, 'she was probably right.'

And then of course later, when she was older, when Edward was dead, well, she had hardly given her mother the opportunity or the encouragement to confide in her, had she? And yet now she realised how much her mother must have always wanted to tell her, to share with her her own pain and need.

'Does he still love her?' Sage asked him simply.

'Yes. He's never stopped loving her.'

'Then why, when my father...when Edward died, why didn't he come to her?'

'Pride, I guess... She'd been pretty brutal with him, telling him she'd never loved him... I guess he told himself that the next time, if there was to be a next time, she could do the running. I guess he never allowed himself to believe that she'd want him to go to her.'

'But he's here now...'

Scott's eyes were sad as he asked emotionally, 'Wouldn't you be, given the circumstances?'

Both of them were silent, sharing their thoughts, their emotions.

Had she known Scott all her life, had she shared this closeness with him, would *she* have been a different person, a more whole person, a gentler person? Sage wondered, and then ruefully made herself admit that she probably would not; that she would all too likely have dominated and bullied him, that she would have been destructively possessive and jealous with him, and that in many ways it was perhaps just as well that they had grown to adulthood separately—that she had learned that it was not possible nor right that one person should ever wholly possess or dominate another, even out of love—before she experienced this closeness, this completeness with another person.

Scott was her brother, her twin, her other half, but he had other important relationships, with his father, his wife... their children, and as he talked to her about them and she heard that love and pride echoing in his voice it underlined her own aloneness, and traitorously it was to Daniel that her thoughts turned. Daniel who infuriated her, aroused her, unnerved her... Daniel who had turned his back on her and walked out on her before she could explain, before she could make him understand that she hadn't been indulging in some foolish reliving of the past, in daydreaming over Scott.

Daniel... her face grew shadowed as she acknowledged how much she wanted him to be here, how much she wanted him to share this special time with her, and emotively she said to Scott, 'You must be missing your wife...your sons... You should have brought them with you.'

The surprised, pleased look he gave her warmed her.

'I wanted to bring them,' he admitted, 'but Averil said that this was a very difficult and special time for the three of us...Dad, you and me... She sends her love, of course, and the boys are dying to meet you. Averil knows all about you, but the boys... Well, as you can imagine, they're thrilled to discover that they have an aunt...'

'I'm looking forward to meeting them already,' Sage laughed, her laughter fading as she added abruptly, 'Did Mother...does Mother...does she know about your wife, your family...?' She thought how painful it must be for her mother knowing that she had a son, grandchildren...and knowing at the same time that she would never be able to get close to them.

'Yes,' Scott told her simply. 'But she's never met them. She and Dad...' He shrugged his shoulders. 'Well, there was so much bitterness there—on Dad's part anyway—that I felt I owed it to him not to...and then there was you. I felt I couldn't ... We all decided that it was best that things remain as they were.'

'And between you, the three of you decided that I couldn't be trusted with the truth,' Sage suggested wryly but without rancour.

What was the point in working herself up into a rage about something which was in the past, something which could not be altered? Perhaps their joint decision had been the right one ... If she had been told the truth then, when she had lacked the maturity to see the sacrifices her mother had made, to be aware of her suffering, she would probably have turned against her ... she would probably in her possessive and immature intensity have demanded and expected from her mother and from Scott a far too intense depth of emotional support. She would have made demands on them which it would have been impossible for them to meet. Idealistic, impossible demands which in the end would have destroyed their relationship and maybe her along with it.

Years ago, when she had accused Daniel of gloating over Scott's desertion of her, he had told her bluntly— and, she had thought, cruelly—that she was emotionally immature, that she was looking to Scott to put right all the perceived wrongs of her childhood ... that she was looking to him to fulfil too many roles in her life and that the real need she was hiding was her need to come to terms with herself, to accept herself ... to like herself.

Then she had been furious ... Now she knew how wisely and truthfully he had spoken.

She smiled wryly to herself. Once, had anyone told her that, alone with Scott, hearing him say how much he loved her and knowing it was the truth, she would have felt this need ... this ache, this hunger for Daniel's company ... well, she would never have believed them. How little she had known about herself, about others.

She was more at peace with herself than she had ever believed possible. She felt only compassion and love for her mother ... respect, too. For her father her feelings were less certain, less settled ... He had believed her mother's denial of her feelings ... He had hurt her ...

And yet she could see that he had suffered greatly himself. It was not, after all, for her to question his actions, his errors, and having seen his face after he had read the last diary she knew how strongly, how unswervingly he had loved and still loved her mother.

Yes, she was more at peace with herself than she had ever been, but she still ached for Daniel. And not just physically... She ached for him emotionally, mentally...hungered for him...wept inside for him...loved him.

Only now did she truly understand what that kind of love meant. She wondered if in her mother's shoes she would ever have had the strength to make the same kind of sacrifices, and shivered as she acknowledged that she most probably would not.

'Someone walk over your grave?' Scott asked her.

She shook her head.

'No, I was just thinking about Mother... marvelling at her strength of character. She's a wonderful person, Scott,' she told him urgently. 'She loved our father... probably still does love him, but she felt that Edward needed her more...'

'I know,' he told her gently. 'I've read the diaries too, now, remember?'

'Mm... I wonder when we'll hear something? She must be out of the operating theatre by now...'

'Not quite yet. They said the operation would take six hours... There's still another hour to go. I'm glad you found out the truth before...'

'Before it was too late...' Sage suggested huskily. 'Oh God, Scott. You don't think she's going to die, do you? I don't think I could bear it... Not now...there's so much I want to tell her, so much I want to ask her...'

'If Dad lets you... It seems to me he's got a lot of catching up to do as well...'

The telephone rang while they were all in the sitting-room, making a pretence of eating the meal which Jenny had insisted on preparing for them.

Faye reached it first, snatching up the receiver and listening.

'It's over,' she told them all quickly. 'Liz came through the operation very well. She's in recovery now and we can go up and see her, although Alaric Ferguson says that she'll be very groggy, that she probably won't even recognise us...'

Scott drove them all to the hospital.

'To be honest I don't feel capable of concentrating on my driving right now,' Sage admitted to him, 'although we all know what happened the last time you drove me anywhere...'

The smile he gave her reassured her that she had long ago been forgiven for that potentially fatal foolishness.

On their way to the hospital they passed a newspaper vendor. The headline splashed across the front page caught Sage's eye and she continued reading it with growing shock.

'Chairman of Cavanagh Construction resigns amid conflict over motorway contract.'

Quickly she darted forwards and bought a copy of the paper. Scott, who had paused to wait for her, watched her anxiously.

'It's Daniel,' she told him shakily. 'I think he's in trouble... I can't explain it all right now...'

Daniel, being forced to resign... Daniel who had come himself to tell her about the change of route. She hadn't stopped to think how difficult that must have been for him, how galling... how potentially financially disastrous. She thought of the house he had bought and the land, the risks he had taken, and, despite the fact that nothing could alter her relief that the village was no longer going to be destroyed, she couldn't help wishing that it could have been achieved without Daniel suffering.

After the noise of the traffic, the silence of the recovery unit carried an awareness of tension and anxiety. An almost spiritual sense of how finely the balance hung here between life and death.

Her mother was in a private room at the end of a short corridor.

Lewis was already there with her. He looked both haggard and elated as he came out to meet them, his voice cracking with emotion as he told them joyfully, 'She's come round. She recognised me...' There were tears in his eyes. 'She's under sedation at the moment...sleeping... But she should be waking up shortly. I've spoken to the specialist. He says she's physically very strong and now that the danger of the blood clot has been removed he has every confidence in her making a full recovery. The danger was that they wouldn't be able to remove the clot, but now that danger's gone it should be just a matter of time——'

'Can we see her?' Sage interrupted him anxiously.

As though he sensed her inability to believe that her mother was actually alive until she had seen her for herself, he nodded. 'Only for a few minutes, mind,' he warned her.

Strange that she, who had always resented authority so deeply and so intensely, did not resent the authority of this man—should almost find it amusing, should regard it with such affection and tolerance.

Her mother's eyes were closed, her body still and small beneath the stiff white sheet, transporting Sage back instantly to that moment when she had first seen her in her hospital bed and realised that she was after all mortal.

Now, as then, she was overwhelmed by a wave of love and fear, but now those emotions were softened by knowledge and maturity.

She had waited a long time to achieve such maturity, Sage recognised grimly. Too long, and, with hindsight, she marvelled at her mother's patience with her.

But then love made great allowances as well as great sacrifices and her mother had made both.

Without knowing she had done so, she discovered that she had reached out and put her hand over her mother's.

'I love you, Ma,' she whispered hesitantly, unconsciously using for the first time the affectionate name only David had called her before.

Was it her imagination, or had the still hand beneath her own moved? She searched her mother's face, her body tensing as she saw her eyelashes flutter... Her eyelids lifted, and she was once again looking into those familiar grey eyes, but where before she had always perceived them as cold and disapproving, as unloving and rejecting, now she saw that in reality they were shadowed with anxiety and concern, that behind the veneer of self-control was love and need.

'I love you, Ma,' she said again. 'But if you ever dare do anything like this to us again I'll never forgive you.'

'Ready, Sage?' Scott asked.

They had agreed between them that it was only fair that, since only one of them could be allowed to remain with Liz, that one should be Lewis.

If Sage had had any doubts about this, they had been banished when she saw the look on her mother's face when she opened her eyes properly and saw Lewis standing beside her bed.

Now Scott was waiting to drive all of them, Sage, Faye, and Camilla, back to Cottingdean, where he and Lewis were going to stay until Liz was well enough to come home from hospital.

'I'm not coming back with you,' she told him. 'I... There's something I need to do...someone I need to see.'

She was still holding the newspaper and she glanced at it betrayingly. Scott followed her glance and his eyes darkened compassionately.

'You're going to see him?' he guessed.

Sage nodded.

'Yes.' She didn't want to explain to Scott about the misunderstanding that had occurred. She didn't need to... It was enough that he knew she loved Daniel.

'You're going to see Daniel Cavanagh?' Faye repeated in astonishment when Sage told her where she was going. 'But I...I thought you didn't like him...?'

'No, I don't,' Sage told her drily. 'In much the same way as you don't like Alaric Ferguson.'

They exchanged mutual looks of self-knowledge, two women who now understood one another a great deal better and who had been united by their mutual voyage of discovery.

Camilla was frowning at both of them, but she was too elated by her grandmother's successful operation to question either of them.

She eyed Scott thoughtfully. He was Sage's twin brother. His father—Sage's father—had been Gran's lover, years and years ago... It was all so romantic...so exciting. She wondered if she'd ever manage to wangle an invitation out to Australia... She'd always wanted to travel...

Sage took a taxi across London, only realising as she climbed out of the cab just how late it was. Daniel might even have gone to bed. It was almost eleven... A *frisson* of sensation curled through her...a softening...an awareness.

Stop it, she warned herself. You're going to apologise and explain. You're going as a friend, not as a potential lover... That's if he'll actually let you in.

He did, but it was plain that he was astonished to see her.

'Sage... What on earth——?'

'I've seen this...' she told him, waving the paper in front of him. 'Oh, Daniel, I'm so sorry... Was it because of the house...was that why they made you resign?'

'*Made* me resign?' To her astonishment he actually started to laugh. 'You thought I'd been *forced* to resign? I *wanted* to resign, Sage. Running a huge corporation, being stuck behind a desk all day bogged down with administration and paperwork—that's not for me. My resignation has been under negotiation for some time. It wasn't easy, I admit, to give up the reins of the company my father built up. I felt I owed it to him to at least try... But in the end I knew he'd understand that I had to be true to myself, my own ideals and ambitions.'

'So what are you going to do?' she asked him blankly. Sage wasn't sure she believed him, but he sounded so confident, so relaxed, so very different from what she had imagined... her visit, like so many of her impulsive gestures, had been unnecessary, foolish even. It seemed that the last thing Daniel needed was her compassion, her concern, her friendship.

'I'm going to do what I've always wanted to do. I'm going to build small, exclusive developments—one-offs, anything that takes my fancy. When the company was originally bought out, financially I did very well. I don't need to work, at least not financially, but mentally, well, that's a different thing... but I'm no workaholic. I want other things in my life besides work. Things like a wife, a family... Why did you come here, Sage?' he asked her abruptly.

She stared at him, her mouth opening and then closing. Why *had* she come here...?

'Suddenly realised you're wasting your life mooning over Scott, is that it? Suddenly realised you need something much more than a mere dream lover can give you?'

Her face went scarlet with temper.

'No, it is not,' she ground out at him. 'And for your information...' She stopped. 'Why did you buy that house?' she asked him obliquely. 'Was it because of the road?'

'No,' he told her shortly, 'it wasn't. I bought it because I want to live in it. Your information wasn't totally accurate. I bought it, not Hever Homes. Now stop trying to change the subject. Why did you come here?'

'Well, it wasn't because I want to go to bed with you, if that's what you think,' she told him dangerously.

'Wasn't it?' he challenged her softly, getting up out of his chair and coming towards her.

When he reached her he didn't touch her but simply asked her conversationally, 'Why are you trembling so much, Sage?'

'Because... because I'm angry,' she told him desperately.

'Angry,' he mused, watching her. 'You've spent a lot of your life being angry, haven't you? Or wasted a lot of your life on it. Are you sure it's anger you feel?'

'Of course I'm sure. After all, if I've spent as much of my life experiencing it as you seem to think, it's hardly something I'm likely to mistake, is it?'

'Not by accident,' he agreed.

He was standing so close to her that she could feel the warmth of his breath stirring her hair. She only had to close her eyes and lean forwards... She trembled violently. This wasn't what she had come for. And besides, Daniel despised her...he thought she still loved Scott.

She took a step back from him and said as firmly as she could, 'It seems I've made a mistake...and it's time I left. The last train...'

Daniel frowned. 'The *what*...? What's happened to your car?'

'Scott brought us up. When we left the hospital, he drove Faye back to Cottingdean... I came straight here...' She stopped abruptly, realising how much she had betrayed...but Daniel seemed to have picked up only on one thing.

'Scott...Scott is here...?'

'Not here... At Cottingdean,' Sage told him, and then as she saw the rejection in his eyes she caught hold of his sleeve and implored, 'Daniel, please listen——'

'Listen...to what? My God, and to think...you realise he's married, don't you...married with two children? Christ, will you never learn? He's not the man for you...'

'And you are, I suppose?' she flamed back at him. 'My God, you're so arrogant... How dare you try to dictate to me? Especially when——'

'Especially when what?' he demanded. 'When both of us know damn well that no matter how much you might cling to some pathetic belief that you still love Scott McLaren you actually want me... Damn you, Sage, when will you——?'

'When will I what? Go to bed with you? Never... Never...'

She turned and headed for the door.

Wrenching it open, she told him shakily, 'And as for Scott... For your information, he's my brother—my twin brother...'

To her disgust she discovered that her voice was so thick with tears and words that they were clogging her throat, burning her eyes. 'Oh, damn!' she swore under her breath, the hallway obscured by her tears.

'What? *What* was that you just said?' she heard Daniel demanding from behind her, his voice rough with anxiety and shock.

She hadn't intended to answer him—she hadn't even intended to stay... but somehow or other she found herself turning towards him and sniffing almost childishly, 'Scott is my brother, my *twin brother*!' and then, almost as though he knew what she was feeling, what she wanted to say to him but couldn't, Daniel's arms came round her and he was hugging her, holding her... giving her the warmth and security, the compassion, the tenderness she had yearned for all her life, as he rocked her gently, and let her howl into the front of his shirt, soaking it with all the abandon of a lost child.

'It was such a shock, and everything happened so fast—Mother, the operation...'

She knew she was not making much sense, but Daniel seemed to grasp what she was trying to say.

'I expect she kept it from you for the best of motives... Did you really think I'd been forced to resign from the company?'

She stiffened in his arms as she heard the indulgent amusement in his voice.

'Yes, as a matter of fact I did,' she told him curtly.

She pushed away from him, holding him at a distance.

'I didn't come here looking for your sympathy, Daniel... or for anything else,' she told him savagely. 'I might want you,' she added bitterly, 'but credit me with the capacity to feel some other emotions besides lust. But then why should you?' she added self-derisively. 'I've never given you any reason to believe that I can feel anything else. If you value me so poorly, it's probably only because that's the way I value myself... but not any longer—not any longer.

'I came here tonight because I was concerned for you, worried about you.' Holding her head high, she looked straight at him, and told him through clenched teeth, 'I came here tonight because... because... because I love you, and stupidly I thought you might need someone, even if that someone was only me... a woman incapable of feeling any emotion other than lust. But you don't need me, do you, Daniel? You don't need anyone, and I now think I've made enough of a fool of myself for one night...'

She pulled herself out of his arms before he could stop her, tugging open the door, running down the steps and flagging down a cruising cab, while Daniel called her name protestingly and muttered under his breath, 'Come back, you stupid woman. I do need you... and I love you, too, damn you!'

He rang her the next day, four times, but on each occasion she refused to take his calls. There was nothing he wanted to do more than to go to her and tell her what he felt, to take advantage of her vulnerability and tie her to him so securely that she'd never be able to tear herself free, but he was right in the middle of the negotiations for the takeover of his successor at Cavanagh's and, no matter how much he might want to do so, there was no way he could behave like an adolescent and walk out on the meetings to go to her.

He couldn't even spare the time to drive down to Cottingdean to see her. Of all the times... If only he had reacted faster last night, kept her with him. By now...

He groaned as he recognised the direction his thoughts were taking, half appalled, half amused by the immediate reaction of his body.

This was not the time to start thinking along those particular lines, not when he had what would potentially be one of the most difficult board meetings of his life to chair... No, much as it galled him, his private life would have to wait... At least for a few days.

A few days. He groaned again. They would feel like a lifetime. Several lifetimes. How the hell was he supposed to concentrate on business when all he really wanted was to be with Sage?

CHAPTER TWENTY-SEVEN

'WHAT'S wrong, darling? You're looking very pensive.'

Sage smiled at her mother. The four of them—Lewis, her mother, Scott and herself—had flown here to this exclusive holiday island in the Caribbean just as soon as her doctors had given her mother the all clear.

They were occupying a villa belonging to a friend of Lewis's and they were to spend a month here, getting to know one another 'as a family', as Lewis had put it.

Sage had only been able to marvel at the patience and wisdom of her unknown sister-in-law, Scott's wife, who had had the understanding and the strength of character to refuse Scott's request for her to join them. Sage had spoken to her by telephone and she had explained to Sage that she believed that the four of them needed this special time together.

'I'm looking forward to meeting you, Sage. But you and Scott and your parents have a lot of private catching up to go through. There'll be time for us later . . . I know Scott's hoping that you and your mother will come out to us for a long holiday . . . And of course Faye and Camilla will be welcome as well.'

But that was for the future . . . For now it was just the four of them. Four people tied by bonds of love and blood, who in so many ways were all strangers to one another.

Sage had witnessed the love between her parents . . . had seen it and recognised it; had been aware of the love Scott felt for his wife, and, despite the happiness she had found in being with these closest members of the family, the joy she had known in at last coming close to her mother, in at last knowing that she had been loved—greatly loved, more loved than she had ever deserved to be—she felt there was still something missing, still a part of her that ached and yearned ... There was still Daniel.

'I was just thinking,' she murmured ...

'About Daniel Cavanagh,' her mother guessed shrewdly. There were no secrets between them now...no need for Liz to conceal any longer the great welling up of love she felt for this, the child Lewis had given her. The child who was so much Lewis's. Gently she pushed the hair off Sage's face, so that she could look at her. 'You love him very much, don't you?'

'Too much,' Sage acknowledged drily. 'Even if he were to love me in return, which he doesn't, I don't know if I'd ever feel happy in that kind of relationship... with that kind of intensity. It makes one so vulnerable.'

'You should never be frightened of love, Sage,' Liz told her gently.

Sage smiled at her. 'Weren't there ever times when you wished you had not loved my father?'

'No,' Liz told her truthfully. 'Because if I hadn't loved him I would never have conceived you. I wanted to be with him, of course, and I was desperately concerned for Scott... Edward allowed me to receive one letter a year from your father, reporting on Scott's progress, and your father was generous enough to make sure that I knew that Scott was growing up healthily and happily. And of course I had you, my precious, wonderful daughter, who was so much her father's child. I was so frightened that Edward would see how much I loved you—that he would insist on separating us...'

'I know,' Sage told her unsteadily, tears filling her eyes as she marvelled at her mother's courage... her steadfastness, her ability to cope with what must have been the most appalling burden of loneliness and fear.

'We'll soon be going home,' Liz reminded her. 'Only another few days.'

'And then you and Dad will cause a riot when you announce that you're getting married. I'm still not sure that I'll be able to cope...with Cottingdean and the mill.'

'You'll cope,' Liz assured her warmly.

'But ultimately Cottingdean must go to Camilla.'

'Yes,' her mother agreed. 'She is, after all, a Danvers, and I did promise Edward...'

'I don't mind,' Sage assured her, knowing that once she would have done—once the knowledge that her niece, no matter how much she loved her, was to inherit the home which she had always felt had somehow rejected her would have hurt unbearably, opening old wounds, recalling old hurts, reinforcing her belief that she was unloved.

'I know you don't.'

'Do you mind—leaving it all, I mean, after all these years?'

'Yes and no... I've achieved as much as I can. It's time that younger, firmer hands took up the reins of control. I was never more than a caretaker for Cottingdean: it knew it and so did I. In some ways Lewis was right when he accused me of wanting Cottingdean more than I wanted him. I didn't want it more than him, and I certainly didn't love it more, but it needed me. Just as Edward needed me, and, perhaps foolishly, I allowed myself to think that I was indispensable... irreplaceable.'

'You were... you are,' Sage assured her. 'I'm still not sure that I——'

'You'll cope... Come on. Lewis and Scott will be wondering what on earth we're doing...'

'You mean that Dad misses you madly every time you're out of his sight for more than ten minutes,' Sage teased her. How well she understood this man who was her father. How well she now understood so much more of herself, of her own emotions and motivations. This time with her mother, her father and her brother was something she would always cherish, a special learning, sharing time which all of them had needed, a special bonding time which had brought them together as a family... a unit. She was delighted that her parents were going to marry. She was delighted that Scott was so happy in his marriage. And yet... and yet despite her happiness she felt alone.

Daniel... It all came back to Daniel... Daniel, whom she loved and who would never love her. What was she doing to herself? Was she deliberately recreating the feeling of rejection, of alienation, of loving hopelessly and helplessly, that she had done with Edward, with her mother, with Scott? It was a depressing thought, and one she did not want to dwell on.

They flew home four days later. Her parents were going to marry, quietly and quickly. It would take a month or so for all the ends to be tied up... for her mother to finally sever her bonds with Cottingdean. But at the end of that time she would be flying out to Australia, to rejoin Scott and his family, and she would be flying out with her new husband... her lover... the father of her two adult children.

Heathrow was busy, crowded with travellers and their families. Faye had come to meet them, along with Camilla. Camilla had an air of suppressed excitement about her. She kept looking at Sage and grinning at her. She, of all of them, seemed to have accepted the changes in their lives the most easily, readily welcoming Scott and Lewis into her family.

Between the welcoming hugs and kisses she told Sage that her mother had been dating Alaric Ferguson. 'He's crazy about her,' she told Sage with a grin. 'Absolutely nuts about her.'

'And do you like him?' Sage asked her niece.

'He's OK,' she said casually. But Sage could tell that she was quite happy with her mother's new relationship. Everyone, it seemed, was happy. Everyone contented and fulfilled. Everyone but her... and then she looked up, and it seemed as though her heart stopped beating.

Daniel was standing less than five yards away from her...just standing there, watching her. She stared back, looking at him with hungry, vulnerable eyes, looking at him as though he had suddenly materialised out of empty space. Daniel... What was he doing here? Where was he going? She looked wildly around her. He wasn't standing in any kind of queue. He wasn't carrying any luggage. Her mother was standing beside her. She gave her a little push.

'Go to him, Sage,' she told her.

Go to him? She opened her mouth to protest, and looked round to discover that her mother and the rest of her family seemed to have disappeared. A wild sensation of having strayed into an unreal world overtook her. She discovered that she couldn't take her eyes off Daniel's face, that she couldn't do anything other than stand there and then stare at him. He wasn't moving. He was looking back at her, watching, waiting...

Go to him, her mother had said... Go to him. She took a step forwards and then another, and suddenly she was in his arms.

'Daniel... Daniel...' The taste of his name mingled with the taste of her tears.

'At last,' she heard him saying roughly. 'At last... Damn you, Sage. Do you *know* how long I've waited to hear you say my name like that—do you?' he demanded, almost shaking her.

'Say it like what?' she asked huskily, while her hands flexed lovingly against his back, absorbing the sensation of his flesh beneath her fingertips...the warmth and reality of him, the maleness. 'Like what?' she repeated dreamily, unaware of the amused and curious glances they were attracting from other travellers.

'As if you'd suddenly discovered you couldn't live without me. As if it tasted of heaven...as if you were handing me your heart and committing yourself to me for the rest of your life...'

'Oh, is that all?' she murmured provocatively. 'I thought you were going to say I said it as though I loved you...'

'And do you?' he demanded when he'd finished kissing her.

'Do I what?'

'Do you love me?'

'Does it matter?'

'More than anything else in this life,' he told her simply. 'I love you, Sage. I want to marry you...I want to spend the rest of my life with you...'

After she had assured him that his feelings were well and truly reciprocated, she asked him, 'How did you know we'd be flying back today?'

'Faye told me...I've been pestering the life out of her, but she finally only gave way when I told her how much I love you. She's one tough lady, that sister-in-law of yours.'

'Yes, she is, isn't she?' Sage agreed with a smile.

'Well, will you marry me, Sage? Will you commit yourself to me?'

She smiled at him, the smile of a sophisticated, knowledgeable woman, but it was the child who looked out of her eyes at him—the child who had known so much rejection, so much pain, the child on the brink of womanhood who had offered herself to him once before, as she was offering herself to him now, when she said seductively, 'I'm not sure. We know so little about one another, Daniel...even sexually.'

'You want us to be lovers now!'

'Only if you do,' she told him unsteadily. And he knew she was remembering that other time she had offered him this gift of her body, of herself, and of how he had rejected it.

'Come with me,' he invited her. 'Come with me, Sage, and let me show you how much...'

It was better than she had expected...better than anything she had experienced before. Not because Daniel was a skilled lover, not even because their bodies were so physically attuned that each caress they shared heightened their pleasure to exquisite levels. No, it was because she loved him and because she knew he loved her in turn that it was so special, Sage recognised...because for the first time in her life she was experiencing not just physical pleasure, but emotional security.

'I love you, Daniel Cavanagh,' she whispered into the musky sweatiness of his skin, as he closed his arms round her. It amused her how much pleasure it gave her to say the words. She was like a teenager...an adolescent in love for the first time, made drunk with the intoxication of it.

'Mmm...I love you too,' Daniel whispered back, and then added gently, 'You're the first woman I've ever wanted to hold in my arms all through the night. The only woman I've ever wanted to love.'

'Liar,' Sage derided him sleepily. 'You *never* wanted to love me...'

'Not at first,' he agreed. 'I fought like hell against what I knew was happening to me.'

'We both did. But the fighting's over now.'

She felt his body shaking and tensed until she realised he was laughing.

'Do you honestly believe that?' he asked her. 'We'll fight all our lives, Sage. And we'll love each other all our lives as well. Loving, fighting, sharing. We were meant to be together, you and I. Only we were both too stupid to admit it.'

'I love you, Daniel, and I never thought I'd say that to any man...'

'Much less me...is that it?'

'Much less you,' Sage agreed. 'Funny how things turn out, isn't it?'

'Hilarious,' Daniel agreed, kissing her tenderly. 'I love you, Sage—no matter what else might change in our lives, that never will.'

'No,' she agreed, and as she looked at him she knew that it was true. His love for her would always be there, supporting her, cherishing her, fulfilling her. She traced the shape of his mouth with her finger and then kissed him. Against his mouth she murmured indistinctly, 'Daniel, do you think I ought to start keeping a diary?'

'Not if you mean to start writing it right at this moment, I don't,' he told her, drawing her against him. 'Not right at this moment.'